THE
JOURNEY TO
THE WEST

THE
JOURNEY TO
THE WEST

VOLUME FOUR

Translated and Edited by Anthony C. Yu

The University of Chicago Press CHICAGO AND LONDON

Preparation of this volume was made possible by a grant
from the Translations Program of the National Endowment
for the Humanities, an independent federal agency.

Publication of this volume has been assisted by a grant
from the National Endowment for the Humanities,
an independent federal agency.

The reprinting of volumes 2, 3, and 4 was made possible
through a grant from the Chiang Ching-Kuo Foundation for
International Scholarly Exchange (USA) and Citibank.

THE UNIVERSITY OF CHICAGO PRESS, CHICAGO 60637
THE UNIVERSITY OF CHICAGO PRESS, LTD., LONDON
© 1983 by The University of Chicago
All rights reserved. Published 1983
Paperback edition 1984
Printed in the United States of America

16 15 14 13 12 11 10   10 11 12 13 14

Library of Congress Cataloging-in-Publication Data

Wu, Ch'eng-en, ca. 1500–ca. 1582.
  The journey to the west.

  Translation of Hsi-yu chi.
  Includes bibliographical references.
  1. Yu, Anthony C., 1938–   II. Title.
PL2697.H75E596   1977   895.1'34   75-27896
ISBN: Vol. I: 978-0-226-97150-6; 0-226-97150-3 (paper)
ISBN: Vol. II: 978-0-226-97151-3; 0-226-97151-1 (paper)
ISBN: Vol. III: 978-0-226-97153-7; 0-226-97153-8 (paper)
ISBN: Vol. IV: 978-0-226-97154-4; 0-226-97154-6 (paper)

For Joseph M. Kitagawa
and
In memoriam Yü Yün

Contents

Acknowledgments

My thanks are due, first of all, to the National Endowment for the Humanities, which has lent me faithful assistance through its Translations Program in the Division of Research Programs. But for such generosity it is most unlikely that I would have been able to finish the last installment of the translation so quickly.

I am fortunate to have in "Joch" Weintraub and "Chris" Gamwell two deans who are eager to provide for their faculty an enabling context. With word and deed they have given me unfailing support.

James Cheng and Ma Tai-loi of Chicago's Far Eastern Library have been invaluable helpers in research and the location of obscure materials. Wen-ching Tsien's exquisite calligraphy validates my belief that reading footnotes can be a pleasure. Susan Fogelson has been a tireless typist and discerning critic, and Charles Hallisey has provided painstaking assistance in the preparation of the index. As was the case with volume 3, Y. W. Ma (Hawaii) gave the manuscript a thorough and searching reading, though I alone am responsible for the final version.

As I bring this lengthy project to its completion, it is fitting for me to pay tribute to my late grandfather, who first introduced me to the wonders of this tale. It was he who, amidst the terrors of the Sino–Japanese war, gave himself unsparingly to teaching me Classical Chinese and English. By precept and example he sought to impart to a young boy his enduring love for literatures east and west. He did not labor in vain.

Seventy-six

Mind-Spirit dwells at home, the demon returns to nature;
Wood Mother subdues together the fiend's true body.

We were telling you about the Great Sage Sun, who dallied inside the belly of the old demon for quite a while until the latter dropped to the ground, hardly breathing or speaking a word. Thinking that the demon might be dead, the Great Sage released his hold somewhat on the demon's innards, and, having caught his breath once more, the demon chief called out, "Most compassionate and merciful Bodhisattva Great Sage, Equal to Heaven!"

When he heard that, Pilgrim said, "Son, don't waste your energy! Spare a few words and just address me as Grandpa Sun!" As he had great regard for his own life, that fiendish demon did indeed cry out, "Grandpa, grandpa! It's my fault! I made a terrible mistake in swallowing you, and now you're in a position to harm me. I beg the Great Sage to be merciful and have regard for the life-seeking wish of an ant. If you spare my life, I'm willing to send your master across this mountain."

Now, though the Great Sage was a warrior, he thought only of the T'ang monk's progress. When he, a person not unreceptive to compliments, heard how pitifully the fiendish demon was begging him, he became kind-hearted again. "Fiend," he cried, "I'll spare you. But how will you send my master off?"

"We have no silver or gold, pearl or jade, cornelian, coral, crystal, amber, tortoiseshell, or any such precious treasure to give to you," said the old demon. "But we three brothers will carry your master on a palanquin made of scented vines, and that's how we will send your master across this mountain."

"If you're going to take him across in a palanquin," said Pilgrim, laughing, "that's better than giving us treasures. Open your mouth wide and I'll come out." The demon chief did open his mouth wide, but the third demon walked up to him and whispered, "Big Brother, when he's about to get out, bite down hard. Chew that little monkey to pieces and swallow him. Then he won't be able to torture you any more."

Pilgrim, however, heard everything. Instead of crawling out himself, he stuck out his golden-hooped rod ahead of him to see if the way was clear. The fiend gave it a terrific bite; with a loud crack, one of his front teeth broke to pieces. Withdrawing his rod, Pilgrim said, "Dear fiend! I have already spared your life, but you want to bite me and kill me instead! I'm not coming out! I'm going to torture you until you drop! No, I'm not coming out!"

"Brother," complained the old demon to the third demon, "you've victimized your own kin! It would have been better if we had invited him to come out. You told me to bite him instead. He has not been bitten, but my teeth have been sorely hurt. What shall we do now?"

When that third demon saw that the blame was put on him, he resorted to the method of "Piquing the General." "Pilgrim Sun," he cried in a loud voice, "Your fame has been so loudly proclaimed that it strikes the ear like a crack of thunder! I have been told how you displayed your power before the South Heavenly Gate, how you showed your form beneath the Hall of Divine Mists, and how you have subdued monsters and bound demons on the way to the Western Heaven. But you are really nothing but an apish small-timer!" "In what way am I a small-timer?" asked Pilgrim. The third fiend said. "As the proverb says,

The valiant stays in the clear;

His fame spreads both far and near.

If you come out and let me fight with you, then you may consider yourself a hero. How can you be satisfied with fooling about in someone's stomach? If you're not a small-timer, what are you?"

When Pilgrim heard these words, he thought to himself, "Yes, yes, yes! If I pull his intestines apart and bust up his bladder, I can finish off this fiend right now. What's so difficult about that? Yet that will truly ruin my reputation. All right! All right! You open your mouth wide, and I'll come out to wage a contest with you. But the entrance to your cave is too narrow for us to use our arms. You must get out to a more spacious area." On hearing this, the third demon called up at once all the fiends; young and old, there were more than thirty thousand of those monster-spirits. Each grasping a sharp weapon, they went out of the cave to arrange themselves in the formation of the Three Forces[1] and do battle with Pilgrim once he came out. The second fiend supported the old demon as he walked out of the door, crying, "Pilgrim

Sun, if you're a hero, come out! There's a fine battlefield right here for you to fight on."

Even inside the demon's stomach the Great Sage could hear the din and hubbub outside, and he knew that they had arrived at a spacious region. He thought to himself: "If I don't go out, it'll mean that I have gone back on my word. If I do, however, I don't know what this monster-spirit with his human face but bestial heart is capable of doing. He said at first that he would send my master across the mountain, but actually he was trying to deceive me and bite me. Now he has even ordered his troops here . . . All right! All right! I'm going to take care of two things at once for him. I'll go out, but I will plant a root firmly in his stomach." He reached behind him and pulled off a piece of hair from his tail, blew his immortal breath on it, and cried, "Change!" It changed at once into a rope no thicker than a piece of hair but some four hundred feet long. (The rope, you see, would grow thicker once it was exposed to wind.) He fastened one end of the rope to the heart of the monstrous fiend, but he left the knot loose enough so as not to hurt the fiend for the moment. Taking hold of the other end, he smiled and said to himself, "Even after I get out, he will have to send my master across the mountain. If he refuses and raises arms against me, I won't even bother to fight with him. All I need to do is to tug at this little rope, and it'll be as if I'm still in his belly."

He then reduced the size of his own body and began to crawl out; when he reached the lower part of the fiend's throat, he saw that the monster-spirit had opened wide his square mouth, with fine teeth standing above and below like rows of sharp swords. Quickly he thought to himself, "That's not good! That's not good! If I leave through his mouth and then try to tug at this rope, he'll bite through it once he begins to hurt. I must get out through some place where he has no teeth." Dear Great Sage! Dragging the rope along, he crawled further up the throat of the fiend until he entered one of the nasal passages. A sudden itch in the old demon's nose caused him to "Ah-choo" loudly, and Pilgrim was sneezed right out.

The moment Pilgrim was exposed to the wind, he stretched his waist once and immediately grew to some thirty feet tall, with one hand holding the rope and the other grasping the iron rod. Not knowing any better, the demon chief, as soon as he saw Pilgrim, lifted up his steel scimitar and hacked away at his opponent's face. Pilgrim parried the blow with one hand holding the iron rod. At the same time, the second fiend using a lance and the third fiend using a halberd both rushed forward and rained blows on him. Putting away his iron rod and letting the rope hang loose, the Great Sage leaped up to the clouds and dashed away. He was afraid, you see, that once the little fiends had surrounded him, he would not be able to carry out his plan. He therefore jumped clear of their camp to reach a spacious spot on the peak of the mountain. Dropping down from the clouds, he grabbed the rope with both hands and tugged with all his strength, and immediately a sharp pain shot through the heart of the old demon. To lessen the pain, the demon clawed his way into the air also, but the Great Sage gave his rope another yank. When the little fiends saw what was happening out there, they all cried out: "O Great King! Don't provoke him any more! Let him go! This little monkey has no sense of the seasons! Clear Brightness[2] hasn't arrived yet, but he's flying a kite over there already!" When he heard this, the Great Sage gave the rope yet another mighty tug: hurtling through the air like a spinning wheel, the old demon fell to the ground with a thud, making a crater about two feet deep in the hardened loess beneath the mountain slope.

The second and the third fiends were so terrified that they both dropped down from the clouds and went forward to take hold of the rope. "Great Sage," they pleaded as they both knelt down, "we thought you were a lenient and magnanimous immortal, but you are no better than a slippery sneak. We wanted to get you out to fight with you, and that's the honest truth. How could we know that you would fasten this rope onto the heart of our elder brother?"

"You bunch of lawless demons," said Pilgrim with a laugh, "you have a lot of nerve! Last time you tried to bite me when you asked me to come out, and this time you bring up all these troops against me. Look at those thousands of fiend soldiers confronting me, and I'm single-handed! That's not quite reasonable, is it? No, I'm yanking you along! I'm yanking you along to see my master!"

Kowtowing along with his brothers, the old demon said, "Be merciful, Great Sage. Spare my life, and I'll be willing to send the Venerable Master across this mountain." "If you want your life," said Pilgrim with another laugh, "all you need to do is to cut the rope with a knife."

"Holy Father!" said the old demon. "I may be able to cut off the rope, but there's still another strip of it fastened to my heart. It's sticking to my throat and making me retch. What shall I do?" "In that case," said Pilgrim, "open wide your mouth and I'll go in again to untie the rope."

Greatly alarmed, the old demon said, "Once you go in, you might refuse to come out again. That's too hard! That's too hard!" Pilgrim said, "I have the ability to untie the rope from the outside. After I have done so, are you really planning to escort my master across this mountain?"

"The moment you untie it," replied the old demon, "we'll escort him at once. I dare not lie." When he ascertained that the old demon was speaking the truth, the Great Sage shook his body once and retrieved his hair; immediately the fiend felt no pain in his heart. (That was the deceptive magic of the Great Sage Sun, you see, when he fastened the demon's heart with a piece of hair. When the hair was retrieved, the fiend's heart no longer ached.)

Leaping up together, the three fiends thanked the Great Sage, saying, "Please go back first, Great Sage, and tell the T'ang monk to pack up his things. We'll bring a palanquin along to escort him." The various fiends all put away their weapons and went back to their cave.

After the Great Sage had put away his rope, he went straight back to the east side of the mountain, where from a great distance he could already see the T'ang monk rolling all over the ground and wailing loudly. Chu Pa-chieh and Sha Monk had the wrap untied and were just in the process of dividing up the contents. "I needn't be told whose doing this is!" sighed Pilgrim to himself. "Pa-chieh must have in-informed Master that I was devoured by the monster-spirit. Master is wailing because he can't bear to part with me, but that Idiot is dividing things up so he can run off. Alas, I wonder if I've got the right interpretation! I'll call Master and see what happens." He dropped down from the clouds and cried, "Master!"

On hearing this, Sha Monk at once began to berate Pa-chieh saying, "You are

A sure coffin-maker

Who does in ev'ry taker!

Elder Brother is still alive, but you said he was dead so you could engage in your shoddy business here. Isn't he the one calling now?"

"I clearly saw him being swallowed by the monster-spirit with one gulp," said Pa-chieh. "This must be an unlucky day, I suppose, and his spirit has returned to haunt us." Going straight up to him, Pilgrim gave Pa-chieh's face a whack that sent him stumbling. "Coolie," he shouted, "am I haunting you?"

Rubbing his face, Pa-chieh said, "Elder Brother, you were devoured by that fiend. You . . . how could you come alive again?"

"I'm no useless moron like you!" replied Pilgrim. "So he ate me, but I scratched his guts and pinched his lungs. I also put a rope through his heart and pulled at him until the pain was unbearable. Everyone of them kowtowed and pleaded with me. Only then did I spare their lives. They are now preparing a palanquin to take our master across this mountain."

When he heard these words, our Tripitaka scrambled up at once and bowed to Pilgrim, saying, "O disciple! I have caused you great inconvenience! If I had believed Wu-nêng's words completely, I would have been finished." Raising his fists to punch at Pa-chieh, Pilgrim scolded him, saying, "This overstuffed coolie! He's so slothful and so callow! Master, please don't worry any more. Those fiends are coming to take you across the mountain." Even Sha Monk felt embarrassed by these words, so much so that he hurriedly offered a few excuses for Pa-chieh. They then gathered up the luggage and loaded it once more onto the horse's back. We shall now leave them for the moment waiting by the wayside.

We tell you instead about those three demon chiefs, who led the flock of spirits to return to their cave. "Elder Brother," said the second fiend, "I thought Pilgrim Sun was someone endowed with nine heads and eight tails, but I can see what he actually is—a puny little ape! Nevertheless, you shouldn't have swallowed him. If we had just fought with him, he could never have withstood you and me. With these thousands of monster-spirits in our cave, we could have drowned him just by spitting. But you had to swallow him into your stomach, where he could exercise his magic to make you suffer. We certainly didn't dare wage any contest with him then. Just now we said we were planning to escort the T'ang monk. That was all pretense, of course, because your life was more important than anything else. Once we tricked him into coming out, we would never escort that monk."

"Worthy brother," said the old demon, "what is your reason for reneging?" "Give me three thousand little fiends," replied the second fiend, "and put them in battle formation. I have ability enough to capture that ape-head!" "Don't ask for a mere three thousand," said the old demon. "You have my permission to call up the whole camp!

Just catch him, and everyone will have made merit."

The second demon at once called up three thousand little fiends and had them spread out by the side of the main road. A blue banner-carrier was sent to convey this message: "Pilgrim Sun, come out quickly and fight with our Second Father Great King."

When Pa-chieh heard this, he laughed and said, "O Elder Brother! As the proverb says,

A liar can't fool his fellow-villager.

What sort of skulduggery, what sort of hanky-panky is this when you tell us that you've subdued the monster-spirits, that they are fetching a palanquin to escort Master? Now they are here to provoke battle. Why?"

"The old fiend," said Pilgrim, "*was* subdued by me. He wouldn't dare show himself, for if he had caught even a whiff of the name Sun, he would have a headache now! This has to be the second fiendish demon, who can't stand the thought of escorting us. That's the reason for this challenge to battle. Let me tell you something, Brother. Those monster-spirits happen to be three brothers, and they all behave gallantly toward each other. We are also three brothers, but there's no gallantry at all among ourselves. I have already subdued the eldest demon. Now that the second demon has shown himself, the least you can do is to fight with him a bit. Is that too much to ask of you?"

"I'm not scared of him," replied Pa-chieh. "Let me go and wage a battle with him." "If you want to go," said Pilgrim, "go!"

Laughing, Pa-chieh said, "O Elder Brother, I'll go. But lend me that little rope of yours." "What for?" asked Pilgrim. "You don't have the ability to crawl inside his stomach, nor are you capable of fastening it to his heart. Why do you want it?"

"I want it fastened around my waist," said Pa-chieh, "as a lifeline! You and Sha Monk should take hold of it at the other end and then let me go out there to do battle. If you see that I'm winning, loosen the rope and I'll be able to capture the monster. If I lose, however, you must pull me back, so that he won't be able to grab me." Pilgrim smiled to himself, saying, "This is going to be some trick on Idiot!" He did indeed tie the rope around Pa-chieh's waist and urged him to do battle.

Lifting high his muckrake, our Idiot ran up to the ledge of the mountain and cried, "Monster-spirit, come out and fight with your ancestor Chu!" The blue banner-carrier went quickly to report: "Great King, a priest with a long snout and big ears has arrived." The second fiend left the camp at once; when he saw Pa-chieh, he did not utter a word but lifted his lance to stab at his opponent's face. Our Idiot went forward to face him with upraised rake, and the two of them joined in battle before the mountain slope. Hardly had they gone for more than seven or eight rounds, however, when Idiot's hands grew weak and could no longer withstand the demon. Turning his head quickly, he shouted, "Elder Brother, it's getting bad! Pull the lifeline! Pull the lifeline!"

When the Great Sage on this side heard those words, he slackened the rope instead and let go of it. Our Idiot was already fleeing in defeat. The rope tied to his waist, you see, was no hindrance when he was going forward. But when he turned back, because it was hanging loose it quickly became a stumbling-block and tripped him up. He scrambled up only to fall down again. At first he only stumbled, but thereafter he fell snout-first to the ground. Catching up with him, the monster-spirit stretched out his dragonlike trunk and wrapped it around Pa-chieh. Then he went back to the cave in triumph, surrounded by the little fiends all singing victory songs.

When Tripitaka below the mountain slope saw what happened, he berated Pilgrim, saying, "Wu-k'ung, I can't blame Wu-nêng for cursing you to death. I see that there's no love or amity between you brothers at all, only mutual hatred and envy! He was yelling for you to pull the lifeline. How could you not do that and let go of the rope instead? Now he's been harmed. What shall we do?"

"Master," replied Pilgrim, laughing, "you're always so protective, so partial! All right, when old Monkey was taken captive, you didn't show much concern. I was quite dispensable! But no sooner had this Idiot been taken captive than you began to blame me. I want him to suffer a little, for only then will he realize how difficult it is to fetch the scriptures."

"O disciple," said Tripitaka, "you think I wasn't concerned about you when you were captured? But you, after all, are most capable of transforming yourself, and I thought that surely you would not be harmed. That Idiot, however, has a rather cumbersome build, and he's not agile at all. When's he's taken like this, he'll meet more ill than good. You must go rescue him." "Master," said Pilgrim, "don't complain any more. Let me go rescue him."

He bounded quickly up the mountain, but he said spitefully to himself, "Since Idiot wanted to curse me to death, I'm not about to gratify him so easily. I'll follow the monster-spirits and see how they plan to treat him. Let him suffer a little first, and then I'll rescue him." Thereupon he recited a magic spell; with one shake of his body, he changed into a tiny mole-cricket. Darting away, he alighted on the base of one of Pa-chieh's ears and went back to the cave with the monster-spirits. The second demon led the three thousand little fiends, all blowing bugles and beating drums, up to the entrance of the cave where they were to be stationed. He himself took Pa-chieh inside and said, "Elder Brother, I've caught one."

The old fiend said, "Bring him here and let me have a look." The second demon loosened his trunk and flung Pa-chieh on the ground, saying, "Isn't this the one?" "This one," said the old fiend, "is quite useless!"

On hearing this, Pa-chieh spoke up: "Great King, let the useless one go. Find the useful one instead and catch him." "Though he may be useless," said the third fiend, "he is still Chu Pa-chieh, a disciple of the T'ang monk. Let's tie him up and send him to soak in the pond in the back. When his hairs are soaked off, we'll rip open his belly, cure him with salt, and sun-dry him. He'll be good with wine when it turns cloudy."

Horrified, Pa-chieh said, "Finished! Finished! I've run into a fiend who's a pickle merchant." The various fiends all joined in and had Idiot hog-tied before hauling him to the edge of the pond. After shoving him out toward the center of the pond, they turned and left.

The Great Sage flew up into the air to have a look, and he found our Idiot half floating and half submerged in the pond, with his four legs turned upward and his snout downward, snorting and blowing water constantly. He was a laughable sight indeed, like one of those huge black lotus roots of late autumn that has cast its seeds after frost. When the Great Sage saw those features, he was moved to both anger and pity. "What am I to do?" he thought to himself. "He is, after all, a member of Buddha's Birthday Feast. But I'm so mad at him, for at the slightest excuse he will divide up the luggage and try to run off. And he's always egging Master on to cast that Tight-Fillet Spell on me. I heard from Sha Monk the other day that he had managed to put away a few private savings. I wonder if it's true. Let me give him a scare!"

Dear Great Sage! Flying near Pa-chieh's ear, he assumed a different voice and called out: "Chu Wu-nêng! Chu Wu-nêng!" "Of all the rotten luck!" mumbled an apprehensive Pa-chieh. "Wu-nêng happens to be a name given to me by the Bodhisattva Kuan-shih-yin. Since I followed the T'ang monk, I have also been called Pa-chieh. How is it that someone at this place should know me as Wu-nêng?" Unable to restrain himself, Idiot asked, "Who is calling me by my religious name?"

"It is I," replied Pilgrim. "Who are you?" asked Idiot, and Pilgrim said, "I'm a summoner."

"Officer," said Idiot, growing more and more alarmed, "where did you come from?"

Pilgrim said, "I've been sent by the Fifth Yama King to summon you." "Officer," said Idiot, "please go back. Inform the Fifth Yama King that, for the excellent friendship he enjoys with my elder brother, Sun Wu-k'ung, I should be spared one more day. Have me summoned tomorrow." "Rubbish!" replied Pilgrim. "As the proverb says,

When Yama at third watch wants you to die,

Who dares detain you till fourth watch goes by?

Hurry up and follow me, so I don't have to put the rope on you and pull you along."

"Officer," said Idiot, "I'm asking no big favor of you. Just look at my face. You think I can live? I know I'm going to die, but I want to wait one more day—until those monster-spirits have my master and the rest of them captured and brought here. We can then enjoy a last reunion before we all expire."

"All right," said Pilgrim, smiling to himself, "I have about thirty other people here to be rounded up. Let me go get them first, and that'll give you another day. You have any travel money? Give me some." Idiot said, "How pitiable! Where does a person who has left home have any travel money?" "If not," said Pilgrim, "I'll rope you up and you can follow me!" "Officer," cried Pa-chieh, horrified, "please don't rope me! I know that little rope of yours has the name of the Life-Dispatching Cord. Once you put it on me, I'll breath my last. Yes! Yes! Yes! I do have a little, but not much." "Where is it?" demanded Pilgrim. "Take it out quickly!"

"Pity! Pity!" replied Pa-chieh. "Since I became a priest, I have bumped into a few philanthropic families who wanted to feed the monks. When they saw that I had a large appetite, they handed me a few pennies more than they gave my companions. Altogether I have managed to save about five mace[3] of silver, but all that loose cash is hard to carry. When I last visited a city, I asked a silversmith to have it forged into a single piece. He turned out to be most unscrupulous, for he stole a few candareen and I was left with a piece of silver weighing but four mace and six candareen. You may take it."

"This Idiot," said Pilgrim to himself, smiling, "doesn't even have a pair of pants on him. Where can he be hiding it?" He said, "Hey, where's your silver?"

"It's stuffed inside my left ear," replied Pa-chieh. "I'm all tied up, and I can't get it for you. Take it out yourself."

On hearing this, Pilgrim reached into the ear and found the piece of silver: shaped like a saddle, it did in fact weigh about four mace and six candareen. When he took hold of it, he could no longer refrain from letting out a loud guffaw. Recognizing at once that it was the voice of Pilgrim, our Idiot, floating in the water, began to let loose a string of abuses. "You damned Pi-ma-wên!" he cried. "I'm in such straits already, and you have to come extort money from me!"

"You overstuffed pig!" said Pilgrim, laughing. "In his attempt to protect Master, old Monkey has undergone who knows how much affliction. But you even manage to stash away private savings!" "Shame on you!" replied Pa-chieh. "What sort of private savings is this? It's something that has been shaved off my teeth! I couldn't bring myself to spend it on my mouth. I was hoping to save it for one garment on my back, but you have to scare it out of me. Give me back a little of that silver!" "Not even half a candareen," answered Pilgrim.

"I'll give it to you as ransom money then," scolded Pa-chieh, "but you'd better rescue me." "Don't be impatient," said Pilgrim. "I'll rescue you."

He put away the silver and changed back into his original form; with the iron rod he teased and guided Idiot in and then hauled him out of the pond by his feet. After he was untied, Pa-chieh leaped up and took off his shirt to wring out the water. Shaking it a couple of times, he draped it on his body again, still dripping wet. "Elder Brother," he said, "open the back door and let's scram!"

"Escaping through the back door," said Pilgrim, "is that manly behavior? Let's fight our way out through the front door." Pa-chieh said, "But my feet are numb from being tied up. I can't move." "Just be quick and follow me," said Pilgrim.

Dear Great Sage! He opened up with his iron rod and fought his way out; Pa-chieh, though still feeling the numbness, had no choice but to follow him. When they reached the second-level door, they found the muckrake standing there. Pushing the little fiends aside, Pa-chieh grabbed his weapon and began to rain blows left and right. After he and Pilgrim went through those three or four levels of door in this manner, they managed to slaughter countless little fiends. When the old demon heard of it, he said to the second demon, "That's some fine person you've caught! Now look at what Pilgrim Sun has done! He has robbed us of Chu Pa-chieh and they have struck down the little fiends at our door!"

Leaping up hurriedly, the second demon grasped the lance and ran out of the main gate. "Brazen ape!" he shouted in a loud voice. "You insolent creature! How dare you insult us like this!"

On hearing this, the Great Sage stood still, while the fiendish creature, without another word, attacked at once with the lance. Pilgrim, the expert (as it were) was not exercised; wielding his iron rod, he faced his opponent head on. Thus the two of them began a magnificent battle outside the cave:

An old, yellow-tusked elephant became a man
And sworn bond-brother to a lion king.
Because the big demon prodded and urged,
They all plotted to eat the priest of T'ang.
Great Sage, Equal to Heav'n, of vast magic powers
Would help the Right to quell the spirits perverse.
Inept Pa-chieh fell to malicious hands,
But Wu-k'ung saved him, got him out the door.
When the fiend king gave chase, flaunting his strength,
Rod and lance joined up, each showing its might.
The lance of that one came like a python slicing through the woods;
The rod of this one soared like a dragon rising from the sea.
The dragon, cloud-shrouded, rose from the sea;
The python, mist-enwrapped, sliced through the woods.
Come to think of it, 'twas for the T'ang monk
That they strove bitterly without restraint.

Though that Pa-chieh saw the Great Sage fighting with the monster-spirit, he did not step forward to help his companion at all. Standing the muckrake on the ground at the mouth of the mountain, he merely stood there and stared dumbly at them. When the monster-spirit saw how heavy Pilgrim's rod was, how tautly executed were his thrusts and parries, without the slightest hint of weakness or mistake, he blocked the rod with his lance and stretched out his trunk to seize his opponent. Pilgrim, however, knew exactly what was happening; raising the golden-hooped rod horizontally high above his own head with both hands, he permitted the monster-spirit to wrap his trunk around his waist, but his hands remained free. Look at him! His two hands played with the rod on top of the monster-spirits' trunk like a drum majorette twirling a baton!

When he saw that, Pa-chieh beat his breast and cried, "Alas, that monster-spirit's so unfortunate! When he caught hold of a ruffian like me, he had even my hands wrapped up so that I could not move at all. But when he caught hold of a slippery creature, he didn't bother to wrap up his hands. All those two hands need to do is to jab the rod into his trunk. There'll be pain and snivel in that nostril. How could he hold on to his prisoner?"

Now Pilgrim actually had not thought of doing that, but this time Pa-chieh managed to give him an idea. Waving the rod once to turn it into a staff over ten feet long and having the thickness of a chicken egg, he jabbed it into the monster's trunk. Horrified, the monster-spirit loosened his hold at once with a loud snort. Pilgrim changed hands and, grabbing hold of the trunk, gave it a mighty tug. To lessen his pain, the monster-spirit walked forward in the direction he was pulled. Only then did Pa-chieh have the courage to approach them and rain blows onto the monster-spirit's side with his muckrake.

"No! No!" cried Pilgrim. "You have sharp teeth on your rake. If you puncture his skin and make him bleed, Master will blame us again for hurting life when he sees this. Just hit him with your rake handle."

Accordingly, our Idiot lifted the rake handle and gave the monster a blow with each step he took, while Pilgrim pulled him in front by the trunk. Like two elephant tenders, they herded the monster down the slope, where Tripitaka stood waiting with unblinking eyes. When he caught sight of them approaching noisily, he called out, "Wu-ching, can you see what it is that Wu-k'ung is dragging along?"

Sha Monk took one look and said, smiling, "Master, Big Brother is pulling a monster-spirit by his trunk. What a lovely sight!"

"My goodness! My goodness!" said Tripitaka. "Such a huge monster-spirit! And what a long nose he has! Go and tell him, if he is gracious enough to escort us across this mountain, we'll spare him. We shouldn't hurt his life."

Hurrying forward to meet them, Sha Monk said in a loud voice, "Master says not to hurt him if that fiend is willing to escort us across this mountain." On hearing this the fiend immediately went to his knees and made a sort of wheezing reply. Since his trunk was gripped by Pilgrim, you see, he sounded as if he had a severe cold. "Venerable Father T'ang," he huffed, "if you're willing to spare my life, we'll fetch a palanquin to escort you."

Pilgrim said, "We master and disciples are all gracious winners. We believe you, and we'll spare your life. Go fetch the palanquin quickly. If you change your mind again, we'll certainly not spare you once we capture you." After he had been freed, the fiend kowtowed and left, while Pilgrim and Pa-chieh gave a full report to the T'ang monk. Overcome by embarrassment, Pa-chieh began sunning his clothes in front of the slope to dry them, and we shall leave them for the moment.

The second demon, trembling all over, went back to the cave. Before he arrived, the little fiends had already made the report that he was taken captive and led away by the trunk. In dismay, the old demon and the third demon were just in the process of leading the troops out when they saw the second demon returning alone. After they had welcomed him back and asked him what had happened, the second demon gave them a complete account of the T'ang monk's kind words and the claim of being a gracious winner. As they stared at each other, no one dared speak up for a long time. Then the second demon said, "Elder Brother, are we ready to escort the T'ang monk?"

"What are you saying, Brother?" said the old demon. "Pilgrim Sun is in truth a kind and benevolent ape. When he was first in my belly, he could have finished me off a thousand times if he wanted to harm me. Just now, when he caught hold of your trunk, he could have given you a lot of trouble if he had refused to set you free and squeezed the tip of your trunk until it was punctured. Let's make the necessary preparations quickly and go escort them."

"Yes, let's escort them! Let's escort them!" said the third demon with a laugh.

"Worthy Brother," said the old demon, "you sound as if you are miffed. If you don't want to escort them, the two of us will go instead."

"Let me inform my two elder brothers," said the third demon, laughing some more. "If those priests did not want us to escort them and simply chose to sneak across this mountain, they would have been lucky. But since they insisted on our escorting them, they would certainly fall into my ploy of 'Seducing the Tiger to Leave Its Mountain.'"

"What do you mean by 'Seducing the Tiger to Leave Its Mountain?'" asked the old fiend.

"Call up all the fiends in our cave," replied the third fiend. "We'll select a thousand from ten thousand of them, a hundred from that thousand, and then sixteen from that hundred. In addition, we want to select thirty more."

"Why is it," asked the old fiend, "that you want to select sixteen little fiends and then thirty more?"

"The thirty little fiends," replied the third demon, "will be selected for their culinary skills. We'll give them some fine rice, thin noodles, bamboo shoots, tea sprouts, fragrant mushrooms, straw mushrooms, bean curds, and wheat glutens, along with the order that they should set up camp at every twenty- or thirty-mile interval to prepare meals for the T'ang monk." "And what do you want the sixteen fiends for?" asked the old fiend.

"Eight of them will haul the palanquin," said the third fiend, "and eight will shout to clear the way. We three brothers will accompany all of them for a distance. Some four hundred miles west of here will be my city, where I will have my men and horses to relieve us. Once we get near the city, all we need do is this, this, and this, so that those master and disciples will have no chance at all to look after each other. If we want to seize the T'ang monk, we'll have to rely on those sixteen demons to bring us success."

When he heard these words, the old fiend could not have been more pleased; it was as if he indeed had snapped out of a hangover or awakened from a dream. "Marvelous! Marvelous! Marvelous!" he cried, and he at once called together all the fiends. He first selected the thirty members to whom he gave the foodstuff. Then he selected sixteen of them and they were told to haul out a palanquin made of fragrant vines. As they walked out the door, he gave them this instruction also: "You are not permitted to wander off somewhere in the mountain. Pilgrim Sun happens to be a monkey full of suspicions. If he sees all of you milling about, he may suspect something and see through our plot."

Leading the throng up to the side of the main road, the old fiend cried out in a loud voice: "Venerable Father T'ang, today does not clash with the dread day of Red Sand.⁴ We are here to invite the Venerable Father to cross this mountain."

On hearing this, Tripitaka said, "Wu-k'ung, who are those people that are calling me?" Pointing with his finger, Pilgrim said, "That's the monster-spirit old Monkey subdued. He has brought a palanquin to escort you."

"My goodness! My goodness!" said Tripitaka, his palms pressed together as he bowed to Heaven. "If it hadn't been for the ability of my worthy disciple, how would I be able to proceed?" He then went forward to salute the various fiends, saying, "I am greatly beholden to your love. When this disciple returns eastward with the scriptures, he will proclaim your virtuous fruits to the multitudes of Ch'ang-an."

As they kowtowed, the fiends said, "Let the Venerable Father ascend the carriage." Being of fleshly eyes and mortal stock, that Tripitaka did not perceive that this was a trick. The Great Sage Sun, too, was a golden immortal of the Great Monad, who was by nature honest and upright. Since he thought that the experience of captivity and release had truly subdued the fiend, he did not expect any intrigue nor did he examine the situation carefully before he complied with his master's wishes. After telling Pa-chieh to load the luggage onto the horse and Sha Monk to follow the rear, he himself took up the lead, his iron rod resting across his shoulders. Eight of the little fiends lifted up the palanquin while eight others shouted to clear the way. With the fiend chiefs supporting the carrying-poles of the palanquin on both sides, the master sat amiably in the middle of the carriage as they took the main road up to the tall mountain.

Little did they realize, however, that once they were under way, sorrow would arrive in the midst of gladness. As a Classic says, "At prosperity's end reversal's born."

They'll meet Jupiter in their fated hour
And baleful spirits of those hung to death!

That group of fiendish demons, of course, were most united in their efforts to gather around Tripitaka and most diligent in their service to him night and day. Hardly had they traveled thirty miles before they presented him with a vegetarian meal, and when they reached fifty miles, they fed him again. They even stopped before it was quite dark so that the master could rest. Throughout this leg of the journey, the fiends behaved most properly, and the pilgrims in their daily meals were fed to their hearts' content. When they paused to rest, they found a nice place where they could sleep soundly.

They proceeded in this manner toward the West for some four hundred miles, and they suddenly found themselves approaching a

city. The Great Sage, his iron rod uplifted, was walking about a mile
ahead of the entourage, when the sight of that city gave him such a
fright that he fell to the ground, hardly able to get up. Since he had
always been so bold, you ask, what was it about the sight of that city
that so terrified him? He discovered, you see, that the city was full of
vicious miasmas. It was

Crowded with fiends and monstrous demons;
At four gates were all rapacious spirits.
Their commander was an old striped tiger;
Their captain, a white-faced, ferocious cat.
Deer with jagged horns did carry their mail,
And wily foxes walked along the roads.
Circling the city were thousand-foot snakes
And huge, long serpents blocked the thoroughfares.
Grey wolves barked orders beneath the towers;
Leopards guarding arbors roared like humans.
Those waving flags and beating drums were fiends all;
Watchmen and patrol, all mountain spirits.
Cunning hares opened doors to ply their trade;
Wild boars toted their loads to do commerce.
This in years past was a great and noble court.
Now it's a city of tigers and wolves.

As the Great Sage lay there nursing his fear, he suddenly heard the
sound of wind behind his ears. He spun around to discover the third
demon with both hands aiming a square-sky halberd directly at his
head. Leaping up, the Great Sage wielded his golden-hooped rod to
face his adversary. The two of them, both thoroughly aroused,

Huffed and puffed, without exchanging a word;
Clenched their teeth, as each wanted to fight.

Then the old demon chief appeared and, after shouting an order, lifted
up his steel scimitar to hack at Pa-chieh. Hurriedly abandoning the
horse, Pa-chieh attacked with his muckrake. The second demon also
grasped his lance to stab at Sha Monk, who parried the blow at once
with his fiend-routing staff. Thus three demon chiefs and three monks,
each engaging the other, began a most bitter battle right on top of that
mountain. Those sixteen little fiends, all obeying the command, immediately went into action: they grabbed the white horse and the
luggage before they overpowered Tripitaka in his palanquin, hauling
him forward until they reached the edge of the city. "By the scheme of

our Father Great Kings," they shouted, "we've caught the T'ang monk here!"

Those monster-spirits in the city, old and young, all ran down and opened wide the city gate. At the same time, they immediately gave the order that all the banners should be rolled up and the drums stopped; there were to be no battle cries or the beating of gongs. "The Great King had told us before," they said, "that we were not to frighten the T'ang monk. The T'ang monk could not withstand fear, for once he was frightened, his flesh would turn sour, and he wouldn't be good to eat." All those fiends,

In great delight, beckoned Tripitaka;
Each bowing, they received the master priest.

They took the T'ang monk and his palanquin and carried him right up to the Hall of Golden Chimes, where they invited him to take a seat in the center and presented him with tea and rice. As they swarmed all over him, the elder was in a daze, for not a single person familiar to him met his sight. We do not know what will happen to his life, and you must listen to the explanation in the next chapter.

Seventy-seven

Various demons prey on native Nature;
Unified Self bows to Bhūtatathatā.

We shall not tell you for the moment about the affliction of the Elder
T'ang. Instead, we shall speak of those three demon chiefs, all united
in their minds and efforts, who were engaged in a strenuous conflict
with the Great Sage and his brothers halfway up the mountain east of
the city, a battle that was something like
    An iron brush scrubbing a copper pan:
    Each party's tough and hard.
What a fight!
    Six substances and forms,[1] six weapons;
    Six body features and six sentiments;
    Six evils of six organs from six desires;[2]
    A contest waged on six ways of rebirth.[3]
    In the comforts of spring of Thirty-six Halls,[4]
    Each of six forms or features[5] had a name.
    This one's golden-hooped rod
    Had thousands of styles;
    That one's square-sky halberd
    Was fierce in a hundred ways.
    Pa-chieh's muckrake was savage and strong;
    The second fiend's lance, able and in good form.
    Young Sha Monk's treasure staff, a wondrous thing,
    Had intent to kill;
    Old demon chief's steel scimitar, fine and sharp,
    Would spare none, once upraised.
    These three were a true monk's guardians whom none could
        withstand;
    Those three were brazen wild spirits who mocked both lord and
        law.
    At first it was so-so,
    Then the battle turned fierce;

When six persons all used the magic of flight,
They each tumbled and turned on the edge of clouds.
In a moment the belched out mist and fog darkened Heaven and
    Earth,
And all you heard were the growls and roars.

The six of them fought for a long time until gradually dusk settled in;
since the sky was already misty and a strong gust was blowing, it
became completely dark in no time at all.

Now Pa-chieh already had huge ears which hovered over his eyes,
making the world seem more opaque than ever to him. His arms and
legs slackened, and he no longer was able to parry the blows. As he
turned to flee in defeat, his muckrake trailing behind him, the old
demon gave him a blow with the scimitar that almost took his life. It
was fortunate that he missed Pa-chieh's head, but a few bristles on
his neck were shaved off. He was, however, chased down by the old
demon, who opened wide his mouth and caught Pa-chieh by the
collar. The demon took his prisoner into the city, threw him to the
little fiends to have him bound in the Hall of Golden Chimes, and then
mounted the clouds once more to join in the battle.

When Sha Monk saw that things were going badly, he turned to
flee after one last halfhearted blow with his treasure staff. The second
fiend flung out his trunk with a snort and wrapped him up, hands and
all. He was brought into the city, where the little fiends were instructed
to have him bound beneath the steps of the hall also. Then the second
fiend rose into the air to try to capture Pilgrim.

When Pilgrim saw that his two brothers had fallen into captivity,
he realized he was unable to oppose three adversaries. As the saying
goes,

Even a good hand can't withstand two fists;
And two fists can't oppose four hands.

With a cry, he broke through the weapons of those three fiendish
demons and fled by mounting the cloud-somersault. When the third
fiend saw Pilgrim somersaulting away, he shook himself and revealed
his original form. Flapping both his wings, he immediately caught up
with the Great Sage.

How could he do so so readily, you ask. When Pilgrim caused great
disturbance in the Celestial Palace, even one hundred thousand warriors from Heaven could not catch hold of him, for a single cloud-
somersault of his would traverse the distance of one hundred and eight

thousand miles. But one flap of this monster-spirit's wing, however, could cover ninety thousand miles, and thus two flaps, in fact, would send him past the Great Sage. That was how the Great Sage fell into his clutches. The grip of the fiend was so firm that he could not move left or right at all, nor could he even exercise his magic power to escape; for when he enlarged himself, the fiend's clutch would loosen somewhat, and when he reduced his size, the fiend tightened his grip accordingly. He was thus taken back to the city, dropped to the ground, and he too was bound and placed together with Pa-chieh and Sha Monk. As the old demon and the second demon came forward to meet him, the third demon joined them to ascend the treasure hall. Ah! Little did they realize that they had not bound Pilgrim; it was more like sending him off!

It was about the hour of the second watch, when all those fiends, after they had greeted each other, pushed the T'ang monk down the steps of the hall. When the lamplight revealed to the elder his three disciples all bound up and lying on the ground, he fell down at Pilgrim's side. "O disciple!" he sobbed. "When we met with an ordeal, it was customary for you to exercise your magic powers outside so that you could seek assistance, when necessary, to subdue the demons. This time even *you* have been taken. How could this poor monk lay claim to his life?"

When Pa-chieh and Sha Monk heard these words of anguish from their master, they, too, began to wail. Pilgrim, however, replied with a smile, "Master, relax! And stop crying, brothers! Let them do what they will, but you will not be harmed. Let the old demons quiet down first, and we'll be on our way."

"O Elder Brother," said Pa-chieh, "you're fibbing again! Look at the way I'm tied up! When the ropes are just the least bit loosened, they immediately spit some water on them to make them tighter. A skinny fellow like you probably doesn't feel a thing, but that's a plague on a fatso like me! If you don't believe me, just look at my shoulders. The ropes have cut at least two inches into my flesh. How could we escape?"

"Not to mention the fact that we're bound by hemp ropes," said Pilgrim with a laugh. "Even if they use coir cables as thick as a rice bowl, I'll treat the matter as lightly as an autumn breeze blowing past my ears! You needn't wonder about that!"

As the three brothers were conversing, they also heard the old demon say: "Our Third Worthy Brother is most capable and most intelligent! His marvelous plan did indeed succeed in capturing the T'ang monk! Little ones, five of you will go bail water; seven of you will scrub the pots; ten of you will start the fire; and twenty of you will go fetch the iron steamer. Let's have those four monks steamed for us brothers to enjoy. We'll give each of you a small piece of their flesh so that you can all attain long life too."

On hearing this, Pa-chieh shook all over and said, "Elder Brother, listen to that! That monster-spirit's planning to have us steamed and eaten!" "Don't be afraid," said Pilgrim. "Let me see if he's a rookie or an old pro of a monster-spirit."

"O Elder Brother," said Sha Monk, "stop this idle chitchat! We're about to become neighbors of King Yama, and you're still talking about rookie or old pro!" He had barely finished speaking when they heard the second fiend say, "It's not easy to steam Chu Pa-chieh."

Delighted, Pa-chieh said, "Amitābha! Who's accumulating secret merit by saying it's not easy to steam me?" "If it isn't," said the third fiend, "let's skin him first before we steam him."

Horrified, Pa-chieh yelled, "Don't skin me! I may be coarse, but the moment the water gurgles, I'll turn soft!" The old fiend said, "The one not easily steamed should be placed in the bottom layer."

"Don't be afraid, Pa-chieh," said Pilgrim, laughing. "He's a rookie, not an old pro." "How d'you know?" said Sha Monk.

Pilgrim said, "Whenever you steam anything, the stuff placed on top always gets done first. That's why you always put the toughest foodstuff in the top layer of the steamer; build up the fire until the hottest steam gets up there, and everything will be fine. But if it is placed in the bottom layer where the steam doesn't get through that easily, you can steam the stuff for half a year and it still may not be cooked. He said just now that Pa-chieh was not easy to steam, but he still wanted to put him in the bottom layer. Isn't he a rookie?"

"O Elder Brother!" said Pa-chieh. "The way you talk, you sound as if you want me to be tortured alive! When they are hard-pressed and see that I'm not fully steamed, they'll pull off the steamer, flip me over, and build up the fire again. I'll then be cooked on both sides but still raw inside, won't I?"

As they were thus conversing, one of the little fiends went up to report: "The water's boiling." The old fiend gave the order at once for the various fiends to haul Pa-chieh into the bottom layer and Sha

Monk into the second. Suspecting that he would be next, Pilgrim decided it was time to leave, saying to himself, "I should be able to do something by this lamplight!" He pulled off a piece of hair and blew his immortal breath onto it, crying, "Change!" It changed at once into a Pilgrim bound by the hemp ropes. His true body rose with his spirit into the air, where he stood still and peered downward. Those fiends, of course, could not tell the true from the false: the moment they came upon the false Pilgrim, they lifted him up and placed him inside the third layer. Only then did they push the T'ang monk to the ground, hog-tie him, and place him in the fourth layer. Fueled by dried wood, a terrific blaze soon flared up.

Perched on the edge of the clouds, the Great Sage sighed to himself: "That Pa-chieh and Sha Monk of mine can still manage to withstand perhaps two seconds of boiling. But my master, all it takes is one second and he'll turn soft! If I don't use magic to save him, he'll perish this instant!" Dear Pilgrim! Making the magic sign in midair, he recited:

Let *Oṁ* and *Ram* purify the dharma realm;

Ch'ien: Origination, Penetration, Harmony, and Firmness.[6]

This spell at once caused the Dragon King of North Sea to arrive in the midst of a dark cloud, crying, "Ao-shun, the little dragon from North Sea, kowtows to you." "Please rise! Please rise!" said Pilgrim. "I wouldn't have bothered you without cause. I came here with Master T'ang, who was caught by these vicious demons. He has been placed inside that iron steamer to be steamed. Please go and give him some protection so that he won't be destroyed." The dragon king immediately changed himself into a cold gust of wind that blew toward the large pan. As it circled around the bottom of the pan, the three inside the steamer felt no heat at all, and that was how their lives were preserved.

Toward the end of the hour of the third watch, the old demon was heard saying, "Subordinates, we plotted and strained ourselves in order to catch the T'ang monk and his three companions, but that effort in escorting them cost us four sleepless days and nights. Now that they are bound inside the steamer, I doubt that they will be able to escape. All of you, however, should take good care in guarding them, and ten of you little fiends should take turns in tending the fire. Let us retire to our bedchambers and rest a little. By the fifth watch, when it's about dawn, they will certainly be softened. You may prepare minced garlic, salt, and vinegar and awake us for the feast." The fiends all obeyed this instruction, while the three demon chiefs went to their bedrooms.

Standing on the edge of the clouds, Pilgrim heard everything clearly. He then lowered the direction of his cloud slightly, but he could hear no voices coming from the steamer. "When the fire is built up," he thought to himself, "there must be heat. Why aren't they afraid of it? And there's not a word from them? Ha, could they be dead already? I'll go nearer and listen again." Dear Great Sage! As he trod the clouds, he shook his body and changed immediately into a little black fly to alight on the trellised frame of the steamer.

"What rotten luck! What rotten luck!" he heard Pa-chieh mumbling inside. "I wonder if we are being steamed the stuffy or the airy way."

"What do you mean by that, Second Elder Brother?" asked Sha Monk. "The stuffy way," replied Pa-chieh, "the cover of the steamer will be put on. The airy way, the cover will not be used."

"Disciples," answered Tripitaka from the very top layer, "the steamer hasn't been covered." "How lucky!" exclaimed Pa-chieh. "We're not going to die yet tonight. This is steaming the airy way."

When Pilgrim heard them speaking like that, he knew that they had not been harmed. Flying up, he picked up the cover of the iron steamer and gently put it on. "Disciples," said a horrified Tripitaka, "it's covered now!"

"We're finished!" said Pa-chieh. "This is steaming the stuffy way. This night we'll die for sure!" Whereupon Sha Monk and the elder began to weep.

"Let's not cry just yet," said Pa-chieh. "I think a fresh batch of fiends have come to tend the fire." "How do you know?" asked Sha Monk. "When we were first placed in the steamer," said Pa-chieh, "it was an ideal situation for me. I'm suffering from a little arthritis, and I want that hot steam. Right now, however, there seems to be cold air coming up from the pan instead. Hey, you officers tending the fire! Why don't you add some wood? What are you good for?"

"This coolie!" said Pilgrim to himself, unable to restrain a giggle. "Doesn't he know that he can withstand the chill, but heat will kill him? If he talks any more like that, everything will be revealed. I must hurry and rescue him. But wait! To rescue him I must change back into my true form. When those ten fiends tending the fire see me, they will certainly make a raucous noise and disturb the old fiends. Wouldn't that be a nuisance? Let me send them a little of my magic; I remember that when I was a Great Sage in Heaven, I once had a game of finger-guessing with Dhṛtarāṣṭra at the North Heavenly Gate.[7] I won some sleep-inducing insects from him, and I still have a few of them here. Let me give them to the fiends." He felt around his waist and found that he had a dozen of those insects left. "I'm going to send them ten of these," he said to himself, "and I'll keep two for breeding."

He flung the insects on the faces of those little fiends; as soon as they crawled into their nostrils, the fiends began to snore and fell asleep. One of them, however, was in charge of the fire fork and could not be induced to sleep soundly. Rubbing his head and face, this little fiend pinched and tweaked his own nose left and right, sneezing constantly. "This fellow," said Pilgrim, "seems to know the business! I'll give him a 'Double-Handled Lamp.'" He threw one more insect on the fiend's face, thinking to himself: "With two insects running in and out of his nostrils, at least one should pacify him!" After two or three huge yawns, that little fiend stretched, abandoned his fire tong, and fell fast asleep without moving again.

"This little magic," said Pilgrim to himself, "is truly both marvelous and efficacious!" He changed back into his original form to walk near the steamer, crying, "Master!"

On hearing this, the T'ang monk said, "Wu-k'ung, save me!" "Elder Brother," said Sha Monk, "are you calling from the outside?"

"If I'm not outside," said Pilgrim, "you think I'm suffering with you inside?" "O Elder Brother," said Pa-chieh, "it's always the same! The slippery one will slip away, but we are left behind to suffocate in here!"

"Don't make so much noise, Idiot," said Pilgrim, laughing. "I'm here to rescue you." "If you want to rescue me, Elder Brother," said Pa-chieh, "you must do a thorough job of it. Don't let them put me back in the steamer!"

Pilgrim then lifted up the cover and untied his master. After shaking himself to retrieve his hair that had changed into the specious Pilgrim, he went through the other two layers to free Sha Monk and Pa-chieh. The moment he was untied, our Idiot wanted to flee. "Don't be in such a hurry! Don't be in such a hurry!" said Pilgrim, and recited a spell to dismiss the dragon god. Finally, he said to Pa-chieh, "There are still tall mountains and rugged peaks in the rest of our journey to the Western Heaven. Without a beast of burden, Master will find it exceedingly difficult to proceed. I must still go get our horse."

Look at him! With nimble hands and feet, he dashed inside the Hall of Golden Chimes, where he saw that the various fiends, old and young, were all asleep. Without disturbing any of them, he managed to untie the reins. Now, that animal was originally a dragon horse; if someone unfamiliar had untied him, he would have let fly both his hind legs and neighed. But Pilgrim, you see, had been a stableman; in fact, he had received the rank of Pi-ma-wên. Moreover, the horse recognized him; so he neither kicked nor neighed. Quietly leading him forward, Pilgrim tightened the girth and fixed up the saddle properly before asking his master to mount. After the elder, still trembling all over, had climbed onto the horse, he too wanted to leave at once.

"Let's not hurry," said Pilgrim. "There are kings out there on the road to the west. We must have our travel rescript before we can proceed. Otherwise, what sort of passport do we have? Let me go find the luggage." "I recall," the T'ang monk said, "that after we entered the door, these fiends placed our luggage to the left of the main hall. Even the pole is standing there below the steps." "I know," replied Pilgrim.

He bounded into the treasure hall to look, and all at once he caught sight of flashes of light, which made him realize that the luggage was there. How did he know, you ask. Because the T'ang monk's brocaded cassock had on it the luminescent pearl[8] that glowed at night. As Pilgrim drew near, he saw that both the luggage and the pole were untouched. He brought them out quickly and told Sha Monk to pick up the pole.

With Pa-chieh leading the horse and Pilgrim the way, they headed straight for the Central Gate of the Sun in front. Soon, however, the loud rattle of sentinel bells could be heard, and they saw that the door had a lock, and a seal was taped over the lock. "How could we penetrate this kind of defense?" said Pilgrim. "Let's go to the back door instead," said Pa-chieh.

Pilgrim led the way toward the back door, only to return with this observation: "I can hear sentinel bells outside the Rear Gate of the Servants as well, and that door too is locked and sealed. What shall we do? In such a situation, if it hadn't been for the mortal frame of the T'ang monk, the three of us could certainly escape by mounting the clouds and wind, regardless of where we were. But the T'ang monk has yet to transcend the three realms, for he still lives within the world of the five phases. His whole body has nothing but carnal bones bequeathed by his parents. He can't rise into the air. It'll be hard for us to escape."

"Elder Brother," said Pa-chieh, "there's no need for further talk. Let's find some place where there are no sentinel bells or guards. We'll lift Master up the wall and let him climb over it."

"That's not so good," replied Pilgrim, laughing. "Right now we may be forced to drag him over the wall like that, but when we return with the scriptures, I'm afraid that your loose idiotic mouth will be spreading word everywhere that we're wall-climbing priests!"⁹ "But you can't worry about behavior now!" said Pa-chieh. "We've got to flee for our lives!" Pilgrim had little choice but to agree with him; they located a section of the wall that was unguarded and began to scale it.

Alas, this was what had to happen! The star of calamity, as it were, had refused to release Tripitaka. As those three demon chiefs slept in their chambers, they were suddenly awakened by some commotion about the T'ang monk having escaped. Dressing hurriedly, they all ascended to the treasure hall and shouted the question, "How many times has the water boiled?"

Those little fiends tending the fire who had been put out by the sleep-inducing insects were sleeping so soundly that they could not be awakened even when beaten. Several others, who had no particular responsibilities, started up and answered confusedly, "Se- . . . se- . . . se- . . . seven times!" As they ran up to the pan, however, they saw that the several layers of the steamer were all thrown on the ground, while those supposed to tend the fire were still fast asleep. Horrified, the little fiends ran back to report, "Great King, they . . . they . . . they have escaped!"

Hurrying down the hall, the three demon chiefs went forward to take a careful look at the pan: indeed they discovered that the layers of the steamer were strewn on the ground while both water and pan had turned cold because the fire was about to die out. Those tending the fire, however, were still snoring away. So astonished were the various fiends that they all shouted: "Seize the T'ang monk quickly! Seize the T'ang monk quickly!"

All that hubbub immediately aroused the rest of the monster-spirits, old and young. Clutching cutlasses and lances, they swarmed from front and back up to the Central Gate of the Sun, where they found that neither lock nor seal had been touched, and heard the continuous rattle of the sentinel bells. They asked those on night patrol outside the door, "Where did the T'ang monk escape?" The reply was that no one had come through the door. When they then rushed to the Rear Gate of the Servants, again they found that the seal, the lock, and the sentinel bells were like those out in front. The entire throng then spread out with torches and lanterns, lighting up the whole place until it was bright as day, and then they caught clear sight of the four pilgrims attempting to scale the wall.

"Where are you running?" roared the old demon as he dashed up to them. His legs weakened and his tendons numbed by fear, the elder fell down at once from the wall and was caught by the old demon. While the second demon seized Sha Monk and the third demon pinned down Pa-chieh, the rest of the fiends took the luggage and the white horse. Only Pilgrim managed to escape. "Damn him! Damn him!" muttered Pa-chieh as he was caught. "I told him to do a thorough job of rescuing us. Now it's back to the steamer for us!"

The various demons took the pilgrims back to the main hall, but they did not want to steam them anymore. Instead, Pa-chieh was tied to a pillar in front of the hall, and Sha Monk was taken to be bound to a pillar at the rear of the hall. The old demon, however, held on to the T'ang monk and refused to let go. "Big Brother," said the third fiend, "why are you holding him like that? Are you going to swallow him alive? But that'll take all the pleasure out of eating, for this creature can't be compared with those foolish, common mortals that you can devour as a meal. He's a rare creature from a superior state. You must take time, when you have the leisure, to prepare him like a gourmet dish. And you eat him to the accompaniment of good game, fine wines, and soft music."

"What you say is quite right, of course, Worthy Brother," said the old demon, smiling, "but in the meantime Pilgrim Sun will sneak back in here to steal him."

"In this palace of mine," said the third demon, "there is a pavilion of brocade-fragrance,[10] inside which there is also an iron chest. Listen to me: hide the T'ang monk in the chest and close up the pavilion. Spread the rumor—so that the little fiends all over our city will be talking about it—that the T'ang monk has been devoured alive by us. Undoubtedly that Pilgrim will come back to snoop around; when he hears the news, he will lose all hope and leave. After four or five days, when he's stopped coming back to harass us, we can then take out the T'ang monk and enjoy him at our leisure. How about that?"

Highly pleased, both the old and second fiends said, "Yes! Yes! Yes! What our brother said makes perfect sense!" And so they put the poor T'ang monk that very night into the iron chest, after which the pavilion was closed. The rumor that he had been eaten alive soon spread through the entire city, and we shall leave that for the moment.

We tell you instead about Pilgrim, who had to abandon the T'ang monk in the middle of the night and mount the clouds to escape. He went straight to the Lion-Camel Cave instead, attacked persistently with his rod, and succeeded in killing all ten thousand plus of those little fiends. Then he hurried back; when he reached the edge of the city, the sun was just rising in the east. He dared not, however, provoke battle. For

One silk fiber is no thread;
A single hand cannot clap.

As he descended from the clouds, he shook his body once and changed into a little fiend to steal into the city. Through large boulevards and small alleys he tried to learn what was happening, and all he heard was: "The T'ang monk has been devoured live by the great kings during the night." Wherever he went in the city, that was the news he was told. Becoming more anxious, Pilgrim strode to the Hall of Golden Chimes to look around, and he saw many spirits in front of the hall, all wearing leather caps dusted with gold, and yellow cloth jackets. With red-lacquered wooden staffs in their hands and ivory plaques dangling from their waists, they were marching back and forth. Pilgrim thought to himself, "These must be monster-spirits authorized to work in the palace. I'll change into one of them to snoop around inside."

Dear Great Sage! He really did change into an exact version of one of those fiends and sneaked inside. As he walked about, he caught sight of Pa-chieh tied to one of the pillars in front of the hall and moaning. Pilgrim drew near and whispered, "Wu-nêng."

Recognizing his voice, our Idiot said, "Elder Brother, are you here? Please rescue me." "I will," replied Pilgrim, "but do you know where Master is?"

"Master's gone!" said Pa-chieh. "Last night he was eaten alive by those monster-spirits." When he heard these words, Pilgrim let out a sob, and tears poured from his eyes.

"Elder Brother, don't cry," said Pa-chieh. "I only heard the wild talk of the little fiends, but I didn't see it with my own eyes. Don't let

yourself be fooled. You should do some more investigating." Only then
did Pilgrim stop weeping and walk further inside to investigate. There
he saw Sha Monk tied to one of the pillars in the rear of the hall. He
approached him at once, rubbed Sha Monk's chest with his hand, and
said "Wu-ching."

Sha Monk, too, recognized his voice and said, "Elder Brother, did
you come in through transformation? Please save me! Save me!"
"Saving you is easy," replied Pilgrim. "But do you know where Master
is?" As tears dripped from his eyes, Sha Monk said, "O Elder Brother!
The monster-spirits couldn't wait to steam Master. He was eaten
alive!"

When the Great Sage heard that the words of both his brothers were
the same, he felt as if a knife had run through his heart. Not even
bothering to rescue Pa-chieh and Sha Monk, he leaped at once into
the air and went back to the mountain east of the city. As he dropped
down from the clouds, he broke into loud wailing, crying, "O Master!

When, mocking Heaven, I landed in the snare,
You came to free me from my great despair.
To seek the Buddha we set our heart and mind;
Ourselves we trained and demons we refined.
I did not know this day you'd meet with harm.
Now I can't take you to the wondrous palm.[11]
It's not your lot to reach the blessèd West.
What can I do when spirit leaves your chest?"

As Pilgrim was grieving in this manner, he thought to himself, ques-
tioning mind with mind: "This has to be all the fault of our Buddha
Tathāgata! Sitting idly in that region of ultimate bliss, he had nothing
better to do than to dream up those three baskets of scriptures! If he
truly cared about the proclamation of virtue, he should have sent the
scriptures to the Land of the East. Wouldn't his name then be an everlasting glory? But he wouldn't part with them so readily, and all he
knew was to ask us to go seek them. Who would expect that Master,
after the painful experience of a thousand mountains, would lose his
life at this miserable place? All right! All right! All right! Let old
Monkey mount his cloud-somersault to visit Tathāgata and tell him
about this. If he's willing to let me send the scriptures to the Land of
the East, it'll still mean the proclamation of the virtuous fruit in the
first place, and the fulfillment of our vow in the second. But if he's unwilling, I'll ask him to recite the Loose-Fillet Spell to release me from

this band. Old Monkey will hand it back to him, go back to his own cave, and play king once more."

Dear Great Sage! Leaping up at once, he mounted his cloud-somersault to head straight for India. It was hardly an hour before the Spirit Mountain came into view. In a moment, he dropped down from the clouds to land on the Vulture Peak, where he was immediately met by the Four Great Diamond Guardians, crying, "Where are you going?"

Bowing to them, Pilgrim said, "I must see Tathāgata on some business."

"This ape," snapped the Diamond Guardian Ever Abiding, the indestructible rāja of the Golden Beam Summit on Kun-lun Mountain, "has a lot of gall! You have yet to thank us for exerting ourselves on your behalf some time ago when we restrained the Bull Demon.[12] But there's hardly even any show of courtesy when you see us today. If you have some business, we must make the report first, and you may enter only when you're summoned. This isn't the same as the South Heavenly Gate, where you can rush in and out at will. Bah! Aren't you going to step aside?" Now the Great Sage was already sorely distressed. When he received this affront, he became so incensed that he thundered forth his protests, which soon reached the ears of Tathāgata.

Our Buddhist Patriarch was sitting solemnly on the lotus throne of nine grades and discussing the sūtras with the Arhats of Eighteen Heavens. He said to them, "Sun Wu-k'ung has arrived. All of you go out and usher him in here." Obeying this decree of Buddha, the arhats with two rows of sacred banners and treasure canopies went outside and intoned: "Great Sage Sun, our Tathāgata has issued a summons for you." Only then did those Four Great Diamond Guardians step aside to allow Pilgrim to enter the monastery. After being led by the arhats up to the treasure lotus platform, he prostrated himself before Tathāgata as two streams of tears coursed down his cheeks.

"Wu-k'ung," said Tathāgata, "why are you weeping so sadly?" "By the grace of your teachings vouchsafed repeatedly to him," replied Pilgrim, "this disciple has entered the gate of Holy Father Buddha. Since I returned to the right fruit, I became the protector of the T'ang monk, honoring him as my teacher and sustaining unspeakable hardships on our journey. The moment we arrived at the Lion-Camel City of the Lion-Camel Mountain, three vicious demons—they're a lion king, an elephant king, and a great roc—had my master captured. Even your disciple became their prisoner, and we were all bound inside a steamer to suffer the affliction of water and fire. Fortunately your disciple managed to escape and call up the dragon king for assistance. That night we stole out with Master, but, unable to shake loose from the star of calamity, we were taken prisoners again. By morning, when I stole into the city to try to get some news, I learned that these vicious demons had devoured my master alive during the night. Not a single piece of his flesh or bone was left behind! I saw only my younger brothers Wu-nêng and Wu-ching, who were bound there also. They too will soon lose their lives, I suppose. Your disciple had no choice but to come here to plead with Tathāgata. I beg you in your great compassion to recite the Loose-Fillet Spell and take off this band from my head. It will be returned to Tathāgata, and your disciple will be released once more to frolic on the Flower-Fruit Mountain." Hardly had he finished speaking when his tears streamed forth, as he sobbed uncontrollably.

"Wu-k'ung," said Tathāgata with a smile, "don't be so sad. You are hurting because one of those monster-spirits has vast magic powers and you can't prevail against him." Kneeling beneath Buddha's throne and pounding his chest, Pilgrim said, "To tell you the truth, this disciple in years past brought great disturbance to the Celestial Palace and assumed the name of Great Sage. Since I acquired the way of humanity, I have never suffered loss, but this time I'm the victim of this vicious demon!"

On hearing this Tathāgata said, "Cease your anguish. I do recognize that monster-spirit."

All at once Pilgrim blurted out: "Tathāgata! I have heard people say that that monster-spirit is related to you!"

"This insolent ape!" said Tathāgata. "How could a monster-spirit be related to me?" "If not," replied Pilgrim with a laugh, "how could you recognize him?"

"By my eyes of wisdom," said Tathāgata, "that's how I recognize all three of them. The old fiend and the second fiend both have their proper masters. Ānanda and Kāśyapa, come! The two of you will mount the clouds and go your separate ways to Mount Five-Platforms and Mount O-mei. Summon Mañjuśrī and Viśvabhadra to come for an audience." The two honored ones departed at once with the decree.

"Mañjuśrī and Viśvabhadra," said Tathāgata, "are the proper

masters of those two fiends. But now that you mention it, the third fiend is indeed somewhat related to me." "On the paternal side," asked Pilgrim, "or the maternal side?"

Tathāgata said, "At the time when Chaos parted, Heaven opened at the epoch of *Tzŭ*, Earth developed at the epoch of *Ch'ou*, and Man came into existence at the epoch of *Yin*.

When Heaven and Earth mated,
Then myriad things were born.

The myriad things consisted of beasts and fowl: of the beasts, the unicorn was the head, and the phoenix was the head of the fowl. After having been fertilized by the aura of procreation, the phoenix also gave birth to the peacock and the great roc. When the peacock first came into the world, it was a most savage creature, able to devour humans. In fact, it could suck in a human being with one breath from a distance of some forty miles. I was on top of the Snow Mountain, having just perfected my sixteen-foot diamond body, when the peacock sucked me into his stomach. I could have escaped through his anal passage, but fearing that my body might be defiled, I cut my way out through his back and rode him back to the Spirit Mountain. I was about to take his life, but the various buddhas stopped me with the observation that to hurt the peacock would be like hurting my own mother. That was why I detained him at the mountain instead and appointed him Buddha-Mother, the Bodhisattva Mahārāja Mayūra.[13] Since the great roc had the same parent as the peacock, it could be said that he was somewhat related to me."

On hearing this, Pilgrim said with a smile, "Tathāgata, according to what you've told me, you should be regarded as the nephew of that monster-spirit!" "Only my presence, I fear, will bring that fiend to submission," said Tathāgata. Touching his head to the ground, Pilgrim said, "I beg you to make this journey at once."

Tathāgata left the lotus throne and went out of the monastery gate with the rest of the buddhas. There they saw Ānanda and Kāśyapa leading Mañjuśrī and Viśvabhadra on their way to the monastery also. As the two bodhisattvas bowed to him, Tathāgata asked, "How long have your beasts of burden been gone from your mountains?"

"Seven days," replied Mañjuśrī. "Seven days in the mountain," said Tathāgata, "are equivalent to several thousand years on earth. I wonder how many lives they have taken down there. You must follow me quickly if we are to retrieve them." With one bodhisattva standing

on each side of him, the Buddha and his followers rose into the air.
You see

Auspicious clouds adrift in all the sky,
As Buddha in mercy his wisdom[14] doth ply:
He shows forth Heaven's law of procreation,
Explaining Earth's patterned transformation.
Before his face five hundred arhats stand;
Behind three thousand guardians form a band.
Ānanda, Kāśyapa follow left and right;
Mañ and Viśva the monstrous fiends will smite.

It was as a peculiar favor granted him that the Great Sage succeeded
in eliciting the assistance of the Buddhist Patriarch and his followers.
In a little while, they caught sight of the city. "Tathāgata," said Pilgrim,
"the spot releasing black vapors over there is the Lion-Camel
Kingdom."

"Go down first," said Tathāgata, "and provoke battle with those
monster-spirits. You are permitted to lose but not to win. When you
retreat back here, I'll bring them to submission."

The Great Sage lowered his cloud and landed on the city wall; his
feet planted on the merlons of the battlement, he shouted, "Damned
lawless beasts! Come out quickly to fight with old Monkey!" Those
little fiends standing on the rampart were so terrified that they dashed
down to report: "Great Kings, Pilgrim Sun is provoking battle on the
battlement!"

"This ape hasn't shown himself for about two days," said the old
fiend. "If he returns to provoke battle this morning, could it be that
he has succeeded in getting some help?"

"We're not afraid of whatever help he has gotten, are we?" said the
third demon. "Let's all go and have a look." Each grasping his weapon,
the three demon chiefs rushed up to the battlement. When they saw
Pilgrim, they raised their arms without a word and attacked. Pilgrim
wielded his iron rod to meet them; after seven or eight rounds, however, he feigned defeat and fled, with the fiend kings all roaring,
"Where are you going?"

The Great Sage shot up to midair with one somersault, but those
three spirits all mounted the clouds to give chase. Immediately Pilgrim
hurled himself into the golden radiance of Father Buddha and vanished
from sight. What did appear were the three images of Buddha—Past,
Present, and Future—together with five hundred arhats and three

thousand guardians, who fanned out on all sides. They had the three fiend kings surrounded so tightly that not even water could have seeped through!

"Brothers, it's bad!" cried the old demon, completely unnerved. "This monkey is truly a devil in the earth! How did he manage to bring our masters here?"

"Don't be frightened, Big Brother," said the third demon. "We'll all go forward together and use our weapons to cut down that Tathāgata and take over his Thunderclap Treasure Monastery."

Not knowing any better, our demon chief accordingly charged forward and tried to attack madly with his scimitar. Mañjuśrī and Viśabhadra, after quickly reciting a magic spell, shouted in unison, "If these cursed beasts do not submit now, are they waiting for another incarnation?" The old fiend and the second fiend were so terror-stricken that they dared not struggle any longer. Dropping their weapons, they rolled over once and changed back into their original forms. The two Bodhisattvas tossed two lotus thrones onto their backs and then leaped up to take their seats on top. In this way, the two fiends lowered their ears and submitted.

Since the two bodhisattvas had thus subdued the green lion and the white elephant, only the third demon refused to surrender. Throwing away his halberd, the fiend spread out his wings and soared into the air, his sharp claws seeking to strike at the Monkey King. The Great Sage was still hiding in the luminosity around the Buddha, and the fiend actually had no way of getting near him, though he would have liked very much to do so. Perceiving the roc's intentions, Tathāgata faced the wind and gave his head (which had once supported the nests of magpies)[15] a shake. The head changed at once into a piece of meat dripping with fresh blood. Stretching out his claws, the monster-spirit drew near and tried to clutch at the piece of meat. Our Father Buddha pointed at him with his finger and immediately the monster-spirit felt such cramps throughout his huge wings that he could not fly away. All he could do was to hover over the Buddha's head in his true form: a golden-winged great roc.

"Tathāgata," he cried, "why did you exercise your mighty dharma power to constrain me?" "Your wickedness," replied Tathāgata, "has incurred for you a heavy debt of retribution in this place. Follow me, and you may acquire merit beneficial to you."

"But your place allows for only a strict vegetarian diet," said the monster-spirit. "It's a condition of extreme poverty and hardship. I can enjoy human flesh here to my endless delight. If you starve and destroy me, you will have sinned, too."

"In the four great continents of my domain," said Tathāgata, "there are countless worshipers. I shall ask those who wish to do good to sacrifice first to your mouth." Since that great roc could neither flee nor escape, though he sorely wished to do so, he had no choice but to make submission.

Only then did Pilgrim step out of the golden radiance to kowtow to Tathāgata, saying, "Father Buddha, you have put away the monster-spirits and eliminated great evils. But my master is gone."

"Wretched ape!" said the great roc through clenched teeth, "You had to find such a tough antagonist to constrain me! Since when did we devour that old priest of yours? He's still hidden in an iron chest at the pavilion of brocade-fragrance." When Pilgrim heard these words, he kowtowed hurriedly to thank the Buddhist Patriarch, who had the roc firmly detained on top of his halo as a guardian. Then the entire entourage left on the clouds to return to the treasure monastery.

Pilgrim lowered himself from the clouds and entered the city, where he could find not a single little fiend. So it was that

A snake without head would not crawl;
A bird without wings could not fly.

When they saw that the fiend kings had made submission to the Buddhist Patriarch, each of them fled for his life. Pilgrim released Pa-chieh and Sha Monk and also found the luggage and the horse. "Master has not been eaten," he said to the two of them. "Follow me!"

He led his two brothers to the interior court and found the pavilion of brocade-fragrance. Opening the door, they located the iron chest, inside of which they could hear the sound of Tripitaka weeping. Wedging open the chest with his fiend-routing staff, Sha Monk called out: "Master!" When he saw them, Tripitaka wailed aloud: "O disciples! How did you manage to subdue the demons? How did you find me here?"

Thereupon Pilgrim gave a thorough rehearsal of what had taken place, from beginning to end, and Tripitaka was filled with gratitude. Master and disciples found some rice and foodstuff in the palace with which they prepared a meal for themselves. After they had eaten their fill, they packed up and set out once more on the main road toward the West. Thus it was that

True scriptures must be by true people sought;
Restless minds and raging wills will come to naught.
We do not know when they will get to face Tathāgata, and you must listen to the next chapter.

Seventy-eight

At Bhikṣu he pities the children and sends for the night gods;
In the royal hall he knows the demon speaking of the way
 and virtue.

> One thought will stir up a demonic crew!
> So bad for training, though what can you do?
> Rely on washing to remove the dust;
> The body harness and refine you must.
> Sweep clean all causations,[1] to stillness return;
> Stamp out every fiend without concern.
> Of shackle and snare you'll surely leap free
> And rise, when merit's done, to Great Canopy.[2]

We were telling you about the Great Sage Sun, who, having exerted every effort, succeeded in eliciting the assistance of Tathāgata to subdue the fiends. When the ordeal finally ended, Tripitaka and his disciples left the Lion-Camel Kingdom and journeyed westward. After several months, it was again the time of winter. You see

> The peak's jadelike plums half-blooming,
> The pond's water slowly icing.
> The red leaves have all dropped away
> And pines turn more verdant and gay.
> The pale clouds are about to snow;
> Dried grass on the mountain lies low.
> What frigid scene now fills the eyes
> As bone-piercing chill multiplies!

Braving the cold and plunging through the chill, resting in the rain and feeding on the wind, master and disciples proceeded until they saw another city. "Wu-k'ung," asked Tripitaka, "what sort of a place is that over there?" "When you get there," replied Pilgrim, "you'll know. If it's a kingdom of the West, we'll have to have our rescript certified. If it's merely a district, county, or prefecture seat, we'll just pass through." Hardly had master and disciples finished speaking than they arrived at the foot of the city gate.

Tripitaka dismounted, and the four of them entered the outer wall of the city, where almost immediately they found an old soldier huddled against the wind and sleeping beneath a wall exposed to sunlight. Pilgrim walked up to him and shook him gently, saying, "Officer." Waking with a start and blinking several times, the old soldier finally caught sight of Pilgrim. Immediately he went to his knees and kowtowed, crying, "Holy Father!"

"Stop making all this fuss!" said Pilgrim. "I'm no evil spirit! Why should you address me as Holy Father?"

"Aren't you Holy Father Thundergod?" asked the old soldier, still kowtowing.

"Certainly not!" said Pilgrim. "I am a priest from the Land of the East on his way to seek scriptures in the Western Heaven. I just arrived, and I came to ask you for the name of your region." Only when he heard those words did the old soldier calm down; with a big yawn he scrambled up to stretch himself and say, "Elder, Elder, pardon me! This place was originally the Bhikṣu Kingdom, but now the name has been changed to the Young Masters' City."

"Is there a king in the city?" asked Pilgrim.

"Yes! Yes! Yes!" replied the old soldier. Pilgrim turned back to say to the T'ang monk, "Master, this place originally was called the Bhikṣu Kingdom, but it has been changed now to the Young Masters' City. I don't know why they changed the name."

"If it was Bhikṣu," said a perplexed T'ang monk, "why then should it be called Young Masters?" Pa-chieh said, "It must be that the Bhikṣu king had died. The one newly occupying the throne is a young master, and that's why it's called the Young Masters' city."

"Nonsense! Nonsense!" said the T'ang monk. "Let's go inside the city first. We may make further inquiry on the streets." "Exactly," said Sha Monk. "That old soldier is probably ignorant, or he may have been frightened into babbling by Big Brother. Let's go into the city to make inquiry." They walked through three levels of city gates before they reached the big thoroughfares. As they paused to look around, they found that the people here all seemed to be good-looking and handsomely dressed. What they came upon were

Wine shops and song bars full of raucous din.
Tall colors adorned teahouses and inns.
Business was good at every gate and door;
Abundant wealth packed both mart and store.
People, like ants, traded brocade and gold;

For fame and for profit they bought and sold.
What solemn manners! Such prosperous scene
Of calm seas and rivers—a year serene!

Toting the luggage and leading the horse, master and disciples walked for a long time on the main boulevards, where the sight of prosperity seemed endless. Then they began to notice that in front of each household was a geese coop.

"O Disciples!" said Tripitaka. "All the people here put a geese coop in front of their house. Why is that?" On hearing this, Pa-chieh looked left and right, and he saw that indeed there were these geese coops lined with silk curtains of five colors.

"Master," said our Idiot with a giggle, "this must be an auspicious day for marriage or for meeting friends. The people must all be performing ceremonies."

"Rubbish!" snapped Pilgrim. "How could every household be performing a ceremony? There must be a reason for this. Let me go and take a look." "You'd better not go," said Tripitaka, tugging at him. "Your hideous features will offend people."

"I'll go in transformation then," replied Pilgrim. Dear Great Sage! Making the magic sign, he recited a spell and changed with one shake of his body into a little bee. Wings outstretched, he flew up to one of the coops and crawled inside the curtains. There he discovered a little child sitting in the middle. When he went to another coop, he found another child also. In fact, he discovered the same thing in front of eight or nine households: they were all little boys, and there were no girls at all. Some of them were playing in the coops; others merely sat and cried; still others were eating fruit or sleeping.

After seeing that, Pilgrim changed back into his original form to report to the T'ang monk: "There are little boys in the coops; the older ones cannot be more than seven years old, and some of the younger ones are barely five. I don't know why they are in there." His words made Tripitaka more perplexed than ever.

A turn on the street brought them all at once up to the gate of an official mansion, the Golden Pavilion Postal Station. "Disciples," said Tripitaka, highly pleased, "let's go inside this postal station. We can ask them about the place, feed our horse, and request lodging for the night."

"Exactly! Exactly!" said Sha Monk. "Let's get inside quickly!" As the four of them entered amiably, the officers on duty at once announced their arrival to the station master, who ushered them inside. After they had exchanged greetings and taken their seats, the station master asked, "Elder, where did you come from?"

"Your humble cleric," replied Tripitaka, "has been sent by the Great T'ang in the Land of the East to go seek scriptures in the Western Heaven. Having arrived in your noble region, we would like to have our travel rescript certified and to beg you to grant us one night's lodging in your lofty mansion."

The station master immediately requested tea and asked those on duty to prepare the tokens of hospitality. Having thanked him, Tripitaka asked again, "Is it possible for me to enter the court today and have an audience with the Throne and get my rescript certified?"

"You can't do it tonight," said the station master. "Wait until early court tomorrow. Please spend the night and rest here in our humble dwelling." In a little while, when the preparation had been finished, the station master invited the four pilgrims to partake of a vegetarian meal. His subordinates were ordered to sweep clean the guest room for the pilgrims to rest. After thanking him repeatedly, Tripitaka sat down and said to the station master, "There is something that this humble cleric must ask you to explain. How do the people of your noble region rear young children?"

The station master said, "As there are no two suns in Heaven, so there are no two rational principles on Earth. The rearing of children begins with the sperm of the father and the blood of the mother. After the tenth month of conception, the child will be born in due time; and after birth, the child will be fed with milk for at least three years, until the bodily features are fully formed. You think we do not know about this?"

"According to what you have just told me," replied Tripitaka, "the people here are no different from those of my humble nation. But when I entered the city just now, I saw that there was placed in front of each household a geese coop, inside of which was placed a little boy. I don't understand this, and that's why I dare request an explanation."

"Elder, don't mind that!" said the station master, at once lowering his voice and whispering into Tripitaka's ear. "Don't ask about that, and don't be concerned with that! Don't speak of it, even! Please rest now, and you can be on your way tomorrow."

On hearing this, however, the elder tugged at the station master and persisted in his request for an explanation. As he shook his head and wagged his finger, all the station master could mutter was, "Be careful with what you say!" Refusing to let go, Tripitaka insisted that he be told the reason. The station master had little choice but to send away all his official attendants, after which he said quietly, alone, by the light of the lamps, "The matter of the geese coops that you mentioned just now happens to be instigated by the unruliness of our lord. Why do you persist in asking about it?"

"What do you mean by unruliness?" asked Tripitaka. "You must help me understand before I can rest."

"This country," said the station master, "used to be called the Bhikṣu Kingdom, but recent folk songs[3] have changed the name to the Young Masters' City. Three years ago, an old man disguised as a Taoist arrived with a young girl, barely sixteen and with a face as beautiful as Kuan-yin's. He presented her as a tribute to our Majesty, who became so infatuated with her that he gave her the title of Queen Beauty. In recent times he would not even look at any of the royal consorts dwelling in the six chambers and three palaces. Night and day he cares only to indulge in amorous dalliance with this one girl until he is reduced to a physical wreck. Constantly fatigued, emaciated, and unable to eat or drink, he has not long to live. The royal hospital has tried all its best prescriptions, but no cure has been found. However, that Taoist, who has been appointed the royal father-in-law, claims to possess a secret formula from beyond the ocean which can lengthen our lord's life. Some time ago he went, in fact, to the Ten Islets and the Three Isles to gather herbs. After his return and the preparation of all the medications, he still requires the terrible medical supplement[4] of one thousand one hundred and eleven hearts of young boys. When the medicine is taken with soup made from boiling these boys' hearts, the king, so the Taoist claims, will live to a thousand years without aging. Those little boys you saw in the geese coops are the selected ones, who are being fed and nurtured before they are slaughtered. Fearing the law of the king, the parents dare not even weep. They can only express their outrage by nicknaming this place the Young Masters' City. When you go to court tomorrow, please confine your business to certifying your travel rescript. You mustn't mention this matter at all." He ended his speech and immediately withdrew.

Our elder was so horrified by what he heard that his bones weakened and his tendons turned numb. Unable to restrain the tears rolling down his cheeks, he blurted out: "Ah, befuddled king! So you grew ill on account of your incontinence and debauchery. But how could you take the lives of so many innocent boys? O misery! O misery! This pain kills me!" For this we have a testimonial poem that says:

One foolish tyrant who misses the truth
Has harmed himself with the pleasure he craves.
He seeks long life by taking lives of boys;
He kills the plebs to lighten Heaven's scourge.
Steadfast in compassion the monk remains;
Unheard-of horror the master reveals.
As he sighs and sheds tears in the lamplight,
Buddha's disciple is o'ercome by pain.

Drawing near to Tripitaka, Pa-chieh said, "Master, what's the matter with you? 'You're always picking up someone's coffin and crying over it in your own house!' Don't be so sad! Remember the adage:

The ruler wants the subject to die,
And the subject who does not is disloyal;
The father wants the son to perish,
And the son who does not is unfilial.

He is hurting his own people, but what does that have to do with you? Come, let's shed our robes and sleep. 'Let's not worry on behalf of the ancients!'"

Still shedding tears, Tripitaka said, "O disciple, you are so hardhearted! Those of us who have left the family must accumulate merit by multiplying our virtuous acts; our very first obligation must be the practice of appropriate means. How could this befuddled king indulge in such a lawless act? I have never heard of such nonsense that eating people's hearts can lengthen one's life. How could I not grieve over something like this?"

"Please do not grieve just yet, Master," said Sha Monk. "Wait till tomorrow when we have our rescript certified. We can boldly discuss the matter with the king, and if he doesn't listen to us, we can also ascertain what kind of person this royal father-in-law is. Perhaps it is a monster-spirit, desirous of devouring human hearts, that has devised such a plan. That may well be the case."

"Wu-ching is perfectly right," said Pilgrim. "Master, you should sleep now. Let old Monkey enter court with you tomorrow and scrutinize the royal father-in-law. If he is a man, he may have embarked on the path of heterodoxy, being ignorant of the proper Way and thinking that only herbs and medicines will achieve realized immortality. Let old Monkey disclose to him the essential themes of cultivation by means of one's natural endowments and enlighten him into embracing the truth. If he's a monster or a fiend, I'll arrest him for the king to see, so that he may learn continence and find out how to nourish his own body. I most certainly will not allow the king to take the lives of those boys."

When Tripitaka heard these words, he quickly bowed to Pilgrim and said, "O disciple, what you've proposed is most marvelous! Most marvelous! When you see that befuddled king, however, you shouldn't ask about this matter right away. For I fear that the befuddled king, without looking properly into the matter, would immediately find us guilty of listening to false rumors. What would we do then?"

"Old Monkey has his own magic power," said Pilgrim, smiling. "First, I will remove these boys in the geese coops from the city, so that tomorrow he will have no one from whom he can take out the hearts. The officials of the land will undoubtedly report to the Throne, and that befuddled king will surely respond by discussing the matter with the royal father-in-law or by asking for more boys to be selected. At that point we will memorialize to him also. Then he will not blame us."

Highly pleased, Tripitaka said again, "How can you make those boys leave the city? If you can, the virtue of my worthy disciple is great as Heaven! You should do this quickly. If you delay, you may be too late." Arousing his spiritual powers, Pilgrim rose at once and gave this instruction to Pa-chieh and Sha Monk: "Sit here with Master and let me act. When you see a gust of cold wind blowing, you'll know that the boys are leaving the city." Whereupon the three of them, Tripitaka and his two disciples, began chanting: "We submit to the Life-Saving Buddha of Medicine![5] We submit to the Life-Saving Buddha of Medicine!"

Once our Great Sage had gone out the door, he rose with a whistle to midair, where he made the magic sign and recited the magic words: "Let *Oṁ* purify the dharma realm!" With this he summoned the god of the city, the local spirit, the god of the soil, and various immortal officials together with the Guardians of Five Quarters, the Four Sentinels, the Six Gods of Darkness and Six Gods of Light, and the Guardians of Monasteries, who arrived in the air to bow to him, saying, "Great Sage, for what urgent business have you summoned us in the thick of night?"

"Because we came upon an unruly king in the Bhikṣu kingdom,"
replied Pilgrim, "who has listened to some monstrous pervert's tale
that the hearts of little boys, when taken as a medical supplement,
would grant him longevity. My master is so disturbed that he has
resolved to save lives and exterminate the fiend. That is why old
Monkey has asked each one of you to come here; I want you to use
your magic powers and move all these boys, including the geese
coops, out of the city. Take them into a mountain valley or deep into
a forest and supply them with fruit to eat so that they won't starve.
You must also provide them with secret protection and prevent them
from crying or being frightened. When I have eliminated the perversity and restored the king to the proper rule of his state, you may
then return the boys just as we are about to leave." When the various
gods heard this command, each of them exercised his magic power as
they dropped down from the clouds. The city immediately was filled
with churning cold wind and spreading fog.

The cold wind darkened a sky full of stars;
The fog spreading bedimmed the radiant moon.
At the very first
They drifted and floated down;
But thereafter
They roared and rumbled through—
Drifting and floating down,
They sought to save the boys from every house;
Roaring and rumbling through,
They found the geese coops to help flesh and blood.
People stayed home for the invading chill,
And piercing cold turned garments iron-hard.
Parents fretted in vain
And kinfolk were aggrieved,
As cold wind churned the earth
To remove the boys in coops.
This night they may be lonely;
By dawn they will all be pleased.

We have also a poem as a testimonial, which says:
Since mercy e'er abounds in Buddha's gate,
Goodness perfected is what's called the Great.[6]
All saints and sages must virtue increase;
The sum of Triratna[7] and five laws[8] is peace.
Had not a king at Bhikṣu state gone bad,

A thousand youngsters' fate would still be sad.
When Pilgrim saves them for his master's sake,
Merit above salvation he will make.

It was about the hour of the third watch during that night when the various deities transported those geese coops to be hidden at another place.

Lowering his auspicious luminosity, Pilgrim went to the courtyard of the posthouse, where he could hear his three companions still chanting, "We submit to the Life-Saving Buddha of Medicine!" In great delight, he drew near and called out: "Master, I've returned! What do you think of the cold wind?"

"That was some cold wind!" replied Pa-chieh.

"But what about rescuing the boys?" asked Tripitaka.

"They have already been taken out one by one," replied Pilgrim, "and will be escorted back to the city by the time we're ready to leave." Tripitaka thanked him again and again before retiring.

By dawn, Tripitaka began to dress the moment he awoke, saying, "Wu-k'ung, I want to attend the morning court so that our travel rescript may be certified." "Master," said Pilgrim, "if you go by yourself, I fear that you may not be able to accomplish much. Let old Monkey go with you to ascertain whether the kingdom is governed by rectitude or perversity."

"But you usually refuse to perform the proper ceremony when you greet a king," said Tripitaka, "and I fear he may be offended."

"I won't show myself," said Pilgrim. "I'll follow you in secret, and I can protect you at the same time."

Highly pleased, Tripitaka instructed Pa-chieh and Sha Monk to watch the luggage and the horse, and then departed. When the station master saw them off, he noticed that the attire of the elder was quite different from that of the day before:

He wore a brocade cassock lined with strange treasures.
A gold-tipped Vairocana hat topped his head.
His hands held up a nine-ringed priestly staff;
His chest enclosed one wondrous, godly spark.
The travel rescript he had on himself,
Packed in a silk purse placed inside the wrap.
He walked like an arhat come down to earth,
With a genuine, living Buddha's face.

After greeting Tripitaka, the station master whispered in his ear and told him to mind his own business. As Tripitaka nodded and murmured his assent, the Great Sage stepped to one side of the door and recited a spell; with one shake of his body he changed into a mole-cricket and flew up to alight on top of Tripitaka's hat. The elder left the postal station and headed straight for the court.

On arriving, he ran into the Custodian of the Yellow Gate, to whom he bowed and said, "This humble priest is someone sent by the Great T'ang of the Land of the East to seek scriptures in the Western Heaven. It is proper for me, after arriving in your noble region, to have my travel rescript certified. I therefore wish to have an audience with the Throne. I beg you to make this known for me." Upon which, that Custodian of the Yellow Gate made his report.

In delight, the king said, "A priest from a distant land must be most accomplished in the Way. Show him in quickly." The Custodian thus summoned the elder to enter the court; after going through the ceremonial greetings beneath the steps, he was granted permission to take a seat in the royal hall. As he thanked the king and sat down, the elder noticed that the king had

Emaciated features
And a listless spirit.
He raised his hands
But could barely salute;
And when he spoke,
His voice started and stopped.

When the elder presented him with the rescript, the king stared at it with unseeing eyes for a long time before he was able to affix his treasure seal on the document and hand it back to the elder.

The king was just about to question our elder further on the reason for seeking scriptures when the official attending the Throne reported, "The royal father-in-law has arrived." At once supporting himself on a young palace eunuch, the king struggled down from the dragon couch in order to receive the visitor. Our elder was so taken aback that he too leaped up and stood to one side. As he turned to look, he discovered an old Taoist swaggering up from the jade steps. The man Tripitaka saw

Had on his head a cloud-patterned, priestly wrap of pale yellow damask,
And he wore a crane-feathered gown of brown silk fretted with plum designs.

A blue sash, braided with three silk and woolen cords, wrapped
  his waist;
His feet trod cloud-patterned slippers woven of grass-linen and
  hemp.
His hand held a nine-jointed staff of dried vine carved like a
  coiling dragon.
Down his chest hung a silk purse embroidered with raised
  dragon-and-phoenix patterns.
His jadelike face was shiny and smooth;
A white beard flowed down his chin;
His pupils blazed golden flames;
His eyes were longer than his brows.
Clouds moved with each step he took,
And fragrant mists encircled him.
Hands folded, all officials beneath the steps
Shouted: "The royal father-in-law has entered court!"

When that royal father-in-law arrived at the front of the treasure hall,
he did not even bother to pay homage to the king. His head held high,
he walked boldly up the steps while the king bowed and said, "We are
delighted that the royal father-in-law has honored us with his divine
presence this morning." He was at once asked to be seated on the
cushioned couch on the left.

Taking a step forward, Tripitaka also bent low to greet him, saying,
"Sir royal father-in-law, this humble cleric salutes you." Sitting loftily
on his couch, the royal father-in-law did not return the greetings at
all; instead, he turned to say to the king, "Where did this monk come
from?"

"He happens to be someone sent by the T'ang court in the Land of
the East to seek scriptures in the Western Heaven," replied the king.
"He's here to have his travel rescript certified."

"The journey leading to the West," said the royal father-in-law with
a laugh, "is shrouded in darkness!⁹ What's so good about that?"
Tripitaka said, "Since ancient times the West has been the noble
region of ultimate bliss. How could it not be good?"

The king asked, "We have heard from the ancients too that monks
are the disciples of Buddha. We would like to know in truth whether
a monk is able to transcend death, whether submission to Buddha can
bring a person longevity."

On hearing this, Tripitaka quickly pressed his palms together in front of his breast to give his reply:

For the person who's a monk,
All causal relations have been abolished;
And to him who understands reality,
All things are but emptiness.
He of great knowledge, both wide and comprehensive,[10]
Exists placidly in the realm of no birth;
The true mysteries perceived in silence,
He roams freely in peace and tranquillity.
With no attachments in the Three Realms, all elementary
    principles are known;
Since his six senses are purged, he has insights into all causes.
He who would strengthen knowledge and consciousness
Must perforce know the mind;
For a mind purified shines in solitary enlightenment,
And a mind preserved pierces all mental projections.
The face of truth, without want or excess,
Can be seen even in a previous life;
But the form of delusion, though manifest, declines at last.
Why seek it beyond bounds?
Sedentary meditation
Is the very source of concentration;
Almsgiving and charity
Are the foundation of austerity.
He who has great wisdom will appear foolish,
For he knows how not to act in every affair;
He who's good at planning will not scheme,
For he needs must let go in every instant.
Once the mind's made immovable,
All your actions are perfected.
But if you dwell on picking the yin to nourish the yang,
You speak but foolish words;
And to bait the eye with long life
Amounts to an empty promise.
You must abandon all particles of defilement,
Regard all phenomena as emptiness.
When you, plain and simple, reduce your desire,

You will with ease an endless life acquire.
When that royal father-in-law heard these words, he smiled sarcasti-
cally and pointed his finger at the T'ang monk. "Ha! Ha! Ha!" he
cried. "Your mouth, monk, is full of balderdash! Those within the fold
of Nirvāṇa all talk about the knowledge of reality. But you don't even
know how reality is to be extinguished! Sedentary meditation—why,
that's nothing but the practice of blind cultivation! As the proverb
says,

'Sit, sit, sit!
Your ass will split!
Play with fire
And you'll land in the pit!'
You have no idea that I,
Who seek immortality,
Possess the hardiest of bones;
Who comprehend the Way,
Am most intelligent in spirit.
I carry basket and gourd to visit friends in the mountain;
I gather a hundred herbs to help people in the world.
Divine flowers I pick to make a hat;
Fragrant orchids I pluck to form a mat.
I sing to clapping of hands
And rest on clouds after I dance.
Explaining the principles of Tao,
I exalt the true teachings of Lao Tzu;
Dispensing amulets and water,
I rid the human world of monstrous miasmas.
I rob Heaven and Earth of their energies
And pluck from the sun and moon their essences.
Yin and yang activated, the elixir gels;
Fire and Water harmonized, the embryo's formed.
When the yin of Two Eights[11] recedes,
It's both dim and blurry;
When the yang of Three Nines[12] expands,
It's both dark and obscure.
In accord with the four seasons I gather herbs;
By nine cylindrical turns my elixir's perfected.
Astride the blue phoenix,
I ascend the purple mansion;

Mounting the white crane,
I reach the capital of jade,
Where I join all Heaven's luminaries
In zealous display of the wondrous Way.
Could this be compared with the quiescence of your Buddhism,
The dark divinity of your tranquillity?
The stinking corpse bequeathed by Nirvāṇa
That can never leave the mortal dust?
Among the Three Teachings mine's the highest mystery.
Tao alone is noble since the dawn of history!"

On hearing this, the king was filled with delight, while the officials of the entire court shouted, "Bravo! Indeed, Tao alone is noble since the dawn of history! Tao alone is noble since the dawn of history!" When the elder saw that everyone had praise for the Taoist, he was terribly embarrassed. The king, nevertheless, asked the Court of Imperial Entertainments to prepare a vegetarian meal so that the priest from distant lands could eat before he departed again for the West.

Tripitaka gave thanks as he withdrew; he descended from the main hall and was just about to walk out when Pilgrim flew down from his hat and whispered in his ear: "Master, this royal father-in-law is a perverse fiend, and the king is under his influence. You go back first to the postal station to wait for the meal. Let old Monkey remain here to learn something more of him." Tripitaka understood and left, and we shall leave him for the moment.

Look at our Pilgrim! He soared up and alighted on one of the king-fisher screens in the Hall of Golden Chimes, when the Commander of Five Military Commissions stepped from the ranks to say, "My lord, there was a gust of cold wind last night which swept away, without a trace, all the little boys lodged in the geese coops in front of the houses."

When the king heard this memorial, he was both frightened and angered. "This means," said he to the royal father-in-law, "that Heaven wants to destroy us! We have been sick for months, and the imperial physician has been wholly ineffectual. It was fortunate that the royal father-in-law has bestowed on us a divine prescription. We were just waiting for the noon hour today to lift the knife and take out these boys' hearts and use them as our medical supplement. How could they all be swept away by a gust of cold wind? What explanation could there be other than that Heaven wanted to destroy us?"

With a smile, the royal father-in-law said, "Your Majesty, please do not worry. The fact that these boys have been swept away means quite the contrary; this is precisely a gift of long life that Heaven is sending to Your Majesty." "How could you say that," asked the king, "when those boys in the coops have all been blown away?"

"When I entered court just now," replied the royal father-in-law, "I noticed an absolutely marvelous medical supplement, far surpassing those one thousand one hundred and eleven young boys' hearts. Those hearts, you see, could only lengthen your life for about a thousand years. But taken with the newfound supplement, my divine medicine will lengthen your Majesty's life for thousands and thousands of years." Since the king, however, did not understand at all what medical supplement the Taoist was referring to, he pressed for an explanation.

Then the royal father-in-law said, "I have noticed that the monk who has been sent by the Land of the East to seek scriptures is possessed of pure and orderly features. They reveal that he has, in fact, a true body which has practiced religion for at least ten incarnations, and that he has been a monk since childhood. He is, in truth, someone who has never dissipated his original yang, someone ten thousand times better than all those little boys put together. If you can get his heart to make soup and take my divine medicine, you will certainly acquire the age of ten thousand years."

Believing completely what he had heard, the befuddled ruler said, "Why didn't you tell us sooner? If it had that kind of efficacy, I would have detained him just now and not let him go."

"But that's not difficult!" said the royal father-in-law. "Just now the Court of Imperial Entertainments was told to prepare a vegetarian meal for him. He will undoubtedly eat first before leaving the city. Issue an edict right now for all the city gates to be closed. Call up the troops, have the Golden Pavilion Postal Station surrounded, and tell them to bring back the monk. First, ask for his heart politely. If he agrees, cut him up and take it out at once. You may promise him an imperial burial and a shrine erected in his honor, so that he may enjoy perpetual sacrifice. If he does not comply with your request, we'll show him the ugly power of force. Tie him up at once, and then cut out his heart. Isn't that easy?" The befuddled ruler indeed followed his suggestion; he gave the decree at once that the city gates should be shut. The imperial guards and their captains were sent to have the postal station surrounded.

When Pilgrim heard this, he spread his wings and darted back to the postal station and changed back to his true form to say to the T'ang monk, "Master, disaster! Disaster!" Tripitaka was just enjoying the imperial banquet with Pa-chieh and Sha Monk. These sudden words so terrified him that the spirits of Three Cadavers left him and smoke poured out of his seven apertures. He fell to the ground at once, his body covered with sweat. All he could do was roll his eyeballs; he could not utter a word. Sha Monk hurried forward to take hold of him, crying, "Master, wake up! Master, wake up!"

"What disaster? What disaster?" said Pa-chieh. "Speak slowly, will you please! Must you frighten Master like that?"

"Since Master left the court," replied Pilgrim, "old Monkey stayed behind and ascertained that that royal father-in-law was indeed a monster-spirit. Soon afterward, the Commander of Five Military Commissions reported that the cold wind had blown away the little boys. The king was frustrated, but the Taoist told him to be happy instead, saying that it was actually Heaven's gift of long life to him. He wanted to ask for Master's heart to be the medical supplement, something he claimed would grant the king an age of ten thousand years. Believing such a perverse suggestion, the befuddled ruler called up his troops to come and surround the postal station. Moreover, the Embroidered-uniform Guards have been sent here to ask for Master's heart."

"You have exercised marvelous compassion!" said Pa-chieh with a laugh. "You have saved marvelous boys! You have called up marvelous cold wind! But this time you have also brought disaster on us!"

Trembling all over, Tripitaka scrambled up to tug at Pilgrim and plead with him, "O worthy disciple! How will we face this?" "If you want to face this," said Pilgrim, "the old must become the young."

"What do you mean by that?" asked Sha Monk. Pilgrim said, "If you want to preserve your life, the master will have to become the disciple, and the disciple will have to become the master." "If you can save my life," said Tripitaka, "I'm willing to be your disciple and grand disciple."

"In that case," said Pilgrim, "no need to hesitate any longer. Pa-chieh, hurry and get me some mud." Idiot immediately used his muck-rake to rake up some dirt; not daring, however, to go outside to fetch water, he hitched up his clothes instead and pissed on the ground. With the urine he managed to mix a lump of stinking mud, which he handed to Pilgrim. Pilgrim, too, had little alternative but to flatten the mud and press it on his own face and, after a little while, succeeded in making an apelike mask. Asking the T'ang monk to stand up but without uttering another word, Pilgrim pasted the mask on his master's face and recited a magic spell. He then blew his immortal breath onto the mask, crying, "Change!" At once the elder took on the appearance of Pilgrim. He was told to take off his own garments and switch clothes with Pilgrim, who made the magic sign and then recited another spell to change into the form of the T'ang monk. The two of them looked so alike their own true selves that even Pa-chieh and Sha Monk could not distinguish them.

As soon as they finished dressing, they heard the sounds of gongs and drums and saw a forest of scimitars and lances approaching. The captains of the imperial guards, you see, had arrived with three thousand troops to have the postal station surrounded. Then an Embroidered-uniform Guard walked into the courtyard to ask, "Where is the elder from the T'ang court in the Land of the East?"

Shaking and quaking, the station master went to his knees and said, pointing with his finger, "In one of those guestrooms down there." The guard walked to the guest room and said, "Elder T'ang, my king invites you to the palace."

While Pa-chieh and Sha Monk stood on two sides to guard the false Pilgrim, the false T'ang monk came out the door and bowed, saying, "Sir Embroidered-uniform, what does His Majesty have to say when he asks for this poor cleric?" Rushing forward to grab him, the guard replied, "I'll go with you into court. He must have some use for you." Also, so it is that

Fiendish lies triumph o'er compassion;

Compassion's met instead with violence.

We do not know what will happen to his life when he leaves, and you must listen to the explanation in the next chapter.

Seventy-nine

Searching the cave for the fiend he meets Long Life;
The proper lord of the court sees the babies.[1]

We were telling you about that Embroidered-uniform Guard, who yanked the spurious T'ang monk out of the postal station. At once the imperial guards had them surrounded before they all headed for the gate of the court. There they said to the Custodian of the Yellow Gate: "We have brought the T'ang monk here. Please report this for us."

The custodian sent in the memorial hurriedly, and the befuddled king sent for the guest at once. While all the officials knelt down at the foot of the steps to bow to the king, the spurious T'ang monk stood erect at the center of the steps and shouted, "King Bhikṣu, why did you ask this humble cleric to come?"

With a smile, the king said, "An illness has afflicted us for many days and no cure has been found. Fortunately, our royal father-in-law has bestowed on us a prescription for which all the medicines have been prepared. All we need now is one particular supplement, which we must seek from you. If we are cured of our illness, we promise that we shall build a shrine for the elder. You will enjoy sacrifices in all four seasons and perpetual incense fires of the state."

"I am a person who has left the family," replied the spurious T'ang monk. "I came here with hardly any possessions on me. Would Your Majesty please ask the royal father-in-law what sort of thing he wants of me for the medical supplement?" "What we need," said the befuddled king, "is the heart of the elder."

The spurious T'ang monk said, "To tell you the truth, Your Majesty, I have quite a few hearts. Which color or shape would you like?"

"Priest," said the royal father-in-law, who was standing on one side, pointing with his finger, "we want your black heart."

"In that case," said the spurious T'ang monk, "bring me the knife quickly, so that I may cut open my chest. If I have a black heart, I'll be pleased to present it to you." Delighted, the befuddled king thanked him and asked the attendant to the Throne to hand the spurious monk a curved dagger. Taking the dagger, the monk untied his robe and stuck out his chest. As he rubbed his belly with his left hand, he plunged the dagger into himself with his right hand and, with a loud ripping noise, tore open his own chest. A mass of hearts rolled out, so terrifying the onlookers that the civil officials paled in fright and the military officers turned numb. When he saw that, the royal father-in-law said in the hall, "This is a monk of many hearts!"[2]

The spurious monk took those bloody hearts and manipulated them one by one for all to see: a red heart, a white heart, a yellow heart, an avaricious heart, a greedy heart, an envious heart, a petty heart, a competitive heart, an ambitious heart, a scornful heart, a murderous heart, a vicious heart, a fearful heart, a cautious heart, a perverse heart, a nameless obscure heart, and all kinds of wicked hearts. There was, however, not one single black heart!

That befuddled king was so stupefied that he could hardly utter a word. Trembling all over, he could only mutter: "Take them away! Take them away!" Unable to hold back any longer, the spurious T'ang monk retrieved his magic. As he changed back into his original form, he said to the befuddled ruler, "Your Majesty, you have no perception whatever. In priests like us there are only good hearts, but your father-in-law is the one who has a black heart that can be used as the medical supplement. If you don't believe me, let me take it out for you to see."

On hearing this, that royal father-in-law opened his eyes wide to take a careful look, and he saw that the monk had quite changed his appearance. He no longer looked the same. Aha!

He recognized the Great Sage Sun of old,

Who had great fame five hundred years ago.

Swirling around, he mounted the clouds to rise up, only to be blocked by Pilgrim, who bounded into the air with one somersault. "Where are you running to?" he bellowed. "Have a taste of my rod!"

The royal father-in-law wielded his coiled-dragon staff to meet his adversary, and the two of them began a marvelous battle in midair.

The compliant rod,

The coiled-dragon staff

Spread out the clouds to fill the airy void.

The father-in-law, a monster-spirit,

Claimed for his fiendish daughter beauteous looks.

The ruler's indulgence brought him disease;

The monster wanted to slaughter young boys.

The Great Sage came to show his magic might:
He seized the fiend and saved the populace.
The iron rod aimed fiercely at the head
Was met by a praiseworthy crooked staff.
They fought till a skyful of mist darkened the city,
Each member of the households paled with fright;
Till souls of all officials left in flight,
All palace girls and consorts changed their looks.
They frightened Bhikṣu's muddled ruler into frantic hiding
And violent trembling, not knowing what to do.
The rod rose like a tiger springing from the mount;
The staff soared like a dragon breaking from the sea.
Now this great disturbance at Bhikṣu state
Would make distinct the righteous and perverse.

That monster-spirit fought bitterly with Pilgrim for some twenty rounds, but the coiled-dragon staff was no match for the golden-hooped rod. After one half-hearted blow, the royal father-in-law changed into a cold beam of light and sped into the inner chamber of the palace to pick up the fiendish queen whom he had presented as a tribute to the king. Both of them changed into cold beams of light and vanished at once.

Dropping down from the clouds, Pilgrim went to the palace to say to the various officials, "You people have some royal father-in-law!" The officials all began to bow to give thanks to the divine monk. "Stop bowing," said Pilgrim. "See where your befuddled lord has gone."

"When our lord saw the fight," one of the officials replied, "he was driven by fear into hiding. We have no idea which palace he has gone to." "Search for him quickly!" commanded Pilgrim. "Don't let Queen Beauty abduct him." When they heard these words, the officials did not care whether they were permitted to enter the inner chambers or not. Together with Pilgrim they headed straight for the room of Queen Beauty, but not a trace of the king could be found. Even Queen Beauty herself had disappeared. Meanwhile, the queen, the girls consort of the Eastern Palace, the consort of the Western Palace, and the concubines of the Six Chambers all came to bow to give thanks to the Great Sage.

"Please rise, all of you," said the Great Sage. "It's not time for you to thank me yet. Let's go find your lord first." In a little while they saw four or five eunuchs support the befuddled ruler walking out from behind the Hall of Careful Conduct.[3] Prostrating themselves on the ground, the various officials said in unison, "Our lord! Our lord! We are indebted to the divine monk, who came to distinguish for us the true from the false. That royal father-in-law is a perverse fiend. Even Queen Beauty has disappeared." When the king heard that, he immediately asked Pilgrim to leave the inner palace and go to the treasure hall with him. "Elder," he said, as he bowed to Pilgrim to thank him, "when you arrived this morning, you looked so handsome. How is it that you've changed your appearance now?"

"To tell you the truth, Your Majesty, the person who came here this morning was my master," replied Pilgrim, laughing. "He is Tripitaka, the bond-brother of the T'ang court, and I'm Sun Wu-k'ung, his disciple. I have two other younger brothers—Chu Wu-nêng and Sha Wu-ching—who are now at the Golden Pavilion Postal Station. Because we knew that you believed in the monstrous suggestion and wanted my master's heart for medical supplement, old Monkey changed into his appearance to come here especially to subdue the fiend." On hearing this, the king at once commanded one of the chief ministers of the Grand Secretariat to go to the postal station and fetch the master and his disciples.

By this time our Tripitaka had learned that Pilgrim, who had changed back to his original form, was trying to subdue the fiend in midair. The elder was frightened out of his wits, and it was fortunate that Pa-chieh and Sha Monk were by his sides to support him. But he was still depressed by that lump of stinking mud that he had to wear on his face. It was then that he heard someone calling, "Master of the Law, we are the chief ministers of the Grand Secretariat sent by the king of the Bhikṣu state. We are here especially to invite you to court so that you may receive our thanks."

"Master, don't be afraid! Don't be afraid!" said Pa-chieh, grinning. "They are not inviting you so that they can demand your heart. I think Elder Brother must have won, and they want to thank you." "That may well be the case," replied Tripitaka, "but how can I face people with this stinking face?"

"You've no choice," said Pa-chieh. "Let's go see Elder Brother first, and we'll find a solution." That elder indeed had little choice but to follow Pa-chieh and Sha Monk, who toted the luggage and led the horse out into the courtyard. When the chief minister caught sight of them, he was aghast, crying, "Holy Father! What a bunch of goblins and monsters!" "Minister, please don't be offended by our ugliness," said Sha Monk. "We were born this way. But when my master sees my elder brother, he'll become handsome."

When the three of them arrived at court, they did not wait for the summons but walked right up to the hall. The moment Pilgrim saw them, he ran down the steps and pulled the lump of mud from his master's face. Blowing his immortal breath on him, Pilgrim cried "Change!" and the T'ang monk at once assumed his original form, feeling more energetic and spirited than before. Meanwhile, the king himself descended the steps to meet them, addressing the T'ang monk as "Venerable Buddha, Master of the Law." After master and disciples had tethered the horse, they all went up to the hall to exchange greetings.

"Your Majesty," said Pilgrim, "do you happen to know where that fiend came from? Let old Monkey go there and seize him, so that any evil consequence will be eliminated." When all those palace ladies and concubines standing behind the kingfisher screens heard Pilgrim speaking of eliminating any evil consequence, they ignored the observance of proper etiquette between men and women and all walked out together to bow to him, saying, "We beg the divine monk, the venerable buddha, to exercise his mighty magic power. Please pull the grass up by the root and exterminate him thoroughly. For this profound act of kindness we shall repay you handsomely."

Returning their bows hurriedly, Pilgrim pressed the king for the address of the Taoist. Somewhat abashed, the king spoke up: "When he arrived three years ago, we did question him, and he told us that he lived not too far from here, in Pure Florescence Village on the Willow Slope south of the city some seventy miles away. Though the royal father-in-law was aged, he had no son, only a daughter by his second wife. Having just turned sixteen, she had not been betrothed to anyone, and he was willing to present her as a tribute to us. Since we loved the girl, we accepted her and took her in as a palace consort. Then we were afflicted by illness, which the repeated efforts of the imperial physician could not alleviate. The royal father-in-law told us that he had a divine formula, which required the hearts of young boys to make soup for supplement. It was our folly to have believed in his words so readily. The boys were selected, and the noon hour today, in fact, was to be the appointed time for their hearts to be gouged out. Little did we anticipate that the divine monk would descend to our realm. When we discovered that the boys in the coops had disappeared, he convinced us that the divine monk, who had practiced the cultivation of realized immortality for ten incarnations, had never permitted his original yang to dissipate. If we could acquire his heart, he said, it would be ten thousand times better than the hearts of the little boys. That was the reason for our misguided affront offered to you. We did not know that the divine monk would recognize the fiendish demon. We beseech you to exercise your vast magic power and eliminate all evil consequences, for which we shall thank you with the wealth of a nation."

"To tell you the honest truth," said Pilgrim smiling, "those boys in the coops were hidden by me on the merciful request of my master. Don't speak of repaying us with any wealth or riches. When I've caught the fiend, that'll be my merit." He then called out: "Pa-chieh, follow me quickly!"

"I'm glad to obey you, Elder Brother," replied Pa-chieh, "but my stomach's so empty I can hardly exert myself." The king immediately asked the Court of Imperial Entertainments to prepare a vegetarian meal, which soon arrived.

After he had eaten his fill, Pa-chieh roused himself and mounted the clouds to rise into the air with Pilgrim. The king, the queens, and all those civil and military officials were so taken aback that they fell to their knees and kowtowed to the sky, all crying, "True immortals, true buddhas have descended to earth!" The Great Sage took Pa-chieh straight to a place some seventy miles south of the city, where they stopped the wind and cloud to look for the fiend's dwelling. All they could see, however, was a clear brook flanked by thousands of willows on both sides, but the Pure Florescence Village was nowhere to be found. Truly

Acres of wild paddies, an endless sight;
Banks of misty willows but no human trace.

After the Great Sage Sun had searched in vain for the fiend, he made the magic sign and recited the immortal word Oṁ, with which he at once summoned into his presence the local spirit. Trembling all over, the deity drew near to kneel down, saying, "Great Sage, the local spirit of Willow Slope kowtows to you." "Don't be frightened," said Pilgrim, "for I'm not going to beat you. I have a question for you instead. This Pure Florescence Village of Willow Slope, where is it?"

"There is here a Pure Florescence Cave," replied the local spirit, "but no Pure Florescence Village. This humble deity now perceives that the

Great Sage perhaps has come here from the Bhikṣu Kingdom?" "Yes, yes!" said Pilgrim. "The Bhikṣu king had been duped by a monster-spirit, but old Monkey recognized the fiend when I reached the city. When that fiend was defeated by me in battle, he changed into a cold beam of light and vanished. I asked the Bhikṣu king, who told us that he did inquire after the fiend's residence three years ago when he presented a beautiful girl as tribute. The fiend claimed then that he used to live in the Pure Florescence Village on Willow Slope, some seventy miles south of the city. Just now I searched my way here and all I saw was the slope. Since I didn't find any village, I thought I would ask you."

"May the Great Sage pardon me!" said the local spirit, kowtowing. "Since the Bhikṣu king, after all, is also the lord of this land, it is the proper duty of this humble deity to take note of his plight. But the monster-spirit has vast magic powers; once I betray his secret, he will come and oppress me. That's why he has not been brought to justice. Now that the Great Sage has arrived, all you need do is to go up to a willow tree with nine branches at the south bank of the brook. Circle around the trunk three times from left to right and then three more times from right to left. Lean on the trunk with both hands and call three times, 'Open the door.' The Pure Florescence Cave will appear."

On hearing this, the Great Sage dismissed the local spirit before leaping over the brook with Pa-chieh to continue their search. Soon they found the tree, which had indeed nine stems forking out from a single trunk. Pilgrim gave this instruction to Pa-chieh: "Stand still at a distance, and let me call the door open. When I find the fiend and chase him out here, you may back me up." Pa-chieh agreed and stood about a quarter mile away.

Following the words of the local spirit, our Great Sage circled the trunk three times from left to right and three times right to left; leaning with both hands on the tree, he cried, "Open the door! Open the door! Open the door!" Instantly two leaves of a door opened with a loud creak while the tree vanished entirely from sight. The inside was lit up by bright, luminous mists, but again there was no hint of any human inhabitant. Rousing his magic powers, Pilgrim dashed into the cave, and he discovered a nice place indeed:

Mist and smoke luminous;
Oblique rays of the sun and moon;
White clouds that often leave the cave;

Green moss that densely coats the yard.
A pathful of strange blossoms vying for glamour;
A stepful of rare grasses most luxuriant.
Warm, temperate air
Makes perpetual spring.
The place seems like Lang-yüan;[4]
It's no worse than P'êng and Ying.[5]
Long creepers spread o'er smooth benches;
Tousled vines dangle from a flat bridge.
Bees, red stamens in their mouths, come to the cave;
Butterflies, playing with orchids, pass a rock screen.

With big strides, Pilgrim dashed forward to take a careful look, and he
saw four big words etched on the rock screen: Pure Florescence Immortal Residence. Unable to restrain himself, he leaped around the
screen to look further, and there he saw the old fiend hugging a
beautiful girl to his bosom. Both panting hard, they were in the midst
of discussing the affairs of the Bhikṣu Kingdom. "What a marvelous
opportunity!" they said together. "Something we've been planning
for three years, and it would have been completed today. But it's
ruined by that ape-head now!"

Darting up to them, Pilgrim whipped out his rod and cried, "You
bunch of hairy lumps! What marvelous opportunity? Have a taste of
my rod!" Abandoning his beauty, the old fiend picked up his coiled-
dragon staff hurriedly to meet him. The two of them began another
fierce battle in front of the cave that was quite different from the one
before.

The upraised rod beamed golden light;
The wielded staff belched viciousness.
The fiend said, "You fool! How dare you barge inside my door?"
Pilgrim said, "I intend to subdue a fiend!"
The fiend said, "My tie to the king's not your concern.
For what reason must you come oppress me?"
Pilgrim said, "The priest's vocation is on mercy based.
We can't bear seeing young boys put to death."
Their words went back and forth, each full of hate.
The staff met the rod, they aimed at the heart.
They snapped strange flowers, watching for their lives;
They kicked up lichens as they slipped and slid.
They fought till the cave's bright mists had lost their glow,

Till the ledge's fine blossoms all collapsed.
The bing-bangs grounded the birds in fear;
Their shoutings scared the beauty into flight.
Only the old fiend and the Monkey King remained
As violent gusts of wind howled through the earth.
They fought on and on till they left the cave,
And Idiot Wu-nêng became all aroused.

Pa-chieh, you see, was standing outside; when he heard them brawling inside, he became so excited that he could hardly contain himself. Whipping out his muckrake, he knocked down the willow tree with nine branches with one terrific blow. As he raked the fallen trunk some more, fresh blood sprouted from the root and it emitted a sort of moaning sound. "This tree has become a spirit!" said Pa-chieh. "This tree has become a spirit!"

He lifted his rake and was about to bring it down again when he saw Pilgrim emerging with the fiend. Without a word our Idiot rushed forward and attacked with the rake. The old fiend was already finding it difficult to withstand Pilgrim; the sight of Pa-chieh's rake, therefore, completely unnerved him. Turning to flee, he shook his body once and changed into a cold beam of light to head for the east. Unwilling to let up at all, the two of them instantly gave chase.

As they shouted to close in for the kill, they suddenly heard the calls of phoenix and crane and saw the glow of auspicious luminosity. Then they caught sight of the Aged Star of South Pole, who had held down the cold beam of light. "Slow down, Great Sage," he cried, "and stop chasing, Heavenly Reeds. This old Taoist salutes you!"

"Brother Aged Star," said Pilgrim, returning his greeting, "where have you come from?"

With a chuckle, Pa-chieh said, "You blubbery codger! Since you've held down the cold beam of light, you must have caught the fiend." "He's here, he's here," replied the Aged Star, smiling back at him "I hope the two of you will spare his life."

"That old fiend's not related to you, old Brother," said Pilgrim. "Why are you speaking up for him?"

"He happens to be my beast of burden," replied the Aged Star with a smile, "and sneaked here to turn into a fiend." "If he's a creature of yours," said Pilgrim, "ask him to change back to his true form for us to see."

When he heard this, the Aged Star released the cold beam of light and shouted, "Cursed beast! Show your true form quickly, and we'll pardon your mortal offense!" Rolling over, the fiend at once revealed himself as a white deer. "This cursed beast!" said the Aged Star as he picked up the staff. "He has even managed to steal my staff!" Prostrate on the ground, the white deer could not utter a word; all he did was kowtow and shed tears. You see

His whole body striped like a token of jade,
Two upthrust horns like seven jagged blades.
In hunger he would the herb garden seek
And drink, in thirst, from the cloud-swollen creek.
Aged, he had the pow'r of flight attained,
And o'er the years a face that changed he gained.
When he at this time hears his master's call,
He'll show his form and in submission fall.

After the Aged Star had thanked Pilgrim, he mounted the deer to leave, only to be grabbed by Pilgrim. "Old Brother," he said, "please don't leave yet. There are two unfinished matters."

"What sort of unfinished matters?" asked the Aged Star, and Pilgrim said, "We have yet to catch the beautiful girl, who must be some kind of fiendish creature, and we must return together to report to that befuddled ruler of the Bhikṣu kingdom."

"If you put it that way," said the Aged Star, "I'll be patient and wait a while. You and Heavenly Reeds go inside the cave and capture the beautiful girl. Then we can go together to let the king see these creatures in their true forms." "Just wait a moment, old Brother," said Pilgrim, "we'll be back soon."

Arousing his spirit, Pa-chieh followed Pilgrim into the Pure Florescence Divine Residence, both shouting, "Catch the monster-spirit! Catch the monster-spirit!" The beautiful girl was still shaking so violently that she could hardly think of fleeing; when she heard the shouts, she dashed behind the rock screen, but there was no back door for her to leave through. "Where are you going?" roared Pa-chieh. "Watch my rake, you stinking, man-deceiving spirit!" As the beautiful girl did not even have a weapon in her hand, she could only step aside and change at once into a cold beam of light to try to flee. She was, however, met by the Great Sage, who slammed his rod down hard on the beam. Immediately the fiend tumbled to the ground and revealed her true form: that of a white-faced vixen.

Unable to hold back his hands, our Idiot raised his rake and gave her head a terrific blow. Alas!

The smile that shakes a city and a state
Into a hairy, lumpish fox is made!
"Don't mash her up!" cried Pilgrim. "Leave her body for that be-fuddled ruler to see."

Not bothered by the filth, our Idiot took her by the tail and yanked her body along to follow Pilgrim out the door. The Aged Star at that moment was just rubbing the deer's head and scolding him. "Dear cursed beast!" he cried. "How could you turn your back on your master and come here to be a spirit? If I hadn't arrived, you would have been struck to death by the Great Sage Sun."

"What are you saying, old Brother?" asked Pilgrim as he bounded out. "Just instructing the deer! Just instructing the deer!" replied the Aged Star. Throwing the dead vixen in front of the deer, Pa-chieh asked, "Is this your daughter?" Nodding his head a few times, the deer stretched out his muzzle to sniff her and bleated several times, as if he could not bear parting with the vixen. He was given a whack on the head by the Aged Star, who said, "Cursed beast! Isn't it enough that you got your life? Why smell her?" He then untied the sash of his robe and fastened it around the neck of the deer to drag him along. "Great Sage," he said, "I'll go see the Bhikṣu king with you." "Just a moment!" replied Pilgrim. "We might as well clean out the inside first, so that this place will not breed any more monstrosity in the years to come."

When he heard this, Pa-chieh lifted up his rake and showered blows on the willow trunk. Pilgrim recited again the magic word Oṁ to summon the local spirit, to whom he gave this instruction: "Find me some dried wood and make a good fire. I am trying to rid this place of monstrous calamity, so that you may be spared from any further oppression."

Turning round, the local spirit mounted gusts of cold winds with his ghostly troops to gather some frost-receiving grass, autumn-green grass, smartweeds, mountain-bud grass, dried southernwood, dried dragon-bones, and dried rushes—all withered plants that had been parched for more than a year and that could feed a fire like oil or fat. "Pa-chieh," Pilgrim cried, "no need to take the tree. Just stuff these things into the cave and light the fire. We'll destroy the place." As soon as the fire started, it did indeed turn the Pure Florescence monster residence into a flaming pit.

He then dismissed the local spirit before returning to face the king in the royal hall, accompanied by the Aged Star leading the deer and Pa-chieh dragging the dead vixen. Pilgrim said to the king, "Here's

your Queen Beauty! You want to dally with her some more?" The
bladder of the king quivered and his heart shook, and then his queens
and consorts were all frightened into bowing by the sight of the Aged
Star leading the white deer. Pilgrim went forward to raise up the king,
saying to him with a chuckle, "Don't bow to me. Here's your father-
in-law. You should bow to him!"

Terribly embarrassed, the king could only murmur, "I thank the
divine monk's Heavenly grace for saving the boys of my nation." He at
once ordered the Court of Imperial Entertainments to prepare a huge
vegetarian banquet. The East Hall was opened wide so that the Old
Man of South Pole, the T'ang monk, and his three disciples could be
seated to receive proper thanks. After Tripitaka and Sha Monk bowed
to greet the Aged Star, they both asked, "If the white deer belonged to
the Venerable Aged Star, how could it get here to harm people?"

The Aged Star answered, smiling, "Sometime Ago the Supreme
Ruler of the East[6] passed by my mountain, and I asked him to stay for
chess. Hardly had we finished one game when this cursed beast ran
away. When we couldn't find him after the guest's departure, I calculated by bending my fingers and realized that he had come to this
place. I came to search for him and ran into the Great Sage just in the
process of demonstrating his power. If I had come a little later, this
beast would have been finished." Hardly had he spoken when the
report came that the banquet was ready. Marvelous vegetarian
banquet!

The doorways decked with five colors;
The seats full of strange fragrance;
Tables draped with glowing brocade damask;
Floors spread with luminous red carpets.
From duck-shaped urns
Curled smoke of sandalwood incense;
Before the royal table
Came the fresh scent of vegetables.
Look at the fruit *crouque-en-bouche* on the dish,
The sweet pastries shaped like dragons or beasts.
Mandarin-duck cakes
And lion candies
All looked so real;
The parrot goblet
And the egret handle

All seemed lifelike.
Every fruit item on display was rich;
Every maigre dish on the table was fine.
Robustly round chestnuts,
Fresh lychees and peaches;
Dates and persimmons with the sweetest flavor;
Pine-seed and grape wines of the mellowest scent.
Several kinds of honey-glazed food
And a few steamed pastries.
Viands deep-fried or sugar-coated,
Made like blossoms or brocade.
Huge buns piled high on golden trays;
Fragrant rice filled many silver bowls.
Hot and spicy—the long rice noodles cooked in soup;
Potently scented—one bowl or dish after another.
You could not describe all the mushrooms,
The wood ears, the tender shoots, the Yellow Sperms;
Vegetables of ten varieties
And a hundred rare delicacies.
Presented back and forth without a pause
Were all kinds, all species of rich fare.

At the time, they took their seats according to rank: the Aged Star occupied the head table, while the elder remained next to him. The king went to the table in front, and Pilgrim, Pa-chieh, and Sha Monk sat on one side. There were three other chief ministers on both sides to keep them company. As the Office of Music was told to begin the serenade, the king held up his purple-mist cup to toast each person in turn, though the T'ang monk was the only one who did not drink. Pa-chieh then said to Pilgrim, "Elder Brother, I'll leave the fruits to you, but you must let us enjoy rice, soup, and the rest." Without regard for good or ill, that Idiot attacked the foodstuff madly and ate it up in no time at all.

After the banquet was over, the Aged Star got up to leave, but the king went forward to kneel to him to beg for a method that would eliminate illness and lengthen his years. With a smile the Aged Star said, "I was looking for my deer and I didn't bring along any elixir or herbs. I would have liked to impart to you the formula for cultivation, but your tendons have so deteriorated and your spirit has been so impaired that it would be impossible for you to accomplish the anablastemic enchymoma.[7] In my sleeve here, however, are three fire dates which were the presents of the Supreme Ruler of the East for my tea. I haven't eaten them yet, and I would like to give them to you now." After the king had swallowed the dates, he felt as if a great weight had been lifted gradually from his body as his illness receded. In fact, the longevity those descendants of his later attained might be traced to this.

When Pa-chieh saw that the king had received such a gift, he cried out, "Old Age, if you have any more fire dates, give me some, too." "I haven't brought any more along," replied the Aged Star. "Another day I'll send you a few pounds." He walked out of the East Hall, and having thanked his host once more, he ordered the white deer to stand up and leaped onto its back. They both rose immediately into the air and left treading on the clouds. The ruler, his consorts, and the populace of the city all bowed to the ground and burned incense.

Then Tripitaka said, "Disciples, start packing so that we may take leave of the king." The king, however, begged them to stay and instruct him. "Your Majesty," said Pilgrim, "from now on you must lessen your sensual pursuits and increase instead your unpublicized good deeds. In all affairs you should allow your strength to compensate for your weakness, and you will find that this is quite sufficient to stave off sickness and lengthen your life. Such is the instruction I have for you." Thereafter the king also presented them with two trays of gold and silver pieces as travel money, but the T'ang monk refused to accept even a penny. The king had no alternative but to send for his imperial cortege and asked the T'ang monk to be seated on the phoenix carriage in the dragon chariot. He and his consorts all put their hands on the carriage and pushed it out of the court. At the same time, all the main boulevards were lined with citizens who added pure water to their sacrificial vases and true incense in the urns to send the pilgrims out of the city.

Just then, a roar of the wind from midair brought down to both sides of the road one thousand, one hundred and eleven geese coops with some crying young boys inside. The local spirit, city god, god of the soil, immortal officials, the Guardians of Five Quarters, the Four Sentinels, the Six Gods of Darkness and Six Gods of Light, and the guardians of monasteries who gave secret protection to the children all announced in a loud voice: "Great Sage, you told us previously to take away these boys in the geese coops. Now that your merit has been achieved and you are about to leave, we have brought them back one by one." The king, the queens, and all the citizens bowed down as Pilgrim said to the air, "I thank you all for your help. Please return to your shrines, and I will ask the people to offer you their thanksgiving sacrifices." Sighing and soughing, the gust of cold wind rose once more and then quickly subsided.

When Pilgrim then asked the households of the city to come retrieve their children, the news was spread abroad at once and all the people came to identify and claim the boys in the coops. In great delight they were lifted out of the cages, hugged, and addressed as "darling" and "precious." Jumping about and laughing, the people all shouted, "We must take hold of the Holy Fathers of the T'ang court and bring them back to our homes. We must thank them for this profound act of kindness!" And so the people went forward, young and old, male and female, without the slightest fear of how ugly the pilgrims might look: they hauled Chu Pa-chieh up bodily, they put Sha Monk on their shoulders, they supported the Great Sage Sun with their heads, and they lifted up Tripitaka with their hands. Leading the horse and toting the luggage, they surged back to the city; not even the king could restrain them.

While one family gave a banquet, another prepared a feast; those who did not have time to take their turns made priestly caps and sandals, clerical robes and cloth stockings, and all manner of inner and outer garments to be presented as gifts. Indeed, the pilgrims had to linger for nearly a month in that city before they could leave. Before their departure, the people also made portraits of them, with their names inscribed on plaques set up below, so that perpetual sacrifices and incense could be offered. Truly it was that

This secret good deed weighty as a mount

Has saved a hundred and a thousand lives.

We do not know what happened thereafter, and you must listen to the explanation in the next chapter.

Eighty

The fair girl, nursing the yang, seeks a mate;
Mind Monkey, guarding his master, knows a monster.

We were telling you about the Bhikṣu king who, along with his sub-jects, escorted the T'ang monk and his disciples out of the city; they journeyed for some twenty miles and still the king refused to turn back. At last Tripitaka insisted on leaving the imperial chariot and mounted the horse to take leave of the escorts, who waited until the pilgrims were out of sight before returning to their own city.

The four pilgrims traveled for some time until both winter and spring faded; there was no end to the sight of wild flowers and moun-tain trees, of lovely and luxuriant scenery. Then they saw in front of them a tall, rugged mountain. Growing alarmed, Tripitaka asked, "Disciples, is there any road on that tall mountain ahead? We must be careful!"

"Your words, Master," said Pilgrim with a laugh, "hardly sound like those of a seasoned traveler! They seem more like those of a prince or nobleman who sits in a well and stares at the sky. As the ancient proverb says,

A mountain does not block a road,

For a road passes through a mountain.

Why ask about whether there is any road or not?"

"Perhaps the mountain does not block the road," replied Tripitaka, "but I fear that such a treacherous region will breed some fiends, or that monster-spirits will emerge from the depth of the mountain." "Relax! Relax!" said Pa-chieh. "This place is probably not too far from the region of ultimate bliss, and it's bound to be peaceful and safe."

As master and disciples were thus conversing, they soon reached the base of the mountain. Taking out his golden-hooped rod, Pilgrim went up a rocky ledge and called out: "Master, this is the way to go around the mountain. It's quite walkable. Come quickly! Come quickly!" The elder had little choice but to banish his worry and urge the horse forward. "Second Elder Brother," said Sha Monk, "you tote

the luggage for a while." Pa-chieh accordingly took over the pole
while Sha Monk held on to the reins so that the old master could sit
firmly on the carved saddle and follow Pilgrim on the main road as
they headed for the mountain. What they saw on the mountain were

Cloud and mist shrouding the summit
And rushing torrent in the brook;
Fragrant flowers clogging the road;
Ten thousand trees both thick and dense;
Blue plums and white pears;
Green willows and red peaches.
The cuckoo weeps for spring's about to leave,
And swallows murmur to end the seedtime rites.[1]
Rugged rocks;
Jade-top pines;
A rough mountain path,
Bumpy and jagged;
Precipitous hanging cliffs
With thickets of creepers and plants.
A thousand peaks noble like halberd rows;
Through countless ravines a grand river flows.

As the old master looked leisurely at this mountain scenery, the sound
of a bird singing filled him again with longing for home. He pulled the
horse to a stop and called out, "Disciples!

Since Heaven's plaque[2] conveyed the royal decree,
The rescript I took beneath brocaded screens.
At Lantern Feast, the fifteenth, I left the East,
From Emperor T'ang parted as Heav'n from Earth.
Just when dragons, tigers met with wind and cloud,
Master and pupils fell to horses and men.
On all twelve summits of Mount Wu I've walked.
When can I face my lord and see my king?"

"Master," said Pilgrim, "you are always so full of longing for home
that you are hardly like someone who has left home. Just relax and
keep moving! Stop worrying so much! As the ancients said,

If wealth in life you wish to see,
Deadly earnest your work must be."

Tripitaka said, "What you say is quite right, disciple, but I wonder how
much more there is of this road that leads to the Western Heaven!"

"Master," Pa-chieh said, "it must be that our Buddha Tathāgata is unwilling to part with those three baskets of scriptures. Knowing that we want to acquire them, he must have moved. If not, why is it that we just can't reach our destination?" "Stop that foolish talk!" said Sha Monk. "Just follow Big Brother. Exert yourself and endure it. There'll be a day when we all arrive at our destination."

As master and disciples chatted in this manner, they came upon a huge, dark pine forest. Becoming frightened, the T'ang monk called out once more, "Wu-k'ung, we've just passed through a rugged mountain path. Why is it that we must face this deep, dark pine forest? We must be on guard."

"What's there to be afraid of?" asked Pilgrim, and Tripitaka said, "Stop talking like that! As the proverb says,

You don't believe the honesty of the honest;
You guard against the unkindness of the kind.

You and I have gone through several pine forests, but none was as deep and wide as this one. Just look at it!

Densely spread out east and west—
In thick columns north and south—
Densely spread out east and west it pierces the clouds;
In thick columns north and south it invades the sky.
Lush thistles and thorns are growing on all sides;
Creepers and weeds wind up and down the trunks.
The vines entwine the tendrils—
The tendrils entwine the vines—
The vines entwine the tendrils
To impede the east-west traveler;
The tendrils entwine the vines
To block the north-south trader.
In this forest
One may spend half a year
Not knowing the seasons,
Or walk a few miles
Without seeing the stars.
Look at those thousand kinds of scenery on the shady side
And ten thousand bouquets in the sunny part.
There are also the millennial *huai*.
The immortal juniper,
The cold-enduring pine,
The mountain peach,

The wild peony,
The dry-land hibiscus—
In layers and clumps they pile together,
So riotous that e'en gods can't portray them.
You hear also a hundred birds:
The parrot's squeal;
The cuckoo's wail;
The magpie darting through the branches;
The crow feeding her parents;
The oriole soaring and dancing;
A hundred tongues making melody;
A call of red partridges,
And the speech of purple swallows.
The mynah learns to speak like a human;
Even the grey thrush can read a sūtra.
You see, too, a big creature[3] wagging its tail
And a tiger grinding its teeth;
An aged fox disguised as a lady,
An old grey wolf growling through the woods.
Even if the devarāja Pagoda-Bearer comes here,
He'll lose his wits though he can subdue a monster!"

Not daunted in the least, however, our Great Sage Sun used his iron rod to open up a wide path and led the T'ang monk deep into the forest. Footloose and carefree, they proceeded for half a day but they had yet to reach the road leading out of the forest.

The T'ang monk called out: "Disciples, our journey to the West has taken us through countless mountains and forests, all rather treacherous. This particular spot, I'm glad to say, is quite nice and the road seems safe enough. The strange flowers and rare plants of this forest are certainly pleasing to behold. I want to sit for a while here—to rest the horse and to relieve my hunger—if you can go somewhere to beg us a vegetarian meal." "Please dismount, Master," said Pilgrim, "and I'll go beg the meal."

That elder indeed dismounted; as Pa-chieh tethered the horse to a tree, Sha Monk put down his load of luggage and took out the alms-bowl to hand to Pilgrim. "Master," said Pilgrim, "you may feel quite safe sitting here. Don't be frightened. Old Monkey will return shortly." While Tripitaka sat solemnly in the pine shade, Pa-chieh and Sha Monk amused themselves by going off to search for flowers and fruits.

We tell you now about our Great Sage, who somersaulted into mid-air. As he paused in his cloudy luminosity to look back, he saw that the pine forest was veiled by hallowed clouds and auspicious mists. So moved was he by the sight that he unwittingly blurted out, "Marvelous! Marvelous!"

Why did he say that, you ask. He was giving praise to the T'ang monk, you see, and recalling to himself the fact that his master was verily the incarnation of the Elder Gold Cicada, a good man who has practiced austerities for ten incarnations. That was why his head was surrounded by such an auspicious halo. "Consider old Monkey," he thought to himself. "At the time when I brought great disturbance to the Celestial Palace five hundred years ago, I toured with the clouds the four corners of the sea and roamed freely the edges of Heaven. I assembled various monster-spirits to call myself the Great Sage, Equal to Heaven; taming the tiger and subduing the dragon, I even removed our names from the register of death. My head wore a triple-decker gold crown, and my body a yellow gold cuirass; my hands held the golden-hooped rod and my feet were shod in cloud-treading shoes. Some forty-seven thousand fiends under my command all addressed me as Venerable Father Great Sage, and that was some life I led. Now that I'm delivered from my Heaven-sent calamity, I must humble myself and serve this man as his disciple. But if my master's head has the protection of such hallowed clouds and auspicious mists, he will, I suppose, end up with something good once he returns to the Land of the East, and old Monkey undoubtedly will also attain the right fruit."

As he thought to himself in this manner and gave praise to his master, he caught sight of a mass of black fumes boiling up from south of the forest. Greatly startled, Pilgrim said, "There must be something perverse in those black fumes! Our Pa-chieh and Sha Monk can't release black fumes like that . . ." In midair our Great Sage at once tried to determine where those black fumes came from, and we shall leave him for the moment.

We tell you instead about Tripitaka, who was sitting in the forest with mind enlightened by the vision of the Buddha-nature in all things. As he recited with utmost concentration the *Mahāprajñā-pāramitāhṛdaya Sūtra*, he suddenly heard a faint cry, "Save me! Save me!" "My goodness! My goodness!" said Tripitaka, highly astonished. "Who would be crying out like that deep in the forest? It must be someone scared by tigers or wolves. Let me take a look." Rising and striding forward, the elder went by the millennial cedars and the immortal pines; he climbed over creepers and vines to take a clear look. Tied to the trunk of a huge tree was a girl: the upper half of her body was bound by vines, while the lower half of her body was buried in the ground.

Stopping before her, the elder asked, "Lady Bodhisattva, for what reason are you bound here?" Alas! She was clearly a monster, but the elder, being of fleshly eyes and mortal stock, could not recognize her. When the fiend heard the question, she released a torrent of tears. Look at her!

As tears dripped from her peachlike cheeks,
She had features that would sink fishes and drop wild geese;
As grief flashed from her starlike eyes,
She had looks that would daunt the moon and shame the flowers.
In truth not daring to approach her, our elder asked again, "Lady Bodhisattva, what possible crime could you have committed? Speak up so that this humble cleric may rescue you."

With clever and deceptive words, with false and specious sentiments, the monster-spirit replied hurriedly, "Master, my home is located in the Bimbāna Kingdom,[4] some two hundred miles from here. My parents, still living and exceedingly devoted to virtue, have in all their lives been kind to friends and peaceable toward relatives. As this is the time of Clear Brightness, they invited various kinfolk and the young and old of our family to sweep clean our ancestral graves and offer sacrifices to the dead. A whole row of carriages and horses went out into the desolate wilds. We had just set up the sacrifices and finished burning paper money and horses when the sound of gongs and drums brought out a band of strong men wielding knives, waving staffs, and screaming to kill as they fell on us. We were scared out of our wits. My parents and my relatives managed to escape on horseback or in the carriages. Being so young and unable to run, I fell in terror to the ground and was abducted by these brigands. The Big Great King wanted me to be his mistress; the Second Great King desired me for his wife; the Third and the Fourth, too, admired my beauty. A heated quarrel thus began among some seventy or eighty of them, and when they could not resolve their anger, they had me tied up in the forest before they scattered. I have been here like this for five whole days and nights, and I expect my life will expire any moment. I don't know which generation of my ancestors accumulated sufficient

merit to acquire for me the good fortune this day of meeting the
venerable master at this place. I beseech you in your great mercy to
save my life. I shall never forget your kindness, even when I reach the
Nine Springs of Hades!" When she finished speaking, her tears fell like
rain.

Always a merciful person, Tripitaka could not refrain from shedding
tears himself. In a choking voice, he called out, "Disciples!"

Our Pa-chieh and Sha Monk were just searching for flowers and
fruits in the forest when they suddenly heard the melancholy cry of
their master. "Sha Monk," said Idiot, "Master must have recognized
one of his relatives here." "You're driveling, Second Elder Brother!"
said Sha Monk, laughing. "We haven't met one good man after walking all this time. Where would this relative come from?"

"If it weren't a relative," replied Pa-chieh, "you think Master would
be weeping with someone else? Let's you and I go take a look." Sha
Monk agreed to go back to the original spot with him. As they drew
near, leading the horse and toting the luggage, they said, "Master,
what's up?"

Pointing to the tree, the T'ang monk said, "Pa-chieh, untie that
lady bodhisattva over there so that we may save her life." Without
regard for good or ill, our Idiot immediately proceeded to do so.

We tell you now about the Great Sage in midair, who saw that the
black fumes were growing thicker all the time until they had the
auspicious luminosity completely covered. "That's bad! That's bad!"
he exclaimed. "When the black fumes have covered the auspicious
luminosity, it may mean that some monstrous perversity has harmed
Master. Begging for vegetarian food is a small matter now. I'd better
go see my master first." Reversing the direction of his cloud, he
dropped down into the forest, where he found Pa-chieh busily trying
to untie the ropes. Pilgrim went forward, grabbed one of his ears, and
flung him with a thud to the ground. As he raised his head to look and
scramble up, Idiot said, "Master told me to rescue this person. Why did
you have to strongarm me and give me this tumble?"

"Brother, don't untie her," said Pilgrim with a laugh. "She is a
monster-spirit who's using some jugglery to deceive us."

"You brazen ape!" snapped Tripitaka. "You're babbling again!
How could you tell that this girl is a fiend?" "Master, you may have
no idea about this," replied Pilgrim, "but it's the kind of business old
Monkey has done before. This is the way monster-spirits try to get

human flesh to eat. How could you know about that?"

Sticking out his snout, Pa-chieh said, "Master, don't believe the lies of this pi-ma-wên. This girl belongs to a family here, whereas we came from the distant Land of the East. We're no acquaintances or kinfolk of hers. How could we say that she is a monster-spirit? He wants us to abandon her and go on our way so that he can use his magic and somersault back here to have a nice time with her. He wants to sneak in through the back door!"

"Coolie, don't you dare mouth such nonsense!" snapped Pilgrim. "During this journey to the West, since when has old Monkey ever been slothful or unruly? I'm no miserable bum like you who loves sex more than life, and who will sell out his friends for a price. Remember how dumb you were when you were deceived by that household's offer to take you in as a son-in-law and ended up being tied to a tree?"[5]

"All right! All right!" said Tripitaka. "Pa-chieh, your elder brother has always been quite right in his perception. If he puts it that way, let's not mind her. Let's leave." "Marvelous!" said Pilgrim, highly pleased. "Master will be able to preserve his life. Please mount up. After we get out of the pine forest, I'll go to some household to beg you a vegetarian meal." The four of them indeed abandoned the fiend and proceeded.

Still bound to the tree, the fiend said to herself through clenched teeth, "I have heard people say for several years that Sun Wu-k'ung has vast magic powers. What I can see of him today certainly confirms the rumor. Since that T'ang monk has begun practicing austerities in his youth, he has never allowed his original yang to leak out. I was hoping that I could seize him and mate with him so that I might become a golden immortal of the Grand Monad. Hardly did I anticipate that this ape would see through my disguise and take him away instead. If he had untied me and let me down, the T'ang monk would have fallen right into my hands. He would have indeed been mine, wouldn't he? If I let him get away now just because of a few casual remarks, it means I have planned and worked in vain. Let me call him a couple more times and see what happens. Still tied up in the ropes, the monster-spirit instead employed a gentle breeze to waft some virtuous sentences faintly into the ears of the T'ang monk. What did she say, you ask. This was how she called out to him: "O Master!

If you a living human passed by and refused to free,
What Buddha or scriptures could such blindness hope to see?"

Hearing a summons like that as he rode along, the T'ang monk immediately reined in the horse and called out, "Wu-k'ung, let's go and free the girl." "Master, you're moving along just fine," said Pilgrim. "What makes you think of her again?"

"She's calling after me!" replied the T'ang monk.

"Did you hear anything, Pa-chieh?" asked Pilgrim. Pa-chieh said, "My oversized ears must have blocked it. I didn't hear a thing."

"Sha Monk, did you hear anything?" asked Pilgrim again. Sha Monk said, "I was walking ahead, toting the luggage, and I didn't pay any attention. I didn't hear anything either." "Nor did old Monkey," said Pilgrim. "Master, what did she say? Why are you the only one who heard the call?"

The T'ang monk said, "The way she called me makes a lot of sense. She said,

If you a living human passed by and refused to free,
What Buddha or scriptures could such blindness hope to see?
As the proverb also puts the matter,
Saving one life
Is better than building a seven-tiered pagoda.
Let's go quickly and rescue her. It'll be as good as fetching scriptures and worshiping Buddha."

"Master," said Pilgrim with a laugh, "when you want to do good, there's no drug in the world that can cure you! Think how many mountains you have crossed since you left the Land of the East and how many monsters you have encountered since you began your journey to the West. Without fail they managed to have you captured and brought into their caves. When old Monkey came to rescue you, the iron rod he used had beaten thousands upon thousands to death. Today there's only one life of a monster-spirit, and you can't leave her. Do you have to rescue her?" "O disciple!" said the T'ang monk. "As the ancients said,

Don't fail to do good even if it's small;
Don't engage in evil even if it's small.
Let's go rescue her."

"If you put it that way, Master," said Pilgrim, "you must assume the responsibility, because old Monkey can't bear it. If you have made up your mind to rescue her, I dare not admonish you too much. For if I do, you'll get mad after a while. You may go and rescue her as you please." "Don't talk so much, ape-head!" said the T'ang monk. "You sit here, while Pa-chieh and I go rescue her."

Returning to the pine forest, the T'ang monk asked Pa-chieh to untie the ropes which had the girl bound to the tree from the waist up, and to use his rake to dig the lower half of her body out from the ground. Stamping her feet and straightening out her skirt, the fiend followed the T'ang monk out of the forest most amiably. When they met up with Pilgrim, he began to snicker uncontrollably.

"Brazen ape!" scolded the T'ang monk. "Why are you laughing?" "I'm laughing replied Pilgrim, "because

Good friends will hail you when times are right;

A fair lady will greet you when fortune fails!"

"Wretched ape!" scolded the T'ang monk again. "What rubbish! The moment I left my mother's belly, I became a priest. Now I'm journeying westward by imperial decree and trying to worship Buddha in all sincerity. I'm no seeker of profit or status. How could there be a time when my fortune fails?"

"Master," replied Pilgrim with a laugh, "though you may have been a monk since your youth, all you know is how to read sūtras and chant the name of Buddha. You aren't familiar with the codes and laws of a state. This girl is both young and pretty, and we are after all persons who have left the family. If we travel with her, we may run into wicked people who will send us to court. Regardless of how we profess to be scripture seekers and Buddha worshipers, they may accuse us of fornication. Even if we are cleared of that charge, they may still have us convicted of kidnaping. You will be expelled from your priesthood and beaten till you're half-dead; Pa-chieh will be sent into the army and Sha Monk will be sentenced to hard labor. Even old Monkey will find it hard to extricate himself from such a messy affair. I may be smart-mouthed, but no amount of haggling on my part will clear us of indiscretion."

"Stop this nonsense!" snapped Tripitaka. "I'm determined to save her life. How could she involve us in any trouble? We're taking her with us. If anything arises, I'll assume the responsibility myself." "You may talk like that, Master," said Pilgrim, "but you don't realize that what you are doing won't save her but will only harm her." Tripitaka said, "I rescued her out of the forest so that she might live. How could she be harmed instead?"

"When she was tied up in the forest," replied Pilgrim, "she might have lasted five to seven days, possibly up to half a month, but without rice to eat, she would have starved to death. Even in that situation, however, she would have died with her body preserved intact. Now you've freed her and brought her with you, without realizing, of course, that you happen to be riding a horse swift as the wind. We may be able to follow you on our feet, not having really any choice in the matter, but the girl has such tiny feet that she moves with great difficulty. How could she possibly keep up with you? If by chance she drops behind, she may well run into a tiger or a leopard, which will swallow her with one gulp. In that case, haven't you harmed her life?"

"Indeed!" said Tripitaka. "It's a good thing you saw things this way. What shall we do?" "Lift her up and let her ride with you," said Pilgrim. "How can I ride with her? . . ." said Tripitaka, and he fell into silent thought.

"How can she proceed?" pressed Pilgrim. "Let Pa-chieh carry her on his back," said Tripitaka, and laughing, Pilgrim said, "Idiot's getting lucky!"

"'A long distance has no light load!'" said Pa-chieh. "How can I be getting lucky if I'm asked to carry someone on my back?"

"But you've such a long snout," said Pilgrim, "long enough, in fact, to stick it behind you to flirt with her once she is on your back. Don't you have an advantage there?" When Pa-chieh heard this, he pounded his chest and jumped up and down. "That's no good! That's no good!" he bellowed. "If Master wants to beat me a few times, I'm willing to take the pain, but it'll be quite messy for me if I put her on my back. All his life, Elder Brother has loved to set people up by planting false evidence. I can't carry her!"

"All right, all right!" said Tripitaka. "I can still manage to walk a few steps. Let me get down and walk slowly with her. Pa-chieh can lead the horse." Breaking into loud guffaws, Pilgrim said, "Idiot is really getting the business. Master's looking after you by asking you to lead the horse!"[6]

"This ape-head is mouthing absurdity again!" said Tripitaka. "The ancients said, 'Though a horse can travel a thousand miles, it can't get there without human guidance.' If I walk slowly on the road, would you like to leave me behind, too? If I move slowly, you must also move slowly; we can certainly walk down the mountain with this lady bodhisattva. When we arrive at some human household, we can leave her there, and that will have completed our task of rescuing her."

"What Master says is quite reasonable," said Pilgrim. "Please proceed quickly." As Tripitaka walked forward, Sha Monk toted the luggage, Pa-chieh led the horse and the girl, and Pilgrim held up his iron rod. They had not covered more than twenty or thirty miles when it was getting late, and there came into their view again a towered building with ornate roof carvings. "Disciples," said Tripitaka, "that must be either a monastery or temple. Let's ask for one night's lodging, and we can proceed tomorrow." "You spoke well, Master," said Pilgrim. "Let's move along, all of us."

As soon as they reached the gate, Tripitaka gave them this instruction: "Stand away from the door, all of you, and let me go ask for lodging. If it's convenient, someone will come to call you." All of them stood beneath the shade of some willow trees, but Pilgrim, gripping his iron rod, stood guard over the girl.

The elder strode forward and saw that the temple gate was so badly rotted that it was all crooked and bent. When he pushed it open to have another look, he was filled with grief, for he found

The long corridors quiet,
An old temple desolate.
Mosses filled the courtyard
And weeds choked the path.
Only the fireflies served as lanterns,
And frog-croaks acted for water clocks.

All at once the elder could not hold back his tears. Truly

The walls were unused and collapsing;
The chambers, forlorn and crumbling.
Over ten piles of broken bricks and tiles;
There were all bent pillars and snapped beams.
Green grasses grew both front and back;
Dust buried the incense alcove.
The bell tower stood in ruin, the drum had no skin;
The crystal chalice was cracked and chipped.
Buddha's gold frame lacked luster;
Arhats lay prone east and west.
Kuan-yin, rain-soaked, was reduced to clay,
Her willow vase fallen to earth.
No priests would enter during the day;
Only foxes rested here by night.
You heard only the wind's thunderous roar
In this tiger and leopard's hiding place.

Walls on all four sides had collapsed,
Leaving no doors to fence in the house.
We have also a testimonial poem that says:
A very old temple in disrepair:
Decayed, declining—no one seems to care.
The fierce wind fractures the guardians' faces,
And heavy rain the buddha-heads defaces.
The arhats have fallen, they're strewn about;
Homeless, a local spirit sleeps without.
Two sorry sights for one to look upon:
The bronze bell's grounded for the belfry's gone.
Forcing himself to be bold, Tripitaka walked through the second-level
door and found that the belfry and the drum tower had both collapsed.
All there was left was a huge bronze bell standing on the ground: the
upper half was white as snow and the lower half was blue-green like
indigo. It had been there for many years, you see: rain had whitened
the upper part of the bell and the dampness of the earth had coated the
lower part with copperas. Rubbing the bell with his hand, Tripitaka
cried out: "O bell! You used to
Make thunderous peal, on a tow'r hung high,
Or boom carved-beam tones to the distant sky,
Or ring in the dawn when the roosters crow'd,
Or send off the twilight when the sun dropp'd low.
The bronze-melter, I wonder where he is,
And whether the smith who forged you still exists.
These two, I think, are now for Hades bound:
They have no traces and you have no sound!"
As the elder loudly lamented in this manner, he unwittingly disturbed
a temple worker who was in charge of incense and fire. When he heard
someone speaking, he scrambled up, picked up a piece of broken brick,
and tossed it at the bell. The loud clang so scared the elder that he fell
to the ground; he struggled up and tried to flee, only to trip over the
root of a tree and stumble a second time. Lying on the ground, the
elder said, "O bell!
While this humble cleric laments your state,
A loud clang suddenly reaches my ears.
No one takes the road to Western Heav'n, I fear,
And thus you've become a spirit o'er the years."
The temple worker rushed forward and raised him up, saying, "Please

rise, Venerable Father. The bell has not turned into a spirit. I struck it, and that is why it clanged."

When he raised his head and saw how ugly and dark the worker looked, he said, "Could you be some sort of goblin or fiend? I'm no ordinary human, but someone from the Great T'ang. Under my command are disciples who can subdue the dragon and tame the tiger. If you run into them, it won't be easy to preserve your life!"

Going to his knees, the temple worker said, "Don't be afraid, Venerable Father. I'm no fiend, only a temple worker in care of the fire and incense in this monastery. When I heard your virtuous lament just now, I was about to step out and receive you. Then I was afraid you might be some kind of perverse demon knocking at our door, so I picked up a piece of brick to toss at the bell—just to calm my own fears before I dared come out. Venerable Father, please rise."

Only then did the T'ang monk collect his wits and say, "Keeper, you nearly frightened me to death! Please take me in." The worker led the T'ang monk straight through the third-level door, the inside of which he found to be quite different from the outside. He saw

Walls of cloud-patterns built by bluish bricks,
And a main hall roofed in green glazed tiles.
Yellow gold trimmed the sages' forms;
White jade slabs made up the steps.
Green light danced on the Great Hero Hall;
Zealous airs rose from the Pure Alcove.
On Mañjuśrī Hall
Colorful designs soared like clouds;
On the Transmigration Hall
Painted flowers heaped up elegance.
A pointed vase tipped the triple-layered eave;
A brocade top lined the Five-Blessings Tower.
A thousand bamboos rocked the priestly beds;
Ten thousand green pines lit up the Buddhist gate.
Golden light shone within the Jade-Cloud Palace;
Auspicious hues fluttered in the purple mists.
With dawn a fragrant breeze blew to all four quarters;
By dusk the painted drum rolled from a tall mountain.
If one could face the sun to mend a cloak,
Would he not by moonlight finish the Book?
They saw, too, lamplight glowing on half the backyard wall

And scented mists flooding the whole of central mall.
When Tripitaka saw all this, he dared not enter. "Worker," he called out, "from the front, your place looks so run down, but it's so nicely maintained back here. How can this be?"

With a laugh the worker said, "Venerable Father, there are many perverse fiends and bandits in this mountain. In fair weather they used to rob and plunder all over the region, but they would seek shelter in this monastery when the skies were grey. They took down holy images and used them for seat cushions, and they pulled up shrubbery and plants for starting fires. As the monks in our monastery are too weak to contend with them, the ruined buildings up front have been turned over to the bandits as their resting place. New patrons were found to build another monastery in the back, so that the pure and the profane could remain distinct. That's how things are in the West!" "I see!" replied Tripitaka.

As they walked inside, Tripitaka saw on top of the monastery gate these five words written large: Sea-Pacifying Zen Grove Monastery. Hardly had they crossed the threshold when they saw a monk approaching. How did he look, you ask.

He wore a cap of wool-silk pinned to the left;
A pair of copper rings dangled from his ears.
He had on himself a robe of Persian wool;
Like silver his two eyes were white and clear.
His hand waving a rattle from Pamirs,
He chanted some scripture barbaric and queer.
Tripitaka could in no way recognize
This lama cleric of the Western sphere.

Coming through the door, the lama priest saw what lovely, refined features Tripitaka possessed: broad forehead and a flat top, shoulder-length ears, hands that reached beyond the knees—so handsome, in fact, that he seemed verily an incarnate arhat. Walking forward to take hold of him, the lama priest, full of smiles, gave Tripitaka's hand and leg a couple of pinches; he also rubbed Tripitaka's nose and pulled at his ear to express his cordial sentiments.

After taking Tripitaka into the abbot's chamber and greeting him, he asked, "Where did the venerable master come from?" "This disciple," replied Tripitaka, "is someone sent by imperial commission of the Great T'ang in the Land of the East to go to the Great Thunderclap Monastery of India in the West to seek scriptures from the Buddha. As we arrive in your precious region at this late hour of the day, I come especially to ask for one night's lodging in your noble temple. Tomorrow we'll set out once more. I beg you to grant us this request."

"Blasphemy! Blasphemy!" said the priest, laughing. "People like you and me didn't leave the family with noble intentions. It's usually because the times of our births happened to have offended the Floriate Canopy.[7] Our families were too poor to rear us, and that gave us the resolve to leave home. Since we have all become the followers of Buddha, we should never speak fraudulent words."

"But mine were honest words!" replied Tripitaka.

"What a distance it is to travel from the Land of the East to the Western Heaven!" said the priest. "There are mountains on the road, there are caves in the mountains, and there are monsters in the caves. You are all by yourself and you seem so young and gentle. You don't look like a scripture seeker!"

"The abbot's perception is quite correct," said Tripitaka. "How could this poor cleric reach this place all by himself? I have three other disciples who are able to open up a road in the mountains and build a bridge across the waters. It is their protection that has enabled me to reach your noble temple."

"Where are your three worthy disciples?" asked the priest.

"Waiting outside the monastery gate," replied Tripitaka.

"Master," said the priest, growing alarmed, "you probably have no idea that there are tigers and wolves, fiendish thieves, and weird goblins out to harm people in this region. Even in daytime we dare not travel very far, and we shut our doors before it gets dark. How could you leave people outside at this hour? Disciples, ask them to come in quickly!"

Two young lamas ran out, but at the sight of Pilgrim they immediately fell down in fright; when they saw Pa-chieh, they stumbled again. Scrambling to their feet, they dashed to the rear, crying, "Holy Father, you've rotten luck! Your disciples have disappeared. There are just three or four fiends standing outside the gate."

"What do they look like?" asked Tripitaka. One of the young priests said, "One had a thundergod beak, another a pestlelike snout, and a third had a blue-green face with fangs. By their side there was a girl, rather heavily made up."

"You could not possibly know that those three ugly creatures happen to be my disciples," said Tripitaka smiling. "The girl, however, is someone whose life I saved back in a pine forest." "O Holy Father!" cried the young priest. "Such a handsome master like yourself, why did you find such ugly disciples?"

"They may be ugly," replied Tripitaka, "but they are all useful. You'd better hurry and invite them inside. If you wait a while longer, that one with the thundergod beak, being no human offspring, loves to cause trouble and he may want to fight his way in."

The young priest hurried out, trembling all over, fell to his knees, and said, "Venerable Fathers, Father T'ang asks you to enter." "O Elder Brother," said Pa-chieh, giggling, "all he has to do is to invite us to enter. Why is he shaking so hard?" "Because he's afraid," replied Pilgrim, "seeing how ugly we are."

"How absurd!" said Pa-chieh. "We were born like this! We don't look ugly just for the fun of it!"

"Let's try to fix up the ugliness somewhat," said Pilgrim. Our Idiot indeed lowered his head to hide his snout in his bosom; while he led the horse and Sha Monk toted the luggage, Pilgrim herded the girl with his rod in the rear as all of them walked inside. Going through the ruined buildings and three levels of doors, they reached the inside, where they tethered the horse and set the luggage on the ground before entering the abbot's chamber to greet the lama priest. When they had taken their proper seats, the priest led out some seventy young lamas who also greeted the pilgrims. Then they began preparing a vegetarian meal to entertain the guests. Truly

Merit must start with a merciful thought;

A priest lauds a monk when Buddhism thrives.

We do not know how they will leave the monastery, and you must listen to the explanation in the next chapter.

Eighty-one

At Sea-Pacifying Monastery Mind Monkey knows the fiend;
In the black pine forest three pupils search for their master.

We were telling you how Tripitaka and his disciples arrived at the Sea-Pacifying Zen Grove Monastery, where they had a vegetarian meal prepared by the local monks. After the four had eaten, and the girl too had received some nourishment, it was getting late and lamps were lit in the abbot's chamber. Because they wanted to ask the T'ang monk the reason for seeking scriptures, and because they coveted a glimpse of the girl, the various monks all crowded into the chamber and stood in rows beneath the lamps. Tripitaka said to the lama he had met earlier, "Abbot, when we leave your treasure temple tomorrow, what's the rest of the journey to the West like?"

At once the priest went to his knees, so startling the elder that he hurriedly tried to raise him, saying, "Please rise, abbot. I am asking you about the journey. Why are you performing ceremony instead?"

"Your journey tomorrow, Master," replied the priest, "should proceed along a smooth and level path, and you need not worry. But at this very moment there is a small but rather embarrassing matter. I wanted to tell you the moment you entered our gate, but I feared that I might offend you. Only after we have served you a meal do I make so bold as to tell you. Since the venerable master has come from such a long way in the East, you must be tired, and it is perfectly all right that you should rest tonight in the room of this humble cleric. But it will not be convenient for this lady bodhisattva, and I wonder where I should send her to sleep."

"Abbot," said Tripitaka, "you needn't suspect that we master and disciples are harboring some perverse intentions. We passed through a black pine forest earlier and found this girl bound to a tree. Sun Wu-k'ung, my disciple, refused to rescue her, but I was moved by my Buddhist compassion to have her released and brought here. Wherever the abbot now wishes to send her to sleep is all right with me."

"Since the master is so kind and generous," said the priest grate-fully, "I'll just ask her to go to the Devarāja Hall. I'll make a bed of straw behind Holy Father Devarāja, and she can sleep there." "Very good! Very good!" said Tripitaka. Thereupon the young priests led the girl to go to sleep at the back of the hall.

After the elder had bidden the other priests good night, everyone left. "You all must be tired," said Tripitaka to Wu-k'ung. "Let's rest now so that we may rise early." All of them thus slept in the same place, for they wanted to guard their master and dared not leave his side. Gradually the night deepened. Truly

All sounds had ceased as the moon rose high;
The temple[1] grew silent for no one walked by.
The silver Stream glistened with starry showers
When tower-drums hastened the change of hours.

Leaving them to rest through the night, we tell you now about Pilgrim, who rose by dawn and at once told Pa-chieh and Sha Monk to pack and ready the horse, so that they might ask their master to set out again. The elder, however, was still sleeping at that moment. Pilgrim walked up to him and called out, "Master."

The master raised his head slightly but did not answer. "Master," asked Pilgrim, "what's the matter with you?"

"I don't know why," replied the elder with a groan, "but my head seems light, my eyes feel puffy, and I ache all over!" On hearing this, Pa-chieh touched him and found him feverish. "I know," said Idiot, giggling. "You saw last night that the rice was free, and you ate one bowl too many and then went to sleep with a blanket over your head. You've got indigestion!"

"Rubbish!" snapped Pilgrim. "Let me find out from master what is the true reason."

"I got up in the middle of the night to relieve myself, and I forgot to put on my cap," said Tripitaka. "I must have been chilled by the wind."

"That's more like it," replied Pilgrim. "Can you travel at all?"

"I can't even sit up," said Tripitaka. "How could I mount the horse? But then, I don't want to delay our journey either!"

"You shouldn't speak like that, Master!" said Pilgrim. "As the proverb says,

Once a teacher,
Always a father.

Since we have become your disciples, we are like your sons. The proverb also says:

You need not rear your children with silver and gold;
That they treat you kindly is good to behold.
If you don't feel well, you needn't mention anything about delaying
our journey. Stay here for a few days. What's wrong with that?" Thus
the brothers all ministered to their master, hardly realizing that

The dawn passed, the noon came, and dusk set in;
The good night withdrew at the break of day.

Time went by swiftly, and two days had passed before the master sat
up on the third day and called out, "Wu-k'ung, I was so sick these last
two days that I did not think of asking you: that lady bodhisattva who
got back her life, did anyone send her some rice to eat?"

"Why worry about her?" said Pilgrim with a laugh. "You should
be concerned with your own illness."

"Indeed! Indeed!" said Tripitaka. "Please help me get up, and bring
out my paper, brush, and ink. Go and borrow an inkstand from the
monastery."

"What for?" asked Pilgrim.

"I want to write a letter," said the elder, "in which I'll also enclose
the travel rescript. You may take that up to Ch'ang-an and ask for an
audience with Emperor T'ai-tsung."

"That's easy," said Pilgrim. "Old Monkey may not be very able in
other matters, but I'm the best postman in the whole wide world.
When you finish your letter, I'll send it to Ch'ang-an and hand-deliver
it to the T'ang emperor with one somersault. Then I'll come back here
with another somersault—before your brush and inkstand are dry!
But why do you want to send a letter? Tell me a little of its contents,
and then you may write." Shedding tears, the elder said, "This is what
I intend to write:

Three times your priestly subject bows his head
To greet my sage ruler, long may he live!
By lords civil and martial let this be read,
Let all four hundred nobles know of it:
When I by decree left the East that year.
I hoped to see Buddha on the Spirit Mount.
I did not such ordeals anticipate
Or in midway such afflictions foresee.
This monk, now gravely ill, cannot proceed,
And Buddha's gate seems far as Heaven's gate.
I've no life for scriptures, my toil is vain;

Some other seeker I beg you ordain."

When Pilgrim heard these words, he could not refrain from breaking into uproarious laughter. "Master," he said, "you're just too weak! A little illness, and you already entertain such thoughts! If you get any worse, if it truly becomes a matter of life and death, all you need is to ask me. Old Monkey has ability enough to pose the following questions: 'Which Yama king dares make this decision? Which judge of Hell has the gall to issue the summons? And which ghostly summoner would come near to take you away?' If I'm the least bit annoyed, I may well bring out that temperament that greatly disturbed the Celestial Palace and, with my rod flying, fight my way into the Region of Darkness. Once I catch hold of the Ten Yama Kings, I'll pull their tendons one by one, and even then I'll not spare them!"

"O Disciple!" said Tripitaka. "I *am* gravely ill! Please don't talk so big!"

Walking up to them, Pa-chieh said, "Elder Brother, Master says the situation is not good, and you insist that it is. That's awfully embarrassing! We should make plans early to sell the horse and hock the luggage so that we can buy a coffin for his funeral before we scatter."

"You're babbling again, Idiot!" said Pilgrim. "You don't realize that Master was the second disciple of our Buddha Tathāgata, and originally he was called Elder Gold Cicada. Because he slighted the Law, he was fated to experience this great ordeal."

"O Elder Brother," said Pa-chieh, "even if Master did slight the Law, he had already been banished back to the Land of the East where he took on human form in the field of slander and the sea of strife. After he made his vow to worship Buddha and seek scriptures in the Western Heaven, he was bound whenever he ran into monster-spirits and he was hung high whenever he met up with demons. Hasn't he suffered enough? Why must he endure sickness as well?"

"You wouldn't know about this," replied Pilgrim. "Our old master fell asleep while listening to Buddha expounding the Law. As he slumped to one side, his left foot kicked down one grain of rice. That is why he is fated to suffer three days' illness after he has arrived at the Region Below."

Horrified, Pa-chieh said, "The way old Hog sprays and splatters things all over when he eats, I wonder how many *years* of illness I'd have to go through!"

"Brother," said Pilgrim, "you have no idea either that the Buddha is not that concerned with you and other creatures. But as people say:

Rice stalks planted in noonday sun

Take root as perspiration runs.

Who knows of this food from the soil

Each grain requires most bitter toil?

Master still has one more day to go, but he'll be better by tomorrow."

Tripitaka said, "I feel quite different from yesterday, for I'm terribly thirsty. Could you find me some cool water to drink?" "That's good!" remarked Pilgrim. "When Master wants to drink, it's a sign that he's getting better. Let me go fetch some water."

Taking out the almsbowl, he went immediately to the incense kitchen at the rear of the monastery to fetch water. There, however, he came upon many priests who were sobbing, their eyes all red-rimmed, though they dared not weep aloud. "How could you priests be so petty?" said Pilgrim. "We stay here for a few days, but we fully intend to thank you and pay you back for the rice and firewood when we leave. Why do you behave in such a low-class manner?"

Greatly flustered, the priests knelt down to say, "We dare not! We dare not!" "What do you mean by you dare not?" said Pilgrim. "I suppose the big appetite of the priest with a long snout has hurt your assets."

"Venerable Father," replied one of the priests. "Even in this desolate temple of ours, there are altogether over a hundred monks, old and young. If one of us were to feed one of you for one day, we could still manage to take care of all of you for over a hundred days. Would we dare be so niggardly and particular about your upkeep?"

"If not," asked Pilgrim, "why are you crying?"

"Venerable Father," said another priest, "we don't know what sort of perverse fiend has invaded this monastery of ours. Two nights ago two young priests were sent to toll the bell and beat the drum, but they never came back. When we searched for them in the morning, we found their caps and sandals abandoned in the rear garden; their skeletons remained, but their flesh was eaten. You have all stayed in our monastery for three days and we have lost six priests. That is why we brothers cannot help fretting and grieving. Since your venerable master is indisposed, however, we dare not make this known to you, though we can't refrain from shedding tears in secret."

On hearing this, Pilgrim was both startled and delighted, saying,

"No need to say any more. There must be a fiendish demon here causing harm to people. Let me exterminate it for you."

"Venerable Father," said a priest, "the monster who is not a spirit will not possess spiritual powers. But those who are will undoubtedly have the ability to soar on the cloud and fog and to penetrate and leave the Region of Darkness. The ancients have put the matter quite well:

Don't believe the honesty of the honest;

Be wary of the unkindness of the kind.

Venerable Father, please forgive me for what I'm about to say: if you could catch this monster for us and rid our desolate temple of this root of calamity, it would indeed be our greatest fortune. But if you cannot catch him, there'll be quite a few inconveniences."

"What do you mean by quite a few inconveniences?" asked Pilgrim.

"To tell you the truth, Venerable Father," replied the priest, "though there are some one hundred monks in our rustic temple, they all left their homes in childhood.

They find knives to cut hair grown long;

They patch often their unlined garments.

Once they rise at dawn and wash their faces,

They bow with pressed palms

To embrace the Great Way;

At night they take pains to burn incense,

Sincere and earnest,

To chant Buddha's name.

Raising their heads to gaze at Buddha's form

On the ninth-grade lotus,

The *Triyāna* means,[2]

And the vessel of mercy afloat on the *dharmamega*,[3]

The world-honored Śākya of Jetavana they vow to see.

Lowering their heads to search their hearts.

Having received the five prohibitions,

Having transcended the world,

Amid the myriad creatures and phenomena

The stubborn void and formless form they would perceive.

When the *dānapatis*[4] are present,

The old and the young,

The tall and the short,

The fat and the thin—

Each one will beat the wooden fish

And strike the golden stone,
Hustling and bustling,
To chant two scrolls of the *Lotus Sūtra*
Or a book of the *Litany of King Liang.*[5]
When the *dānapatis* are absent,
The new and the old,
The unfamiliar and the familiar,
The rustic and the urbane—
Each one will press his palms together
And close his eyes,
In silence and darkness,
To meditate on the rush mat
And bolt the gate beneath the moon.[6]
We leave those orioles and birds to chatter and bicker by
    themselves:
They have no place in our convenient, compassionate *Mahāyāna.*
That is why
We are not able to tame tigers,
Nor are we able to subdue dragons;
We have no knowledge of fiends,
Nor can we recognize spirits.
If you, Venerable Father, manage to annoy that fiendish demon,
He may find a hundred of us priests barely sufficient for one meal.
Then we'll all fall upon the Wheel of Transmigration;
Second, our zen grove and old temple will be destroyed;
And third, at Tathāgata's assembly
We'll not enjoy even half a mite of glory.
These are some of those inconveniences!"
When Pilgrim heard the priest delivering a speech like that,
    Anger flared up from his heart,
    And wrath sprouted by his bladder.
"How stupid can you monks be?" he shouted. "All you know is about
the monster-spirit. Haven't you any idea of old Monkey's exploits?"

"In truth we do not," replied the priests softly.

"I'll give you only a brief summary today," said Pilgrim. "Listen to
me, all of you!

    I did tame tigers and subdue dragons on Mount Flower-Fruit;
    I did ascend to Heaven's Palace to cause great havoc.
    In hunger I picked up Lord Lao's elixir

And chewed up—not many—just two or three pellets!
In thirst I took up the Jade Emperor's wine
And drank—so lightly—six or seven cups!
When my gold-pupil eyes, not black or white, flare wide open,
The sky will pale
And the moon darken;
When I hold up one golden-hooped rod, not too long or short,
I'll come and go
Without a trace.
Why mention big spirits or small fiends!
Who's afraid of their hex or devilry!
The moment when I give chase,
The fleeing will flee,
The shaking will shake,
The hiding will hide,
And the fearful will fear;
The moment when I catch them,
They will be sawed,
They will be burned,
They will be ground,
And they will be pounded.
Something like Eight Immortals crossing the sea,
Each revealing magic ability.
Monks and priests,
I'll seize this monster-spirit for you to see.
Only then will you realize I'm old Monkey!"

When those various monks heard this, they all nodded and said to themselves, "There has to be some basis for this villainous bonze to open his big mouth and utter these big words!" Each of them, therefore, responded to Pilgrim agreeably, but the lama priest spoke up: "Wait a moment! Since your master is indisposed, you shouldn't feel so eager to catch this monster-spirit. As the proverb says,

A prince at a banquet
Will either be drunk or fed;
A hero on the field
Will either be hurt or dead.

If the two of you engage in battle, you may well involve your master in some difficulty, and that's not too appropriate."

"Right you are!" replied Pilgrim. "Let me take some cold water to my master first and then I'll return." Picking up the almsbowl and

filling it with water, he left the incense kitchen and went directly back
to the abbot's chamber. "Master," he cried, "drink some cold water."

Racked by thirst, Tripitaka raised his head, held the water to his
mouth, and took a mighty draught. Truly

In thirst one drop of liquid's like sweet dew;
The true cure arrives and the illness heals.

When Pilgrim saw that the elder was gradually regaining his strength
and that his features seemed to brighten, he asked, "Master, can you
take some rice soup?"

"This cold water," replied Tripitaka, "is so much like an efficacious
elixir that at least half of my illness is gone. If there is any rice soup, I
can eat some." At once Pilgrim shouted repeatedly, "My master's well.
He wants some soup and rice." His cries sent those monks scampering
to wash the rice, cook it, make noodles, bake biscuits, steam breads,
and make rice-noodle soup. They brought in, in fact, four or five tables
of food, but the T'ang monk could take only half a bowl of rice soup.
Pilgrim and Sha Monk managed to finish one tableful, while the rest
all went into Pa-chieh's stomach. After they had cleared away the
utensils and lighted the lamps, the monks retired.

"How many days have we stayed here?" asked Tripitaka.

Pilgrim said. "Three whole days. By dusk tomorrow, it'll be the
fourth day." "How much have we fallen behind in our journey?"
asked Tripitaka again. "Master," said Pilgrim, "you can't make that
sort of calculation. Let's leave tomorrow." "Exactly," said Tripitaka.
"Even if I'm still not quite well, I'd better get going."

"In that case," said Pilgrim, "I'd better catch a monster-spirit
tonight."

"What sort of monster-spirit do you want to catch this time?" asked
Tripitaka, growing alarmed.

"There's a monster-spirit in this monastery," said Pilgrim. "Let old
Monkey catch it for them."

"O Disciple!" said the T'ang monk. "I'm not even recovered yet,
and you want to start something like this already! Suppose that fiend
has great magic powers and you can't catch it. Wouldn't you put me
in jeopardy?"

"You do love to put me down!" said Pilgrim. "As old Monkey goes
about subduing fiends everywhere, have you ever seen him an under-
dog? I may not move my hands, but the moment I do, I'll win." Tugging at him, Tripitaka said, "Disciple, the proverb puts the matter well:

Do someone a favor when you have that favor;

Spare a person when you can afford to spare.
Can restiveness compare with contentedness?
Is tolerance nobler than belligerence?"

When the Great Sage Sun heard his master pleading so passionately with him, refusing to let him subdue a fiend, he had little choice but to tell the truth, saying, "Master, I don't want to hide this from you, but the fiend has devoured humans at this place."

Horrified, the T'ang monk asked, "What humans has the fiend devoured?" "We have stayed in this monastery for three days," replied Pilgrim, "and six young priests of the monastery have been devoured."

The elder said, "'When a hare dies, the fox grieves; for a creature will mourn its own kind.' If a fiend has devoured the priests of this monastery, I too am a priest. I'll let you go, but you must be careful." "No need to tell me that," said Pilgrim. "Old Monkey will eliminate it the moment he raises his hands."

Look at him! In the lamplight he gave instructions for Pa-chieh and Sha Monk to guard their master, and then leaped out of the abbot's chamber jubilantly. When he reached the main Buddha hall to look around, he found that there were stars in the sky though the moon had not yet risen. The hall was completely dark, so he exhaled some immortal fire from within himself to light the crystal chalice; then he went to strike the bell on the east and toll the bell on the west. Thereafter with one shake of his body he changed into a young priest no more than twelve or thirteen years of age. Draped in a clerical robe of yellow silk and wearing a white cloth shirt, he chanted scriptures as his hand struck a wooden fish. He waited there in the hall till about the hour of the first watch and nothing happened. By the hour of the second watch, when the waning moon had just risen, he heard all at once a loud roar of the wind. Marvelous wind!

Its black fog blotted out the sky;
Its somber clouds bedimmed the earth.
All four quarters seemed splashed with ink
Or coated with some indigo paint.
At first it lifted up dust and sprayed dirt;
Afterwards it toppled trees and felled forests.
Though stars glistened through lifted dust and sprayed dirt,
The moon paled as trees toppled and forests fell.
It blew till Ch'ang-o tightly hugged the *sha-lo* tree,[7]
The jade hare spinning searched for its dish of herbs;
Nine Star Officials all shut their doors,

Dragon Kings of Four Seas all closed their gates;
City gods looked for young demons in their shrines,
But midair divines could not soar on clouds.
Yama of Hades sought to find horse-faces,
As judges dashed madly to run down their wraps.
It rocked the boulders on K'un-lun summit
And churned up the waves in rivers and lakes.

When the wind subsided, he immediately felt the fragrance of orchids and perfumes and he heard the tinkling of girdle jade. He rose slightly and raised his head to look. Ah! It was a beautiful young girl, walking straight up the hall.

"Oo-li, oo-la!" chanted Pilgrim, pretending to recite scriptures. The girl walked up to him and hugged him, saying, "Little elder, what sort of scriptures are you chanting?"

"What I vowed to chant!" replied Pilgrim. "Everyone's enjoying his sleep," said the girl. "Why are you still chanting?"

"I made a vow!" replied Pilgrim. "How could I not do so?"

Hugging him once more, the girl kissed him and said, "Let's go out back and play." Turning his face aside deliberately, Pilgrim said, "You are kind of dumb!"

"Do you know physiognomy?" asked the girl.

"A little," replied Pilgrim. "Read my face," said the girl, "and see what sort of a person I am." "I can see," said Pilgrim, "that you are somewhat of a slut or debauchee driven out by your in-laws!" "You haven't seen a thing!" said the girl. "You haven't seen a thing!

I am no slut or debauchee
Whom my in-laws compelled to flee.
By my former life's poor fate
I was given too young a mate,
Who knew nothing of marriage rite
And drove me to leave him this night.

But the stars and the moon, so luminous this evening, have created the affinity for you and me to meet. Let's go into the rear garden and make love."

On hearing this, Pilgrim nodded and said to himself, "So those several stupid monks all succumbed to lust and that was how they lost their lives. Now she's trying to fool even *me*!" He said to her, "Lady, this priest is still very young, and he doesn't know much about lovemaking."

"Follow me," said the girl, "and I'll teach you." Pilgrim smiled and said to himself, "All right! I'll follow her and see what she wants to do with me."

They put their arms around each other's shoulders, and, hand in hand, the two of them left the hall to walk to the rear garden. Immediately tripping Pilgrim up with her leg so that he fell to the ground, the fiend began crying "Sweetheart" madly as she tried to pinch his stinky member.[8]

"My dear child!" exclaimed Pilgrim. "You do want to devour old Monkey!" He caught her hand and, using a little tumbling method, flipped the fiend on to the ground also. Even then, the fiend cried out, "Sweetheart, you certainly know how to make your old lady fall!"

Pilgrim thought to himself, "If I don't move against her now, what am I waiting for? As the saying goes,

Strike first and you're the stronger;

Delay and you won't live longer!"

Hands on his hips, he snapped his torso erect and leaped up to change into the magic appearance of his true form. Wielding his golden-hooped iron rod, he struck at the girl's head.

The fiend, too, was somewhat startled, thinking to herself, "This young priest is quite formidable!" She opened her eyes wide to take a careful look and found that her opponent was in fact the disciple of Elder T'ang, the one with the surname of Sun. She was, however, not the least intimidated. What kind of spirit was she, you ask. She has

A nose of gold

And fur like snow.

She dwells in tunnels underground

Where every part's both safe and sound.

A breath she nourished three hundred years before

Had sent her a few times to Mount Spirit's shore.

Of candles and flowers once she ate her fill,

She was banished by Tathāgata's will

To be Pagoda-Bearer's cherished child;

Prince Naṭa took her as his sister mild.

She's no mythic, sea-filling bird[9] of the air

Nor a turtle[10] that a sacred mountain bears.

Of Lei Huan's magic sword[11] she has no fear;

To her, Lü Ch'ien's cutlass[12] cannot go near.

Scurrying here and there,

She defies the River Han or Yangtze's breadth and length;

Scampering up and down
The heights of Mount T'ai or Hêng is her special strength.
When you behold her looks seductive and sweet,
Who'd think that she's a rodent-spirit in heat?
Proud of her own vast magic powers, she casually picked up a pair of
swords and began to parry left and right, to slash east and west, causing loud janglings and clangings. Though Pilgrim was somewhat
stronger, he could not quite overtake her. A cold gust rose everywhere, and thé waning moon had now lost its light. Look at the two
of them engaged in this marvelous battle in the rear garden!

A cold wind rose from the ground;
The waning moon released faint light.
Quiet was the Buddhist palace
And forlorn the spirit porch.
But the rear garden was some battlefield!
Great Master Sun,
A sage from Heav'n,
And the furry girl,
A queen of women,
They took up a contest in magic powers.
One hardened a woman's heart to scold this black bonze;
One widened his eyes of wisdom to glower at a girl.
When the swords in both hands flew,
Who'd recognize a "lady bodhisattva"?
When the single rod attacked,
He was more vicious than a live vajra-guardian.
The golden-hooped crackled like thunderbolts;
The white steel flashed forth like luminous stars.
Kingfishers dropped from jade towers;
Mandarin ducks broke on the golden hall.
Apes wailed as the Szechwan moon dimmed;
Wild geese called from the vast Ch'u sky.
The eighteen arhats
All shouted bravos in secret;
The thirty-two devas
All became terror-stricken.

As the Great Sage Sun became more and more energetic, the blows of
his rod hardly ever slackening, the monster-spirit suspected that she
would not be able to withstand him much longer. All at once her

knitted brows gave her a plan, and she turned to flee.

"Lawless wench!" shouted Pilgrim. "Where are you going? Surrender instantly!" But the monster-spirit refused to answer and kept retreating. She waited until Pilgrim was about to catch up with her and then ripped off her flower slipper from her left foot. Reciting a spell and blowing a mouthful of magic breath on it, she cried "Change!" and it changed into her appearance, both hands wielding the swords to attack. Her true self in a flash turned into a clear gust and disappeared. Alas! Is she not once more the star of calamity for Tripitaka? She swept into the abbot's chamber and immediately abducted Tripitaka T'ang. Silently and invisibly they rose straight to the clouds, and in a twinkling of an eye they reached Mount Void-Entrapping. After they entered the Bottomless Cave, she asked her little ones to prepare a vegetarian wedding feast, and there we shall leave them for the moment.

We tell you now about Pilgrim, who fought on anxiously till he found an opening and struck down the monster-spirit with one blow of the rod. Only then did he discover that it was merely a flower slipper. Realizing that he had been duped, Pilgrim rushed back to see his master, but he was nowhere to be found. Only Idiot and Sha Monk were there, chattering noisily about something. Maddened, Pilgrim lost all regard for good or ill as he raised high his rod and screamed, "I'm going to slaughter both of you! I'm going to slaughter both of you!"

Our Idiot was so terrified that he did not know where to flee. Sha Monk, however, was a general from Mount Spirit after all. When he saw that things had become complicated, he turned gentle and mild as he walked forward and went to his knees. "Elder Brother," he said, "I think I know what the matter is. You want to strike both of us dead so that you can go home and not go rescue Master."

"I'll slaughter both of you," replied Pilgrim, "and then I'll go rescue him by myself."

"Elder Brother, how can you speak like that?" said Sha Monk with a smile. "Without the two of us, you'll be reduced to the condition of the proverb:

One silk fiber is no thread;
A single hand cannot clap.

O Elder Brother! Who's going to look after the luggage and the horse for you?

Better that we emulate Kuan and Pao[13] dividing their gold
Than to imitate Sun and P'ang[14] in their matching of wits.
As the ancients said,
To fight the tiger you need brothers of the same blood;
To go to war requires a troop of fathers and sons.
I beg you to spare us from this beating. By morning we'll unite with
you in mind and effort to go search for Master."

Though Pilgrim had vast magic powers, he was also a most sensible
person. When he saw Sha Monk pleading like that, he at once relented,
saying, "Pa-chieh, Sha Monk, get up, both of you. We have to exert
ourselves tomorrow to find Master." When Idiot learned that he was
spared, he was ready to promise Pilgrim half of the sky! "O Elder
Brother," he said, "let old Hog take care of everything!" With so much
on their minds the three brothers, of course, could hardly sleep. How
they wished that
One nod of their heads would bring forth the rising sun,
One blow of their breaths would scatter all the stars!
Sitting up till dawn, the three of them immediately prepared to leave.
Some of the monks in the monastery soon appeared, asking, "Where
are the venerable fathers going?"

"It's hard for me to say this!" replied Pilgrim, chuckling. "I boasted
yesterday that I would catch the monster-spirit for you. I haven't succeeded, but I have lost our master instead. We're about to go find
him."

Growing fearful, the monks said, "Venerable Father, such a small
matter of ours has now caused your master trouble. Where do you
plan to go to look for him?" "There'll be a place for us to look," replied
Pilgrim.

"In that case," said one of the monks quickly, "there's no need to
hurry. Please have some breakfast first." Thereupon they brought in
several bowls of rice soup, and Pa-chieh finished them all. "Good
monks!" he cried. "After we have found our master, we'll return for
some more fun!"

"So you still want to come back here to eat!" said Pilgrim. "Why
don't you go to the Devarāja Hall instead and see if that girl is still
around?"

"No, she isn't, she isn't!" said another priest hurriedly. "She stayed
there for one night, but she vanished the next day."

In great delight Pilgrim at once took leave of the monks and asked

Pa-chieh and Sha Monk to tote the luggage and lead the horse to head for the east. "You've made a mistake, Elder Brother," said Pa-chieh. "Why do you want to head for the east instead?"

"How could you know?" said Pilgrim. "That girl who was tied up the black pine forest the other day—these fiery eyes and diamond pupils of old Monkey have long seen through her. All of you thought that she was such a fine person! It was she who devoured the monks, and it was she who abducted Master. You rescued a fine lady Bodhisattva indeed! Now that Master is taken, we have to search for him on the road we came from."

"Very good! Very good!" said the two of them, sighing with admiration. "Truly there's finesse in your roughness! Let's go! Let's go!" The three of them hurried back to the forest, and all they saw were

Endless clouds,
Boundless fog,
Layered rocks,
Winding path;
Criss-crossing tracks of foxes and hare;
Tigers, wolves, and leopards crowding there.
With not a trace of the fiend in the woods,
They knew not where Tripitaka was at all.

Growing more anxious, Pilgrim whipped out his rod and, with one shake of his body, changed into that appearance that had greatly disturbed the Celestial Palace: with three heads and six arms wielding three rods, he delivered blows madly all over the forest.

When he saw that, Pa-chieh said, "Sha Monk, Elder Brother has gone berserk. Unable to locate Master, he's having a fit of anger!" Pilgrim's rampage, however, managed to turn up two old men; one was the mountain god, and the other the local spirit. "Great Sage," they said as they went to their knees, "the mountain god and the local spirit have come to see you."

"What a miraculous stick!" exclaimed Pa-chieh. "He waved it around and beat out both this mountain god and this local spirit. If he beat it around some more, he might even get himself Jupiter!"

"Mountain god, local spirit," said Pilgrim as he began his interrogation. "How ill-behaved you are! You have persisted in making bandits your allies in this place, and when they succeed, they undoubtedly sacrifice livestock in your honor. Now you even band together with a monster-spirit and join her in abducting my master.

Where have you hidden him? Confess at once, and I'll spare you a beating!"

Horrified, the two deities said, "The Great Sage has wrongly blamed us. That monster-spirit is not in this mountain, nor is she subject to our dominion. But these minor deities do happen to know a little about the source of the wind last night." "If you know," said Pilgrim, "tell it all!"

The local spirit said, "That monster-spirit has abducted your master to a place about one thousand miles due south of here. There is a mountain there by the name of Void-Entrapping, in which there is a cave called Bottomless. The mistress of the cave is the monster-spirit who took your master."

Startled by what he heard, Pilgrim dismissed the deities and retrieved his magic appearance. In his true form he said to Pa-chieh and Sha Monk, "Master is very far away." "If he's very far," said Pa-chieh, "let's soar on the clouds to get there."

Dear Idiot! He mounted a violent gust to rise first, followed by Sha Monk astride the clouds. Since the white horse was originally a dragon prince, he too trod on the wind and fog with the luggage on his back. Then the Great Sage also mounted his cloud-somersault, and they all headed straight for the south. In a little while they saw a huge mountain blocking their path. Pulling back the horse, the three of them stopped their clouds to find that the mountain had

A peak rubbing the blue sky,
A top joining the green void.
Divers trees by the thousands grew all around;
Birds and fowl, cacophonous, flew here and there.
Tigers, leopards walked in bands;
Deer, antelope moved in herds.
Where it faced the sun,
Rare flowers and plants grew fragrant;
On the shady parts
The ice and snow stayed stubborn.
The rugged summits;
Steep precipices;
A tall peak erect;
A deep winding brook.
Dark pine trees
And scaly rocks—

A sight that struck fear in a traveler's heart!
No shadow of one woodsman was ever seen,
Nor a trace of an herb-gathering youth.
Wild beasts before you could raise the fog
As foxes all around called up the wind.

Pa-chieh said, "O Elder Brother! Such a rugged mountain must harbor fiends!" "That goes without saying!" replied Pilgrim. "For as the proverb puts it,

A tall mountain will always have fiends.
Could rugged peaks be without spirits?

Sha Monk, you and I will remain here, and Pa-chieh can go down to the mountain fold to see which is the better road to take. He should also find out whether there is in fact a cave, and whether its doors are open, and after he has made a thorough investigation, we can then go find Master and rescue him."

"Old Hog's so unlucky!" said Pa-chieh. "You always put me up to something first!"

Pilgrim said, "You said last night that you would take care of everything. How could you go back on your word now?" "No need to start a quarrel!" said Pa-chieh. "I'll go." Putting down his muckrake, Idiot shook loose his clothes and leaped down the mountain empty-handed. As he left, we do not know whether good or ill would befall him, and you must listen to the explanation in the next chapter.

Eighty-two

The fair girl seeks the yang;
Primary spirit guards the Way.

We were telling you about Pa-chieh, who, having bounded down the mountain, discovered a narrow path, which he followed for some five or six miles. Suddenly he caught sight of two female fiends bailing water from a well. How did he know so readily, you ask, that they were female fiends? Because he saw that each of them had a chignon on her head about fifteen inches tall and adorned with tiny bamboo strips. It was a most unfashionable style! Our Idiot walked up to them and cried, "Monstrous fiends!"

Infuriated by what they heard, the fiends said to each other, "This monk is such a rogue! We don't know him, nor have we ever tittle-tattled with him. How can he address us as monstrous fiends just like that?" Greatly annoyed, the fiends picked up the poles they had brought along for carrying water and brought them down on Pa-chieh's head.

Since Idiot had no weapons to ward off the blows, they succeeded in whacking him quite a few times. Holding his head, he ran back up the mountain, crying, "O Elder Brother, let's go back! Those fiends are fierce!"

"How fierce?" asked Pilgrim. Pa-chieh replied, "In the mountain valley there were two female monster-spirits bailing water from a well. I called them once and they beat me several times with poles."

"What did you call them?" said Pilgrim. "I called them monstrous fiends," answered Pa-chieh.

"That," said Pilgrim, chuckling, "was too small a beating!"

"Thanks for looking after me!" said Pa-chieh. "My head's swollen, and you claim that it's too small a beating!" Pilgrim said, "Haven't you heard of the proverb?

Gentility gets through the world;
Obduracy takes you nowhere.

They are monsters of this region, but we are monks who came from afar. Even if you possessed arms all over your body, you would still have to be more tactful. You walk up to them and immediately call them monstrous fiends! Would they overlook you and want to hit me instead? 'A human person must put propriety and music first.'"

"I'm even more ignorant of that!" said Pa-chieh.

Pilgrim said, "When you were devouring humans in the mountain during your youth, did you have any knowledge of two kinds of wood?" "No, what are they?" asked Pa-chieh. "One is poplar, and the other's rosewood," said Pilgrim. "Poplar is quite pliant by nature, and it is used by craftsmen for carving holy images or making Tathāgatas. The wood is dressed in gold and painted; it is decorated with jade and other ornaments. Tens of thousands of people burn incense before it in their worship, and it enjoys countless blessings. Rosewood, on the other hand, is hardy and tough by nature. Oil factories, therefore, take it to make caskets: they bind the planks with iron rings, and then they hammer them with mallets. The wood's toughness, you see, is what causes it to suffer like that."

"O Elder Brother!" said Pa-chieh. "If you had told me a story like that a bit sooner, I would not have been beaten by them."

"You must go back and question them further," said Pilgrim. "But they'll recognize me," protested Pa-chieh. "You may go in transformation," Pilgrim answered, and Pa-chieh said, "Even if I go in transformation, Elder Brother, how should I question them?"

Pilgrim said, "After you have transformed yourself, walk up to them and give them a proper greeting. See how old they are. If they're about the same age as we are, address them as Ladies. If they are somewhat older, then call them Mesdames."

"What poppycock!" said Pa-chieh, chuckling. "This place is so far from home. Why bother to be so intimate?" "It's not a matter of intimacy," said Pilgrim, "but of getting information from them. If they had indeed abducted Master, we could move against them immediately. If not, we certainly don't want to be delayed from going elsewhere to finish our business, do we?" "You're right," said Pa-chieh, "I'll go back."

Dear Idiot! Stuffing the rake inside the sash around his waist, he walked down to the mountain valley, where with one shake of his body he changed into a dark, stoutish priest. He swaggered up to the fiends and bowed deeply, saying, "Mesdames, this humble cleric salutes you."

Delighted, the two of them said to each other, "Now this priest is quite nice! He knows how to bow, and he knows how to greet people properly." "Elder," asked one of them, "Where did you come from?"

"Where did I come from," said Pa-chieh.

"Where are you going to?" she asked again.

"Where am I going to," he replied again.

"What is your name?" she asked a third time.

"What is my name," he replied a third time.

Laughing, the fiend said, "This priest is nice all right, but he doesn't seem to know anything, not even his own history, except to repeat what people say."

"Mesdames," asked Pa-chieh, "why are you bailing water?" The fiend said, "You may not know this, priest, but last night the mistress of our house abducted a T'ang monk into our cave whom she wanted to entertain. Since the water in our cave is not clean enough, she sent the two of us here to fetch fine water that is a product of yin-yang copulation.[1] She is also having a vegetarian banquet prepared for the T'ang monk, for she wants to marry him this evening."

When he heard this, our Idiot turned quickly to race up the mountain, crying, "Sha Monk, bring out the luggage quickly and let's divide it up!" "Second Elder Brother," asked Sha Monk, "why do you want to divide it up again?" "After we've divided it up," replied Pa-chieh, "you may return to the River of Flowing Sand to devour humans, and I'll go back to the Kao Village to see my in-laws. Big Brother can go to Mount Flower-Fruit to call himself a sage, while the white horse can return to the ocean to become a dragon. Master, you see, has already married the monster-spirit in the cave. We should all scatter to pursue our own livelihood."

Pilgrim said, "This Idiot is babbling again!" "Only your son's babbling!" replied Pa-chieh. "Just now, those two monster-spirits bailing water told me that they were preparing a vegetarian banquet for the T'ang monk. After he has been fed, they will be married."

"That monster-spirit may have Master imprisoned in the cave," said Pilgrim, "but he must be waiting with bulging eyes for us to go rescue him. And you are speaking in this manner!" "How are we going to rescue him?" asked Pa-chieh. Pilgrim said, "The two of you can lead the horse and pole the luggage while we follow those two female fiends. We'll let them lead us up to their door, and then we'll begin the attack together."

Our Idiot had little choice but to comply. From a great distance Pilgrim trained his eyes on those two fiends, who walked deep into the mountain for some twenty miles and then vanished from sight. "Master must have been seized by daytime ghosts!" exclaimed a startled Pa-chieh.

"What fine perception!" said Pilgrim. "How could you tell their true forms so readily?" Pa-chieh said, "Those fiends were carrying their water as they walked along, and then they suddenly disappeared. Aren't they daytime ghosts?"

"I think they have crawled inside a cave instead," said Pilgrim. "Let me take a look."

Dear Great Sage! He opened wide his fiery eyes and diamond pupils to scan the entire mountain, but he saw no movement whatsoever. Below a sheer cliff, however, there was a small terrace with elegant openwork carvings decorated with floral patterns of five colors and a towered gate with triple eaves and white banners. When he walked up to the terrace with Pa-chieh and Sha Monk to look, he saw these large words inscribed on the gate: Mount Void-Entrapping, Bottomless Cave.

"Brothers," said Pilgrim, "that monster-spirit has erected this edifice here, but I wonder where she has put the door." "It can't be very far," said Sha Monk. "Let's make a careful search." As they turned to look around, they discovered a huge boulder, the surface area of which had to be over ten square miles, beneath the towered gate at the foot of the mountain. In the center of this boulder there was an opening to a cave, roughly the size of a large earthen vat, which had been crawled over so frequently that the surface of the entrance had grown shiny and smooth.

"O Elder Brother!" said Pa-chieh. "This is the entrance through which the monster-spirit goes in and out."

When he looked at it, Pilgrim said, "How strange! Both of you know that old Monkey has captured quite a few monster-spirits since he became a guardian of the T'ang monk. But I have never seen a cave-dwelling quite like this. Pa-chieh, you go down first and see how deep it is. Then I can go in and try to rescue Master."

Shaking his head, Pa-chieh said, "This is hard! Very hard! Old Hog is quite ponderous. If I trip and fall in, I wonder if I can reach bottom after two or three years!" "Is it that deep?" asked Pilgrim. "Just look!" said Pa-chieh.

The Great Sage prostrated himself at the rim of the cave opening and peered downward. Egads! It was deep! All around it had to be more than three hundred miles. "Brothers," he said, turning around, "it's very deep indeed!"

"You may as well go back!" said Pa-chieh. "You can't rescue Master!"

"How can you talk like that!" replied Pilgrim. "You must not be lazy, nor should you be slothful. Let's put the luggage down and tether the horse to the pillar of the towered gate. Use your rake and Sha Monk can use his staff to bar the entrance. I'll go in to investigate. If Master is indeed inside, I'll use my iron rod to attack the monster-spirit and chase her out. When she reaches the entrance up here, you two can cut off her escape route. That's cooperation from within and without. Only after we have slaughtered the spirits in this way can we hope to rescue Master." The two of them obeyed. With a bound, Pilgrim leaped into the cave, as

Ten thousand colored clouds rose beneath his feet;
Auspicious air, in layers, veiled his side.

In a little while, he reached the depths of the cave, which, however, he found to be bright and clear. Like the outside world, this place had sunlight, the rustle of wind, flowers, fruits, and trees. Delighted, Pilgrim said to himself, "What a marvelous place! It makes me think of the Water-Curtain Cave, which Heaven bestowed on old Monkey when he came into the world. But this place is also a cave-Heaven, a blessed region!"

As he looked about, he saw also a double-eaved towered gate surrounded by pines and bamboos. Inside the gate there were many buildings, and he thought to himself again, "This has to be the residence of the monster-spirit. Let me go in and do a little detection. But wait! If I enter like this, she'd recognize me. I'll go in transformation." Making the magic sign and shaking himself, he changed at once into a fly and flew silently up to the towered gate to spy on the monster-spirit. There he could see that the fiend was sitting in the center of a thatched pavilion. She appeared vastly different from the way she looked at the time when she was rescued in the pine forest or when Pilgrim fought with her in the monastery. Her makeup was lovelier than ever:

Her tresses piled high in a crow-nest bun,
She wore a flow'ry jacket of green wool.
A pair of tiny feet like lily hooks;

Like spring's tender shoots her ten fingers looked.
Her round, powdered face was a silver disc;
Smooth like a cherry were her lips of rouge.
Solemn and proper seemed her beauteous form,
More delightful than Ch'ang-o of the moon.
This day she caught the scripture-seeking monk,
With whom at once she would share her bed.

Pilgrim did not make any noise so that he could hear what she had to say.

After a little while, she parted her cherry lips and called out in a most amiable manner: "Little ones, prepare the vegetarian feast quickly! After Brother T'ang monk has been fed, he and I will be married."

"So, she means business!" said Pilgrim, smiling to himself. "I thought that Pa-chieh was talking nonsense, just for fun. I'll fly in there and search around for Master. I wonder how stable his mind is at this time. If he has been moved by this fiend, I'll leave him here." He spread his wings at once and flew in; there beyond the east corridor, in a room shuttered with red, translucent paper on top and opaque ones at the bottom, the T'ang monk was seated.

Crashing headfirst right through the papered trellis, Pilgrim darted onto the bald head of the T'ang monk and cried, "Master!" Tripitaka recognized his voice immediately and said, "Disciple, save me!"

"I can't do that, Master!" replied Pilgrim. "That monster-spirit is preparing a banquet for you, after which she plans to marry you. If she bears you a boy or a girl, that will be your priestly posterity. Why are you so sad?"

On hearing this, the elder spoke through clenched teeth: "Disciple, after I left Ch'ang-an, I took you in at the Mountain of the Two Frontiers. Since we began our journey westward, when did I ever use meat? On which day did I ever harbor a perverse thought? Now I am caught by this monster-spirit who wants me as her mate. If I lose my true yang, let me fall upon the Wheel of Transmigration and be banished to the rear of the Mountain of Darkness! Let me never find release!"

"Don't swear!" said Pilgrim, chuckling. "If you truly desire to seek scriptures in the Western Heaven, old Monkey will take you there."

"But I have quite forgotten the way we came in," said Tripitaka.

Pilgrim said, "Don't tell me that *you* have quite forgotten the way!

This cave of hers is not a place where you can walk in and out casually. It's a cave you crawl in from above; after I rescue you, we must crawl back out from below. If we're lucky, we'll find the mouth of the cave and get out. If we're unlucky, we may not find the entrance and we may suffocate."

"If it's so difficult, what are we going to do?" asked Tripitaka, his eyes brimming with tears.

"That's nothing! That's nothing!" said Pilgrim. "The monster-spirit wants to drink with you, and you have no choice but to comply. But when you pour for her, do it rather quickly so that there will be bubbles. I'll change into a mole-cricket and fly into the wine bubbles. When she swallows me inside her stomach, I'll squeeze through her heart and tear her guts apart. After I kill the monster-spirit like that, you'll be able to get out."

"Disciple," said Tripitaka, "what you tell me is rather inhuman." "If all you want to practice is virtue," said Pilgrim, "your life will be finished. A monster-spirit is the very cause of harm for humans. How can you pity her?" "All right! All right!" said Tripitaka. "But you must stay close to me." Truly

That Great Sage Sun firmly guarded Tripitaka T'ang;
The scripture monk relied solely on Handsome Monkey King.

Hardly had the master and disciple finished their discussion than the monster-spirit, having completed her preparations, walked near the east corridor and opened the locked door. "Elder," she called out, but the T'ang monk dared not reply. She called him again, but he still did not dare reply.

Why is it that he dared not reply, you ask. Because he thought of the proverb:

The mouth parts, and energy disperses;
The tongue moves, and strife comes to birth.

Then he reflected further on the fact that if he absolutely refused to open his mouth, she might grow violent and instantly end his life. Truly it was that

Caught between two ills, his mind asked his mouth;
Patient, thinking hard, his mouth asked his mind.

As he pondered his dilemma, she called out to him once more, "Elder!"

The T'ang monk had little choice but to answer her, saying, "Lady, I'm here." When the elder gave a reply like that, he felt as if his flesh had been drawn down to Hell by the weight of a thousand pounds!

Now, everyone has been saying that the T'ang monk was a priest wholly sincere in his determination to go worship Buddha and seek scriptures in the Western Heaven. How could he answer a monster like that? Well, you who ask such a question must not realize that this was a moment of the gravest danger, a time of life and death. He did this because he simply had no alternative. Though he gave such a reply on the outside, he was not in any way swayed by lust within.

When the monster-spirit heard such a reply from the elder, how-ever, she pushed open the door and raised up the T'ang monk with her hands. She then held his hand and put her arm around his back, nuzzling him with her head and whispering into his ear. Look at her! She put on a thousand kinds of coy looks and romantic airs, hardly realizing that Tripitaka was filled up to his neck with annoyance! Smiling secretly to himself, Pilgrim said, "I wonder if Master will be swayed by such seductive behavior of hers!" Truly

The true monk meets beauty, for he's demon-chased.
This lissome fiend is most worthy of praise!
Like willow leaves part her faintly drawn brows;
Her pink cheeks match peach-blossoms on the boughs.
Two tiny feet her embroidered shoes half show;
Chignons, on both sides, rise like nests of crow.
When she, all smiles, takes up the master's hand,
The cassock's perfumed by sweet orchid-gland.[2]

The monster-spirit led Tripitaka near the thatched pavilion and said, "Elder, I've prepared a cup of wine which I'd like to drink with you."

"Lady," replied the T'ang monk, "this humble cleric keeps a special diet."

"I know that," said the monster-spirit. "Since the water in our cave is unclean, I have sent specially for the pure water from the summit, a product of the copulation of yin and yang. I have also ordered a vegetarian banquet for your enjoyment." The T'ang monk stepped inside the pavilion with her to look around. Indeed he saw

Beneath the door
Drapes of colorful silk,
And filling the court
Incense from golden beasts.
Laid out there were black enameled tables
And black lacquered bamboo trays.

On the black enameled tables
Were many fine dainties;
The bamboo trays
Had rare vegetarian goods.
Crabapples, olives, lotus meat, and grapes;
Muskberries, hazelnuts, lychees, and lungans;
Chestnuts, water chestnuts, dates, and persimmons;
Walnuts, almonds, kumquats, and oranges;
The fruits of one whole mountain,
And vegetables most in season.
Bean curds, wheat glutens, wood ears,
Fresh bamboo shoots, button mushrooms,
Flat mushrooms, mountain herbs,
Yellow Sperms, white and yellow-flowered
Vegetables sauteed in clear oil;
Flat and round string beans
Mixed in mellow sauces;
Cucumbers, calabashes,
Gingko nuts, and rape-turnips.
Skinned eggplants made like partridges,
And winter melons carved like *fang-tan*.[3]
Taros cooked till soft and sugar-coated,
And white turnips boiled with vinegar.
Hot peppers and gingers, best of every kind;
The salty and plain well balanced one will find.

Revealing her slender, jadelike fingers and holding high a shiny gold
cup, she filled it with fine wine and handed it to the T'ang monk, saying, "Brother Elder, you wonderful man, please drink this cup of
love!"

Terribly embarrassed, Tripitaka took the wine, sprayed a few drops
of it toward the air with his fingers, and said this silent prayer: "Those
various guardian devas, the Guardians of Five Quarters, the Four
Sentinels, hear me. This disciple, Ch'ên Hsüan-tsang, since leaving the
Land of the East, has been indebted to the Bodhisattva Kuan-shih-yin
for sending you deities to give me secret protection so that I may bow
at Thunderclap and seek scriptures from the Buddha. Now I'm caught
on the way by a monster-spirit who wants to force me to marry her.
She's handing this cup of wine to drink. If this wine is indeed fit to
drink by someone keeping a vegetarian diet, your disciple will make

an effort to drink it, in hopes that he will still be able to see Buddha and achieve his merit. If it is unfit to drink, if the wine indeed causes this disciple to transgress his commandment, may he fall into eternal perdition!"

The Great Sage Sun, however, had taken on a delicate transformation, and at that critical moment he was whispering into his master's ear. His words, of course, could be heard only by Tripitaka and no one else. Since he knew that his master was rather fond of dietary wine made of grapes, he told him now to drink it. Having no choice but to follow his disciple's prompting, the master drank it and hurriedly poured another cup to present to the fiend. Indeed, he poured it so quickly that there were some bubbles. Pilgrim changed at once into a tiny mole-cricket and flew right into the bubbles.

The monster-spirit, however, took the cup in her hand and, instead of drinking immediately, bowed a couple of times to the T'ang monk. Only after she had bashfully said a few words of love to him did she raise the cup. By now the bubbles had already dissipated and the insect was fully visible. Not able to recognize that it was a transformation of Pilgrim, the monster-spirit thought that it was a mere insect and immediately scooped it up with her little finger and tried to throw it away. When Pilgrim saw that things were not turning out as he had hoped, he knew that it would be difficult to get inside her stomach. At once he changed into a hungry old hawk. Truly he has

Jade claws, golden eyes, and iron quills;
A brave, fierce form for battling the clouds.
The sly fox, the wily hare on seeing him
Will swiftly flee to farthest land.
Hungry, he hunts birds in the wind;
Sated, he soars to Heaven's gate.
His old fists, most deadly, are hard as steel;
E'en the sky he finds too low in flight.

He darted up and stretched out his jadelike claws; with a loud crash he overturned the banquet tables and smashed to pieces all those fruits and vegetables, all those saucers and cups. Then he flew out of the place, abandoning the T'ang monk.

The heart and bladder of the monster-spirit almost burst with fear, and the bones and flesh of the T'ang monk too turned numb. Trembling all over, the monster-spirit embraced him and said, "Brother Elder, where did this creature come from?"

"Your poor monk has no idea," replied Tripitaka.

"I have taken great pains," said the fiend, "to prepare this vegetarian banquet for your enjoyment. But I wonder where this wretched hairy beast came from to smash up all my utensils."

"Mistress," said the various little fiends, "smashing the utensils is not half as bad as spilling all those dietary foods on the ground. How can they be used now that they are defiled?" Tripitaka, of course, knew that this was the power of Pilgrim, but he dared not reveal it.

That monster-spirit said, "Little ones, I know. It must be that Heaven and Earth are displeased by my seizure of the T'ang monk and they send down this creature. Take away the broken utensils and prepare some other wine and food. It doesn't matter whether they are dietary or not. I'll ask Heaven to be the marriage go-between and Earth to be the witness. Then the T'ang monk and I will be married." Thereupon they sent the elder back to the room in the east corridor, and we shall leave him there for the moment.

We tell you now about Pilgrim, who flew up out of the place and changed into his true form as he reached the entrance of the cave. "Open up," he cried. Pa-chieh laughed and said, "Sha Monk, Elder Brother's here." The two of them lowered their weapons for Pilgrim to jump out.

Pa-chieh walked forward to tug at him, saying, "Is there a monster-spirit? Is our master there?" "Yes! Yes! Yes!" replied Pilgrim.

"Master must be suffering in there," said Pa-chieh. "Is he tied up or is he trussed up? Do they want to steam him or boil him?"

"Nothing of that sort," said Pilgrim. "She only wants to prepare a vegetarian banquet so that she can do that thing with him."

"Lucky you! Lucky you!" said Pa-chieh. "You must have drunk some wedding wine!" "O Idiot!" said Pilgrim. "Master's life is in danger! What wedding wine have I drunk?" "Why did you come back then?" asked Pa-chieh.

Pilgrim gave a thorough account of how he found the T'ang monk and how he went into transformation. Then he said, "Brothers, no more of these foolish thoughts. Master *is* here. When old Monkey goes back this time, he will certainly rescue him."

At once he entered the cave once more and changed into a fly to alight on the towered gate. There he heard the fiend panting hard and giving the following instruction: "Little ones, just bring me some food for the offering. I don't care whether it's vegetarian or not. I'll entreat

Heaven and Earth to be my go-between and witness, for I am determined to marry that priest." On hearing this, Pilgrim smiled and said to himself, "This monster-spirit is completely shameless! She has a priest locked up at home in broad daylight for fun and games! But let's not rush things. Let old Monkey go inside to have a look first."

With a buzz he flew to the east corridor, where he saw his master sitting in the room with clear teardrops rolling down his cheeks. Pilgrim crawled in there and landed on his bald head, crying, "Master!" Recognizing his voice, the elder jumped up all at once and said spitefully through clenched teeth, "Wretched ape! Any other person who has the *gall* to do something, at least the gall is wrapped inside the person's body. But in your case, it's your gall that has you wrapped inside! How much could those utensils that you smashed by flaunting your magic transformation be worth? But if you provoke the monster-spirit and arouse her lechery, she won't bother about dietary laws and will insist on copulating with me. What am I to do then?"

"Master," said Pilgrim softly, trying to placate him, "please don't be offended. I have a plan to rescue you."

"How will you rescue me?" asked the T'ang monk.

"When I flew up just now," replied Pilgrim, "I noticed that she has a garden in the rear. Trick her to go play with you in the garden. I'll rescue you then."

"How will you rescue me in the garden?" asked the T'ang monk once more.

Pilgrim said, "When you get to the garden with her, you should stop walking once you reach the peach trees. Let me fly up to one of the branches and change into a red peach. You pretend that you want to eat a fruit and pluck off the red one that I change into. Undoubtedly she will want to pluck one off also. Insist on giving yours to her. The moment she takes a bite, I'll enter her stomach. Then I'll punch through her belly and tear her guts apart. When she's dead, you'll be free."

"If you have the ability," said Tripitaka, "all you need is to fight with her. Why must you want to get inside her belly?"

"Master, you're just not too sensible!" said Pilgrim. "If this cave of hers were easy to get into and out of, then I could fight with her. But it is not; in fact, the crooked paths here are exceedingly hard to negotiate. If I move against her, the whole nest of them, old and young, may have me bogged down. What shall I do then? I have to use this underhanded method to mop things up!"

Nodding his head in belief, Tripitaka said only, "You must stay close to me." "I know! I know!" said Pilgrim. "I'm on your head!"

After master and disciple had formulated their plan, Tripitaka got up and, supporting himself on the shutters, called out: "Lady! Lady!" When the monster-spirit heard him, she ran near to him and said, giggling, "Dear⁴ Wonderful Man, what do you want?"

"Lady," said Tripitaka, "Since I left Ch'ang-an to journey westward, there was not a day when I did not have to climb a mountain or ford a river. When I stayed at the Sea-Pacifying Monastery the other day, I caught a bad cold. Only today has my condition improved some-what, for I have been perspiring. I am grateful to you for bringing me to your immortal residence, but having sat here all day I feel sickly again. Is there a place where you can take me for some relaxation?"

Highly pleased, the fiend said, "If dear Wonderful Man shows this kind of interest, I'll be delighted to take you strolling in the garden." She then cried out: "Little ones, bring me the key to open the garden. Sweep out the path."

Pushing open the shutters, this monster-spirit led the T'ang monk out by the hand. Look at those many little fiends of hers, all with oiled heads and powdered faces, all sinuous and lissome! They surged around the T'ang monk and headed straight for the garden. Dear monk!

He found no ease in this troop of satin and silk;
He played deaf and dumb in such brocaded grove.
He only could face Buddha, who had an iron mind and heart;
No mortal fond of wine and sex would in scripture-seeking succeed.

When they reached the entrance of the garden, the monster-spirit whispered lovingly to him, saying, "Dear Wonderful Man, enjoy your-self here. You may truly relax and unwind." Walking hand in hand with her into the garden, the T'ang monk raised his head to look around. It was indeed a lovely place. What he saw were

Paths twisting and turning,
Profusely coated with specks of green moss;
Handsome silk-gauze windows,
Each faintly enclosed by embroidered screens.
When a gentle breeze rises,
Western silk and eastern damask spread out fluttering;
When a fine rain recedes,
Ice-flesh and jade-substance appear seductive.
The sun warms fresh apricots,

Red like the skirts that immortals hang out to dry;
The moon illumes the plantain,
Green like feathered fans whirled by a goddess.
By the painted walls on four sides
Orioles sing amid ten thousand willows;
Around the leisure cottage
Butterflies swirl through the yard's cherry-apples.
Look further at the fragrance-holding alcove,
The green-moth alcove,
The wine-dispelling alcove,
And the romance alcove,
One on top of the other where
The rolled-up red curtains
Are drawn by hooks like shrimp-whiskers.
Look also at the grief-relieving kiosk,
The purity-draped kiosk,
The brow-painting kiosk,
And the four rains kiosk,
Each a noble edifice
With floriate plaques
Inscribed with seal scripts.
Look at the crane-bathing pool,
The goblet-washing pool,
The moon-pleasing pool,
And the tassel-cleansing pool,
Where golden scales glisten among green lilies and reeds;
There are, too, the ink-flower arbor,
The strange-chest arbor,
The proper-weal arbor,
And the cloud-adoring arbor,
Where mellow wine floats within jade flasks and cups.
Beyond and before the pools and kiosks
There are rocks from Lake T'ai,
Purple-blooming rocks,
Parrot-falling rocks,
And rocks of Szechuan rivers,
Around which the green tiger-whisker rush are planted.
East and west of the alcoves and arbors,
There are false wooden hills,

Kingfisher-screen hills,
Wind-whistling hills,
Jade-agaric hills,
On each grow thickets of phoenix-tail bamboos.
The *t'u-mi*[5] props
And the cinnamon rose props
Near the stand of swing.
They all seem like brocade curtains and silk drapes.
The pine-and-cypress kiosk,
The *hsin-i*[6] kiosk,
Facing the *mu-hsiang*[7] kiosk,
Both resemble a green city's embroidered veils.
The *shao-yao*[8] rails,
The peony groves,
Their flowers vie for denseness in purple and red;
The *yeh-ho*[9] terrace,
The white jasmine fence,
Both bring forth grace and glamor year after year.
The magnolia adorned with drops of dew
Should be sketched or drawn;
The hibiscus blazing red toward the sky
Should be hymned or sung.
Speaking of scenery,
Let's not boast of Lang yüan or P'êng-lai;
To compare such beauty
One need not count Yao's yellow or Wei's purple.[10]
In late spring when one fences with grass,
This garden lacks only divine blooms of jade.

The elder, walking hand in hand with the fiend to enjoy the garden, could hardly look at all the rare flowers and exotic plants. After going past many arbors and kiosks and entering gradually, as it were, the lovely scenery, he saw all at once that they had arrived in front of the peach orchard. Pilgrim gave his master's head a pinch and the elder knew immediately what he meant.

Flying up to one of the branches, Pilgrim with one shake of his body changed into a peach, a lovely red one. The elder said to the monster-spirit, "Lady, you have here

Fragrant blooms in the yard,
Ripened fruits on the boughs—

Fragrant blooms in the yard which bees vie to sip;
Ripened fruits on the boughs that birds fight to pluck.
But why is it that on this particular peach tree the peaches are both
red and green?"

With a giggle the monster-spirit said, "When Heaven is lacking in
yin and yang, the sun and the moon will not shine; when the Earth
is lacking in yin and yang, male and female cannot be distinguished.
The same principle applies to the fruits of this peach tree. Those on the
sunny side are ripened first by the warmth, and that's why they are
red; those on the shady side will grow but without the benefit of the
sun, and that's why they are still green. This is the principle of yin and
yang."

"I thank my lady for the instruction," said Tripitaka, "for this
humble cleric indeed had no idea this was so." He immediately reached
forward and plucked a red peach, and the monster-spirit too went and
plucked a green one. Bowing, Tripitaka presented the red peach to the
fiend, saying, "Lady, you are fond of colors, so please take this red
peach. Give me the green one to eat."

The monster-spirit indeed exchanged it with him, saying in secret
delight to herself, "Dear monk! A true man indeed! We aren't even
married yet, and he's already so affectionate!" Her delight, in fact,
caused her to behave more cordially than ever to the T'ang monk.
When he took the green peach and began eating it at once, the monster-
spirit was only too pleased to keep him company. Opening her cherry
lips to reveal her silvery teeth, she was about to take a bite. But Pilgrim
Sun had always been impetuous. Before she could sink her teeth into
the fruit, he immediately rolled inside her mouth and somersaulted
through her throat down to her stomach. Terribly frightened, the
monster-spirit said to Tripitaka, "O Elder, this fruit is really something!
How could it roll down there before I even bit it?"

"Lady," said Tripitaka, "a newly ripened fruit is most edible. That's
why it goes quickly." "But I haven't even spat out the pit," said the
monster-spirit, "and it has gone down already." "When you're in such
an excellent mood, Lady," replied Tripitaka, "you have a good appetite.
That's why it goes down even before you manage to spit out the pit."

In her stomach, Pilgrim changed back to his true form and cried,
"Master, don't banter with her. Old Monkey has succeeded!"

"Disciple, do try not to be too harsh," replied Tripitaka. Hearing
that, the monster-spirit said, "Whom are you talking to?"

"To my disciple, Sun Wu-k'ung," replied Tripitaka.

"Where is Sun Wu-k'ung?" asked the monster-spirit.

"In your stomach, of course!" replied Tripitaka. "He's the red peach you just ate."

Horrified, the monster-spirit said, "Finished! Finished! If this ape-head has crawled inside my belly, I'm as good as dead! Pilgrim Sun, what do you plan to do after using all your schemes and plots to get inside my belly?" "Not much!" replied Pilgrim spitefully inside her. "I'll just devour

Your six loaves of liver and lung,[11]
Your triple-haired and seven-holed heart.
All five viscera I'll clean out,
One rattling spirit you'll become!"

On hearing this, the monster-spirit was scared out of her wits. Trembling all over, she embraced the T'ang monk to say, "O Elder! I thought we were

Fated to be by one scarlet thread[12] bound,
Two hearts as one like fish in water found.
Who knows birds of love will thus be parted,
That spouses will sever brokenhearted?
Our courtship fails for Blue Bridge tide[13] is high;
Our meeting's vain as temple incense[14] dies.
Drawn to each other we must now disperse.
Which year will I once more with you converse?"

Inside her belly Pilgrim heard her speaking in this manner, and he was afraid that the compassionate elder might be deceived again. At once he began to wave his fists and stamp his feet, to assume boxing postures and do gymnastic exercises, nearly punching through her leather bag in the process. Unable to endure the pain, the monster-spirit dropped to the ground and dared not speak for a long time.

When Pilgrim found that she was silent, he thought that she might be dead and decided to ease up somewhat. Catching her breath, she cried, "Little ones, where are you?" When those little fiends, you see, entered the garden, they all knew how to behave. Instead of congregating in one place, they scattered to play—plucking flowers or fencing with grasses—so as to allow the monster-spirit to flirt freely with the T'ang monk. When they suddenly heard the summons, they ran to the spot and found the monster-spirit fallen to the ground, pale and groaning, hardly able even to crawl. Hurriedly they tried to raise her as they crowded around, all asking, "Mistress, what's wrong? Are you having a heart attack?"

"No! No!" replied the monster-spirit. "Don't ask, but I have someone in my stomach! Just get this monk out, quickly, so that my life may be preserved." Those little fiends indeed went forward and tried to pull the elder out.

"Don't any of you dare raise your hand!" yelled Pilgrim inside her belly. "If you want to, you yourself must present my master to the outside world. When we get there, I'll spare you."

The monster-spirit, of course, had no other motivation than pity for her own life. Struggling to her feet, she swiftly placed the T'ang monk on her back and strode toward the outside. Running after her, the little fiends asked, "Mistress, where are you going?" The monster-spirit said, "Let's get this fellow outside!

If we the moon above the five lakes retain,

There's always a spot to drop the hook again!
Let me find someone else instead."

Dear monster-spirit! She mounted the cloudy luminosity and immediately reached the entrance of the cave, where a loud clangor of arms could be heard. "Disciple," said Tripitaka, "I can hear the sound of weapons outside."

Pilgrim said, "It has to be Pa-chieh wielding his muckrake. Call him." Tripitaka at once called out: "Pa-chieh!"

Pa-chieh heard him and said, "Sha Monk, Master has come out!" The two of them removed the rake and the staff, and the monster-spirit carried the T'ang monk outside. Aha! Truly it is that

Mind Monkey, working within, subdues a fiend;

Wood and Earth guarding the door receive a sage monk.
We do not know whether the monster-spirit will preserve her life, and you must listen to the explanation in the next chapter.

Eighty-three
Mind Monkey knows the elixir source;
Fair girl returns to her true nature.

We were telling you about Tripitaka, who was escorted out of the cave by the monster-spirit. Sha Monk drew near and asked, "Master, you've come out, but where's Elder Brother?" "He's calculating enough," said Pa-chieh, "so he must have accompanied Master out here somehow."

Pointing at the monster-spirit, Tripitaka said, "Your Elder Brother is in her belly."

"How dirty and smelly!" said Pa-chieh with a giggle. "What's he doing in her belly? Come out!"

Pilgrim cried out from within: "Open wide your mouth and let me come out!" The fiend opened her mouth as bidden. Pilgrim reduced his size and crawled up to her throat; he was about to go out, but fearing that she might bite him, he took out the iron rod and blew his immortal breath onto it, crying, "Change!" It changed into a small nail, which propped up the roof of her mouth. With a bound he leaped clear of her mouth, taking along with him the iron rod as he jumped. One stretch of his torso helped him to assume his characteristic appearance, as he struck with uplifted rod. The monster-spirit also picked up her pair of treasure swords and blocked his blow with a loud clang. The two of them thus began a fierce battle on the top of the mountain:

Double swords flying that slash at the face;
A golden-hooped rod that aims at the head.
One is a Heav'n-born ape with a mind-monkey frame;
One is an Earth-born spirit with a fair-girl form.
The two of them
Are full of hate;
Gladness breeds rancor, causing a mighty bout.
That one desires primal yang to be her mate;
This one fights pure yin to form the holy babe.[1]
The upraised rod fills the sky with chilly fog;

123

The sword goes forth, the land roils with black dirt.
Because the elder's
In quest of Buddha,
They strive bitterly, showing great power.
Water wars with fire to hurt the basic way;[2]
Yin-yang cannot unite, each drifting free.
The two engage in such a lengthy brawl
That mountain and earth quake as forests sprawl.

When Pa-chieh saw them battling in this manner, he began to murmur against Pilgrim. Turning to Sha Monk, he said, "Brother, Elder
Brother's twiddling! When he was in her just now, he could have sent
her a belly-full-of-red with his fists and crawled out by punching
through her stomach. That way he would have had done with her,
wouldn't he? Why did he have to come out through her mouth and
fight with her, allowing her to be so insolent?"

"You're quite right," replied Sha Monk, "but Elder Brother, after
all, has worked very hard to have Master rescued from a deep cave.
Now that he has to fight some more with the monster-spirit, I think
Master should sit by himself while you and I go with our weapons to
lend some assistance to Elder Brother. Let's go and knock down that
monster-spirit."

"No! No! No!" said Pa-chieh, waving his hand. "He has magic
powers, but we're quite useless."

"What are you saying?" said Sha Monk. "That's something that
will benefit everyone. We may be useless, but even our fart can add to
the wind!" That Idiot did become aroused for the moment; whipping
out his rake, he cried, "Let's go then!"

Abandoning their master, they both mounted the wind and rushed
forward to battle, madly delivering blows to the monster-spirit with
their rake and staff. The monster-spirit was already having difficulty
withstanding Pilgrim by herself; when she saw the two of them, she
knew that defeat was certain. Twirling around, she tried to flee.

"Brothers, catch her!" snapped Pilgrim. When the monster-spirit
saw that they were pressing, she yanked off the flower slipper from her
right foot and blew her immortal breath on it, crying, "Change!" It
at once took on her appearance, attacking her pursuers with two
swords. She herself, with one shake of her body, changed into a clear
gust of wind and sped away. Now, you may think that we were only
speaking of her defeat and of her retreat out of regard for her own life.

How could you know that *this* had to be the turn of events? It must be that the star of calamity had not withdrawn its influence over Tripitaka. As the monster-spirit sped by the cave entrance, she saw Tripitaka sitting all alone beneath the towered gate. Rushing up to him, she snatched him and the luggage as well and bit through the reins; she succeeded in abducting both person and horse into the cave, where we shall leave them for the moment.

We tell you instead about Pa-chieh, who found an opening and struck down the monster-spirit with one blow of his rake. Then he discovered that it was only a flower slipper. "You two idiots!" said Pilgrim. "It's enough for you to look after Master. Who asked you to come and help?"

"There you are, Sha Monk!" said Pa-chieh. "Didn't I tell you not to come? This monkey's sick in his brains! We help him to subdue the fiend, but he blames us instead!"

"Where on earth did you subdue a fiend?" Pilgrim said. "When she fought with me yesterday, that fiend tricked me by this ploy of dropping her slipper. I wonder how Master is faring now that you two have left his side. Let's hurry back and look!"

The three of them hurried back, but their master indeed had vanished. There was not even a trace of the luggage or the white horse. So astonished was Pa-chieh that he dashed back and forth in confusion, while Sha Monk searched hither and yon. The Great Sage Sun too was racked by anxiety as he looked everywhere, and then he saw half a rein lying by the side of the road. Picking it up, he could not stop the tears flowing from his eyes. "O Master!" he cried aloud. "When I left I took leave of both man and horse; when I returned I could see only this rope!" Thus it was that

Seeing the saddle he recalled the horse;
Shedding tears he thought of his kin.

When Pa-chieh saw him shedding tears, however, he broke into loud guffaws with face raised toward the sky.

"You coolie!" scolded Pilgrim. "You want to disband again!"

"O Elder Brother!" said Pa-chieh, still laughing. "It's not like that. Master must have been abducted into the cave once more by the monster-spirit. As the proverb says, 'Success comes only with a third try.' You have entered the cave twice. Now go in a third time, and I'm sure that you'll be able to bring out Master."

Wiping away his tears, Pilgrim replied, "All right! Since things are this way, I have little choice but to go in again. Now that you don't even have to worry about the luggage and the horse, you must take care to guard the entrance."

Dear Great Sage! He turned and leaped into the cave; not undergoing transformation, he merely retained his characteristic appearance. Truly

Of strange-looking cheeks and a valiant mind,
He grew up a fiend with great magic strength.
His face like a saddle curved up and down;
His eyes flashed gold beams that blazed like fire.
Hard like needles were his whole body's furs;
His tiger-skin kilt jingled with loud floral bells.
In Heav'n he crashed through ten thousand clouds;
His rod in the sea lifted mountainous waves.
That day his might beat up the devarājas
And repelled one hundred and eight thousand foes.
Appointed Great Sage, the Handsome Monkey Sprite,
He used, by custom, a golden-hooped rod,
Going in again to help Tripitaka.

Look at him! He stopped the cloud luminosity after he reached the residence of the monster-spirit, where he found the towered gates were all shut. Without regard for good or ill, he broke through with one blow of his rod and barged in. It was completely quiet and not a trace of the inhabitants could be found. The T'ang monk was no longer seen by the east corridor; the furniture in the pavilion and the various utensils had all disappeared.

There were, you see, some three hundred miles of living space inside the cave, and the monster-spirit had many residences. When she had brought the T'ang monk to this particular spot the time before, Pilgrim had found them. Now that she had abducted the T'ang monk again, she feared that Pilgrim would return to the same place, and so she immediately moved somewhere else. Our Pilgrim was so exasperated that he pounded his chest and stamped his feet, crying, "O Master! You are a misfortune-begotten Tripitaka T'ang, a scripture monk forged by calamity! Alas! This road is familiar enough to me. Why aren't you here? Where should old Monkey look for you?"

As he was shouting like this in great annoyance, his nose suddenly caught a whiff of scented breeze. Calming down all at once, he said to himself, "This incense drifted out from the rear. They must be back

there." Gripping the iron rod, he strode in but found no movement
whatever—only three small chambers. At the back of one of these
chambers was a lacquered sacrificial table with open-mouthed dragons
carved on both sides. On the table was a huge incense urn of melted
gold from which fragrant incense smoke curled upward. Above the
urn was hung a large plaque with the following inscription in gold
letters: The Tablet of Honored Father, Devarāja Li. Slightly below it to
one side was another inscription: The Tablet of Honored Brother Naṭa,
the Third Prince.

Filled with delight by what he saw, Pilgrim immediately abandoned
his search for the fiend or the T'ang monk. He gave his iron rod a
squeeze to change it back into an embroidery needle, which he could
store in his ear. Stretching forth his hands, he took the plaque and the
urn and trod on his cloudy luminosity to go back out to the entrance
of the cave, hee-hawing in continuous laughter on the way.

When Pa-chieh and Sha Monk heard him, they stepped aside to
meet him, saying, "Elder Brother, you must have succeeded in rescuing Master, and that's why you're so happy."

"No need for us to go rescue Master," said Pilgrim, still guffawing,
"just make our demand known to this plaque." "O Elder Brother!"
said Pa-chieh. "This plaque is no monster-spirit, nor does it know how
to speak. Why should we make our demand known to it?"

"Take a look, both of you," said Pilgrim as he placed the plaque on
the ground. Sha Monk approached and saw the inscriptions: The
Tablet of Honored Father Devarāja Li, and The Tablet of Honored
Brother Naṭa, the Third Prince. "What's the meaning of this?" he
asked.

"It's something to which the monster-spirit makes offerings," replied Pilgrim. "When I broke into her residence, I found that both
persons and things had disappeared. There was only this plaque. She
has to be the daughter of Devarāja Li, the younger sister of the third
prince, who has descended to the Region Below out of profane longings. Disguised as a fiend, she has abducted our master. If we don't
demand of the persons whose names appear on this plaque, whom
should we ask? While the two of you stand guard here, let old Monkey
take the plaque and go up to Heaven to file charges before the Jade
Emperor. That'll make Devarāja Li and his son return our master."

"O Elder Brother!" said Pa-chieh. "As the proverb says, 'To charge
someone with a mortal offense is itself a mortal offense.' You can't do

it unless your cause is just. Besides, do you think that filing charges before the Throne is an easy thing? You'd better tell me how you plan to go about it."

"I have my way," said Pilgrim with a laugh. "This plaque and this urn I shall use as evidence. In addition, I shall file a formal, written complaint."

"What are you going to put in that complaint?" said Pa-chieh. "Let's hear it." Pilgrim said, "This is what I plan to say:

The plaintiff Sun Wu-k'ung, whose age and birthday are recorded here in the document, is the disciple of the priest, Tripitaka T'ang, who has been sent by the T'ang Court in the Land of the East to seek scriptures in the Western Heaven. The complaint I lodge concerns the crime of abetting a monster in kidnaping a human. I hereby accuse Li Ching, the Pagoda-Bearer Devarāja, along with Prince Naṭa, his son, for gross negligence in domestic affairs, which caused his own daughter to become a runaway. At the Region Below she had assumed the form of monstrous perversity in the Bottomless Cave of Mount Void-Entrapping, bringing vexation and harm to countless humans. She has, at the moment, abducted my master into the crooked recesses of her habitation, where he cannot be found at all. I have no choice but to charge father and son with an act of great atrocity, for allowing the daughter to become a spirit and to harm people. I beg you, there-fore, to sustain in your great mercy my complaint and arrest the culprits, so that perversity may be brought to submission, my master may be rescued, and the guilt of the offenders may be clearly established. In anticipation of your kind assistance, I hereby submit my complaint.

On hearing these words, Pa-chieh and Sha Monk were terribly pleased, both saying, "O Elder Brother, your complaint is most reasonable! You will undoubtedly win the case. You'd better go there at once, for we fear that a little delay may result in the monster-spirit's taking our master's life."

"I'll hurry! I'll hurry!" said Pilgrim. "It'll take me no more than the time needed for boiling tea, or at most for rice to be cooked, to get back here."

Dear Great Sage! Holding the plaque and the urn, he leaped up to mount the auspicious cloud and went straight before the South Heavenly Gate. When Devarājas Powerful and Dhṛtarāṣṭra, who were standing guard at the gate, saw him, both bent low to bow to him and dared not bar his way. He was permitted to go straight up to the Hall of Perfect Light, where he was greeted by Chang, Ko, Hsü, and Ch'iu, the four Heavenly Preceptors. "Why has the Great Sage come?" they asked.

"I have a document here," replied Pilgrim, "which I intend to file as a formal complaint."

"This caster of blame!" said one of the astonished preceptors. "I wonder whom he plans to accuse." They had no choice but to lead him into the Hall of Divine Mists to announce his arrival. He was then summoned into the presence of the Jade Emperor.

After putting down the plaque and the urn and paying homage to the Throne, he presented his plaint, which the Immortal Ko received and spread out on the imperial desk. When the Jade Emperor had read its content from beginning to end, he signed the document and endorsed it as an imperial decree. Then he commanded Gold Star Venus, Longevity of the West, to take the decree and go to the Cloud-Tower Palace to summon Devarāja Li, the Pagoda-Bearer, to appear before the Throne.

"I beg the Heavenly Lord to punish him properly," said Pilgrim, walking forward, "or else he may start some other trouble."

The Jade Emperor gave this order also: "Let the plaintiff go along."

"Should old Monkey really go along?" asked Pilgrim.

"Since His Majesty has already issued the decree," said one of the Heavenly Preceptors, "you may go with the Gold Star."

Pilgrim indeed mounted the clouds with the Gold Star to reach the Cloud-Tower Palace, which was, you see, the residence of the devarāja. There was a divine youth standing in front of the gate who recognized the Gold Star. He went inside at once and announced, "The Holy Father Gold Star Venus has arrived." The devarāja went out to meet his guest; when he saw that the Gold Star was bearing an imperial decree, he asked immediately for incense to be lighted. Then he caught sight of Pilgrim following the Gold Star in, and the devarāja stirred with anger.

Why was he angered, you ask. During the time when Pilgrim caused great disturbance at the Celestial Palace, the Jade Emperor once appointed the devarāja as the Demon-Subduing Grand Marshal and Prince Naṭa as the God of the Three Charities Grand Assembly. They were to lead the heavenly hosts against Pilgrim, but they could not prevail even after several engagements. The defeat of five hundred years ago, you see, still rankled him, and that was why he became angry. Unable to restrain himself, he asked, "Old Longevity, what's that decree you're bearing?"

"It happens to be a complaint," replied the Gold Star, "lodged against you by the Great Sage Sun."

The devarāja was already sorely annoyed; when he heard this, he became enraged, saying, "What's he accusing me of?"

"The crime of abetting a monster in kidnaping a human," replied the Gold Star. "After you've lit the incense, you may read it for yourself."

Panting hard, the devarāja hurriedly set out the incense table; after he had expressed his gratitude toward the sky and kowtowed, he spread out the decree. A careful reading of the document, however, sent him into such a rage that he gripped the table with both hands and said, "This ape-head! He has so wrongly accused me!"

The Gold Star said, "Don't get so mad! He happens to have a plaque and an urn for evidence before the Throne, and he claims that all those objects point to your own daughter."

"But I have only three sons and a daughter," said the devarāja. "The eldest is Suvarnaṭa, who serves Tathāgata as the vanguard of the Law. My second son is Mokṣa, who is the disciple of Kuan-shih-yin at South Sea. My third son Naṭa is with me and attends court night and day as an imperial guardsman. My only daughter, named Chên-ying, happens to be only seven years old. She doesn't even know much of human affairs. How could she be a monster-spirit? If you don't believe me, let me carry her out for you to see. This ape-head is mighty insolent! Let's not say that I am a marshal in Heaven, who has received such a high appointment that I'm permitted to execute someone first before memorializing to the Throne. Even if I were one of the common people in the Region Below, I should not be falsely accused. The Law says, 'A false accusation should receive a thrice-heavy penalty.'" He turned to his subordinates with the order: "Tie up this ape-head with the fiend-binding rope!"

The Mighty-Spirit God, General Fish-Belly, and Marshal Vajrayakṣa, who were standing in a row down at the courtyard, immediately surged forward and tied up Pilgrim.

"Devarāja Li," said the Gold Star, "you'd better not start any trouble! He is one of the two persons decreed by the Throne to come here to summon you. That rope of yours is quite heavy. If you hurt him in any way, you'll be the loser!"

"O Gold Star!" said the devarāja. "How could you allow him to file false charges and disturb the peace like that? Please be seated, while I cut off this ape-head with the fiend-hacking scimitar. Then I'll return with you to see the Throne."

When the Gold Star learned that he was about to raise the scimitar, his heart quivered and his bladder shook as he said to Pilgrim, "You've made a mistake! Filing charges before the Throne is no light thing! Why didn't you try to ascertain the truth first? All your foolish doings now may cause you to lose your life. What'll you do?"

Not frightened in the least, Pilgrim said, full of smiles, "Relax, old Minister, it's nothing! Old Monkey has to do his own business this way: he must lose first, and then he'll win."

Hardly had he finished speaking when the devarāja wielded his scimitar and brought it down hard on Pilgrim's head. All at once the third prince rushed forward and parried the blow with the fiend-hacking sword, crying, "Father King, please calm your anger!" The devarāja turned pale with alarm.

Ah! When the father saw the son parrying the scimitar with his own sword, he should have commanded the son to turn back. Why should he turn pale with alarm? This is the reason, you see:

When this child was born to the devarāja,[3] he had on his left hand the word Na, and on his right the word Ṭa, and that was why he was named Naṭa. On the third morning after he was born, this prince already decided to bathe in the ocean and caused a great disaster. He overturned the water-crystal palace and wanted to pull out the tendons of one of the dragons to use them for a belt. When the devarāja learned of the incident, he feared that his son might prove to be a calamity afterward and sought to have him killed. Naṭa became enraged; knife in hand, he cut off his own flesh to give it back to his mother and carved up his bones to give them back to his father. After he had, as it were, repaid his father's sperm and his mother's blood, his soul went to the region of ultimate bliss in the West to complain to Buddha.

Buddha at the time was lecturing to the various bodhisattvas when he heard someone on the sacred banners and parasol calling, "Save me!" One look with his eyes of wisdom and Buddha knew it was the soul of Naṭa. Using the root of the lotus for bones and its leaves for garment, he recited the magic words of revivification and restored Naṭa to life. With his newfound divine strength, Naṭa succeeded in subduing the fiendish demons of ninety-six caves. His magic powers were so great that he later wanted to kill the devarāja in order to exact vengeance for self-immolation.

The devarāja had little choice but to plead with Tathāgata, who, of course, was an advocate of peace. He therefore bestowed on the devarāja a compliant, yellow-gold treasure pagoda of the finest open-work carving and filled with śārī-relics; the pagoda, in fact, symbolized Buddha on each level, and the entire edifice was bathed in luminosity. The sight of the pagoda thus would remind Naṭa of Buddha, who was to be revered as the prince's true father, and that is how the enmity was dissolved. This is the reason also for Li Ching to be named the Devarāja Pagoda-Bearer.

Since he was at home today, at leisure, the devarāja had not been carrying his pagoda, and he thought that Naṭa had been seized by the desire for vengeance again. That was the reason he paled with fear. Immediately reaching for the gold treasure pagoda on the stand and holding it high, he asked Naṭa, "Child, you've parried my scimitar with your sword. What do you want to say to me?"

Abandoning his sword and kowtowing, Naṭa replied, "Father King, you do have a daughter at the Region Below."

"Child," said the devarāja, "I have had only the four of you. What other daughter do I have?"

"You have quite forgotten, Father King," said Naṭa. "That other daughter was originally a monster-spirit. Some three hundred years ago she became a fiend who stole and devoured the fragrant flowers and treasure candles of Tathāgata at Spirit Mountain. Tathāgata sent us, father and son, to lead an expedition against her. When she was caught, she should have been beaten to death, but Tathāgata gave us this instruction:

For fishes reared in the ponds you never fish;

For deer fed in the mountains long life's your wish.

At that time, therefore, we spared her life, and in gratitude she took you as her father and your child as her elder brother. She was to set up our tablets down below, to which she would offer perpetual incense fires. Who would have expected her to become a spirit again and conspire to harm the T'ang monk? When Pilgrim Sun searched through her lair, the tablets were found and charges were thus filed before the Throne. This is your daughter by the bond of grace, not a sister of mine by blood."

Astounded by what he heard, the devarāja said, "My child, I have indeed forgotten the whole matter. What's her name?"

"She has three of them," replied the prince. "At her birthplace she was originally called the Golden-Nosed White-Haired Rodent-Spirit. Because she had stolen the fragrant flowers and treasure candles, her name was changed to Bisected Kuan-yin. When she was spared and sent to the Region Below, she changed her name again to Mistress Ground-Rushing."

Only then did the devarāja realize what had happened. Immediately he wanted to untie Pilgrim with his own hands, but Pilgrim had turned rowdy. "Who dares untie me?" he cried. "You can take me in ropes to see the Throne! Old Monkey will then win his litigation!" The hands of the devarāja turned numb with fear, the prince became speechless, and the various subordinate officers retreated shamefacedly.

Rolling all over the place in a tantrum, the Great Sage insisted that the devarāja appear before the Throne with him. Having no alternative, the devarāja could only plead pitifully with the Gold Star to speak on his behalf. The Gold Star said, "As the ancients put the matter, 'One should be lenient in all things.' The way you do things, however, is rather hasty! You've bound him, and you even wanted to kill him. This monkey happens to be notorious in casting blame. Now what do you want me to do? According to what your son has told us, she is not your daughter by blood but only by bond. Nonetheless, that is still an important tie of kinship. No matter how you dispute the matter, you are somewhat guilty."

The devarāja said, "If the venerable Star would speak on my behalf, then my guilt will be absolved." "I would like indeed to pacify you both," said the Gold Star, "but I don't quite know how to plead for you."

"Why don't you," said the devarāja, "just mention the former incident, when you went to him on your mission of pacification and gave him his appointment?" The Gold Star did indeed go forward to touch Pilgrim and said, "Great Sage, for my sake let us untie you so that we may all go see the Throne."

"Old Minister," said Pilgrim, "you needn't untie me. I know how to roll, and I'll roll my way there!"

"Monkey, you're quite unfeeling!" said the Gold Star, chuckling. "I was, after all, rather kind to you in times past. Now you refuse me even in a trivial matter like this." "What sort of kindness have you shown me?" asked Pilgrim.

The Gold Star said, "In those years when you were a fiend in Mount Flower-Fruit, when you tamed tigers and subdued dragons, when you abolished the register of death by force, and when you assembled various monsters to perpetrate your delinquency, Heaven above wanted to arrest you. It was this old man who boldly memorialized to the Throne to issue a decree of pacification and have you summoned to the Celestial Palace and appointed you a pi-ma-wên. After you had drunk the immortal wine of the Jade Emperor and needed pacification once more, it was this old man's bold memorial also that got you the appointment of Great Sage, Equal to Heaven. But you did not behave and went on to steal peaches, filch wine, and rifle elixir from Lord Lao. Only after this and that did you attain a state of birthlessness and deathlessness. But if it hadn't been for me, would you have reached this day?"

Pilgrim said, "The ancients truly had put the matter well: even in death you should not share a grave with an old man! Like it or not, he knows how to carp! What's so big that I did? I merely disturbed the Celestial Palace as pi-ma-wên. All right! All right! For your sake, Venerable Sir, I'll relent, but he himself must untie me." Only then did the devarāja dare approach and untie the rope. Pilgrim was then invited to tidy his clothes and take the honored seat, after which the various deities went forward one by one to pay their respects.

Facing the Gold Star, Pilgrim said, "Old Minister, how about it? Didn't I tell you that I would lose first, and then win? That's how one should do business! Let's urge him to go see the Throne quickly, lest my master is harmed." "Let's not rush things," said the Gold Star. "Having squandered all this time already, let's have a cup of tea first."

"If you drink his tea," said Pilgrim, "you're, in fact, accepting his bribe. What sort of crime should you be charged with, when you free the felon on a bribe and slight the imperial decree?"

"I won't drink his tea! I won't drink his tea!" exclaimed the Gold Star. "Now you're even casting blame on me! Devarāja Li, go quickly! Go quickly!" But the devarāja, of course, dared not go with Pilgrim to see the Throne, for he was terribly afraid that the ape might turn rowdy once more. If he were to mouth all kinds of accusations before

the Jade Emperor, how could the devarāja hope to refute them? He
had no choice but again to plead with the Gold Star to speak up for
him.

At length the Gold Star said to Pilgrim, "I have just one word for
you! Will you agree to it?"

"I have already overlooked for *your* sake the affront of being bound
and hacked by the scimitar," said Pilgrim. "Do you have anything
more to say? Speak up! Speak up! If it's good, I'll listen; if not, don't
blame me!"

The Gold Star said, "Remember the proverb, 'One day's litigation
will take ten days to settle.' You file a charge before the Throne, claim-
ing that the monster-spirit is the daughter of the devarāja, and he
denies it. The two of you can argue this matter back and forth before
the Jade Emperor. Meanwhile, let me remind you that one day in
Heaven is equivalent to one year in the Region Below. For this whole
year the monster-spirit has had your master imprisoned in the cave.
Let's not mention a wedding ceremony. Even if it's a makeshift affair,
by now she must have produced a little monk for him! Hasn't your
delay upset the great enterprise?"

Lowering his head, Pilgrim thought to himself, "Yes, indeed! When
I left Pa-chieh and Sha Monk, I told them that I would return after a
time no longer than it takes tea to boil, or at most for rice to be cooked.
I've messed around here all this while. Am I too late?" He said thereby
to the Gold Star, "Old Minister, how should we return this imperial
decree?"

"Let's ask Devarāja Li to summon his troops to go down with you
to subdue the fiend," replied the Gold Star. "I'll return the decree."

"What will you say as your report?" asked Pilgrim.

"That the plaintiff has fled," said the Gold Star, "and that the
defendant has been dismissed from the case."

"How nice!" said Pilgrim with a laugh. "For *your* sake I'm dropping
my charges, and you claim instead that *I* have fled! Tell him to call
up the troops and wait for me outside the South Heavenly Gate. I'll go
with you to return the decree."

Growing alarmed once more, the devarāja said, "If he starts talking
once he gets inside the palace, I may end up with the crime of
treason."

"What sort of person do you take old Monkey for?" said Pilgrim.
"I, too, am a true man! 'Once my word is given, horses can't retrieve

it.' You think I would smear you with slander?"

The devarāja then thanked Pilgrim, who left with the Gold Star to return the decree. The devarāja at once called up the troops under his command and had them stationed outside the South Heavenly Gate. Going before the Throne with Pilgrim, the Gold Star said to the Jade Emperor, "The person who has imprisoned the T'ang monk happens to be a gold-nosed, white-furred rodent which has become a spirit. She is also the one who has set up the tablets of Devarāja Li and his son. Since learning of this, the devarāja has already called up his troops for an expedition against the fiend. I beg the Celestial-Honored One to pardon him."

Since the Jade Emperor had already known of this, he at once extended his heavenly grace and pardon. Pilgrim turned back his cloudy luminosity to go out of the South Heavenly Gate, where he found the devarāja, the prince, and the heavenly hosts waiting in smart formation. Behold! Those divine warriors, in churning wind and fog, received the Great Sage and then lowered their clouds to descend to Mount Void-Entrapping.

Pa-chieh and Sha Monk, with bulging eyes, were waiting on the mountain when they saw Pilgrim arriving with the heavenly hosts. Bowing to the devarāja, Idiot said to him, "We've troubled you!" "Marshal Heavenly Reeds," said the devarāja, "we have something to tell you: we, father and son, may have enjoyed one stick of her incense, but the monster-spirit has thereby grown audacious enough to have your master imprisoned. Please don't blame us for this tardy arrival. Is this Mount Void-Entrapping? I wonder which direction the entrance of her cave faces."

"I'm familiar enough with the way in," said Pilgrim. "Her cave here is named the Bottomless Cave, and its inside is about three hundred miles in circumference. The monster-spirit actually must have many lairs. Previously she had my master detained within a double-eaved towered gate. Now it's so quiet there that you won't see even the shadow of a ghost! I have no idea where she has moved to." The devarāja said, "No matter.

Let her maneuver in a thousand ways;
She'll n'er escape the net of Heav'n and Earth.
Let's approach the entrance first, and then we'll decide what to do."
All of them immediately proceeded. Ah! After some ten miles they reached the big boulder. Pointing to the entrance about the size of a huge barrel, Pilgrim said, "That's it."

"'Without entering the tiger's lair,'" said the devarāja, "'how could one capture the tiger cubs?' Who dares lead the way?"

"I do," said Pilgrim.

"Since I'm to subdue a fiend by imperial decree," said the prince, "I'll lead the way."

At that moment our Idiot became even more impetuous. "Old Hog will be the one to lead the way!" he shouted.

"No need to make so much noise!" said the devarāja. "Let me give the order: the Great Sage Sun and the prince will lead the troops down there. We three will stand guard up here at the entrance. We shall coordinate our efforts within and without, so that she will have no route to flee to Heaven and no door to enter Earth. Only then will we truly show our power." All of them responded with a resounding "Yes!"

Look at Pilgrim and the prince! Leading the captains and troops, they slid inside the cave and immediately mounted the cloudy luminosity. As they looked about, it was a fine cave indeed!

The sun and moon's familiar orbs
Shine on the same mountains and streams;
Pearly deeps, jade wells warmed and sheathed in mist,
And many lovely sights.
Red painted towers in layers,
Scarlet walls and green fields endless.
Late autumn lotus and willows of spring
Such a cave-heaven's rarely seen.

In a moment, they stopped their cloudy luminosity right before the old residence of the monster-spirit. Noisily the celestial warriors began a door-to-door search; they looked everywhere, spreading out through all those three hundred miles, but neither a single monster-spirit nor a Tripitaka could be seen at all.

"This cursed beast," said the warriors, "must have left the cave and removed herself far away." Little did they know that there was another tiny cave at the dark southeast corner; there was a tiny door in the cave and a house built rather low, surrounded by a few pots of flowers and several stalks of bamboo. It was a place shrouded in darkness and faint fragrance. Here the old fiend had brought Tripitaka and wanted to force him to marry her, thinking that Pilgrim would never be able to find them. She did not realize, of course, that her fate was about to overtake her. As those little fiends crowded together inside, you see, one of the more courageous ones stuck out his head to take a peek outside, and he ran directly into the celestial warriors.

"They're here!" they cried, and Pilgrim became so aroused that he went crashing in, his hand gripping the golden-hooped rod. The whole nest of monster-spirits was packed in that small and narrow place. When the prince and his troops surged forward, where could any of the fiends run to hide?

Pilgrim soon located the T'ang monk, the luggage, and the dragon horse. When the old fiend realized that there was no way for her to flee, she faced Prince Naṭa and kowtowed repeatedly, begging for her life. The prince said, "Our expedition here to arrest you is decreed by the Jade Emperor, and it's no small thing. We, father and son, by enjoying one stick of your incense, nearly brought on ourselves colossal calamity!" Thereupon he bellowed: "Celestial soldiers, take out the fiend-binding ropes and tie up all those monster-spirits!" The old fiend, you see, could not avoid a little suffering.

The company then turned around their cloudy luminosity and went outside the cave, with Pilgrim chortling loudly all the way. The devarāja left his post at the entrance to meet Pilgrim, saying, "This time you've seen your master!"

"Thank you! Thank you!" replied Pilgrim, and at once led Tripitaka to bow to thank the devarāja and the prince. Sha Monk and Pa-chieh would have liked very much to hack the old spirit into tiny pieces, but the devarāja said, "Since she was arrested by imperial decree, she should not be easily disposed of. We have yet to return to make a report to the Throne."

So the devarāja and the third prince led the divine warriors and celestial soldiers to guard the monster-spirit and take her back to face judgment before Heaven's tribunal. Meanwhile Pilgrim and Sha Monk scurried around the T'ang monk to pack as Pa-chieh steadied the horse for him to mount. They headed for the main road together. Thus it is that

The silk threads are sundered to dry the golden sea;

The jade lock's broken and he leaves the bird-cage.

We do not know what happens as they journey forth, and you must listen to the explanation in the next chapter.

Eighty-four

It's hard to destroy the priests[1] to reach great enlightenment;
The Dharma-king perfects the right, his body's naturalized.

We were telling you how Tripitaka T'ang had safeguarded his primal yang and escaped from the bitter trap of the fair sex. As he followed Pilgrim to head for the West, it was soon again the time of summer, when warm breezes freshly stirred, and rain of the plum season drizzled down in fine strands. Marvelous scenery, it is:

Lush and dense is the green shade;
In light breeze young swallows parade.
New lilies unfold on the ponds;
Old bamboos spread slowly their fronds.
The sky joins the meadows in green;
Mountain blooms o'er the ground are seen.
Swordlike, rushes stand by the brook;
Pomegranates redden this sketchbook.

Master and disciples, the four of them, had to endure the heat, of course.

As they proceeded, they came upon two rows of tall willows flanking the road; from within the willow shade an old woman suddenly walked out, leading a young child by the hand. "Priest," she cried aloud to the T'ang monk, "you must stop right now! Turn your horse around and return to the East quickly! The road to the West leads only to death!"

So startled was Tripitaka that he leaped down from the horse and bowed to her, saying, "Old Bodhisattva, as the ancients have said,

The ocean is wide so fishes may leap;
The sky is empty so birds may fly.

Why do you tell me that there's no further road to the West?"

Pointing westward with her finger, the old woman said, "About five or six miles from here is the Dharma-Destroying Kingdom. In some previous incarnation somewhere the king must have contracted evil karma so that in this life he sins without cause. Two years ago he

139

made a stupendous vow that he would kill ten thousand Buddhist priests. Until now he has succeeded in slaughtering nine thousand, nine hundred, and ninety-six nameless monks. All he is waiting for now are four more monks, preferably with names, and the perfect score of ten thousand will be reached. If you people arrive at his city, you will all become life-giving bodhisattvas!"

Terror-stricken by these words, Tripitaka said, trembling all over, "Old Bodhisattva, I'm profoundly grateful for your kindness, and I can't thank you enough. May I ask whether there is another road which conveniently bypasses the city? This poor monk will gladly take such a road and proceed."

With a giggle, the old woman replied, "You can't bypass the city! You simply can't! You might do so only if you could fly!"

At once Pa-chieh began to wag his tongue and said, "Mama, don't speak such scary words! We're all able to fly!" With his fiery eyes and diamond pupils, however, Pilgrim was the only one who could discern the truth: the old woman and the child were actually the Bodhisattva Kuan-yin and the Boy of Goodly Wealth. So alarmed was he that he went to his knees immediately and cried, "Bodhisattva, pardon your disciples for failing to meet you!"

Gently the bodhisattva rose on a petal of pink cloud, so astounding the Elder T'ang that he did not quite know where to stand. All he could do was to fall on his knees to kowtow, and Pa-chieh and Sha Monk too went hurriedly to their knees to bow to the sky. In a moment, the auspicious cloud drifted away to return to South Sea. Pilgrim got up and raised his master, saying, "Please rise, the bodhisattva has returned to her treasure mountain."

As he got up, Tripitaka said, "Wu-k'ung, if you recognized the bodhisattva, why didn't you tell us sooner?"

"You couldn't stop asking questions," replied Pilgrim, laughing, "while I immediately went to my knees. Wasn't that soon enough?" Pa-chieh and Sha Monk then said to Pilgrim, "Thanks to the bodhisattva's revelation, what lies before us has to be the Dharma-Destroying Kingdom. What are we all going to do when there's this determination to kill monks?"

"Idiot, don't be afraid!" said Pilgrim. "We have met quite a few vicious demons and savage fiends, and we have gone through tiger lairs and dragon lagoons, but we have never been hurt. What we have to face here is a kingdom of common people. Why should we fear them? Our only trouble right now is that this is no place to stay. Besides, it's getting late, and if any villagers returning from business in the city catch sight of us priests and begin to spread the news, that won't be very convenient. Let's lead Master away from the main road and find a more secluded spot. We can then make further plans."

Tripitaka indeed followed his suggestion; all of them left the main road and went over to a small ditch, in which they sat down. "Brothers," said Pilgrim, "the two of you stay here and guard Master. Let old Monkey go in transformation to look over the city. Perhaps I can find a road that's out of the way, which will take us through the region this very night."

"O Disciple!" urged the T'ang monk. "Don't take this lightly, for you're going against the law of a king. Do be careful!"

"Relax! Relax!" replied Pilgrim with a smile. "Old Monkey will manage!" Dear Great Sage! When he finished speaking, he leaped into the air with a loud whistle. How fantastic!

Neither pulled from above by strings,
Nor supported below by canes,
Like us all, two parents he owns,
But only he has lighter bones.

Standing at the edge of the clouds, he peered below and saw that the city was flooded by airs of gladness and auspicious luminosity. "What a lovely place!" Pilgrim said. "Why does it want to destroy the dharma?" As he stared at the place, it gradually grew dark. He saw that

At letter-ten crossings[2] lamps flared brightly;
At nine-tiered halls incense rose and bells tolled.
Seven glowing stars lit up the blue sky;
In eight quarters travelers dropped their gear.
From the six-corps camps
The painted bugles just faintly sounded;
In the five-watch tower,
Drop by drop the copper pot 'gan dripping.
On four sides night fog thickened;
At three marts chilly mist spread out.
Spouses, in twos, entered the silken drapes,
When one bright moon ascended the east.

He thought to himself: "I would like to go down to the business districts to look over the roadways, but with a face like this, people will undoubtedly holler that I'm a priest if they see me. I'll transform myself." Making the magic sign and reciting a spell, he changed with one shake of his body into a moth:

A small shape with light, agile wings,
He dives to snuff candles and lamps.
By metamorphosis he gains his true form,
Most active midst rotted grasses.
He strikes flames for love of hot light,
Flying, circling without ceasing.
Purple-robed, fragrant-winged, chasing the fireflies,
He likes most the deep windless night.

You see him soaring and turning as he flew toward those six boulevards and three marts, passing eaves and rafters. As he proceeded, he suddenly caught sight of a row of houses at the corner of the street ahead, each house having a lantern hung above its door.

"These families," he thought to himself, "must be celebrating the Lantern Feast. Why would they have lighted lanterns by the row?" Stiffening his wings, he flew near and looked carefully. The house in the very middle had a square lantern, on which these words were written: Rest for the Traveling Merchant. Below there were also the words: Steward Wang's Inn. Pilgrim knew therefore that it was a hotel.

When he stretched out his neck to look further, he saw that there were some eight or nine people, who had all finished their dinner. Having loosened their clothes, taken off their head wraps, and washed their hands and feet, they had taken to their beds to sleep. Secretly pleased, Pilgrim said, "Master may pass through!" How did he know so readily that his master might pass through, you ask. He was about to follow a wicked design: waiting until those people were asleep, he would steal their clothes and wraps so that master and disciples could disguise themselves as secular folks to enter the city.

Alas! There had to be this disagreeable development! As he was deliberating by himself, the steward went forward and gave this instruction to his guests: "Sirs, do be careful, for our place caters to both gentlemen and rogues. I'd like to ask each of you to take care of your clothing and luggage." Think of it! People doing business abroad, would they not be careful about everything? When they heard such instruction from the innkeeper, they became more cautious than ever. Hastening to their feet, they said, "The proprietor is quite right. Those of us fatigued by travel may not easily wake up once we're asleep. If we lose our things, what are we going to do? Please take our clothes, our head wraps, and our money bags inside. When we get up in the morning, you may return them to us." Steward Wang accordingly took all of their clothes and belongings into his own residence.

By nature impulsive, Pilgrim at once spread his wings to fly there also and alighted on one of the head-wrap stands. Then he saw Steward Wang going to the front door to take down the lantern, lower the cloth curtain, and close the door and windows. Only then did Wang return to his room to take off his clothes and lie down. The steward, however, also had a wife sleeping with two children, and they were still making so much noise that none of them could go to sleep right away. The wife, too, was patching some garment and refused to retire.

"If I wait until this woman sleeps," thought Pilgrim to himself, "won't Master be delayed?" Fearing also that the city gates might be closed later in the night, he could no longer refrain from flying down there and threw himself on the taper. Truly

He risked his life to dive into flames;
He scorched his brow to tempt his fate.

The taper immediately went out. With one shake of his body he changed again into a rat. After a squeak or two he leaped down, took the garments and head wraps, and began to drag them out. Panic-stricken, the woman said, "Old man, things are bad! A rat has turned into a spirit!"

On hearing this, Pilgrim flaunted his abilities some more. Stopping at the door, he cried out in a loud voice, "Steward Wang, don't listen to the babblings of your woman. I'm no rodent-spirit. Since a man of light does not engage in shady dealings, I must tell you that I'm the Great Sage, Equal to Heaven, who has descended to Earth to accompany the T'ang monk on his way to seek scriptures in the Western Heaven. Because your king is without principles, I've come especially to borrow these caps and gowns to adorn my master. Once we've got through the city, I'll return them." Hearing that, Steward Wang scrambled up at once. It was, of course, pitch black, and he was in a hurry besides. He grabbed his pants, thinking he had his shirt; but no matter how hard he tried, slipping them on this way and that, he could not put them on.

Using his magic of abduction, the Great Sage had already mounted the clouds to leave the city and get back to the ditch by the road. In the bright light of the stars and moon, Tripitaka was standing there staring when he saw Pilgrim approaching. "Disciple," he asked, "can we go through the Dharma-Destroying Kingdom?"

Walking forward and putting down the garments, Pilgrim said, "Master, if you want to go through the Dharma-Destroying Kingdom, you can't remain a priest."

"Elder Brother," said Pa-chieh, "who are you trying to fool? It's easy not to remain a priest: just don't shave your head for half a year, and your hair will grow."

"We can't wait for half a year!" said Pilgrim. "We must become laymen right now!"

Horrified, our Idiot said, "The way you talk is most unreasonable, as always! We are all priests, and you want us to become laymen this instant! How could we even wear a head wrap? Even if we tighten the edges, we have nothing on our heads to tie the strings with!"

"Stop the wisecracks!" snapped Tripitaka. "Let's do what's proper! Wu-k'ung, what *is* your plan?"

"Master," said Pilgrim, "I have inspected the city here. Though the king is unprincipled enough to slaughter monks, he is nevertheless a genuine son of Heaven, for his city is filled with joyful and auspicious air. I can recognize the streets in the city, and I can converse in the local dialect. A moment ago I borrowed several garments and head wraps from a hotel. We must disguise ourselves as laymen and enter the city to ask for lodging. At the fourth watch we should rise and ask the innkeeper to prepare us a meal—vegetarian, of course. By about the hour of the fifth watch, we will walk close to the wall of the city-gate and find the main road to the West. If we run into anyone who tries to detain us, we can still give the explanation that we have been commissioned by the court of a superior state. The Dharma-Destroying King would not dare hinder us. He'll let us go." Sha Monk said, "Elder Brother's plan is most proper. Let's do as he tells us."

Indeed, the elder had little choice but to shed his monk's robe and his clerical cap and to put on the garment and head wrap of a layman. Sha Monk, too, changed his clothes. Pa-chieh, however, had such a huge head that he could not wear the wrap as it was. Pilgrim had to rip open two wraps and sew them together with needle and thread to make one wrap and drape it over his head. A larger garment was selected for him to put on, after which Pilgrim himself also changed into a different set of clothing. "Once we get moving," he said, "you all must put away the words 'master and disciples.'"

"Without these words," said Pa-chieh, "how shall we address ourselves?"

Pilgrim said, "We should do so as if we were in a fraternal order: Master shall be called Grand Master T'ang, you shall be called Third Master Chu, Sha Monk shall be called Fourth Master Sha, and I shall be called Second Master Sun. When we reach the hotel, however, none of you should talk; let me do all the talking. If they ask us what sort of business we're in, I'll say that we're horse traders, using this white horse of ours as a sample. I'll tell them that there are altogether ten of us in this fraternal order, but the four of us have come first to rent a room in the hotel and sell our horse. The innkeeper will certainly take care of us. If we receive his hospitality, I'll pick up by the time we leave some bits or pieces of broken tiles and change them into silver to thank him. Then we'll get on with our journey." The elder had no alternative but to comply reluctantly.

The four of them, leading the horse and toting the luggage, hurried into the city. It was fortunate that this happened to be a peaceful region, so that the city gates had not yet been closed even at the time the night watch began. When they reached the door of the Steward Wang's Hotel, they heard noises from inside, crying, "I've lost my head wrap!" Another person said, "I've lost my clothes!" Feigning ignorance, Pilgrim led them to another hotel, catercorner from this one. Since that hotel had not yet even taken down its lantern, Pilgrim walked up to the door and called out: "Innkeeper, do you have a room for us to stay in?"

Some woman inside replied at once, "Yes! Yes! Yes! Let the masters go up to the second floor." She had hardly finished speaking when a man arrived to take the horse, which Pilgrim handed over to him. He himself led his master behind the lamplight and up to the door of the second floor, where lounge tables and chairs had been placed. He pushed open the shutters, and moonlight streamed in as they took their seats. Someone came up with lighted lamps, but Pilgrim barred the door and blew out the lamps with one breath. "We don't need lamps when the moon's so bright," he said.

After the person with the lamps had been sent away, another maid brought up four bowls of pure tea, which Pilgrim accepted. From below, a woman about fifty-seven or fifty-eight years old came straight up to the second floor. Standing to one side, she asked, "Gentlemen, where have you come from? What treasure merchandise do you have?"

"We came from the north," replied Pilgrim, "and we have a few ordinary horses to sell."

"Well," said the woman, "we haven't seen many guests who sell horses."

"This one is Grand Master T'ang," said Pilgrim, "this one is Third Master Chu, and this one is Fourth Master Sha. Your humble student here is Second Master Sun."

"All different surnames," said the woman with a giggle.

"Indeed, all different surnames but living together," said Pilgrim. "There are altogether ten of us in our fraternal order; we four have come first to seek lodging at your hotel, and the six others are resting outside the city. With a herd of horses, they don't dare enter the city at such a late hour. When we have located the proper place for them to stay, they'll come in tomorrow morning. Once we have sold the horses, we'll leave."

"How many horses are there in your herd?" asked the woman.

"Big and small, there are over a hundred," said Pilgrim, "all very much like the horse we have here. Only their colors vary."

Giggling some more, the woman said, "Second Master Sun is indeed a merchant in every way! It's a good thing that you've come to our place, for any other household would not dare receive you. We happen to have a large courtyard here, complete with stalls and stocked with feed. Even if you had several hundred horses, we can take care of them. You should be aware, too, that our hotel has been here for years and has gained quite a reputation. My late husband, who unfortunately died long ago, had the surname of Chao, and that's why this hotel is named Widow Chao's Inn. We have three classes of accommodation here. If you will kindly allow impoliteness to precede courtesy, I will discuss the room rates with you, so I'll know what to charge you."

"What you say is quite right," said Pilgrim. "What three classes of accommodation do you have in your hotel? As the saying goes,

High, medium, and low, are three prices of goods,

Guests, far and near, are not treated the same.

Tell me a little of your three classes of accommodation."

Widow Chao said, "What we have here are the superior, moderate,

and inferior classes of accommodation. For the superior, we will prepare a banquet of five kinds of fruits and five courses, topped by lion-
head puddings and peck-candies. There will be two persons per table,
and young hostesses will be invited to drink and rest with you. The
charge per person is five mace of silver, and this includes the room."

"What a bargain!" said Pilgrim, chuckling. "Where I came from,
five mace of silver won't even pay for the young ladies!"

"For the moderate," said the widow again, "all of you will share
one table, and you'll get only fruits and hot wine. You yourselves may
establish your drinking rules and play your finger-guessing games,
but no young hostesses will be present. For this, we charge two mace
of silver per person."

"That's even more of a bargain," said Pilgrim. "What's the inferior
class like?"

"I dare not describe that in front of honored guests," replied the
woman.

"You may tell us," said Pilgrim. "We'll find our bargain and do our
thing!"

The woman said, "In the inferior class there's no one to serve you.
You may eat whatever rice there is in the pot, and when you've had
your fill, you can get some straw and make yourself a bed on the
ground. Find yourself a place to sleep, and in the morning you may
give us a few pennies for the rice. We won't haggle with you."

On hearing this, Pa-chieh said, "Lucky! Lucky! That's old Hog's
kind of business! Let me stand in front of the pot and stuff myself with
rice. Then I'll have a nice damn snooze in front of the hearth!"

"Brother," said Pilgrim, "what are you saying? You and I, after
all, have managed to earn a few taels of silver here and there in the
world, haven't we? Give us the superior class!"

Filled with delight, the woman cried, "Bring some fine tea! Tell the
chefs to start their preparations." She dashed downstairs and shouted
some more: "Slaughter some chickens and geese. Have them cooked
or cured to go with the rice. Slaughter a pig and a lamb too; even if
we can't use them today, we may use them tomorrow. Get the good
wine. Cook white-grain rice, and take bleached flour to make biscuits."

When he heard her from upstairs, Tripitaka said, "Second Master
Sun, what shall we do? She is planning to slaughter chickens, geese,
a pig, and a lamb. When she brings these things up, which one of us,

keepers of a perpetual vegetarian diet as we are, dare take one bite?"

"I know what to do," replied Pilgrim, and he went to the head of the stairs and tapped the floor with his foot. "Mama Chao, please come up," he said.

The mama came up and said, "What instructions do you have for me, Second Master?" "Don't slaughter anything today," said Pilgrim, "for we're keeping a vegetarian diet."

Astonished, the widow said, "Do the masters keep a perpetual diet or a monthly diet?" "Neither," replied Pilgrim, "for ours is named the *kêng-shên* diet. Since the cyclical combination for today is, in fact, *kêng-shên*, we must keep the diet. Once the hour of the third watch is past, it will be the day of *hsin-yu*, and we'll be able to eat meat. You may do the slaughtering tomorrow. Please go now and prepare us some vegetarian dishes. We'll pay you the price of the superior class just the same."

The woman was more delighted than ever. She dashed downstairs to say, "Don't slaughter anything! Don't slaughter anything! Take some woodears, Fukien bamboo-shoots, bean curds, wheat glutens, and pull some greens from our garden to make vermicelli soup. Let the dough rise so that we can steam some rolls. We can cook the white-grain rice and brew fragrant tea also." Aha! Those chefs in the kitchen, accustomed to doing this every day, finished their preparations in no time at all. The food was brought upstairs, along with ready-made lion-puddings and candied fruits, so that the four could enjoy themselves to their hearts' content.

"Do you take dietary wine?" the woman asked again. Pilgrim said, "Only Grand Master T'ang doesn't drink, but the rest of us can use a few cups." The widow then brought up a bottle of hot wine. Hardly had the three of them finished pouring when they heard loud bangings on the floor down below.

"Mama," said Pilgrim, "did something fall downstairs?"

"No," replied the widow. "A few hired hands from our humble village who arrived rather late tonight with their monthly payment of rice were told to sleep downstairs. Since you masters have come, and we haven't enough help right now, I've asked them to take the carriages to go fetch the young hostesses here to keep you company. The poles on the carriages must have accidentally backed into the boards of the staircase."

"It's a good thing that you mention this," said Pilgrim. "Quickly tell them not to go. For one thing we're still keeping the diet, and for another our brothers have not yet arrived. Wait till they come in tomorrow, then we'll invite some call girls for the whole order to have some fun right here. After we've sold our horses, we'll leave."

"Good man! Good man!" said the widow. "You've not destroyed the peace, but you've saved your own energy at the same time!" She called out, "Bring back the carriages. No need to fetch the girls." After the four had finished the wine and rice, the utensils were taken away, and the attendants left.

Tripitaka whispered behind Pilgrim's ear, "Where shall we sleep?" "Up here," replied Pilgrim.

"It's not quite safe," said Tripitaka. "All of us are rather tired. When we're asleep, if someone from this household chances to come by to fix things up and notices our bald heads if our caps roll off, they will see that we're monks. What shall we do if they begin yelling?"

"Indeed!" replied Pilgrim. He went again to the head of the stairs to tap his foot, and the widow came up once more to ask: "What does Master Sun want?"

"Where shall we sleep?" asked Pilgrim.

"Why, up here, of course!" said the woman. "There are no mosquitoes. You may open wide the windows, and with a nice southerly breeze, it's perfect for you to sleep upstairs."

"No, we can't," said Pilgrim. "Our Third Master Chu here is somewhat allergic to dampness, and Fourth Master Sha has arthritic shoulders. Big Brother T'ang can only sleep in the dark, and I, too, am rather sensitive to light. This is no place to sleep."

The mama walked downstairs and, leaning on the counter, began to sigh. A daughter of hers, carrying a child, approached and said, "Mother, as the proverb says,

For ten days you sit on the beach;
In one day you may pass nine beaches.

Since this is the hot season, we haven't much business, but by the time of the fall, business may increase so much that we can't even cope with it. Why are you sighing?"

"Child," replied the woman, "I'm not worrying about lack of business, for at dusk today I was ready to close shop. But at the hour when the night watch began, four horse traders came to rent a room. Since they wanted the superior-class accommodation, I was hoping to make a few pennies profit from them. But they keep a vegetarian diet, and that completely dashes my hopes. That's why I'm sighing."

Her daughter said, "If they have eaten our rice, they can't leave and go to another household. Tomorrow we can prepare meat and wine for them. Why can't we make our profit then?"

"But they are all sick," said the woman again, "afraid of draft, sensitive to light; they all want to sleep in a dark place. Come to think of it, all the buildings in our household are covered by single-tiered transparent tiles. Where are we going to find a dark enough place for them? I think we'd better consider donating the meal to them and ask them to go to some place else."

"Mother," said her daughter, "there's a dark place in my building, and it has no draft. It's perfect!"

"Where is that?" asked the woman. The daughter said, "When father was alive, he made a huge cupboard about four feet wide, seven feet long, and at least three feet deep. Six or seven people can probably sleep in it. Tell them to go into the cupboard and sleep there."

"I wonder if it's acceptable," said the woman. "Let me ask them. Hey, Master Sun, our humble dwelling is terribly small, and there is no dark place. We have only a huge cupboard which neither wind nor light can get through. How about sleeping in that?"

"Fine! Fine! Fine!" replied Pilgrim. Several of the hired hands were asked at once to haul out the cupboard and remove the door before they were told to go downstairs. With Pilgrim leading his master and Sha Monk picking up the pole of luggage, they walked behind the lamplight to the cupboard. Without regard for good or ill, Pa-chieh immediately crawled in. After handing him the luggage, Sha Monk helped the T'ang monk in before entering himself.

"Where's our horse?" said Pilgrim. One of the attendants on the side said, "It's tethered at the rear of the house and feeding."

"Bring it, along with the feed," said Pilgrim, "and tether it tightly beside the cupboard." Only then did he himself enter the cupboard. He cried, "Mama Chao, put on the door, stick in the bolt and lock it up. Then take a look for us and see whether there are any holes anywhere that light may get through. Paste them up with paper. Tomorrow, come early and open the cupboard." "You're much too careful!" said the widow. Thereafter everyone left to close the doors and sleep, and we shall leave those people for the moment.

We tell you now about the four of them inside the cupboard. How pitiful! For one thing, it was the first time they had worn head wraps;

for another, the weather was hot. Moreover, it was very stuffy because no breeze could get in. They all took off their wraps and their clothes, but without fans they could only wave their monk caps a little. Crowding and leaning on one another, they all began to doze by about the hour of the second watch.

Pilgrim, however, was determined to be mischievous! As he was the only one who could not sleep, he stretched out his hand and gave Pa-chieh's leg a pinch. Pulling back his leg, our Idiot mumbled, "Go to sleep! Look how miserable we are! And you still find it interesting to pinch people's arms and legs for fun?"

As a lark, Pilgrim began to say, "We originally had five thousand taels of silver. We sold some horses previously for three thousand taels, and right now, there are still four thousand taels left in the money bags. We can also sell our present herd of horses for three thousand taels, and we'll have both capital and profit. That's enough! That's enough!" Pa-chieh, of course, was a man intent on sleeping, and he refused to answer him.

Little did they know that the waiters, the water haulers, and the fire tenders of this hotel had always been part of a band of thieves. When they heard Pilgrim speaking of so much silver, some of them slipped out at once and called up some twenty other thieves, who arrived with torches and staffs to rob the horse traders. As they rushed in, Widow Chao and her daughter were so terrified that they slammed shut the door of their own building and let the thieves do what they pleased. Those bandits, you see, did not want anything from the hotel; all they desired was to find the guests. When they saw no trace of them upstairs, they searched everywhere with torches and came upon the huge cupboard in the courtyard. To one of the legs a white horse was tethered. The cupboard was tightly locked, and they could not pry open the door.

The thieves said, "People of the world like us have to be observant! If this cupboard is so heavy, there must be luggage and riches locked inside. What if we steal the horse, haul the cupboard outside the city, break it up, and divide the contents among ourselves—wouldn't that be nice?" Indeed, those thieves did find some ropes and poles, with which they proceeded to haul the cupboard out of the hotel. As they walked, the load swayed from side to side.

Waking up with a start, Pa-chieh said, "O Elder Brother, please go to sleep! Why are you shaking us?"

"Don't talk!" said Pilgrim. "No one's shaking you."

Tripitaka and Sha Monk also woke up and cried, "Who is carrying us?"

"Don't shout! Don't shout!" said Pilgrim. "Let them carry us. If they haul us all the way to the Western Heaven, it'll save us some walking!"

When those thieves succeeded in getting away from the hotel, they did not head for the West; instead, they hauled the chest toward the east of the city, where they broke out after killing some of the guards at the city gate. That disturbance, of course, alerted people in the six boulevards and three marts, the firemen and guards living in various stations. The reports went quickly to the Regional Patrol Commander and the East City Warden's Office. Since this was an affair for which they had to assume responsibility, the commander and the warden at once summoned the cavalry and archers to pursue the thieves out of the city. When the thieves saw how strong the government troops were, they dared not contend with them. Putting down the huge cupboard and abandoning the white horse, they fled in every direction. The government troops did not manage even to catch half a thief, but they did take the cupboard and caught the horse, and returned in triumph. As he looked at the horse beneath the lights, the commander saw that it was a fine creature indeed:

Its mane parts like silver threads;
Its tail dangles as strips of jade.
Why mention the Eight Noble Dragon Steeds?[3]
This one surpasses Su-hsiang's[4] slow trotting.
Its bones would fetch a thousand gold,
This wind-chaser through ten thousand miles.
He climbs mountains oft to join the green clouds,
Neighs at the moon, and fuses with white snow.
Truly a dragon that has left the isles,
A jade unicorn that man loves to own!

The commander, instead of riding his own horse, mounted this white horse to lead his troops back into the city. The cupboard was hauled into his official residence, where it was then sealed with an official tape issued jointly by him and the warden. The soldiers were to guard it until dawn, when they could memorialize to the king to see about its disposal. As the other troops retired, we shall leave them for the moment.

We tell you instead about the Elder T'ang, inside the cupboard, who complained to Pilgrim, saying, "You ape-head! You've just about put me to death! If we had stayed outside and been caught and sent before the king of the Dharma-Destroying Kingdom, we could still argue with him. Now we are locked up in a cupboard, abducted by thieves, and then recovered by government troops. When we see the king tomorrow, we'll be ready-made victims for him to complete his number of ten thousand!"

Pilgrim said, "There are people outside right now! If they open the cupboard and take us out, we'll either be bound or hanged! Do try to be more patient, so that we don't have to face the ropes. When we see that befuddled king tomorrow, old Monkey has his own way of answering him. I promise you that you'll not be harmed one whit. Now relax and sleep."

By about the hour of the third watch, Pilgrim exercised his ability and eased his rod out. Blowing his immortal breath on it, he cried, "Change!" and it changed into a three-pointed drill. He drilled along the bottom edge of the cupboard two or three times and made a small hole. Retrieving the drill, he changed with one shake of his body into an ant, and crawled out. Then he changed back into his original form to soar on the clouds into the royal palace. The king at that moment was sleeping soundly.

Using the Grand Magic of Body-Division and the Assembly of Gods, he ripped off all the hairs on his left arm. He blew his immortal breath on them, crying, "Change!" They all changed into tiny Pilgrims. From his right arm he pulled off all the hairs, too, and blew his immortal breath on them, crying, "Change!" They changed into sleep-inducing insects. Then he recited another magic spell, which began with the letter, Oṁ, to summon the local spirits of the region into his presence. They were told to lead the small Pilgrims so that they would scatter throughout the royal palace, the Five Military Commissions, the Six Ministries, and the residences of officials high and low. Anyone with rank and appointment would be given a sleep-inducing insect, so that he would sleep soundly without even turning over.

Pilgrim also took up his golden-hooped rod; with a squeeze and a wave, he cried, "Treasure, change!" It changed at once into hundreds and thousands of razor blades. He took one of them, and he told the tiny Pilgrims each to take one, so that they could go into the palace, the commissions, and the ministries to shave heads. Ah! This is how it was:

Dharma-king would the boundless dharma destroy,
Which fills the world and reaches the great Way.

All dharma-causes are of substance one;
Triyana's wondrous forms are all the same.
The jade cupboard's drilled through, the truth[5] is known;
Gold hairs are scattered and blindness is removed.
Dharma-king will surely the right fruit attain:
Birthless and deathless, he'll live in the void.

The shaving activities which went on for half the night were completely successful. Thereafter Pilgrim recited his spell to dismiss the local spirits. With one shake of his body he retrieved the hairs of both his arms. The razor blades he squeezed back into their true and original form—one golden-hooped rod—which he then reduced in size to store in his ear once more. He next assumed the form of an ant to crawl back into the cupboard before changing into his original appearance to accompany the T'ang monk in his confinement. There we shall leave them for the moment.

We tell you now about those palace maidens and harem girls in the inner chambers of the royal palace, who rose before dawn to wash and do their hair. Everyone of them had lost her hair. The hair of all the palace eunuchs, young and old, had also vanished. They crowded outside the palatial bedchambers to start the music for waking the royal couple, all fighting hard to hold back their tears and daring not report their mishap.

In a little while, the queen of the three palaces awoke, and she too found that her hair was gone. Hurriedly she moved a lamp to glance at the dragon bed: there in the midst of the silk coverlets a monk was sleeping! Unable to contain herself, the queen began to talk and her words awoke the king. When the king opened his eyes, all he saw was the bald head of the queen. Sitting bolt upright, he said, "My queen, why do you look like this?"

"But my lord is also like this!" replied the queen. One touch of his own head sent the king into sheer panic, crying, "What has become of us?" In that moment of desperation, the consorts of six halls, the palace maidens, and the eunuchs young and old all entered with bald heads. They knelt down and said, "Our lord, we have all become priests!"

Seeing them, the king began to shed tears. "It must be the result of our slaughtering the monks," he said. Then he gave this decree: "You are forbidden, all of you, to mention your loss of hair, for we fear that the civil and military officials would criticize the unrighteousness of the state. Let's prepare to hold court at the main hall."

We tell you now about all those officials, high and low, in the Five Commissions and Six Ministries, who were about to have an audience with the Throne at dawn. As each one of them, you see, had also lost his hair during the night, they were all busily preparing memorials to report the incident. Thus you could hear that

Three times the whip struck as they faced the king;

The cause of their hair being shorn they would make known.

We do not know what has happened to the stolen goods recovered by the commander of the government troops, and you must listen to the explanation in the next chapter.

Eighty-five

Mind Monkey envies Wood Mother;
The demon lord plots to devour Zen.

We were telling you about the morning court of the king, during which many civil and military officials presented their memorials, saying, "Our lord, please pardon your subjects for being remiss in their manners."

"Our worthy ministers have not departed from their customary good deportment," replied the king. "What is remiss in your manners?"

"O Our Lord!" said the various ministers; "we do not know the reason, but during the night all your subjects lost their hair." Clutching those memorials that complained of loss of hair, the king descended from his dragon couch to say to his subjects, "Indeed we do not know the reason either, but we and the other members of the royal palace, high and low, also lost all our hair." As tears gushed from their eyes, ruler and subjects said to one another, "From now on, we wouldn't dare slaughter monks!"

Then the king ascended his dragon couch once more as the officials returned to standing in ranks. The king said, "Let those who have any business leave their ranks to present their memorials; if there is no further business, let the screen be rolled up so that the court may retire." From the ranks of military officials the city patrol commander stepped out, and from the ranks of the civil officials the east city warden walked forward. Both came up to the steps to kowtow and say, "By your sage decree your subjects were on patrol last night, and we succeeded in recovering the stolen goods of one cupboard and one white horse. Your lowly subjects dare not dispose of these by our own authority, and we beg you to render a decision." Highly pleased, the king said, "Bring us both horse and cupboard."

As soon as the two officials went back to their offices, they immediately summoned their troops to haul out the cupboard. Locked inside, Tripitaka became so terrified that his soul was about to leave his body. "Disciples," he said, "what do we say once we appear before the king?"

Laughing, Pilgrim said, "Stop fussing! I have made the proper arrangements! When they open the cupboard, they'll bow to us as their teachers. Just tell Pa-chieh not to wrangle over seniority!" "To be spared from execution," said Pa-chieh, "is already boundless blessing! You think I dare wrangle?" Hardly had they finished talking when the cupboard was hauled to the court; the soldiers carried it inside the Five-Phoenix Tower and placed it before the vermilion steps.

When the subjects asked the king to inspect the cupboard, he immediately commanded that it be opened. The moment the cover was lifted, however, Chu Pa-chieh could not refrain from leaping out, so terrifying the various officials that they were all struck dumb. Then they saw the T'ang monk emerging, supported by Pilgrim Sun, while Sha Monk brought out the luggage. When Pa-chieh caught sight of the commander holding the horse, he rushed forward and bellowed, "The horse is ours! Give it to me!" The commander was so scared that he fell backward head over heels.

As the four of them stood on the steps, the king noticed that they were all Buddhist priests. Hurrying down from his dragon couch, the king asked all his consorts of the three palaces to join his subjects in descending from the Treasure Hall of Golden Chimes and bowing with him to the clerics. "Where did the elders come from?" the king asked.

Tripitaka said, "We are those sent by the Throne of the Great T'ang in the Land of the East to go to India's Great Thunderclap Monastery in the West to seek true scriptures from the living Buddha."

"If the Venerable Master had come from such a great distance," said the king, "for what reason did you choose to rest in a cupboard?"

"Your humble cleric," replied Tripitaka, "had learned of Your Majesty's vow to slaughter monks. We therefore dared not approach your superior state openly. Disguising ourselves as laymen, we came by night to an inn in your treasure region to ask for lodging. As we were afraid that people might still recognize our true identity, we chose to sleep in the cupboard, which unfortunately was stolen by thieves. It was then recovered by the commander and brought here. Now that I am privileged to behold the dragon countenance of Your Majesty, I feel as if I had caught sight of the sun after the clouds had parted. I beg Your Majesty to extend your grace and favor wide as the sea to pardon and release this humble cleric."

"The Venerable Master is a noble priest from the heavenly court of a superior state," replied the king, "and it is we who have been remiss in our welcome. The reason for our vow to slaughter monks stems from the fact that we were slandered by certain priests in years past. We therefore vowed to Heaven to kill ten thousand monks as a figure of perfection. Little did we anticipate that we would be forced to become monks instead, for all of us—ruler and subjects, king and consorts—now have had our hair shorn off. We, in turn, beg the Venerable Master not to be sparing in your great virtue and accept us as your disciples."

When Pa-chieh heard these words, he roared with laughter, saying, "If you want to be our disciples, what sort of presentation gifts do you have for us?"

"If the Master is willing," said the king, "we would be prepared to offer you the treasures and wealth of the state."

"Don't mention treasures and wealth," said Pilgrim, "for we are the sort of monks who keep to our principles. Only certify our travel rescript and escort us out of the city. We promise you that your kingdom will be secure forever, and you will be endowed with blessings and long life in abundance."

When the king heard that, he at once ordered the Court of Imperial Entertainments to prepare a huge banquet. Ruler and subjects, meanwhile, prostrated themselves to return to the One. The travel rescript was certified immediately, and then the king requested the masters to change the name of his kingdom. "Your Majesty," said Pilgrim, "the name of Dharma Kingdom is an excellent one; it's only the word 'Destroying' that's inadequate. Since we have passed through this region, you may change its name to Dharma-Honoring Kingdom. I promise that you will

In calm sea and river prosper a thousand years

With rain and wind in season and in all quarters peace."

After thanking Pilgrim, the king asked for the imperial cortege and the entire court to escort master and disciples out of the city so they could leave for the West. Then ruler and subjects held fast to virtue to return to the truth, and we shall speak no more of them.

We tell you now about the elder, who took leave of the king of the Dharma-Honoring Kingdom. As he rode along, he said in great delight, "Wu-k'ung, you've employed an excellent method this time, and you've achieved a great merit."

"O Elder Brother," said Sha Monk, "where did you find so many barbers to shave off so many heads during the night?" Thereupon Pilgrim gave a thorough account of how he underwent transformations and exercised magic powers. Master and disciples laughed so hard they could hardly get their mouths shut.

In that very moment of gaiety, they suddenly saw a tall mountain blocking their path. Reining in his horse, the T'ang monk said, "Disciples, look how rugged that mountain is. We must be careful!"

"Relax! Relax!" said Pilgrim with a laugh. "I guarantee you there's nothing to be afraid of!"

"Stop saying there's nothing!" replied Tripitaka. "I can see how precipitous the mountain peak is, and even from a great distance there appear to be violent vapors and savage clouds soaring up from it. I'm getting more and more apprehensive; my whole body's turning numb, and I'm filled with troubled thoughts."

Still laughing, Pilgrim said, "And you've long forgotten the Heart Sūtra of the Crow's Nest Zen Master." "I do remember it," said Tripitaka. "You may remember the sūtra," said Pilgrim, "but there are four lines of gāthā which you have forgotten." "Which four lines?" asked Tripitaka. Pilgrim said,

Seek not afar for Buddha on Spirit Mount;
Mount Spirit lives only in your mind.
There's in each man a Spirit Mount stūpa;
Beneath there the Great Art must be refined.

"Disciple," said Tripitaka, "you think I don't know this? According to these four lines, the lesson of all scriptures concerns only the cultivation of the mind."

"Of course, that goes without saying," said Pilgrim. "For when the mind is pure, it shines forth as a solitary lamp, and when the mind is secure, the entire phenomenal world becomes clarified. The tiniest error, however, makes for the way to slothfulness, and then you'll never succeed even in ten thousand years. Maintain your vigilance with the utmost sincerity, and Thunderclap will be right before your eyes. But when you afflict yourself like that with fears and troubled thoughts, then the Great Way and, indeed, Thunderclap seem far away. Let's stop all these wild guesses. Follow me." When the elder heard these words, his mind and spirit immediately cheered up as all worries subsided.

The four of them proceeded, and a few steps brought them into the mountain. This was what met their eyes:

The mountain's truly a good mountain.
Look closely, it's mixed colors show!

On top the clouds wander and drift;
Tree shades are cool before the cliff.
Birds screechy and shrill;
Beasts savage and fierce.
A thousand pines in the forest;
A few bamboos on the summit.
Those snarling are grey wolves fighting for food;
Those growling are tigers struggling for feed.
Wild apes wail long as they search for fresh fruits;
The deer climb o'er flowers to reach the peak.
A soughing breeze
And gurgling stream,
Where oft you hear the coos of birds unseen.
In a few places creepers pull and tug;
By the brook orchids mix with fine grasses.
Strange rocks sharply etched;
Hanging cliffs sheer and straight.
Foxes and raccoons dash by in packs;
Badgers and gibbons frolic in bands.
The traveler, troubled by such ruggedness,
Can do little with an old path's curviness!

Wary and cautious, master and disciples walked along, and all at once they heard the howling of a strong gust. Becoming fearful, Tripitaka said, "A wind has risen!"

Pilgrim said, "Spring has a temperate wind, summer a warm one. Autumn has a west wind, and winter has a north wind. There are winds in all four seasons. Why fear a gust of wind now?"

"But this wind has blown up so quickly," replied Tripitaka, "that it cannot possibly be a natural wind." "From ancient times," said Pilgrim, "wind has risen from the ground and clouds have emerged from mountains. How could there be such a thing as a natural wind?" Hardly had he finished speaking when they also saw fog rising. That fog truly

Spreads out to make the sky opaque
As darkness the earth overtakes.
The sun wholly loses its light;
All singing birds vanish from sight.
It seems like Chaos returning,
Like dust both flying and churning.
When summit trees all disappear,

Could one an herb-picker go near?

Becoming more alarmed than ever, Tripitaka said, "Wu-k'ung, the wind has hardly subsided. Why is there such fog rising?"

"Let's not jump to any conclusion," replied Pilgrim. "Let our master dismount, and the two brothers can stand guard here. I'll go look over the situation to see if it's good or bad."

Dear Great Sage! One snap of his torso shot him up to midair: shading his brows with his hand, he opened wide his fiery eyes to peer downward and at once discovered that there was, indeed, a monster-spirit sitting by a hanging cliff. Look how he appears:

A burly body swathed in colored hues,
Stalwart and tall, he seems most spirited.
His fangs push through his mouth like drills of steel;
His nose in the center's a hook of jade.
His golden eyes flaring, fowl and beasts take fright.
His silver beard bristling, god and ghosts grow sad.
Perched firmly by the ledge he flaunts his might;
By belching wind and fog he plies his wiles.

Standing in rows to the left and right of him were some thirty or forty little fiends, all watching his magic exercise as he belched out wind and spat out fog.

Chuckling to himself, Pilgrim said, "My master does have a little prescience! He said it was no natural wind, and indeed it was a stunt of this monster's that brought it forth. If old Monkey uses his iron rod now to deliver a blow downward, it will be nothing but a 'Garlic Pounder.' I'll strike him dead, but it'll also ruin old Monkey's reputation." Valiant all his life, Pilgrim never quite knew how to stab people in the back. He said to himself instead, "I'll go back and give some business to Chu Pa-chieh. Let him come first to do battle with this monster-spirit. If Pa-chieh is capable of defeating this monster, it'll be his good fortune. If he's not strong enough and gets himself captured, then I'll go rescue him. That's the proper way to enlarge my fame. But wait! Usually he's quite lazy and refuses to take the initiative in anything. Nonetheless he's hoggish and loves to eat. Let me trick him a little and see what he'll say."

Instantly dropping down from the clouds, he went before Tripitaka, who asked, "Wu-k'ung, how's the situation in the wind and fog?" "It seems to have cleared up right now," replied Pilgrim, "for there's hardly any wind or fog."

"Yes," said Tripitaka, "they do seem to have subsided."

"Master," said Pilgrim with a chuckle, "my eyesight is usually quite good, but this time I've made a mistake. I had thought that there might be a monster in the wind and fog, but there wasn't." "What is it then?" asked Tripitaka.

"There's a village not too far ahead," said Pilgrim, "and the families there are quite devoted to good works. They are steaming white-grain rice and bleached-flour buns to feed the monks. The fog, I suppose, could have been the steam coming from their steamers, a sure sign of their good works."

When Pa-chieh heard this, he thought it was the truth. Pulling Pilgrim aside, he said softly, "Elder Brother, did you take a meal with them before you came back?"

"I didn't eat much," said Pilgrim, "for the vegetable dishes were a bit too salty for my taste."

"Bah!" exclaimed Pa-chieh. "No matter how salty they might be, I would have eaten until my stomach was filled. If I'm too thirsty, I'll come back and drink water."

"Do you want to eat?" asked Pilgrim.

"Of course," replied Pa-chieh, "because I'm just feeling a little hungry! I would like very much to go and eat something. What do you think?"

"Brother," said Pilgrim, "you shouldn't mention this. An ancient book said, 'When the father is present, the son should not act on his own.'[1] If Master remains here, who dares go there first?"

"If you don't speak up," said Pa-chieh, giggling, "I'll be able to go."

"I won't," said Pilgrim; "I'd like to see how you manage to get away." That Idiot, you see, was peculiarly endowed with gluttonish intelligence. Walking forward, he bowed deeply and said, "Master, just now Elder Brother told us that there are families in the village ahead who are feeding the monks. Our horse here, however, is bound to bother people once we get there. Won't it be a nuisance when we have to find feed or hay for him? It's a good thing that the sky is now cleared of wind and fog. Why don't you sit here for a while and let me go find some nice, tender grass to feed the horse. Then we may proceed to beg for our meal from those households."

"Marvelous!" said a delighted T'ang monk. "How is it that you're so industrious today? Go, and return quickly!"

Chuckling to himself, that Idiot left at once, only to be pulled back by Pilgrim, saying, "Brother, those families there will feed only handsome monks, not ugly ones."

"If you put it that way," said Pa-chieh, "it means I have to undergo transformation again."

"Exactly," said Pilgrim, "you'd better change a little." Dear Idiot! He too had the ability of thirty-six transformations. After he walked into the fold of the mountain, he made the magic sign and recited a spell; with one shake of his body he changed into a rather thin and short priest. His hand striking a wooden fish, he began to mutter something as he walked. He knew nothing of chanting scriptures, of course, and all he could mumble was "Noble Eminence!"

We tell you now about that fiend who, after he had retrieved the wind and fog, ordered the various fiends to form a circle at the entrance of the main road and wait for the travelers. Our Idiot had the misfortune to walk right into the circle. The various fiends at once had him surrounded; some tugged at his clothes while others pulled at his sash. As they surged around him, Pa-chieh said, "Stop pulling! I'll eat from you, house by house!"

"Monk," said the fiends, "what do you want to eat?"

"You people want to feed the monks," said Pa-chieh, "and I have come to take my meal."

"So, you think we're feeding the monks," said one of the monsters. "You don't know that we specialize in eating monks here. Since we are monstrous immortals who have attained the Way in the mountain, we are particularly fond of catching monks and bringing them into our house to have them steamed in steamers. And you want to eat our meals instead!"

On hearing this, Pa-chieh was so horrified that he began to castigate Pilgrim, saying, "This pi-ma-wên is such a rogue! He lied to me about the feeding of monks in this village. What village is there, and what feeding of monks? These are monster-spirits!" Exasperated by their pulling, our Idiot at once changed back into his original form and took out his muckrake from his waist. A few wild blows sent those little monsters retreating.

They dashed back, in fact, to report to the old fiend: "Great King, disaster!" "What sort of disaster?" asked the old fiend. One of the little monsters said, "From the front of the mountain arrived a monk who looked quite neat. I said that we should take him home to be steamed, and if we couldn't finish him immediately, we could have parts of him cured and left for bad weather. I didn't expect him to know how to change."

"What did he change into?" asked the old monster.

"Nothing that looks human!" said the little monster. "Long snout, huge ears, and a tuft of hair behind his head. Wielding a muckrake with both his hands, he delivered blows madly at us. We were so scared that we ran back to report to the great king."

"Don't be afraid," said the old fiend. "Let me go look." He held up an iron club and walked forward, only to discover that Idiot was ugly indeed. This was how he appeared:

A snout, pestlelike, over three feet long
And teeth protruding like silver prongs.
Bright like lightning a pair of eyeballs round,
Two ears that whip the wind in *hu-hu* sound.
Arrowlike hairs behind his head are seen;
His whole body's skin is both coarse and green.
His hands hold up a thing bizarre and queer:
A muckrake of nine prongs which all men fear.

Forcing himself to be bold, the monster-spirit shouted: "Where did you come from? What is your name? Tell me quickly, and I'll spare your life!"

With a chuckle Pa-chieh said, "My child, so you don't recognize your Ancestor Chu! Come up here and I'll recite for you:

I've huge mouth and fangs and great magic might.
Emperor Jade made me Marshal Heavenly Reeds.
The boss of Heaven's eighty-thousand marines,
Comforts and joys I had in the halls of light.
Because I mocked Ch'ang-o when I was drunk
And flaunted my strength at a wrongful hour—
One shove of my snout toppled Tushita;
Queen Mother's divine herbs I then devoured—
Emperor Jade pounded me two thousand times
And banished me from the Three Heavens realm.
Though told to nourish my primal spirit,
I became again a monster down below.
About to marry at the Village Kao,
I met Brother Sun—'twas my wretched fate!
Quite defeated by his golden-hooped rod,
I had to bow and take the Buddhist vow:
A coolie who bears luggage and leads the horse,
Who owes the T'ang monk in former life a debt!
This iron-legged Heavenly Reed's name is Chu;
And my religious name is Chu Pa-chieh."

On hearing these words, the monster-spirit snapped, "So you're the disciple of the T'ang monk. I've always heard that the flesh of the T'ang monk is most edible. Now that you've barged in here, you think I'll spare you? Don't run away! Watch my club!"

"Cursed beast!" said Pa-chieh. "So you used to be a Doctor in Dyeing!"

"Why was I a Doctor in Dyeing?" asked the monster-spirit.

"If you weren't," replied Pa-chieh, "how would you know the use of a stirring club?" The fiend, of course, did not permit any further chatter; he drew near and struck madly. The two of them thus began quite a furious battle in the fold of the mountain:

The nine-pronged muckrake,
One single iron club—
The rake in motion churned like violent wind;
The club used deftly flew like sudden rain.
One was a nameless, vile fiend blocking the mountain path;
One was sinful Heavenly Reeds helping Nature's lord.
With Nature righted, why fear demons or fiends?
On tall mountains, earth would not gold beget.
That one's club parried like a serpent bolting from the deep;
This one's rake came like a dragon breaking from the banks.
Their shouts, thunderous, rocked mountains and streams;
Their cries, heroic, stirred the depths of earth.
Two valiant fighters each showing his power
To wage a life-risking contest of might.

Summoning his own powers, Pa-chieh engaged the monster-spirit, who also shouted for the little fiends to have his opponent encircled.

We shall leave them for the moment and tell you instead about Pilgrim, who, standing behind the T'ang monk, burst out laughing. "Elder Brother," asked Sha Monk, "why are you snickering?"

"Chu Pa-chieh is truly idiotic!" said Pilgrim. "When he heard that people were feeding monks, he was deceived into leaving immediately and still hasn't returned after all this time. If his rake managed to beat back a monster-spirit, you would be able to watch him come back in triumph and clamor for merit. But if he could not withstand him and got himself captured, then that would be my misfortune also, for I don't know how many times, backward and forward, he would castigate me as pi-ma-wên. Wu-ching, stop talking to me for a while. Let me go see what's happening."

Dear Great Sage! Without letting the elder know, he quietly pulled a hair from the back of his head and blew his immortal breath on it, crying, "Change!" It changed into his appearance to accompany both Sha Monk and the elder. His true body left with his spirit to shoot up into the air and look: he soon discovered that Idiot, surrounded by the fiends, was gradually losing ground, the movements of his muckrake slackening.

Pilgrim could no longer restrain himself; lowering his cloud, he cried out in a loud voice, "Don't worry Pa-chieh! Old Monkey's here!" When that Idiot heard Pilgrim's voice, he was stirred to greater strength than ever as he attacked madly with his rake. Unable to withstand him, the monster-spirit said, "A moment ago this monk was beginning to weaken. Why is it that he has turned more ferocious all at once?"

"My child," said Pa-chieh, "you shouldn't try to oppress me! Someone from my family has arrived!" Ever more fiercely he delivered blows at his opponent's head and face, until the monster-spirit could hardly parry his blows and led the other monsters to retreat in defeat. When Pilgrim saw the monster-spirit flee, however, he did not draw near. Turning his cloud around, he went back to where he had been, and with one shake retrieved his hair. Being of fleshly eyes and mortal stock, the elder did not perceive what had taken place.

In a little while, Idiot also returned; though he was the winner, he had been so exercised that he was sniveling from the nose and foaming at the mouth. Panting hard, he walked near to call out, "Master!" Astonished by the sight of him, the elder said, "Pa-chieh, you went to cut some grass for the horse. How is it that you're returning in such terrible shape? Could it be that people on the mountain are guarding the grass and refuse to let you cut it?"

Putting down his rake, Idiot began to slap his head and stamp his feet, saying, "Master, don't ask! If I told you, I'd be embarrassed to death!"

"Why?" asked the elder.

Pa-chieh said, "Elder Brother tricked me! He said at first that there was no monster-spirit in the wind and fog, that there was no evil omen. It was, he said, a village, and its families were devoted to virtue. They were steaming white-grain rice and bleached-flour buns to feed the monks. Since I thought it was the truth and was feeling so hungry, I wanted to get there and beg some first, on the excuse that I was cutting grass for the horse. Little did I expect that there would be quite a few fiends, who had me surrounded. I have been fighting bitterly with them all this time. If it hadn't been for the assistance lent by Elder Brother's mourning staff, I would have never escaped the net and come back here."

On one side Pilgrim began to laugh, saying, "This Idiot's babbling! The moment you become a thief, you like to shift the blame on a whole bunch of people. I was watching Master right here. Since when did I leave his side?"

"That's right!" said the elder. "Wu-k'ung hasn't left me at all."

Jumping up and down, Pa-chieh screamed, "Master, you just don't know. He has an alibi!"

The elder said, "Wu-k'ung, are there really fiends?" Knowing that he could no longer fool him, Pilgrim bowed and said, chuckling, "There are a few small ones, but they don't dare bother us. Pa-chieh, come over here. I want to entrust you with something truly worthwhile. When we escort Master through this rugged mountain road, we should act as if we were on military maneuvers."

"What would we do if we were?" asked Pa-chieh.

"You can be the path-finding general and open up the road in front," replied Pilgrim. "You needn't do anything if the monster-spirit doesn't show up, but if he appears, you fight with him. If you prevail, it will be regarded as your meritorious fruit." Pa-chieh calculated that the monster-spirit's abilities were about the same as his, and so he said, "I don't mind dying at his hands! Let me lead the way!"

"This Idiot!" said Pilgrim with a chuckle, "If he mouths such unlucky words first, how can he make any progress?" Pa-chieh said, "Elder Brother, do you know the proverb?

A prince at a banquet
Will either be drunk or fed;
A fighter on the field
Will either be hurt or dead.

I want to say something amiss first, and then I may prove to be the stronger afterward." Delighted, Pilgrim saddled the horse at once and asked the master to mount. With Sha Monk toting the luggage, they all followed Pa-chieh into the mountain, and we shall leave them for the moment.

We tell you instead about that monster-spirit, who led those several defeated little fiends back to their own cave. Taking a seat high on a rocky edge, he fell completely silent. Many of the little fiends who had remained behind as household guards crowded around him to ask,

"Great King, when you go out, you frequently return in a happy mood. Why are you so troubled today?"

"Little ones," replied the old monster, "normally when I go out to patrol the mountain, I grab a few humans or beasts—regardless of where they are from—to take back home for you to feast on. Today my luck's rather poor, for I ran into an adversary."

"What adversary?" asked the little monsters.

"He happens to be a monk," replied the old monster, "a disciple of the scripture-seeker T'ang monk from the Land of the East, whose name is Chu Pa-chieh. I was defeated by blows from his muckrake. I'm damn mad! For years I've heard people say that the T'ang monk is an arhat who has practiced austerities in ten incarnations. If someone eats a piece of his flesh, his age will be lengthened, and he'll attain longevity. Little did I expect him to arrive this day at our mountain. I wanted so badly to seize him and have him steamed for food, but I didn't know he had a disciple like that under him."

He had hardly finished speaking when a little monster stepped forward from the ranks. Facing the old monster above, he sobbed three times aloud and then he laughed three times. "Why are you weeping and crying?" snapped the old monster. The little monster knelt down to say, "Just now the great king says that he wants to eat the T'ang monk, but I would like to tell you that this monk's flesh is impossible to eat."

The old monster said, "People everywhere claim that one piece of his flesh will enable one to live long without growing old, to acquire an age as lasting as Heaven's. Why do you say that it's impossible to eat?"

"If it were possible," replied the little monster, "he wouldn't have made it here, for he would have been devoured by monster-spirits elsewhere. He has three disciples under him, you see." "Do you know which three?" asked the old monster. "His eldest disciple is Pilgrim Sun," said the little monster, "and his third disciple is Sha Monk. This Chu Pa-chieh is his second disciple."

"How strong is Sha Monk when compared with Chu Pa-chieh?" asked the old monster.

"About the same," replied the little monster.

"What about that Pilgrim Sun? How does he compare with Chu?"

Sticking out his tongue, the little monster said, "I dare not speak! That Pilgrim Sun has vast magic powers and knows many ways of transformation! Five hundred years ago, he caused great disturbance at the Celestial Palace. Those Twenty-eight Constellations[2] from the Region Above, the Nine Luminaries, the Twelve Horary Branches, the Five Nobles and Four Ministers, the Stars of East and West, the Gods of North and South, the Deities of the Five Mountains and the Four Rivers, and the divine warriors of entire Heaven could not tangle successfully with him. How could you have the nerve to want to eat the T'ang monk?"

"How do you know so much about him?" asked the old monster.

The little monster said, "I used to live with the great kings of the Lion-Camel Cave at the Lion-Camel Ridge. Those great kings, not knowing anything better, wanted to devour the T'ang monk. When Pilgrim Sun used his golden-hooped rod to fight inside our door, alas, he reduced us to the condition like the title of a domino combination: Minus One, Abolish Six! I was intelligent enough, fortunately, to slip out the back door and come here to be received by the great king. That's how I found out about his abilities!" When the old monster heard these words, he paled with fright, for as the saying goes, "Even a great general is afraid of augury." When he heard a member of his own household speaking like that, how could he not be frightened?

At that anxious moment, another little monster went forward to say, "Great King, don't be upset, and don't be frightened. The proverb tells us that 'Haste does not breed success.' If you desire to devour the T'ang monk, let me offer you a plan to seize him."

"What sort of plan do you have?" asked the old monster.

"One called 'The Plan of Plum Blossoms with Parted Petals,'" answered the little monster. "What do you mean by that?" asked the old monster.

The little monster said, "Take a roll call of all the monsters in the cave, young and old; select a hundred out of the thousands, ten out of the hundred, and finally three out of those ten. These three must all have abilities and the capacity for transformation. They will all change into the great king's appearance, wearing his armor and holding his club, and then be placed in ambush. The first one will engage Chu Pa-chieh in battle; the next, Pilgrim Sun; and the third, Sha Monk. We shall risk these three little monsters to induce those three brothers to leave their master. Then the great king will be able to stretch forth his hand from midair to seize the T'ang monk like 'Fetching Things from One's Pocket,' like 'Squeezing a Fly in the Fish Bowl.' That's not too difficult, is it?"

On hearing this the old monster was filled with delight. "This is a

most marvelous plan!" said he. "When we set out, I won't do anything if we can't catch the T'ang monk. But if we do catch him, I'll not
treat you lightly. I'll appoint you as our vanguard officer." The little
monster kowtowed to thank him before giving the order for the roll
call. When all the monster-spirits of the cave, young and old, were
summoned into their presence, three able little monsters were indeed
selected. All of them were told to change into the form of the old
monster; each holding the iron club, they were placed in ambuscade
to wait for the T'ang monk, and we shall leave them there for the
moment.

We tell you now about our Elder T'ang who, free of cares and
worries, followed Pa-chieh up the main road. After they had proceeded
for a long time, a loud pop from the side of the road suddenly brought
out a little monster, who rushed forward and attempted to seize the
elder. "Pa-chieh," cried Pilgrim Sun, "the monster-spirit is here! Why
don't you do something?"

Without bothering to distinguish one from the other, our Idiot
whipped out his muckrake and dashed forward to attack madly the
monster-spirit, who met his blows with an iron club. Back and forth,
the two of them fought beneath the mountain slope, when another
fiend leaped out from some bushes with a pop and headed straight for
the T'ang monk.

"Master, things are going wrong!" cried Pilgrim. "Pa-chieh's so
blind that he has allowed the monster-spirit to slip by him to come
here to grab you. Let old Monkey go beat him off!" Hurriedly he
wielded his rod and rushed forward, bellowing, "Where are you going?
Watch my rod!" Without uttering a word, the monster-spirit lifted his
club to meet him. Beneath the grassy knoll the two of them thus rushed
together, and as they fought, another monster-spirit leaped out from
behind the mountain to the howling of a strong gust and headed
straight for the T'ang monk.

When Sha Monk saw him, he was horrified. "Master!" he cried.
"Both Big Brother and Second Elder Brother must be so dim of sight
that they allowed the monster-spirit to slip past them and come to
grab you! Sit here on the horse, and let old Sand go capture him!"
This monk, without distinguishing between good and ill either, immediately wielded the staff to block the iron club of the monster-spirit.
They strove together most bitterly, shouting and screaming at each
other as they gradually drifted away. When the old fiend, flying

through the air, discovered the T'ang monk sitting all alone on the horse, he reached down with his five steellike claws; with one grasp he lifted the master away from the horse and stirrup. The monster-spirit then took him away in a gust of wind. How pitiful! This is why it's hard for

Zen-nature plagued by demons to reach right fruit.

River Float meets again his Ill-luck Star!

Lowering the wind, the old monster brought the T'ang monk into the cave, shouting, "Vanguard!" The little fiend who planned all this ran forward to kneel down, saying, "I dare not accept the title! I dare not accept the title!"

"Why do you say this?" said the old monster. "When a great general gives his word, it's as if the white has been dyed black! Just now I told you that I wouldn't do anything if we couldn't catch the T'ang monk, but if we did, you would be appointed vanguard of our forces. Today your marvelous plan indeed succeeded. How could I betray you? You may bring the T'ang monk over here, and ask the little ones to fetch water and scrub the pan, to haul in the wood and start a fire. Steam him a bit, so you and I can eat a piece of his flesh to lengthen our age."

"Great King," said the vanguard, "let's not eat him just yet."

The old fiend said, "We've captured him. Why shouldn't we eat him?" The vanguard replied, "Of course the great king may eat him, and if you do, both Chu Pa-chieh and Sha Monk even may be persuaded that they should overlook the matter. But that bossy Pilgrim Sun, I fear, may let loose his viciousness once he learns that we have devoured his master. He doesn't even have to come fight with us. All he needs do is plunge that golden-hooped rod of his into the midriff of our mountain; it'll create such a gaping hole that the mountain itself will topple over. Then we won't even have a place to stay."

"Vanguard," said the old fiend, "what sort of noble opinion do you have?"

"As I see the matter," replied the vanguard, "you should send the T'ang monk into the back garden and tie him to a tree. Don't feed him any rice for two or three days. That'll clean up his inside, for one thing, and for another, it should give us the time we need until his three disciples stop searching for him at our door. When we know for certain that they have left, we'll then take him out and enjoy him at our leisure. Isn't that better?"

"It is, it is!" said the old fiend, laughing. "What the vanguard says makes perfect sense!" The order was immediately given that the T'ang monk would be brought into the back garden, where he was bound to a tree with a rope. Then the little fiends all went back to the front to wait on the old monster.

Look at that elder! Enduring most bitterly the tight fetter and the restraint of ropes, he could not stop the tears from rolling down his cheeks. "O disciples!" he cried. "In which mountain are you trying to capture fiends, and on what road are you chasing monsters? I have been brought by a brazen demon to suffer here. When will we ever meet again? The pain's killing me!" As tears streamed from both his eyes, he heard someone calling from a tree opposite him, saying, "Elder, so you, too, have entered here!"

Calming down, the elder said, "Who are you?"

The man said, "I'm a woodcutter from this mountain who was captured by that mountain lord and brought here. I have been bound for three days, and I imagine that they want to eat me."

"O woodcutter!" said the elder, as tears began to flow once more. "If you die, you are all by yourself and you don't have any worries. I, however, cannot die in such a carefree manner."

"Elder," said the woodcutter, "you are someone who has left home. You have neither parents above you nor wife and children below you. If you die, you die. What cares or concerns do you have?"

The elder said, "I am someone sent by the Land of the East to seek scriptures in the Western Heaven. By the decree of Emperor T'ai-tsung of the T'ang court, I am to bow to the living Buddha and acquire from him the true scriptures, which will be used for the redemption of those orphaned lost souls in the Region of Darkness. If I lose my life here, would that not have dashed the expectation of the emperor and the high hopes of his ministers. Would that not grievously disappoint those countless wronged souls in the City of Unjust Death? They would never be redeemed, and all this attempt at meritorious fruit would be reduced to wind and dust! How could I die carefree and without concern?"

When the woodcutter heard these words, he too began to shed tears as he said, "Elder, if you must die in this manner, then my death is even more grievous. I lost my father in childhood, and I have lived all my life with my widowed mother. We have no other livelihood except my gathering firewood. My old mother is now eighty-three and

I'm her sole support. If I lose my life, who will take care of her or bury her? O misery! O misery! This pain is killing me." On hearing this, the elder wailed aloud, crying, "How pitiful! How pitiful!

If e'en a rustic has longings for his kin.

Has not this poor priest chanted sūtras in vain?

To serve the ruler or to serve one's parents follows the same principle. You live by the kindness of your parents, and I live by the kindness of my ruler." Truly it is that

The tearful eye beholds a tearful eye;

A broken heart escorts a broken heart!

We shall leave for the moment Tripitaka in suffering and confinement. We tell you instead about Pilgrim Sun, who, having defeated the little monster beneath the grassy knoll, hurried back to the side of the main road. His master had vanished; only the white horse and the luggage remained. He was so horrified that he began searching toward the summit at once, leading the horse and poling the luggage. Alas! This is how

Woe-beset River Float keeps meeting more woes!

The demon-routing Great Sage is by demons plagued!

We do not know whether he finally succeeds in locating his master, and you must listen to the explanation in the next chapter.

Eighty-six

Wood Mother, lending its power, conquers the fiendish
    creature;
Gold Squire, using his magic, extirpates the deviates.

We were telling you about the Great Sage Sun who, as he led the horse
and toted the luggage, was searching and calling for his master all
over the summit. It was then that he saw Chu Pa-chieh run up to him,
panting hard and saying, "Elder Brother, why are you hollering?"

"Master has disappeared," replied Pilgrim, "Have you seen him?"

"Originally," said Pa-chieh, "I followed the T'ang monk to be a
priest. But you have to make fun of me again, telling me to play
the general! I took enormous risk to fight with that monster-spirit
for quite some time before I came back here with my life. You and Sha
Monk, however, were supposed to be guarding Master. How is it that
you're asking me instead?"

Pilgrim said, "Brother, I'm not blaming you. Perhaps you were a
little dazed and didn't realize that you had allowed the monster-spirit
to slip back here to seize Master. I went to strike at the monster-spirit,
relying on Sha Monk to guard Master. Now even Sha Monk has disappeared!"

"Sha Monk," said Pa-chieh with a giggle, "must have taken Master
somewhere to drop his load!" Hardly had he finished speaking when
Sha Monk appeared. "Sha Monk," asked Pilgrim, "where has Master
gone?"

"Both of you must have been seeing double," said Sha Monk, "and
that's why you allowed the monster-spirit to slip back here to try to
seize Master. Old Sand took off to fight with him, but Master should be
sitting by himself on the horse." All at once Pilgrim became so enraged
that he jumped up and down as he cried, "We've fallen for their plan!
We've fallen for their plan!"

"What sort of a plan?" asked Sha Monk.

"This," replied Pilgrim, "is called 'The Plan of Plum Blossoms with
Parted Petals,' which they used to split us brothers apart before they
dashed right into our midst to haul Master away. Good Heavens!

174

Good Heavens! What shall we do?" As he spoke, he could hardly hold back the tears rolling down his cheeks.

"Don't cry!" said Pa-chieh. "Once you cry, you turn into a namby-pamby! He can't be very far, for he has to be somewhere in this mountain. Let's go search for him."

With no better alternative, the three of them had to enter the mountain to begin their search. After they had journeyed some twenty miles, they reached a cave-dwelling beneath a hanging cliff, with

Steep summits half appearing,
And strange rocks so rugged;
Rare blossoms and plants most fragrant,
Red apricots, green peaches most luscious.
The old tree before the ledge,
Its skin, forty spans, is frost-white and rain-resistant;
The hoary pine beyond the door,
Its jadegreen hues rise skyward two thousand feet.
Wild cranes in pairs
Come oft before the cave to dance in the breeze;
Mountain fowl in twos
Would perch on the boughs to sing in the sun.
Clusters of yellow vines like hanging ropes;
Rows of misty willows like dripping gold.
A square pond storing up water—
A deep cave close to the mountain—
A square pond storing up water
Conceals an aged dragon which has yet to change;
In a deep cave close to the mountain
Lives one man-eating old fiend of many years.
In truth no less than an immortal's lair,
This place that gathers in the wind and air.

On seeing the cave-dwelling, Pilgrim in two or three steps bounded right up to the door to examine it more closely. The stone door was tightly closed, but across the top of the door was a slab of stone bearing this inscription in large letters: The Mist-Concealing Mountain, the Broken-Peak, Joined-Ring Cave.

"Pa-chieh," said Pilgrim, "let's move! This is where the monster-spirit lives, and Master has to be in the house." Strengthened by the presence of his companions, our Idiot unleashed his violence and delivered as hard a blow as he could on the stone door, making a huge, gaping hole in it. "Fiend," he cried, "send my master out quickly, lest this muckrake tear down the door and finish off your entire household!"

Those little monsters guarding the door hurried inside to report: "Great King, we've brought on a disaster!"

"What disaster?" asked the old fiend.

"Someone has broken through our front door," replied one of the little monsters, "yelling for his master." Astounded, the old fiend said, "I wonder whoever could have found his way here."

"Don't be afraid!" said the vanguard. "Let me go out and have a look." This little fiend dashed up to the front door and stuck his head out sideways through the hole to look around. When he saw the huge snout and large ears, he at once turned back and called out, "Great King, don't be afraid of him! This is Chu Pa-chieh, who has not much ability and won't dare be unruly. If he does, we'll open our door and take him in here to be prepared and steamed. The only person we need fear is the monk with a hairy face and a thundergod beak."

When he heard this through the door, Pa-chieh said, "O Elder Brother! He's not afraid of me but only of you. Master has to be in his house. You go forward quickly."

"Lawless cursed beast!" shouted Pilgrim. "Your Grandpa Sun is here! Send out my master and I'll spare your life!"

"Great King," said the vanguard, "it's bad! Pilgrim Sun has found his way here!" The old fiend began to reprehend him, saying, "It's all because of that so-called 'Parted Petals' plan of yours that disaster has descended on our door! How will this end?"

"Please relax, Great King," said the vanguard, "and don't find fault with me. I recall that Pilgrim Sun happens to be a kind and forbearing ape. Though he may possess vast magic powers, he also loves flattery. Let us take out a fake human head to deceive him a little, and flatter him a little, too, with a few words. Just tell him that we have devoured his master. If we can deceive him, the T'ang monk will be ours for enjoyment. If we can't, we'll try something else." "Where shall we find a fake human head?" asked the old fiend. The vanguard said, "Let's see if I could make one."

Marvelous fiend! Using a steel ax, he cut off a lump of willow root, shaped it into a skull, and threw some human blood on it. In this gory fashion the head was taken out to the door on a lacquered tray by a small fiend, who called out: "Holy Father Great Sage, please calm your anger and allow me to report to you."

Pilgrim Sun was indeed susceptible to flattery; when he heard the 'Holy Father Great Sage,' he stopped Pa-chieh, saying, "Let's not move yet and see what they have to say."

"After your master had been taken into the cave by our Great King," said the little fiend holding the tray, "those uncouth young fiends of ours did not know any better than to try to swallow him at once. Some tore at him, while others gnawed at him. Your master was thus devoured, and all we have left here is his head."

"It's all right if he's been devoured," said Pilgrim, "but show me the head and let me see if it's real." The little fiend threw out the head through the hole in the door. The moment Chu Pa-chieh saw it, he began to weep, saying, "How pitiful! We had one kind of master entering through this door, but now we have this kind of master coming out."

"Idiot," said Pilgrim, "why don't you try to determine whether this is a real human head before you start weeping?" "Aren't you ashamed of yourself?" said Pa-chieh. "Could there be a false human head?"

"*This* happens to be a false one," replied Pilgrim. "How can you tell?" asked Pa-chieh. "If you threw down a real human head," said Pilgrim, "it would fall on the ground with a dull thud, whereas a false head would make a loud rattle. If you don't believe me, let me throw it down for you to hear." He took it up and hurled it against a boulder, and it produced a loud clang.

"Elder Brother," said Sha Monk, "it rattles all right."

"If it rattles," said Pilgrim, "it's a false one. Let me bring out its true form." Whipping out his golden-hooped rod, he cracked it open with one blow. Pa-chieh looked more closely and discovered that it was only a lump of willow root. Unable to contain himself, Pa-chieh began to utter a string of abuses, crying, "You bunch of hairy clods! You have already hidden my master in the cave, and yet you dare use a lump of willow root to deceive your Ancestor Chu! Could my master have been a willow spirit?"

The little fiend who held the tray was so horrified that he shook all over as he ran back to report: "Hard! Hard! Hard! Hard! Hard! Hard!"

"Why so many hards?" asked the old fiend.

The little fiend said, "Both Chu Pa-chieh and Sha Monk were deceived, but Pilgrim Sun happens to be an antique dealer who knows his stuff! He recognized the fact that it was a false human head. If you could find a real head for him, you might be able to send him away."

"Where could I find one?" said the old fiend. "Ah, I know! In our skinning pavilion we still have several human heads which haven't been eaten yet. Go pick one out for us." A few of the fiends went immediately to the pavilion and selected a fresh head, which they then gnawed at until it was slick and smooth. The little fiend carried it out to the front again on a tray, crying, "Holy Father Great Sage, the previous one was indeed a false head. This one, however, is the true head of Father T'ang. Our Great King has kept it as a talisman for the house, but we're presenting it to you now." With a thud, the head was thrown out through the hole in the door, and it rolled all over, still dripping blood.

When Pilgrim Sun saw that it was a real human head, he had no choice but to weep. Pa-chieh and Sha Monk, too, joined in the loud wailing. As he tried to hold back his tears, Pa-chieh said, "Elder Brother, let's not cry just yet. The weather isn't so good right now, and I fear that it may stink. Let me take it somewhere to have it buried while it's still fresh. Then we can cry some more." "You're quite right," replied Pilgrim.

Not revolted, our Idiot hugged the head to his bosom and ran up the mountain ledge. Having found a spot facing the sun where the wind and air would be collected, he used his rake to dig a hole to try to bury the head. Then he built a grave mound, and called out to Sha Monk, "You and Elder Brother can stay here and weep. Let me go find something to use for offering." Going over to the side of the brook, he selected several large twigs of willow and picked up some egg-shaped pebbles, which he brought back to the graveside. The willow twigs were planted on both sides, and the pebbles were placed in a pile in front.

"What do you mean by this?" asked Pilgrim.

"We can pretend that these twigs are pines and cypresses," replied Pa-chieh, "so that Master will have a bit of shade on top. The pebbles may be taken as pastries, so that Master will enjoy a small offering."

"Coolie!" snapped Pilgrim. "The man's dead! And you still want to offer him pebbles?" Pa-chieh said,

Mere sentiment of the living
To show our filial feeling.

"Let's stop this horseplay!" said Pilgrim. "Sha Monk can remain here to guard the grave, the horse, and the luggage. You and I will go and tear down the cave-dwelling. When we capture the fiendish demon, we'll cut him into ten thousand pieces to avenge our master."

"What Elder Brother says is perfectly right," said Sha Monk, still shedding tears. "The two of you should put your hearts to this. I'll stand guard here."

Marvelous Pa-chieh! He took off his black silk shirt and tightened his undergarment before lifting his rake high to follow Pilgrim. Striding forward, the two of them, without waiting for further discussion, smashed down the stone door. "Give us back a living T'ang monk!" they thundered so loudly that the heavens shook.

Those various fiends inside the cave, old and young, were so terrified that they all cast their blame on the vanguard as the old fiend asked him, "These monks have smashed their way inside our door. What shall we do?" The vanguard replied, "The ancients have put the matter well:

Put your hand in the fish basket
And you can't avoid the stink!

Never retreat once you start something! Let's call up the left and right commanders to lead our soldiers out to slaughter those monks!"

As he had no better plan than what he heard, the old fiend thereupon gave the order: "Little ones, be of one mind and pick up your best weapons. Follow me out to battle." With a roar, they stormed out of the cave.

Our Great Sage and Pa-chieh quickly retreated a few steps down to a level spot in the mountain. As they faced the various fiends, they shouted, "Who is the leader who has a name? Who is the fiend who has captured our master?"

The various fiends pitched camp immediately and unfurled an embroidered floral banner. Grasping an iron club, the old fiend answered the call in a loud voice, saying, "Brazen monk, don't you recognize me? I am the Great King of South Mountain, and I have held this place in my sway for several centuries. I've captured and devoured your T'ang monk. What do you propose to do about that?"

"You audacious hairy clod!" scolded Pilgrim. "How many years have you lived that you dare assume the title, South Mountain? Old Ruler Li happens to be the patriarch of creation, but he still sits to the right of Supreme Purity. The Buddha Tathāgata is the honored one who governs the world, and yet he still sits beneath the great roc. K'ung the Sage is the founder of Confucianism, but he assumes the mere title of Master. And you, a cursed beast, dare call yourself some Great King of South Mountain, holding this place in your sway! Don't try to escape! Have a taste of your Grandfather's rod!"

Stepping aside to dodge the blow, the monster-spirit wielded his club to parry the iron rod and said, his eyes glowering, "Your features are those of an ape, and yet you dare insult me with so many words! What abilities do you have that you dare behave in such a rowdy manner in front of my door?"

"You nameless cursed beast!" said Pilgrim, laughing. "Of course, you don't know anything of old Monkey! Stand still, be brave, and listen to my recital:

At Pūrvavideha, my ancestral home,
Through thousands of years conceived of Heav'n and Earth
One stone egg immortal on Mount Flower-Fruit
Did break and beget me, its progeny.
By birth I thus was not of mortal stock,
For sun and moon did this sage body forge.
Myself, cultivated, was no small thing—
Alert and keen, a great elixir source.
Named the Great Sage, I lived among the clouds
And fought the stars, relying on my power.
Ten thousand gods could not approach me even;
T'was easy to beat all planets of Heaven.
My fame was known in the world's every part;
My wiles left a trail through the universe.
By luck I've now embraced the Buddhist faith
To help an elder on his westward way.
No one blocks the path I open on the mount
Though fiends worry when I build a bridge.
I'll seize the forest tigers with my might;
My hands will tame leopards before the cliff.
The East's Right Fruit is coming to the West:
Which monstrous deviate dares show his head?
Since you, cursed beast, dare my master devour,
Your life will surely perish within this hour."

Alarmed and angered by these words, the fiend clenched his teeth, leaped forward, and struck out at Pilgrim with his iron club. Casually parrying the blow with his rod, Pilgrim wanted to talk some more with him, but our Pa-chieh could not hold back any longer. He lifted his rake and madly attacked the vanguard of the fiend, who met him head-on with the other monsters. This was some brawl on the mountain meadow, truly a marvelous battle:

A priest from an eastern superior state
Went seeking true scriptures from the blissful West.
The South Mount's great leopard belched wind and mist
And blocked the path; showing alone his might,
With a clever plan
And a wily scheme,
He bagged in ignorance the Great T'ang monk.
He met then the Pilgrim of vast magic power
And Pa-chieh also of great renown.
When fiends on the mountain meadow fought,
Dust and dirt flew up to bedim the sky.
Little fiends shouted over there,
Madly raising their swords and spears;
Divine monks bellowed over here,
Lifting up both rake and rod.
The Great Sage was a hero without match;
Wu-nêng was both stalwart and strong in years.
The South Mountain old fiend
And his subject, the vanguard,
All because of the T'ang monk's one piece of flesh,
Had quite forgotten the fear of life or death.
These two turned hostile for their master's sake;
Those two grew violent, desiring the T'ang monk.
Back and forth they battled for quite a while;
Clashing and bumping, they fought to a draw.

When the Great Sage Sun saw how ferocious those little fiends were, how they refused to step back even when they were repeatedly attacked, he resorted to his Magic of Body-Division. Ripping out a bunch of his own hairs, he chewed them to pieces before spitting them out, crying, "Change!" At once they all assumed his appearance, each wielding a golden-hooped rod, and began to push in from the front line of the battle. Those one or two hundred little fiends found it difficult, of course, to look after both their front and their rear. Parrying the blows from the left, they could not attend to those coming from their right, and so all of them fled for their lives and retreated to the cave. As our Pilgrim and Pa-chieh also fought their way out from the center of the battle, pity those monster-spirits who did not know any better: those running into the rake received nine bleeding holes, while those hugged by the rod had their bones and flesh turned into putty. That Great King of South Mountain was so terrified that he fled for his life by mounting fog and wind. The vanguard, however, could not transform, and he was struck down by one blow of Pilgrim's rod. His original form emerged as an iron-backed gray wolf. Dragging him closer and flipping him over for another look, Pa-chieh said, "I wonder how many piglets and lambkins this fellow has stolen from people and eaten since his youth!"

With one shake of his body Pilgrim retrieved his hair, saying, "Idiot, we must not delay! Let's chase down the old fiend quickly and ask him to pay for Master's life." When he turned his head and did not see those little Pilgrims, Pa-chieh said, "The magic forms of Elder Brother have all disappeared?"

"I've retrieved them," said Pilgrim.

"Marvelous! Marvelous!" said Pa-chieh, and the two of them returned in delight and triumph.

We tell you now about that old fiend, who, when he fled back into his cave with his life, ordered the little fiends to move boulders and pole mud to the front door. Trembling all over, those fiends who managed to save their lives did indeed barricade the door and dared not show their heads at all. When our Pilgrim led Pa-chieh to chase up to the front door, their shouts brought no answer from within, and when Pa-chieh used his rake to strike at the barrier of mud, he could not budge it one whit. Realizing what had happened, Pilgrim said, "Pa-chieh, don't waste your strength. They have barricaded the door."

"In that case," said Pa-chieh, "how shall we avenge our master?"

"Let's go back to the grave to see how Sha Monk's doing," said Pilgrim.

The two of them went back to the site and found Sha Monk still weeping. Ever more grief-stricken, Pa-chieh abandoned his rake and flung himself on the grave. As he pounded the dirt with his hands, he wailed, "O ill-fated Master! O far-removed Master! Where shall I ever get to see you again?"

"Brother, please calm your sorrow," said Pilgrim. "If this monster-spirit has his front door stopped up, there must be a back door for him to go in and out. The two of you remain here, and let me go back to have another look around."

"O Elder Brother," said Pa-chieh, shedding tears. "Do be careful! If they manage to grab even you, it'll be difficult for us to weep. A sob for Master and a sob for Elder brother—we'll be all confused!" "Don't worry!" replied Pilgrim. "I'll be able to take care of myself."

Dear Great Sage! Putting away his rod and tightening his skirt, he went past the mountain slope and immediately heard the sound of gurgling water. He saw, turning his head, that it came from a brook tumbling down from the peak. Then he discovered a little entrance on the other side of the brook, to the left of which there seemed to be a drainage sewer. "It goes without saying," he thought to himself, "that this must be the back door. If I present my face like this, some little fiends opening the door might recognize me. I'll change into a little water snake to get through—but wait! If the ghost of Master knew that I'd changed into a snake, he would blame me because a serpentine creature would ill become a priest. Why not a little crab then? That's no good either, for Master'll blame me for being a busybody priest." Finally he changed into a water rat and, with a whoosh, darted across the brook. Through the drainage sewer he crawled into the courtyard and looked around: at the spot facing the sun were several little fiends hanging up, piece by piece, slabs of human flesh to be dried.

"O my dear children!" said Pilgrim to himself. "That has to be Master's flesh! They couldn't finish all of him, and so they want to cure some strips for inclement weather. I would like to reveal my true form, rush up there, and slaughter them all with one stroke of my rod, but that'll only show that I have courage but little wisdom. I'll change again and go inside to find the old fiend to see what's happening." He leaped out of the sewer and with one shake of his body changed into a tiny, winged ant. Truly

His name's Dark Horse,[1] a small and feeble thing,
But long cultivation has formed his wings.
In idle moments by a bridge he'd flit
Or roam beneath a bed to test his wit.
He seals his hole, knowing when rain would come;
Weighed down by dust he would ashes become.
So airy and agile he can quickly soar
A few times, unknown, past the wooden door.

Stretching his wings, without a shadow or sound, he flew directly into the center hall, where he found the old fiend sitting dejectedly. From behind him a small monster leaped out to say, "Great King, ten thousand delights attend you!"

"Where do these delights come from?" asked the old monster.

The little monster said, "Just now I was doing a bit of intelligence work by the brook at our rear entrance, and I heard someone wailing. When I climbed up the peak to take a further look, I found that it was Chu Pa-chieh, Pilgrim Sun, and Sha Monk who were mourning before a grave. They must have believed that human head was the T'ang monk's and buried it. Now they are weeping beside the grave they dug."

When Pilgrim heard this, he was secretly pleased, saying to himself, "If he could say this, my master must still be hidden here somewhere. He hasn't been devoured. Let me go search further to find out indeed whether Master is dead or alive before I discuss the matter with these monsters."

Dear Great Sage! Soaring high in the center hall, he looked this way and that and discovered to one side a little door, which was tightly shut. Crawling through a crack in the door, he found a large garden inside, from the center of which faint sounds of grief could be heard. When he flew deep into the garden, he came upon a clump of tall trees, beneath which two persons were tied: one of them was none other than the T'ang monk. Pilgrim was so excited by the sight that he could not refrain from changing back into his original form and approaching to say, "Master."

Recognizing him, the elder said, as his tears fell, "Wu-k'ung, so you've come! Save me quickly! Wu-k'ung! Wu-k'ung!"

"Stop calling my name, Master!" said Pilgrim. "There are still people up front, and I fear that they may get wind of this. As long as you're still alive, I can save you. That fiend told us that you had been devoured, using a false human head to deceive us. We have already fought bitterly with him. Please relax, Master. Just bear with me a bit longer. When I've toppled that monster-spirit, I'll be able to come back here to free you."

Reciting a spell, the Great Sage at once changed back into an ant to return to the center hall and alight on the main beam. A crowd of those little monsters who had not lost their lives were milling about noisily. From their midst one little monster suddenly dashed out to say, "Great King, when they see that the door is barricaded and that they cannot break it open, they must also give up all hopes of recovering the T'ang monk. After all, the false human head has been turned into a grave. They'll mourn for a day today and for another tomorrow.

By the day after tomorrow, they should have fulfilled the obligation of three-day mourning and they will leave. When we have made sure that they have scattered, we can then bring out the T'ang monk and have him finely diced. Pan-fry him with some star anise and Szechwan pepper, and we can enjoy a nice fragrant piece to lengthen our lives."

"Stop talking like that!" said another little monster, clapping his hands. "He'll taste much better if we steam him."

"But not as economical as plain boiling," said another. "At least we can save some firewood that way."

"He is, after all, a rare thing," another spoke up. "We really should cure him with salt, so that we may enjoy him much longer."

When he heard this, perched on the beam, Pilgrim was filled with rage, saying to himself, "What sort of enmity do you have against my master that you should make such elaborate plans to devour him?" Pulling out a bunch of his own hairs and chewing them to pieces, he spat them out lightly and recited in silence a magic spell. The hairs all changed into sleep-inducing insects, which he threw onto the faces of the monsters. As the insects crawled into their noses one by one, the little monsters gradually dropped off until, in no time at all, they had all fallen fast asleep. Only the old monster, however, remained restless as he continued to scratch his head and rub his face with both hands. He was sneezing repeatedly so that he kept pinching his nose.

"Could it be that he has found out something?" said Pilgrim. "Let's give him a double-wick lamp!" Pulling off another piece of hair, he fashioned another creature like the ones before and threw it onto his face. Now he had two insects, one entering through his left nostril and the other through his right. Struggling up for a moment, the old monster stretched and yawned a couple of times, and then he too fell into a snoring slumber.

Delighted, Pilgrim leaped down and changed back into his original form. Taking out his rod from his ear, he waved it once and it attained the thickness of a duck egg. With a loud clang he smashed the side door to pieces and ran into the rear garden, shouting, "Master!"

"Disciple, untie me quickly," said the elder, "for I'm about to be ruined!"

"Don't hurry, Master," Pilgrim said. "Let me slay the monster-spirit first before I come rescue you." He turned and dashed back into the center hall. As he was about to strike with upraised rod, he stopped and said, "No good! Let me untie Master first before I strike at him."

He rushed back into the garden, only to think to himself, "I'll slay him first before the rescue." He went back and forth like this two or three times before finally dancing his way into the garden. This sight of him gave the elder some delight even in his sorrow. "Monkey," he said, "it must be that you are overjoyed by the sight of my being still alive, and that is why you are dancing in this manner."

Pilgrim then walked up to him to untie his ropes. As he led his master away, they heard the person tied to another tree facing them call out, "Venerable Father, please exercise your great mercy and save my life, too!"

Standing still, the elder said, "Wu-k'ung, please untie that person also." "Who is he?" asked Pilgrim. "He's a woodcutter," replied the elder, "who had been captured a day before I was seized. He told me that he has an aged mother, whom he thinks of constantly. He's a most filial person, and we might as well rescue him, too."

Pilgrim agreed and untied the man's ropes also; they went out through the rear entrance together and ascended the cliff to cross the swift-flowing brook. "Worthy disciple," said the elder, "I thank you for saving his life and mine! Wu-nêng and Wu-ching, where are they?" "The two of them are mourning you," replied Pilgrim. "You may call out to them now." And the elder cried out in a loud voice: "Pa-chieh! Pa-chieh!"

As he had been weeping till he was half dazed, our Idiot wiped his snout and eyes and said, "Sha Monk, Master must have come home to show his spirit! Isn't it he who's calling us from somewhere?"

Rushing forward, Pilgrim shouted, "Coolie! Who's showing any spirit? Isn't this Master who has returned?" When Sha Monk lifted his head and saw them, he fell to his knees and said, "Master, how you must have suffered! How did Elder Brother manage to rescue you?" Whereupon Pilgrim gave a thorough account of what had taken place.

When he heard this, Pa-chieh grew so infuriated that he raised his rake, clenched his teeth, and hacked away the grave mound. Digging out the head, he pounded it to pieces. "Why did you beat it up?" asked the T'ang monk.

"O Master!" said Pa-chieh. "I don't know which family this outcast belongs to, but he has caused me to weep for him for a long time."

"You should thank him instead for saving my life," said the T'ang monk. "When you brothers fought your way to their door and demanded my return, the monsters used him as a substitute to ward you off. If it hadn't been for him, I would have been killed. You should have him buried, simply as an expression of our priestly gratitude." When he heard these words of the elder, our Idiot indeed packed up the mess of flesh and bones and buried it again by digging another grave.

With a chuckle Pilgrim said, "Master, please sit here for a moment, and let me go and finish them off." He leaped down from the cliff and crossed the brook to return to the cave. Taking into the center hall the ropes which had been used to tie the T'ang monk and the woodcutter, he found the old monster still sleeping. After having hog-tied him, Pilgrim used his golden-hooped rod to lift the bundle up and carried it on his shoulder to leave by the rear entrance. When Pa-chieh caught sight of them from a distance, he said, "Elder Brother just loves this lopsided business! Wouldn't it be better if he had found another monster to give him a balanced load?"

Pilgrim drew near and dropped down the old monster, and Pa-chieh was about to strike with his rake. "Wait a moment!" said Pilgrim. "We haven't seized the little monsters in the cave yet."

"O Elder Brother," said Pa-chieh, "lead me to them so I can hit them!"

"Hitting them is such a waste of energy," said Pilgrim. "It's better to find some firewood and finish them off that way." On hearing this, the woodcutter immediately led Pa-chieh to the eastern valley to find some broken bamboos, leafless pines, hollow willows, snapped-off vines, yellow artemisia, old reeds, rushes, and parched mulberry. After they had hauled bundles of these into the rear entrance, Pilgrim lit a fire while Pa-chieh fanned up a breeze with his ears. As he leaped out of the cave, our Great Sage shook his body once to retrieve his hairs. By the time those little monsters awoke, both smoke and fire were pouring out. Alas! Not even half a monster managed to escape, for the cave-dwelling was completely burned out.

When the disciples returned to their master, the elder saw that the old monster was stirring, and he called out: "Disciples, the monster-spirit is awake." Going forward, Pa-chieh slew the old fiend with one blow of his rake; its original form appeared to be that of a spotted leopard. "This sort of spotted leopard," said Pilgrim, "can even devour a tiger. Now it has managed to assume human form. Putting it to death will prevent it from causing any further trouble." The elder thanked them over and over again before climbing once more into the saddle.

"Venerable Father," said the woodcutter, "toward the southwest not far from here is my humble abode. I would like to invite you there to meet my mother, so that she may bow to thank you all for saving my life. Then we will escort you to the main road."

Delighted, the elder dismounted and headed southwest with the woodcutter and the three disciples. After a short distance they came upon

A path of flagstones moss-lined
And wood gates wistaria-entwined.
On four sides are mountains lambent
And trees filled with birdsong strident.
Pines and bamboos join in thick green;
Profusive rare blossoms are seen.
Deep in the clouds and out of the way
Is a bamboo-fenced thatched hut to stay.

From a long way away they caught sight of an old woman, leaning on the wooden gate and weeping bitterly, crying out for her son all the while. When the woodcutter saw his own mother, he abandoned the elder and rushed up to the wooden gate. As he went to his knees, he cried, "Mother, your son's here!"

Embracing him, the old woman said, "O my child! When you did not return home these last few days, I supposed that you were seized by the mountain lord and killed, and the very thought of it gave me unbearable pain. If you weren't harmed, why did you wait till today before returning? Where are your ropes, your pole, and your ax?"

The woodcutter kowtowed before replying, "Mother, your son indeed was taken away by the mountain lord and tied to a tree. It would have been truly difficult to preserve my life if it hadn't been for these several venerable fathers. That one happens to be an arhat sent by the T'ang court of the Land of the East to go seek scriptures in the Western Heaven. He too was captured by the mountain lord and bound to a tree. His three disciples, however, possess vast magic powers. They succeeded in slaying the mountain lord, who turned out to be the spirit of a spotted leopard. Then they burned to death a great number of the little monsters. When they freed and rescued that old venerable father, they rescued your child as well. Their kindness to me is high as Heaven and thick as Earth! If it hadn't been for them, your child would certainly have perished. Now the mountain is quite safe, and even if your child journeys through the night, there'll be no danger."

When the old woman heard these words, she bowed with each step she took to receive the elder and the three disciples into her thatched cottage. After they were seated, mother and son kowtowed repeatedly to thank them before rushing into the kitchen to prepare a vegetarian meal.

"Brother woodcutter," said Pa-chieh, "I realize that yours is a humble livelihood. You may feed us a simple meal, but please don't go to the trouble of making any elaborate preparation."

"To tell you the truth, Venerable Father," replied the woodcutter, "ours indeed is a lowly abode in the mountains. There are no large black mushrooms, button mushrooms, Szechwan peppers, or star anise. We have only a few items of wild vegetation to present to you all as a mere token of our gratitude."

"Sorry to have caused you such inconvenience!" said Pa-chieh, chuckling. "Just make it snappy, for we're getting awfully hungry!"

"In a moment! In a moment!" said the woodcutter. Indeed, in a moment the tables and chairs were spread out and wiped clean, and several dishes of wild vegetation were brought out. What you see[2] are the

Yellow cabbage lightly blanched
And white beans pickled and minced.
Water polygonum and purslane,
Shepherd's purse and Wild-goose-intestine.[3]
The Swallow-not-coming[4] both fragrant and tender;
Bean sprouts with small buds both crisp and green.
Horse-blue[5] roots cooked till soft;
Dog-footprints[6] plainly toasted.
Cat's-ears[7]
And pi[8] dropped in the wilds.
The Ashen-stalk,[9] cooked very soft, is esculent.
The Scissors'-handle[10]
And Cow's-pool-profit,[11]
The Hollow-snail[12] upturned and filled, the broomlike shepherd's
    purse.
The broken-rice-chi,[13]
The Wo-ts'ai-chi[14] —
These few items are both fragrant and smooth.
Niao-ying[15] flowers fried in oil
And most praiseworthy water-chestnuts.

Rushes' stems and tender watercress—
Four aqueous plants truly rich and pure.
The Wheat-wearing-lady[16]
Is coy and good;
The Torn-worn-cassock,[17]
No need to wear it;
Below the bitter hemp are bamboo props.
The Little-bird's-cotton-coat[18]
And the Monkey's-footprints[19]
Are so oily when fried that you have to eat them.
The Slanted *hao*,[20] the Green *hao*,[21] and the Mother-hugging
    hao;[22]
Some tiny moths have flown atop the flat buckwheat.
To bare Goat-ears[23]
And *Kou-chi*[24] roots
You add but Black-blue[25] and there's no need for oil.
These few wild vegetations and a meal of rice
The woodman sincerely offers as a gift of thanks.

After master and disciples had eaten their fill, they at once made
preparation to leave. Not daring to detain them for long, the woodcutter asked his mother to come out to thank and bow to their visitors
once more while he kowtowed repeatedly. Having tidied his clothes,
the woodcutter then took up a staff made from the trunk of a date
tree to escort the pilgrims out the door. While Sha Monk led the horse,
Pa-chieh toted the luggage, and Pilgrim followed closely to one side,
the elder, riding the horse, folded his hands before his chest and said,
"Brother woodcutter, please lead the way. We shall take proper leave
of you when we reach the main road." They then descended from the
heights and headed for the slope, following the turns of the brook.
Musing as he rode, the elder said, "O disciples!

Since leaving my lord to go to the West,
I've walked the path of an unending quest.
In mountains and streams disasters await;
My life has been the fiends and monsters' bait.
Tripitaka's the sole thought on my mind;
The Ninefold Heaven's all I hope to find.
When will I from such toil my respite earn
And, merit done, to the T'ang court return?"

On hearing this, the woodcutter said, "Venerable Father, please cast aside your worries. In less than a thousand miles on this main road to the West will be the Kingdom of India, the home of ultimate bliss."

When he heard this, the elder at once dismounted and said, "We've caused you inconvenience to come this far. If that is the main road before us, let me urge you to return to your house, brother woodcutter, and do thank your honored mother for us for that sumptuous vegetarian repast. This humble cleric has few tokens of gratitude to offer except the promise of reciting scriptures morning and evening on your behalf, so that both of you, mother and son, will be blessed with peace and long life of a hundred years." The woodcutter respectfully agreed and walked back, while master and disciples headed straight for the West. Truly,

The fiend subdued, they leave their bitter ordeal;

The kindness received, they're earnestly on their way.

We do not know how many more days it will take them to reach the Western Heaven, and you must listen to the explanation in the next chapter.

Eighty-seven

The Phoenix-Immortal Prefecture offends Heaven and suffers
  drought;
The Great Sage Sun advocates virtue and provides rain.

The Great Way's deep and mysterious—
How it waxes and wanes,
Once told, will astonish both gods and spirits.
Enfolding the universe,
Cutting through one's native light,[1]
The true bliss is matchless in the world.
Before the Spirit Vulture Peak,
The treasure pearl, when taken out,
Will blaze forth five kinds of radiance
To illumine all the living of the cosmos;
The enlightened lives long as mountains and seas.

We were telling you about Tripitaka and his three disciples, who took
leave of the woodcutter and descended the Mist-Concealing Mountain
to proceed on the main road. After traveling for several days, they
found themselves approaching a city.

"Wu-k'ung," said Tripitaka, "can you see whether the city ahead
of us is the Kingdom of India?"

"No! No!" replied Pilgrim, waving his hands, "Though the place of
Tathāgata is named Ultimate Bliss, there is no city as such, only a
large mountain in which there are terraces and towered buildings.
The name there is the Great Thunderclap Monastery of the Spirit
Mountain. Even if we have arrived at the Kingdom of India, it doesn't
mean that that's where Tathāgata lives. Heaven knows how great a
distance there is between the kingdom and the Spirit Mountain! The
city over there, I suppose, must be some sort of outer prefecture of
India, but we'll know more once we get near it."

In a little while they reached the outside of the city. Dismounting,
Tripitaka and his disciples walked through the triple gates. Inside they
found little human activity, and the streets seemed rather desolate.
When they reached the edge of the market, they saw many people

wearing blue robes standing in rows left and right; a few who had on
official caps and belts were standing beneath the eaves of a building.
The four pilgrims proceeded along the street, but the people would not
step aside for them at all. As Chu Pa-chieh had always been a country
bumpkin, he stuck out his long snout and yelled, "Get out of the way!
Get out of the way!"

When those people raised their heads and caught sight of a shape
like that, they turned numb with fear and fell all over the place. "A
monster-spirit's here! A monster-spirit's here!" they yelled.

Trembling all over, those with official caps and belts bowed and
said, "Where are you people from?"

Fearing that his disciples might cause trouble, Tripitaka immediately
went to the front to answer the question. "This humble priest," he
said, "is the subject of the Great T'ang in the Land of the East and has
been sent to the Great Thunderclap Monastery in the Kingdom of
India to seek scriptures from the Buddhist Patriarch. As we pass
through your treasure region, we have yet to learn of your country's
name and seek shelter from a household. Having just entered the city,
we fail to give right of way to others, and I beg you various officials to
pardon us."

One of the officials returned the greetings and said, "This is the
outer prefecture of India, and the name of the region is Phoenix-
Immortal. Because we have had a severe drought for several years,
the prefect ordered us to put up here a public notice seeking a priest to
pray for rain and save the people."

On hearing this, Pilgrim said, "Where's your notice?" "Right
here," replied the officials. "We've been sweeping clean the wall and
the eave just now, and we have yet to hang it up."

"Bring it here and let me have a look," said Pilgrim, and the various
officials rolled out the notice at once and hung it beneath the eave. As
Pilgrim and his companions drew near, this was the notice they found:

The Prefect Shang-kuan of the Phoenix-Immortal Prefecture in
the Great Kingdom of India hereby promulgates a public notice
to seek an enlightened master for the performance of a mighty
religious deed. Though the territory of our prefecture is spacious,
and though both our military and civilians have been affluent, we
have suffered drought and famine for several consecutive years.
The fields of the people are unplowed, and the military lands are
infertile; the rivers have receded and the ditches have dried out.

There is neither water in the wells nor liquid in the streams. The wealthy can barely subsist, but the poor can hardly remain alive. A bushel of grain costs a hundred gold, while five ounces of silver is the price of one bundle of wood. A ten-year-old girl is given in exchange for three pints of rice, while a five-year-old boy is taken away at will. Those fearful of the law in the city would pawn their clothes and possessions to preserve themselves, but those abusing the public in the countryside will rob and plunder to save their lives. For this reason we have promulgated this notice to plead with the worthy and wise of all quarters to pray for rain and save the people. Such kindness will be heavily rewarded with the payment of a thousand gold, and this is a sure promise.

After he had read it, Pilgrim asked the various officials, "What does the Prefect Shang-kuan² mean?"

"Shang-kuan happens to be his surname, and it's also the name of our prefecture," they replied. "But that's quite a rare name," said Pilgrim, chuckling.

"So Elder Brother hasn't gone to school, after all!" Pa-chieh said. "Don't you know that toward the end of *The Book of Family Names* there is the phrase, Shang-kuan Ou-yang?"

"Disciples," Tripitaka said, "let's stop this idle chatter. Whichever one of you knows how to pray for rain should do so on their behalf in order to bring relief to the populace. This is a most virtuous deed. If you cannot, we should leave and not delay our journey."

"What's so difficult about praying for rain?" said Pilgrim. "Old Monkey can overturn rivers and seas, alter the course of the planets, topple Heaven and upturn a well, belch out fog and cloud, chase down the moon while carrying a mountain, call up the wind and the rain. Which one of these things, in fact, has not been the sport of my youth? There's nothing to marvel at!"

When the various officials heard what he said, two of them quickly went to the prefectural office to report, "Venerable Father, ten thousand happinesses have arrived!"

The prefect was just in the midst of uttering a silent prayer before stalks of lighted incense. When he heard the announcement, he asked, "What happinesses?" One of the officials replied, "Having received the public notice today, we were about to mount it at the entrance of the market when four monks arrived. They claimed to be pilgrims sent by the Great T'ang in the Land of the East to seek scriptures from Buddha in the Great Thunderclap Monastery of the Kingdom of India. When they saw the notice, they also told us of their ability to pray for rain, and that is why we came especially to report to you."

The prefect immediately tidied his clothing and began walking toward the market, not even waiting for carriage or horses to be summoned, in order that he might solicit with great courtesy the help of these priests. When someone on the street announced, "The Venerable Father Prefect has arrived," the crowd stepped aside. As soon as he caught sight of the T'ang monk, the prefect started bowing low in the middle of the street, not intimidated at all by the hideous appearances of the monk's disciples. "Your lowly official named Shangkuan," he said, "is the prefect of the Phoenix-Immortal Prefecture. With burned incense, and having ritually cleansed myself, I bow to implore the master to pray for rain and save the people. I beg the master to dispense widely his mercy, exercise his magic potency, and answer our needs!"

Returning his salutation, Tripitaka said, "This is hardly the place for conversation. Allow this humble cleric to reach a monastery or temple, where it'll be easier for us to do what we must do." "Let the master come to our humble residence," said the prefect. "There will be an unsullied area for you to stay."

Master and disciples thereupon led the horse and toted the luggage to the official residence. After he had greeted each one of them, the prefect at once ordered tea and a vegetarian meal to be served. When the food arrived in a little while, our Pa-chieh ate with abandon like a hungry tiger, so terrifying those holding dishes and trays that their hearts quivered and their gallbladders shook. Back and forth they scurried about to fetch more soup and rice, moving like revolving lanterns. They could barely keep up with the demand, but they did not stop until the pilgrims had satisfied themselves. After the meal, the T'ang monk expressed his thanks and then asked, "Sir Prefect, for how long has your noble region been afflicted with drought?" The prefect said,

At India's Kingdom, this, our nation great,
Of Phoenix-Immortal I'm the magistrate.
For three long years a drought has laid us low:
The five grains perished—not even grass would grow!
Commerce is hard for households big and small;
Ten doors or nine portals are tearful all.

Two-thirds of us have been by hunger slain,
While one-third like a wind-blown torch remains.
When I this public notice promulgate,
It's our luck that true monks have reached our state.
If you with one inch of rain the people bless,
A thousand gold I'll give for such kindness.

On hearing this, Pilgrim showed great delight and said, with a roar of laughter, "Don't say that! Don't say that! If you mention a thousand gold as repayment, you'll not receive even half a drop of rain. But if you wish to accumulate merit and virtue, old Monkey will present you with a torrential shower."

That prefect, you see, was indeed an upright and honest official who had great love for his people. He immediately asked Pilgrim to take the honored seat; he bowed low and said, "Master, if you would indeed extend your mercy, this lowly official will never dare turn my back on virtue."

"Let's not talk any more," said Pilgrim, "and please rise. May I trouble you to take good care of my master, so that old Monkey can act."

"Elder Brother," said Sha Monk, "how will you act?"

"You and Pa-chieh come over here," replied Pilgrim. "Stand at the foot of the steps of the hall there and serve as my ritual assistants. Let old Monkey summon the dragon here to make rain." Pa-chieh and Sha Monk obeyed; when the three of them all stood at the foot of the steps of the hall, the prefect burned incense and worshipped, while Tripitaka sat and recited a sūtra.

As Pilgrim recited a magic spell, immediately a dark cloud arose from east and gradually drifted down to the courtyard in front of the hall; it was actually Ao-kuang, the old Dragon King of the Eastern Ocean. After the cloud had been retrieved, Ao-kuang took on human form and walked forward to bow and salute Pilgrim, saying, "In what capacity may this humble dragon serve the Great Sage who has summoned me?"

"Please rise," said Pilgrim. "I've troubled you to come from a great distance only for one purpose, and that is to ask you why you have not provided rain to relieve a drought of several years here at the Prefecture of Phoenix-Immortal."

"Let me humbly inform the Great Sage," said the old dragon. "Though I may be able to make rain, I am subject to the will of

Heaven. If Heaven above has not authorized me, how could I dare come here to make rain?"

Pilgrim said, "Because I passed through this region and saw how the people suffered from such a prolonged drought, I asked you especially to come and bring relief. Why are you making excuses?"

"Would I dare do that?" said the dragon king. "When the Great Sage recited his magic spell, I would never dare not show up. But I have not been authorized by Heaven in the first place, and, second, I have not brought along the divine warriors in charge of making rain. How could I start anything? If the Great Sage indeed has such elee-mosynary intentions, allow this little dragon to return to the sea and summon his troops. Meanwhile, let the Great Sage make a memorial at the Celestial Palace and ask for an imperial decree authorizing the descent of rain. Request the aquatic officials to let loose the dragons, and then I'll be able to make rain according to the amount specified by the decree."

As Pilgrim could not quite controvert this proper argument which the old dragon offered, he had to let him return to the sea. He himself then jumped out of the star-treading pattern to give the T'ang monk a thorough account of what had happened. "In that case," said the T'ang monk, "you may go and do your duty, but you must not utter even a word of falsehood." Pilgrim at once gave this injunction to Pa-chieh and Sha Monk: "Guard the master, for I'm going up to the Celestial Palace."

Dear Great Sage! He said he was leaving and at once vanished from sight. Quaking with fear, the prefect said, "Where has Venerable Father Sun gone to?"

"He mounted the clouds to ascend to Heaven," said Pa-chieh, chuckling. The prefect became more respectful than ever. An order was hurriedly dispatched to the broad boulevards and narrow alleys, asking all the people—whether they be nobles or plebeians, civilian or military—to set up a placard for the dragon king in front of each household. Clean water jars with willow twigs stuck inside were to be placed by the doors, and incense was to be burned so that all could worship Heaven. Here we shall leave them for the moment.

We tell you instead about Pilgrim, who reached the West Heavenly Gate with a single cloud-somersault. The Devarāja Dhṛtarāṣṭra led a group of Heavenly soldiers and *vīra* to greet him with the question: "Great Sage, have you completed the enterprise of scripture seeking?"

"The end can't be too far off," replied Pilgrim. "We have reached the border of the Kingdom of India, where there is an outer prefecture by the name of Phoenix-Immortal. That place has not had rain for three years, and the people are in terrible straits. Old Monkey wanted to pray for rain to bring relief, but when I summoned the dragon king there, he claimed that he dared not do it on his own authority. I have come here, therefore, to request a decree from the Jade Emperor."

"I am quite sure that rain is forbidden at that particular place," said the devarāja, "for I have heard that the prefect, because of some mischief, has offended Heaven and Earth. As a punishment, the Jade Emperor established a rice mountain, a noodle mountain, and a huge square lock of gold. Until these three things are overturned, there will be no rain for the region." Not knowing, however, what the devarāja was speaking of, Pilgrim insisted on an audience with the Jade Emperor. The devarāja dared not bar his way, and he was permitted to go inside till he reached the Hall of Perfect Light. He was then met by the Four Heavenly Preceptors, who asked: "What is the Great Sage doing here?"

"While escorting the T'ang monk," said Pilgrim, "I arrived at the border of the Kingdom of India. Because of a severe drought at the Prefecture of Phoenix-Immortal, the prefect sought magicians to make rain. When old Monkey managed to summon the dragon king and ask him to make rain, he said that he dared not do it without the explicit decree of the Jade Emperor. Hence I've come to request a decree to relieve the people's suffering." "But it should not rain at that region," said the Heavenly Preceptors.

With a laugh, Pilgrim said, "Whether it should or not, please announce my presence and see whether old Monkey can win this favor."

The Immortal Ko said, "As the proverb has it, 'A fly wraps around a net—what a large countenance!'"[3] "Stop this babbling!" said Hsü Ching-yang. "Let's take him inside." Thereupon Ch'iu Hung-chih, Chang Tao-ling, Ko, and Hsü, these four realized immortals, led the visitor into the Hall of Divine Mists to memorialize, saying, "Your Majesty, we have here Sun Wu-k'ung, who is passing through the Phoenix-Immortal Prefecture of the Kingdom of India. Wishing rain for the people, he has come especially to seek your decree."

"On the twenty-fifth day of the twelfth month three years ago," said the Jade Emperor, "we were out on tour to inspect the myriad heavens and float through the Three Realms. When we arrived at that particular region, we had occasion to witness that Shang-kuan right in the midst of his wickedness. He pushed over the sacrificial maigre intended for offering to Heaven and fed it to dogs instead. Furthermore, he even made obscene utterances and committed the sin of blasphemy. For this reason, we established three things in the Fragrance-Draping Hall, to which all of you should lead Sun Wu-k'ung to see. If these things have been overturned, we shall grant him a decree; if not, he should be told to mind his own business."

The four Heavenly Preceptors at once led Pilgrim to the hall to look around. There they came upon a mountain of rice, about one hundred feet tall, and a mountain of noodles, about two hundred feet in height. At the side of the rice mountain was a chicken no larger than a human fist, which was pecking at the rice at a rather irregular pace—now speeding up, now slowing down. Over at the noodle mountain was a golden-haired puppy, a Peking pug, which, with an occasional flick of his tongue, was lapping up some of the noodles. On the left side of the hall, moreover, there was an iron rack with a large square lock, at least fifteen inches in length, hanging from it. Beneath the key of the lock, which was at least as thick as a human finger, was a small lamp, its tiny flame barely touching the key.

Not knowing what to make of the sight, Pilgrim turned to ask the Heavenly Preceptors, "What does this mean?" One of them replied, "Because that fellow has offended Heaven, the Jade Emperor established these three things. Not until the chicken has finished pecking the rice, the dog has lapped up all the noodles, and the lamp has burned through the key of the lock will there be rain in that region."

When he heard these words, Pilgrim was so taken aback that he paled with fright. Not daring to present another memorial to the Emperor, he walked out of the hall, visibly embarrassed. "The Great Sage need not be overly perplexed," said one of the preceptors. "This affair can only be resolved by virtue, for if there is a single thought of kindness and mercy to stir up Heaven above, the rice and noodle mountains will topple immediately, and the lock key too will snap at once. You must go and persuade that prefect to do good, and blessing will be on its way." Pilgrim agreed.

Not taking leave of the Jade Emperor at Divine Mists,

He went straightaway below to answer a mortal man.

In a moment he arrived at the West Heavenly Gate, where he saw Devarāja Dhṛtarāṣṭra again. "Did you succeed in getting a decree?"

asked the devarāja. Having given an account of the matter of the rice mountain, the noodle mountain, and the golden lock, Pilgrim said, "He did refuse to grant me a decree, as you told me he would. But when the Heavenly Preceptors sent me off just now, they also instructed me to persuade that fellow to return to virtue, and blessing would come to him as before." Thus they parted, and Pilgrim descended on a cloud to the Region Below.

When he arrived, the prefect, Tripitaka, Pa-chieh, Sha Monk, and all the officials, great and small, crowded around him to question him about his journey. Pilgrim singled out the prefect and bellowed at him, "Because you offended Heaven and Earth three years ago, on the twenty-fifth day of the twelfth month, you brought a great ordeal on your people, for Heaven now refuses to grant you rain." These words so astonished the prefect that he fell prostrate on the ground, asking, "How did the master learn of the incident three years ago?"

"How could you," said Pilgrim, "push down sacrificial maigre intended for offering to Heaven and feed it to dogs? You'd better give us an honest account!"

Not daring to conceal anything, the prefect said, "On the twenty-fifth day of the twelfth month three years ago, we indeed offered sacrificial maigre to Heaven in our residence. Because of my wife's ill behavior—she taunted me, in fact, with some nasty words—I was momentarily blinded by anger and pushed down the votive table, spilling all the vegetarian food. At that point I did in fact get the dogs to come and eat it up. Since then this incident has lingered in my memory and often driven me to distraction, but I know of no way to present an explanation. I hadn't realized that Heaven Above took offense and brought harm to the people on my account. Now that the master has descended again to this region, I beg you to reveal to me how Heaven intends to reckon with me."

Pilgrim said, "That day happened to be the epiphany of the Jade Emperor to the Region Below. When he saw you feeding the sacrificial maigre to dogs and mouthing obscene words, he at once set up three things as reminders of your transgression."

"What three things?" asked Pa-chieh.

"At the Fragrance-Draping Hall," replied Pilgrim, "a rice mountain approximately a hundred feet tall and a noodle mountain about two hundred feet in height were set up. By the rice mountain there was a chicken no larger than a fist, pecking away rather leisurely at the rice.

At the noodle mountain there was a golden-haired Peking pug, lapping up some of the noodles with an occasional flick of his tongue. On the left side of the hall, moreover, there was an iron rack with a huge lock made of yellow gold hanging from it, its key as thick as a finger. Below the key is a lamp, but the flame is barely touching the key. Not until the chicken has finished pecking the rice, the dog lapping up the noodles, and the lamp burning through the key is there to be rain in this region."

Chuckling, Pa-chieh said, "No problem! No problem! If Elder Brother is willing to take me there, I'll undergo magical transformation and finish off all that rice and noodle in a single meal. We'll break the key, too, and there'll be rain."

"Stop babbling, Idiot!" said Pilgrim. "This happens to be a device of Heaven. How could you undo it?"

"In that case," said Tripitaka, "what shall we do?"

"It's not too difficult! It's not too difficult!" said Pilgrim. "When I was about to come back, the Four Heavenly Preceptors told me that this matter could be resolved only by doing good."

Prostrating himself on the ground, the prefect pleaded: "I beg the master to inform me. This lowly official will obey all your instructions."

"If you indeed repent and return to virtue," said Pilgrim, "and make it your early practice to worship Buddha and read scriptures, I shall see what I can do for you. But if you refuse to change, even I cannot undo your miseries. Before long Heaven will decree your execution, and your life will not be spared."

Touching his head to the ground, the prefect vowed that he would submit to religion. At once he gave the order for Buddhist and Taoist clerics of his region to begin performing services for three days, about which they had to write up detailed documents, burn them, and send them to Heaven above. The prefect himself personally led his subjects in worship and in the presentation of incense in order to appease Heaven and Earth and do penance. Tripitaka, too, also recited sūtras for him. In the meantime, another order was dispatched with all speed to every household within and without the city: each man and woman was to burn incense and chant the name of Buddha. From that moment on the sound of good works could be heard everywhere.

Highly pleased by what he saw and heard, Pilgrim said to Pa-chieh and Sha Monk, "The two of you should take care to guard our master.

Let old Monkey make another trip for him."

"Elder Brother," asked Pa-chieh, "where do you want to go this time?"

"Since this prefect has believed the words of old Monkey," replied Pilgrim, "and has received indeed our teachings, and since he is now chanting the name of Buddha with due reverence, compassion, and sincerity, I will go again to memorialize to the Jade Emperor and beg some rain for him."

"If you wish to go, Elder Brother," said Sha Monk, "you need not hesitate so that our journey will not be delayed. Do finish this rain service for them in order that our right fruit, too, may be perfected."

Dear Great Sage! Mounting the clouds, he reached the Heavenly Gate, where he was greeted by the question of Devarāja Dhṛtarāṣṭra, "Why are you here again?" "That prefect," replied Pilgrim, "has already returned to virtue." The devarāja, too, was delighted.

As they conversed, they saw the Messenger of Direct Talismans arrive, holding Taoist documents and Buddhist rescripts to be sent through the Heavenly Gate. When the messenger saw Pilgrim, he saluted him, saying, "This is the merit of the Great Sage in his evangelical work."

"Where are you sending these documents?" asked Pilgrim.

"To the Hall of Perfect Light," replied the messenger, "so that the Heavenly Preceptors may present them before the Jade Emperor, the Great Celestial Honored One." "In that case," Pilgrim said, "you walk ahead, and I'll follow you."

As the talismans messenger entered the gate, Devarāja Dhṛtarāṣṭra said, "Great Sage, there's no need for you to have an audience with the Jade Emperor. You need only to go to the Bureau of Appointed Seasons of the Ninefold Heaven and ask for the thunder deities. When you have started the thunder and lightning, rain will be on its way."

Indeed Pilgrim followed his advice; after entering the Heavenly Gate, he did not proceed to seek another decree at the Hall of Divine Mists. Instead, turning his step on the clouds, he went straight to the Bureau of Appointed Seasons of the Ninefold Heaven. He was met by the Thunder Gate Messenger, the Recorder of Collective Registry, and the Recorder of the Provincial Judicial Commission, who saluted him and asked, "To what do we owe this visit, Great Sage?"

"There's something," replied Pilgrim, "for which I must have an audience with the Celestial-Honored One." The three messengers at once went in to make the announcement, and the Celestial-Honored One walked out from behind the royal cinnabar screen adorned with nine phoenixes. After having tidied his attire, he met his visitor. When they had finished their exchange of greetings, Pilgrim said, "I've come with a special request."

"What is it?" asked the Celestial-Honored One. Pilgrim said, "I escorted the T'ang monk to the Prefecture of Phoenix-Immortal. When he saw how severe a drought they have been having, I promised the people that I would seek rain on their behalf. Now I've come specially to request the assistance of your officers to go there and provide thunder."

"I happen to know that the prefect has offended Heaven," said the Celestial-Honored One, "as a result of which three conditions have been established. I wonder if it should rain in that region." Pilgrim said, "Yesterday I went to request a decree from the Jade Emperor, and he told the Heavenly Preceptors to lead me to the Fragrance-Draping Hall to look at those three conditions. They were actually a rice mountain, a noodle mountain, and a golden lock. The condition was that only when the mountains topple and the key snaps would there be rain. I was deeply troubled by the difficulty of meeting these conditions, but the Heavenly Preceptors instructed me to go and persuade the prefect and his subjects to do good. Their idea was that

When man has a virtuous thought,

Heaven will grant him support.

They assured me, in fact, that the works of virtue would alter the Mind of Heaven and bring deliverance to the people's suffering. Now that a virtuous thought has indeed sprung up in the prefect and that the sound of virtue can be heard everywhere in that region, the Messenger of Direct Talismans has already reported to the Jade Emperor with documents recording such deeds of repentance and penance. That is the reason old Monkey has come to your honored residence to request the assistance of your thunder officials."

"In that case," said the Celestial-Honored One, "I'll send the Squires of Thunder—Têng, Hsin, Chang, and T'ao—who will lead the Mother of Lightning to follow the Great Sage to the Prefecture of Phoenix-Immortal to sound the thunder."

In a little while, the four warriors, on arriving at the region of Phoenix-Immortal with the Great Sage, immediately began to exercise their magic in midair. All you could hear were powerful peals of thunder, and all you could see were blinding flashes of lightning. Truly

Electric flash like purple-gold snake,
And thunder like all creatures aroused.
Ablaze are the flying flames;
The cracks topple mountain caves.
The lightning lights up the heavens;
The tumult unhinges the earth.
One scarlet gold flash the seedlings quickens;
A whole, large empire is rocked and shaken.

For three full years the people at the Prefecture of Phoenix-Immortal, regardless of whether they were civilians or military personnel, or whether they lived inside or outside of the city, had not heard the sound of thunder. When they encountered both thunder and lightning this day, all of them fell to their knees. Some of them held up incense braziers on their heads, while others picked up willow twigs; all of them chanted, "Namo Amitābha! Namo Amitābha!" Such a cry of virtue indeed alerted Heaven Above, just as the ancient poem said:

One wish born in the heart of man
Is known throughout Heaven and Earth.
If vice or virtue lacks reward,
Unjust must be the universe.

Let us leave the Great Sage for a moment, as he directed the deities who were producing thunder and lightning at the Prefecture of Phoenix-Immortal. We tell you instead of the Messenger of Direct Talismans in the Region Above, who escorted the documents of both Buddhists and Taoists up to the Hall of Perfect Light. They were then taken by the Four Heavenly Preceptors to present to the Jade Emperor. The Emperor said, "If those fellows down there have turned their thoughts to good, we should take a look at the three conditions." Even as he was speaking, a guard from the Fragrance-Draping Hall arrived to make this report: "Not only have the rice and noodle mountains toppled, but all the rice and noodles have vanished in an instant. The key to the lock is also broken."

No sooner had he finished this memorial when a celestial court attendant arrived, leading the local spirit, the city deity, and the spirits of land and grain at the Prefecture of Phoenix-Immortal. All the gods bowed to the Jade Emperor and memorialized, "The prefect and the entire population of our region have repented. There is not a single household, indeed not a single person, which has not embraced the fruit of virtue by worshiping Buddha and revering Heaven. We beg you now, therefore, to extend your mercy and let the sweet dew descend to succor the people."

Filled with delight by what he heard, the Jade Emperor at once issued this decree: "Let the Bureau of Wind, the Bureau of Clouds, and the Bureau of Rain follow our instruction to go to the Region Below. Within the territory of the Prefecture of Phoenix-Immortal at this day and hour, let them sound the thunder, deploy the clouds, and lower three feet and forty-two drops of rain." The Four Heavenly Preceptors transmitted this decree to the various bureaus, the deities of which all roused themselves to exercise their divine power in the world below.

Pilgrim and the thundergods, meanwhile, were telling the Mother of Lightning to ply her tricks in midair when they were joined by the other arriving deities. In no time at all, clouds and wind came together and sweet rain descended in torrents. Marvelous rain!

Endless dense clouds,
Boundless black fog,
Thunder cracking,
Lightning flashing,
Violent wind churning,
Sudden rain pouring.
This is how one thought could move Heaven
And all people realize their hopes.
Since the Great Sage has caused decisive change,
The empire grows dark for ten thousand miles—
A good rain likes seas and rivers upturned,
Obscuring land and sky.
A cascade hangs before the eaves,
And chimes resound beyond the screens.
In every door people chant the Buddha's name,
And water runs wild through six streets and marts.
Rivers, east and west, are filled to the brim;
Streams are flowing freely both north and south.
Shriveled sprouts are moistened;
Withered woods now revive.
In the fields hemp and wheat flourish;
In the village grains and beans increase.
The traders find joy in commerce;

The farmers once more love their plowing.
From henceforth millet and grain will prosper,
Their tillage yield naturally rich harvests.
With rain and wind in season the people rest
And in calm seas and rivers enjoy peace.

In a single day there descended the full measure of three feet and forty-two drops of rain. As the various deities gradually halted their activities, the Great Sage cried out in a loud voice: "Let the deities of the Four Bureaus temporarily stay their cloudy attendants. Allow old Monkey to go ask the prefect to make his proper expression of thanks. All of you can then sweep aside the mist and cloud to reveal your true forms. When these common mortals have seen you with their own eyes, they will then believe and sacrifice to you with constancy." On hearing this, the gods had no choice but to remain in midair.

Lowering the direction of his cloud, Pilgrim went to the prefecture, where he was met by Tripitaka, Pa-chieh, and Sha Monk. The prefect made a bow with each step he took to express his gratitude. "You shouldn't thank me," said Pilgrim, "but I have managed to detain the deities of the Four Bureaus here for the moment. Assemble many of your people quickly and thank them, so that they will return in the future to grant you rain." The prefect accordingly sent out an immediate dispatch to all the people that they should hold lighted incense and bow to the sky. When the mist and clouds moved apart, what the people saw were the revealed true forms of the deities of the Four Bureaus, these being the Rain Bureau, the Thunder Bureau, the Cloud Bureau, and the Wind Bureau. This was what they saw:

The dragon king's revealed form,
The thundergod's exposed body.
The Cloud-Boy's appearance,
The Earl of Wind's true image.
The dragon king's revealed form:
Such silver beard and hoary face matchless in the world.
The thundergod's exposed body:
Such incomparable hooked mouth and forceful mien.
The Cloud-Boy's appearance:
Who could rival his jadelike face and head of gold?
The Earl of Wind's true image:
Who resembles his round eyes and bushy brows?
Jointly they emerge in the blue heavens,

Each showing in turn his holy presence.
Phoenix-Immortal people then believe,
Worship with incense, and their evil leave.
Once they have seen Heaven's warriors this day,
They cleanse their hearts and virtue now obey.

The various deities lingered for an hour, and the people did not cease in their worship. Pilgrim Sun rose again into the air to salute them, saying, "We've troubled you! We've troubled you! Please return to your bureaus, all of you. Old Monkey will make certain that the households in this prefecture are faithful in their offerings and make oblation in due season to thank you. From now on, please return every fifth day to give the people wind, and every tenth day to give them rain. Do come back, all of you, and vouchsafe your salvation to them." The deities agreed, and they all returned to their bureaus, where we shall leave them.

We tell you instead about the Great Sage, who dropped down from the clouds and said to Tripitaka, "Our affair's concluded, and the people are safe. We can pack and move on." On hearing this, the prefect quickly saluted them, saying, "How could you say that, Venerable Father Sun? What you have accomplished here are kindness and merit without limits. This lowly official has already asked for a small banquet to be prepared as a token of our gratitude for your great kindness. We intend also to buy some land from the people so that we may build a monastery, in truth, to establish a living shrine to you. Your names will be inscribed on plaques so that you may enjoy our offerings in all four seasons. But even if I were to engrave your deed on my bones and carve it on my heart, I could not repay a fraction of your kindness. How can you say, then, that you want to leave?"

"Though you may find it appropriate to say what you said, Your Excellency," said Tripitaka, "you must realize also that we are but mendicants journeying to the West. We dare not stay long. In a day or two we shall certainly leave." The prefect, of course, would not let them go. He gave the order that preparations for the banquet be made immediately, and also that work begin that very night for the building of the shrine.

The next day a grand banquet was given, in which the T'ang monk was asked to take the honored seat. The Great Sage Sun, Pa-chieh, and Sha Monk all had their own tables, while the prefect and his subordinates, high and low officials, all took turns to present food and drinks to the accompaniment of fine music. The entertainment lasted one whole day, and it was a delightful occasion indeed, for which we have a testimonial poem:

After a long drought the fields meet sweet rain.
Commerce and rivers freely flow again.
We have to thank the divine monks' advent
And the Great Sage who to Heav'n's Palace went.
Three things of former evil now undone,
One thought contrite has fruits of virtue won.
Henceforth may it e'er be like Yao-Shun times:
Rich harvests and rains due in all four climes.

There was a party one day, and there was a banquet the next—it went on like that for almost half a month, during which time they were also waiting for the monastery to be built and the living shrine to be finished.

One day the prefect asked the four pilgrims to go look at the building. "It's an enormous labor," said an astonished T'ang monk. "How can you get it finished so quickly?"

"This lowly official," replied the prefect, "has ordered the laborers to work night and day in order that they might complete their task speedily. Now I'm inviting the Venerable Fathers especially to go see it." "You're indeed a worthy prefect," said Pilgrim with a smile, "one who has not only virtue but ability as well!"

They thus went to the new monastery. When they saw the towering edifices and the magnificent gates, they were full of praise. Pilgrim then requested his master to name the monastery, and Tripitaka said, "Yes, let us call it the Monastery of Salvific Rain." "Very good! Very good!" exclaimed the prefect. Brushed gold notices were then set up to recruit qualified priests to attend the fires and incense. On the left of the main hall, living shrines were erected to the four pilgrims, at which offerings would be made in all four seasons. There were plans also to build shrines to the thunder deities and dragon deities as tokens of gratitude for their divine works. After witnessing all of this, the pilgrims decided to leave.

Knowing that their benefactors could no longer be detained, the populace of the entire prefecture came with gifts and cash, but not even a penny was accepted. Thereupon the officials and the civilians of the entire region formed a huge entourage, with the waving of banners and the beating of drums, to escort the pilgrims out of the

city. Even after some thirty miles they could not quite bring themselves to part with the pilgrims, whom they escorted yet another
distance with tearful eyes. Only when the pilgrims disappeared from
sight did the people turn back. Thus it is that

A virtuous divine monk leaves Salvation behind;

The Great Sage, Equal to Heaven, spreads his kindness wide.

We do not know how many days must pass before they get to see
Tathāgata, and you must listen to the explanation in the next chapter.

Eighty-eight

Zen, reaching Jade-Flower, convenes an assembly;
Mind Monkey, Wood, and Earth take in disciples.

We were telling you about the T'ang monk, who took leave of the prefect. Riding along, he spoke most amiably to Pilgrim: "Worthy disciple, your virtuous fruit this time far surpasses even that of the occasion when you rescued the children of the Bhikṣu Kingdom. This is entirely your merit!"

"At the Bhikṣu Kingdom," said Sha Monk, "only one thousand, one hundred and eleven young boys were saved. How can that compare with this torrential rain, which provided moisture everywhere and revived hundreds and thousands of lives? This disciple, too, has been secretly admiring Elder Brother for his great magic strength which can move Heaven and for his compassion which covers the Earth."

With a giggle, Pa-chieh said, "Yes, Elder Brother has kindness, and he has virtue! Unfortunately, he practices benevolence and righteousness only on the outside, and he harbors malicious designs within. Whenever he walks with old Hog, he steps on people!"

"When did I ever step on you?" asked Pilgrim.

"Enough! Enough!" said Pa-chieh. "Frequently you took care to see that I was bound, that I was hung up, that I was cooked, that I was steamed! Since you have extended your kindness and mercy to hundreds and thousands of people at the Phoenix-Immortal Prefecture, you should have stayed there at least half a year. That way I would have been able to enjoy a few leisurely meals, eating my fill. But all you did was hurry us on our way!"

On hearing this, the elder snapped at him, "This Idiot! All you can think of is something to stuff down your throat! Get moving quickly, and don't you dare talk back!" Not daring to utter a word, Pa-chieh pouted a little; he toted the luggage and guffawed a few times as master and disciples headed down the main road. Time went by like a weaver's shuttle, and soon it was late autumn. You see

Water lines recede,
Mountain rocks turn bare.

Red leaves flutter about,
A time of yellow blossoms.
The frost glows, you feel the night lengthen;
The white moon pierces the paper screens.
Fire and smoke in all households, the twilight's long;
The lake surfaces a cold gleam everywhere.
Fragrant white duckweeds,
And dense red smartweeds.
Oranges yellow and green,
Droopy willows and handsome grains.
The wild geese drop by a hamlet midst rush like snow;
Soy beans are reaped as the inn's roosters crow.

After the four of them had journeyed for a long time, they again saw the shadow of city walls looming. Lifting his crop to point toward the distance, the elder called out: "Wu-k'ung, look! There's another city over there. I wonder what sort of a place it is?"

"You and I haven't even reached it," said Pilgrim. "How could we know? Let's walk up and ask some people." Just as he finished speaking, an old man walked out from a clump of trees. Holding a bamboo staff in his hands, he wore a light garment on his body, a pair of coir sandals on his feet, and a thin belt around his waist. The T'ang monk was so startled that he rolled down from his saddle at once, walked up to him, and saluted him. Leaning on his staff, the old man returned his greetings and asked, "Where have you come from, Elder?"

Pressing his palms together in front of him, the T'ang monk said, "This humble cleric is someone sent by the T'ang court in the Land of the East to Thunderclap to seek scriptures from Buddha. Arriving at your treasure region, I see a rampart ahead of us. Since I do not know what place it is, I ask the old patron especially for instruction."

On hearing this, the old man exclaimed, "A Zen Master who possesses the Way! Our humble region here happens to be the lower prefecture of the Kingdom of India. The name of this place is the Jade-Flower District. As the county magistrate is a member of the royal household of the King of India, he has been appointed the Jade-Flower Prince. He is a most virtuous ruler, one who pays special reverence to Buddhists and Taoists and loves the common people dearly. If the old Zen Master goes to have an audience with him, he will undoubtedly grant you special honor." Tripitaka thanked him, and the old man left by walking through the forest.

Then Tripitaka turned to give a thorough account to his three disciples, who were all delighted and tried to help their master to mount. "It's not too far," said Tripitaka, "I need not ride the horse." The four of them, therefore, walked up to the city streets to look around. Most of the households over there, you see, were busily engaged in buying and selling. The place seemed to be densely populated, and business too seemed to be flourishing. Listen to their voices and look at their features: they seem no different from those of China. "Disciples," admonished Tripitaka, "do be careful and don't be rowdy."

Pa-chieh at once lowered his head and Sha Monk put a hand over his face. Pilgrim, however, took his master's arm to give him support, and soon people on both sides began to crowd them, vying to take a look at these strange travelers. "We have here noble priests who can tame dragons and subdue tigers," they cried, "but we have never seen such hog-taming and monkey-subduing monks!"

Unable to contain himself, Pa-chieh stuck out his snout and said, "Have you ever seen a hog-taming king of a priest?" He so scared those people on the street that they stumbled and fell, scattering right and left. "Idiot," said Pilgrim, laughing, "hide your snout quickly. Stop being so histrionic, and watch your steps. You're about to cross a bridge." Lowering his head, our Idiot kept giggling as they crossed the drawbridge to enter the city gates. On the big boulevards they could see many wine shops and song houses, all prospering and bustling in activities. It was indeed a capital city right out of China, for which we have a testimonial poem. The poem says:

A royal city and fortress ever strong
Where all things seem fresh near hills and rivers long.
The marts with a hundred goods the lake-boats ply;
To sell wine a thousand shops their banners fly.
On each tower and terrace the people bustle;
In every street and lane the traders hustle.
This scene's as lovely as that of Ch'ang-an's fame:
Roosters crow, dogs bark—they all sound the same.

Secretly delighted, Tripitaka thought to himself, "I have heard people speaking of the various barbarians in the Western Territories, but I have never been here. When I look carefully at the place, however, I find that it's no different from our Great T'ang. It certainly lives up to its name of Ultimate Bliss!" He overheard, moreover, that a picul of white rice cost no more than four mace of silver, and that a mere penny would fetch a catty of sesame oil. It was truly a region blessed with bountiful harvests of the five grains.

They walked for a long time before they reached the residence of the Jade-Flower Prince. On both sides of the residence, there were also the residence of the Administrator of a Princely Establishment, the Investigative Hall, the Refectory, and the Guest Hostel. "Disciples," said Tripitaka, "this is the royal residence. Let me go in to have an audience with the prince and have our rescript certified."

"If Master is going inside," said Pa-chieh, "should we stand in front of this official residence?"

"Don't you see the sign on the door here?" replied Tripitaka. "It says, Guest Hostel. You may enter and take a seat inside. Find some hay to feed our horse. After I have seen the prince, and if he bestows some food on us, I'll call you to share it with me."

"You may go in without worry, Master," said Pilgrim. "Old Monkey will take care of things." Sha Monk then toted the luggage into the hostel. When the attendants inside saw how hideous they looked, they dared not question the visitors, nor were they bold enough to ask them to leave. They had, in fact, to permit the pilgrims to sit down, and there we shall leave them for the moment.

We tell you instead about the old master, who changed his attire, took up the travel rescript, and went to the royal residence. He was met by a protocol officer, who asked, "Where has the elder come from?"

Tripitaka answered, "I'm a priest sent by the Great T'ang in the Land of the East to seek scriptures from the Buddhist Patriarch at the Great Thunderclap. Having arrived at your treasure region, I would like to have my travel rescript certified, and that is why I have come especially to have an audience with His Highness." The protocol officer immediately announced his arrival.

The prince, who was indeed an upright and knowledgeable person, at once asked his visitor to enter. After Tripitaka had saluted him at the foot of the steps to the main hall, the prince invited him to take a seat inside. Tripitaka then presented the rescript. When the prince read it and noticed the seals of various kingdoms and their rulers' signatures, he too applied the treasure seal amiably and affixed his own signature. Folding it up again and placing it on the desk, the prince asked, "Elder National Preceptor, I see you have gone through many nations. Exactly how far is it from your Great T'ang to this place?"

"This humble cleric does not quite remember the exact distance," replied Tripitaka. "Years ago, however, the Bodhisattva Kuan-yin revealed herself to our emperor and left his line of the *sung*:[1] 'The way: a hundred and eight thousand miles.' On his journey, this humble cleric has already gone through fourteen summers and winters."

"That means fourteen years!" said the prince with a smile. "You must have had some delays on the way, I suppose."

"I can't even give you a brief account of them—those ten thousand beasts and a thousand demons!" replied Tripitaka. "You have no idea, Your Highness, how much I have suffered before reaching your treasure region." Highly pleased, the prince immediately asked the royal chef to prepare a vegetarian meal for his visitor.

"Your Highness," said Tripitaka again. "This humble cleric has three disciples waiting outside. I dare not receive the maigre, for I fear that our journey might be delayed." The prince said to the court attendant, "Go quickly to invite the three disciples of the elder to come in and have a meal."

The officer went out with the invitation, but he was greeted by the remark: "We haven't see them! We haven't seen them!" Then one of the followers said, "There are three ugly priests sitting in the Guest Hostel. They must be the ones."

The court attendant went with his followers to the hostel and asked the official in charge, "Which ones are the noble disciples of the scripture-seeking priest of the Great T'ang? Our lord has commanded that they be invited for a meal."

Pa-chieh was just seated there, dozing. The moment he heard the word *meal* he could not refrain from leaping up and replying, "We're the ones! We're the ones!" The sight of him so terrified the court attendant that he screamed, shaking all over, "It's a hog-demon! A hog-demon!"

When Pilgrim heard the commotion, he tugged at Pa-chieh and said, "Brother, try to be a little more civilized, and stop being such a village brute!" When those officials saw Pilgrim, they cried, "It's a monkey-spirit! A monkey-spirit!"

Folding his hands in his sleeve before his chest, Sha Monk said, "Please do not be frightened, all of you! We three are all disciples of the T'ang monk." On seeing him, the various officials all cried, "The god of the hearth! The god of the hearth!" Pilgrim Sun then asked Pa-chieh to lead the horse and Sha Monk to tote the luggage so that they could all enter the Jade-Flower Royal Residence. The court attendant meanwhile went ahead to announce their arrival.

When the prince's eyes beheld such ugliness, he, too, became quite frightened. Pressing his palms together, Tripitaka said, "Please have no fear, Your Highness. Though my disciples look ugly, they are all good-hearted." Pa-chieh walked forward and bowed, saying, "This humble cleric salutes you!" The prince grew even more apprehensive.

"My disciples," Tripitaka said again, "were all recruited from the wilds. They are untutored in proper etiquette, and I beg you to forgive them." Suppressing his fear, the prince told the royal chef to take the monks to the Gauze-Drying Pavilion for the vegetarian meal. After thanking him, Tripitaka left the prince and went with his disciples to the pavilion, where he immediately berated Pa-chich. "You coolie!" he said. "You have no manners at all! You should have kept your mouth shut, and that would have been all right. How could you be so rude! One word, and you nearly knocked down the T'ai Mountain!"

"It's a good thing I neither spoke nor bowed," said Pilgrim, chuckling. "I've managed to save some energy!"

"He should have waited for us to bow together," said Sha Monk. "Instead, he went ahead and started hollering with his snout jutting!"

"What a fuss! What a fuss!" said Pa-chieh. "You told me some days ago, Master, that I should bow and make a salutation when I met someone. I did that today, and you say now that it's no good. What am I supposed to do?"

"I told you to bow and greet people," said Tripitaka, "but I didn't tell you to fool with the prince! As the proverb says,

There are different kinds of things

And different grades of people.

How could you not distinguish between the noble and the lowly?" As they spoke, the royal chef led the servants to spread out tables and chairs and serve the maigre. Master and disciples stopped talking as each ate his meal.

We tell you instead about the prince, who left the main hall and went inside the palace. When his three young princes saw how pale he looked, they asked: "Why does Father King seem so frightened today?"

The prince said, "Just now there was a priest sent by the Great T'ang in the Land of the East to seek scriptures from Buddha. He came to have his travel rescript certified, and he seemed a rather comely person. When I asked him to stay for a meal, he told me that he had disciples waiting in front of our residence. I ordered them invited also, but when they came in after a little while, they did not pay me the respect of performing the grand ceremony. All they did was bow, and I was already displeased. But when I managed to take a look at them, each one was ugly as a monstrous demon. I grew quite frightened, and that's why I look pale." Now those three young princes, you see, were quite different from other people, for each of them was fond of martial arts. So they rolled up their sleeves at once and clenched their fists, saying, "Could these be monster-spirits from the mountain who have assumed human forms? Let us take our weapons out and have a look!"

Dear princes! The eldest took up a rod tall as his eyebrows; the second wielded a nine-pronged rake; and the third picked up a staff coated with black enamel. In big heroic strides, they walked out of the palace and shouted, "Who are the monks seeking scriptures? Where are they?" The chef and other officials all went to their knees and said, "Young princes, they are having their vegetarian meal at the Gauze-Drying Pavilion."

Without regard for good or ill, the young princes barged right in and bellowed: "Are you fiends or humans? Speak up quickly, and we'll spare your lives." Tripitaka was so terrified that he paled with fright. Abandoning his rice bowl, he stood bowing and said, "Your humble cleric is someone sent by the T'ang court to seek scriptures. I'm a human, not a fiend."

"You seem like a human all right," said one of the princes, "but those three hideous ones have to be fiends!" Pa-chieh kept right on gorging himself with rice and refused to pay them any attention. Sha Monk and Pilgrim, however, rose slightly and said, "We too are humans. Our features may seem ugly, but our hearts are good; our bodies may seem cumbersome but our natures are kind. Where have you three come from? Why are you so brash with your words?"

The royal chef, standing at their side, said, "These three are our prince's heirs." Dropping down his bowl, Pa-chieh said, "Your Highnesses, why are you each holding your weapon? Could it be that you want to fight with us?"

The second prince strode forward and raised his rake with both hands, about to strike Pa-chieh. "That rake of yours," said Pa-chieh, giggling loudly, "only deserves to be the grandson of *my* rake!" He at once lifted up his garment and took out his own rake from his waist.

One wave of it and there were ten thousand shafts of golden light; he moved it a few times and there were a thousand strands of auspicious air. The prince was so terrified that his hands weakened and his tendons turned numb; he did not dare wield his own weapon any further.

When Pilgrim saw the eldest using a rod and hopping about, he took out from his ear the golden-hooped rod. One wave of it and it had the thickness of a rice bowl and the length of about thirteen feet. He gave the ground a stab with it and it went in about three feet. As it stood there, Pilgrim said with a chuckle, "Allow me to present you with this rod of mine!"

When he heard that, the prince threw away his own rod and went to take hold of the other. He used all his strength to try to pull it out of the ground, but he could not move it one whit. He then tried to give it a shove and a shake, but it remained there as if it had taken root. Growing impatient, the third prince attacked with his black-enameled staff, only to be brushed aside with one hand by Sha Monk. With his other, Sha Monk took out his fiend-routing staff, and with a little twirl it created luminous colors and radiant mists. The royal chef and other officials were struck dumb and numb with fright, while the three young princes all knelt down and said, "Divine masters! Divine masters! Being mortals we did not recognize you. We beg you to show us your abilities, so that we may honor you as our teachers." Walking forward, Pilgrim lifted up his own rod with no effort at all and said, "It's too cramped here. I can't stretch my hands. Let me leap into the air and show you a little of how the rod should be used."

Marvelous Great Sage! With a loud whistle he somersaulted right up into midair, his two feet treading the auspicious cloud of five colors. At about three hundred paces above ground, he let loose his rod to make Sprinkling Flowers over the Top[2] and the Yellow Dragon Entwining the Body. Up and down he moved, circling left and right. In the beginning his person and the rod so complemented each other that they seemed, as the adage had it, like flowers added to brocade. By and by even the person disappeared, and all one could see was a sky full of twirling rods!

Shouting a "Bravo!" down below, Pa-chieh could not contain himself any longer. "Let old Hog go and sport a little too!" he cried. Dear Idiot! Mounting on a gust of wind, he rose also to midair and let loose his rake: three strokes up and four down, five strokes left and six strokes right, seven strokes in front and eight behind. All these bodily movements made one hear only a loud continuous swish. When the performance reached its most exciting moment, Sha Monk said to the elder, "Master, let old Sand go also and exercise!"

Dear Monk! With one leap he, too, rose into the air and wielded his staff. Now an ardent fighter swathed in golden radiance, he used both hands to make with his staff the Scarlet Phoenix Facing the Sun and the Hungry Tiger Leaping on its Prey. A tight parry and a slow block were followed by swift turns and quick lunges. The three brothers thus made a tremendous display of their magic potency, showing off their prowess and martial ability in midair. Thus it is that

The image of true Zen's no common view:
The Great Way's causes[3] the cosmos imbue.
In power Gold and Wood fill the dharma-sphere;
Tossing Spatula and ubiquity[4] cohere.
At all times divine arms can their might lay bare;
Elixir vessels are honored everywhere.
Though India's lofty, one must nature coerce;
Jade-Flower princes all to the mean reverse.[5]

So astounded were the three young princes that they went to their knees in the dust. Those officials, of high rank or low, around the Gauze-Drying Pavilion, the old prince in the royal residence, and the entire population of the city—whether military or civilian, male or female, Buddhist, Taoist, or laymen—all began chanting the name of Buddha and kowtowing. Each household, moreover, took up lighted incense and worshipped. Truly

The image revealed returns us to the real,
For priests bring to mankind both peace and weal.
Henceforth the fruit will on Bodhi's way ripen,
Where all worship Buddha and practice Zen.

After the three disciples had made a thorough display of their heroic ability, they lowered their auspicious clouds and put away their weapons. Going before the T'ang monk, they bowed and thanked their master for permission before taking their seats again. There we shall leave them for the moment.

We tell you instead about those three young princes, who hurried back to the palace to report to the old prince, saying, "Father King, ten thousand happinesses have come upon you! Unsurpassable merit may be ours this very moment! Have you seen the display in midair?"

"I only saw colorful mists in the sky," replied the old prince, "and immediately your mother and I burned incense to worship along with the rest of the residents of the palace. We have no idea what immortals have come down and congregated at this place."

"They weren't immortals from anywhere," said one of the young princes; "they were just those very ugly disciples of the scripture-seeking priest. One of them used a golden-hooped iron rod, one a nine-pronged muckrake, and the third a fiend-routing treasure staff. Though the weapons we three use may resemble theirs, ours can in no way be compared with those three weapons. We asked them to exercise for us, and they told us that it was too cramped for them to perform on the ground. They wanted to rise to the air to give us an exhibition. When they mounted the clouds, the sky was filled with auspicious clouds meandering and hallowed air circling. They finally dropped down only a moment ago to take their seats once more in the Gauze-Drying Pavilion. Your sons are so delighted that they would like very much to honor them as teachers. If we could learn their ability to protect our nation, this would be indeed our unsurpassable merit. We wonder what our Father King thinks of this?" The old prince at once gave his consent to what he heard.

And so father and sons, the four of them, did not ask for the royal carriage or the imperial panoply. Instead, they walked to the Gauze-Drying Pavilion, where they found the four pilgrims packing their belongings and just about to enter the royal palace to give thanks for the meal. No sooner had the Jade-Flower and his sons entered the pavilion than they all bowed low, so startling the elder that he, too, hugged the earth to return the salutation. Pilgrim and his two brothers, however, stepped to one side and only gave a slight smile. After the bows, the prince invited the four priests to enter the main hall to take a seat, and the four amiably agreed. Then the old prince stood up and said, "Old Master T'ang, we have a request to make. Do you think that your noble disciples will grant it?"

"Please tell us, Your Highness," said Tripitaka. "My humble disciples would not dare refuse you."

"When we first met you," said the old prince, "we thought that you were merely mendicants from the distant T'ang court. In fact, our eyes of flesh and our mortal disposition prevented us from recognizing you, and we might have greatly offended you. Just now when we beheld how Master Sun, Master Chu, and Master Sha performed in the air, we realized that you are immortals and buddhas. As our three unworthy sons have always been fond of martial arts, they are now most eager to become disciples in order to learn the art well. We, therefore, beg the masters to open their hearts wide as Heaven and Earth. Spread afar your vessels of mercy and transmit your mysteries to our humble offspring. We shall thank you with the wealth of our entire city."

On hearing this, Pilgrim could not refrain from laughing uproariously. "Your Highness!" he said. "You're so benighted! We are people who have left the family, and we're only too anxious to take on a few disciples. If your sons have the desire to follow virtue, you think we'd turn them down? Just don't bother with even the merest hint of payment or profit. Treat us with kindness—that shall be our sufficient reward."

The prince was delighted by Pilgrim's words, and he immediately gave the order for a huge banquet to be laid out right there in the main hall of his residence. Behold! No sooner had the decree been issued than it was carried out. You see

Colors aflutter,
Curls of fragrant smoke,
And gold inlaid tables festooned in bright silk
To dazzle one's eyes.
Gay lacquered chairs with brocade spread out
Add stylishness to the seats.
Fresh fruits from the trees
And aromatic teas.
Four or five dishes of pastries so light and sweet;
One or two panfuls of breads both rich and neat.
More marvelous are those steamed crispies and honey-glazed;
The oily-dips and sugar-roasted are truly great!
A few bottles of fragrant glutinous rice wine
Which, when poured,
Surpasses the juice of jade;
And those several cups of Yang-shan[6] divine tea,
Once held in hand,
Its scent o'erpowers the cassia.
There's food of every variety—
Each item is extraordinary!

During this time the court entertainers were ordered to sing, to dance, and to play their woodwind and string instruments. Master and disciples spent a happy day together with the prince and his princes.

When night fell, the food and wine were taken away and bedding was laid out at the Gauze-Drying Pavilion for the pilgrims to rest. By morning, the prince said, the young princes would burn incense and return with all sincerity to receive instruction in martial arts. As each person obeyed the royal command, scented liquid was prepared for the masters to bathe in before retiring. At this time

The birds rest aloft and all seems at peace;
He leaves the couch, the poet's chantings cease.
The Milky Way shines as the heavens brighten;
The wild path's forlorn where grasses heighten.
Washing flails jangle in a yard nearby;
Dark, distant hills where homeward longings lie.
To know one's feelings the cold cricket seems:
Its loud plaint by bedside would pierce your dreams!

The night went by, and early in the morning, the old prince and his sons arrived once more to visit. When they were received by the elder, they greeted the priests as their teachers, even though they themselves had been honored as royalty the day before. Thus the young princes kowtowed to Pilgrim, Pa-chieh, and Sha Monk as they made this request: "We beg the honorable teachers to take out their weapons and allow their disciples to look at them once more."

On hearing this, Pa-chieh took out amiably his muckrake and laid it on the ground, while Sha Monk leaned his treasure staff against a wall. The second and third princes leaped up at once and tried to pick up the weapons. It was, however, as if dragonflies were pummeling pillars of rock! Though both princes struggled till their heads reddened and their faces turned scarlet, they could not budge the weapons one whit. When the eldest prince saw this, he called out: "Brothers, stop wasting your energy! You should know that the masters' are all divine weapons, but I wonder how heavy they are."

With a chuckle, Pa-chieh said, "My rake's not too heavy! No more, in fact, than the weight of a single canon.[7] Including the handle, it weighs five thousand and forty-eight pounds."

Turning to Sha Monk, the third prince asked, "Master, how heavy is your treasure staff?"

"It's also five thousand and forty-eight pounds," replied Sha Monk. The eldest prince then asked Pilgrim to show him his golden-hooped rod. Pilgrim at once took out a tiny needle from his ear; one wave of it in the wind and it acquired the thickness of a rice bowl. As it stood there erect before their eyes, all the princes were frightened and all the officials grew apprehensive. Bowing, the three young princes said, "The weapons of Master Chu and Master Sha are all carried on their persons and are taken out from beneath their clothes. Why is it that only Master Sun takes out his from his ear? Why does it grow the moment it's exposed to the wind?"

Smiling, Pilgrim said, "You don't seem to realize that my rod isn't just something you can pick up anywhere in this mortal world. This happens to be

An iron rod forged at Creation's dawn
By Great Yü himself, the man like a god.
The depths of all oceans, rivers, and lakes
Were tested and fixed by this very rod.
Having bored through mountains and conquered floods,
It stayed in East Ocean and ruled the seas,
Where after long years it turned luminous,
Able to grow or shrink or radiate.
To call it my own was old Monkey's fate,
To make it change in any way I wish.
I want it big, it'll fill the universe;
I want it small, it'll be a tiny pin.
It's name's Compliant, its style, Golden-hooped—
In Heaven and Earth something quite unique!
Its weight, thirteen thousand and five hundred pounds,
It can grow thick or thin, can wane or wax.
It helped me to havoc the House of Heav'n;
It followed me to crush the halls of Earth.
It tames tigers and dragons everywhere;
It smelts at all places demons and fiends.
One jab upward will make the sun grow dim
And daunt the gods and ghosts of Heav'n and Earth.
A treasure handed down from Chaos' time:
No worldly iron is this rod sublime!"

When those princes heard this declaration, every one of them bowed again and again and begged with all sincerity for instruction. "What sort of martial arts do you three want to learn?" asked Pilgrim.

One of the princes said, "The one used to wielding a rod will study the rod. The one accustomed to using a rake will study the rake, and the one fond of using the staff will study the staff."

"It's easy enough to give instruction," said Pilgrim with a smile, "but none of you has any strength, and you can't wield our weapons. I fear that you will not be able to attain mastery, and then the result will be something like

A poorly drawn tiger that looks like a dog!
As the ancients aptly put it,

Instruction lacking sternness is the teacher's sloth;

Learning without accomplishment is the student's fault.
If the three of you are indeed sincere about the matter, you may burn some incense to worship Heaven and Earth. Let me then transmit some divine strength to you first, and only there after can we teach you the martial arts."

Filled with delight by these words, the three young princes went to find an incense table and carried it back themselves. Having purified their hands and lighted sticks of incense, they bowed deeply to Heaven. After the ceremony, they then asked for instruction from their masters.

Turning around, Pilgrim saluted the T'ang monk in turn and said, "Let me inform the honored master and ask for his pardon. Since I was delivered by your great virtue that year in the Mountain of Two Frontiers, and since I embraced the faith of Buddhism, I have followed you in your westward journey. Though I have yet to repay all the kindness of my master, I have nonetheless served you with all my heart and all my strength. Now that we have arrived at a region in Buddha's kingdom, we have the good fortune of meeting three worthy princes who have made submission to us and are desirous of learning the martial arts. If they become our disciples, they will be the grand-disciples of my master. I want to make this special report to you before I begin instruction." Tripitaka was exceedingly pleased.

When Pa-chieh and Sha Monk saw Pilgrim saluting their master, they, too, went to their knees and kowtowed to Tripitaka, saying, "Master, we are foolish persons, slow of speech and dull-witted, and we don't know how to speak. We simply beg you to take the lofty seat of dharma and allow also the two of us the pleasure of taking disciples. They'll add to our remembrance of the journey to the West." In delight Tripitaka gave his consent.

In a secluded room behind the Gauze-Drying Pavilion, Pilgrim traced out on the ground a diagram of the Big Dipper. Then he asked the three princes to prostrate themselves inside the diagram and, with eyes closed, exercise the utmost concentration. Behind them he himself intoned in silence the mantras and recited the true words of realized immortality as he blew divine breaths into their visceral cavities. Their interior gods were thus brought back into their original abodes. Then he transmitted secret oral formulas to them so that each of the princes received the strength of a thousand arms. He next helped them to circulate and fill up the fire-phases, just as if they were carrying out the technique for expulsion from the womb and changing the bones. Only when the circulation of the vital force had gone through all the circuits of their bodies (modelled on planetary movements) did the young princes regain consciousness. When they jumped to their feet and gave their own faces a wipe, they felt more energetic than ever. Each of them, in fact, had become so strong and sturdy that the eldest prince could handle the golden-hooped rod, the second prince could wield the nine-pronged muckrake, and the third prince could lift the fiend-routing staff.

When the old prince saw this, he could not have been more pleased, and another vegetarian banquet was laid out to thank the master and his three disciples. Right before the banquet tables, however, they began their instruction. The one studying the rod performed with the rod; the one studying the rake performed with the rake; and the one studying the staff performed with the staff. The princes thus succeeded in making a few turns and several movements, but they were, after all, mortals, and they found the goings rather strenuous. After exercising for a while, they began to pant heavily. Indeed, they could not last long, though their weapons might have the ability to undergo transformation. In their advances and retreats, their attacks and offenses, the princes simply could not attain the wonder of natural transformation. Later that day the banquet came to an end.

The next day the three princes came again to thank their masters and to say: "We thank the divine master for endowing us with strength in our arms. Though we are now able to hold the weapons of our masters, however, we find it difficult to wield and turn them. We propose, therefore, that artisans be asked to duplicate the three weapons. They will use your weapons as models but take some of the weight off. Would the masters grant us permission?"

"Fine! Fine! Fine!" said Pa-chieh. "That's a remarkable proposal! You really can't use our weapons in the first place, and besides, we need them for the protection of the Law and the subjugation of demons. You should indeed make three other weapons." The young princes immediately ordered the ironsmiths to purchase ten thousand pounds of raw iron. A tent was pitched in the front courtyard of the royal residence to serve as a temporary factory, and furnace and forge were set up. First, the iron was refined into steel in one day; the next day they asked Pilgrim and his two brothers to place the golden-hooped rod, the nine-pronged rake, and the fiend-routing staff in the tent so that the smiths could make copies of them. The weapons were thus left there day and night.

Alas! These weapons originally were treasures meant to be carried by the pilgrims on their persons and not separated from them for a moment. Even when concealed by the pilgrims' bodies, they would exude great radiance to protect their owners. Now that they had been placed in the tent factory for several days, the myriad shafts of luminous mist and auspicious air emitted by these weapons flooded the sky and covered the earth. One night, a monster-spirit sat up in his abode, which happened to be some seventy miles away from the city, in a mountain called Leopard's-Head and a cave named Tiger's-Mouth. When he suddenly caught sight of the luminous mist and auspicious air, he mounted the clouds to investigate and found that the radiance was coming from the royal palace. Lowering his cloud to draw near, the monster-spirit discovered the three weapons and was moved to delight and desire. "Marvelous treasures! Marvelous treasures!" he exclaimed. "I wonder who uses them, and why they are placed here? Hmmmmm! This has to be my affinity! Let's take them away! Let's take them away!" As his affection grew, he at once summoned a powerful gust and swept away all three weapons and returned to his own cave. Thus it is that

Tao can't be left for a moment;[8]
What can be left is not the Tao.
When weapons divine are stolen,
The seekers have labored in vain.

In the end we don't know how those weapons will be found, and you must listen to the explanation in the next chapter.

Eighty-nine

The yellow lion-spirit in vain gives the Muckrake Feast;
Gold, Wood, and Earth disturb with a scheme Mount
   Leopard's-Head.

We were telling you about those several ironsmiths, who had been
hard at work for several days and therefore slept soundly at night. By
morning, when they rose to resume their heating and hammering,
they discovered that the three weapons in the tent had vanished.
Dumbfounded and panic-stricken, they searched all over the place and
ran into the three young princes, who were walking out from the
palace to inspect the work. The ironsmiths all kowtowed and said, "O
young lords! We do not know where the weapons of the divine masters
have gone!"

Shaken by the words, the young princes said, "Perhaps the masters
themselves put the weapons away at night." They dashed over to the
Gauze-Drying Pavilion and saw that the white horse was still tethered
at the corridor. Unable to contain themselves, they cried, "Masters,
are you still sleeping?"

"We're up," replied Sha Monk as he opened the door to let the
princes in. When they looked around and did not see the weapons,
one of them asked nervously, "Did the masters take back their
weapons?"

"No, we didn't!" said Pilgrim, jumping up.

"Those three weapons of yours," said another prince, "all vanished
during the night."

Scrambling up in haste, Pa-chieh asked, "Is my rake there?"
Another young prince said, "When we three came out just now, we
saw people searching all over but they couldn't find them. Your disciples suspect that the weapons may already have been taken back
by the masters, and that's why we've come to ask you. Since the
treasures of our teachers can grow or shrink, I wonder if you haven't
concealed them on your bodies again, just to make fun of your disciples."

"Really, we have not taken them back," said Pilgrim. "Let's all go look for them." They all went to the tent in the courtyard, but there was no trace of the weapons.

"Those ironsmiths must have stolen them!" said Pa-chieh. "Bring out the weapons quickly! A moment's delay and you'll be beaten to death! Beaten to death!"

Horrified, the ironsmiths kowtowed and shed tears, saying, "Holy Fathers! We have been working so hard these last few days that we all slept through the night. By morning when we got up, the weapons were gone. We are all mortal men. How could we even have moved them? We beg you, Holy Father, to spare our lives! Please spare our lives!"

Pilgrim said nothing in reply. Greatly annoyed, he muttered to himself, "This is our fault! Once they had copied the forms, we should have taken the weapons back. Why did we leave them here like that? Those treasures generate tremendous radiance and luminous colors. That must have disturbed some wicked person, who came and stole them during the night."

"What are you saying, Elder Brother?" said Pa-chieh, refusing to believe him. "It's such a peaceful region here! This is no hollow mountain on the rustic countryside! How could there be any wicked people? It has to be the greed of those ironsmiths. When they saw the radiance of our weapons, they knew that these were treasures. They must have left the palace during the night and banded together with others. They must have dragged and hauled our weapons away. Let's seize them now! Let's beat them!" The ironsmiths could only kowtow and swear their denial.

In the midst of all this commotion the old prince came out. When he learned what had taken place, his face, too, was drained of color. He brooded for a long time and then said, "The weapons of the divine masters are not like those of common mortals. Scores or even hundreds of men could not unlodge them or move them. Moreover, we have governed this city for almost five generations already. Not that we wish to brag or boast, but we do enjoy quite a virtuous reputation beyond these palace walls. The people of this city, be they civilians, soldiers, or artisans, do have respect for the laws of ours. They'd never dare be so unscrupulous. I beg the divine masters to reexamine the matter."

"There's no need to reexamine anything!" replied Pilgrim, laughing. "Nor need we persist in putting the blame on the ironsmiths. Let me ask Your Highness, are there any mountain forests and monstrous fiends around this city of yours?"

"This question of the divine master is most reasonable," said the prince. "There is a Leopard's-Head Mountain north of our city, and there is also a Tiger's-Mouth Cave in it. People have frequently claimed that there are immortals in the cave, but some say also that tigers, wolves, and monstrous fiends live there. We have not been able to determine exactly what creatures there are."

"No need to say any more," said Pilgrim, chuckling. "It must be some wicked creatures there who, having discovered our treasures, stole them during the night." He then called out: "Pa-chieh, Sha Monk, stay here to guard Master and protect the city. Let old Monkey go and look for our weapons." He also instructed the ironsmiths not to put out the fire in the furnace so that they could continue to forge the princes' weapons.

Dear Monkey King! After taking leave of Tripitaka, he vanished completely from sight. Instantly he was standing on the Leopard's-Head Mountain, for it was, you see, no more than thirty miles from the city. When he looked around on the peak, he saw that indeed there was a certain aura of monsters. Truly

A lengthy dragon pulse,[1]
A region vast and wide;
Pointed peaks, erect, that puncture the sky;
Sloping streams, dark and deep, that swiftly flow.
Before the mount's a carpet of jade grass;
Behind the mount's the brocade of rare blooms.
Aged pines and cypresses;
Ancient trees and bamboos.
Crows and magpies in confusion fly and cry;
Wild apes and cranes all screech and squall.
Below the hanging ledge,
Pairs and pairs of deer;
Before the sheer cliff,
Badgers and foxes in twos.
The dragon approaching rises and falls;
With nine turns and bends comes the earthly pulse.
Jade-Flower District is where the ranges meet,
A place that prospers in ten thousand years.

As Pilgrim stared at the scenery, he suddenly heard someone speaking from behind the mountain. Turning quickly to look, he found two wolf-headed fiends walking toward the northwest, chatting loudly.

"These have to be fiendish creatures out patrolling the mountain," mused Pilgrim. "Let old Monkey follow them and hear what they have to say." Making the magic sign with his fingers, he recited a spell and, with one shake of his torso, changed into a little butterfly. With outstretched wings he soared and turned to catch up with them. In truth it was quite a model of transformation!

Two wings gossamery,
Twin feelers silvery.
Aloft the wind he darts away
Or dances slowly through the day.
The waters and walls so nimbly he'll skirt;
With fragrant catkins his delight's to flirt.
Scents of fresh flowers his airy self most please;
His graceful form unfolds with greatest ease.

Wings aflutter, he alighted on the head of one of the monster-spirits to eavesdrop on them. All of a sudden, the monster said, "Second Elder Brother, our Great King has had several pieces of good luck. Last month he got himself a beautiful lady, who has been giving him a good time in the cave. Then last night he acquired these three weapons, and they're truly priceless treasures. Tomorrow he plans to give a banquet at this so-called Muckrake Festival. All of us are going to enjoy ourselves."

"We're quite lucky, too!" said the other one. "We have these twenty taels of silver to take to buy hogs and sheep. When we reach the Northwest Market, let's have a few bottles of wine first. Let's skim two or three taels off the top so that we can buy a cotton jacket for winter. Won't that be nice?" The two fiends thus chatted and giggled as they sped along the main road.

When Pilgrim heard that there was to be a Muckrake Festival, he was secretly pleased. He would have slain the fiends, but he had no weapon, and in any case he felt that they were not responsible for the theft. Flying ahead of them, therefore, he resumed his original form and stood still by the road. He waited until those two fiends had almost reached him and then suddenly spat a mouthful of magic saliva onto them, crying, *"Oṃ Hūm Ta Li!"* At once this magic of immobilization rendered those two wolf-headed spirits completely motionless: eyes unblinking, they could not even open the mouths; body upright, their two legs stood absolutely still. Then Pilgrim pushed both of them over, searched through their clothes, and did indeed find the twenty taels of silver wrapped in a little bag tied to the belt around one of their waists. Each of them also had a white lacquered tablet hanging on his belt; on one was the inscription Shifty-and-Freaky, and on the other, Freaky-and-Shifty.

Dear Great Sage! He took their silver and untied their tablets, then strode back to the city. When he arrived at the royal residence, he gave a thorough account to the prince, the T'ang monk, the various officials, and the artisans. "It must be," said Pa-chieh, chuckling, "old Hog's treasure that is emitting such great radiance that they have to buy hogs and sheep to feast and celebrate. Now how are we going to get it back?"

Pilgrim said, "All three of us brothers ought to go there. The silver should be given to our own artisans as a reward. Let's ask His Highness for a few sheep and hogs. Pa-chieh, you change into the form of Shifty-and-Freaky, and I'll change into the form of Freaky-and-Shifty. Sha Monk can disguise himself as a trader of sheep and hogs. We'll enter the Tiger's-Mouth Cave that way. When we have the chance, each of us will grab our own weapon and finish off those monstrous deviates. Then we can be on our way."

"Marvelous! Marvelous! Marvelous!" laughed Sha Monk. "We shouldn't delay! Let's go!" The old prince indeed agreed to his scheme and asked one of his stewards to purchase about seven hogs and four or five sheep.

The three brothers took leave of their master and went out of the city to exercise their magic powers. "Elder Brother," said Pa-chieh, "since I have never laid eyes on that Shifty-and-Freaky, how could I change into his form?"

"That fiend has been rendered motionless by old Monkey's magic of immobilization," said Pilgrim, "and he won't come out of it until this time tomorrow. But I remember how he looks. Stand still, and let me show you what to change into. Like this . . . and this . . . and you'll look like him." Instantly he was transformed into an exact image of Shifty-and-Freaky. The fiend's tablet was then hung on his waist. Pilgrim also changed into the form of Freaky-and-Shifty with the proper tablet hanging on his waist. Sha Monk then disguised himself as a trader; herding the hogs and sheep, the three of them took the main road heading straight for the mountain.

In a little while they entered the fold of the mountain and again ran into a little monster. He had some vicious features indeed! Look at those

Two round, rolling eyes
Like lamps aglow;
And red, bristling hair
Like flames ablaze.
Bottled nose,
Gaping mouth,
And sharp teeth protruding;
Biforked ears,
Caved-in brow,
And puffed up blue face.
He wore a light yellow garment
And trod a pair of rush sandals—
Strong and sturdy like a savage god,
Brash and hasty like a wicked demon.

With a colored lacquered box for invitations tucked under his left arm, the fiend yelled at Pilgrim, "Freaky-and-Shifty, have you two returned? How many animals did you buy?"

"Just look at what we're herding," replied Pilgrim.

"And who is this?" asked the fiend, facing Sha Monk. "He's an animal trader," said Pilgrim. "We still owe him a few taels of silver, and we're taking him home so that he can be paid. Where are you going?"

The fiend said, "I'm heading for the Bamboo-Knot Mountain to invite the venerable great king to attend a festival tomorrow." Following the drift of the conversation, Pilgrim immediately asked him, "How many people are invited altogether?"

"The venerable great king will head the table, of course," said the fiend. "Including our great king and the captains of our mountain, there'll be some forty persons." They were conversing like that when Pa-chieh spoke up, "Let's get going! The animals have scattered!"

"You round them up," said Pilgrim, "while I ask him for the invitation so I can have a look." Because he thought that Pilgrim was a member of their own family, the fiend opened the box and took out the invitation card to hand over to Pilgrim. Pilgrim unfolded it and found this message written on it:

Tomorrow morning a banquet will be reverently prepared for you so that we may celebrate the Fine Festival of the Muckrake. I pray that you will visit our mountain with your chariot and attendants. It will be our good fortune if you do not refuse. With profound gratitude I submit this invitation to my Venerable Grandmaster, the Ninefold-Numina Primal Sage. Your grand-disciple, Yellow Lion, kowtows a hundred times.

After reading it, Pilgrim handed the card back to the fiend, who put it back in the box and took off toward the southeast.

"Elder Brother," asked Sha Monk, "what does the card say?" "It's an invitation to celebrate a festival of the muckrake. The sender identifies himself as such: 'Your granddisciple, Yellow Lion, kowtows a hundred times.' The one to whom the invitation is addressed happens to be the grandmaster, one 'Ninefold Numina Primal Sage.'" On hearing this, Pa-chieh laughed and said, "This has to be old Hog's property!"

"How can you tell that it's your property?" asked Pilgrim.

Pa-chieh said, "The ancients have a saying that 'A scabby sow is the special foe of the golden-haired lion.' That's why I say that this is old Hog's property."

As the three of them chatted and laughed, they herded the hogs and sheep along. Soon they caught sight of the Tiger's-Mouth Cave. Outside the door this was the scenery they saw:

Emerald mountains all around
Like cities in one row bound.
Green creepers the crags entwine;
From tall cliffs hang purple vines.
Birdsongs the woods invade;
Flowers the cave's entrance shade.
A Peach Blossom Cave[2] no less,
Such that hermits would possess.

When they approached the cave, they found a motley crew of monster-spirits, old and young, cavorting beneath the blossoms and trees. The "Ho! Ho!" snortings of Pa-chieh as he herded the animals caught their attention, and they all came forward to meet members of their own household. As they went after the hogs and sheep and began trussing them, the commotion alerted the monster-king inside, who led a dozen of little monsters to come out and asked, "So, you two have returned? How many hogs and sheep did you buy?"

"Eight hogs and seven sheep," replied Pilgrim, "altogether fifteen animals. The price of hogs should be sixteen taels of silver, the price of sheep, nine taels. We received twenty taels before. Now we still owe five taels. This is the trader, who came along to get his money."

On hearing this, the monster-king gave the order: "Little ones, fetch five taels of silver and send the man off."

Pilgrim said, "This trader didn't just come for his money. He wanted to observe the festival too."

Enraged, the monster-king rebuked him, saying, "What a rogue you are, Freaky Child! You were supposed just to make the purchase. Why did you have to mention the festival to anyone?" Pa-chieh drew near and said, "My lord, the treasures you acquired are indeed rare in the world. What's wrong with letting him take a look at them?"

"You're a pest, too, Shifty Child!" snapped the monster. "I got my treasures from the city in the Jade-Flower District. If this trader sees them and spreads the news in the district, the prince may hear about it. If he then comes here to look, what am I going to do?"

"My Lord," said Pilgrim, "this trader comes from behind the Northwest Market. He's not a resident of the city. How could he go there and spread the word? Besides, he's a little hungry, and neither of us has eaten. If there's any wine and food in the house, please give him some, and then send him off." He had hardly finished speaking when a little monster handed over five taels of silver to him. Passing the silver to Sha Monk, Pilgrim said, "Trader, take the silver. I'll take you to the back to have some food."

Forcing himself to be bold, Sha Monk went inside the cave with Pa-chieh and Pilgrim. When they reached the second-level hall, they found a votive table set up in the center, on which the nine-pronged muckrake was laid, its colorful radiance truly blinding. Leaning on the east wall was the golden-hooped rod, and on the west a fiend-routing staff. The monster-king, who had followed them in, said, "Trader, the luminous thing in the center is the muckrake. You may look at it, but don't ever mention this to anyone after you leave." Sha Monk nodded and thanked him. Alas!

When someone sees his property,

He will go for it certainly.

For his entire life that Pa-chieh had been an impetuous person. When he saw the muckrake, he was not about to engage in any more small talk. Running up to the table and seizing it with both hands, he changed back into his true form and struck at the face of the monster-spirit. Our Pilgrim and Sha Monk, too, dashed to both walls to grab their own weapons and change back into their true forms. As the three brothers began to attack madly, the fiendish king retreated hastily to the back, where he picked up a four-lights shovel[3] with a long handle and a sharp blade. Rushing back out into the courtyard, he blocked the three weapons and shouted, "Who are you that you dare use a trick to wangle my treasures from me?"

"You larcenous hairy lump!" scolded Pilgrim. "So you don't recognize us! We are the disciples of Tripitaka T'ang, a sage monk from the Land of the East. When we had our travel rescripts certified at the Jade-Flower District, the noble prince there asked his three sons to submit to us as teachers and learn martial arts from us. Because our treasures were to serve as models for their weapons, which were being forged, we left them in the yard, and they were stolen by you larcenous hairy lump during the night. And you say instead that we use a trick to wangle your treasures! Don't run away! Have a taste of what our three weapons can dish up for you!" The monster-spirit immediately raised his shovel to oppose him. Thus began a battle that moved from the courtyard to beyond the front door. Look at those three monks crowding one fiend. A marvelous fight it was!

The rod swishes like the wind;
The rake descends like the rain.
The staff lifts up to fill the sky with mist;
The shovel extends to color the clouds.
Like three gods refining great cinnabar—
The flames, the colors would awe ghosts and gods.
Pilgrim's most able to exert his pow'r.
The monster stole treasures, how insolent!
Pa-chieh, Heavenly Reeds, now shows his might;
Sha Monk, the great warrior, is good and strong.
Brothers, united, use their smart device
And stir up a fight in Tiger's-Mouth Cave.
That fiend is tough and he exploits his wiles:
Four sturdy heroes thus have quite a match.
They brawl this time till the sun's heading west,
When the monster grows weak and fails to stand.

After they fought for a long time on the Leopard's-Head Mountain, the monster-spirit could no longer withstand his opponents. He shouted at Sha Monk, "Watch my shovel!" and, as Sha Monk stepped aside to dodge the blow, he escaped through the hole thus created. Mounting the wind, he sped toward the southeast. Pa-chieh was about to give chase when Pilgrim said, "Let him go. As the ancient proverb has it, 'The desperate bandit should not be pursued.' Let's cut off his way of retreat instead." Pa-chieh agreed.

Going up to the entrance of the cave, the three of them slaughtered all of those hundred-odd monster-spirits, old and young alike. They were actually tigers, wolves, leopards, horses, deer, and mountain goats. Then the Great Sage used his magic to haul up all the valuable belongings from the cave, the carcasses of the slain monsters, and the hogs and sheep which had been herded there. With dried wood Sha Monk started a fire, and Pa-chieh wagged his ears to fan up a strong gust. The entire lair was thus gutted, after which, they took the stuff brought out of the cave and returned to the city.

At that time the city gates had not been closed for people had not yet retired. The old prince and his sons were waiting with the T'ang monk at the Gauze-Drying Pavilion when they suddenly found the courtyard littered with dead beasts, live hogs and sheep, and some fine jewels and clothing thrown down from midair. Then they heard the cry, "Master, we have returned in triumph!"

The prince gave thanks immediately, and Elder T'ang was filled with delight. When the three young princes went to their knees, Sha Monk raised them and said, "Don't thank us yet. Let's take a look at what we have here."

"Where do they all come from?" asked the old prince.

"Those tigers, wolves, leopards, horses, deer, and mountain goats," said Pilgrim with a smile, "happen to be spirits who have become fiends. We succeeded in recovering our weapons and fought our way out of their door. The old monster is actually a golden-haired lion. Using a four-lights shovel, he fought with us till dusk before fleeing for his life toward the southeast. Instead of giving him pursuit, we eliminated his way of retreat by slaughtering all the rest of the fiends and bringing back these valuable belongings of his."

The old prince was both delighted and alarmed by what he heard: he was delighted by the victory, but he was also alarmed by the possibility that the monster might return to exact vengeance.

"Please do not worry, Your Highness," said Pilgrim. "I have considered the matter also, and I will take appropriate action. We will certainly clean up the whole affair for you before we depart, so that no harm will come to you afterward. When we went there this noon, we ran into a red-haired, blue-faced little monster on his way to deliver an invitation. This was what I saw written on the card:

> Tomorrow morning a banquet will be reverently prepared for
> you so that we may celebrate the Fine Festival of the Muckrake.
> I pray that you will visit our mountain with your chariot and
> attendants. It will be our good fortune if you do not refuse. With
> profound gratitude I submit this invitation to my Venerable
> Grandmaster, the Ninefold-Numina Primal Sage.

The sender was identified as 'Your granddisciple, Yellow Lion.' When that monster-spirit fled in defeat just now, he must have gone to his grandfather's place to talk. Tomorrow they will certainly come looking for us to exact vengeance. We will then make a clean sweep of these monsters for you." The old prince thanked him and asked for the evening maigre to be served. After master and disciples had eaten, they retired, and we shall leave them for the moment.

We tell you instead about the monster-spirit, who headed southeast and did indeed flee to the Bamboo-Knot Mountain. In that mountain was a cave-dwelling with the name of Nine-Bends Curvate Cave. The Ninefold-Numina Primal Sage living there was the grandfather of the monster-spirit, whose legs that night never descended from the wind. By the time of the fifth watch, he arrived at the entrance of the cave and was admitted after knocking on the door. One little monster said to him, "Great King, Little Blue Face arrived last night to deliver your invitation, and Venerable Father asked him to stay till this morning, so that he could go with him to attend your muckrake festival. How is it that you also have come at such an early hour to deliver another invitation in person?"

"I don't know what to say," replied the monster-spirit, "but there isn't going to be any festival!"

As he spoke, Little Blue Face came out and said, "Great King, why are you here? Once Venerable Father Great King gets up, he'll go with me to attend your festival." The monster-spirit, however, could only wave his hand nervously without uttering a word.

In a little while, the old monster arose and summoned his visitor in. As the monster-spirit abandoned his weapon and went to his knees, he could not stop the tears rolling down his cheeks.

"Worthy grandchild," said the old monster, "you sent me an invitation yesterday, and I was about to go attend your festival this morning.

Now you have even come in person. But why are you so sad and troubled?"

Kowtowing, the monster-spirit said, "Your granddisciple was taking a leisurely stroll the other night in the moonlight when he saw radiance flooding the sky over the Jade-Flower District. When I hastened to investigate, I found three luminous weapons in the courtyard of the royal residence: a muckrake with nine prongs dipped in gold, a treasure staff, and a golden-hooped rod. After your granddisciple brought them back with magic, he wanted to have a Fine Festival of the Muckrake. The little ones were told to purchase hogs, sheep, and various fruits to prepare a banquet for celebration and for the enjoyment of our grandfather. After I sent off Blue Face yesterday to deliver the invitation to you, Child Freaky whom I asked to go buy the hogs and sheep returned herding a few animals. He brought a trader along, who came to collect some money we owed him and insisted on being an observer of the festival. At first your granddisciple refused, for I feared that he might spread the news to the wrong person outside. Then he claimed he was hungry and asked for food. So I told him to go inside to eat. When they walked in and saw the weapons, they claimed they were theirs. Each of them, in fact, seized one of the weapons and then changed into his original form: one was a priest with a hairy face and a thundergod beak, one was a priest with a long snout and huge ears, and one was a priest with dark, gloomy complexion. Without regard for good or ill, they all shouted madly that they wanted to fight. Your humble grandson took up the four-lights shovel quickly to oppose them, trying at the same time to find out who they were that they dared used such deception. They claimed that they were disciples of the T'ang monk, who had been sent by the Great T'ang in the Land of the East to go to the Western Heaven. They were passing through the city and having their rescript certified when they were detained by the young princes, who wanted to learn martial arts from them. Their three weapons were placed in the yard as models to be copied, and I stole them. That was the explanation for their angry attack on me. But I don't know the names of those three priests, who all seem very able. Your grandson alone could not withstand the three of them. So I fled in defeat to my grandfather, in hopes that you would take up arms to assist me and seize those monks to exact vengeance. That would be a great token of your love for your grandson."

On hearing these words, the old monster reflected in silence for a while. With a chuckle, he said, "So, it's they! My worthy grandchild, you made a mistake when you got *them* involved!"

"Do you know who they are, grandmaster?" asked the monster-spirit.

"The one with a long snout and huge ears," said the old monster, "happens to be Chu Pa-chieh, and the one with dark, gloomy complexion is Sha Monk. These two are still all right. But the one who has a hairy face and a thundergod beak goes by the name of Pilgrim Sun. This person truly has vast magic powers. When he caused great disturbance in the Celestial Palace five hundred years ago, not even a hundred thousand warriors from Heaven could capture him. Moreover, he devotes himself to mischief-making. Whether it's ransacking a mountain or overturning an ocean, breaking down a cave or besieging a city, he's a real champion at creating troubles! How could you provoke *him*? All right, I'll go with you. I'll capture that fellow and those princes of Jade-Flower as well, just to relieve your feelings." The monster-spirit kowtowed to give thanks.

Immediately the old monster summoned into his presence his various grandsons: Gibbon-Lion,[4] Snow Lion, Suan-i,[5] Pai-tsê,[6] Wildcat, and Elephant-Baiter. Led by Yellow Lion, each of them took up a sharp weapon and mounted a gust of violent wind to reach the Leopard's-Head Mountain. There they encountered the powerful odor of fire and smoke and heard the sound of weeping. When they looked more carefully, they found Freaky and Shifty sobbing and crying for their lord.

"Are you the real Freaky Child or the false Freaky Child? snapped the monster-spirit as he walked up to them.

The two fiends fell on their knees. As they kowtowed and tried to hold back their tears, the two fiends said, "How could we be false? Yesterday we took the money to go purchase hogs and sheep. When we got to the main road west of the mountain, we ran into a priest with a hairy face and a thundergod beak. He spat on us once and immediately our legs grew weak and our mouths clamped shut. We could neither talk nor walk. He pushed us over and searched out our silver. He took our tablets, too. Neither of us snapped out of our stupor until just now. When we got home, the smoke and fire had not yet died but all our buildings had been burned out. Because we couldn't see our lord or any of the captains and officers, we stayed here and wept. How did this fire start anyway?"

When he heard this, the monster-spirit could not stop the tears gushing from his eyes. As he stamped the ground with both feet, he railed spitefully, "Baldie! You're so wicked! How could you do such a vicious thing? You have gutted my cave-dwelling, burned my pretty lady to death, and robbed me of all my family and belongings! You kill me! You really kill me!"

The old monster asked Gibbon-Lion to drag him over and said to him, "Worthy grandchild, when things have reached this stage, getting mad won't do you any good. Let's conserve our vitality instead so that we may go seize those monks in the prefectural city."

Refusing to stop his wailing, the monster-spirit said, "Venerable Father! That mountain home of mine wasn't built in a day! Now it's completely wrecked by that baldpate! What do I have to live for?" He struggled up and would have rammed his head against a boulder to kill himself had not Snow Lion and Gibbon-Lion stopped him with their earnest pleadings. After a while, they left the mountain and headed for the city.

When their churning wind and looming fog drew near, the people outside all parts of the capital were so terrified that men and women alike fled into the city with scant regard for their homes or possessions. After they had entered, the gates were shut tightly; meanwhile, someone had sped to the palace to cry, "Disaster! Disaster!" The princes and the T'ang monk were just enjoying breakfast in the Gauze-Drying Pavilion when they heard this report. When they stepped out to inquire, the people said, "A large band of monster-spirits are approaching the city, kicking up sand and stone and belching wind and fog."

"What shall we do?" exclaimed the old prince, horrified.

"Relax, all of you!" said Pilgrim, chuckling. "This must be the monster-spirit from the Tiger's-Mouth Cave who fled in defeat yesterday toward the southeast. Now he has banded together with that so-called Ninefold-Numina Primal Sage to come here. Let us brothers go out to meet them. Order the four gates closed and call up men to guard the city." The prince indeed gave the order for the city gates to be closed and armed men were summoned to ascend the rampart. On the city tower the prince together with his three sons and the T'ang monk made the roll call. Amid fluttering banners that blotted out the sun and cannon fire that filled the sky, Pilgrim and his two brothers left the city midway between cloud and fog to face their enemies. Thus it was that

Affinity's lack had caused wise weapons' loss

And stirred up the demons, their perverse foes.
We do not know how this battle will turn out, and you must listen to
the explanation in the next chapter.

Ninety

Masters and lions,[1] teachers and pupils, all return to the One;
Thieves and the Tao, bandits and Buddhists, quiet
  Ninefold-Numina.

We were telling you about the Great Sage Sun, who went out of the
city with Pa-chieh and Sha Monk. When they met the monster-spirits
face to face, they found them to be a bunch of lions of various colors:
Yellow Lion Spirit led in front, with Suan-i Lion and Elephant-Baiter
on his left, Pai-tsê Lion and Wildcat on his right, Gibbon-Lion and
Snow Lion at the back. In the middle of the group was a nine-headed
lion, and by his side was the fiend, Child Blue Face, holding a brocade
pennant with raised floral patterns. Child Shifty-and-Freaky and
Child Freaky-and-Shifty held high two red banners as they all stood
in an orderly fashion to the north.

Pa-chieh, always foolhardy, walked up to them and began to abuse
them, saying, "You larcenous fiend! Where did you go to collect these
several hairy lumps to come here?"

"You lawless and vicious bonze!" cried the Yellow Lion Spirit, bar-
ing his teeth. "Yesterday three of you attacked one of me, and I was
defeated. Wasn't that enough that you had the upper hand? Why did
you have to be so cruel as to burn down my cave-dwelling, ruin my
mountain home, and harm all my relatives? My animosity toward
you is deep as the sea! Don't run away! Have a taste of your venerable
father's shovel." Dear Pa-chieh! He met the lion with upraised rake.

The two of them had just come together, and no decision could yet
be reached when the Gibbon-Lion, wielding an iron caltrop, and the
Snow Lion Spirit, using a three-cornered club,[2] also advanced to
attack. "Welcome!" shouted Pa-chieh, and on his side, Sha Monk
quickly took out his fiend-routing staff to lend his assistance. Then
Suan-i Spirit, Pai-tsê Spirit, Elephant-Baiter, and Wildcat all surged
forward, and they were met by the Great Sage Sun grasping his golden-
hooped rod. Suan-i used a cudgel, Pai-tsê a bronze mallet, Elephant-
Baiter, a steel lance, and Wildcat a battle ax. Those seven lion-spirits
and these three savage priests thus had quite a battle!

Mallet, cudgel, lance, and three-cornered club,
Four-lights shovel, iron caltrop, and an ax[3] —
Seven lions with seven weapons sharp
Encircle three priests as they roar and shout.
Vicious is the Great Sage's iron rod
And rare among men, Sha Monk's treasure staff.
Pa-chieh, as if plague-ridden, sallies forth
With a radiant muckrake that terrifies.
Back and front they parry as they ply their might;
Left and right they charge for they're all fearless.
Princes on the rampart now lend their strength
By beating gongs and drums to rouse their hearts.
Pressing back and forth they use magic power
And fight till Heaven and Earth grow obscure.

Those monster-spirits fought for half a day with the Great Sage and his two companions, and it became late. Pa-chieh was foaming at the mouth, and his legs were gradually weakening. With a last half-hearted wave of his rake, he turned to flee.

"Where are you off to? Watch out!" cried Snow Lion and Gibbon-Lion. Our Idiot did not dodge quickly enough and received a blow to his spine from the club. As he lay flat on the ground, all he could mumble was "Finished! Finished!" Seizing him by the bristles and the tail, the two spirits hauled Pa-chieh away to show him to the nine-headed lion, saying, "Grandmaster, we've caught one."

They had hardly finished speaking when Sha Monk and Pilgrim, too, were defeated. As the various monster-spirits gave chase together, however, Pilgrim pulled off a bunch of hairs, chewed them to pieces, and spat them out, crying, "Change!" They changed at once to hundreds of little Pilgrims who had Pai-tsê, Suan-i, Elephant-Baiter, Wildcat, and the golden-haired lion-fiend completely surrounded. Sha Monk and Pilgrim then returned and also plunged into the fray. When night fell, they captured Suan-i and Pai-tsê, though Wildcat, Elephant-Baiter, and Golden Hair managed to escape. When the old fiend learned from his grandsons that two lions were lost, he gave this instruction: "Tie up Chu Pa-chieh, but don't take his life. Wait till they return our two lions, and we'll give Pa-chieh back to them. If they're foolish enough to harm our two lions, we'll make Pa-chieh pay with his life." That night the various monsters rested outside the city, and there we shall leave them for the moment.

We tell you now about the Great Sage Sun, who had the two lion-spirits hauled near the city. When the old prince saw them, he ordered the city gates open and sent out some thirty guards with ropes to truss up the lion-spirits and take them inside. After he had retrieved his magic hairs, the Great Sage Sun went with Sha Monk up to the city tower to see the T'ang monk.

"That was quite a fierce battle!" said the T'ang monk. "You think Wu-nêng will live?"

"Relax!" replied Pilgrim. "Since we've caught these two monster-spirits, they will never dare harm him. Let's have these two spirits firmly bound, so that they may be exchanged for Pa-chieh tomorrow."

Kowtowing to Pilgrim, the three young princes said, "When our master first went into battle, we saw only one of you. But when you feigned defeat later, over a hundred of you suddenly appeared. By the time you had the monster-spirits captured and returned to the side of the city, you became a single person once more. What sort of magic was that?"

"On my body," replied Pilgrim with a chuckle, "there are eighty-four thousand hairs. One of them can change into ten of me, and the ten can also change into a hundred. In fact, the transformation can grow to millions and billions. This is the magic of the body beyond the body." One after another, the princes touched their heads to the ground to show their reverence, after which, food was brought up to the tower for them to dine right there. At each crenel on the battlement were set up lanterns and flags, watch rattles, gongs, and drums. The soldiers were told to be diligent in announcing the watches, sending communication arrows, firing cannons, and shouting battle cries.

Soon it was dawn. The old fiend summoned the Yellow Lion Spirit into his presence to give him this plan: "All of you today should exert yourselves and try to capture Pilgrim and Sha Monk. Let me secretly soar through the air to ascend the city and seize their master along with the old prince and his sons. After that, I'll go back first to the Nine-bends Curvate Cave to wait for your triumphal return." Accepting the plan, Yellow Lion led Gibbon-Lion, Snow Lion, Elephant-Baiter, and Wildcat, each grasping his weapon, approached the city to provoke battle, in the midst churning wind and roiling mist. On this side Pilgrim and Sha Monk leaped down from the parapet and shouted, "Lawless fiends! Return our brother Pa-chieh quickly, and we'll spare your lives! Otherwise, we'll pulverize you!"

Those monster-spirits, of course, did not permit further conversation. As they rushed forward, our Great Sage and his companion
both exercised their intelligence to oppose those five lions. This battle
was quite different from that of yesterday:

A vicious, howling wind that scrubs the earth,
A dark, heavy fog that blots out the sky.
Flying dirt and stone dismay ghosts and gods;
Toppling trees and woods alarm tigers and wolves.
The lance is cruel, the ax, luminous;
Caltrop, club, and shovel are all ruthless.
How they wish they could swallow Pilgrim whole!
Or capture alive that little Sha Monk!
This one compliant rod of our Great Sage
Can thrust, turn, toss, and twist most cleverly.
That fiend-routing staff of bold Sha Monk
Has great fame beyond the Divine Mists Hall.
This time in motion's their vast magic power
To sweep away the spirits of the West.

When that battle between those five lion-spirits with coats of more
than one color and Sha Monk and Pilgrim reached its most feverish
moment, the old fiend mounted a dark cloud to ascend the city tower.
All he had to do was to give his heads a shake, and those on the rampart—the various officials and the guards—became so terrified that
they all tumbled down from the battlement. He sped inside the tower,
and with wide-open mouths, caught hold of Tripitaka, the old prince,
and his sons. He then went back to the spot at the north and seized
Pa-chieh with another mouth. He had, you see, altogether nine heads,
and he therefore had nine mouths. One mouth held the T'ang monk,
the second one Pa-chieh, the third one the old prince, the fourth one
the eldest young prince, the fifth one the second young prince, and
the sixth one the third young prince. With six persons in six mouths,
he still had three empty ones! "I'm leaving first!" he roared. When
these five young lion-spirits saw the triumph of their grandmaster,
they became more aggressive than ever.

Pilgrim, too, heard the commotion on the rampart, and he knew at
once that he had fallen for their scheme. Quickly admonishing Sha
Monk to be careful, he ripped off all his hairs from both arms and
chewed them to pieces before spitting them out: they changed instantly into hundreds and thousands of little Pilgrims. As they surged

forward to attack, they dragged down the Gibbon-Lion, captured live Snow Lion, caught hold of Elephant-Baiter, overturned Wildcat, and beat to death Yellow Lion. From this wild melee, however, Child Blue Face, Shifty-and-Freaky, and Freaky-and-Shifty managed to escape.

When the officials on the rampart saw what was happening, they opened the city gates once more and brought out ropes to tie up the five lion-spirits. After they had been dragged inside and before they had even been disposed of, a tearful queen came to bow to Pilgrim, saying, "O divine master! Our Royal Highness, his sons, and your master may have lost their lives! What is to become of this deserted city?"

"Worthy Queen, please do not grieve," said the Great Sage, bowing to her as he retrieved his magic hairs. "Because I have caught these seven lion-spirits, I don't think that my master or His Highness and his heirs will be harmed, even though they have been abducted by the magic of the old monster. Early next morning, we two brothers will go to that mountain. We promise you that we shall capture the old monster and return four princes to you." When the queen and other court ladies heard this, all of them kowtowed to Pilgrim and said, "We pray earnestly that the lives of His Highness and his heirs be preserved and that his royal dominion be established forever!" After their bows, each of them returned to the palace, struggling to hold back her tears.

Pilgrim gave this instruction to the various officials: "Skin that Yellow Lion Spirit that we have beaten to death, and lock up the rest of the six living ones. Bring us some vegetarian food so that we may take a rest after the meal. You can all relax, for I promise you nothing serious will occur."

On the following day, the Great Sage led Sha Monk to mount the auspicious cloud, and in a little while, they arrived at the summit of the Bamboo-Knot Mountain. As they lowered the direction of their cloud to look around, they saw a marvelous tall mountain indeed, with

A row of peaks rugged
And summits most jagged.
Deep in the stream flows a gurgling torrent;
Below the cliff blooms the ornate fragrance.
Winding ranges one after one
And ancient paths encircling.
Truly the cranes arrive to squire the pines,

But the clouds depart to make the rocks forlorn.
The apes face the sunlight to search for fruits,
And deer enjoy the warmth to find their flowers.
The bluebird's reedy songs,
The oriole's murmurous notes.
Spring peaches and plums vie for glamor;
Summer elms and willows both prosper;
Autumn spreads brocades of yellow flowers;
Winter comes with white snow aflutter.
A splendid scene in all four seasons,
As good as the immortal Isle Ying-chou.

As they enjoyed the scenery on the summit, they suddenly caught sight of that Child Blue Face dashing out of a little valley down below, his hand gripping a small cudgel.

"Where do you think you're going?" bellowed Pilgrim. "Old Monkey's here!" The little monster was so terrified that he tumbled down the slope, while the two brothers eagerly gave chase. In a moment, however, Blue Face disappeared. A few steps more brought them to the front of a cave-dwelling, where they found tightly shut two doors of veined rocks. Across the top of the door was a stone placard, with the following inscription in clerkly script: Myriad-Numina Bamboo-Knot Mountain, Nine-Bends Curvate Cave.

The little monster, you see, had dashed in and closed the doors, and had gone to the center of the cave to say to the old monster, "Venerable Father, there are two monks outside again."

The old monster said, "Did your great king and the rest return—Gibbon-Lion, Snow Lion, Elephant-Baiter, and Wildcat?"

"I haven't seen any of them! I haven't seen any of them!" replied the little monster. "Only two monks high on the peak scanning the region. When I saw them, I turned and ran. They chased me back here, and I quickly bolted the door."

On hearing this, the old monster fell silent for a long time; then all at once he shed a few tears. "Woe!" he cried. "My Yellow Lion grand-disciple is dead, and the others have all been taken captive into the city by those priests. How am I to avenge myself?"

Lying on one side, a melancholy Pa-chieh, who had been trussed up along with the T'ang monk, the old prince, and his sons and left there to suffer, was gladdened by this statement of the old monster about his grandsons. "Master, don't be afraid!" he whispered. "And

Your Highness, don't worry! My elder brother has won a victory and caught several monsters. He'll soon find his way here to rescue us." He finished speaking, and then he heard the old monster say, "Little ones, stand guard here. Let me go out and capture those two monks and bring them in here also for punishment."

Look at him! With neither armor on his body nor weapons in his hands, he walked in big strides up to the front, where he could hear the shoutings of Pilgrim Sun. Flinging wide the doors, he did not wait for the exchange of even one word before heading straight for Pilgrim. As Pilgrim wielded his iron rod to meet him, Sha Monk brandished his treasure staff and struck. All the old monster did was to give his head one shake, and eight others heads with open mouths appeared, four on each side. Ever so gently they caught Pilgrim and Sha Monk and brought them inside the cave. "Bring me some ropes!" he cried.

Shifty-and-Freaky, Freaky-and-Shifty, and Child Blue Face were the three who had escaped with their lives the night before. Taking out two ropes, they bound up the priests firmly.

"You wretched ape!" said the old monster. "You've taken my seven grandsons, but I've caught four of you priests and four princes. That should be a fair exchange for my grandsons' lives! Little ones, select some thorny willow canes. Let's give this monkey-head a flogging, so that my Yellow Lion granddisciple may be avenged."

Each picking up a willow cane, those three little monsters began to rain blows on Pilgrim. Pilgrim's body, however, was one that had undergone prolonged cultivation and refinement. The effect of those willow canes on him was no more severe than scratching an itch! No matter how hard they flogged him, he neither showed concern nor made a sound. Pa-chieh, the T'ang monk, and the princes, however, were petrified at the sight. After a little while, even the canes broke from the flogging and had to be replaced.

It went on like this until evening. The blows Pilgrim received were numberless. When Sha Monk saw how long Pilgrim had been beaten, he felt guilty and said, "Let me take a hundred strokes or so for him!"

"Don't be so impatient!" said the old monster. "You'll be beaten tomorrow! Each of you will have your turn!" Horrified, Pa-chieh said, "Then the day after tomorrow will be old Hog's turn!"

The flogging continued for yet another while until it grew dark. "Little one's, let's stop!" cried the old monster. "Light the lamps, and take some food and drink, all of you. I'm going to my brocade den to take a nap. All three of you have suffered before in the hands of these monks, and you should therefore guard them carefully. Wait till tomorrow before we flog them some more."

Moving the lamps over, the three little monsters took up the willow canes and began beating Pilgrim's skull: tick-tick-tock, tock-tock-tick, now fast, now slow, it sounded as if they were beating a rattle. As the night deepened, however, the monsters all fell sound asleep.

Immediately Pilgrim exercised his magic of Passage. He shrank his body and climbed out of the ropes. Having shaken loose his fur and straightened out his clothes, he whipped out his rod from his ear. One wave of it and it acquired the thickness of a bucket and the length of twenty feet. "You cursed beasts!" he said to the three little monsters. "You have beaten your Venerable Father umpteen times, but he hasn't changed a bit. Let your Venerable Father drop this rod on you a little, and see what happens!" Ever so lightly he dropped the rod on those three little fiends, and at once they turned into three meat patties.

Then Pilgrim pulled up the wick in a lamp and began to untie Sha Monk. As he had been hurting from the ropes, Pa-chieh could not refrain from saying in a loud voice, "Elder Brother, my hands and feet are swollen! Why can't you untie me first?" This one yell of Idiot's aroused the old monster, who scrambled up immediately, saying, "Who's untying . . . ?"

When he heard that, Pilgrim blew out the lamp immediately and abandoned Sha Monk. With his iron rod he punched through several doors and escaped. The old monster went out to the center hall and called out: "Little ones, why are the lights out? Has someone escaped?"

He shouted like that once, but no one answered him. He cried again, but still there was no answer. By the time he lit a lamp himself, the first thing he saw were three bloody meat patties on the ground. Then he saw that the old prince, his sons, the T'ang monk and Pa-chieh were still there; only Pilgrim and Sha Monk had disappeared. With a lighted torch, he rushed to the back and front to search for them, and he found Sha Monk sidling along a wall in one of the porches. The old monster grabbed him, threw him on the ground, and tied him up as before. Then he continued to search for Pilgrim. When he saw that several of the doors had been smashed, he knew that Pilgrim had managed to escape. Instead of giving chase, he tried to patch up and repair the doors to guard his property. There we shall leave him for the moment.

We tell you instead about the Great Sage Sun who, having emerged from the Nine-Bends Curvate Cave, went straight back to the Jade-Flower County astride the auspicious cloud. In the air above the city he was met by several local spirits of the region and the tutelary deities of the city, all bowing.

"Why did you all wait until now to come to see me?" said Pilgrim.

"These humble deities," replied the city god, "knew already that the Great Sage had descended upon the Jade-Flower County. Since you have been entertained by a worthy prince, we dared not intrude upon you. Now we have learned that the princes encountered fiends and that the Great Sage is in the process of subduing demons. We have therefore come especially to bow to receive you."

Pilgrim was still annoyed and was beginning to berate them when the Golden-Headed Guardian, the Six Gods of Darkness, and the Six Gods of Light appeared with another local spirit in their custody. As they knelt down, they said, "Great Sage, we have captured this devil-in-the-earth and brought him here."

"Why aren't you all protecting my master at the Bamboo-Knot Mountain?" snapped Pilgrim. "Why are you milling about at this place?"

One of the Gods of Darkness and Light said, "Great Sage, after you had escaped, the monster-spirit re-captured the Curtain-Raising General and had him tied up once more. When we saw how powerful his magic was, we rounded up the local spirit of the Bamboo-Knot Mountain and marched him here. He should know the origin of this monster-spirit. Let the Great Sage question him, so that he may devise the proper means to rescue the sage monk and deliver the worthy prince from his suffering."

Pilgrim was delighted by what he heard. Trembling all over, the local spirit kowtowed and said, "The year before last that old monster descended upon the Bamboo-Knot Mountain. The Nine-Bends Curvate Cave was originally a den for six lions. Since the old monster's arrival, however, the six lions all honored him as their grandsire, who is actually a nine-headed lion. He styles himself the Nine-Numina Primal Sage. If you want to vanquish him, you must go to the Wondrous-Cliff Palace at the East Pole and fetch his master. Only that person and no one else has the power to subdue him."

When he heard this, Pilgrim thought for quite some time, musing to himself: "The Wondrous-Cliff Palace at the East Pole, that's the Salvific Celestial-Honored One of the Great Monad. His beast of burden is precisely a nine-headed lion. In that case . . ." He at once gave this instruction: "Let the Guardian and the Gods of Darkness and Light return with the local spirit to their proper stations to provide secret protection for my master, my brothers, and the princes of the district. The city deities should take up their post to guard the city." The various deities obeyed and left.

Mounting the cloud-somersault, our Great Sage journeyed through the night. By about the hour of the Tiger,[4] he arrived at the East Heavenly Gate, where he ran into Devarāja Virūpākṣa and an entourage of Heavenly guards and *vīra*. They all stopped and, folding their hands in their sleeves to salute him, asked, "Where are you going, Great Sage?"

After returning their salutation, Pilgrim said, "Making a trip to Wondrous-Cliff Palace."

"Why aren't you on your way to the Western Heaven?" asked the devarāja. "Why have you come to the Eastern Heaven?"

"When we arrived at the Jade-Flower County," replied Pilgrim, "we were royally entertained by the prince. His three sons, in fact, took us three brothers in and honored us as teachers of martial arts. Little did we expect that we would end up with a bunch of lion-fiends. I've just found out that the Salvific Celestial-Honored One of the Great Monad at the Wondrous-Cliff Palace is the lion master, and I would like to ask him to subdue the fiend and rescue my master."

"It's precisely because you desired to be someone's teacher,"[5] said the devarāja, "that you got into trouble with a den of lions."

"No doubt that's the reason! No doubt that's the reason!" chuckled Pilgrim. All the soldiers and *vīra* saluted him again with folded hands and stepped aside to let him pass. After the Great Sage entered the East Heavenly Gate, he reached in a little while the Wondrous-Cliff Palace. He saw

Colored clouds in tiers,
Billows of purple mist,
Tiles shimmering in golden flames,
Doors guarded by rows of jade-beasts.
Flowers fill a double arch swathed in red mist;
Tall trees, sun-drenched, are encased in green dew.
Truly myriad gods surround the place
Where all sages flourish.
The buildings are layers of brocade,

All joined through windows and porches,
Watched by an old dragon circling in light
Divine and charged with thick, auspicious air.
This is the realm of everlasting bliss,
The Palace of Wondrous-Cliff.

Inside the gate of the palace stood a divine lad wearing a garment of rainbow hues. When he caught sight of the Great Sage Sun, he went inside to announce, "Holy Father, the Great Sage, Equal to Heaven, who caused great havoc in the Celestial Palace, has arrived."

The Salvific Celestial-Honored One of the Great Monad at once asked his guards and attendants to usher his visitor in. When they entered the palace, the Celestial-Honored One left his lofty lotus throne of nine colors enshrouded in countless beams of auspicious radiance to greet them. Pilgrim bowed low, and the Celestial-Honored One returned his salutation, saying, "Great Sage, we haven't seen you these few years. I heard some time ago that you left the Tao to embrace Buddha in order to escort the T'ang monk to acquire scriptures in the Western Heaven. Your merit and work must have been accomplished."

"Not quite," replied Pilgrim, "but they are near completion. At this moment, however, my accompanying the T'ang monk has taken us to the Jade-Flower County, where the local prince was kind enough to have his three sons take old Monkey and his brothers as teachers of martial arts. New weapons were being forged, using ours as models, but they were stolen by a thief at night. When we looked for them in the morning, we learned that the thief was a golden-haired lion-spirit residing in the Tiger's-Mouth Cave on the Leopard's-Head Mountain north of the city. A ploy of old Monkey got back our weapons, but that spirit banded together with a considerable number of other lion-spirits to brawl with me. In their midst was a nine-headed lion who possessed vast magic powers. He caught with his mouths my master, Pa-chieh, and the four princes and took them to the Nine-Bends Curvate Cave of the Bamboo-Knot Mountain. The next day old Monkey and Sha Monk followed them there, and we too were captured. Old Monkey was bound and beaten by him countless times, but I was fortunate enough to have escaped, using my magic. They are still suffering at that place. Not until I questioned the local spirit of the region did I find out that the Celestial-Honored One happens to be his master. I've come especially to ask you to subdue the monster and grant deliverance."

On hearing this, the Celestial-Honored One immediately ordered his subordinates to fetch the lion page from the lion room and bring him forward for interrogation. The page, however, was sleeping soundly and did not wake up until some of the gods had given him a few shakes. They dragged him up to the center hall, and the Celestial-Honored One asked, "Where's the lion?"

Shedding tears and kowtowing, the page boy could only mutter, "Spare me! Spare me!"

"In the Great Sage Sun's presence you will not be beaten," said the Heavenly-Honored One. "But you'd better confess quickly how you carelessly allowed the nine-headed lion to run away."

"Holy Father," said the page, "the day before yesterday I came upon a bottle of wine in the Hall of Universal Sweet Dew. Not knowing any better, I stole it and drank it, and I fell fast asleep. I must not have locked up the beast properly, and that's why he escaped."

The Celestial-Honored One said, "That wine happened to be a gift of Lao Tzu called Jade Liquid of Transmigration. If you drank it, you'd stay drunk for three whole days. How many days has it been since the lion ran away?"

"According to the local spirit," said the Great Sage, "he descended to earth the year before last. By now it's almost three years."

"Yes! Yes!" said the Celestial-Honored One with a smile. "A day in Heaven is a year in the mortal world." Then he said to the lion page, "Get up. We'll spare you for the moment. Follow me and the Great Sage to the Region Below to retrieve him. The rest of the immortals may go back. There's no need for all of you to accompany us."

The Celestial-Honored One trod the clouds with the lion page and the Great Sage to reach the Bamboo-Knot Mountain, where they were met by the Guardians of Five Quarters, the Six Gods of Darkness and the Six Gods of Light, and the local spirit of the mountain. "You who are supposed to be guardians, has my master been harmed?" asked Pilgrim.

"The monster-spirit," replied the deities, "has been rather upset and has gone to sleep. He has not inflicted punishment on anyone." "After all," said the Celestial-Honored One, "that Child Primal Sage of mine is a true spirit who has attained the Way through prolonged cultivation. One roar of his can reach the Three Sages above and penetrate the Nine Springs down below. He will not take a life casually. Great Sage Sun, please go and provoke battle at his door. Entice him to come out so that I may subdue him."

Hearing this, Pilgrim indeed whipped out his rod and leaped toward the cave's entrance, shouting, "Brazen monster-spirit! Return my people! Brazen monster-spirit! Return my people!" He shouted several times, but there was no answer at all, for the old monster had fallen fast asleep. Growing impatient, Pilgrim wielded his iron rod and fought his way inside, shouting abuses as he moved along. Only then was the old monster roused from his sleep. Startled and enraged, he scrambled up and roared, "To battle!" At once he shook his head and attacked with open mouths.

Pilgrim turned back and leaped out of the cave. The monster-spirit followed him out, crying, "Monkey thief! Where are you going?"

Standing on a cliff, Pilgrim said, chuckling, "You still dare be so audacious and unruly! You have no idea what's coming to you in a moment! Don't you realize that your Venerable Father Master is here?"

The monster-spirit rushed up to the cliff, only to find a Celestial-Honored One reciting a spell and shouting, "Child Primal Sage, I'm here!" The monster recognized his master, and he dared not struggle at all. Falling prostrate on all fours, he could only kowtow repeatedly. From one side the lion page dashed out and, seizing his hair on the neck with one hand, rained blows on his head with the other. "You beast!" he scolded him. "Why did you run away and make me suffer?"

The lion dared neither move nor utter a word. Only when his fist grew tired did the lion page stop punching and put the brocade saddle on. The Celestial-Honored One mounted him, gave the order to leave, and the lion rode the colored clouds to return to the Wondrous-Cliff Palace.

After giving thanks toward the sky, the Great Sage entered the cave. He untied the Jade-Flower prince first, then Tripitaka T'ang, and finally, Pa-chieh, Sha Monk, and the three princes. Together they looted the cave's valuables before stepping outside. Pa-chieh piled up dried wood front and back and started a blaze. The entire Nine-Bends Curvate Cave was reduced to a charred and gutted kiln! Then the Great Sage dismissed the other deities, though he ordered the local spirit to remain there and guard the region. Pa-chieh and Sha Monk were told to exercise their magic and carry the princes back to the prefectural city on their backs, while Pilgrim himself took hold of the T'ang monk by the hands to transport him. In a short while, when the sky darkened, they all arrived at the capital and were met by the queen, the palace ladies, and various officials. Evening maigre was served at once, and they all sat down to enjoy the fare. The elder and his disciples again rested in the Gauze-Drying Pavilion, while the prince retired to the palace. They all had a peaceful night.

The next day the prince ordered another huge vegetarian banquet, for which all the officials of the palace, high and low, gave thanks. Pilgrim also asked the butchers to slaughter the six lions and skin them, as they had done to the yellow lion. Their meat was to be prepared for the people's enjoyment. Delighted by this suggestion, the prince at once gave this command: the meat of one lion was to be saved for the residents of the palace, and that of another would be given to the Administrator of a Princely Establishment and other district officials. The rest of the five lions would be cut into small pieces, about two to three ounces each, and distributed by palace guards to the civilian and military populace in and out of the city, so that they might have a taste of lion meat to calm their fears. All the households thus acknowledged the gift with gratitude.

In the meantime, the ironsmiths had finished forging the three weapons. As they kowtowed to Pilgrim, they said, "Holy Father, our work is done."

"What's the weight of each of the weapons?" asked Pilgrim.

"The golden-hooped rod weighs a thousand pounds," replied one of the ironsmiths. "The nine-pronged rake and the fiend-routing staff both weigh eight hundred pounds."

"All right," said Pilgrim, and he asked the three princes to come out and pick up their weapons.

"Father Prince," said the three princes to the old prince, "today the weapons are perfected." "Because of them," said the old prince, "my sons and I almost lost our lives."

"It was fortunate that the divine master did exercise his magic to have us rescued," said the young princes, "and to have the monstrous deviates dispersed. With all evil consequences removed, we may truly expect a peaceful world of calm seas and clear rivers." At once the old prince rewarded the ironsmiths; then father and sons went to the Gauze-Drying Pavilion to thank the masters.

In order that their journey would not be delayed, Tripitaka urged Pilgrim and his companions to hasten in giving lessons in martial arts to the princes. Right in the palace courtyard, therefore, each of the brothers wielded his weapon and began instructing the princes one by one. In a few days those three princes became thoroughly familiar with their drills and exercises. All the methods of offense and defense, fast and slow, indeed all seventy-two styles of movement that belonged to each weapon were mastered. The three princes, after all, were most determined to learn, and, moreover, the Great Sage Sun had endowed them with divine strength. For this reason they could now raise and move a thousand-pound rod or an eight-hundred-pound muckrake. Compared with the martial arts they formerly practiced by themselves, this was something else indeed! We have a testimonial poem, which says:

Good luck for them has three teachers convened.
Why should martial arts bestir a lion fiend?
The empire's safe when perverts are wiped out;
They yield to one substance and pariahs[6] rout.
Nine[7] fits the principle of primal *yang*;
From such perfection the Tao truly sprang.
A mind informed these teachings e'er release
And grant Jade-Flower lasting joy and peace.

Once more the princes gave a huge banquet to thank their teachers for the instruction. A large platter of silver and gold was also presented as token of their gratitude.

"Take it away! Quickly!" said Pilgrim, laughing. "We are people who have left home. What do we need it for?"

Pa-chieh, sitting to one side, said, "We really can't take the gold and silver. But this robe of mine has been torn almost to shreds by those lion-spirits. If you could provide us with a change of clothing, it would be received as a token of your great love for us." The princes at once asked the tailors to take several bales of blue silk, red silk, and brown silk and, following the styles and colors of what the priests were wearing, make three suits of clothing. The three pilgrims gladly received their gifts and put on their new cassocks of silk before packing to leave.

At this time there was not a single person in and out of the city who did not address them as incarnate arhats or living buddhas. All the streets were filled with the sounds of drums and music and clogged with the colors of banners and pennants. Truly

Outside each household the incense fires burned;
Before each door colorful lanterns turned.

Only after escorting the pilgrims a long distance would the people permit the four of them to resume their journey toward the West. Their departure signaled their escape from the various lions and their devotion to attaining the right fruit. Truly

Without a worry they'd reach Buddha's realm

And, with hearts unfeigned, ascend Thunderclap.

We do not know, however, how great a distance remains for them to reach Spirit Mountain, or when they will arrive, and you must listen to the explanation in the next chapter.

Ninety-one

At Gold-Level Prefecture they watch lanterns on the
    fifteenth night;
In Mysterious Flower Cave the T'ang monk makes a
    deposition.

How should one strive in the practice of Zen?
Cut off quickly the wily horse and ape.
Binding them firmly will five colors beget;
A moment's stop will land you on Three Ways.
If the sovereign elixir's caused to leak,
Then jade nature withers for leisure's released.[1]
Joy, wrath, care, and thought must be swept away:
Like nothingness is wondrous mystery gained.

We were just telling you about the T'ang monk and his three disciples,
who left the Jade-Flower city and proceeded along a path safe and
sound. In truth the region befitted the name of Ultimate Bliss. After
five or six days, they again caught sight of a city.

"What sort of a place is this again?" the T'ang monk asked Pilgrim.

"It's a city," replied Pilgrim, "but the flagpole on the rampart has
no pennant. We can't tell the name of this region. Let's wait till we
get near, and ask."

When they reached the suburb outside the eastern gate, they saw
bustling teahouses and wine shops on both sides of the street, and
flourishing rice markets and oil stores. On the streets there were a few
vagabonds; when they saw the long snout of Chu Pa-chieh, the
gloomy countenance of Sha Monk, and the red-rimmed eyes of Pilgrim
Sun, they had the travelers surrounded. Struggling to get a closer look
at these strange visitors, they nonetheless did not have the courage to
question them. The T'ang monk was so nervous that he was, as it
were, clinging onto his own sweat, for he feared that his disciples
might cause trouble. They walked past several more alley entrances,
but still they had not reached the city. It was then that they came upon
the gate of a monastery with this inscription: Mercy Cloud Temple.

"How about going in there to rest the horse," said the T'ang monk,
"and beg for a meal?"

"Good! Good!" said Pilgrim, and the four of them all walked in. They saw

Noble treasure towers,
Soaring bejeweled thrones,
A Buddha alcove above the clouds
And priestly chambers within the moon.[2]
Misty red swirls about tall pagodas;
Dark green trees enshroud clean praying-wheels.
A true pure land,
A false dragon place,
A Great Hero Hall encased in purple cloud.
Along two porches endless visitors play;
Guests climb a stūpa that's often open.
Incense in the censers is e'er ablaze;
Fragrant lamps nightly on the platforms glow.
When one strikes an abbot hall's golden bell,
Priests on duty will sūtras recite.

As the four of them looked at the place, they caught sight of a priest walking out from one of the corridors. "Master, where did you come from?" he saluted the T'ang monk.

"This disciple happens to be someone who came from the T'ang court of China," replied the T'ang monk. At once the monk fell on his knees to make a bow, so startling the T'ang monk that he hurriedly tried to raise him with his hands. "Abbot," he asked, "why do you honor me with such a grand ceremony?"

Pressing his palms together in front of him, the monk said, "When those people inclined to virtue at our region study the sūtras and chant the name of Buddha, their ardent hope invariably is to find incarnation at your land of China. Just now when I beheld the bearing and clothing of the venerable master, I realized at once that only the cultivation of a previous life could provide you with such noble endowment. It is fitting, therefore, for me to kneel and bow to you."

"I'm terribly embarrassed!" said the T'ang monk with a smile. "This disciple is but a mendicant. What endowment could he claim? The abbot here is able to enjoy a quiet and comfortable existence. That's true blessing!"

The monk thereupon led the T'ang monk to the main hall to worship the images of Buddha. Only after that did the T'ang monk summon his disciples to enter. Pilgrim and his two companions, you see, had been standing with their faces turned away to watch the horse and luggage since their master had begun conversing with the priest. The priest thus did not pay them much attention. Not until they heard their master calling "Disciples!" did they turn around. When the priest saw them, he was so aghast that he cried, "O Holy Father! Why is it that your noble disciples are so ugly?"

"Though they may be ugly," replied the T'ang monk, "they do possess considerable magic power. Throughout our journey I have been quite dependent on their protection."

As they chatted, several more priests walked out to salute them. The one who appeared previously said to the ones who just arrived, "This master is a person who came from the Great T'ang of China. These three are his noble disciples." Both pleased and alarmed, the monks said, "Master, why did you come here from your great nation of China?"

"By the sage decree of our T'ang emperor," declared the T'ang monk, "I am seeking scriptures from the Buddha at Spirit Mountain. Passing through your treasure region, I have come especially to your superior temple, merely to inquire about the place and to beg for a meal. Thereafter we shall leave."

Each one of those monks was delighted. They invited the pilgrims into the abbot's quarters, where there were several more priests conducting business with some donors of a vegetarian feast. One of those monks who walked in first cried, "All of you come and look at people from China. Now we know there are both handsome people and ugly people in China. The handsome is too handsome to be sketched or painted, but the ugly ones are exceedingly bizarre."

Many of those monks and feast donors came to greet them. They then took their seats, and, after tea, the T'ang monk asked, "What is the name of your honored region?"

"Our is the outer prefecture of the Kingdom of India," replied one of the monks, "the Gold-Level Prefecture."

"How far is it from your honored prefecture to the Spirit Mountain?" asked the T'ang monk.

"It is about two thousand miles from here to the capital," said the monk, "and this is a journey we ourselves have taken before. But we have never gone westward to the Spirit Mountain, and, not knowing the distance, we dare not offer you a fraudulent reply." The T'ang monk thanked him.

In a little while, they brought out a vegetarian meal, after which, the T'ang monk wanted to leave. He was, however, detained by the donors and the monks, who said to him, "Please feel free to stay for a couple of days, Venerable Master. Enjoy yourself till we have passed the Lantern Festival. Then you may go."

Somewhat taken aback, the T'ang monk said, "All this disciple knows on the road is that there are mountains and waters. What I fear most is running into fiends and demons. I have quite lost track of time. When is the fine Lantern Festival?"

Smiling, one of the monks said, "The venerable master is preoccupied with the worship of Buddha and the realization of Zen, and that is why you have no concept of time. Today happens to be the thirteenth of the first month. By night the people will be trying out the lanterns. The day after tomorrow is the fifteenth proper. We don't put away the lanterns until the eighteenth or nineteenth. The households of our region here are quite active and fond of excitement. Moreover, our prefect holds the people in great affection. So lanterns and lights will be set up high all over the place, and there'll be music all night long. We have also a Golden-Lamp Bridge, a relic of antiquity but still a prosperous site. Let the venerable fathers stay here for a few days. Our humble monastery can certainly take care of you." The T'ang monk had no choice but to remain.

That night a great salvo of drums and bells could be heard coming from the main hall of Buddha when the faithful and the local residents arrived with their gifts and votive lanterns for Buddha. The T'ang monk and his companions all left the abbot's quarters to watch these lanterns before retiring.

The next day temple priests brought in more food. When they had finished eating, they took a stroll together through the rear garden. A fine place indeed!

The time is the first month;
The season, a new spring.
A fine, wooded garden
Of charms luxuriant.
Rare blooms and plants of four seasons;
Rows upon rows of summits.[3]
Before the steps lovely grasses stir;
On old plum boughs fragrance rises.
The red enters young peach blossoms;

The green returns to fresh willows.
Boast not of Gold-Valley's[4] opulence
Speak not of Felloe-Spring's[5] soft breezes.
Here's one flowing stream
Where wild ducks appear now and then;
We have a thousand bamboos planted
On which the writers make no end of verses.
The peony,
The tree-peony,
The crape flower,
The magnolia—
Their natures have just awakened.
The camelia,
The red plum,
The jasmine,
The most fragrant plant[6]—
They first display their glamor.
Though snow left on shady ledges retains its chill,
Distant trees with mist afloat are brushed with spring.
You see, too, deer glancing at their pond-reflections
And cranes listening to strings beneath the pines.
A few buildings to the east,
A few buildings to the west,
Where guests may come to stay;
A few halls to the south,
A few stūpas to the north,
Where monks in silence meditate.
In the midst of flowers
There are a couple of towers for cultivation,
Their double eaves curving high up;
Amid hills and streams
Are three or four demon-smelting rooms
With neat tables and bright lattices.
Truly a natural place of reclusion,
There's no need to look elsewhere for P'êng and Ying.

After enjoying the garden for a day, master and disciples also looked
at the lanterns in the halls before going to watch the lantern shows.
What they saw were
Cornelian floral cities,

Glass immortal-caves,
Palaces of crystal and mother-of-pearl
Like layers of brocade
And tiers of openwork carvings.
As the star-bridge sways and the cosmos moves,
See how a few flaming trees waver.
Pipes and drums along the six streets,
A bright moon atop a thousand doors,
And scented breeze from all households.
Here and there scorpaenid humps rear up;
There are dragons leaving the ocean
And phoenixes soaring.
Admire both lamplight and moonlight—
What harmonious blend!
Those troops of satin and silk
All enjoy the sounds of pipe and song;
Atop both chariots and horses
There is no end of flower and jadelike faces,
Or of gallant knights,
Or of lovely scenes.

After Tripitaka and the monks had watched the lanterns in the monastery, they also took to the streets of the suburb by the east gate to see the sights. Not until the time of the second watch did they turn back to retire.

The next day the T'ang monk said to the priests, "This disciple once made a vow[7] to sweep a pagoda whenever I came upon a pagoda. Since this day is the fine festival of the first full moon, let me request the abbot to open the pagoda for me to fulfill my vow." The priests accordingly opened the door, as Sha Monk took out the cassock to attend to the T'ang monk. When they reached the first level, the elder put on the cassock to worship Buddha and say prayers. Thereafter he swept out that level with a broom before taking off the cassock to hand back to Sha Monk. He then swept clean the second level and went through each one in that manner until he reached the very top. On each level of that pagoda, you see, there were images of Buddha and open windows. When one level was swept clean, the T'ang monk and his companions would remain a while to enjoy and commend the scenery. By the time the work was done, and they descended from the pagoda, it was already late, and lamps had to be lit.

This was the night of the fifteenth, the first full moon. "Venerable Master," said the priests, "we have been watching the lanterns with you these last two nights in our monastery and in the suburb. Tonight is the festival proper. How about going into the city with us to watch the lanterns there?" In delight the T'ang monk agreed. With the monks of the monastery, he and his three disciples all entered the city. Truly it is

Fifteenth, a lovely night and feast;
Spring hues blend with the first full moon.
Floral lights o'erhang busy shops
As people sing the songs of peace.
You see only bright lights in the six streets and three marts
When a mirror rises in midair.
The moon seems like a silver dish the River God pushed up;
The lights look like brocade carpets woven by divine maidens.
The lights in moonlight
Add one measure of light;
The moon shines on the lights,
Enhancing their brilliance.
There are countless iron chains and star-bridges to see,
And endless lamp wicks and flaming torches to watch.
The snowflake lantern
And the plum-flower lantern
Seem to be chiseled from spring ice.
The silk-screen lantern
And the painted-screen lantern
Are constructed with five colors.
The walnut lantern
And the lily lantern
Hang high on the tower.
The green-lion lantern
And the white-elephant lantern
Frolic high by the awnings.
The little-lamb lantern
And the rabbit lantern
Sparkle beneath the eaves.
The hawk lantern
And the phoenix lantern
Are joined side by side.

The tiger lantern
And the horse lantern
Walk and run together.
The divine-crane lantern
And the white-deer lantern,
These Longevity Star rides on.
The goldfish lantern
And the long-whale lantern,
These Li Po will sit on.
The scorpaenid-hump lantern—
A congregation of immortals.
A revolving-horse lantern—
Where generals do battle.
A thousand households of glittering towers;
Many miles of a world of cloud and smoke.
Over there
Clippety-clop come the jade saddles flying;
Over here
The rumbling wheels of scented chariots pass by.
Look at those in red-trimmed towers:
Leaning on the rails
Behind the screens
Shoulder to shoulder
Pairs and pairs of beauties eager for pleasure.
Or those by the bridge o'er green waters:
Noisily cavorting
All bundled in silk
Besotted and soused
In loud guffaws
Two by two the tourists play in gay garments.
Flutes and drums resound in the whole city;
Pipes and songs rend the air throughout the night.
We have also a testimonial poem, which says:
From fields of brocade comes the lotus song.
To this peaceful region flocks a great throng.
With bright lights and moon on this fifteenth eve,
Rain and wind timely the year will receive.
Since this was precisely the time the nocturnal curfew was to be lifted,
countless people mingled and milled about the place. Some were

dancing, some were walking on stilts, there were people disguised as ghosts, and others riding on elephants—a bunch here and a cluster there. You could hardly watch them all.

When the T'ang monk and the other priests finally made their way to the Golden-Lamp Bridge, they came upon three lamps with bases the size of cisterns. The coverings on top were actually two artificial towered edifices knit in the most elegant and delicate fashion with fine gold threads. Suspended inside the edifices were thin pieces of glass. The light of these lamps could rival the moon's, while their oil emitted powerful aromas.

The T'ang monk turned to ask the priests, "What sort of oil do these lamps use? Why does it have such a powerful, strange fragrance?"

"I should tell you, Venerable Master," replied one of the priests, "about the district behind our prefecture, which is called Compassionate-Heaven. This district covers some two hundred and forty square miles. Supporting the annual land taxes of this district are two hundred and forty so-called oil families. Mind you, the other taxes of the district are manageable, but the ones levied on these families are quite burdensome. Each household, in fact, must spend over two hundred taels of silver on the oil for these lamps, which is no ordinary oil. It is a specially blended fragrant oil, and each tael is worth two taels of silver. Each catty of oil thus would cost thirty-six taels of silver. The cistern of each of those three lamps holds up to five hundred catties, so three lamps would require one thousand and five hundred catties of oil. The fuel itself, therefore, would cost forty-eight thousand taels of silver. Other miscellaneous expenses would push the total sum to over fifty thousand. The lamps, however, can only last three nights."

"How could you burn up so much oil in just three nights?" asked Pilgrim.

The priest answered, "There are forty-nine large wicks in each of the cisterns. They are made of wick-straw tied together and wrapped in fine cotton. Each wick is actually about as thick as a chicken egg, but they can last only through this night. After Father Buddha has revealed himself, the oil will have disappeared by tomorrow evening and the lamps will go dim."

"It must be," giggled Pa-chieh, from the side, "that Father Buddha takes away even the oil!"

"Exactly!" replied the priest. "This has been the belief handed down from antiquity by the people of the entire city. Because the oil dries up, people all say that the Buddhist Patriarch himself has put away the lamps, and that ensures a rich harvest of the five grains. If, however, there is a year when the oil does not dry up, then there will be droughts or poor harvests or wind and rain out of season. That is the reason why all the families feel compelled to make these sacrifices."

As they spoke, the howl of wind could suddenly be heard up in the sky, so terrifying the lamp spectators that they all scattered. The priests, too, found it difficult to stand on their feet. "Venerable Master," they said, "let's go back. The wind has arrived. It must be Father Buddha's auspicious descent, coming here to watch the lamps."

"How do you know it's Buddha coming to watch the lamps?" asked the T'ang monk.

"It's like this every year," replied one of the monks. "Hardly past the hour of the third watch the wind arrives. Knowing that it is the auspicious descent of the various Buddhas, people all get out of the way."

"This disciple," said the T'ang monk, "happens to be a person who thinks of Buddha, who chants the name of Buddha, and who worships Buddha. If there are indeed Buddhas making their descent on this fine occasion, I will certainly pay them homage. Even a small gesture is desirable."

The priests begged in vain for him to leave. In a little while, three figures of Buddha indeed appeared in the wind, coming toward the lamps. The T'ang monk was so astonished that he rushed up to the top of the bridge and fell on his knees to bow to them. Hurrying forward to try to pull him up, Pilgrim shouted, "Master, these are not good people! They have to be monstrous deviates!" Hardly had he finished speaking than the lamp light suddenly grew dim. With a loud whoosh, they scooped up the T'ang monk and left astride the wind. Alas! We do not know

Of which mountain or cave are these real fiends,

False Buddhas who for years have watched the gold lamps.

So terrified were Pa-chieh and Sha Monk that they searched and hollered left and right.

"Brothers!" Pilgrim cried. "No need to call for Master at this place. His extreme pleasure has turned to grief, and Master has been abducted by monster-spirits."

"Holy Father!" said those few frightened monks. "How could you tell that monster-spirits abducted him?"

With a chuckle, Pilgrim said, "All of you are a bunch of mortals. You have no perception all these years, for you were deluded by those monstrous deviates. All you thought of were true Buddhas making their auspicious descent to enjoy these offerings of the lamps. Just now when the wind passed by, those apparitions of Buddha were actually three monster-spirits. Unable to recognize them either, my master dashed to the top of the bridge and immediately bowed down. They managed to dim the lights, took away the oil with some vessels, and even abducted our master. I was a bit slow in getting up there, and that's why the three of them could escape by changing into the wind."

"Elder Brother," said Sha Monk, "what are we going to do, then?"

"No need for hesitation," replied Pilgrim. "The two of you go back to the temple with the rest of them to guard our horse and luggage. Let old Monkey make use of this wind and track them down."

Dear Great Sage! Swiftly mounting the cloud-somersault, he rose to midair and, catching a whiff of putrid odor from that wind, sped toward the northeast. He chased it till dawn, and all at once the wind died down. Then he came upon a huge mountain that appeared most treacherous and truly rugged. Marvelous mountain!

Canyons in layers,
And torrents tortuous.
From sheer cliffs hang vines and creepers;
On hollow heights stand cypress and pine.
The cranes cackle in morning mist
And geese call from the clouds of dawn.
Tall and erect like halberds are the peaks;
Jagged and rough huge boulders pile up.
The summit soars ten thousand feet;
The peak rises in a thousand turns.
Conscious of spring, wild woods and flowers bloom;
Moved by the sights, nightjars and orioles sing.
It may seem lofty and grand,
It's in truth a precipice
That's bizarre, rugged, treacherous, and hard.
Stop and enjoy it, but no man's in sight:
You hear only tigers and leopards growl.
Musk and white deer will wander as they please;
Jade hare and green wolves will come and go.
A deep brook flows out to a thousand miles,

Its eddies gurgling as they strike the rocks.

On the mountain ledge the Great Sage was searching for his way when he caught sight of four persons herding three goats down the western slope and shouting, "Begins Prosperity!" Blinking his fiery eyes with diamond pupils, the Great Sage stared more carefully and perceived that they were the Four Sentinels of Year, Month, Day, and Hour approaching in disguises.

Immediately whipping out his iron rod which, with one wave, attained the thickness of a rice bowl and a length of about twelve feet, the Great Sage leaped down from the ledge and shouted, "Where do you dirty sneaks think you are going?"

When the Four Sentinels saw that he had penetrated their disguises, they were so terrified that they shooed away the goats and changed back into their true forms. Stepping to the side of the road to make their bows, they said, "Great Sage, please forgive us!"

"Because I haven't asked for your services for a long time," said Pilgrim, "you think Old Monkey has become indulgent. Every one of you, in fact, has turned slothful, since you haven't shown up once to present yourself to me. What have you got to say to that? Why aren't you all giving secret protection to my master? Where are you off to?"

"Your master has backslid a little," replied one of the Sentinels. "Because he has been indulging in pleasures at the Mercy Cloud Temple of the Gold-Level Prefecture, his extreme prosperity has produced negativity, and the fullness of his happiness has become grief. Now he has been captured by some monstrous deviates, but at least he has the Guardians of Monastery at his side to give him protection. We know that the Great Sage has been giving chase all through the night. Fearing that the Great Sage might not know his way in this mountain forest, we have come especially to make it known to you."

"If you wanted to do that," said Pilgrim, "why did you do it in such a secretive manner? Herding three goats and shouting this and that— what for?"

The Sentinel said, "We brought along these three goats in order to symbolize the saying, 'With three *yang* begins prosperity.'[8] That symbol should break up and dispel your master's misfortune."

Pilgrim was angrily threatening to beat them, but when he heard their intention, his anger turned to delight, and he decided to spare them. Putting away his rod, he said, "Is this the mountain where the monster-spirit lives?"

"Indeed, it is," replied the Sentinel. "This is the Green Dragon Mountain, in which there is a Mysterious Flower Cave. Inside the Cave are three monster-spirits: the eldest is named Great King Cold-Deterrent; the second, Great King Heat-Deterrent; and the third, Great King Dust-Deterrent. They have lived here for a thousand years. Since their youth they have been fond of eating that specially blended fragrant oil. When they became spirits in years past, they came here disguised as the images of Buddha to dupe the officials and people of the Gold-Level Prefecture into setting up these golden lamps and using that specially blended fragrant oil as fuel. By mid-month of the first month every year, they would assume the forms of Buddha to collect oil. When they saw your master this year, they recognized that he had the body of a sage monk and they abducted him into their cave. In no time they will want to cut off your master's flesh and sauté it with that fragrant oil for food. You must work quickly to rescue him."

On hearing this, Pilgrim dismissed the Four Sentinels and went past the mountain ledge to search for the cave. He had not gone more than a few miles when he came upon a huge boulder, beneath which was a stone house with two half-closed stone doors. By the side of the door was a stone tablet with these six words: Green Dragon Mountain, Mysterious Flower Cave. Not daring to walk straight in, Pilgrim stood still and called out, "Monstrous fiend, send my master out quickly!"

With a loud creak the doors were flung open and out ran several bull-headed spirits. Rather glumly and stupidly, they asked, "Who are you that you dare make all these noises here?"

"I'm the senior disciple of the sage monk, Tripitaka T'ang," replied Pilgrim, "who was sent by the Great T'ang in the Land of the East to seek scriptures. We passed through the Gold-Level Prefecture, and while we were watching the lanterns, my master was kidnaped by your household's demon chieftains. Return him early, and I'll spare your lives! If you don't, I'll overturn your den and reduce you spirits to pus and blood!"

On hearing this, those little monsters hurried inside to say, "Great Kings, disaster! Disaster!" The three old monsters had brought the T'ang monk deep into the cave, where without any further interrogation they were ordering their subordinates to have him stripped and scrubbed clean by water pumped from the well. They were making plans, too, to cut him or dice him so that his flesh could be sautéed for food with that specially blended fragrant oil. When they suddenly heard this announcement of disaster, Number One was astonished enough to ask why.

"In front of our main door," replied one of the little monsters, "there is a monk with a hairy face and a thundergod beak. He claims that our Great Kings have abducted his master to this place and demands that he be sent out at once. Then he'll spare our lives. But if we don't do that, he will overturn our den and reduce us all to pus and blood."

All alarmed by what they heard, the older monsters said, "We just caught this fellow, and we haven't yet had a chance to question him about his name or where he came from. Little ones, put his clothes back on him and bring him over here for us to interrogate him. Who is he anyway, and where does he come from?"

The monsters rushed forward and untied the T'ang monk. After they had dressed him, they pushed him before the seats of the old monsters. Trembling all over, the T'ang monk knelt down and could only cry, "Great Kings, spare me! Please spare me!"

"Where did you come from, monk?" asked the three monster-spirits in unison. "When you saw the forms of Buddha, why did you not step aside? Why did you impede our cloudy path?"

As he kowtowed, the T'ang monk said, "This humble cleric is some-one sent by the Throne of the Great T'ang in the Land of the East, someone on his way to seek scriptures from the Buddhist Patriarch at the Great Thunderclap Monastery in the Kingdom of India. Because I went to the Mercy Cloud Temple at the Gold-Level Prefecture to beg for a meal, I was asked by the priests of that temple to stay through the Lantern Festival and enjoy the lights. When the Great Kings re-vealed themselves in the forms of Buddha on the Golden-Lamp Bridge, this humble cleric, who has only fleshly eyes and mortal frame, none-theless has the desire to worship Buddha whenever he beholds his image. That is the reason why I impeded your cloudy path."

"It is a long way from your Land of the East to this place," said those monster-spirits. "How many people are there altogether in your entourage? Tell us quickly, and we'll spare your life."

"My secular name is Ch'ên Hsüan-tsang," replied the T'ang monk, "and I have been raised a monk in the Gold Mountain Monastery since my youth. Later I was appointed a monk official by the T'ang emperor at the Temple of Great Blessing. On account of prime minister Wei Chêng's execution of an old dragon of the Ching River in his dream, the T'ang emperor made a tour of Hades and then returned to life.

To provide redemption for the lost souls of darkness, he convened the Grand Mass of Land and Water and graciously selected me as the chief priest in charge of the ceremony and the exposition of scriptures. It was at that time that the Bodhisattva Kuan-shih-yin revealed herself to enlighten this humble cleric, announcing to us that there were three canons of true scriptures at the Great Thunderclap Monastery in the Western Heaven. These scriptures, she said, could provide deliverance for the deceased and enable them to ascend to Heaven. The T'ang emperor therefore sent this humble cleric to fetch the scriptures. He bestowed on me the style, Tripitaka, and the surname of T'ang. That's why people all address me as Tripitaka T'ang. I have three disciples. The first one's surname is Sun, and his names are Wu-k'ung and Pilgrim. He is actually the converted Great Sage, Equal to Heaven."

Greatly startled by the last name they heard, the monsters said, "Is this Great Sage, Equal to Heaven, the person who caused great disturbance in the Celestial Palace five hundred years ago?"

"Indeed, he is," said the T'ang monk. "My second disciple has the surname of Chu, and his given names are Wu-nêng and Pa-chieh. He is the incarnation of the Marshal of Heavenly Reeds. My third disciple has the surname of Sha, and his given names are Wu-ching and Monk. He is the Curtain-Raising General who has descended to Earth."

When they heard this, all three of those monster-kings were alarmed. "It's a good thing we haven't eaten him yet," they said. "Little ones, let's chain the T'ang monk in the rear. Let's wait till we capture his three disciples so that we can eat them together." Then they called up a herd of spirits, all mountain buffaloes, water buffaloes, and yellow buffaloes. Each grasping a weapon, they walked out of the front door where with a trumpet signal, they waved their banners and rolled the drums.

In full battle dress, the three monsters went out the door also and cried, "What person is bold enough to shout and yell in front of our door?" Half concealed up on the boulder, Pilgrim stared at them. The monster-spirits all had

Colored faces, round eyes
And two rugged horns;
Four ears[9] most pointed,
And sparkling intelligence;
A body full of patterns like a colored painting

Or a large piece of brocade with floral designs.
The first one
Wears on his head a cap of warm fox fur;
His face is steamy and covered with hair.
The second one
Has draped on himself thin gauze flaming red,
His four patterned hooves resemble chunks of jade.
The third one
Has a mighty roar like a thunderclap,
His jutting teeth seem sharper than silver picks.
Each one bold and fierce,
They hold three kinds of arms:
One uses a battle-ax,
And one, a huge cutlass.
But the third one, look again!
Across his shoulders rests a knotty cane.

He saw, moreover, many monster-spirits: tall and short, fat and thin, old and young, they were all bull-heads or demonic fiends holding spears and clubs. There were three huge banners on which these titles were clearly inscribed: Great King Cold-Deterrent, Great King Heat-Deterrent, and Great King Dust-Deterrent.

After he had stared for a while, Pilgrim could wait no longer. He went forward and shouted: "You lawless thieves and fiends! Do you recognize old Monkey?"

"So you are the Sun Wu-k'ung who disturbed Heaven!" snapped one of the monsters. "Truly,

Though your face is preceded by your fame,
A god who sees you would die with shame!
You are nothing but a puny ape!"

"You oil-stealing thieves!" scolded Pilgrim, enraged. "You greasy-mouthed fiends! Stop babbling! Return my master instantly!" He rushed forward and struck out with his iron rod. Those three old monsters met him swiftly with three kinds of weapon. That was some battle in the fold of the mountain!

Battle-ax, cutlass, and a knotty cane
The Monkey King dares oppose with one rod.
The fiends—Cold-, Heat-, and Dust-Deterrent—now
Recognise the Great Sage Equal to Heaven's name.
The rod rises to frighten gods and ghosts;

The ax and cutlass madly fly and slash.
What an image of true void magically fused,
Which resists three monstrous, false Buddha-forms!
Those three felons of this year who wet their noses with stolen
    oil
Are eager to seize the priest commissioned by a king.
This one for his master fears not mountains or distance;
Those ones for their mouths' sake want annual offerings.
Bing-bang: only ax and cutlass are heard.
P'i-p'o: now only the rod makes the sounds.
Charging and bumping, three go against one;
Each parries and blocks to display his might.
From morning they fight till the time of night.
Who knows who will suffer and who will win?

With that single rod of his Pilgrim Sun fought the three demons for some one hundred and fifty rounds, but no decision had been reached when the sky began to darken. After a rather feeble blow of his knotty cane, the Great King Dust-Deterrent leaped across the battle line to wave his banner. Immediately that band of bull-headed fiends surged forward and had Pilgrim surrounded in the middle. Each wielding a weapon, they madly attacked him.

Seeing that the tide was turning against him, Pilgrim mounted the cloud-somersault and fled in defeat. Those monsters did not pursue him; calling back their subordinates, they prepared dinner instead and ate it. A little monster was ordered to give a bowlful to the T'ang monk, who would not be prepared for cooking until Pilgrim was captured also. Because he had always kept a vegetarian diet and because he was racked by sorrow, the master did not even allow the food to touch his lips. For the moment we shall leave him there, weeping.

We tell you instead about Pilgrim, who mounted the clouds to return to the Mercy Cloud Temple. "Brothers!" he called out.

Pa-chieh and Sha Monk were waiting for him. When they heard the call they came out together to meet him, saying, "Elder Brother, why did you go for a whole day before you came back? What actually happened to Master?"

"I followed the scent of the wind to give chase last night," replied Pilgrim with a smile, "and by morning, I arrived at a mountain. The wind vanished, but luckily the Four Sentinels reported to me that the mountain was called the Green Dragon Mountain. In the mountain was a cave with the name of Mysterious Flower, with three monster-spirits living inside it. They had the names of Great King Cold-Deterrent, Great King Heat-Deterrent, and Great King Dust-Deterrent. They had been stealing oil from this place for years, falsely assuming the form of Buddha to deceive the officials and people of the Gold-Level Prefecture. This year they happened to bump into us, and, not knowing any better, went so far as to abduct Master. After old Monkey had acquired this information, I ordered the Sentinels to give secret protection to Master while I provoked battle before the door. Those three fiends came out together, and they all seemed like bull-headed demons. One used a battle-ax, one a huge cutlass, and the third a cane. Behind them came a whole den of bull-headed demons, waving their banners and rolling their drums. Old Monkey battled the three chieftains for an entire day, and we fought to a draw. Then one of the monster-kings waved his banner, and the little monsters all came at me. When I saw that it was getting late, I feared that I could not prevail and I somersaulted back here."

"It must be demon kings from the Capital of Darkness causing trouble," said Pa-chieh.

"What led you to make such a guess?" asked Sha Monk.

Chuckling, Pa-chieh said, "Elder Brother told us that these were all bull-headed demons. That's how I know."

"No! No!" said Pilgrim. "As old Monkey sees the matter, they are spirits of three rhinoceroses."

"If they are," said Pa-chieh, "let's capture them and saw off their horns. They are worth quite a few taels of silver!"

As they were speaking, the monks of the temple came to ask whether Father Sun would like dinner. "If it's convenient, I'll have some," replied Pilgrim. "If not, I can pass."

"Father Sun has fought for an entire day," said a priest. "Aren't you hungry?"

"Just a day or so, how could I be hungry?" said Pilgrim, chuckling. "Old Monkey once had no taste of food or drink for five hundred years!" Those priests, however, thought he was only joking and presently they brought him food. After he had eaten, Pilgrim said, "Let's get ready to retire. Tomorrow we can all go together to do battle. When we capture the monster-kings, we can rescue Master."

"What are you saying, Elder Brother?" said Sha Monk. "As the proverb has it, 'A pause makes one smarter!' If that monster-spirit could not sleep tonight and brought harm to Master, what would we do then? I think it's better for us to try to rescue Master now, and catch them off their guard. Further delay may prove to be a mistake."

When he heard that, Pa-chieh became more spirited. "Brother Sha is quite right!" he said. "We should take advantage of this moonlight to go subdue the demons." Pilgrim agreed and gave this instruction to the temple priests: "Guard our luggage and our horse. Wait till we capture the monster-spirits and bring them back here. We shall prove to the magistrate of this prefecture that they are specious Buddhas. The levy of oil can then be eliminated to bring relief to all the common folk of the region. Won't that be nice?" The priests obeyed. The three pilgrims at once mounted their auspicious clouds to leave the city. Truly

Shiftless and slothful, Zen nature's confused;

Fated for dangers, the mind of Tao's obscured.

We do not know whether they will meet victory or defeat when they get there, and you must listen to the explanation in the next chapter.

Ninety-two

Three priests fight mightily at Green Dragon Mountain;
Four Stars help to capture rhinoceros fiends.

We were telling you about the Great Sage Sun, who trod the wind and mounted the clouds with his two brothers and headed toward the northeast. Soon they arrived at the entrance to the Mysterious Flower Cave in the Green Dragon Mountain. As soon as they had dropped down from the clouds, Pa-chieh wanted to tear down the doors with his rake. "Wait a moment!" said Pilgrim. "Let me go in and find out whether Master is dead or alive. Then we can do battle with them."

"These doors are tightly shut," said Sha Monk. "How can you get in?"

"With my magic power, of course," replied Pilgrim.

Dear Great Sage! Putting away his rod, he made the magic sign with his fingers and recited a spell, crying, "Change!" At once he changed into a little firefly, truly quick and agile. Look at him!

Wings outstretched he soars like a comet.
"Grasses decayed become fireflies."[1]
One should not take lightly such magic change:
His is a nature that endures.
Flying near the stone door to look
Through the drafty crack on one side,
With one leap he reaches the quiet yard
To spy on the demons' conduct.

He flew inside and immediately found several buffalo sprawling all over the place. Snoring thunderously, they were all fast asleep. Even when he reached the center hall, he did not come across any activity. The doors on all sides were closed, and he had no idea where the three monster-spirits were sleeping. Passing through the hall, he headed for the rear, his tail glowing, and he heard the sound of weeping. There he discovered the T'ang monk, who had been chained to a pillar in a back room. As Pilgrim flew quietly up to him, he heard his master sob out:

276

Since leaving Ch'ang-an o'er ten years ago,
Mountains and streams I've passed in bitter woe.
Happy to find one gala in the West,
To reach at Gold-Level the Lanternfest,
I cannot discern the lamps' false Buddha-forms,
For tribulations are my poor life's norms.
If my good pupils come in strong pursuit,
Let their heroic powers soon bear fruit!

On hearing this, Pilgrim was filled with delight and at once spread his wings to fly in front of his master.

"Ah!" said the T'ang monk, wiping away his tears. "The West is truly different! This is only the first month, a time when most insects are just beginning to stir. How can there be fireflies already?"

Unable to contain himself, Pilgrim called out, "Master, I'm here!"

"Wu-k'ung," said the T'ang monk, delighted, "I was just saying, how can there be fireflies in the first month. So, it's you!"

"O Master!" said Pilgrim as he changed back to his original form. "Because you could not distinguish the true from the specious, you have caused such delay in your journey and wasted so much effort. I shouted at you repeatedly, trying to tell you that these were not good people, but you were already making your bows. Those fiends were allowed to dim the lamps, steal the specially blended fragrant oil, and even kidnap you. I instructed Pa-chieh and Sha Monk to remain in the monastery to guard our belongings. I myself followed the scent of the wind here. I didn't know, of course, the name of this region, but luckily the Sentinels came to report that this was the Mysterious Flower Cave of the Green Dragon Mountain. Yesterday I fought with those fiends until nightfall and then went back to tell my younger brothers what had happened. We didn't sleep, but we all came here instead. Fearing that it's not easy to do battle deep in the night, and not knowing either how Master is faring, I used transformation to get in here to do a bit of detection."

Highly pleased, the T'ang monk said, "So, Pa-chieh and Sha Monk are outside?"

"Yes, they are," replied Pilgrim. "Just now old Monkey saw that all the monster-spirits had fallen asleep. Let me open the lock, bash down the door, and lead you out." The T'ang monk nodded his head to thank him.

Using his lock-opening magic, Pilgrim brushed the instrument with his hand, and the lock snapped open at once by itself. As he led his master out, he suddenly heard one of the monster-kings calling out from one of the chambers by the side of the main hall, "Little ones, shut the doors tightly, and be careful with the candles and torches. How is it that there is no patrol or watch announcement? Why aren't the rattles sounded?"

That bunch of little fiends, you see, had been fighting strenuously all day and had therefore all fallen asleep. They were awakened only by these words of the old monster. When the rattle sounded, some of them picked up their weapons, struck up a gong, and headed for the rear. They ran smack into both master and disciple.

"My good monk!" shouted the little monsters in unison. "You may have twisted open the lock, but where do you think you're going?"

Without permitting further explanation, Pilgrim whipped out his rod, which, with one sweep, attained the thickness of a rice bowl. He struck, and immediately slew two of them with one blow. The rest of the little monsters abandoned their weapons and dashed back to the center hall. Hammering on the door of the bedroom, they shouted: "Great Kings! It's bad! It's bad! The hairy-faced monk has killed right in our house!"

Scrambling to their feet when they heard this, the three fiends cried, "Seize him! Seize him!" So terrified was the T'ang monk that his arms and legs turned numb.

Unable to care for his master any longer, Pilgrim wielded his rod and charged ahead. Those little monsters were in no way able to block him or stop him; he struck down a few here, pushed over several there, and escaped after smashing through several doors. "Brothers, where are you?" he cried as he emerged.

With upraised rake and staff, Pa-chieh and Sha Monk were waiting. "Elder Brother," they said, "how are things?" Thereupon Pilgrim gave a thorough account of what had taken place after he had entered the cave through transformation—how he had freed his master and begun to slip out when the monsters discovered them, and how he had to leave his master behind and fight his way out. We shall leave them for the moment.

The monster-kings, having captured again the T'ang monk, had him chained as before. Gripping their cutlass and ax, with torches ablaze, they asked, "How did you open the lock? How did that monkey get in here? Confess at once, and we'll spare your life! If you don't, we'll carve you in two!"

Trembling all over, the T'ang monk fell on his knees and said, "Father Great Kings, my disciple Sun Wu-k'ung knows seventy-two ways of transformation. Just now he changed into a little firefly and flew in here to try to rescue me. We didn't expect to wake up the Great Kings or to run into the little Great Kings. Not knowing any better, my disciple wounded two of them. When they all shouted with upraised weapons and lighted torches, he abandoned me and ran out."

Laughing uproariously, the three monster-kings said, "It's a good, thing we woke up! We haven't let *you* escape!" They ordered their little ones to shut the doors tightly front and back, and they were to do this in complete silence.

"If they shut the doors tightly without making a noise," said Sha Monk, "they might secretly be plotting against our master. We should get moving!"

"You are right," said Pilgrim. "Let's knock down the door quickly!" Our Idiot at once sought to display his magic powers. Raising his rake, he delivered a blow with all his strength and smashed the stone doors to pieces.

"You oil-stealing fiends!" he cried in a loud voice. "Send out my master instantly!"

Those little monsters were so terrified that they rolled back inside to report, "Great Kings, it's bad! It's bad! Our front doors have been smashed by those priests."

Greatly annoyed, those three monster-kings said, "These fellows are impudent indeed!" They immediately sent for their armor and, grasping their weapons, led the little monsters out the door to battle. It was then about the hour of the third watch, and a radiant moon in the sky made it almost bright as day. Once outside, they wielded their weapons without exchanging one word. On this side, Pilgrim went for the battle-ax, Pa-chieh opposed the huge cutlass, and Sha Monk met the large cane. This was a magnificent battle!

Three Buddhist priests
With rod, staff, and rake,
And three monstrous demons with added spunk.
From battle-ax, cutlass, and knotty cane
One hears only the sound of wind and dust.

The first few rounds stir up such grievous fog;
Colored mists soar and scatter thereafter.
Around the body the rake's movements churn;
Still more praiseworthy's the brave iron rod.
A world's rarity is the treasure staff,
To which the fiends are too stubborn to yield.
The blade of the ax is both bright and sharp;
The cane is knotty and covered with dots.
The cutlass shimmers like a single-leaf door,
Opposed no less by priestly magic might.
On this side they strike fiercely for their master's life;
On that side they claw at faces to keep the T'ang monk.
The ax and the rod both strive hard to win;
The rake and the cutlass both clash and meet.
The knotty cane and the fiend-routing staff
Go back and forth to display their power.

Three priests and three fiends fought for a long time, and neither side proved to be the stronger.

Then that Great King Cold-Deterrent shouted, "Little ones, come up here!" The various spirits rushed up with their weapons, and almost immediately Pa-chieh tripped and fell to the ground. Tugging and pulling, several water-buffalo spirits hauled him inside the cave and tied him up. When Sha Monk saw that they had lost Pa-chieh to a bellowing herd of bulls, he struck weakly at the Great King Dust-Deterrent and then turned to flee. He was, however, thrown face first to the ground by the spirits swarming over him. Struggling in vain to get up, he too was taken captive and tied up. Pilgrim knew then that it would be difficult for him to continue fighting by himself; mounting the cloud-somersault, he managed to escape.

At the sight of Pa-chieh and Sha Monk who were brought before him, the eyes of the T'ang monk brimmed with tears. "What a pity," he said, "that you two have also fallen into the clutches of these vicious hands! Where's Wu-k'ung?"

"When Elder Brother saw that we were captured," replied Sha Monk, "he fled."

"If he escaped," said the T'ang monk, "he most certainly went somewhere to seek help. But I wonder when we might go free." Master and disciples were overcome by sadness, and we shall leave them for the moment.

We tell you now about Pilgrim, who mounted his cloud-somersault to return to the Mercy Cloud Temple. As the priests there met him, they asked, "Have you rescued Father T'ang?"

"It's hard to do that!" said Pilgrim. "Very hard indeed! Those monster-spirits had vast magic powers. We three brothers fought those three for a long time. Then they summoned the little monsters to capture Pa-chieh first and seize Sha Monk afterward. Old Monkey was lucky enough to escape."

Greatly frightened, the priests said, "If someone like you, Holy Father, who could mount the clouds and ride the fog, still could not arrest them, the old master will certainly be harmed."

"Not necessarily!" replied Pilgrim. "My master himself enjoys the secret protection of the Guardians of Monastery, the Guardians of Five Quarters, and the Six Gods of Darkness and Light. Then, too, he once tasted the Grass of the Reverted Cinnabar.[2] I doubt that his life will be harmed. It's just that the monster-spirits are quite able, which makes it necessary for old Monkey to seek help in Heaven. You all must take good care to guard the horse and the luggage."

Even more intimidated, the priests said, "Can Holy Father go up to Heaven?"

With a chuckle, Pilgrim said, "The Celestial Palace used to be my homestead, in those years when I was the Great Sage, Equal to Heaven. Because I disrupted the Festival of Immortal Peaches, I was subjugated by our Buddha. I had no choice but to escort the T'ang monk in his quest for scriptures, using my merit to atone for my sins. Throughout the journey, I have been assisting the right by dispelling the deviates. It is my master's lot, however, that he should suffer this ordeal, something none of you know anything about." These words moved the priests to kowtow and worship. Stepping out, Pilgrim gave a loud whistle and at once vanished.

Marvelous Great Sage! He soon arrived at the West Heavenly Gate, where he ran into the Gold Star Venus conversing with the Devarāja Virūḍhaka and the Four Spirit Officers Yin, Chu, T'ao and Hsü. When they saw Pilgrim arrive, they hurriedly saluted him and asked, "Where's the Great Sage going?"

"As the guardian of the T'ang monk," replied Pilgrim, "I have reached the Compassionate Heaven District of the Gold-Level Prefecture, which is located on the eastern border of the Kingdom of India. My master was asked by the priests of the Mercy Cloud Temple to stay and enjoy the Lantern Festival. When we went to see the Golden-Lamp Bridge, we saw three golden lamps, in fact, which used as fuel a specially blended fragrant oil. Though that oil has the worth of some fifty thousand taels of white gold, it is nonetheless presented for the enjoyment of some Buddhas who make an auspicious descent every year. As we were looking at those lamps, three images of Buddha indeed appeared. Not knowing good or ill, my master immediately rushed up to the top of the bridge to make his bow, while I was trying to tell him they were no good. But they had already dimmed the lamps and abducted both the oil and my master in a gust of wind. I set off in pursuit of the wind and by dawn came upon a mountain. The Four Sentinels reported to me that it was the Green Dragon Mountain. The Mysterious Flower Cave of that mountain had three fiends with the names of Great King Cold-Deterrent, Great King Heat-Deterrent, and Great King Dust-Deterrent. Old Monkey quickly demanded my master's return at their door, fought with the monster-spirits, but did not gain the upper hand. Then I used transformation to gain entrance. When I saw that my master was chained but unharmed, I freed him and tried to lead him out. But we were detected, and I had to flee. Thereafter, Pa-chieh and Sha Monk joined me to wage a bitter battle with them, which ended with the capture of my two brothers. For this reason, old Monkey has come to request the Jade Emperor's assistance in locating their origin and in bringing them to submission."

"If the Great Sage had already fought with them," said the Gold Star, chuckling sardonically, "couldn't he tell where they came from?"

"Of course! Of course!" replied Pilgrim. "I could tell they were a herd of bovine spirits. But because of their great magic powers, they are difficult to subdue quickly."

The Gold Star said, "Those are indeed three rhinoceros spirits. Because their bodily designs bear the patterns of Heaven, long years of cultivation have wrought immortality for them, so that they too, are able to soar on the clouds and tread on the fog. Those fiends also have a penchant for cleanliness. Invariably offended by their own reflection, they would want to leap into water to take a bath. They have various names, too: like female rhinoceros,[3] male rhinoceros, bull rhinoceros, striped rhinoceros, barbarian-hat rhinoceros,[4] to-lo rhinoceros,[5] and Heaven-reaching patterned rhinoceros. They are all endowed with a single aperture, triple hair, and two horns. When they move through rivers and seas, they are able to open a path in the water. As for your Cold-Deterrent, Heat-Deterrent, and Dust-Deterrent, they are so named because of certain precious vital forces stored in their horns. That's why they have given themselves such titles as Great King so-and-so. If you want to catch them, you must seek help from the Four Wood-Creature Stars. Their mere presence will bring these beasts to submission."

Bowing hurriedly, Pilgrim asked, "And who are the Four Wood-Creature Stars? I beg Longevity to tell me plainly."

"These stars," replied the Gold Star with a smile, "are stationed at that part of the universe just outside the Dipper Palace. When you have memorialized to the Jade Emperor, you will learn the truth." After folding his hands in front of him to indicate his gratitude, Pilgrim went inside the Heavenly Gate.

In a moment, he reached the lower level of the Hall of Perfect Light, where he met first with Ko, Ch'iu, Chang, and Hsü, the Four Heavenly Preceptors. "Where are you heading?" they asked.

"Recently we arrived at Gold-Level Prefecture," replied Pilgrim. "Because my master has loosened slightly his hold on the nature of Zen, he was abducted by monstrous demons while watching the lights during the Lantern Festival. Old Monkey cannot bring them to submission, and I have come especially to make this known to the Jade Emperor and request assistance."

The Four Preceptors led Pilgrim immediately into the Hall of Divine Mists to present his memorial. After the exchange of greetings and a complete rehearsal of what took place, the Jade Emperor was about to issue a decree to call up some celestial warriors. Pilgrim went forward and said, "Just now when old Monkey arrived at the West Heavenly Gate, Star Longevity told me that those fiends were rhinoceroses who had become spirits. Only the Four Wood-Creature Stars are able to bring them to submission." The Jade Emperor at once ordered Heavenly Preceptor Hsü to go to the Dipper Palace and summon the Four Wood-Creature Stars to descend with Pilgrim to the Region Below.

When they arrived outside the palace, the Twenty-Eight Constellations were there to meet them. "By the sage decree," said the Heavenly Preceptor, "I am to command the Four Wood-Creature Stars to descend to the Region Below with the Great Sage Sun in order to subdue certain monsters." Immediately Horn the Wood Dragon,

Dipper the Wood Unicorn, Straddler the Wood Wolf, and Well the Wood Hound stepped forward to answer the call. "Great Sage Sun," they said, "where do you want us to go to subdue monsters?"

"So, it's you four!" said Pilgrim, laughing. "That old Longevity is so cryptic that I can't understand him! If he had told me that I should see the Four Woods of the Twenty-Eight Constellations, I would have come directly to issue the invitation. There would have been no need for any imperial decree."

"How can you say that, Great Sage?" said the Four Woods. "Without the decree, which one of us dares leave his station? Where is this place you want us to go to? Let's get there quickly."

"It's a spot northeast of the Gold-Level Prefecture," replied Pilgrim, "at the Mysterious Flower Cave in the Green Dragon Mountain. We have some rhinoceroses there who have become spirits."

"If rhinoceroses have become spirits," said Dipper the Wood Unicorn, Straddler the Wood Wolf, and Horn the Wood Dragon together, "you don't need all of us. Just ask Constellation Well to go with you. He can climb mountains to devour tigers, and go down to the seas to catch rhinoceroses."

"These are no moon-gazing rhinoceroses!" said Pilgrim. "They are ones who have attained the Way through prolonged cultivation, all enjoying the age of a thousand years. We have to have the four of you, and please do not refuse. If only one of you went along with me, you might not be able to catch them. Wouldn't that be a waste of our efforts again?"

"Look at the way you people talk!" said the Heavenly Preceptor. "The decree orders all four of you to go. How could you not go? Let's start flying at once, so I can go back to make my report." Thereupon the Heavenly Preceptor took leave of Pilgrim and left.

"There's no need for you to wait any longer," said the Four Woods. "You go provoke battle first and entice them to come out. We'll then attack."

Rushing forward, Pilgrim shouted, "You oil-stealing fiends! Return my master!" The doors, you see, had been smashed by Pa-chieh, but now they had been boarded up with planks by the little monsters. When they heard Pilgrim reviling them outside, they dashed in to report, "Great Kings, the monk Sun is reviling us outside!"

"He has already fled in defeat," said Dust-Deterrent. "Why is he returning a day later? Could it be that he has found some help somewhere?"

"Who's afraid of any help he might get?" said Cold-Deterrent. "Bring our armor quickly. Little ones, make sure that you surround him this time and don't let him get away."

Not knowing any better, that herd of spirits all walked out of the cave, all holding spears and knives, waving banners, and rolling drums. "Aren't you afraid of a beating, ape? You dare show up again?" they snapped at him.

Now the word "ape" was most irksome to Pilgrim. Clenching his teeth in fury, he raised the iron rod to strike. The three monster-kings ordered the little monsters to fan out and had Pilgrim entirely surrounded. On this side, however, the Four Wood-Creature Stars all brandished their weapons and shouted, "Cursed beasts, don't you dare move!"

When those three monster-kings saw the Four Stars, they naturally became frightened. "It's bad! It's bad!" they all cried. "He has found our conquerors! Little ones, run for your lives!" With loud snorts and bellows, all the little monsters changed back into their original forms: they were all mountain-buffalo spirits, water-buffalo spirits, and yellow-buffalo spirits, madly stampeding all over the mountain. The three monster-kings, too, revealed their true forms. When they lowered their two hands, they had four legs once more. Their hooves thundering like iron cannons, they fled toward the northeast, closely pursued by the Great Sage leading Well the Wood Hound and Horn the Wood Dragon. Dipper the Wood Unicorn and Straddler the Wood Wolf, however, remained on the eastern slope, where they succeeded in either beating to death or capturing live all the rest of the buffalo spirits stranded on the summit, in the stream, or in the valley. Then they proceeded to the Mysterious Flower Cave and freed the T'ang monk, Pa-chieh, and Sha Monk.

Recognizing the two Stars, Sha Monk bowed with his companions to thank them. "How did the two of you manage to come and rescue us?" he asked.

"We were ordered here by the Jade Emperor's decree to bring those fiends to submission and rescue you," replied the two Stars, "after the Great Sage Sun presented a memorial."

"Why, then," asked the T'ang monk, shedding tears again, "didn't my disciple Wu-k'ung come here?"

"Those three old fiends happen to be three rhinoceroses," said the Star. "When they saw us, they fled for their lives toward the northeast. The Great Sage Sun led Well the Wood Hound and Horn the

Wood Dragon to give chase. Having mopped up the herd of buffalo, we two came here especially to free the sage monk." The T'ang monk again touched his forehead to the ground to thank them. Then he prostrated himself once more to thank Heaven.

Raising him, Pa-chieh said, "Master, excessive ceremony becomes insincerity. There's no need for you to keep on bowing. The Four Star Officers have done this partly because of the imperial decree of the Jade Emperor, and partly because of their regard for Elder Brother. We may have done away with the various fiends, but we have yet to find out whether those old monsters have been brought to submission. Let us take out some of the valuables in this place and then tear down the cave so that they will be permanently uprooted. Afterward we should return to the temple to wait for Elder Brother."

"Marshal Heavenly Reeds is quite right," said Straddler the Wood Wolf. "You and the Curtain-Raising General should protect your master and return to rest in the temple. Let us go to the north-east to fight."

"Exactly! Exactly!" said Pa-chieh. "You two must join them in pursuit. You must exterminate all of the monsters before you go back to report to the Throne." The two star officers at once left in pursuit.

Ransacking the cave, Pa-chieh and Sha Monk took out a pile of valuables—all coral, cornelian, pearls, amber, ornamental gems, precious stones, fine jade, and gold. They asked their master to sit on the mountain ledge before starting a fire that had the entire cave reduced to ashes. Only then did they help the T'ang monk find their way back to the Mercy Cloud Temple. Truly,

"Good's limit begets evil,"[6] the classics say.
Fair fortune ends in mishap? Well it may!
Zen nature's confused for love of floral lights;
Pretty scenes have led the mind of Tao astray.
The great elixir you must always guard;
One slip and you're rewarded with dismay.
Never slacken your firm and tight control.
A little indolence brings on disarray.

We'll speak no more for the moment about those three, who returned to the temple with their lives. Let us tell you instead about Dipper the Wood Unicorn and Straddler the Wood Wolf, those two star officers, who mounted the clouds and pursued the fiends toward the northeast. They looked this way and that in midair but could see no one. Then they looked toward the great Western Ocean and caught sight of the Great Sage Sun in the distance, hollering above the water. Lowering the direction of their clouds, the two of them said, "Great Sage, where have the fiends gone?"

"Why didn't the two of you join us in pursuit?" asked Pilgrim angrily. "Why do you wait till now to ask your addle-headed questions?"

"When I saw that the Great Sage with Well and Horn had defeated the fiendish demons," said Dipper the Wood Unicorn, "I thought that you would surely capture them. We two, therefore, made a clean sweep of the other monster-spirits, and then entered the Mysterious Flower Cave to rescue your master and brothers. We ransacked the mountain, burned down the cave, and entrusted your master to the care of your two brothers, who were going to bring him back to the Mercy Cloud Temple in the city. When we saw, however, that you did not return after all this while, we found our way here."

Moved to delight and gratitude by these words, Pilgrim said, "In that case, you have achieved merit. Thanks for all your trouble! Thanks for all your trouble! Those three monstrous demons, however, crawled into the ocean after we chased them here. Well and Horn went after them, but they told old Monkey to remain by the shore to stand guard. Since the two of you have arrived, you can head them off here. Let old Monkey go in too."

Dear Great Sage! Gripping his iron rod and making the magic sign with his fingers, he opened up a pathway in the water and went into the depths of the ocean. There he found those three monstrous demons waging the most bitter battle with Well the Wood Hound and Horn the Wood Dragon. Leaping near, he shouted, "Old Monkey's here!"

Those monster-spirits were already hard pressed when they had to confront the two star officers. When they heard Pilgrim's cry, they turned immediately and fled for their lives toward the center of the ocean. The horns on the fiends' heads, you see, were excellent instruments for dividing the water. All you could hear were a loud splatter as they knifed through the billows, with the Great Sage Sun and the two star officers hard on their heels.

We tell you now that in the Western Ocean, there were a yaksa and a seaman out on patrol. When they saw from a distance the rhinoceroses opening up the water, and, moreover, when they caught sight of the Great Sage Sun and the two celestial constellations, whom they recognized, they hurried to the Water Crystal Palace to report to the dragon king. "Great King," they said, somewhat apprehensively, "there are three rhinoceroses being chased by the Great Sage, Equal to Heaven, and two celestial constellations!"

On hearing this, the old dragon king, Ao-shun, summoned Prince Mo-ang and said to him, "Call up the aquatic soldiers at once! It must be that Cold-Deterrent, Heat-Deterrent, and Dust-Deterrent, those three rhinoceros spirits, have offended Pilgrim Sun. Since they have now arrived in our ocean, we should give Sun some armed assistance." This order immediately made Ao Mo-ang call up the troops.

In an instant, tortoises, sea-turtles, sea-dragons, breams, carps, shrimp soldiers, and crab privates all gave their battle cries and rushed out of the Water Crystal Palace, each wielding spear or sword, to block the path of the rhinoceros spirits. Unable to advance, the spirits retreated hurriedly, only to find the Great Sage closing in with Well and Horn, the two stars. They became so flustered that they were no longer able to stay together as a herd. Scattering in three directions, each tried to flee for his life.

Soon Dust-Deterrent was surrounded by the old dragon king and his troops. Delighted by what he saw, the Great Sage Sun cried, "Hold it! Hold it! We want him alive! We don't want to catch a carcass!" Hearing this, Mo-ang led his troops to rush forward and pull Dust-Deterrent down. An iron hook was thrust through his nose and then he was hog-tied.

Then the old dragon king gave the command for his troops to track down the other two spirits and lend assistance to the star officers for their capture. When the young prince led his troops forward, they saw Well the Wood Hound had changed into his original form. He had Cold-Deterrent pinned down and was, in fact, devouring him with great bites. "Constellation Well! Constellation Well!" cried Mo-ang. "Don't bite him! The Great Sage Sun wants him alive, not dead!" He shouted several times, but the monster's neck had already been bitten through.

Mo-ang ordered the shrimp soldiers and crab privates to haul the dead rhinoceros back to the Water Crystal Palace, while he and other soldiers set off in pursuit again with Well the Wood Hound. They ran right into Horn the Wood Dragon, who was chasing Heat-Deterrent back toward them. Ordering the tortoises and turtles to fan out, Mo-ang led his troops to encircle the spirit completely. "Spare my life!

Spare my life!" the fiend could only say. Well the Wood Hound walked forward and grabbed one of his ears. Taking away his cutlass, the star officer said, "We're not going to kill you. We'll turn you over to the Great Sage Sun for his disposal."

They all lowered their weapons and went back to the Water Crystal Palace, crying, "We've caught them all!"

Pilgrim saw that one of the spirits had been beheaded; still dripping blood, the corpse lay on the ground. Another was pushed to his knees, his ear still grasped by Well the Wood Hound. As he walked forward to look more carefully, Pilgrim said, "It wasn't a blade that cut this head off!"

"If I hadn't yelled out," said Mo-ang, chuckling, "Star Officer Well would have devoured the body as well!"

"It's all right," said Pilgrim. "Let's saw off his two horns and skin him. We'll take those things along, but the meat will be left here for the enjoyment of the worthy dragon king and his prince."

A rope was threaded through the iron hook in the nose of Dust-Deterrent, so that Horn the Wood Dragon could lead him. The same treatment was given Heat-Deterrent, and Well the Wood Hound held onto the rope. "Let's bring them up to see the chief of the Gold-Level Prefecture, so that he can make a thorough investigation of how they have impersonated Buddha to hurt the people all these years. Then we'll decide what to do with them." All of them agreed.

They took leave of the dragon king and his prince and left the Western Ocean, leading the two rhinoceroses. After rejoining Straddler and Dipper, the two stars, they mounted the cloud and fog to return to the Gold-Level Prefecture. Treading the auspicious luminosity, Pilgrim cried aloud in midair: "Chief of the Gold-Level Prefecture, subordinate officials, and all you people of this region, hear me! We are sage monks sent by the Great T'ang in the Land of the East to seek scriptures in the Western Heaven. The creatures who pretended to be various Buddhas making their auspicious descent and who demanded sacrifices of the golden lamps each year from the households of this district and prefecture are actually these rhinoceros fiends. When we passed through here and went to look at the lamps on the night of the fifteenth, these fiends abducted both my master and the lamp oil. I, therefore, asked the gods of Heaven to bring them to submission. We have now cleaned up their mountain cave, and all the monstrous demons have been exterminated. From now on your district and

prefecture should not make any sacrifice of the golden lamps, for it
only taxes the people and drains their wealth."

Inside the Mercy Cloud Temple, Pa-chieh and Sha Monk had just
escorted the T'ang monk through the gate. When they heard Pilgrim
speaking up in midair, they abandoned their master and their luggage
to mount the wind and cloud and rise to the sky. When they questioned him, Pilgrim said, "One has been bitten to death by Constellation Well, but we have taken along its skin and the sawed-off horns.
The two captured alive are here."

"We might as well push these two down to the city for the officials
and the people to see," said Pa-chieh, "so that they'll know that we
are sages and deities. Moreover, we must trouble the four star officers
to lower their clouds to the ground and go with us to the prefectural
hall for the disposal of these fiends. The truth and their guilt have been
firmly established. There's nothing more we should discuss!"

"Of late," said one of the four stars, "Marshal Heavenly Reeds
seems to be quite knowledgeable about principles and shows good
understanding of the law. That's marvelous!"

"Being a priest for some years has taught me a few things!" replied
Pa-chieh.

So the various deities pushed the rhinoceroses toward the earth.
When they all descended to the prefectural residence on a bouquet of
colored clouds, the officials of this district and prefecture along with
the populace in and out of the city were so terrified that each household set up incense tables and bowed to receive the gods from Heaven.
In a little while, the priests of the Mercy Cloud Temple could be seen
entering the prefectural residence also, carrying the elder in a palanquin. When he met Pilgrim, he thanked him profusely.

"I was beholden to the noble Constellation officers," said the T'ang
monk, "for having us rescued. But not having seen my worthy disciple has caused me unending concern. Now I truly rejoice in your
return in triumph. I would like to know, however, where you chased
these fiends before they were captured."

"Since I took leave of my honored master day before yesterday,"
replied Pilgrim, "old Monkey ascended to Heaven to make his investigation. The Gold Star Venus was kind enough to reveal to me that
these monstrous demons were actually rhinoceroses, and that I
should solicit the help of the Four Wood Creature Stars. Immediately
I memorialized to the Jade Emperor, who gave his permission and his

decree for the stars to descend to the cave. We fought there and they fled. Dipper and Straddler, the two Constellations, kindly rescued you, while old Monkey joined Well and Horn, the two other Constellations, to pursue the monsters. When we reached the Great Western Ocean, we were also indebted to the assistance of the dragon king, who sent his son to help us with his troops. That's why we were able to capture them and bring them back for trial." The elder could not stop his thanksgiving and commendation. They also saw the magistrate of the district and his various subordinate officials, who were all burning tall precious candles and filling their braziers with incense as they bowed to the sky.

After a little while, Pa-chieh became so aroused that he whipped out the ritual razor. With one stroke he cut off the head of Dust-Deterrent and with another, the head of Heat-Deterrent. Then he took up a saw to saw off their four horns. The Great Sage Sun was even more resolute. He at once gave this order: "Let the four star officers take these four rhinoceros horns up to the Region Above and present them as tribute to the Jade Emperor when you hand back the imperial decree. As for the two horns we brought along, we shall deposit one at the prefectural hall, so that it may be used as a perpetual witness to posterity that the lamp-oil levy has been eliminated. We ourselves will take along one horn to present to the Buddhist Patriarch at the Spirit Mountain." The four stars were enormously pleased. Bowing immediately to take leave of the Great Sage, they mounted the colored clouds to go back.

The chief official, however, would not permit the master and his three disciples to leave. He ordered a huge vegetarian banquet, and asked various village officials to bear the visitors company. Meanwhile, he issued a public proclamation informing the civil and military population that no golden lamps are permitted for the following year, and that the necessity for oil purchases levied on the big households was forever removed. The butchers, too, were told to slaughter the two rhinoceroses; their hides were to be treated and dried so that they could be used to make armor, while their meat was distributed to both officials and the common people. In addition, he appropriated some of the funds already collected for oil purchases to buy land from the people. A temple commemorating the four stars subjugating the monsters was to be erected, along with living shrines to the T'ang monk and his three disciples. Placards with proper inscriptions were set up, so that their good deeds could forever be transmitted and grate-fully acknowledged.

Since they could not leave at once, master and disciples made up their mind to enjoy themselves. Each of those two hundred and forty lamp-oil households took turns to entertain them; after a banquet was given by one family, another would be offered by a different house-hold without pause. Pa-chieh was determined to have complete satis-faction. Stuffing up his sleeve a few of those treasures that he had looted from the monsters' cave, he used them as tips for each of the vegetarian banquets. They lived there thus for over a month, and still they could not set out on their journey. Finally, the elder gave this instruction: "Wu-k'ung, take the rest of the precious jewels and give them all to the priests of the Mercy Cloud Temple as a token of our thanks. Let's not tell those big households, but let's slip away to-morrow before dawn. If we indulge in pleasure like this, our enter-prise of scripture-seeking will be delayed, and I fear that we shall offend the Buddhist Patriarch and bring on further calamities. That will be most inconvenient." Pilgrim carried out his master's instruc-tions one by one.

By the hour of the fifth watch next morning he was already up, and at once asked Pa-chieh to prepare the horse. Having enjoyed his food and drink in great comfort, our Idiot slept so soundly that he was still half-dazed when he said, "Why prepare the horse so early in the morning?"

"Master tells us to get moving!" snapped Pilgrim.

Rubbing his face, Idiot said, "That elder should behave himself! All two hundred and forty of those big households have sent us invita-tions, but we've managed to enjoy a full meal barely thirty times. Why does he want to make old Hog endure hunger so soon?"

On hearing this, the elder scolded him, saying, "Overstuffed coolie! Stop babbling! Get up quickly! If you keep up this ruckus, I'll ask Wu-k'ung to knock out your teeth with his golden-hooped rod!"

When Idiot heard that, he became completely flustered. "This time Master has changed!" he cried. "Usually he cares for me, loves me, and, knowing that I am stupid, protects me. Whenever Elder Brother wants to hit me, he pleads for me. Why should he turn so vicious today as to want to beat me?"

"Because Master's offended by your gluttony," said Pilgrim, "which has delayed our journey. Hurry up! Pack the luggage and get the

horse ready. You'll be spared a beating!" As our Idiot was truly fearful
of being beaten, he leaped up and put on his clothes. Then he shouted
at Sha Monk: "Get up quickly! A beating's on its way!"

Sha Monk, too, leaped up, and each of them finished his preparation. Waving his hand, the elder said, "Quiet! Let's not disturb the
temple priests." He mounted the horse hurriedly. After opening the
gate, they found their way and left. As they went forth this time, it
was truly like

Opening the jade cage to let the phoenix out,

Or breaking the gold lock to set the dragon free.

We do not know how those households would react by morning, and
you must listen to the explanation in the next chapter.

Ninety-three

At Jetavana Park he asks the aged about the cause;

At the Kingdom of India he sees the king and meets his mate.

Memory's awakening has to be love;
Leniency will surely beget mishap.
For what reason does discernment distinguish three images?
Merit done returns you to the primal sea.
Whether you become an immortal or buddha,
You must prepare yourself accordingly:
Be clean, pure, and removed from dust entirely.
Fruition yields ascent to the Region Above.

We were telling you about the priests in the temple, who discovered by dawn that Tripitaka and his disciples had vanished. "We didn't detain them," they all said, "we didn't take leave of them, and we didn't beg them! And that's how we allowed a living bodhisattva to walk away before our very eyes!"

As they were saying this, a few members of the wealthy households in the south suburb arrived to deliver their invitations. Clapping their hands, the various priests said, "We were caught off-guard last evening, and they all mounted the clouds and left in the night." The people all bowed to the sky to express their gratitude. Because of what the monks had said, however, the entire population of the city—officials and commons—all learned of it. They at once requested the wealthy households to purchase the five beasts, flowers, and fruits to sacrifice at the living shrine as an expression of their gratitude. Of this we shall speak no more.

We tell you instead about the T'ang monk and his disciples, who fed on the wind and slept by the waters as they journeyed peacefully for over half a month. One day they found themselves again before a tall mountain. Growing apprehensive, the T'ang monk said, "Disciples, with that tall rugged mountain before us, we must be careful!"

Laughing, Pilgrim said, "This road taking us near the land of Buddha surely does not harbor any monster or deviate. Master, you should relax and not worry."

"Disciple," said the T'ang monk, "it may be true that the land of Buddha is not far away. But remember what the temple priests told us the other day: the distance to the capital of the Kingdom of India is still some two thousand miles. I wonder how far have we gone already."

"Master," said Pilgrim, "could it be that you have quite forgotten again the *Heart Sūtra* of the Crow's Nest Zen Master?"

Tripitaka said, "That *Prajñā-pāramitā* is like a cassock or an alms bowl that accompanies my very body. Since it was taught me by that Crow's Nest Zen Master, has there been a day that I didn't recite it? Indeed, has there been a single hour that I didn't have it in mind? I could recite the piece backward! How could I have forgotten it?"

"Master, you may be able to recite it," said Pilgrim, "but you haven't begged that Zen Master for its proper interpretation."

"Ape-head!" snapped Tripitaka. "How dare you say that I don't know its interpretation! Do you?"

"Yes, I know its interpretation!" replied Pilgrim. After that response, neither Tripitaka nor Pilgrim uttered another word.

At their sides, Pa-chieh nearly collapsed with giggles and Sha Monk nearly broke up with amusement. "What brassiness!" said Pa-chieh. "Like me, he began his career as a monster-spirit. He wasn't an acolyte who had heard lectures on the sutras, nor was he a seminarian who had seen the law expounded. It's sheer flimflam and pettifoggery to say that he knows how to interpret the sūtra! Hey, why is he silent now? Let's hear the lecture! Please give us the interpretation!"

"Second Elder Brother," said Sha Monk, "do you believe him? Big Brother is giving us a nice tall tale, just to egg Master on his journey. He may know how to play with a rod. He doesn't know anything about explaining a sūtra!"

"Wu-nêng and Wu-ching," said Tripitaka, "stop this claptrap! Wu-k'ung's interpretation is made in a speechless language. That's true interpretation."

As master and disciples conversed like that, they managed to cover quite a distance and walk past several mountain ridges. Then they came upon a huge monastery by the side of the road. "Wu-k'ung, that's a monastery ahead of us," said Tripitaka. "Look at it. Though

Not overly big or small,

It has the roof of glazed green tiles;
Half old and half new.
It's enclosed with red eight-word brick walls.[1]
Vaguely one can see the canopies of green pines,
Aged things of who knows how many hundred or thousand
    years that have lived till now;
And one can hear a stream's soft murmur,
A waterway dug out in some distant dynasty that has still
    remained.
On the gates
'Gold-Spreading Monastery' in large letters;
On a hanging plaque
'The Ruins of Antiquity' is inscribed."

Pilgrim replied that indeed he too saw that it was the Gold-Spreading
Monastery, and Pa-chieh said the same thing.

"Gold-Spreading, Gold-Spreading," mused Tripitaka as he rode,
"could this be the territory of the Kingdom of Śrāvasti?"

"This is quite strange, Master!" said Pa-chieh. "I have followed you
now for several years, and I have never known you to recognize the
way before. Today you seem to know where you are."

"It's not quite like that," replied Tripitaka. "It's just that in studying
the sūtras I have frequently read this account, which tells of the
Buddha's experience in the Jetavana Park of the city, Śrāvasti. The
park was said to be something that the Elder Anāthapiṇḍika wanted
to purchase from Prince Jeta, so that it could be used as the place for
Buddha to lecture on the sūtras. The prince, however, said, 'My park
is not for sale. The only way you can buy it is for you to cover the
whole park with gold. When Elder Anāthapiṇḍika heard this, he took
gold bricks and spread them throughout the park. Only then did he
succeed in purchasing the Jetavana Park from the prince and in inviting the World-Honored One to expound the Law. When I saw the
Gold-Spreading Monastery just now, I thought this could be the one
described in the story."[2]

"How fortunate!" said Pa-chieh, chuckling. "If indeed it's the one
in the story, we should go and dig up a few bricks to give to people."
They all laughed at this for a while before Tripitaka dismounted.

When they entered the monastery, they discovered sitting by the
main gates a few cartfuls of people—some luggage toters, some cart
pushers, and some with bags on their backs. Some were sleeping and

others were chatting when they caught sight of master and disciples. The handsome features of the elder along with the hideous ones of his disciples made the people somewhat fearful, and they all stepped aside for the pilgrims to pass through. Fearing that they might stir up trouble, Tripitaka kept calling out, "Gently! Gently!" and all his disciples seemed to be behaving themselves.

After passing through the Vajra Hall, they were met by a priest whose whole bearing seemed quite devout. Truly

His face like a full moon shone;
His body was the wisdom-tree.
His wind-swept sleeves hugged his staff
And sandals trod the pebbled path.

Tripitaka saluted the moment he caught sight of him, and the priest hurriedly returned his greeting, saying, "Master, where do you come from?"

"This disciple is Ch'ên Hsüan-tsang," replied Tripitaka, "who has been sent by the decree of the Great T'ang emperor to go worship Buddha in the Western Heaven and seek scriptures. Our journey takes us past your treasure monastery, and I have taken the liberty of visiting you to ask for one night's lodging. We'll leave tomorrow."

"Our humble monastery," said the priest, "is inhabited frequently by visitors from all over the world for as long as they please. The elder, moreover, is a divine monk from the Land of the East, and it will be our very good fortune to serve you." Tripitaka thanked him, and then asked his three companions to follow him. They went past the winding corridor and the donation boxes to reach the abbot's quarters. After exchanging greetings with the abbot, they took their seats proper to hosts and guests. Pilgrim and his two brothers, too, sat down with hands lowered at their sides.

We tell you that when the monastery had heard the news of scripture priests sent by the Great T'ang in the Land of the East, all the monks—whether they were old or young, long-term residents or temporary guests, elders or altar boys—came to present themselves. After tea had been offered, a vegetarian meal was served.

Our elder presently was still reciting his grace, but Pa-chieh was impatient enough to send the buns, vegetarian foods, and vermicelli soups tumbling down his throat. The abbot's quarters by now were filled with people; the more intelligent ones were admiring the features of Tripitaka, but the sportier persons were all staring at the way

Pa-chieh ate. As Sha Monk was rather observant, he saw immediately what was happening and furtively gave Pa-chieh a pinch, saying, "Gently!"

Pa-chieh became so exasperated that he yelled, "Gently! Gently! But my stomach's empty!"

Chuckling, Sha Monk said, "Second Elder Brother, you may not realize this. There are many so-called gentlemen in the world, but when it concerns the stomach, they are no different from you and me." These words quieted Pa-chieh, while Tripitaka said a short grace to end the meal. After the eating utensils had been removed, Tripitaka thanked his hosts.

One of the priests of the monastery inquired about the history of the Land of the East. When Tripitaka spoke of certain historical ruins, he in turn asked for the reason for the name of the Gold-Spreading Monastery. That priest replied, "This originally was the Monastery of the Anāthapiṇḍika Garden in the Kingdom of Śrāvastī. It also goes by the name of the Jetavana Park. Because the Elder Anāthapiṇḍika spread gold bricks on the ground to enable the Buddha to expound the sūtras, the name was changed again to the present one. About a generation ago, this whole region was the Kingdom of Śrāvastī, and Elder Anāthapiṇḍika was living here at the time. Our monastery originally was the elder's Jetavana Park, and that is why the full name should be Benefactor-of-Orphans Gold-Spreading Monastery. Behind our monastery we still have the foundation of the Jetavana Park. In recent years, a great rainstorm would on occasion wash out some gold or silver or pearls. Those lucky enough would be able to pick them up."

"So it's not a false rumor but the truth!" said Tripitaka. Then he asked again, "When I entered your treasured monastery just now, I saw inside the twin corridors by the gate many merchants with their mules and horses, their luggage and carts. Why are they staying here?"

"Our mountain here is named the Hundred-Legs Mountain," replied the priest. "In previous years it had been quite safe. Recently, however, we don't quite know what has taken place, but it may be that the seasonal cycles have produced a few centipede spirits, which have frequently injured people on the road. Though the wounds they inflict may not be lethal, they have certainly inhibited the travelers' movement. Beneath our mountain is a pass by the name of Cock-Crow.

People dare not walk through it until the cock has crowed. Because it's getting late now, those merchants you saw don't want to take an unnecessary risk. So they use our humble monastery for lodging, and they'll leave after the cock has crowed."

"We, too, will wait till the cock crows before we leave," said Tripitaka. As they chatted, more vegetarian food was brought in, so that the T'ang monk and his disciples dined again. Afterwards, Tripitaka and Pilgrim went out for a leisurely stroll to enjoy a bright moon in her first quarter. A workman approached them and said, "Our venerable father teacher would like to meet the visitors from China."

Turning quickly, Tripitaka saw an old monk, a bamboo staff in his hand, who saluted him, saying, "Is this the master who has come from China?"

"I dare not accept such honor," replied Tripitaka, returning his salutation, as the old monk began to compliment him effusively.

"What is the old master's lofty age?" he asked.

"I have passed my forty-fifth year in vain," said Tripitaka, "and may I ask what is the honorable age of the old abbot?"

With a chuckle, the old monk said, "Rather fruitlessly I have exceeded the venerable master's age by a sexagenary cycle."

"You're a hundred and five years old now," said Pilgrim. "Can you tell how old *I* am?"

"Though the countenance of this master is aged," said the old priest, "your spirit is most clear. My eyes are quite dim in the moonlight, and it's hard for me to tell your age right away." After talking for a while, they went to look at the rear corridor. "Just now the old foundation of the Jetavana Park was mentioned," said Tripitaka. "Where exactly is it?"

"Just beyond our rear gate," replied the old monk, and asked that it be opened immediately. All they saw was a vacant lot with a few piles of rubble remaining as the foundation of the walls. Pressing his palms together, the elder sighed and said,

The good giver, Sudatta, I call to mind;
With jewels and gold he relieved poor mankind.
For all times Jetavana has its fame.
With which arhat can we the elder find?

They all walked slowly, enjoying the sight of the moon. Having gone out of the rear gate, they reached a terrace where they sat for a while. Suddenly they heard the sound of weeping. Tripitaka listened

attentively, and found that the person weeping was also making
protest, something about her parents not comprehending her pain. So
moved was he by the words that he himself began to shed tears also.

"Who is this person grieving here?" he turned to ask the other
monks. On hearing this question, the old monk ordered the other
priests to go back first to make tea. After everyone had left, he at once
bowed low to Tripitaka and Pilgrim. Raising him, Tripitaka said, "Old
abbot, why are you doing this?"

"Since this disciple has now exceeded a hundred years of age,"
replied the old monk, "he is somewhat knowledgeable in human
affairs. In the quiet hours of meditation, moreover, he has seen a few
visions. And that is why this disciple can perceive that the venerable
master and his disciple are quite different from other people. For only
this young master here can bring to light this grievous matter."

"Let's hear you tell us what the problem is," said Pilgrim.

The old monk said, "Exactly on this day a year ago, your disciple
was just in the midst of meditation on the dialectical relation between
our nature and the moon[3] when a soft breeze brought to me the
sounds of grief and protest. I descended from my couch to go to the
foundation of the Jetavana Park to look around. There I found a pretty,
comely girl. I asked her: 'What family do you belong to? Why are you
here?' The girl replied, 'I'm the princess of the King of India. I was
enjoying the sight of flowers beneath the moon when I was blown
here by a strong gust.' Immediately I had her locked up in an empty
room, which I sealed with bricks until it looked like a prison. There
was only a small hole left in the door, through which one could pass
a rice bowl. The next day I told this story to the other priests—that I
had imprisoned a monstrous deviate. Since we priests were men of
mercy, I said, I would not take its life, and I would give the prisoner
two meals of coarse rice and tea daily for sustenance. The girl was
clever enough to understand my intentions. Fearing that she might be
violated by the priests, she pretends to be mad, sleeping in her own
piss and lying in her own shit. During the day she babbles all the time
and puts on a dumb, stupid look. In the quiet of the night, however,
she weeps and yearns for her parents. Several times I myself have
tried to enter the city to make inquiry about the princess, but I have
had no success whatever. For this reason I have kept her tightly
locked up and dare not release her. Now that we have the good fortune
of seeing the venerable master's arrival at our kingdom, I beg you

enter the capital and exercise your vast dharma power to shed light on this matter. Not only will you thus be able to rescue the virtuous, but you will also make manifest your divine potency."

Pilgrim and Tripitaka firmly committed to their memory what they had heard. As they spoke, however, two young priests came to invite them to tea before retiring, and so they all returned to the monastery.

In the abbot's quarters Pa-chieh was grumbling to Sha Monk, saying, "We have to be on our way by dawn when the cock crows. And they still won't come to bed!"

"Idiot," said Pilgrim, "what are you mumbling?"

"Go to sleep!" said Pa-chieh. "It's so late already. What's there to look at?" Thereupon the old monk walked away, and the T'ang monk retired. This is precisely the time when

The moon fades, the flowers dream, and all sounds cease.

The window screens let in a soft, warm breeze.

Thrice has the clepsydra dropped low in sight;[4]

The Milky Way glows like the brightest light.[5]

They had not slept for very long that night when they heard the cock crow. In the front the traveling merchants all rose in a clamor as they lit their lamps and began to cook their rice. Our elder, too, woke up Pa-chieh and Sha Monk so that they could saddle the horse and pack. When Pilgrim asked for lights, the priests of the monastery had already risen earlier to prepare tea and breakfast, which they waited to serve in the rear. Delighted, Pa-chieh ate an entire platter of buns. Thereafter he and Sha Monk brought out the horse and the luggage, while Pilgrim and Tripitaka thanked their hosts.

Again the old monk said to Pilgrim, "Don't forget that matter of the weeping girl!"

"Indeed, I shall not!" laughed Pilgrim. "When I get to the city, I'll be able to establish the fundamental principles by listening to sounds and determine the emotions by scrutinizing countenances."

Those traveling merchants, noisy and boisterous, also followed them to the main road. By about the hour of the Tiger[6] they passed the Cock-Crow Pass, but not until the hour of the Serpent[7] did they catch sight of the city rampart. The city itself was truly like an iron cistern or a citadel of metal, a divine islet and a Heavenly prefecture. It has the noble form of

A dragon coiled or a tiger sitting,

With colors from phoenix towers emitting.

The royal moat flows like a circling band;
Mountains, flaglike, surround this blessed land.
Banners at dawn light up the imperial way;
Pipes and drums of springtime by bridges play.
The people prosper for the king is good:
Five grains in abundance they have for food.

As they moved along the street of the eastern suburb, the various merchants went off one by one to their hotels and inns. Master and disciples walked inside the city, where they came upon a College of Interpreters and its posthouse. When Tripitaka and his companions walked in, the steward at once made this report to the clerk of the posthouse: "There are four strange-looking priests leading a white horse in here."

When the posthouse clerk heard that there was a horse, he knew that these visitors had to be on some sort of official business. He therefore went out to the main hall to greet them. Saluting him, Tripitaka said, "This humble cleric has been sent by imperial decree of the Great T'ang to go see Buddha at the Great Thunderclap of the Spirit Mountain and seek scriptures. I carry with me a travel rescript which I would like to have certified at your court. I would like also to borrow your noble residence for a short rest. We shall leave the moment our affair's concluded."

Returning his bow, the clerk of the posthouse said, "This official residence was established precisely for the entertainment of honored guests and messengers. It is my responsibility to extend our hospitality to you. Please come in. Please come in."

A highly pleased Tripitaka at once asked his disciples to come and present their greetings. When the posthouse clerk encountered their hideous visages, he was secretly horrified, not knowing whether these beings were human or demonic. Trembling all over, he forced himself to oversee the service of tea and maigre. Tripitaka, seeing how frightened he was, said to him, "Sir, please don't be afraid! Though my three disciples look ugly, they all have good hearts. As the saying goes, 'A savage face but a kindly person.' Nothing to be afraid of!"

Calmed by these words, the posthouse clerk asked, "National Master, where is the T'ang court?"

"In the land of China," replied Tripitaka, "at the South Jambūdvīpa Continent."

"When did you leave?" the clerk asked again.

"In the thirteenth year of the reign period, Chên-kuan," said Tripitaka. "I've gone through fourteen years and the bitter experience of
ten thousand waters and a thousand mountains before arriving at
this region."

"Truly a divine monk, a divine monk!" exclaimed the posthouse
clerk.

Then Tripitaka asked, "And what is the Heaven-allotted age of your
noble state?"

"Ours is the Great Kingdom of India," replied the posthouse clerk.
"Since the time of the founder of our kingdom, T'ai-tsung, it has been
some five hundred years already. The father who occupies the throne
at present is a person who has peculiar fondness for mountains and
streams, flowers and plants. His dynastic name is King I-tsung, and
the title of his reign period is Ching-yen. He has been ruling for
twenty-eight years."

"This humble cleric," said Tripitaka, "would like to have an audience with him today to have our travel rescript certified. Do you know
whether court is still being held?"

"Good! Good! This is precisely a good time!" said the posthouse
clerk. "Our princess, the daughter of the king, has recently celebrated
her twentieth birthday. At the intersection of the major thoroughfares, a festooned tower has been erected from which she will throw
down an embroidered ball in order to determine which person she
will take for her husband, the man ordained of Heaven. Today happens to be the very day of that exciting event, and I believe our father
the king has yet to retire from court. If you wish to have your rescript
certified, this would be a good time to go do so."

Tripitaka was pleased, and he would have left at once had not he
seen that a vegetarian meal was being served. He stayed, therefore,
and ate it with the posthouse clerk and his three disciples.

It was past noon, and Tripitaka said, "I should go now."

"I'll escort you, Master," said Pilgrim.

"I'll go too," said Pa-chieh, but Sha Monk said, "Second Elder
Brother, you shouldn't. Your features aren't the most attractive. What
will you do when you arrive at the court gate? Pretend that you are
fat? Let Big Brother go."

"Wu-ching is quite right," said Tripitaka. "Our Idiot is rough and
coarse. Wu-k'ung still has a little refinement."

Pouting his snout, that Idiot said, "With the exception of Master,

there's not that much difference in the way the three of us look!"
Tripitaka put on his cassock, and Pilgrim picked up the document
satchel to go with him. On the street they saw all the people—scholars,
farmers, laborers, merchants, writers, the learned and the ignorant—
saying to one another, "Let's go see the tossing of the embroidered
ball!"

Standing by the side of the road, Tripitaka said to Pilgrim, "The
people in this place—their clothing, their buildings, their utensils, their
manner of speech and behavior—are all the same as those of our Great
T'ang. I'm thinking now about the deceased mother of my secular
home who met the man she was destined to marry, by throwing an
embroidered ball, and they became man and wife. To think that they
should have this custom here also!"

"Let us go, too, to have a look! How about it?" said Pilgrim.

"No! No!" said Tripitaka. "You and I are dressed improperly, as
priests. People may get suspicious."

"Master," said Pilgrim, "have you quite forgotten the words of that
old monk at the Benefactor-of-Orphans Gold-Spreading Monastery?
We should go see the festooned tower because at the same time we
can distinguish truth from falsehood. In the midst of all this hurly-
burly, that king must be concerned with the happy doings of his
daughter. How could he be bothered with the affairs of the court at
this time? There's no harm in you and me going to the crossroads."

On hearing this, Tripitaka did indeed follow Pilgrim to go watch the
various people waiting for the embroidered ball to be tossed. Ah! Little
did they realize that their going there was like

The fisher, casting down both hook and thread,

Would henceforth haul up some intrigues instead!

We tell you now about that King of India, who, because of his love for
mountains and streams, flowers and plants, led his queen and princess
into the imperial garden last year one night to enjoy the moonlight.
Their outing aroused a monstrous deviate, who abducted the true
princess while she herself falsely assumed the princess's form. Knowing that the T'ang monk would reach this region at that particular
hour, day, month, and year, she wangled the wealth of the state to
erect a festooned tower in order to take him as her mate. She was, you
see, desirous of picking the vital energy of his true yang so that she
would become a superior immortal of the Great Monad.

It was now the third quarter past the hour of noon. Pilgrim and

Tripitaka pushed through the crowd and approached the tower. Just then the princess, flanked by some seventy maidens all colorfully attired, held up high the lighted stalks of incense to pray to Heaven and Earth, while an attendant stood by her holding the embroidered ball. That tower had eight exquisite windows; through one of them, the princess gazed at the crowd. When she saw the T'ang monk draw near, she picked up the ball with her own hands and tossed it at him. The ball landed on his head, knocking his Vairocana hat to one side. The T'ang monk was so startled that he tried to hold on to the ball with his hands. All at once the ball rolled into one of his sleeves.

"It hit a priest! It hit a priest!" Those standing on the tower all began to shout.

Aha! Those merchants and tradesmen at the crossroads all pressed forward to try to take the embroidered ball away. With a thunderous roar, Pilgrim gave his torso a stretch, teeth clenched, and immediately became an imposing figure some thirty feet tall and with a most ugly face. Those people became so terrified that they tumbled and fell, not daring at all to come near. In a moment they dispersed, and Pilgrim changed back into his original form. Meanwhile, the palace maidens and eunuchs, young and old, all descended from the tower to bow to the T'ang monk, saying, "Honorable man! Honorable man! Please enter the hall of the court to be congratulated!"

Tripitaka hurriedly returned their salutations and tried to raise them with his hands before turning to grumble at Pilgrim. "You ape-head!" he said. "You are making a fool of me again!"

"The embroidered ball hit *your* head," said Pilgrim, chuckling, "and it rolled into *your* sleeve. What has that to do with me? Why blame me?"

"What am I supposed to do now?" asked Tripitaka.

"Master, please relax," said Pilgrim. "Go into the court to have an audience with the Throne, while I return to the posthouse to tell Pa-chieh and Sha Monk. We shall wait for your news. If the princess does not desire to take you for a husband, you'll simply have your travel rescript certified and leave. If she insists on taking you, you say to the king, 'Summon my disciples so that I may give them some instructions.' When we three are summoned into the court, I'll be able to distinguish the true from the false. This is my plot of Subduing the Fiend through Marriage." The T'ang monk had no choice but to agree, and Pilgrim turned to go back to the posthouse.

That elder, surrounded by the various palace maidens, was brought to the tower. The princess came down and led him by the hand to the imperial chariot, which they then rode together. The entire entourage departed for the gate of the court. The Custodian of the Yellow Gate proceeded first to memorialize to the king, saying, "Your Majesty, the princess is leading back a monk, who probably has been hit by the ball. They are now outside the gate awaiting your summons."

The king was not pleased by what he heard. He would have liked to send the priest away, but not knowing the wishes of the princess, he felt obliged to summon them inside. The princess and the T'ang monk thus went up to the Hall of Golden Chimes. Truly, this was what happened:

Husband and wife both cried, "Your Majesty!"

Both Good and Evil bowed most solemnly.

After the ceremony, the king asked them to ascend the hall as he posed this question, "Where did you come from, priest, and how were you hit by our daughter's ball?"

Prostrating himself on the ground, the T'ang monk said, "This humble cleric is someone sent by the Great T'ang emperor in the South Jambūdvīpa Continent to go worship Buddha and seek scriptures from the Great Thunderclap in the Western Heaven. Since I carry with me a rescript for this lengthy journey, I have come especially to have an audience with the king to have it certified. My path took me past the crossing beneath the festooned tower, and I did not expect that I would be hit on the head by the ball that the princess tossed. This humble cleric is someone who has left the family and who belongs to a strange religion. How could I dare become the spouse of royalty? I beg you, therefore, to pardon the mortal offense of this humble cleric, certify my rescript, and send me off quickly to the Spirit Mountain. When I have faced Buddha and succeeded in acquiring scriptures to return to my homeland, I shall establish a perpetual memorial to Your Majesty's Heavenly kindness."

The king said, "If you are a sage monk from the Land of the East, you must have been, as it were, 'Drawn through a thousand miles to marriage by a thread.' Our princess has just celebrated her twentieth birthday and not yet married. Because it was determined that the year, month, day, and hour of this very day are all auspicious, we erected that festooned tower for tossing the ball to seek a good match for her. It just happened that you were hit. We are not pleased, but we do not know how our princess feels."

"Father King," said the princess as she kowtowed, "there is a proverb which says,

If you wed a chicken, you follow a chicken;

If you marry a dog, you follow a dog.

Your daughter, after all, made a vow earlier, when this embroidered ball was knitted. I made known to the deities of Heaven and Earth that I would marry whomever the ball struck, for that would be the foreordained person. Today the ball struck the sage monk. This has to be the affinity of a past life which makes possible our meeting in this one. Dare I alter fate? I am willing to take him as our royal son-in-law."

Only then did the king show pleasure. At once he commanded the president of the Imperial Board of Astronomy to select the proper day for the wedding. He also asked for the preparation of the dowry and issued a proclamation to notify the entire kingdom.

When he heard this, however, Tripitaka did not express his gratitude. All he could say instead was, "Release me and pardon me!"

"This monk is most unreasonable!" said the king. "We are using the wealth of an entire nation to take him in as a royal son-in-law. Why doesn't he want to stay here and enjoy it? Why must every thought of his dwell on seeking scriptures? If he persists in his refusal, let the Embroidered-Uniform Guards push him out and have him beheaded!"

Scared out of his wits, the elder shook all over as he knelt down to kowtow and said, "I thank Your Majesty for your Heavenly kindness! But there are four of us altogether in our company, for this humble cleric has three disciples outside. I know I should accept your gracious proposal, but I have not yet had a chance to give them a word of instruction. I beg you, therefore, to summon them to court and certify this travel rescript, so that they may leave early and not be delayed in their journey to the West."

The king consented and asked, "Where are your disciples?"

"They are all in the posthouse of the College of Interpreters," replied Tripitaka. Immediately the king ordered the officials to summon the disciples to court so that they could pick up the travel rescript and and leave for the West. The sage monk, however, was to remain and become the royal son-in-law. The elder had little choice but to rise and stand in waiting to one side. For this situation we have the following testimonial poem:

The no-leak[8] great elixir requires three perfections.[9]

Austere works are not built on hateful relations.

A sage must teach the Tao, you the self cultivate;
Blessings are Heaven's, man must virtue aggregate.
Let not the six organs[10] take their indulgent course.
Nature, suddenly enlightened, reveals your source.
Without love, without thought, you're naturally pure—
Transcendence you'll gain for deliverance is sure.

We tell you now about Pilgrim, who took leave of the T'ang monk beneath the festooned tower and walked back to the posthouse, giggling happily with each step he took. He was met by Pa-chieh and Sha Monk, who asked him, "Elder Brother, why are you laughing so happily? Where's Master?"

"Master has met great happiness!" replied Pilgrim.

"We haven't reached our destination yet," said Pa-chieh, "nor have we seen the Buddha and acquired scriptures. Where does this happiness come from?"

Giggling some more, Pilgrim said, "Master and I walked to the crossroads where the festooned tower was erected. Right there he was hit directly by the embroidered ball tossed down by the princess of this dynasty. He was then taken by the palace maidens and eunuchs to meet the princess, who rode the imperial chariot with him to court. He will be taken in as the royal son-in-law. Isn't that happiness?"

On hearing this, Pa-chieh stamped his feet and thumped his chest, saying, "I knew I should have gone there myself! It was all because of Sha Monk's roguery! If you hadn't stopped me, I would have headed straight for the festooned tower. When the embroidered ball struck old Hog, the princess would have had to take me in. Wouldn't that be nice? Wouldn't that be marvelous? What a handsome, comely, and proper arrangement! We'd play and play! What fun!"

Sha Monk walked forward and scratched Pa-chieh's face with his finger, saying, "Aren't you ashamed of yourself? What a magniloquent mouth!

With three coins you buy an old donkey
And brag about its ridability!

If that embroidered ball struck you, a letter of annulment sent overnight wouldn't be fast enough! Would anyone dare take a catastrophe like you inside the door?"

"A blackguard like you has no feeling for anything!" said Pa-chieh. "I may be ugly, but my person still exudes a certain flavor! As the ancients said, 'Though the flesh and bones are coarse, the constitution is sturdy. Each characteristic, in fact, has its own desirability.'"

"Stop babbling like that, Idiot!" said Pilgrim. "Let's get our luggage together. I fear that Master may be so harried that he will soon be summoning us to the court to protect him."

"You are wrong again, Elder Brother," said Pa-chieh. "If Master has become the royal son-in-law, he will go into the palace to make love to the king's daughter. He is not going to climb mountains or traipse along the roads, where he could meet fiends or encounter demons. Who needs your protection? At his age, you think he's so ignorant of what goes on in bed that he requires your assistance?"

Grabbing him by the ears, Pilgrim shook his fist at Pa-chieh and scolded him, saying, "You lecherous coolie! What sort of bunk is this?"

As they were thus quarreling, the clerk of the posthouse arrived and said, "His Majesty has issued a decree and sent an official with an invitation for you three divine monks." "For what specific purpose?" asked Pa-chieh. The posthouse clerk said, "The old divine monk was fortunate enough to be struck by the princess's embroidered ball and to have been taken in as the royal son-in-law. That is why an official has come with an invitation." "Where is this official?" said Pilgrim. "Tell him to come in."

The official, when he saw Pilgrim, at once saluted him. After the ceremony, however, he dared not raise his eyes to look at him. All he could say to himself was, "Is this a demon or a fiend? A thunder squire or a yakṣa?"

"Official," said Pilgrim, "why don't you speak up? What are you thinking of?" Trembling all over, the official held up the imperial decree with both hands and blurted out, "My princess invites you to meet her kin! My princess's kin invite you to meet her!"

"We have no instruments of torture here," said Pa-chieh, "and we have no intention to beat you. Speak slowly. Don't be afraid."

"You think he's afraid of a beating?" said Pilgrim. "It's your face he's afraid of. Pick up the pole and the luggage quickly, and lead the horse along. We must go into court to discuss this affair." Truly

It's hard to sidestep for the way is strait;
Love will certainly be turned into hate.

We do not know what they have to say after they have seen the king, and you must listen to the explanation in the next chapter.

Ninety-four

Four priests are feted at the imperial garden;
One fiend vainly seeks the sensual joys.

We were telling you about Pilgrim Sun and his two companions, who followed the summons official to the gate of the court. The custodian of the Yellow Gate immediately notified them to enter. The three of them walked in together and stood still, without, however, even bowing.

"Which three are the noble disciples of the sage monk, our royal son-in-law?" asked the king. "What are your names? Where do you live? For what reason did you become priests? What scriptures are you seeking?"

Pilgrim strode forward and wanted to ascend to the main hall. The guardians of the Throne at once shouted, "Stop! If you have anything to say, speak up at once!"

"We people who have left the family," said Pilgrim, smiling, "will advance one step when we have the chance to take one step." After him Pa-chieh and Sha Monk also drew near. Fearing that their vulgarity might upset the Throne, the elder, standing on one side, stepped forward and said, "Disciples, His Majesty is asking for your origins. You should present a proper reply."

When Pilgrim saw that his master was standing in waiting on one side, he could not refrain from yelling, "Your Majesty, you slight others and you slight yourself! If you have taken in my master as the royal son-in-law, why do you make him stand? The world addresses your daughter's husband as 'Honorable Man.' How can an honorable man not be allowed to sit?"

When he heard that, the king paled with fright. He would have withdrawn himself immediately from the hall had he not been afraid of impropriety. Forcing himself to be bold, he asked his attendants to bring out an embroidered cushion for the T'ang monk to sit on. Only then did Pilgrim memorialize to him, saying,

Old Monkey's ancestral home is located at the Water Curtain

Cave of the Flower-Fruit Mountain, in the Ao-lai Kingdom of
the East Pūrvavideha Continent.
My father was Heaven, my mother, Earth:
I was born when a stone burst.
Once a perfected man's pupil,
I mastered the Great Way
Ere returning to my divine home
To congregate with my kind in the cave-heaven of a blessed
    land.
In the ocean I subdued dragons;
On the mountains I captured beasts.
Having abolished the register of death
And placed our names in the book of life,
I was appointed the Great Sage, Equal to Heaven,
To enjoy the towers of Jade
And roam the treasure lofts.
I joined the celestial immortals
To sing and revel every day;
Living in the sages' realm,
I had great pleasures each morning.
For disrupting the Peaches Festival
And causing great havoc in Heaven,
I was subjugated by Buddha
And pinned beneath the Mountain of Five Phases,
With but iron pellets for my hunger
And copper juice for my thirst,
And not a drop of tea or rice for five hundred years.
Fortunately my master left the Land of the East;
As he headed for the West,
Kuan-yin delivered me from Heaven's calamity.
Free of my great ordeal,
I made submission as a student of Yoga.
My old name's Wu-k'ung,
But people address me as Pilgrim.

When the king heard such an important pedigree, he was so im-
pressed that he left the dragon couch immediately to walk forward
and take the elder's arm. "Royal son-in-law," he said, "this must be
our affinity ordained of Heaven that we may have you as a divine
kinsman."

Tripitaka thanked him profusely and asked him to ascend his throne once more. Then the king asked, "Who is your second noble disciple?" Sticking out his snout to display his authority, Pa-chieh said,

In his previous incarnation old Hog
Was most fond of pleasure and sloth;
My whole life was chaotic,
My nature confused and my mind deluded.
I never knew Heaven's height or Earth's thickness,
Nor could I perceive this world's breadth and length.
In that leisurely existence
I met suddenly a realized immortal
Who, with half a sentence
Untied my net of retribution,
And with two or three words
Punched through my door of calamity.
Immediately coming to myself,
I took him at once as a teacher.
With care I cultivated the work of two-eights,[1]
And smelted fore and after the time of three times three.[2]
My work done I ascended
Into the palace of Heaven.
By the great kindness of the Jade Emperor
I was appointed Marshal of Heavenly Reeds,
In command of the troops of Heaven's river,
Roaming freely throughout the cosmos.
For getting drunk at the Peaches Festival
And dallying with Ch'ang-o,
I was stripped of my rank
And exiled to this mortal world.
An erroneous incarnation
Made me born in the form of a hog.
A resident of Mount Fu-ling,
I committed boundless evils
When I met Kuan-yin,
Who pointed out the way of virtue.
I submitted to the Buddhist faith
To give the T'ang monk protection
On his way to the Western Heaven
To bow and seek the wondrous texts.

My religious name's Wu-nêng,
But they call me Pa-chieh.

These words made the king's spleen shake and his heart quiver, and he hardly dared look at the speaker.

Our Idiot, however, became more energetic than ever; shaking his head, sticking out his snout, and raising both ears, he laughed uproariously. Fearing again that the Throne might be terrified, Tripitaka snapped, "Pa-chieh, behave!" Only then did Pa-chieh lower his hands, putting one over the other, and stand there pretending to be a gentleman.

Then the king asked once more, "For what reason did the third noble disciple become a priest?" Pressing his palms together, Sha Monk said,

Old Sand was originally a mortal man.
Fear of the karmic wheel made me seek the Way,
Roaming cloudlike to the corners of the sea
And wandering throughout the edges of Heaven.
As always my frock and almsbowl followed me;
Long I taught my mind and spirit to concentrate.
Because of such sincerity
I found an immortal partner;
I nurtured the baby[3]
And married the fair girl.
When my merit reached three thousand
My work harmonized with the Four Signs,[4]
I went beyond the limit of Heaven
To bow at the mysterious height.
Made the Great Curtain-Raising Warrior,
I attended the phoenix-and-dragon chariot,
Appointed to the rank of general.
At the Peaches Festival also
I dropped and broke a crystal chalice,
For which I was exiled to the Flowing-Sand River.
My head and features transformed,
I sinned by taking lives.
Fortunately the Bodhisattva on her journey to the Land of the
    East
Persuaded me to repent
And wait for a Buddhist son of the T'ang court,

Who would go seek scriptures at the Western Heaven.
Henceforth I stood in this renewal
And sought once more the great awakening.
I use the river as my surname;
My religious name's Wu-ching,
And they address me as Monk.

When the king heard that, he was filled with great joy but also great
terror. What brought him joy was the fact that his daughter had taken
a living Buddha in for a husband, but what brought him terror was
that the man's disciples were actually three monstrous deities. In that
very moment, the chief imperial astronomer arrived to say, "The date
of the wedding has been set for the fine day of *jên-tzŭ*, the twelfth day
of this month in this year. That day ought to be felicitous for the entire
family, and it is thus fitting for a marriage to take place."

"What day is today?" asked the king.

"Today is the eighth," replied the astronomer, "the day of *mou-
shên*, when the apes come to present fruits. It is thus a day appropriate
for receiving the worthies and setting appointments."

Exceedingly pleased, the king immediately asked the attendants to
sweep out some towered buildings in the imperial garden, so that the
royal son-in-law and his three disciples could use them for lodging.
Thereafter he asked for the preparation of the wedding banquet so
that the princess could get married. All his subjects reverently obeyed.
After the king had retired from court, the various officials dispersed,
and we shall leave them for the moment.

We tell you now instead about Tripitaka and his disciples, who
went together to the imperial garden. As it was getting late, a vegetarian meal was set out. Delighted, Pa-chieh said, "It's about time
we ate after one whole day!" Those in charge toted in whole loads of
rice and noodles. Pa-chieh ate and ate; the more they brought, the
more he ate. He did not stop till his guts were stuffed and his stomach
was bloated. In a little while, lights were brought in and bedding
spread out for each of them, so that they could sleep.

When the elder saw that they were by themselves, he shouted
angrily at Pilgrim, "Wu-k'ung! You wretched ape! You put me in a
bind every time! I told you that all I wanted was to have the rescript
certified, and I told you not to go near the festooned tower. Why did
you insist on taking me there to look? Now, have you seen anything

good? We've ended up in this pickle. What are we going to do now?"

Trying to placate him with a smile, Pilgrim said, "The master's statement that his deceased mother, who also met the person destined for her by the tossing of an embroidered ball, whereupon the two of them became man and wife, seems to indicate a longing for the past. Only because of that did old Monkey lead you to the tower. Moreover, I thought of the words of that abbot from the Benefactor-of-Orphans Gold-Spreading Monastery, and I wanted to use this occasion to examine the true and the false. Just now when I looked at the king, I noticed that his complexion was somewhat dark and swarthy. But I haven't been able to look at the princess to determine what she was like."

"What would you be able to do if you saw the princess?" asked the elder.

Pilgrim said, "The moment these fiery eyes and diamond pupils of old Monkey see her face, they will be able to discern truth and falsehood, good and evil, wealth and poverty. Then I will be able to act to distinguish the right from the deviant."

With loud giggles, both Pa-chieh and Sha Monk said, "Elder Brother must have recently learned the art of physiognomy!"

"Those physiognomists," said Pilgrim, "ought to be regarded only as my grandsons!"

"Stop gabbing!" snapped Tripitaka. "It appears now that they are bent on taking me in. What should we do, really?"

Pilgrim said, "Let's wait till the twelfth, the day of the wedding ceremony, when the princess undoubtedly will appear to pay homage to her parents. Let old Monkey take a look at her from the side. If she were a real woman, it wouldn't be too bad for you to become the royal son-in-law and enjoy the glory of a nation."

These words sent Tripitaka into greater fury. "You wretched ape!" he cried. "You still want to injure me! As Wu-nêng puts it, nine-tenths of our journey has been covered already, and you still stab me with your hot tongue! Stop wagging it, and don't you dare open that stinking mouth of yours! If you behave with such insolence just one more time, I'll recite that spell to make life intolerable for you!"

When Pilgrim heard that he wanted to recite the spell, he was so horrified that he immediately went to his knees and said, "Don't do that! Don't do that! If she were a real woman, we'd wait till the time

of the mutual bows, and then we would create havoc in the palace
and get you out." As master and disciples conversed, the announcement of the night watches began. Truly

The palace clock drips slowly;
The floral scent spreads softly.
The boudoir drops its pearly screen;
In empty yards no lights are seen.
The swings stand idle, showing only their shades;
All is quiet as a Tangut flute fades.
The moon on the blossoms confers her grace;
The stars seem brighter in a treeless space.
The nightjar ends her song;
The butterfly-dream is long.
The Milky Way crosses the sky
As white clouds to one's homeland fly:
A time when travelers feel the keenest pain,
Saddened by the wind-swept young willow-skein.

"Master," said Pa-chieh, "it's late. If there's anything important, discuss it tomorrow. Let's go to sleep! Let's go to sleep." Master and disciples indeed enjoyed a restful night.

Soon the golden rooster announced the arrival of dawn, and the
king ascended the main hall for his early audience. You see

The palace open, the purple aura high;
Wind-blown, the king's music rends the blue sky.
Clouds move the leopard's-tails[5] and banners shake;
The sun hits carved dragons[6] and girdle-jades quake.
Fragrant mist heightens the palace willow green;
Dew drops moisten the flowers' imperial sheen.
Midst shouts and dances the ministers stand,
For peace and harmony reign o'er the land.

After the hundred officials, both civil and military, had paid their
homage, the king gave this order: "Let the Court of Imperial Entertainments prepare the wedding banquet for the twelfth. For today,
however, let us make ready some spring wine and entertain our royal
son-in-law in the imperial garden." He also instructed the Director of
the Bureau of Ceremonies to take the three worthy kinsmen back to
the College of Interpreters. There they would be served a vegetarian
feast by the Court of Imperial Entertainments. The staff from the Office
of Music would be asked to play at both the college and the garden,

so that all could be entertained while they spent time enjoying the sight of spring.

When Pa-chieh heard all this, he at once spoke up and said, "Your Majesty, since we, master and disciples, made each other's acquaintance, we have not been separated for a single moment. Today, if you plan to eat and drink in the imperial garden, take us along and let us play for a couple of days. That's the way for you to make my master your royal son-in-law. Otherwise, I fear that you may find it hard to carry out this scheme."

The king had already noticed Pa-chieh's hideous appearance and vulgar manner of speech. And when he saw him sticking out his snout and wagging his ears, constantly twisting his head and kneading his neck, he thought the speaker was showing signs of madness. Fearing that the marriage might be ruined, the king had no choice but to agree to the demands. "Prepare two tables," said the king, "in the Eternal Pacification of the Chinese and Barbarian Loft, where we shall sit with our royal son-in-law. Three other tables are to be set up in the Spring-Detaining Arbor for those three guests. Master and disciples, we fear, may not find it convenient to sit together."

Only then did our Idiot bow and say, "Thank you!" before each person withdrew. The king also issued this order that the official in charge of the inner palace prepare another banquet, so that the queen and the consorts of three palaces and six chambers could assist the princess in putting on her headgear and present her with her dowry, in anticipation of the fine match set for the twelfth.

By about the hour of the Serpent,[7] the king called for his carriage and invited the T'ang monk and his companions to go to the imperial garden. As they looked around, they saw a marvelous place indeed.

The path's made of colored stones—
The railings bear carved patterns—
The path's made of colored stones,
By the side of which rare blossoms grow.
The railings bear carved patterns,
Within and beyond which strange flora flourish.
Lush peaches bewitch the kingfishers;
Young willows display the orioles.
A walk brings quiet fragrance to fill your sleeves;
A stroll makes much pure scent cling to your robe.
A phoenix terrace and a dragon pool;

A bamboo garret and a pine arbor.
On the phoenix terrace,
A flute makes the phoenix come with its measured gamboling;[8]
In the dragon pool,
Fishes raised there change into dragons to leave.
The bamboo garret has poems,
All lofty rhymes composed with utmost skill;
The pine arbor has essays,
A noble collection of pearl and jade.
Green rocks form artificial hills;
The winding stream's azure and deep.
The true-peony arbor,
The cinnamon rose props,
Seem like thick damask and brocade spread out;
The mo-li[9] fence,
The pyrus patch,
Appear as mist or jade piled up.
The peony has exotic scent;
The Szechuan mallow shows rare glamor;
White pears vie with red apricots for fragrance;
Purple orchids strive with gold day-lilies for brilliance.
The li-ch'un flower,[10]
The "wood-brush" flower,[11]
And the azalea
Are all fresh and fiery;
The crape-flower,
The fêng-hsien flower,[12]
And the "jade-pin" flower[13]
Are all tall and trembly.
Each spot of red ripeness seems like moistened rouge;
Each clump of dense fragrance is a brocade round.
A joy's the east wind recalling the warm sun;
The whole garden's lit up and with charms o'errun.

The king and his several guests viewed this scenery for a long time.
Then the Director of Ceremonies came to invite Pilgrim and his two
brothers to go to the Spring-Detaining Arbor, while the king took the
T'ang monk to the Chinese and Barbarian Loft, each party being
served separately. The music and dance, the decorations and appointments, were quite extraordinary. Truly

The Heaven-gate's[14] rugged in the morning light.
On dragon towers auspicious mists alight.
The soft hues of spring the flora adorn;
Silk robes shimmer, struck by the rays of dawn.
Like feastings of gods pipes and songs resound;
With juices of jade the cups make their rounds.
Joined in their fun are both subjects and king;
A world at peace must prosperity bring.

When the elder saw what great esteem the king showed him, he had
little choice but to force himself to participate in the revelry. Truly he
showed delight without but harbored anxiety within.

At the place where they were sitting, there were four gilded screens
hanging on the wall, on which were painted the scenes of the four
seasons. Inscribed on these paintings were poems, all compositions by
noted scholars of the Han-lin Academy.

The Poem of Spring says:
The cycle of nature has made its turn.
The great earth quickens and all things seem new.
Plums vie with peaches in their beauteous blooms;
Swallows pile on carved beams their scented dust.

The Poem of Summer says:
The south wind blows to cause our thoughts delay;
The sun beams on *k'uei*[15] and pomegranate.
A jade flute's soft notes stir our midday dream,
When scent of water lily spreads to the drapes.

The Poem of Autumn says:
Of golden well's *wu-t'ung*[16] one leaf's yellow.
Draw not the pearl screen for the night has frost.
The swallows know it's time to leave their nests,
As wild geese depart for another land.

The Poem of Winter says:
The rain clouds make the sky both dark and cold,
And wind blows the snow to build a thousand hills.
The palace, of course, has a warm, red stove
When plum blossoms o'erlay with jade the rails.

When the king saw how intently the T'ang monk was staring at the poems, he said, "If the royal son-in-law finds the flavor of poetry so attractive, he too must be skilled in the art of chanting and composition. If you are not parsimonious with your pearl and jade, please give a reply in kind to each of the poems, using the same rhymes. Will you do that?"

Now the elder was someone who could lose himself in such scenery, for his mind was enlightened by the vision of seeing the Buddha-nature in all things. When he heard the king favoring him with such a request, he blurted out the sentence,

The sun melts the ice as the great earth turns.

Exceedingly pleased, the king said to one of the palace attendants, "Bring out the library's four treasures.[17] Record the poetic replies of our royal son-in-law, so that we may savor them leisurely." The elder did not refuse. In delight he took up the brush to write

> *A Reply to the Poem of Spring:*
> The sun melts the ice as the great earth turns.
> This day the king's garden blossoms anew.
> The people are blessed with such clement clime,
> For rivers and seas are rid of worldly dust.
>
> *A Reply to the Poem of Summer:*
> The dipper points south to cause the days delay.
> Ablaze are the *huai*[18] and pomegranate.
> Orioles and swallows midst the willow sing
> And send their lovely duet through the drapes.
>
> *A Reply to the Poem of Autumn:*
> Fragrant's the orange—green and yellow.
> The verdant pine and cypress love their frost.
> Brocadelike, the crysanthemum's half in bloom.
> Our songs resound through cloud and water land.
>
> *A Reply to the Poem of Winter:*
> The snow has stopped but still the air is cold,
> When jagged rocks like jade surround the hills.
> The stove's beast-shaped charcoals have warmed the milk.[19]
> We sing, hands in sleeves, and lean on the rails.

The king read the poems and he could not have been more pleased. "What a marvelous line!" he chanted. "'We sing, hands in sleeves, and lean on the rails!'" At once he asked the Office of Music to set the poems to music and perform them. They spent the day that way before dispersing.

Meanwhile Pilgrim and his two companions also abandoned themselves to enjoyment at the Spring-Detaining Arbor. Growing somewhat tipsy from the several cups of wine they each consumed, they were about to leave to look for the elder when they spotted him in a distant room with the king. His silly nature aroused, Pa-chieh shouted, "What a ball! What comfort! Today I've had some enjoyment! As long as I'm full, it's time to take a snooze!"

"Second Elder Brother," said Sha Monk, chuckling, "that's not very dignified of you! With such a full stomach, how can you sleep?" Pa-chieh said, "You wouldn't know about this. The proverb says,

If after a meal you don't lie flat,

Your belly won't get fat!"

The T'ang monk took leave of the king and went to the arbor, where he rebuked Pa-chieh, saying, "You coolie! You're getting rowdier! What sort of a place is this that you dare to shout and holler? If the king takes offense, you may lose your life!"

"It's nothing! It's nothing!" replied Pa-chieh. "After all, we are related to him as in-laws, properly speaking, and he can't be offended by us. As the saying goes,

You can't cut off your kin with beating,

Nor can you your neighbor with scolding.

We're all having some fun. Why worry about him?"

"Bring that Idiot over here!" snapped the elder. "Let me give him twenty strokes with my priestly staff!" So Pilgrim pulled him over and bent him down, while the elder raised his staff to strike.

"Father royal son-in-law!" cried Idiot. "Please pardon me! Please pardon me!"

Those officials who had borne them company during the party persuaded the T'ang monk to stop. Scrambling up, our Idiot could be heard muttering, "Dear honorable man! Dear royal son-in-law. The wedding hasn't even taken place, and you're administering royal law already!"

Putting his hand over Pa-chieh's mouth, Pilgrim said, "Stop jabbering! Stop jabbering! Hurry and go to sleep!" They spent another night in the Spring-Detaining Arbor, and by dawn, they feasted once more.

They spent three or four days in such pleasure, and the happy day

of the twelfth arrived. The officials from the three departments of the
Court of Imperial Entertainments came to say, "Since receiving your
decree on the eighth, your subjects have now finished building the
royal son-in-law's residence, though we are still waiting for the dowry
to furnish the place. The wedding banquet, too, is prepared. Altogether,
both vegetarian and nondietary, there are some five hundred tables."
Delighted, the king wanted to ask his son-in-law at once to attend the
banquet, when an official of the inner palace suddenly appeared and
said, "Your Majesty, the queen wishes to have an audience."

The king went inside, and found the queens of the three palaces and
the ladies of six chambers chatting merrily with the princess at the
Chao-yang Palace. Truly they were like bouquets of flowers and
rounds of brocade! All that opulence could rival even that of the lunar
palace in Heaven, and it certainly was not inferior to the divine jasper
residence. As a testimonial, we have four new songs based on the
words of Joy, Meet, Fine, and Mate.

The Song of Joy says:
Joy! Joy! Joy!
This happiness enjoy.
A matrimony
Of love most seemly.
Such smart palace fashion
Would rouse Ch'ang-o's passion.
Those dragon and phoenix hairpins
Of luminous gold threads thin;
Those lustrous teeth and cherry lips,
A body light as flower-slips.
Layers of silk
Within the five-colored groves;
Lovely fragrance
Rising from beauties in droves.

The Song of Meet says:
Meet! Meet! Meet!
One seductive and sweet.
Mao Ch'iang[20] she rivals
And sister Ch'u[21] equals.
A wrecker of city and state,
Fair like flower and jade.

Her makeup is fresh and charming;
Her jewels are more disarming.
An orchid mind and nature lofty,
And ice-white flesh and face most stately.
Like distant hills her dark brows are painted thin;
The regiment of silk she's fairest therein.

The Song of Fine says:
Fine! Fine! Fine!
A maiden divine.
Profoundly lovely,
Truly praiseworthy.
Rare fragrances combine
With powder and carmine.
The blessed T'ien-t'ai's off somewhere.
Could it with a royal house compare?
She speaks and smiles in form so fair,
As pipes and music both rend the air.
Pretty are a thousand forms of flower and silk.
Scan the whole world but none is in her ilk.

The Song of Mate says:
Mate! Mate! Mate!
The orchid scents dilate.
Immortal crowd
And beauties proud.
The maidens' colors fresh-born.
The princess newly adorned:
Her coiffure rises like a crow's nest;
Phoenix skirt beneath a rainbow vest.
Celestial sonorities ahead;
Two rows of lovely purple and red.
In years past she had fixed a nuptial date;
This day she's happy to meet her fine mate.

We tell you now about that king, who arrived in his carriage. The
queen led the princess along with the consorts and palace maidens to
meet him. Cheerfully the king entered the Chao-yang Palace to take
his seat. After the ladies had bowed to him, the king said, "Princess,
our worthy daughter, we trust that the happy meeting with the sage

monk when you tossed the ball from the festooned tower on the eighth has given you great satisfaction. The officials of various bureaus and departments, moreover, have been so considerate of our interests that all the preparations are now completed. Today is the auspicious day. You must make haste to attend the wedding feast, so that the goodly hour will not be forfeited."

Stepping forward, the princess went to her knees to bow low and said, "Father King, please pardon your daughter's ten thousand offenses! There is a matter about which I must speak to you. For several days I have heard the palace officials say that the T'ang monk has three disciples, who are exceedingly ugly. Your daughter dares not face them, for they will surely cause me great fear and dread. I beg the Father King to send them out of the city so that my feeble body will not be harmed by fright nor our happiness ruined."

"If our child hadn't spoken of this matter," replied the king, "we would have overlooked it. They are indeed quite hideous and wild. These past few days we've entertained them at the Spring-Detaining Arbor in the royal garden. We'll take this opportunity today to go up to the hall and certify their rescript. After they have been sent out of the city, we'll then hold our banquet." The princess kowtowed to express her thanks. The king at once rode his carriage to the main hall, where he issued a summons for the royal son-in-law and his three disciples.

Now the T'ang monk too had been counting the days with his fingers. When he reached the twelfth, he began even before dawn to discuss the matter with his disciples, saying, "Today's the twelfth. How are we to settle this affair?"

"I could tell," said Pilgrim, "that the king has a certain gloomy aura about him. It has not, however, penetrated his body yet, and I don't think it will cause him any great harm. But I still haven't had a chance to see the princess. If only she would come out! With one glance old Monkey can tell us whether she is real or not, and only then can we do anything. You shouldn't worry, though. Today they will certainly call for us in order to send us three out of the city. You should accept the summons without fear. In the twinkling of an eye I'll be back at your side to give you protection."

As master and disciples talked, the attendant to the Throne and the Director of Ceremonies indeed arrived with a summons. Chuckling,

Pilgrim said, "Let's go! Let's go! We are about to be sent off, while Master will remain for the marriage."

"To send us off," said Pa-chieh, "they must present some thousand taels of gold or silver. That'll be enough for me to get some gifts to go back to *my* in-laws. We'll have another wedding and a little fun!"

"Clamp your mouth, Second Elder Brother, and stop blabbering!" said Sha Monk. "Just let Big Brother make the decision."

They took the luggage and the horse to follow the various officials to the vermilion steps. When he saw them, the king asked the three disciples to approach him, saying, "Bring us your travel rescript. We shall use our treasure seal on it. In addition, we shall increase your travel allowance and wish you a speedy arrival at the Spirit Mountain to see Buddha. When you return with the scriptures, there will be further reward. The royal son-in-law will remain here, and you need not worry about him."

Thanking him, Pilgrim asked Sha Monk to take out the rescript to hand over to the king. The king read it before applying his seal and affixing his signature. Then he presented them with ten ingots of yellow gold and twenty ingots of white gold as wedding gifts. As he had always been both lecherous and greedy, Pa-chieh immediately took them, while Pilgrim gave a bow and said, "Much obliged! Much obliged!"

He turned and began to walk out. Tripitaka was so startled that he scrambled up and caught hold of Pilgrim. Teeth grinding audibly, he said, "Are you all abandoning me?"

Squeezing Tripitaka's palm with his hand, Pilgrim winked at him and said, "Relax and enjoy your union here. When we have acquired the scriptures, we'll return to see you." The elder seemed not to believe him and refused to let go. The other officials, however, thought that master and disciples were indeed bidding each other farewell. Then the king asked the royal son-in-law to ascend to the hall once more, while the other officials were to see the disciples off outside the city. The elder had to loosen his grip and went back to the hall.

Pilgrim and his two companions went out of the gate of the court and took leave of the officials. "Are we really leaving?" said Pa-chieh. Without saying a word, Pilgrim walked back to the posthouse, where they were received by the posthouse clerk. As he went to prepare rice and tea, Pilgrim said to Pa-chieh and Sha Monk, "You two stay here and don't show yourselves. If the posthouse clerk questions you, just muddle through with some answer. Don't speak to me at all, for I'm leaving to go protect Master."

Dear Great Sage! He pulled off a piece of hair, blew his immortal breath on it, and cried, "Change!" It changed at once into a form of himself, which remained with Pa-chieh and Sha Monk in the posthouse. His true self leaped into midair and changed into a bee. You see his

> Yellow wings, sweet mouth, and sharp tail—
> A mad dancer lost in the gale,
> Most able to pick the buds and steal their scent,
> To make through willows his descent.
> He submits to both stains and dyes;
> Hither and yon vainly he flies,
> N'er tasting that sweetness he helps distill.
> He has only his name for a will.

Look at him! Ever so lightly he flew into the court, where he found the T'ang monk sitting most dejectedly and with furrowed brow on a brocade cushion to the left of the king. Alighting on his Vairocana hat, he crawled near his ear to whisper, "Master, I'm here. Please don't worry."

Those few words, of course, were audible only to the T'ang monk and to none of those other mortals. When the T'ang monk heard them, he felt more reassured. In a little while, a palace official came to say, "Your Majesty, the wedding banquet has been laid out in the Magpie Palace. The queen and the princess are waiting there for the presence of Your Majesty and the honorable man." The king could not have been more pleased. At once he took the royal son-in-law inside the palace. Thus it is that

> The deviant lord loves flowers, but flowers bring woe;
> The Zen-mind stirs to thought, but thought begets sorrow.

We do not know how the T'ang monk in the palace will find deliverance, and you must listen to the explanation in the next chapter.

Ninety-five

The jade hare, which falsely assumes the true form, is
    captured;
True yin returns to the right and meets Numinous Source.[1]

We tell you now about that T'ang monk, who dolefully followed the
king into the inner palace, where he heard the loud noise of music
and drums and encountered strong whiffs of rare perfume. Lowering
his head, he dared not look up at all. Pilgrim, however, was secretly
delighted. Perched on his master's Vairocana hat, he exercised his
magic perception and stared everywhere with his fiery eyes and
diamond pupils. Two rows of palace maidens, colorfully dressed, stood
in waiting, so enhancing the place that it seemed like a flower palace
or divine residence and more attractive than the silken drapes in the
breeze of spring. Truly

They are both graceful and lissome,
With substance like jade and flesh like ice.
Pairs and pairs, more charming than Ch'u maidens;
Two by two they rival Hsi Shih in beauty.
Phoenixes rear up from coiffures piled high;
Like distant hills are moth brows faintly drawn.
That graceful playing of reeds,
That frequent blowing of flutes—
The tones—*kung, shang, chüeh, chih,* and *yü*—[2]
High and low make their lyric flow.
Wondrous songs and dances e'er lovable;
Silk and floral clusters all agreeable.

When Pilgrim saw that his master was completely unmoved, he said
to himself in silent praise, "Marvelous monk! Marvelous monk!

Living midst silk and satin he's not enticed;
Walking through opulence he's not beguiled."

In a little while, the princess, with the queen and the concubines
thronging around her, walked out of the Magpie Palace to receive the
king, all crying, "Long live Your Majesty! Long live Your Majesty!"

The elder became so flustered that he shook all over, not knowing

what to do at all. Pilgrim, on the other hand, at once perceived that
there was a slight manifestation of monstrous aura on top of the
princess's head, though it did not seem too virulent. He quickly crawled
near his master's ear to whisper: "Master, that princess is a false one."

"If she is not a true princess," said the elder, "how can we make her
reveal her true form?"

"By showing my magic body," replied Pilgrim, "I'll capture her
immediately."

"No! No!" said the elder. "You might frighten the Throne. Let the
monarch and the queen retire first. Then you may exercise your magic
power."

That Pilgrim, however, had been impetuous all his life. How could
he permit this? With a roar he revealed his original form and dashed
forward. Grabbing the princess, he cried, "You cursed beast! You
make the false become real here! Isn't it enough for you to enjoy yourself at this place? Why must you be so greedy as to want to deceive
my master and ruin his true yang to satisfy your lust?" These words
rendered the king dumb and stupid with fear, and sent the queen and
concubines tumbling all over. Every one of those gaily attired girls
and palace maidens darted east and west, fleeing for her life. This was
what their condition was like:

A spring wind breezy—
Autumn air blustery—
The breezy spring wind passes garden and wood
And a thousand blossoms quiver;
The blustery autumn air comes to the courts
And myriad leaves flutter.
The blasted peony falls beneath the fence,
And blown-up peony lies beside the rails.
The shore's hibiscus trembles;
The steps' crysanthemum heaps up.
The pyrus turns feeble and sinks to the dust;
The rose, still fragrant, lies in the wilds.
The spring wind severs the lotus stalks;
The winter snow crushes the plum's young buds.
Pomegranate petals
Scatter east and west in the inner palace;
Willow twigs by the shore
Dangle north and south of the royal mansion.

In one night a wild storm of wind and rain
Does with dying redness the landscape stain.

More flustered than ever and shaking all over, Tripitaka embraced the
king and said only, "Your Majesty, please don't be afraid. Please don't
be afraid! This is how my mischievous disciple must work his magic
power to distinguish truth and falsehood."

We tell you now about that monster-spirit, who saw that things
were going badly. She struggled free, ripped off her clothes, and flung
away her earrings, bracelets, and jewels. Dashing into the shrine of
the local spirit at the imperial garden, she took out a short, pestlelike
club, turned and struck madly at Pilgrim. Pilgrim caught up with her
and faced her with the iron rod. The two of them, screaming and
shouting, started a battle in the garden, which continued in midair
when both of them displayed their magic powers and mounted cloud
and fog. In this very conflict,

The golden-hooped rod has both name and fame,
But a club like a pestle no one knows.
One seeking true scriptures has reached this place;
One for love of strange blossoms has come to stay.
The fiend, long knowing of the T'ang sage monk,
Desires to unite with his primal sperm.
Abducting the true princess the year before,
She took human form as the king's belov'd.
The Great Sage now perceives her monstrous air;
He would save life by making known the truth.
The short club works violence, bashing the head;
The iron rod with power hits the face.
Loud and boisterous the two of them fight
As mist and cloud remove the sun from sight.

As the two of them waged a fierce battle in midair, they filled the populace of the whole city with horror and terrified the officials of the
entire court.

Supporting the king with his hands, the elder could only say,
"Please don't be afraid! Please tell our lady, the queen, and the rest
not to fear. Your princess is actually someone specious who has taken
on the true princess' form. When my disciple captures her, you will
know the difference."

Several of the more courageous palace ladies took the clothing and
jewels to show to the queen, saying, "These were worn by the princess.

Now she has abandoned everything. Stark naked, she is fighting that monk in the sky. She must be a monstrous deviate." By then the king, the queen, and the royal concubines had grown calmer and began to stare at the sky. We shall leave them for the moment.

We tell you now about that monster-spirit, who battled the Great Sage for half a day, and they fought to a draw. Tossing the rod up into the air, Pilgrim cried, "Change!" The single rod changed into ten rods; the ten became a hundred, and the hundred turned into thousands. Like slithering snakes and gliding dragons in midair, these rods madly attacked the monstrous deviate. Completely flustered, the monstrous deviate transformed herself into a clear breeze and fled toward the region above the blue sky. Pilgrim recited a spell, which reduced the iron rods to a single piece, before mounting the auspicious luminosity to give chase. When they approached the West Heavenly Gate, they could see gleaming banners fluttering.

"Those guarding the Heavenly Gate," shouted Pilgrim, "block the monster-spirit! Don't let her escape!" The Devarāja Dhṛtarāṣṭra indeed led the Four Grand Marshals P'ang, Liu, Kou, and Pi to bar the way, each wielding his weapon. Unable to proceed, the monstrous deviate spun around and began to battle with Pilgrim once more, brandishing her short club.

As he wielded his iron rod to meet her, the Great Sage stared at the club and saw that it was thick on one end and thin on the other. It resembled, in fact, a pestle used for hulling grain. "Cursed beast!" he cried. "What sort of weapon is that you have there that you dare oppose old Monkey? Submit at once, lest one blow of my rod smash your skull!"

Clenching her teeth, the monstrous deviate said, "So, you don't know about this weapon of mine! Listen to my recital!

This divine root's a piece of mutton jade,
Its form cut and polished for countless years.
I owned it already when Chaos parted;
'Twas my possession when the world began.
No mortal thing could with its source compare,
For its nature came from Heaven above.
Its golden-light frame with Four Signs accords,
Three Primaries[3] fused with Five Phases' breaths.
In Toad Palace[4] it has long stayed with me,
A frequent companion by Cassia Hall.[5]

For love of flowers I came down to Earth
And went to India, posing as a girl.
I shared the king's joys with no other wish
Than wedding the T'ang monk to seal my fate.
How wicked you are that you wreck our match!
So savage that you hunt me down to fight!
This weapon of mine has tremendous fame,
Surpassing greatly your golden-hooped rod.
A pestle for herbs in Vast-Cold Palace,[6]
Its one blow will send one to Yellow Spring."

On hearing this, Pilgrim laughed scornfully and said, "Dear cursed
beast! If you had lived in the Toad Palace, you couldn't be ignorant
of old Monkey's abilities, could you? And you still dare take a stand
here? Reveal your form and surrender at once, and I'll spare your
life!"

"I recognize that you are the Pi-ma-wên," said the fiend, "who
greatly disturbed the Celestial Palace five hundred years ago. I should
defer to you, I suppose. But ruining one's marriage is an act of bitter
enmity like murdering one's parents. Neither reason nor sentiment
would allow me to give in, and that's why I'm going to fight you
Heaven-defying Pi-ma-wên!"

Now, those three words, Pi-ma-wên, were most irksome to the
Great Sage. When he heard them, he became enraged and immediately
raised his iron rod to strike at her face. The monstrous deviate wielded
her club to meet him, and right before the West Heavenly Gate they
locked in savage combat once more. In this battle,

The golden-hooped rod,
The pestle for herbs,
Two weapons divine formed a worthy match
That one for marriage descended to Earth;
This one protecting the T'ang monk arrived here.
The king, actually, was not quite upright—
His love of flowers won a fiend's delight
And brought on this moment a bitter fight,
Both parties stirred to stubbornness and hate.
They charged and sallied to see who would win;
With taunts and slurs they waged a war of words.
The mighty pestle was rare in the world;
The rod's divine strength had e'en more appeal.

Golden beams flashing lit up Heaven's gate;
Cold mists lambent spread throughout the Earth.
They fought back and forth for over ten rounds.
The monster, growing weak, now lost her ground.

That monster-spirit fought more than ten rounds with Pilgrim. When
she saw how taut and fast was the style of the rod, she realized that it
would be difficult for her to prevail. After one feeble blow with her
club, she shook her body and changed into myriad shafts of golden
light to flee toward the south. The Great Sage gave chase, and they
suddenly reached a huge mountain. The monster's golden light
lowered and entered a mountain cave, completely disappearing from
sight. Fearing that she might sneak back to the kingdom to harm the
T'ang monk, Pilgrim took careful note of the shape of that mountain
before reversing the direction of his cloud to return to the kingdom
himself.

This was about the hour of the Monkey. The king, tugging at Tripitaka, was still shaking all over. "Sage monk, please save me!" was all
he could say. Those concubines and the queen, too, were quite apprehensive when they saw the Great Sage dropping down from the edge
of the clouds.

"Master," he cried, "I'm back!"

"Stand still, Wu-k'ung," said Tripitaka, "and don't alarm His
Majesty. Let me ask you what, in fact, has become of the princess?"

Standing outside the gate to the Magpie Palace, with hands folded
across his chest, Pilgrim said, "The false princess is a monstrous
deviate. At first I fought with her for half a day. When she found that
she could not prevail, she changed into a clear breeze and fled toward
the gate of Heaven. I shouted for the celestial deities to bar her way.
She changed back to her form and again fought over ten rounds with
me. Once more she changed into shafts of golden light to flee to a
mountain due south of here. I chased her there but couldn't find her.
Fearing that she may come back here to harm you, I came back to
look after you."

When the king heard this, he tugged at the T'ang monk to ask, "If
the false princess is a monstrous deviate, where is our real princess?"

"Let me catch the false princess first," Pilgrim responded at once,
"and your real princess will naturally return to you."

When the queen and palace ladies heard this declaration, their
fears were lifted. Each one of them went forward, bowed low, and

said, "I beg the sage monk to rescue our real princess and bring her back. When this whole affair has been cleared up, you will be amply rewarded."

"This is no place for us to talk," said Pilgrim. "Let His Majesty go to the main hall with my master. And let the queen and her companions return to their palaces. Have my brothers Pa-chieh and Sha Monk summoned to the palace so that they may give my master protection. I can then leave to subdue the monster. In that way, proper etiquette for what is public and private will be observed, and I shall be spared from worry. Please take note of what I have said, for it betokens a great deal of energy expended."

The king was most grateful to follow his suggestion. Hand in hand, he walked with the T'ang monk to the main hall, while the queen and the ladies returned to their own palaces. The king then asked for the preparation of a vegetarian meal and sent for Pa-chieh and Sha Monk. In a little while the two of them arrived, and Pilgrim gave them a thorough account of what had taken place and enjoined them to protect their master with all diligence. Mounting the cloud-somersault, our Great Sage hurtled through the air and left. All those officials before the main hall bowed low to the sky, and we shall leave them there for the moment.

The Great Sage Sun headed straight for the mountain to the south of the kingdom to begin his search. The monstrous deviate, you see, had fled there in defeat; on reaching the mountain, she crawled inside her hole and used pieces of rock to stop up its entrance. Terribly dismayed, she hid herself and kept totally out of sight. Pilgrim searched for a while, but he could detect no movement whatever. Growing anxious, he made the magic sign with his fingers and recited a spell to summon into his presence the local spirit and the mountain deity for interrogation. The two gods arrived and immediately kowtowed, both crying, "We didn't know! We didn't know! If we had known, we would have gone far to receive you. We beg you to pardon us."

"I'll not hit you just yet," said Pilgrim. "Let me question you instead. What's the name of this mountain? How many monster-spirits are to be found here? Tell me the truth and I'll pardon you."

"Great Sage," those two deities said, "this mountain is named Mount Hairbrush. It has three rabbit holes in it.[7] From antiquity till now there has never been any monster-spirit, for it is a blessed land of complete circularity. If the Great Sage wishes to find monster-spirits, he'd better stick to the road to the Western Heaven."

Pilgrim said, "When old Monkey arrived at the Kingdom of India in the Western Heaven, he discovered that the princess, the daughter of the king, had been abducted by a monster-spirit and left in the wilds. The monster-spirit assumed the form of the princess to deceive the king into erecting a festooned tower, from which she would toss an embroidered ball to select her husband. When I escorted my master beneath the tower, she purposely threw the ball on the T'ang monk, for she wanted to become his mate so that she could steal his primal yang through temptation. I saw through all that and revealed myself in the palace to capture her. Stripping off her human clothes and jewelry, she fought with me for half a day, wielding a short club called a pestle for herbs. Then she changed into a clear breeze to flee, but old Monkey caught up with her before the West Heavenly Gate, and we fought for another ten rounds or more. Realizing that she could not prevail, she changed into beams of golden light and fled here. Why is it that she can't be seen now?"

When the two deities heard this, they led Pilgrim at once to search the three rabbit holes. They began with the one at the foot of the mountain; looking there, they could see only a few wild rabbits, which were frightened away. When they searched their way up to the hole on the peak, however, they at once spotted two huge slabs of stone blocking its entrance. "This has to be where the monstrous deviate is," said the local spirit. "She must have crawled in there to evade your pursuit."

Pilgrim lifted away the stones with his iron rod. The monstrous deviate was indeed hiding in there. With a loud whoosh, she leaped out and attacked with upraised pestle. Pilgrim wielded his iron rod to parry the blow, so terrifying the two deities that the mountain god backed up and the local spirit darted away. "Who asked you two," whined the monster to the two of them, "to bring him here to look for me?" Barely able to withstand the iron rod, she fought as she retreated, rising to midair.

It was getting late, and the situation became more precarious. Growing more and more violent, Pilgrim was about to give her the coup de grace. Suddenly a voice rang out from the azure air of the Ninefold Heaven: "Great Sage, don't raise your hand! Don't raise your hand! Be lenient with your rod!"

Pilgrim turned to look and discovered the Star Lord of Supreme Yin, followed by the immortal Ch'ang-o and other lunar goddesses, all descending in front of him on a pink cloud. Pilgrim was so startled that he quickly put away his iron rod and bowed to receive them, saying, "Old Supreme Yin, where are you going? Pardon old Monkey for not stepping out of the way!"

"The monstrous deviate opposing you," said Supreme Yin, "happens to be the jade hare of my Vast-Cold Palace, the one who helps me pound the immortal drug of mysterious frost. On her own she picked open the gold lock and jade bolt and fled the palace for a year. I calculated that she might be in mortal danger at this moment, and that's why I have come to save her life. I beg the Great Sage to spare her for this old man's sake."

"Yes! Yes! Yes!" said Pilgrim. "I dare not refuse you, of course! No wonder she knows how to use a pestle for herbs! So, she is the little jade hare! But I wonder whether the old Supreme Yin knows of her kidnaping the princess of the Kingdom of India. She speciously assumed the form of the princess in order to ruin the primal yang of a sage monk, my master. Her desire and her offense are really intolerable. How could she be spared so lightly?"

"You have no knowledge of this either," said Supreme Yin. "The daughter of the king is no ordinary mortal. Originally she was the White Lady[8] of the Toad Palace. Eighteen years ago, after giving a slap to the little jade hare, she was overcome by mortal longings and went to the Region Below. The light of her soul found conception in the belly of the queen, and she was born to the royal family. Nursing the grudge of that single slap, this little jade hare ran away from our palace last year so that she could send the White Lady into the wilds. But she should not have wanted to marry the T'ang monk, and this offense is certainly unforgivable. Fortunately you were alert enough to discern the true and the false, so that she did not have a chance to ruin your master. I beg you, therefore, to pardon her for my sake. I'll take her back now."

"When you present me with this sort of karma," said Pilgrim, chuckling, "old Monkey dares not go against your wishes. But if you take away the little jade hare now, I fear that the king may not believe me. I hope, therefore, that Lord Supreme Yin and my immortal sisters will take the trouble of bringing the little jade hare to the kingdom and giving a clear testimony. In that way, not only the ability of old Monkey will be made known, but the reason for the descent of the

White Lady can also be told. Then we may ask the king to send for Princess White Lady, so that the purpose of manifest retribution may be clearly established."

Consenting to what he said, Lord Supreme Yin pointed at the monstrous deviate and snapped, "Cursed beast! Aren't you returning to what is right?" Rolling over on the ground, the little jade hare revealed her true form. Truly she has

Sharp teeth and divided lips,
Long ears with little hair.
Her body is a ball of furlike jade;
She can fly through mountains with paws outstretched.
The creamy straight nose
Seems brightly frosted or thickly powdered;
The shining red eyes
Can rival e'en white snow dotted with rouge.
Hugging the ground,
She's all fleecy like a bundle of silk;
Torso stretched out,
She's argent like a silver-threaded frame.
A number of times
She drinks at dawn the clear dew of Heaven's air,
And pounds long-life drug with a jade pestle rare.

Delighted by the sight, the Great Sage trod the cloudy luminosity, leading the way, followed by Lord Supreme Yin, Ch'ang-o and other lunar goddesses, and the jade hare.

They arrived at the Kingdom of India about dusk, and the moon was just rising. When they neared the city, they could hear the roll of drums on the watchtower. The king and the T'ang monk were still in the main hall, while Pa-chieh and Sha Monk, along with many officials at the foot of the steps, were discussing the cessation of court. They saw a glowing sheen of colored mists approaching from due south, its luminosity making the whole place bright as day. As they stared into the sky, they heard the Great Sage Sun crying out in a loud voice: "Your Majesty of India, please ask your queen and concubines to come out and look. Beneath this treasure canopy is the Star Lord of Supreme Yin, and the immortal sisters on both sides of him are the lunar goddesses and Ch'ang-o. This little jade hare is the false princess of your household; she has now revealed her true form."

The king hurriedly assembled the queen, his concubines, the palace maidens, and gaily-attired girls to bow to the sky and worship. He himself and the T'ang monk also expressed their thanks toward the sky by bowing low. All the households in the city also set up incense tables and kowtowed, chanting the name of Buddha.

As they looked up into the air, Chu Pa-chieh was moved to lust. Unable to contain himself, he leaped into the air and embraced a rainbow-skirted immortal, crying, "Sister, you and I are old acquaintances! Let's go play!"

Walking forward to grab hold of him, Pilgrim gave him a couple of slaps on the face and a scolding. "You vulgar Idiot!" he said. "Where do you think you are, that you dare vent your lust?"

"It's just a bit of slapstick," replied Pa-chieh, "to dispel my boredom and have some fun! That's all!" That Lord Supreme Yin ordered the entourage to turn. With the goddesses, they took the jade hare back to the Lunar Palace, while Pilgrim yanked Pa-chieh back to the ground.

After thanking Pilgrim in the main hall, the king asked, "Since the false princess has been captured by the mighty magic power of the divine monk, where is our true princess to be found?"

"That true princess of yours," replied Pilgrim, "did not come from mortal stock either. She was actually the immortal White Lady of the Lunar Palace. Because she slapped the jade hare once eighteen years ago, she thought of this world and descended to the Region Below, where she was conceived in your queen, who gave birth to her. Nursing this former enmity, the little jade hare last year picked open the jade bolt and gold lock and escaped to this place also. She kidnaped the White Lady and left her in the wilds before assuming her form to deceive you. This entire karmic process was told to me personally by Lord Supreme Yin himself. Today the false one has been removed; tomorrow you will be asked to go search for the real one."

On hearing this, the king became both embarrassed and alarmed, hardly able to hold back the tears flowing down his cheeks. "Child!" he said. "Since I was enthroned in my youth, I have never even left the gate of the city. Where should I go look for you?"

With a smile, Pilgrim said, "No need to be upset. Right now your princess is feigning madness at the Benefactor-of-Orphans Gold-Spreading Monastery. Let's retire. By morning I promise you I'll return your true princess." The other officials, too, prostrated themselves and said, "Let our king put his worries to rest. These several divine monks are buddhas who are able to soar on the clouds and ride the fog. Most certainly they possess the knowledge of past and future. Let the divine monks go make a search tomorrow, and undoubtedly they will get to the end of the matter." The king agreed, and ordered the pilgrims again taken to the Spring-Detaining Arbor for their meals and lodging. By then it was almost the hour of the second watch. Truly

The moon is fair, the copper pots mark their times
As wind wafts the tinklings of golden chimes.
Spring has half faded and the nightjars weep;
Petals shroud the path for the night is deep.
An idle swing the royal garden shades;
The silver stream a jade-blue sky invades.
None walks the streets or visits the bazaars
When night's aglow with a sky full of stars.

They all rested that night, and we shall leave them for the moment.

Because his demonic aura had been dispelled, the king's energy revived during the night. By the third quarter of the fifth watch, he appeared again to hold his morning court, after which he asked for the T'ang monk and his three disciples to come and discuss the matter of finding his daughter. The elder arrived and greeted him, while the Great Sage and his two brothers also bowed.

Returning their bows, the king said, "We spoke of our child, the princess, yesterday. May I trouble the divine monks to look for her?"

The elder said, "The day before your humble cleric came from the East, by nightfall we had entered a Benefactor-of-Orphans Gold-Spreading Monastery to ask for lodging. The priests there were good enough to accommodate our request. After dinner we took a stroll in the moonlight to go to look at the foundation of the old Gold-Spreading garden. Suddenly we heard the sound of lament. When we inquired into the matter, a priest of the monastery, who was already over a hundred years of age, sent away his attendants and told us, 'This is the source of that lament: Late spring last year, I was just meditating on the dialectical relation of the moon and our nature when a breeze brought to me the sounds of weeping and lament. When I arose from my mat and went down to the foundation of the Jetavana garden to look, I found a girl. On being questioned, she told me that she was the daughter of the King of India, blown to that place by a strong gust when she was enjoying the sight of flowers in the moonlight.' Since that old priest was quite knowledgeable in human propriety, he locked the princess in a quiet room. Fearing that she might be defiled by other priests in the monastery, he only told them that a monster-spirit had been locked up by him. The princess, too, understood his intentions; during the day she would babble absurdities just to win some sustenance of tea and rice for herself. During the night, however, with no one present, she would think of her parents and weep. That old priest had journeyed to the capital several times to try to ascertain the truth. When he learned that the princess, to all appearance, was in the palace and unharmed, he dared not present a memorial on the matter. When he learned, however, that my disciple had some magic powers, he urged us repeatedly to make a thorough investigation. Little did we expect that the jade hare of the Toad Palace had become a monster and, falsely fused with the true form, had taken on the appearance of the princess. The monster, moreover, was hoping to ruin my primal yang, and it was fortunate that my disciple exercised his magic power to distinguish the true from the specious. Now the hare has been taken back by the Star of Supreme Yin, but your worthy daughter may still be seen feigning madness at the Gold-Spreading Monastery."

When the king heard this meticulous account, he gave voice to loud weeping, so disturbing those in three palaces and six chambers that they arrived to make inquiry. When they learned of the cause, everyone wept profusely. After a long while, the king asked again, "How far is the Gold-Spreading Monastery from the city?"

"No more than sixty miles," replied Tripitaka.

The king at once issued this decree: "Let the consorts of the East and the West Palaces guard the main hall, while the court's Grand Preceptor will defend the kingdom. We and the queen herself will take the many officials and the four divine monks to the monastery and bring our princess home."

Immediately carriages were lined up and they all went out of the court. Look at that Pilgrim! He leaped into the air and, with one twist of his torso, arrived at the monastery before them. The priests there hurriedly knelt down to receive him, saying, "When the Venerable Father left, he walked with the rest of his companions. Why did you descend from the sky today?"

"Where is that old master of yours?" asked Pilgrim, laughing. "Ask him to come out quickly, so that you may set up incense tables to receive the royal carriage. The king and queen of India, along with many officials and my master, are about to arrive." The various monks could not quite comprehend what he was saying, and they asked the old priest to come out.

When the old priest caught sight of Pilgrim, he bent low and said, "Venerable Father, what have you found out about the princess?" Thereupon Pilgrim gave a thorough rehearsal of how the false princess tossed an embroidered ball to try to wed the T'ang monk, how he fought and chased her, and how Lord Supreme Yin appeared to take away the jade hare. The old priest again kowtowed to express his thanks.

Raising him with his hands, Pilgrim said, "Stop bowing! Stop bowing! Prepare quickly to receive the imperial carriage." Only then did those priests discover that a girl had been locked up in the back room. In amazement, they all went to help set up incense tables beyond the monastery gate. After putting on the cassocks, they began to toll the bells and roll the drums as they waited. In a little while the imperial carriage did indeed arrive. Truly

Auspicious mists and fragrance fill the sky
When to this rustic temple Grace draws nigh—
Like a timeless rainbow cleansing streams and seas,
Like springtime lightnings of sage kings' dynasties.
Such kindness the sylvan beauty advances;
Such moisture the wild floral scent enhances.
For relics left by an ancient elder,
This precious hall receives a wise ruler.

The king reached the monastery gate and was met outside by those monks in orderly rows. They all prostrated themselves to receive him. Then he saw Pilgrim standing in their midst.

"How did the divine monk manage to get here first?" asked the king.

"Old Monkey arrived here with a mere twist of his torso!" said Pilgrim, chuckling. "Why did you people take half a day to do it?" Thereafter the T'ang monk and the others arrived. With the elder leading the way, they went to the room at the back of the monastery, where they found the princess still babbling and feigning madness. Going to his knees, the old priest pointed to the room and said, "Inside this room is the lady princess who was blown here last year by the wind."

The king at once ordered the door opened, and they removed the iron lock from the door. When the king and queen caught sight of the princess and recognized her face, they rushed forward to embrace her, not at all bothered by the filth. "Our poor child!" they cried. What bitter fate has caused you to suffer like this here!" Truly the reunion of parents and child is not the same as any other kind of reunion. The three of them hugged each other and wailed. After they had cried for a while and had given expression to how greatly they missed each other, the king ordered scented liquid to be sent in for the princess so that she could bathe and change her clothing. They then climbed onto the imperial chariot together to return to the capital.

Afterward Pilgrim greeted the king once more with hands folded in front of him and said, "Old Monkey has another matter to bring to your attention."

Returning his greeting, the king said, "We shall obey whatever instruction the divine monk has for us."

Pilgrim said, "They told me that in your mountain here, the one named Hundred-Legs, there are centipedes which have become spirits recently and have harmed people during the night. The travelers and merchants have found that a great inconvenience. Since roosters are the natural foes of centipedes, I think you should select a thousand huge roosters and scatter them throughout the mountain so that these poisonous insects will be eliminated. You should change the name of this mountain also, and you should bestow a building decree to this monastery as a token of your gratitude for this monk's care for the princess."

Exceedingly pleased, the king immediately sent officials into the city to fetch the roosters. The name of the mountain was changed to Precious Flower. The Bureau of Labor was told to provide the necessary materials for the repair and renovation of the monastery, and its name was changed to the Royal Benefactor-of-Orphans Gold-Spreading Monastery of the Precious Flower Mountain. The priest was appointed a monk-official, with the perpetual title of Patriotic and an official salary of thirty-six stones. The monks, after giving thanks, saw the imperial carriage return to court, where the princess entered the various palaces to be reunited with her kinfolk. Large banquets were prepared for celebrating her homecoming and reunion with her family. The king and his subjects also joined in the revelry, drinking and feasting all evening.

The next morning the king issued the decree for portraits to be made of the four sage monks and mounted in the Chinese and

Barbarian Loft. The princess, with fresh clothing and makeup, was asked to come out to thank the T'ang monk and his three disciples once more for her deliverance. After that, the T'ang monk wanted to take leave of the king to journey westward, but the king, of course, refused to let them go. Again they were feted for five or six days, thus providing excellent opportunities for our Idiot to stuff himself repeatedly.

When the king saw, however, how eager they were in their desire to worship Buddha, rejecting all entreaties for them to stay, he presented them with two hundred ingots of gold and silver and a platter of treasures. Master and disciples refused to take even a penny. The king then ordered the imperial carriage for the old master to ride in and many officials to escort him to a great distance. The queen, the concubines, the officials, and the people all kowtowed without ceasing to express their thanks. When they reached the outskirts of the city, they saw the priests of the temple, too, had come to bow and see them off, reluctant to take leave of the pilgrims. When Pilgrim saw that all the people were unwilling to turn back, he had no choice but to make the magic sign with his fingers and blew a mouthful of immortal breath toward the ground on the southwest. Immediately a gust of dark wind blinded the people's eyes, and only then could the pilgrims proceed. Truly,

Cleansed by the gracious waves they returned to the revealing
    cause;[9]
Leaving the sea of metal they awaked to the true void.

We do not know what the journey ahead was like, and you should listen to the explanation in the next chapter.

Ninety-six

Squire K'ou gladly entertains a noble priest;
The elder T'ang does not covet riches.

Form's not originally form,
Nor is emptiness emptiness.
Quiet, noise, speech, and silence are all the same;
A dream in a dream needn't be told.[1]
The useful is useless in use;
No power is power applied to power.
It's like ripened fruits which redden naturally.
Don't ask how they're cultivated!
We were telling you about the disciple of the T'ang monk, who used his magic power to stop those priests from the Gold-Spreading Monastery. After the dark wind subsided, the priests, no longer able to see the master pilgrim and his disciples, thought that they had witnessed the descent of living buddhas. They therefore kowtowed and returned to their own monastery, and we shall speak no more of them.

Master and disciples proceeded toward the West, and once more it was the time of late spring and early summer.

The weather is pleasant and bright
With pond-lotus coming in sight.
Plums ripen after the rains;
Wheat in the wind its height attains.
With their young river swallows fly;
To feed their offspring pheasants cry.
The Dipper's south, the day's at its longest;
Fair and gay all things seem strongest.
Countless times they rested at night and dined at dawn, fording the streams and climbing the slopes. On a peaceful road they journeyed for half a month, and then they saw again a city ahead of them;

"Disciples," asked Tripitaka, "what sort of place is this again?"

"I don't know! I don't know!" replied Pilgrim.

"You have taken this road before," said Pa-chieh, giggling. "How could you say you don't know? There must be something uncanny about this place. You're deliberately pretending to be ignorant just to play a trick on us."

"This Idiot is completely unreasonable!" said Pilgrim. "Though I have traveled several times on this road, I did it in the air. I mounted the clouds to go back and forth. Since when did I ever make a stop on the ground? There was no reason for me to investigate what was of no concern to me. That's why I am ignorant. There's nothing uncanny here. Who wants to play a trick on you?"

As they talked, they came up to the edge of the city. Tripitaka dismounted to walk over the drawbridge and enter the gate. In a corridor by a long street, two old men were seated and conversing. "Disciples," said Tripitaka, "stand out in the middle of the road. Lower your heads and behave yourselves. Let me go up to the corridor to ask what place this is." Pilgrim and the rest indeed obeyed him and stood still.

The elder drew near, pressed his palms together, and called out, "Old patrons, this humble cleric salutes you."

Those two old men were just having a leisurely discussion—about the rise and fall, the gains and losses of past dynasties, about who were the sages and worthies, and about the great, lamentable fact that what had once been a heroic enterprise was now reduced to nothing —when they suddenly heard this salutation. They at once returned the greeting and said, "What does the elder wish to say?"

"This humble cleric came from afar to worship Buddha," said Tripitaka. "Having just reached your treasure region, I do not know its name. I would like to know also where I might find a family inclined to charity, so that I might beg a meal there."

One of the old men said, "This is the Bronze Terrace Prefecture, behind which is the Numinous Earth District. If the elder wishes to have vegetarian meal, there is no need for you to beg. Go past this archway, and on the street running north and south, you'll come to a towered-gate facing east guarded by figures of sitting tigers. This is the home of Squire K'ou; before his door there's also a plaque with the inscription, Ten Thousand Monks Will Not Be Barred. A distant traveler like you can enjoy all you want. Go! Go! Go! And don't interrupt our conversation!"

Having thanked them, Tripitaka turned and said to Pilgrim, "This is the Numinous Earth District of the Bronze Terrace Prefecture. The two old men told me that beyond the archway on the street running north and south, there is a tiger-guarded towered gate facing east. That's the home of Squire K'ou, where before the door there is a plaque bearing the inscription, Ten Thousand Monks Will Not Be Barred. They told us to go to that household to have a meal."

"The region of the West," said Sha Monk, "is the land of Buddha, so there must be people who wish to feed the monks. If this is only a district or a prefecture, there's no need for us to have our rescript certified. Let's go beg some food, and we can leave after the meal."

As the elder walked slowly through the long street with his three followers, they aroused again such alarm and suspicion of those people in the markets that they all crowded around the pilgrims to stare at their features. Telling his disciples to remain silent, the elder kept saying, "Behave yourselves! Behave yourselves!" The three of them indeed lowered their heads and dared not look up. After they turned a corner, they came upon a broad street running north and south.

As they walked along, they saw a tiger-guarded towered-gate, on the other side of which there was hung on the wall, a huge plaque with the inscription, Ten Thousand Monks Will Not Be Barred. "In this Buddha land of the West," said Tripitaka, "there's no deception in either the foolish or the wise. I was not prepared to believe what the two aged men told me, but what I see here confirms their story."

Always rude and impulsive, Pa-chieh wanted to go in at once. Pilgrim said, "Idiot, let's stop a moment. Wait till someone comes out. When we have obtained permission, then you may enter."

"What Big Brother says is quite right," said Sha Monk. "If we do not observe proper etiquette, we may offend the patron." They rested the horse and the luggage before the gate. In a little while, an old retainer appeared, carrying in his hands a scale and a basket. When he suddenly caught sight of the four, he was so startled that he abandoned his possessions and ran inside to report, "My lord, there are four strange-looking priests outside!"

The squire, leaning on his staff, was just taking a leisurely stroll in the courtyard, chanting repeatedly the name of Buddha. The moment he heard this report, he threw away his staff and hurried out to receive his visitors. When he saw the four pilgrims, he was not intimidated by their ugliness. All he said was, "Please come in! Please come in!"

With modesty Tripitaka entered with his disciples. After going through a little alley, the squire led them to a building and said, "This building houses the Buddha hall, the sūtra hall, and the dining hall which will entertain the Venerable Fathers. The building to the left is where this disciple and his family live." Tripitaka was full of compliments as he put on his cassock to worship Buddha. They ascended the hall to look around, and they saw

Fragrant clouds of incense,
And bright flames of candles;
A hall filled with bundles of silk and flowers,
Four corners festooned with gilt and colors.
On a vermilion prop
A bell of purple gold hangs high;
On colored lacquered frames
A pair of patterned drums are mounted.
A few pairs of banners
All embroidered with the eight jewels;
A thousand Buddhas
All gilded in gold.
An old bronze censer,
And an old bronze vase;
A carved lacquered table,
And a carved lacquered box.
From the old bronze censer
Arise unending curls of smoky fragrance;
Within the old bronze vase
Now and then the lotus displays its colors.
Five-colored clouds[2] fresh on the carved lacquered table;
Mounds of scented petals in the carved lacquered box.
In a crystal chalice,
The holy water's clear and clean;
In a lamp of glass,
The fragrant oil burns brightly.
The gold stone-chime's one note
Lingers and resonates.
Truly unsoiled by red dust in this precious tower,
A household Buddha-hall nobler than a temple.

Having purified his hands, the elder took up incense to kowtow and worship. Then he turned to go through the proper ceremony of greeting the squire, who said, however, "Just a moment! We shall do that

in the sūtra room." There they saw
  Square and erect cases—
  Jade and gold boxes—
  In square and erect cases
  Countless volumes of sūtra pile up;
  In jade and gold boxes
  Many notes and letters are collected.
  On the colored lacquered table
  Are paper, ink, brush, and inkstone—
  All exquisite items of the study.
  Before the pepper-dusted screens
  Are books, paintings, a psaltery, and chess—
  All marvelous objects of real pleasure.
  A divine stone-chime of jade o'erlaid with gold is placed there;
  A grapevine mat that shields the moon and wind is hung there.
  The pure air makes one cheerful and bright;
  A chaste mind sets free the mind of Tao.

Having reached the place, the elder was about to go through the ceremony when he was stopped again by the squire, saying, "Please take off your Buddha robe." Tripitaka doffed his cassock, and only then was he allowed to give his host the proper greeting. Then the squire also exchanged greetings with Pilgrim and his two brothers. He asked his servants to feed the horse and to place the luggage in the corridor. Only then did he inquire about the pilgrims' origin.

Tripitaka said, "Your humble cleric has been sent by royal decree of the Great T'ang in the Land of the East to visit the Spirit Mountain of your treasure region in order to seek true scriptures from the Buddhist Patriarch. I heard that your honored household reveres the monks, and that's why I came bowing. I would like to beg for a meal, and then we shall leave."

His face beaming with pleasure, the squire smiled broadly and said, "Your disciple's surname is K'ou. My given name is Hung (Great), and my style is Ta-k'uan (Liberality). I'm sixty-four years old. At the age of forty, I made a vow which would not be fulfilled until I had fed ten thousand monks. This has been going on for twenty-four years. I have kept a record of all those I have fed. Recently in my leisure hours, I went through the names of the monks and discovered that I have fed nine thousand, nine hundred, and ninety-six persons. Only four more remain before I reach the number of perfection. It is indeed my good fortune that Heaven has sent me today you four old masters to complete this number. Please leave me your honored titles, and you must stay here for a month also. Please wait until we have performed the ceremony of the completion of a vow. Your disciple will then escort you all to the mountain with horses and carriages. Our region is only some eight hundred miles from the Spirit Mountain. It's not very far." Exceedingly pleased by what he heard, Tripitaka agreed to what he proposed, and we shall leave them for the moment.

Several houseboys, old and young, went into the squire's residence to haul firewood and bail water. They also took out rice, noodles, and vegetables in order to prepare the dietary meal. All these activities led the aged wife of the squire to ask, "Where do these monks come from, that they have to receive such special treatment?"

"When our master asked these four noble priests about their origin," replied the houseboys, "one of them said that they were sent by the Great T'ang emperor to worship our Holy Father Buddha in the Spirit Mountain. Who knows how great a distance they have covered to reach our place, but our master said that they came from Heaven. He told us to prepare a vegetarian meal quickly to entertain them."

Delighted also by what she heard, the old woman said to her maid, "Get me some clothes. I want to go meet them also."

"Madam," said one of the houseboys, "you want to meet only one of them, not the other three. Their features are extremely ugly!"

"You people are just ignorant," said the old woman. "When the features are ugly, strange, or extraordinary, they must belong to celestial beings descending to the Region Below. Run along now and announce my presence to your master."

The houseboys dashed out to the sūtra hall to say to the squire, "Madam is here. She wishes to meet the venerable fathers of the Land of the East." On hearing this, Tripitaka rose from his seat as the old woman arrived at the hall. She raised her eyes and scrutinized the dignified and handsome features of the T'ang monk. Then she turned to look at Pilgrim and his two companions, whose appearances were extraordinary indeed! Though she thought that they were celestial beings descended to Earth, she did feel a little nervous as she went to her knees to bow to them.

Hurriedly returning her salutation, Tripitaka said, "The Lady Bodhisattva has erroneously paid us great homage."

The old woman asked the squire, "Why aren't these four masters

sitting together?" Sticking out his snout, Pa-chieh said, "We three are
only disciples!" Eeeee! That one declaration of his seemed like a tiger's
roar deep in the mountain! The old woman became more frightened
than ever.

As they spoke, another houseboy came to say, "The two uncles
have arrived." Turning quickly to look, Tripitaka found two young
hsiu-ts'ai,[3] who walked up the sūtra hall and bent low toward the
elder. Tripitaka hastily returned their greetings, while the squire
tugged at him and said, "These are my two sons, named K'ou Liang
and K'ou Tung. They have just returned from school and haven't had
their lunch yet. Learning of the master's arrival, they have come to
bow to you." Delighted, Tripitaka said, "Excellent! Excellent! Truly

To exalt your house doing good's the rule.

To have good sons you must send them to school."
"Where did this Venerable Father come from?" the two young men
asked their father.

"From a great distance," replied the squire, laughing. "He is some-
one sent by the Great T'ang emperor in the Land of the East, at the
South Jambūdvīpa Continent, to go see the Holy Father Buddha at
Spirit Mountain and acquire scriptures."

One *hsiu-ts'ai* said, "I read in *A Guide through the Forest of Affairs*[4]
that the world is divided into four continents. Our region here belongs
to the West Aparagodānīya Continent, and there is also an East
Pūrvavideha Continent. I wonder how many years it took him to
travel from South Jambūdvīpa to this place?"

With a smile, Tripitaka said, "This humble cleric on his journey has
spent more days in being delayed than in traveling. Frequently I fell
to poisonous demons and savage fiends, to thousands of bitter ordeals.
I am fortunate to have the protection of my three disciples. Altogether
I have experienced fourteen summers and winters before arriving at
your treasure region."

When they heard this, the two *hsiu-ts'ai* paid him effusive compliments, saying, "Truly a divine monk! Truly a divine monk!" Hardly
had they finished speaking when a young boy came to say, "The
maigre has been spread out. We invite the Venerable Fathers to partake." The squire asked his wife to return to their residence with his
sons. He himself accompanied the four pilgrims to the dining hall for
the meal.

The appointments in the hall were arranged in a most orderly manner, with gilded lacquered tabletops and black-lacquered arm chairs. The front row of food consisted of a crouque-en-bouche of five colors, created in the latest fashion by the most skillful and artistic hands. In the second row there were five platters of little dishes, while the third row had five plates of fruits. The fourth row had five big platters of snacks, every item delicious and fragrant. The vegetarian soups, the rice, the steamed dumplings and buns were all steaming hot and most appetizing. Seven or eight houseboys dashed back and forth to serve them, and four or five chefs never stopped working. Look at them! Some brought in soup while others added rice; coming and going, they were like meteors chasing the moon. Our Chu Pa-chieh swallowed a bowl with one gulp, and he went after the food like wind sweeping away the clouds. Master and disciples thus enjoyed a full meal.

The elder rose and, having thanked the squire for the maigre, was about to leave immediately. Stopping him, the squire said, "Old teacher, please relax and stay for a few days. As the proverb says, Beginning is easy but the end is hard. Please wait till I have performed the rite of completion. Only then would I dare escort you on your way." When Tripitaka saw how sincere and earnest he was, he had no choice but to remain.

Not until six or seven days had gone by did the squire invite some twenty-four local Buddhist priests to conduct a service of the completion of a vow. The priests spent three or four days to compose the service, and, having selected an auspicious date, they began the sacrifice. Their manner, of course, was no different from that of the Great T'ang. They too

Unfurled the huge banners
And set up the gilded images;
Lifted high the tall candles
And burned incense to worship.
They rolled drums and tapped cymbals;
They blew on reeds and kneaded pipes.
The little gongs
And the flute's pure tones
All followed the *kung-ch'ê* notations.[5]
They struck up the music
And played for a while
Before beginning to chant the sūtras aloud.

First they pacified the local spirits;
Next they called on divine warriors.
They burned and sent off the documents,
And they bowed to Buddha's images.
They recited the *Peacock Sūtra*,
Each sentence woe-dispelling;
They lighted the Bhaiṣajya Lamp,
Its flame both bright and blazing.
They did the *Water Penitential*
To dissolve guilt and enmity;
They proclaimed the *Garland Sūtra*
To remove slander and strife.
Triyāna's wondrous law had the finest aim;
One or two Śramaṇa were all the same.

For three days and nights it went on like that, and at last the service was over. Thinking of Thunderclap, the T'ang monk wanted to leave. As he tried to thank his host, the squire said, "The old teacher is so eager to leave! It must be that my preoccupation with the service these last few days has caused me to slight you in some manner, and you are offended."

"I have greatly disturbed your noble residence," replied Tripitaka, "and I do not know how I can repay you. Dare I even speak of offense? It's just that when my sage ruler escorted me out of the imperial pass, he asked me when I would return. By mistake I replied that I should be back in three years. Little did I expect that I would be on the road for fourteen years! And I still don't know whether I'd be able to acquire the scriptures! By the time I have taken them back, it will probably be another twelve or thirteen years. Would I not have violated the sage decree? What unbearable crime would that be? I beg the old squire to let this humble cleric proceed. Wait till I have acquired the scriptures; then I'll come back to stay a little longer at your mansion. That should be permissible."

Unable to contain himself, Pa-chieh shouted, "Master, you're too insensitive to human wishes! You've no regard for human sentiments! The old squire must be a very rich man if he has been able to make such a vow to feed priests. Now that it is completed, and now that he is urging us so earnestly to stay, there's no harm in our remaining a year or so. Why must you insist on leaving? Why should we abandon such ready-made provisions and resume begging from someone else?

What old father or mother's family do you have ahead of you?"

"You coolie!" snapped the elder. "All you know is eating! You never have a thought for returning to your origin. Truly you're a beast who cares only for

Eating in the trough

To ease your belly's itch!

Since you crave so much to indulge in this deluded passion, I'll leave tomorrow by myself."

When Pilgrim saw that even the color of his master's face had changed, he grabbed Pa-chieh and pounded him with his fists. "This Idiot," he cried, "without knowing any better, has caused Master to blame even *us*!"

"That's a good beating! That's a good beating!" said Sha Monk, chuckling. "Even when he's silent, as he is now, he annoys people! Wait till he butts in again with his mouth!" In a huff, our Idiot stood to one side and dared not utter another word. When the squire saw that master and disciples had become agitated, he tried to placate them with a broad smile, saying, "Please calm yourself, old teacher, and bear with us for one more day. Tomorrow I shall prepare some banners and drums and invite a few relatives and neighbors to see you off."

As they conversed, the old woman appeared and said, "Old Master, if you have come to our house, there is no need for you to rush off so eagerly. How many days have you been staying, anyway?"

"Already half a month," replied Tripitaka.

"Let that half-month be counted as the meritorious service of the squire," said the old woman. "I too have accumulated a little cash from sewing, and I have hopes also of feeding the old master for half a month."

She had barely finished speaking when K'ou Tung and his brother also came out and said, "Please hear us, you four Venerable Masters. Our father fed the monks for over twenty years, but he had never come upon a good person. Now he is lucky enough to reach the number of perfection only because of your arrival, which has, as it were, brought radiance to a thatched hut. Your students are too young to know much about karma, but we do know the proverb:

What pa sows pa reaps;

What ma sows ma reaps;

One who sows not, reaps not.

The reason our father and mother wish to extend their hospitality is just so that they may each attain certain karmic reward. Why must you refuse them so bitterly? Even we foolish brothers have saved up a small sum from our school allowances, with which we, too, would like to entertain the Venerable Masters for half a month before we see you off."

"Already I dare not accept the great kindness of your mother, the old Bodhisattva," said Tripitaka. "How could I presume upon the affection of you worthy brothers? I truly dare not. I must leave this day, and I implore all of you to pardon me. If I remained, I would have exceeded the imperial limit, and my crime would be even greater than one punishable by execution."

When the old woman and her two sons saw that he was adamant, they grew angry and said, "Out of good intentions we wanted him to stay, but he's bent on leaving. All right! He wants to go, let him go! No need to chatter any more!" Mother and sons thereupon got up and went inside.

Unable to restrain himself, Pa-chieh spoke again to the T'ang monk, "Master, don't overdo your playacting! As the proverb says,

To stay's appropriate.
Loitering irritates!

Let us stay here for one more month, just to satisfy the wishes of mother and sons. What's the hurry?"

"Oh?" snapped the T'ang monk, and immediately our Idiot gave his own mouth a couple of slaps, saying, "Shhhhh! Shhhhh! Don't talk! You're making noises again!" On one side Pilgrim and Sha Monk began to giggle uncontrollably.

"What are you laughing at?" said the T'ang monk to Pilgrim, sorely annoyed. Making the magic sign with his fingers, he was about to recite the Tight-Fillet Spell. So horrified was Pilgrim that he at once went to his knees to say, "Master, I wasn't laughing! I wasn't laughing! Don't recite that spell, I beg you!"

When the squire saw that master and disciples were becoming more and more rancorous, he dared not insist on their staying any longer. All he said was, "The Venerable Masters need not quarrel. I promise you that I shall escort you on your way tomorrow." He went out of the sūtra hall and told his secretary to send over a hundred invitations to his relatives and neighbors to join him in sending off in the morning the old master from the T'ang court in his westward

journey. In the meantime, he ordered the chefs to prepare a farewell
banquet, and his steward to have twenty pairs of colored banners
made up and to find a band of musicians and drummers. A group of
monks from the South Advent Monastery and a group of Taoists from
the East Mountain Temple were to be ready to join the party by the
hour of the Serpent in the morning. His domestic staff obeyed and left.
In a little while, it was nightfall. After the evening meal, they all
retired. You see

A few crows to the village homeward fly.
Drums and bells toll from distant towers high.
Human traffic ceases in the street and mart;
From all households lights and fires now depart.
In moonlight and wind blossoms show their shade;
The stars the obscure silver stream pervade.
The night has deepened for the nightjars weep;
The heavens grow silent when the earth's asleep.

At the time it was no more than the hour between the third and fourth
watch when those houseboys in charge of various affairs all rose early
in order to complete their tasks. Look at them!

Those preparing the banquet
Rushed about in the kitchen;
Those making the colored banners
Clamored before the hall;
Those beckoning monks and priests
Sprinted on their two legs;
Those calling for musicians
Hurled themselves forward;
Those sending out invitations
Darted east and west;
Those readying horse and carriage
Shouted back and forth.

From the hour of midnight, the tumult lasted till dawn. By about the
hour of the Serpent, every business was concluded—with money, of
course!

We tell you now about the T'ang monk and his disciples, who also
rose early, attended by all those people. The elder at once gave the
instruction to pack and to hitch up the horse. When our Idiot heard
that they were truly about to leave, he pouted his fat lips some more
and grumbled incessantly, but he had no choice other than to pack

up the cassock and almsbowl and pick up the pole and its load. Having
brushed and scrubbed down the horse, Sha Monk saddled it and
waited. Pilgrim handed the nine-ringed priestly staff to his master and
hung the satchel containing his travel rescript on his own chest. They
were about to walk out together when the squire came to invite them
to a large sitting room in the rear, where a huge banquet was spread
out. The hospitality they encountered here was quite different from
what they received in the dining hall in front. They saw

Curtains loftily hung
And screens on all four sides.
Hung in the center
Was a painting with the aged mountain and blessed sea motif;
Displayed on two walls
Were the scenes of spring, summer, autumn, and winter.
From dragon-veined tripods rose incense smoke;
Auspicious air grew in crow-tortoise urns.
The display-plates' many colors
Showed vivid bejeweled floral patterns;
The side tables' mounds of gold
Held orderly rows of lion-god candies.
Drums and dances followed the graceful notes;
Brocadelike food and fruits were placed in the hall.
Such refined vegetarian soup and rice!
Such attractive fragrant tea and wine!
Though this was a home of a commoner,
It was not different from a noble's house.
You could hear only a joyous hubbub
That truly disturbed Heaven and Earth.

The elder was just greeting the squire when a houseboy appeared and
said, "The guests have all arrived."

These were all neighbours left and right, the wife's brothers, the
cousins, and the sisters' husbands. There were also squires who had
jointly pledged to keep a diet, and Buddhist believers. After all of them
bowed ceremoniously to the elder, they took their proper seats as
pipes and strings played below the steps and the feasting went on
inside the hall.

This sumptuous spread had the undivided attention of Pa-chieh,
who said to Sha Monk, "Brother, let yourself go and eat! When we
leave the K'ou home, there'll be no more rich fare like this!"

"What are you saying, Second Elder Brother!" said Sha Monk, chuckling. "As the proverb puts the matter

The hundred flavors of rare dainties

Are no more once you've eaten your fill.

You may accumulate private savings

But not in your stomach private hoardings!"

"You're much too feeble! Too feeble!" replied Pa-chieh. "When I have eaten to the limits in one meal, I won't be hungry again even after three days!"

Hearing him, Pilgrim said, "Idiot, don't puncture your belly! We have to be on the road!"

Hardly had they finished speaking when it was almost noon. The elder, in his seat of honor, lifted his chopsticks to recite the Sūtra for the End of Maigre. So alarmed was Pa-chieh that he took up the rice, downed one bowl with a gulp, and put away five or six more bowls. Next he picked up those buns, rolls, cakes, and baked goods and stuffed both his sleeves full of them, regardless of whether they were good or bad. Only then did he leave the table, following his master. Having thanked the squire and the other guests, the elder walked out of the door, encountering many colorful banners and treasure canopies, drummers and musicians, on the other side. The two bands of Taoist priests and Buddhist monks were just arriving.

With a smile the squire said to them, "All of you are late, and the old master is eager to leave. There is no time for me to present you with the maigre. Allow me to thank you when we come back." Those pulling the carriages, riding horses, or walking all stepped aside for the four pilgrims to proceed. As they went forward, loud strains of music and the roll of drums drifted skyward while banners and flags blotted out the sun. The whole place was clogged by people, chariots, and horses, as everyone came to see Squire K'ou sending off the T'ang monk. The wealth and riches so displayed.

Surpassed the enclosures of pearl and jade,

And rivaled those silken drapes of love.

Those monks played a Buddhist tune, after which the priests struck up a Taoist melody, as they all escorted the pilgrims out of the prefectural city. When they reached the tenth-mile wayside station,[6] food and drink were served, and they toasted each other once more as they bade farewell.

The squire, however, still could not bear to part with his guests.

Blinking back his tears, he said, "When the Venerable Master returns after acquiring the scriptures, he must come to our house to stay for a few days. That'll be the fulfillment of K'ou Hung's wish."

Deeply moved, Tripitaka thanked him repeatedly, saying, "If I reach the Spirit Mountain and get to see the Buddhist Patriarch, your great virtue will be the first to be told. On my return, I shall surely stop at your door to express my thanks!" Speaking in this manner, they went on for two or three more miles. The elder earnestly bowed to take leave of his host, and the squire had to turn back, wailing loudly. Truly

Vowing to feed monks, he'd return to wondrous knowledge;
But with no affinity he could not see Tathāgata.

We shall speak no more of Squire K'ou, who escorted the pilgrims to the tenth-mile wayside station and then returned with his other companions to his house. We tell you instead about the master and his three disciples, who journeyed for some forty or fifty miles, when the sky darkened. "It's getting late," said the elder. "Where shall we ask for lodging?"

Toting the luggage, Pa-chieh pouted and said, "There's ready-made rice, but you won't eat it! There's a house built with cool tiles but you won't live in it! All you want is to hurry on some journey, like a lost soul going to a funeral! Now it's getting late. If it rains, what are we going to do then?"

"You brazen cursed beast!" scolded the T'ang monk. "You're complaining again! As the proverb says,

Ch'ang-an may be fine,
But it's no place to linger in.

Wait till we reach the affinity of seeing the Buddhist Patriarch and acquire the true scriptures. When we return to the Great T'ang and report to our lord, we will let you eat the rice from the imperial kitchen for several years. I hope, you cursed beast, you'll become so bloated that you'll die and become an overstuffed ghost!" Our Idiot giggled silently and dared not utter another word.

Pilgrim peered into the distance and discovered several buildings by the main road. He said quickly to his master, "Let's rest over there! Let's rest over there!" The elder drew near and saw that it was shrine which had collapsed. On top of the shrine was an old plaque, on which there was an inscription written in dust-covered, faded letters: The Temporary Court of Bright Radiance.

Dismounting, the elder said, "The Bodhisattva Bright Radiance was the disciple of the Buddha of Flames and Five Lights. Because of his expedition against the Demon King of Poisonous Fire, he was demoted and changed into the Spirit Officer of Five Manifestations. They must have a shrine keeper here." They all went inside, but they discovered that both rooms and corridors had toppled and there was no sign of any human person. They would have turned and gone back out were it not for the fact that dark clouds suddenly had gathered above and a torrential rain descended. They had little choice but to find whatever shelter they could in that dilapidated building and remain there in stealthy silence, fearing that they might otherwise disturb some monstrous deviates. Either sitting or standing, they endured a sleepless night. Ah! Truly

Prosperity's limit begets negativity;

In the midst of pleasure they encounter grief.

We do not know what was their condition when they proceeded in the morning, and you must listen to the explanation in the next chapter.

Ninety-seven

Gold-dispensing External aid[1] meets demonic harm;
The sage reveals his soul to bring restoration.

Let us not speak for the moment of the T'ang monk and his disciples,
who spent a night of discomfort in the dilapidated shrine of Bright
Radiance to seek shelter from the rain. We tell you now instead
about a group of violent men in the city located at the Numinous
Earth District of the Bronze Terrace Prefecture, who had squandered
away their possessions through sleeping with prostitutes, drinking,
and gambling. Without any other means of livelihood, those men—
more than a dozen of them—banded together to become thieves. As
they deliberated on which family in the city might be considered the
richest and which the second richest for them to rob, one of them said,
"There's no need for investigation or calculation. There's only one
man here who is very rich, and he's that Squire K'ou who sent off
today the priest from the T'ang court. In this rainstorm tonight,
people won't be out in the streets, and the police won't make their
rounds. We should strike now and take some capital from him. Then
we can go and have some more fun, whoring and gambling. Won't
that be nice?"

Delighted, the thieves all agreed. Taking up daggers, caltrops, staffs,
clubs, ropes, and torches, they set out in the rain. Having broken
through the gates of the K'ou home, they rushed in with a shout. The
members of his family, young and old, male and female, were so
terrified that they all fled. The squire's wife cowered under their bed,
while the old man hid behind a door. K'ou Liang, K'ou Tung, and his
other children all scattered in every direction.

Grasping weapons and torches, the thieves broke open the chests
and trunks in the house and ransacked them for gold, silver, treasures,
jewels, clothing, utensils, and other household goods. Agonized at
parting with all his possessions, the squire risked his life to walk outside his house and plead with the robbers, saying, "Great Kings, please
take what you need. But leave this old man a few things and some

359

garments for his remaining years."

Those robbers, of course, would not permit such discussion. They rushed forward, and one kick at the groin sent Squire K'ou tumbling to the ground. Alas!

His three spirits[2] gloomily drifted back to Hades;
His seven souls slowly took leave of mankind.

After their success, the thieves left the K'ou residence and climbed out of the city by means of rope ladders they set up along the rampart walls. They then fled toward the west through the night rain.

Only when they saw that the thieves had left did the houseboys and servants of the K'ou household dare show themselves. They immediately discovered the old squire lying dead on the ground. "O Heavens! Our master has been slain!" they cried, bursting into tears as they fell on the corpse to mourn him.

By about the hour of the fourth watch, the old woman began to think spitefully of the T'ang monk. Because of his refusal to stay and enjoy their hospitality, she thought, they had to make such lavish arrangements to send him off and brought on themselves instead this terrible calamity. Her rancor thus aroused her desire to plot against the four pilgrims. As she leaned on K'ou Liang for support, she said, "Child, there's no need for you to weep anymore. Your old man used to be so eager to feed monks. He wanted to do it one day after another. Little did he know that when he achieved perfection, he would run into a bunch of murderous monks!"

"Mother," said the two brothers, "what do you mean by murderous monks?"

"When those savage robbers broke into our room," replied their mother, "I hid under our bed. Though I was shaking all over, I managed to take a good look at them under the glare of torches and lights. Do you know who they were? The one holding a torch was the T'ang monk. Chu Pa-chieh was holding a knife and Sha Monk was dragging out our silver and gold. The one who slew your old man was Pilgrim Sun."

Thinking that what they heard was the truth, her two sons said, "If mother caught a clear glimpse of them, they had to be the robbers. After all, the four of them spent over half a month here, and they must be completely familiar with the layout of our house—with the entrances, the walls, the casements, and the alleys. Wealth is a big temptation. That's why they have taken advantage of this night's rain to return here. Not only have they robbed us of our possessions, but they have also slain our father. How vicious can they be? In the morning we must go to the prefecture to file charges against them."

"How shall we word the complaint?" asked K'ou Tung.

"Exactly as mother told us," replied K'ou Liang, and this was what he wrote:

Pa-chieh cried for slaughter;
The T'ang monk held the fire.
Sha Monk removed our silver and gold
While Pilgrim Sun beat to death our sire.

The whole family was in uproar, and soon it was dawn. They sent word immediately to their relatives to prepare for the funeral and purchase the coffin. Meanwhile, K'ou Liang and his brother went to the prefectural hall to file their plaint. Now, the magistrate of this Bronze Terrace Prefecture, you see, was

Upright all his life,
And his nature, virtuous.
In his youth he had studied studiously
And had been examined at Golden Chimes.
At all times, he had been a patriot,
A man full of mercy and kindness.
His fame would spread in history for a thousand years
As if Kung and Huang[3] reappeared;
His name would resound forever in the halls of justice
As if Cho and Lu[4] were reborn.

After he had ascended the prefectural hall and disposed of routine affairs, he ordered the display of the placard which announced that he was ready to hear and decide cases. The K'ou brothers placed the placard in one of their bosoms and entered the hall. Falling to their knees, they cried, "Venerable Father, these little ones wish to file a complaint on the weighty matter of robbery and murder."

The complaint was handed over to the magistrate, who, having read its content, said, "People said yesterday that your family, by feeding four noble priests, had fulfilled a vow. Those four, we were told, happened to be arhats from the T'ang court, and they were sent off by you with a lavish band of drummers and musicians clogging the streets. How could such a thing happen to you last night?"

Kowtowing, the two brothers said, "Venerable Father, K'ou Hung, our father, had been feeding monks for some twenty-four years. It happened that these four monks coming from a great distance would just make up the number of ten thousand. That was why we had a ceremony of perfection and asked them to stay for half a month. They thereby became thoroughly acquainted with the layout of our house. After we had sent them off yesterday, however, they returned during the night, taking advantage of the darkness and the rainstorm. With lighted torches and weapons, they broke into our home and took away our silver and gold, our treasures and jewels, and our clothing. Moreover, they slew our father and left him on the ground. We beg the Venerable Father to grant us humble folks justice!"

When the magistrate heard these words, he at once called up both cavalry and foot soldiers. Including other recruits and conscripts, they formed a posse of some hundred and fifty men. Each wielding sharp weapons, they went out of the western gate to pursue the T'ang monk and his three companions.

We tell you now about master and disciples, who waited patiently till dawn in the dilapidated building of the Bright Radiance Temporary Court before emerging and setting out again toward the West. It so happened that those thieves who had robbed the K'ou family the night before also took this same road after getting out of the city. By morning they had walked some twenty miles past the shrine. Hiding in a valley, they were dividing up their booty and had not quite finished when they saw the four pilgrims moving up the road.

Still unsatisfied, the thieves pointed at the T'ang monk and said, "Isn't that the monk who was sent off yesterday?" Then they laughed and said, "Welcome! Welcome! After all we are engaged in this ruthless business! These monks have traveled quite a distance. And then they stayed for a long time in the K'ou house. We wonder how much stuff they have on them. We might as well cut them off and take their belongings and the white horse. We'll split the heist, too. Won't that be a satisfying thing?"

Picking up their arms, the thieves ran up the main road with a shout. They stood in a single file across the road and cried, "Monks, don't run away! Quickly give us some toll money, and your lives will be spared! If only half a no escapes from your mouth, each of you will face the cutlass. None will be spared!"

The T'ang monk, riding the horse, shook violently, while Sha Monk and Pa-chieh were filled with fear. "What shall we do? What shall we do?" they said to Pilgrim. "After half a night's misery through the rain, we now face bandits blocking our path. Truly, 'Calamity always knocks twice!'"

"Master, don't be afraid!" said Pilgrim with laughter. "And don't worry, Brothers! Let old Monkey question them a bit."

Dear Great Sage! Tightening his tigerskin skirt and giving his silk shirt a shake, he walked up there with folded arms and said, "What do you all do?"

"This fellow has no idea of life or death!" bellowed one of the bandits. "How dare you question me? Don't you have eyes beneath your skull? Can't you recognize that we're all Father Great Kings? Hand us the toll money quickly, and we'll let you through!"

On hearing this, Pilgrim smiled broadly·and said, "So you are bandits who pillage on the road!"

"Kill him!" shouted the bandits, turning savage.

Pretending to be frightened, Pilgrim said, "Great Kings! Great Kings! I'm a village priest, and I don't know how to talk. If I've offended you, please pardon me. If you want toll money, you needn't ask those three. All you need is to ask me for it, for I'm the book-keeper. Whatever cash we have collected from reciting sūtras or holding services, whatever we've acquired through begging or charity, they're all in the wrap. I'm in charge of all incomes and expenditures. Though he's my master, the one riding the horse only knows how to recite sūtras. He has no other concern, for he has quite forgotten about wealth or sex, and he doesn't own a penny. The one with the black face is a laborer I took in halfway in our journey, and he only knows how to care for the horse. The one with a long snout is a long-term laborer I hired, and all he knows is how to tote the luggage. If you let those three past, I'll give you all our possessions, including the cassock and the almsbowl."

When they heard this, the thieves said, "This monk is quite honest after all. Tell those three to drop the luggage, and we'll let them go by." Pilgrim turned and winked at his companions. Immediately, Sha Monk dropped the pole and the luggage. He and Pa-chieh led the horse and proceeded westward with their master. As Pilgrim lowered his head to untie the luggage, he managed quickly to scoop up a fist-ful of dirt, which he tossed into the air. Reciting a spell, he exercised the magic of immobilization. "Stop!" he cried, and those bandits—

altogether some thirty of them—all stood erect. Each of them with teeth clenched, eyes wide open, and hands lowered, they could neither talk nor move.

Leaping clear from them into the road, Pilgrim shouted, "Master, come back! Come back!"

"That's bad! Bad!" said Pa-chieh, horrified. "Elder Brother is sacrificing us! He has no money on him, and there is neither silver nor gold in the wrap. He must be calling back Master for the horse. And he may be asking us to strip."

"Second Elder Brother, stop that nonsense!" said Sha Monk, chuckling. "Big Brother is an able person. Previously he could subdue even vicious demons and fierce fiends. You think he's afraid of these few clumsy bandits? When he calls, he must have something to say. Let's go back quick to have a look."

The elder agreed; turning around the horse, he went back amiably and said, "Wu-k'ung, why do you call me back?"

"All of you see what these bandits have to say," said Pilgrim. Pa-chieh walked up to one of them and gave him a shove, saying, "Bandit, why can't you move?" That man, however, was completely oblivious and speechless.

"He must be numb and dumb!" said Pa-chieh.

Chuckling, Pilgrim said, "They have been stopped by the magic of Immobilization of old Monkey." "You might have stopped their bodies, but not their mouths," said Pa-chieh. "Why can't they make even a noise?"

Pilgrim said, "Master, please dismount and take a seat. As the proverb says,

There's erroneous arrest
But no mistaken release.

Brothers, push these bandits over and tie them up. We'll tell them to confess, to see if they are new thieves or experienced bandits."

"But we have no ropes!" said Sha Monk. Pilgrim pulled off some hairs and blew his immortal breath on them. At once they changed into some thirty ropes. All the brothers worked together: they pushed over the bandits and hog-tied them. Then Pilgrim recited the spell of release, and the bandits gradually regained consciousness.

Pilgrim asked the T'ang monk to take a seat above them before the three brothers, each holding his weapon, and shouted at the thieves, "Clumsy thieves, how many of you are there altogether? For how many years have you engaged in this business? How much stuff have you plundered? Have you killed anyone? Is this the first transgression? The second? Or the third?"

"Fathers, please spare our lives," the thieves cried.

"Don't yell!" said Pilgrim. "Make an honest confession."

"Venerable Father," said the thieves, "we are not accustomed to thievery, for we are all sons of good families. Because we are stupid enough to drink, gamble, and sleep with prostitutes, we have completely squandered our inheritances and properties. We have neither abilities nor money for our livelihood. Since we learned that Squire K'ou in the prefectural city of Bronze Terrace had vast possessions, we banded together yesterday and went to pillage his household last night, taking advantage of the rain and darkness. We took silver, gold, clothing, and jewels. Just now, we were dividing the loot in the valley north of the road here when we saw you coming. Someone among us recognized that you were those priests whom Squire K'ou sent off, and we thought that you must have great possessions also. When we saw, moreover, how heavy the luggage was and how swiftly the white horse trotted, we grew so greedy that we were going to try to hold you up. We didn't know that Venerable Father had such tremendous magic power to imprison us. We beg you to be merciful. Please take away the things we stole, but spare our lives."

When Tripitaka heard that the K'ou family had been robbed, he was so taken aback that he stood up immediately. "Wu-k'ung," he said, "the old Squire K'ou is so kind and virtuous. How could he bring on himself such a terrible calamity?"

"All because of his desire to see us on our way," replied Pilgrim, chuckling. "Those color drapes and floral banners, that extravagant display of drums and music, all attracted people's attention. That's why these scoundrels moved against his house. It's fortunate that they ran into us, so that we could rob them of this great amount of silver and gold, clothing and jewelery."

"Since we have bothered the K'ous for half a month but have nothing to repay their great kindness with," said Tripitaka, "we should take these belongings back to their house. Wouldn't that be a good deed?" Pilgrim agreed. With Pa-chieh and Sha Monk, he went to the mountain valley and, having packed up the stolen goods, put them on the horse. Pa-chieh was asked to tote another load of gold and silver, while Sha Monk toted their own luggage. Pilgrim would have

liked to slaughter all those bandits with one blow of his rod, but fearing
that the T'ang monk would blame him for taking human lives, he
had no choice but to shake his body once to retrieve his hairs. With
their hands and legs freed, those bandits scrambled up and fled for
their lives. Our T'ang monk then retraced his steps to escort the stolen
property back to the squire. This act of his, however, was like a moth
darting into fire, a self-induced disaster! We have a testimonial poem
for him, which says:

Kindness repaying kindness is a rarity,
For kindness can change into enmity.
To save the drowning you may go amiss.
Think thrice before acting, you'll live in bliss.

As Tripitaka and his disciples proceeded to take back the stolen goods,
they suddenly caught sight of a forest of swords and spears approaching them. Greatly alarmed, Tripitaka said, "Disciples, look at those
weapons coming at us! What do they mean?"

"Disaster's here! Disaster's here!" Pa-chieh said. "These must be
the bandits we let go. They have taken up arms and banded together
with more people so that they could return to contend with us."

"Second Elder Brother," said Sha Monk, "they do not look like
bandits. Big Brother, take a careful look."

"The evil star has descended once more on Master," whispered
Pilgrim to Sha Monk. "These are government troops out to catch
bandits." Hardly had he finished speaking when the soldiers rushed
up to them and had master and disciples completely surrounded.

"Dear monks!" they cried. "After you've robbed and plundered,
you are still swaggering around here!" They surged forward and
yanked the T'ang monk off the horse. He was immediately tied up
with ropes, after which Pilgrim and his two companions were also
bound and hog-tied. Poles were inserted through the loops so that two
soldiers could carry one prisoner on their shoulders. As the entire
troop went back to the prefectural city, hauling the luggage and herding the horse, this was the condition of the pilgrims:

The T'ang monk
Shook all over,
Speechless and shedding tears;
Chu Pa-chieh
Mumbled and grumbled,
His feelings grievous and sour;

Sha Monk
Muttered and murmured,
Uncertain what to do;
Pilgrim Sun
Giggled and tittered,
About to show his power.

In a little while, the throng of government troops hauled their prisoners and recovered booty back into the city. They then proceeded to the yellow hall to make this report: "Venerable Father, the recruits have captured the bandits." Sitting solemnly in the hall, the magistrate first rewarded his troops. Then he examined the recovered property before he sent for members of the K'ou family to take it back. Finally, he ordered Tripitaka and his companions brought before the hall for interrogation.

"You priests," he said, "you claim that you have come from the distant Land of the East and that you are on your way to the Western Heaven to worship Buddha. Actually, however, you are thieves who resort to clever devices to get to know the layout of a place in order to plunder and pillage!"

"Your Excellency, allow me to speak," said Tripitaka. "This humble cleric is in truth not a thief. This is no lie, for I have with me a travel rescript which you may look at. All this came about because of our regard for the great kindness of Squire K'ou, who fed us for half a month. When we ran into the bandits on our way who had robbed the squire's household, we took the stolen property and were about to return it to the K'ou family as a gesture of our gratitude. Little did we expect that the soldiers would arrest us, thinking that we were the thieves. Truly we are not thieves, and I beg Your Excellency to exercise careful discernment."

"Now that you are caught by government troops," said the magistrate, "you resort to this clever talk of your gesture of gratitude. If you met the bandits on the way, why didn't you seize them also, so that you could report to the proper official and repay the squire's kindness? Why were there only four of you? Look! This is the plaint filed by K'ou Liang, who named you specifically as the accused. You still dare to struggle?"

When he heard these words, Tripitaka was scared out of his wits, like someone on a boat in a boiling sea. "Wu-k'ung," he cried, "why don't you come up here to defend us?"

"The booty is real," replied Pilgrim. "What's the use of defense?"

"Exactly!" said the magistrate. "With such evidence before you, you still dare to deny the charge?" He said to his subordinates, "Bring the head clamp. We'll give this thief's bald head a taste of the clamp before we flog him."

Terribly flustered, Pilgrim thought to himself, "Though my master is fated to meet this ordeal, he should not be allowed to suffer too much." When he saw, therefore, that the bailiffs were preparing the ropes to make the head clamp, he said, "Your Excellency, please don't clamp that monk. During the robbery of the K'ou home last night, it was I who held the light and the knife, and it was I who robbed and murdered. I'm the chieftain of the thieves. If you want flogging, flog me. They have nothing to do with this. Just don't release me."

On hearing this, the magistrate gave the order: "Let's clamp the head of this one first." Together the bailiffs looped the head clamp onto Pilgrim. When they suddenly tightened the rope, it snapped with a loud crack. They joined the rope and clamped again, and once more it snapped with a loud crack. After three or four times of clamping like this, the skin on Pilgrim's head did not even show a wrinkle. When they wanted to change ropes and make another clamp, someone came in to report, "Venerable Father, Father Junior Guardian Ch'ên from the capital has arrived. Please go out of the city to meet him."

The magistrate immediately gave this order to the clerk of justice: "Take the thieves into the jail and guard them carefully. Wait until I have received my superior. We'll interrogate them some more." The clerk pushed the T'ang monk and his three disciples into the jailhouse. Pa-chieh and Sha Monk, however, had to carry their own luggage in.

"Disciples," said Tripitaka, "how did this thing come to be?"

"Master, get in! Get in!" said Pilgrim, laughing. "There are no dogs barking here. It's rather good fun!" Alas! The four of them were taken inside and they were all pushed onto the rack. Then belly compressors, head prongs, and chest straps were fastened to each of them. The prison guards then arrived and began a severe flogging. Hardly able to endure the pain, Tripitaka could only cry, "Wu-k'ung, what shall we do? What shall we do?"

Pilgrim said, "They want to beat some money out of us! As the saying goes,

Settle down if you a nice place find;
Spend money when you're in a bind.

They'll probably ease up on us if we give them some money."

"Where do I have any money?" asked Tripitaka.

"If we have no money," said Pilgrim, "even clothing is all right. Give him that cassock of yours." On hearing this, Tripitaka felt as if a dagger had stabbed his heart. Since, however, he could not endure the flogging any longer, he had little choice but to say, "Wu-k'ung, do as you wish."

Immediately Pilgrim cried out, "Officers, no need for you to beat us any more. Inside of one of those two wraps we carried in, there is a brocade cassock worth a thousand gold. Untie the wrap and take it. Please leave us." When those prison guards heard this, they all went to untie the two wraps. There were indeed several cloth garments and a satchel, which were of no value at all. Then they came upon an object wrapped in several layers of oiled paper, with shafts of luminous radiance coming through. They knew it had to be a good thing. When they shook it loose to examine it, they saw a garment of

Bright, wonderful pearl appliqués,

Sequins of rare Buddhist treasures;

With coiled-dragon knots of brocade,

And silk pipings of phoenix made.

As they fought to have a look at such a marvel, they disturbed the prison warden, who came to say, "Why are you all making such noises here?"

Going to their knees, the guards said, "Just now the old sire indicted these four priests, who all belonged to a large group of bandits. When we gave them a little flogging, they offered us these two wraps. We found this object after we untied the wraps, and we didn't know what to do with it. To tear up the robe and divide it would be a great pity, but if only one of us owned it, the others would receive no benefit. Fortunately the old sire has come along. We'll leave it up to you to decide for us."

The warden recognized that it was a cassock. He then examined the other items of clothing and the satchel. Next, he unfolded the travel rescript to have a look. When he saw the signatures and treasure seals of various nations, he said, "I'm glad I saw this in time! Otherwise you people might have brought a terrible disaster on yourselves. These monks are no bandits. Don't you dare touch their clothing! Wait till the grand sire interrogates them tomorrow, and we'll probably learn the real truth." When the guards heard this, they handed the wraps over to him. The warden tied them up as before and put them away for safe-keeping.

Gradually the night deepened; the drum-roll began on the towers as the night patrol shouted the watches. By about the third quarter of the fourth watch, Pilgrim saw that his companions had stopped moaning and had all fallen asleep. He thought to himself, "It was fated that Master should have this one night of prison ordeal. That's the reason why old Monkey did not bother to dispute the judge or use magic power. Now that the fourth watch is almost over and the calamity is nearly completed, I must leave to make some plans so that we can get out of prison in the morning."

Look at the way he exercises his abilities! Reducing the size of his body, he at once got out of the rack and, with one shake, changed into a midge to fly out through a crack between the roof tiles. It was a fair and quiet night of stars and a bright moon in the sky. Having determined the direction of the K'ou house, he flew toward it. Soon he saw the bright flares of light coming from a house to the west. When he flew near it to look more closely, he discovered that it belonged to a family of bean-curd makers. An old man was tending fire, while his aged wife was squeezing out the soybean milk.

Presently he heard the old man say, "Mother, Mr. K'ou might have sons and wealth, but he had no age. He was, you know, a schoolmate of mine when we were young. I am five years his senior. His father's name was K'ou Ming, and at that time, they had no more than a thousand acres of farm land, which they had leased out, but they couldn't even collect the proper rental. By the time the son was twenty years old, the father died and it was up to him to manage their property. It was a stroke of luck that he took for his wife the daughter of Chang Wang (Prosperity). Her nickname was Needle-Pusher, but she certainly brought prosperity to her husband. Since her entrance into his family, their lands yielded rich harvests and their rentals excellent returns. What they bought accrued value and what they sold made profits. Their assets by now must be worth a hundred thousand cash. When he reached his fortieth year, he began to devote himself to good deeds and managed to feed ten thousand monks. Who would have thought that he would be kicked to death by bandits last night! How pitiable! He was only sixty-four years old and had reached just the right age to enjoy himself. Who would expect a person of such virtuous inclination to be rewarded by such a violent death? It's most lamentable! Most lamentable!" Every word of this statement was heard by Pilgrim.

By then it was the first quarter of the fifth watch, and Pilgrim flew right into the house of the K'ou family. The squire's coffin had been placed in the main hall so that the family could hold a wake over the dead man. Lamps were lit at the head of the coffin, flowers and fruit arranged around it. On one side his weeping wife kept vigil, and his two sons also were kneeling there and weeping. Two of his daughters-in-law were bringing in two bowls of rice for offering.

Pilgrim landed on the head of the coffin and gave a cough. The two daughters-in-law were so terrified that they ran outside, their arms and legs flailing the air. Prostrating themselves on the floor, the K'ou brothers dared not move at all. All they could mutter was, "Father! Looooo! Loooo! . . ."

The old woman, however, was courageous enough to give the head of the coffin a tap and said, "Old Squire, have you come back to life?"

Imitating the voice of the squire, Pilgrim replied, "No, I haven't!" More frightened than ever, the two sons continued to kowtow and shed tears. All they could mutter was, "Father! Looo! Looo! . . ." Forcing herself to be bold, the woman asked again, "Squire, if you haven't come back to life, why are you speaking?"

"I have been sent back by King Yama in the custody of a ghost guardian," said Pilgrim, "so that I can speak to all of you. I am supposed to tell you that Needle-Pusher Chang has used her foul mouth and slanderous tongue to injure the innocent."

When the old woman heard her own nickname, she became so flustered that she fell to her knees and kowtowed, saying, "Dear old man! You're so old already, and you still want to address me by my nickname! What do you mean by my foul mouth and slanderous tongue? Which innocent have I injured?" Pilgrim bellowed, "Didn't you say something like this?

Pa-chieh cried for slaughter;
The T'ang monk held the fire.
Sha Monk removed our silver and gold
While Pilgrim Sun beat to death our sire.

Because of your slanderous words, good people have been made to suffer. Those four masters of the T'ang court, when they ran into the brigands on the road, took back our stolen property. They wanted to return that to us as a token of their gratitude. What an expression of goodwill! You, however, drew up this specious plaint and asked your sons to file it with the official. Without carefully examining the case either, he sent them to prison. Now the god of the jailhouse, the local spirit, and the city deity are all so overwrought that they have reported the matter to King Yama. He in turn sent his ghost guardian to take me back home to tell you this: that you should work for the monks' release at once. Otherwise, I have been authorized to cause trouble for a solid month here in the house. The entire household, old and young, including chickens and dogs, will not be spared!"

Again kowtowing, the K'ou brothers pleaded with him, saying, "Daddy, please go back. Please don't ever harm the old and the young of this house. We will hasten to the prefecture in the morning and file a petition for release and make our confession. All we want is peace for both the living and the deceased."

On hearing this, Pilgrim cried, "Burn paper money! I'm going!" The whole family gathered at once to burn paper money.

With outstretched wings Pilgrim flew up and soared straight to the magistrate's house. As he looked down, he perceived light, for the magistrate had already risen. When he flew into the central hall to look around, he saw a painting hanging in the middle, the subject of which was an official riding a horse with black spots. Behind him were several attendants, one carrying a blue umbrella and another an armchair. Pilgrim, of course, could not tell what was the story behind the painting, but he flew up to it and settled in the middle of the scroll. Presently the magistrate emerged from his room and bent low to wash his face.

Suddenly Pilgrim gave a loud cough, so scaring the magistrate that he dashed back into his room. After finishing his washing and combing his hair, he donned a long coat and came out once more to burn incense before the painting and intone this petition: "To the divine tablet of my deceased uncle, Duke Chiang Ch'ien-i. Blessed by ancestral virtue, your filial nephew, Chiang K'un-san, succeeded in passing the second and third degrees. He is now favored with the appointment to the magistrate of the Bronze Terrace Prefecture. To you we have offered night and day without ceasing incense and fires. Why, therefore, do you make a sound this day? I beg you not to work the work of a monster or evil spirit, lest the family members be terrified."

Chuckling secretly to himself, Pilgrim said, "So, this is the picture

of his father's elder brother!" He made use of the opportunity, however, to say to the magistrate, "K'un-san, my worthy nephew, you
have honored your ancestral inheritance by ever being a clean and
upright official. How could you, therefore, be so foolish yesterday as
to have regarded four sage monks as bandits? Without making a
thorough investigation, you sent them to jail. Now the god of the
jailhouse, the local spirit, and the city deity are highly disturbed. They
have reported the matter to King Yama, who sent me in the custody
of a ghost guardian to inform you that you should examine every
aspect of the case and quickly release them. If you don't do this, you
will be asked to go and answer for yourself in the Region of Darkness."

Alarmed by what he heard, the magistrate said, "Let my uncle
withdraw his presence. When your humble nephew ascends the hall,
he will immediately release them."

"In that case," said Pilgrim, "go burn paper money. I'll go back to
report to King Yama." The magistrate thus added incense and burned
paper money to offer his thanks.

Pilgrim flew out of the hall, and he found that it was beginning to
grow light in the east. By the time he reached the Numinous Earth
District, he saw that the district magistrate had already seated himself
in the official hall. "If a midge speaks," thought Pilgrim to himself,
"and someone sees it, my identity may be revealed. That's no good."
He changed, therefore, into the huge magic body: from midair he
lowered a giant leg, which completely filled the district hall. "Hear me,
you officials," he cried, "I'm the Wandering Spirit sent by the Jade
Emperor. I charge you that a son of Buddha has been wrongfully
beaten in the jail of your prefecture, thus greatly disturbing the peace
of the deities in the Three Regions. I am told to impart this message to
you, that you should give him an early release. If there is any delay,
my other leg will descend. It will first kick to death all the district
officials of this prefecture. Then it will stamp to death the entire population of the region. Your cities finally will be trodden into dust and
ashes!"

All the officials of the district were so terrified that they knelt down
together to kowtow and worship, saying, "Let the noble sage withdraw his presence. We will go into the prefecture at once and report
this to the magistrate. The prisoner will be released immediately. We
beg you not to move your leg, for it will frighten these humble officials
to death." Only then did Pilgrim retrieve his magic body. Changing

once more into a midge, he flew back inside the jail through the crack between the roof tiles and crawled back to sleep in the rack.

We now tell you about the magistrate, who went up to the hall. No sooner had he displayed the placard announcing his readiness to hear a case than the K'ou brothers took it in one of their bosoms and cried aloud on bended knees. The magistrate summoned them inside, where they submitted their petition for release. When the magistrate saw it, he grew angry and said, "It was only yesterday that you filed a complaint of loss. We caught the thieves for you and the stolen property was returned to you. Why did you come today to submit petition for release?"

Shedding tears, the two of them said, "Venerable Father, the spirit of your humble subjects' father manifested itself last night to say to us, 'The sage monks from the T'ang court were the ones who had originally captured the bandits. It was they who recovered our possessions and released the bandits. Out of goodwill they decided to send back in person the stolen goods in order to repay our hospitality. How could you turn them into thieves and send them to jail to suffer? So overwrought were the local spirit and the city deity that they reported the matter to King Yama. King Yama told me to come in the custody of a ghost guardian to tell you to file another petition with the prefecture for the release of the T'ang monk. Only that will avert further disasters. If you don't do this, both the old and the young of the family will perish.' For this reason, we have come to submit our petition for release. We beg the Venerable Father to grant us our request."

When the magistrate heard this, he thought to himself, "Their father happens to be a corpse that's still warm. A newly departed showing itself is not an unusual phenomenon. But my uncle has been dead five or six years. Why did he too show his spirit last night and ask me to release the prisoners? Hmmm . . .! They must be wrongfully accused."

As he deliberated with himself, the district magistrate of the Numinous Earth District came running up the hall, yelling, "Your Honor! It's bad! It's bad! Just now the Jade Emperor sent the Wandering Spirit down here to order you to release quickly some good people from prison. Those monks you caught yesterday were not bandits. They are all sons of Buddha on their way to acquire scriptures. If there is any further delay, all of us officials will be kicked to death. Our cities, including the entire population, will be trodden to dust and ashes." Paling with fright, the magistrate at once commanded the clerk of justice to issue a placard for the prisoners to be brought out. When this was done immediately, Pa-chieh said sadly, "I wonder what sort of beating they'll give us today!"

With a laugh, Pilgrim said, "I promise you that you won't receive a single stroke. Old Monkey has settled everything. When you go up to the hall, don't you kneel, for he will step down to ask us to take the seats of honor. Let me demand from him the return of our horse and luggage. If anything is missing, I'll beat him up for you to see."

Just as they finished speaking, they arrived at the entrance to the hall. The magistrate, the district magistrate, and the officials of the prefecture and district all descended the hall to meet them, saying, "When the sage monks arrived yesterday, we did not manage to question you carefully, partly because of the urgent necessity to go meet our superiors, and partly because we were distracted by the sight of the stolen booty."

Pressing his palms together in front of him and bowing, the T'ang monk gave another thorough account of what had happened. The various officials all confessed, saying, "We've made a mistake! We've made a mistake! Please do not blame us! Please do not blame us!" Then they asked the T'ang monk whether he had lost anything in jail. Pilgrim now walked forward, glowering, and declared in a loud voice, "Our white horse was taken away by someone in this hall. Our luggage was snatched by the people in jail. Return them to us quickly! It's our turn today to interrogate you all. You have wrongly seized common folks and accused them of thievery! What sort of crime should you be charged with?"

When the officials saw how violent he had become, there was not a single one of them that was not scared. They immediately told those who had taken the horse to bring it back, and those who had taken the luggage to return it. Even after all these items were turned over piece by piece, the three disciples continued to display their pique. Look at them! The various officials could only use the K'ou family as their excuse.

Trying to be the peacemaker, the T'ang monk said, "Disciples, we won't get to the bottom of this here. Let's go to the K'ou household. There we can confront and interrogate any witness. Let's find out who it was who saw me as a robber."

"You are right," said Pilgrim. "Let old Monkey call up the dead

and ask him to identify his murderer." Sha Monk at once helped the
T'ang monk to mount the horse right there in the prefectural hall. In
a body, they rushed out, shouting and bellowing. The various officials
of the prefecture and the district all went to the K'ou house also.

K'ou Liang and his brother were so terrified that they went to their
front door and kowtowed without ceasing. When the visitors were
received into the living room, they could see that inside the mourning
parlor members of the family were still weeping behind the funeral
drapes.

Pilgrim called out: "That old woman who used slander to injure
common people, stop crying! Let old Monkey summon your husband
here. Let him tell us who the real person was who slew him. That
ought to put a little shame in you!" Those officials thought that Pilgrim Sun was only jesting, but he said to them, "Sirs, please keep my
master company by sitting here for a moment. Pa-chieh, Sha Monk,
take care to stand guard. I'll be back soon."

Dear Great Sage! He vaulted through the door and rose immediately into the air. All that the people could see were
Colored mists everywhere shrouding the house;
The sky's hallowed air shielding primal spirit.
When they finally realized that this was an immortal who could
mount the clouds and ride the fog, a sage who could bring life out of
death, they all burned incense to worship. There we shall leave them
for the moment.

With a series of cloud-somersaults, that Great Sage went to the
Region Below and crashed right into the Hall of Darkness. So startled
were they that
Ten Yama Kings, hands joined, saluted him;
Five Quarters ghost judges kowtowed to him.
Sword-trees, a thousand stalks, were all askew;
Dagger-hills, ten thousandfold, were all made plain.
Goblins were saved in the Wrongful-Dead City;
Ghosts revived by No Alternative Bridge.[5]
Truly like Heaven's reprieve was one beam of divine light:
The whole Region of Darkness now turned bright.
The Ten Yama Kings received the Great Sage; after having exchanged
greetings, they asked the reason for his visit.

Pilgrim said, "Which one of you took away the soul of K'ou Hung,
the person who fed the monks in the Numinous Earth District of the

Bronze Terrace Prefecture? Find out instantly and bring him to me."

"K'ou Hung is a virtuous person," said the Ten Yama Kings. "We did not have to use a ghost guardian to summon him. He came by himself, but when the Golden-Robed Youth of King Kṣitigarbha met him, he led him to see the king." Pilgrim at once took leave of them to head for the Jade Cloud Palace, where he greeted the Bodhisattva King Kṣitigarbha and gave a thorough account of what took place.

In delight the Bodhisattva said, "It was foreordained that K'ou Hung should leave the world without touching a bed or a mat when his allotted age reached its end. Because he had been a person of virtue who fed the monks, I took him in and made him the secretary in charge of the records of good karma. Since the Great Sage has come to ask for him, I shall lengthen his age by another dozen years. He may leave with you."

The Golden-Robed Youth led out K'ou Hung, who, on seeing Pilgrim, cried out, "Master! Master! Save me!" "You were kicked to death by a robber," said Pilgrim. "This is the place of the Bodhisattva King Kṣitigarbha in the Region of Darkness. Old Monkey has come especially to take you back to the world of light so that you may give your testimony. The Bodhisattva is kind enough to release you and lengthen your age for another dozen years. Thereafter you'll return here." The squire bowed again and again.

Having thanked the Bodhisattva, Pilgrim changed the soul of the squire into ether by blowing on him. The ether was stored in his sleeve so that they could leave the house of darkness and go back to the world of light together. Astride the clouds, he soon arrived at the K'ou house. Pa-chieh was told to pry open the lid of the coffin, and the soul of the squire was pushed into his body. In a moment, he began to breathe once more and revived. Scrambling out of the coffin, the squire kowtowed to the T'ang monk and his three disciples, saying, "Masters! Masters! Having suffered a violent death, I am much obliged for this master's arrival at the Region of Darkness and returning me to life. His is the kindness of a new creation!" After thanking them repeatedly, he turned and saw all the officials standing there. Touching his head to the ground once more, he said, "Why are all the Venerable Fathers in the house?"

"Your sons at first filed a complaint of loss," replied the magistrate, "which accused the sage monks by name. I sent people to arrest them, not realizing that the sage monks on their journey had run into those bandits who murdered you and robbed your house. They took back your possessions and were about to send them back to your home in person. My subordinates arrested them by mistake, and I sent them to jail without careful examination. Last night your soul made an appearance, and my deceased uncle also revealed himself at our home. The Wandering Spirit, too, made a descent into the district. All these epiphanies at one time led us to release the sage monks, after which that particular one went to bring you back to life."

Remaining on his knees, the squire said, "Venerable Father, you have truly wronged these four sage monks. There were some thirty bandits that night who broke into our house with torches and rods. When they took away our belongings, I couldn't bear it and tried to reason with the thieves. One of them killed me with a kick at my lower parts. These four had absolutely nothing to do with the crime!" Then he summoned his wife and sons into his presence to say, "Didn't you know who kicked me to death? How dare you file false charges? I'm going to ask the Venerable Father to convict you."

All the family members, old and young, could only kowtow at that time, but the magistrate was magnanimous enough to pardon all of them. K'ou Hung then ordered a banquet to thank this great kindness of the prefecture and the district, but each of the officials returned to his official residence without lingering. The next day the squire once more displayed his plaque announcing his desire to feed monks and wanted to entertain Tripitaka some more. Tripitaka, however, steadfastly refused to stay, whereupon the squire invited his relatives and friends and prepared banners and canopies to send off the pilgrims as he had done before. Lo! Truly

The wide earth may harbor vicious affairs,
But high Heaven will a good man vindicate.
Footloose they're safe on Tathāgata's way,
Certain to reach Mount Spirit's paradise gate.

We do not know what will become of them when they see Buddha, and you must listen to the explanation in the next chapter.

Ninety-eight

Only when ape and horse are tamed will they cast their shells;
When merit and work are perfected, they see the Real.

Since Squire K'ou was able to return to life, he again prepared banners
and canopies, drums and music, and invited relatives and friends,
Buddhists and Taoists, to escort the pilgrims on their way. We shall
now leave them and tell you instead about the T'ang monk and his
three disciples, who set out on the main road.

In truth the land of Buddha in the West was quite different from
other regions. What they saw everywhere were gemlike flowers and
jasperlike grasses, aged cypresses and hoary pines. In the regions
they passed through, every family was devoted to good works, and
every household would feed the monks.

They met people in cultivation beneath the hills.
And saw those reciting sūtras in the woods.
Resting at night and journeying at dawn, master and disciples proceeded for some six or seven days when they suddenly caught sight
of a row of tall buildings and noble lofts. Truly

They soar skyward a hundred feet,
Tall and towering in the air.
You look down to see the setting sun
And reach out to pluck the shooting stars.
Spacious windows engulf the universe;
Lofty pillars join with the cloudy screens.
Yellow cranes bring letters[1] as autumn trees age;
Phoenix-sheets come with the cool evening breeze.
These are the treasure arches of a spirit palace,
The pearly courts and jeweled edifices,
The immortal hall where Tao is preached,
The cosmos where sūtras are taught.
The flowers bloom in the spring;
Pines grow green after the rain.
Purple agaric and divine fruits, fresh every year.

Phoenixes gambol, potent in every manner.

Lifting his whip to point ahead, Tripitaka said, "Wu-k'ung, what a lovely place!"

"Master," said Pilgrim, "you insisted on bowing down even in a specious region, before false images of Buddha. Today you have arrived at a true region with real images of Buddha, and you still haven't dismounted. What's your excuse?"

So taken aback was Tripitaka when he heard these words that he leaped down from the horse. Soon they arrived at the entrance to the buildings. A Taoist lad, standing before the gate, called out, "Are you the scripture seeker from the Land of the East?"

Hurriedly tidying his clothes, the elder raised his head and looked at his interrogator.

He wore a robe of silk
And held a jade duster.
He wore a robe of silk
Often to feast at treasure lofts and jasper pools;
He held a jade yak's-tail
To wave and dust in the purple mansions.
A sacred registry hangs from his wrist,
And his feet are shod in sandals.
Floating along, he's a true feathered-one;[2]
Attractive, he's indeed exceptional!
Long life attained, he lives in this fine place;
Immortal, he can leave the world of dust.
The sage monk knows not our Mount Spirit guest:
The Immortal Golden Head of former years.[3]

The Great Sage, however, recognized the person. "Master," he cried, "this is the Great Immortal of the Golden Head, who resides in the Yü-chên Taoist Temple at the foot of the Spirit Mountain."

Only then did Tripitaka realize the truth, and he walked forward to make his bow. With laughter, the great immortal said, "So the sage monk has finally arrived this year. I have been deceived by the Bodhisattva Kuan-yin. When she received the gold decree from Buddha over ten years ago to find a scripture seeker in the Land of the East, she told me that he would be here after two or three years. I waited year after year for you, but no news came at all. Hardly have I anticipated that I would meet you this year!"

Pressing his palms together, Tripitaka said, "I'm greatly indebted

to the great immortal's kindness. Thank you! Thank you!" The four
pilgrims, leading the horse and toting the luggage, all went inside the
temple before each of them greeted the great immortal once more.
Tea and a vegetarian meal were ordered. The immortal also asked the
lads to heat some scented liquid for the sage monk to bathe, so that he
could ascend the land of Buddha. Truly,

> It's good to bathe when merit and work are done,
> When nature's tamed and the natural state is won.
> All toils and labors are now at rest;
> Law and obedience have renewed their zest.
> At *mara*'s end they reach indeed Buddha-land;
> Their woes dispelled, before Śramaṇa they stand.
> Unstained, they are washed of all filth and dust.
> To a diamond body[4] return they must.

After master and disciples had bathed, it became late and they rested
in the Yü-chên Temple.

Next morning the T'ang monk changed his clothing and put on
his brocade cassock and his Vairocana hat. Holding the priestly staff,
he ascended the main hall to take leave of the great immortal. "Yesterday you seemed rather dowdy," said the great immortal, chuckling,
"but today everything is fresh and bright. As I look at you now, you
are a true of son of Buddha!" After a bow, Tripitaka wanted to set out
at once.

"Wait a moment," said the great immortal. "Allow me to escort
you."

"There's no need for that," said Pilgrim. "Old Monkey knows the
way."

"What you know happens to be the way in the clouds," said the
great immortal, "a means of travel to which the sage monk has not
yet been elevated. You must still stick to the main road."

"What you say is quite right," replied Pilgrim. "Though old Monkey
has been to this place several times, he has always come and gone on
the clouds and he has never stepped on the ground. If we must stick
to the main road, we must trouble you to escort us a distance. My
master's most eager to bow to Buddha. Let's not dally." Smiling
broadly, the great immortal held the T'ang monk's hand

> To lead Candana[5] up the gate of Law.

The way that they had to go, you see, did not lead back to the front
gate. Instead, they had to go through the central hall of the temple

to go out the rear door. Immediately behind the temple, in fact, was the Spirit Mountain, to which the great immortal pointed and said, "Sage Monk, look at the spot halfway up the sky, shrouded by auspicious luminosity of five colors and a thousand folds of hallowed mists. That's the tall Spirit Vulture Peak, the holy region of the Buddhist Patriarch."

The moment the T'ang monk saw it, he began to bend low. With a chuckle, Pilgrim said, "Master, you haven't reached that place where you should bow down. As the proverb says, 'Even within sight of a mountain you can ride a horse to death!' You are still quite far from that principality. Why do you want to bow down now? How many times does your head need to touch the ground if you kowtow all the way to the summit?"

"Sage Monk," said the great immortal, "you, along with the Great Sage, Heavenly Reeds, and Curtain-Raising, have arrived at the blessed land when you can see Mount Spirit. I'm going back." Thereupon Tripitaka bowed to take leave of him.

The Great Sage led the T'ang monk and his disciples slowly up the mountain. They had not gone for more than five or six miles when they came upon a torrent of water, eight or nine miles wide. There was no trace of human activity all around. Alarmed by the sight, Tripitaka said, "Wu-k'ung, this must be the wrong way! Could the great immortal have made a mistake? Look how wide and swift this river is! Without a boat, how could we get across?"

"There's no mistake!" said Pilgrim, chuckling. "Look over there! Isn't that a large bridge? You have to walk across that bridge before you can perfect the right fruit." The elder walked up to the bridge and saw beside it a tablet, on which was the inscription, Cloud-Transcending Stream. The bridge was actually a single log. Truly

Afar off, it's like a jade beam in the sky;
Near, a dried stump that o'er the water lies.
To bind up oceans it would easier seem.
How could one walk a single log or beam,
Shrouded by rainbows of ten thousand feet,
By a thousand layers of silk-white sheet?
Too slipp'ry and small for all to cross its spread
Except those who on colored mists can tread.

Quivering all over, Tripitaka said, "Wu-k'ung, this bridge is not for human beings to cross. Let's find some other way."

"This *is* the way! This *is* the way!" said Pilgrim, laughing.

"If this is the way," said Pa-chieh, horrified, "who dares walk on it? The water's so wide and rough. There's only a single log here, and it's so narrow and slippery. How could I move my legs?"

"Stand still, all of you," said Pilgrim. "Let old Monkey take a walk for you to see." Dear Great Sage! In big strides he bounded on to the single-log bridge. Swaying from side to side, he ran across it in no time at all. On the other side he shouted: "Come across! Come across!"

The T'ang monk waved his hands, while Pa-chieh and Sha Monk bit their fingers, all crying, "Hard! Hard! Hard!"

Pilgrim dashed back from the other side and pulled at Pa-chieh, saying, "Idiot! Follow me! Follow me!" Lying flat on the ground, Pa-chieh said, "It's much too slippery! Much too slippery! Let me go, please! Let me mount the wind and fog to get over there."

Pushing him down, Pilgrim said, "What sort of a place do you think this is that you are permitted to mount wind and fog! Unless you walk across this bridge, you'll never become a Buddha."

"O Elder Brother!" said Pa-chieh. "It's okay with me if I don't become a Buddha. But I'm not going on that bridge!"

Right beside the bridge, the two of them started a tug-of-war. Only Sha Monk's admonitions managed to separate them. Tripitaka happened to turn his head, and he suddenly caught sight of someone punting a boat upstream and crying, "Ahoy! Ahoy!"

Highly pleased, the elder said, "Disciples, stop your frivolity! There's a boat coming." The three of them leaped up and stood still to stare at the boat. When it drew near, they found that it was a bottomless one. With his fiery eyes and diamond pupils, Pilgrim at once recognized that the ferryman was in fact the Conductor Buddha, also named the Light of Ratnadhvaja. Without revealing the Buddha's identity, however, Pilgrim simply said, "Over here! Punt it this way!"

Immediately the boatman punted it up to the shore. "Ahoy! Ahoy!" he cried. Terrified by what he saw, Tripitaka said, "How could this bottomless boat of yours carry anybody?" The Buddhist Patriarch said, "This boat of mine

Since creation's dawn has achieved great fame;
Punted by me, it has e'er been the same.
Upon the wind and wave it's still secure;
With no end or beginning its joy is sure.
It can return to One, completely clean,

Through ten thousand kalpas a sail serene.
Though bottomless boats may ne'er cross the sea,
This ferries all souls through eternity."

Pressing his palms together to thank him, the Great Sage Sun said, "I thank you for your great kindness in coming to receive and lead my master. Master, get on the boat. Though it is bottomless, it is safe. Even if there are wind and waves, it will not capsize."

The elder still hesistated, but Pilgrim took him by the shoulder and gave him a shove. With nothing to stand on, that master tumbled straight into the water, but the boatman swiftly pulled him out. As he stood on the side of the boat, the master kept shaking out his clothes and stamping his feet as he grumbled at Pilgrim. Pilgrim, however, helped Sha Monk and Pa-chieh to lead the horse and tote the luggage into the boat. As they all stood on the gunwale, the Buddhist Patriarch gently punted the vessel away from shore. All at once they saw a corpse floating down the upstream, the sight of which filled the elder with terror.

"Don't be afraid, Master," said Pilgrim, laughing. "It's actually you!"

"It's you! It's you!" said Pa-chieh also.

Clapping his hands, Sha Monk also said, "It's you! It's you!"

Adding his voice to the chorus, the boatman also said, "That's you! Congratulations! Congratulations!" Then the three disciples repeated this chanting in unison as the boat was punted across the water. In no time at all, they crossed the Divine Cloud-Transcending Stream all safe and sound. Only then did Tripitaka turn and skip lightly on to the other shore. We have here a testimonial poem, which says:

Delivered from their mortal flesh and bone,
A primal spirit of mutual love has grown.
Their work done, they become Buddhas this day,
Free of their former six-six senses'[6] sway.

Truly this is what is meant by the profound wisdom and the boundless Dharma which enable one to reach the other shore.

The moment the four pilgrims went ashore and turned around, the boatman and even the bottomless boat had disappeared. Only then did Pilgrim point out that it was the Conductor Buddha, and immediately Tripitaka awoke to the truth. Turning quickly, he thanked his three disciples instead.

Pilgrim said, "We two parties need not thank each other, for we are meant to support each other. We are indebted to our master for our liberation, through which we have found the gateway to the making of merit, and fortunately we have achieved the right fruit. Our master also has to rely on our protection so that he may be firm in keeping both law and faith to find the happy deliverance from this mortal stock. Master, look at this surpassing scenery of flowers and grass, pines and bamboos, phoenixes, cranes, and deer. Compared with those places of illusion manufactured by monsters and deviates, which ones do you think are pleasant and which ones bad? Which ones are good and which evil?" Tripitaka expressed his thanks repeatedly as every one of them with lightness and agility walked up the Spirit Mountain. Soon this was the aged Thunderclap Monastery which came into view:

Its top touches the firmament;
Its root joins the Sumeru range.
Wondrous peaks in rows;
Strange boulders rugged.
Beneath the cliffs, jade-grass and jasper-flowers;
By the path, purple agaric and scented orchid.
Divine apes plucking fruits in the peach orchard
Seem like fire-burnished gold;
White cranes perching on the tips of pine branches
Resemble mist-shrouded jade.
Male phoenixes in pairs—
Female phoenixes in twos—
Male phoenixes in pairs
Make one call facing the sun to bless the world;
Female phoenixes in twos
Whose radiant dance in the wind is rarely seen.
You see too those mandarin duck tiles of lustrous gold,
And luminous, patterned bricks cornelian-gilt.
In the east
And in the west
Stand rows of scented halls and pearly arches;
To the north
And to the south,
An endless sight of treasure lofts and precious towers.
The Devarāja Hall emits lambent mists;
The Dharma-guarding Hall sends forth purple flames.

The stūpa's clear form;
The Utpala's fragrance.
Truly a fine place similar to Heaven
With lazy clouds to make the day long.
The causes cease, red dust can't come at all:
Safe from all kalpas is this great Dharma Hall.

Footloose and carefree, master and disciples walked to the summit of
Mount Spirit, where under a forest of green pines they saw a group of
upāsikās and rows of worshipers in the midst of verdant cypresses.
Immediately the elder bowed to them, so startling the upāsakas and
upāsikās, the monks and the nuns, that they all pressed their palms
together, saying, "Sage monk, you should not render us such homage.
Wait till you see Śākyamuni, and then you may come to exchange
greetings with us."

"He is *always* in such a hurry!" said Pilgrim, laughing. "Let's go to
bow to those seated at the top!"

His arms and legs dancing with excitement, the elder followed
Pilgrim straight up to the gate of the Thunderclap Monastery. There
they were met by the Four Great Vajra Guardians, who said, "Has the
sage monk arrived?"

Bending low, Tripitaka said, "Yes, your disciple Hsüan-tsang has
arrived." No sooner had he given this reply than he wanted to go
inside. "Please wait a moment, Sage Monk," said the Vajra Guardians.
"Allow us to announce your arrival first before you enter."

One of the Vajra Guardians was asked to report to the other Four
Great Vajra Guardians stationed at the second gate, and one of those
porters passed the news of the T'ang monk's arrival to the third gate.
Those guarding the third gate happened to be divine monks who
served at the great altar. When they heard the news, they quickly
went to the Great Hero Hall to announce to Tathāgata, the Most
Honored One, also named Buddha Śākyamuni, "The sage monk from
the T'ang court has arrived in this treasure monastery. He has come
to fetch the scriptures."

Highly pleased, Holy Father Buddha at once asked the Eight
Bodhisattvas, the Four Vajra Guardians, the Five Hundred Arhats,
the Three Thousand Guardians, the Eleven Great Orbs, and the
Eighteen Guardians of Monasteries to form two rows for the reception.
Then he issued the golden decree to summon in the T'ang monk.

Again the word was passed from section to section, from gate to gate: "Let the sage monk enter." Meticulously observing the rules of etiquette, our T'ang monk walked through the monastery gate with Wu-k'ung, Wu-nêng, and Wu-ching, still leading the horse and toting the luggage. Thus it was that

Commissioned that year, a resolve he made
To leave with rescript the royal steps of jade.
The hills he'd climb to face the morning dew
Or rest on a boulder when the twilight fades.
He totes his faith to ford three thousand streams,
His staff trailing o'er endless palisades.
His every thought's on seeking the right fruit.
Homage to Buddha will this day be paid.

The four pilgrims, on reaching the Great Hero Treasure Hall, prostrated themselves before Tathāgata. Thereafter, they bowed to all the attendants of Buddha on the left and right. This they repeated three times before kneeling again before the Buddhist Patriarch to present their traveling rescript to him. After reading it carefully, Tathāgata handed it back to Tripitaka, who touched his head to the ground once more to say, "By the decree of the Great T'ang emperor in the Land of the East, your disciple Hsüan-tsang has come to this treasure monastery to beg you for the true scriptures for the redemption of the multitude. I implore the Buddhist Patriarch to vouchsafe his grace and grant me my wish, so that I may soon return to my country."

To express the compassion of his heart, Tathāgata opened his mouth of mercy and said to Tripitaka, "Your Land of the East belongs to the South Jambūdvīpa Continent. Because of your size and your fertile land, your prosperity and population, there is a great deal of greed and killing, lust and lying, oppression and deceit. People neither honor the teachings of Buddha nor cultivate virtuous karma; they neither revere the three lights nor respect the five grains. They are disloyal and unfilial, unrighteous and unkind, unscrupulous and self-deceiving. Through all manners of injustice and taking of lives, they have committed boundless transgressions. The fullness of their iniquities therefore has brought on them the ordeal of hell and sent them into eternal darkness and perdition to suffer the pains of pounding and grinding and of being transformed into beasts. Many of them will assume the forms of creatures with fur and horns; in this manner they will repay their debts by having their flesh made for food for mankind. These are the reasons for their eternal perdition in Avīci without deliverance.

"Though Confucius had promoted his teachings of benevolence, righteousness, ritual, and wisdom, and though a succession of kings and emperors had established such penalties as transportation, banishment, hanging, and beheading, these institutions had little effect on the foolish and the blind, the reckless, and the antinomian.

"Now, I have here three baskets of scriptures which can deliver humanity from its afflictions and dispel its calamities. There is one basket of vinaya, which speak of Heaven; a basket of śāstras, which tell of the Earth; and a basket of sūtras, which redeem the damned. Altogether these three baskets of scriptures contain thirty-five titles written in fifteen thousand one hundred and forty-four scrolls. They are truly the pathway to the realization of immortality and the gate to ultimate virtue. Every concern of astronomy, geography, biography, flora and fauna, utensils, and human affairs within the Four Great Continents of this world is recorded therein. Since all of you have traveled such a great distance to come here, I would have liked to give the entire set to you. Unfortunately, the people of your region are both stupid and headstrong. Mocking the true words, they refuse to recognize the profound significance of our teachings of Śramaṇa."

Then Buddha turned to call out: "Ānanda and Kāśyapa, take the four of them to the space beneath the precious tower. Give them a vegetarian meal first. After the maigre, open our treasure loft for them and select a few scrolls from each of the thirty-five divisions of our three canons, so that they may take them back to the Land of the East as a perpetual token of grace."

The two Honored Ones obeyed and took the four pilgrims to the space beneath the tower, where countless rare dainties and exotic treasures were laid out in a seemingly endless spread. Those deities in charge of offerings and sacrifices began to serve a magnificent feast of divine food, tea, and fruit—viands of a hundred flavors completely different from those of the mortal world. After master and disciples had bowed to give thanks to Buddha, they abandoned themselves to enjoyment. In truth

Treasure flames, gold beams on their eyes have shined;
Strange fragrance and feed even more refined.
Boundlessly fair the tow'r of gold appears,

And immortal music that clears the ears.
Such divine fare and flower humans rarely see;
Long life's attained through strange food and fragrant tea.
Long have they endured a thousand forms of pain.
This day in glory the Tao they're glad to gain.

This time it was Pa-chieh who was in luck and Sha Monk who had the advantage, for what the Buddhist Patriarch had provided for their complete enjoyment was nothing less than such viands as could grant them longevity and health and enable them to transform their mortal substance into immortal flesh and bones.

When the four pilgrims had finished their meal, the two Honored Ones who had kept them company led them up to the treasure loft. The moment the door was opened, they found the room enveloped in a thousand layers of auspicious air and magic beams, in ten thousand folds of colored fog and hallowed clouds. On the sūtra cases and jeweled chests red labels were attached, on which the titles of the books were written in clerkly script, as follows:[7]

1.	*The Nirvāṇa Sūtra,* 1 title	748 scrolls
2.	*The Ākāśagarbha-bodhisattva-dharmi Sūtra,* 1 title	400 scrolls
3.	*The Gracious Will Sūtra,* Major Collection, 1 title	50 scrolls
4.	*The Prajñāpāramitā-saṁkaya gāthā Sūtra,* 1 title	45 scrolls
5.	*The Homage to Bhūtatathātā Sūtra,* 1 title	90 scrolls
6.	*The Anakṣara-granthaka-rocana-garbha Sūtra,* 1 title	300 scrolls
7.	*The Vimalakīrti-nirdeśa Sūtra,* 1 title	170 scrolls
8.	*The Vajracchedika-prajñāpāramitā Sūtra,* 1 title	100 scrolls
9.	*The Buddha-carita-kāvya Sūtra,* 1 title	800 scrolls
10.	*The Bodhisattva-piṭaka Sūtra,* 1 title	1,021 scrolls
11.	*The Sūraṅgama-samādhi Sūtra,* 1 title	110 scrolls
12.	*The Arthaviniścaya-dharmaparyāya Sūtra,* 1 title	140 scrolls
13.	*The Avataṁsaka Sūtra,* 1 title	500 scrolls
14.	*The Mahāprajñā-pāramitā Sūtra,* 1 title	916 scrolls
15.	*The Abhūta-dharma Sūtra,* 1 title	1,110 scrolls
16.	*The Other Mādhyamika Sūtra,* 1 title	270 scrolls
17.	*The Kāśyapa-parivarta Sūtra,* 1 title	120 scrolls
18.	*The Pañca-nāga Sūtra,* 1 title	32 scrolls
19.	*The Bodhisattva-caryā-nirdeśa Sūtra,* 1 title	116 scrolls
20.	*The Magadha Sūtra,* 1 title	350 scrolls

21. The *Māyā-dālamahātantra mahāyāna-gambhīra nāya-guhya-paraśi Sūtra*, 1 title	100 scrolls
22. The *Western Heaven Śāstra*, 1 title	130 scrolls
23. The *Buddha-kṣetra Sūtra*, 1 title	1,950 scrolls
24. The *Mahāprajñāpāramitā Śāstra*, 1 title	1,080 scrolls
25. The *Original Loft Sūtra*, 1 title	850 scrolls
26. The *Mahāmayūrī-vidyārajñī Sūtra*, 1 title	220 scrolls
27. The *Abhidharma-kośa Śāstra*, 1 title	200 scrolls
28. The *Mahāsaṃghaṭa Sūtra*, 1 title	130 scrolls
29. The *Saddharma-puṇḍarika Sūtra*, 1 title	100 scrolls
30. The *Precious Permanence Sūtra*, 1 title	220 scrolls
31. The *Sāṅghika-vinaya Sūtra*, 1 title	157 scrolls
32. The *Mahāyāna-śraddhotpāda Śāstra*, 1 title	1,000 scrolls
33. The *Precious Authority Sūtra*, 1 title	1,280 scrolls
34. The *Correct Commandment Sūtra*, 1 title	200 scrolls
35. The *Vidyā-mātra-siddhi Śāstra*, 1 title	100 scrolls

After Ānanda and Kāśyapa had shown all the titles to the T'ang monk, they said to him, "Sage Monk, having come all this distance from the Land of the East, what sort of small gifts have you brought for us? Take them out quickly! We'll be pleased to hand over the scriptures to you."

On hearing this, Tripitaka said, "Because of the great distance, your disciple, Hsüan-tsang, has not been able to make such preparation."

"How nice! How nice!" said the two Honored Ones, snickering. "If we imparted the scriptures to you gratis, our posterity would starve to death!"

When Pilgrim saw them fidgeting and fussing, refusing to hand over the scriptures, he could not refrain from yelling, "Master, let's go tell Tathāgata about this! Let's make him come himself and hand over the scriptures to old Monkey!"

"Stop shouting!" said Ānanda. "Where do you think you are that you dare indulge in such mischief and waggery? Get over here and receive the scriptures!" Controlling their annoyance, Pa-chieh and Sha Monk managed to restrain Pilgrim before they turned to receive the books. Scroll after scroll were wrapped and laid on the horse. Four additional luggage wraps were bundled up for Pa-chieh and Sha Monk to tote, after which the pilgrims went before the jeweled throne again to kowtow and thank Tathāgata. As they walked out the gates

of the monastery, they bowed twice whenever they came upon a
Buddhist Patriarch or a Bodhisattva. When they reached the main
gate, they also bowed to take leave of the priests and nuns, the upāsakas and upāsikās, before descending the mountain. We shall now
leave them for the moment.

We tell you now that there was up in the treasure loft the aged
Dīpaṁkara, also named the Buddha of the Past, who overheard
everything and understood immediately that Ānanda and Kāśyapa
had handed over to the pilgrims scrolls of scriptures that were wordless. Chuckling to himself, he said, "Most of the priests in the Land of
the East are so stupid and blind that they will not recognize the value
of these wordless scriptures. When that happens, won't it have made
this long trek of our sage monk completely worthless?" Then he
asked, "Who is here beside my throne?"

The White Heroic Honored One at once stepped forth, and the aged
Buddha gave him this instruction: "You must exercise your magic
powers and catch up with the T'ang monk immediately. Take away
those wordless scriptures from him, so that he will be forced to return
for the true scriptures with words." Mounting a violent gust of wind,
the White Heroic Honored One swept out of the gate of the Thunderclap Monastery. As he called up his vast magic powers, the wind was
strong indeed! Truly

A stalwart Servant of Buddha
Is not like any common wind god;
The wrathful cries of an immortal
Far surpass a young girl's whistle!
This mighty gust
Causes fishes and dragons to lose their lairs
And angry waves in the rivers and seas.
Black apes find it hard to present their fruits;
Yellow cranes turn around to seek their nests.
The phoenix's pure cries have lost their songs;
The pheasant's callings turn most boisterous.
Green pine-branches snap;
Blue lotus-blossoms soar.
Stalk by stalk, verdant bamboos fall;
Petal by petal, gold lotus quakes.
Bell tones drift away to three thousand miles;
The scripture chants o'er countless gorges fly.

Beneath the cliff rare flowers' colors fade;
Fresh, jadelike grasses lie down by the road.
Phoenixes can't stretch their wings;
White deer hide on the ledge.
Vast waves of strange fragrance now fill the world
As cool, clear breezes penetrate the heavens.

The elder T'ang was walking along when he encountered this churning fragrant wind. Thinking that this was only an auspicious portent sent by the Buddhist Patriarch, he was completely off guard when, with a loud crack in midair, a hand descended. The scriptures that were loaded on the horse were lifted away with no effort at all. The sight left Tripitaka yelling in terror and beating his breast, while Pachieh rolled off in pursuit on the ground and Sha Monk stood rigid to guard the empty pannier. Pilgrim Sun vaulted into the air. When that White Heroic Honored saw him closing in rapidly, he feared that Pilgrim's rod might strike out blindly without regard for good or ill to cause him injury. He therefore ripped the scriptures open and threw them toward the ground.

When Pilgrim saw that the scripture wrappers were torn and their contents scattered all over by the fragrant wind, he lowered the direction of his cloud to go after the books instead and stopped his pursuit. The White Heroic Honored One retrieved the wind and fog and returned to report to the Buddha of the Past.

As Pa-chieh sped along, he saw the holy books dropping down from the sky. Soon he was joined by Pilgrim, and the two of them gathered up the scrolls to go back to the T'ang monk. His eyes brimming with tears, the T'ang monk said, "O Disciples! We are bullied by vicious demons even in this land of ultimate bliss!"

When Sha Monk opened up a scroll of scripture which the other two disciples were clutching, his eyes perceived only snow-white paper without a trace of so much as half a letter on it. Hurriedly he presented it to Tripitaka, saying, "Master, this scroll is wordless!"

Pilgrim also opened a scroll and it, too, was wordless. Then Pa-chieh opened still another scroll, and it was also wordless. "Open all of them!" cried Tripitaka. Every scroll had only blank paper.

Heaving big sighs, the elder said, "Our people in the Land of the East simply have no luck! What good is it to take back a wordless, empty volume like this? How could I possibly face the T'ang emperor? The crime of mocking one's ruler is greater than one punishable by execution!"

Already perceiving the truth of the matter, Pilgrim said to the T'ang monk, "Master, there's no need for further talk. This has all come about because we had no gifts for these fellows, Ānanda and Kāśyapa. That's why we were given these wordless texts. Let's go back quickly to Tathagata and charge them with fraud and solicitation for a bribe."

"Exactly! Exactly!" yelled Pa-chieh. "Let's go and charge them!" The four pilgrims turned and, with painful steps, once more ascended Thunderclap.

In a little while they reached the temple gates, where they were met by the multitude with hands folded in their sleeves. "Has the sage monk returned to ask for an exchange of scriptures?" they asked, laughing. Tripitaka nodded his affirmation, and the Vajra Guardians permitted them to go straight inside. When they arrived before the Great Hero Hall, Pilgrim shouted, "Tathāgata, we master and disciples had to experience ten thousand stings and a thousand demons in order to come bowing from the Land of the East. After you had specifically ordered the scriptures to be given to us, Ānanda and Kāśyapa sought a bribe from us; when they didn't succeed, they conspired in fraud and deliberately handed over wordless texts to us. Even if we took them, what good would they do? Pardon me, Tathāgata, but you must deal with this matter!"

"Stop shouting!" said the Buddhist Patriarch with a chuckle. "I knew already that the two of them would ask you for a little present. After all, the holy scriptures are not to be given lightly, nor are they to be received gratis. Some time ago, in fact, a few of our sage priests went down the mountain and recited these scriptures in the house of one Elder Chao in the Kingdom of Śrāvasti, so that the living in his family would all be protected from harm and the deceased redeemed from perdition. For all that service they managed to charge him only three pecks and three pints of rice. I told them that they had made far to cheap a sale and that their posterity would have no money to spend. Since you people came with empty hands to acquire scriptures, blank texts were handed over to you. But these blank texts are actually true, wordless scriptures, and they are just as good as those with words. However, those creatures in your Land of the East are so foolish and unenlightened that I have no choice but to impart to you now the texts with words."

"Ānanda and Kāśyapa," he then called out, "quickly select for them a few scrolls from each of the titles of true scriptures with words, and then come back to me to report the total number."

The two Honored Ones again led the four pilgrims to the treasure loft, where they once more demanded a gift from the T'ang monk. Since he had virtually nothing to offer, Tripitaka told Sha Monk to take out the alms bowl of purple gold. With both hands he presented it to the Honored Ones, saying, "Your disciple in truth has not brought with him any gift, owing to the great distance and my own poverty. This alms bowl, however, was bestowed by the T'ang emperor in person, in order that I could use it to beg for my maigre throughout the journey. As the humblest token of my gratitude, I am presenting it to you now, and I beg the Honored Ones to accept it. When I return to the court and make my report to the T'ang emperor, a generous reward will certainly be forthcoming. Only grant us the true scriptures with words, so that His Majesty's goodwill will not be thwarted nor the labor of this lengthy journey be wasted." With a gentle smile, Ānanda took the alms bowl. All those vīra who guarded the precious towers, the kitchen helpers in charge of sacrifices and incense, and the Honored Ones who worked in the treasure loft began to clap one another on the back and tickle one another on the face. Snapping their fingers and curling their lips, every one of them said, "How shameless! How shameless! Asking the scripture seeker for a present!"

After a while, the two Honored Ones became rather embarrassed, though Ānanda continued to clutch firmly at the alms bowl. Kāśyapa, however, went into the loft to select the scrolls and handed them item by item to Tripitaka. "Disciples," said Tripitaka, "take a good look at these, and make sure that they are not like the earlier ones."

The three disciples examined each scroll as they received it, and this time all the scrolls had words written on them. Altogether they were given five thousand and forty-eight scrolls, making up the number of a single canon.[8] After being properly packed, the scriptures were loaded onto the horse. An additional load was made for Pa-chieh to tote, while their own luggage was toted by Sha Monk. As Pilgrim led the horse, the T'ang monk took up his priestly staff and gave his Vairocana hat a press and his brocade cassock a shake. In delight they once more went before our Buddha Tathāgata. Thus it is that

Sweet is the taste of the Great Piṭaka,
Product most refined of Tathāgata.
Note how Hsüan-tsang has climbed the mount with pain.
Pity Ānanda who has but love of gain.

Their blindness removed by Buddha of the Past,
The truth now received peace they have at last—
Glad to bring scriptures back to the East,
Where all may partake of this gracious feast.

Ānanda and Kāśyapa led the T'ang monk before Tathāgata, who ascended the lofty lotus throne. He ordered Dragon-Tamer and Tiger-Subduer, the two arhats, to strike up the cloudy stone-chime to assemble all the divinities, including the three thousand Buddhas, the three thousand guardians, the Eight Vajra Guardians, the five hundred arhats, the eight hundred nuns and priests, the upāsakas and upāsikās, the Honored Ones from every Heaven and cave-dwelling, from every blessed land and spirit mountain. Those who ought to be seated were asked to ascend their treasure thrones, while those who should stand were told to make two columns on both sides. In a moment celestial music filled the air as layers of auspicious luminosity and hallowed mist loomed up in the sky. After all the Buddhas had assembled, they bowed to greet Tathāgata.

Then Tathāgata asked, "Ānanda and Kāśyapa, how many scrolls of scriptures have you passed on to him? Give me an itemized report."

The two Honored Ones said, "We have turned over to the T'ang court the following:

1.	*The Nirvāṇa Sūtra*	400 scrolls
2.	*The Ākāśagarbha-bodhisattva-dharmi Sūtra*	20 scrolls
3.	*The Gracious Will Sūtra*, Major Collection	40 scrolls
4.	*The Prajñāpāramitā-saṃkaya gāthā Sūtra*	20 scrolls
5.	*The Homage to Bhūtatathātā Sūtra*	30 scrolls
6.	*The Anakṣara-granthaka-rocana-garbha Sūtra*	50 scrolls
7.	*The Vimalakīrti-nirdeśa Sūtra*	30 scrolls
8.	*The Vajracchedika-prajñāpāramitā Sūtra*	1 scroll
9.	*The Buddha-carita-kāvya Sūtra*	116 scrolls
10.	*The Bodhisattva-piṭaka Sūtra*	360 scrolls
11.	*The Sūraṅgama-samādhi Sūtra*	30 scrolls
12.	*The Arthaviniścaya-dharmaparyāya Sūtra*	40 scrolls
13.	*The Avataṁsaka Sūtra*	81 scrolls
14.	*The Mahāprajñā-pāramitā Sūtra*	600 scrolls
15.	*The Abhūta-dharma Sūtra*	550 scrolls
16.	*The Other Mādhyamika Sūtra*	42 scrolls
17.	*The Kāśyapa-parivarta Sūtra*	20 scrolls
18.	*The Pañca-nāga Sūtra*	20 scrolls

19. The *Bodhisattva-caryā-nirdeśa Sūtra*	60 scrolls
20. The *Magadha Sūtra*	140 scrolls
21. The *Māyā-dālamahātantra mahāyāna-gambhira nāya-guhya-paraśi Sūtra*	30 scrolls
22. The *Western Heaven Śāstra*	30 scrolls
23. The *Buddha-kṣetra Sūtra*	1,638 scrolls
24. The *Mahāprajñāpāramitā Śāstra*	90 scrolls
25. The *Original Loft Sūtra*	56 scrolls
26. The *Mahāmayūrī-vidyārajñī Sūtra*	14 scrolls
27. The *Abhidharma-kośa Śāstra*	10 scrolls
28. The *Mahāsaṃghaṭa Sūtra*	30 scrolls
29. The *Saddharma-puṇḍarika Sūtra*	10 scrolls
30. The *Precious Permanence Sūtra*	170 scrolls
31. The *Sāṅghika-vinaya Sūtra*	110 scrolls
32. The *Mahāyāna-śraddhotpāda Śāstra*	50 scrolls
33. The *Precious Authority Sūtra*	140 scrolls
34. The *Correct Commandment Sūtra*	10 scrolls
35. The *Vidyā-mātra-siddhi Śāstra*	10 scrolls

From the thirty-five titles of scriptures that are in the treasury, we have selected altogether five thousand and forty-eight scrolls for the sage monk to take back to the T'ang in the Land of the East. Most of these have been properly packed and loaded on the horse, and a few have also been arranged in a pannier. The pilgrims now wish to express their thanks to you."

Having tethered the horse and set down the poles, Tripitaka led his three disciples to bow to Buddha, each pressing his palms together in front of him. Tathāgata said to the T'ang monk, "The efficacy of these scriptures cannot be measured. Not only are they the mirror of our faith, but they are also the source of the Three Teachings. They must not be lightly handled, especially when you return to your South Jambūdvīpa Continent and display them to the multitude. No one should open a scroll without fasting and bathing first. Treasure them! Honor them! Therein will be found the mysteries of gaining immortality and comprehending the Tao, the wondrous formulas for the execution of the thousand transformations." Tripitaka kowtowed to thank him and to express his faith and obedience. As before, he prostrated himself in homage three times to the Buddhist Patriarch with all earnestness and sincerity before he took the scriptures and left. As he went through the three monastery gates, he again thanked each of the sages, and we shall speak no more of him for the moment.

After he had sent away the T'ang monk, Tathāgata dismissed the assembly for the transmission of scriptures. From one side stepped forth the Bodhisattva Kuan-shih-yin, who pressed her palms together to say to the Buddhist Patriarch, "This disciple received your golden decree that year to search for someone in the Land of the East to be a scripture seeker. Today he has succeeded. Altogether, his journey took fourteen years or five thousand and forty days. Eight more days and the perfect canonical number will be attained. Would you permit me to surrender in return your golden decree?"

Highly pleased, Tathāgata said, "What you said is most appropriate. You are certainly permitted to surrender my golden decree." He then gave this instruction to the Eight Vajra Guardians: "Quickly exercise your magic powers to lift the sage monk back to the East. As soon as he has imparted the true scriptures to the people there, bring him back here to the West. You must accomplish all this within eight days, so as to fulfill the perfect canonical number of five thousand and forty-eight. Do not delay." The Vajra Guardians at once caught up with the T'ang monk, crying, "Scripture seekers, follow us!" The T'ang monk and his companions, all with healthy frames and buoyant bodies, followed the Vajra Guardians to rise in the air astride the clouds. Truly

Their minds enlightened, they bowed to Buddha;
Merit perfected, they ascended on high.

We do not know how they will pass on the scriptures after they have returned to the Land of the East, and you must listen to the explanation in the next chapter.

Ninety-nine

Nine times nine is the perfect number and *māra*'s
  extinguished;
The work of Double Three[1] ended, the Tao returns to its root.

We shall not speak of the Eight Vajra Guardians escorting the T'ang
monk back to his nation. We turn instead to those Guardians of the
Five Quarters, the Four Sentinels, the Six Gods of Darkness and the
Six Gods of Light, and the Guardians of Monasteries, who appeared
before the triple gates and said to the Bodhisattva Kuan-yin, "Your
disciples had received the Bodhisattva's dharma decree to give secret
protection to the sage monk. Now that the work of the sage monk is
completed, and the Bodhisattva has returned the Buddhist Patriarch's
golden decree to him, we too request permission from the Bodhisattva
to return your dharma decree to you."

Highly pleased also, the Bodhisattva said, "Yes, yes! You have my
permission." Then she asked, "What was the disposition of the four
pilgrims during their journey?"

"They showed genuine devotion and determination," replied the
various deities, "which could hardly have escaped the penetrating
observation of the Bodhisattva. The T'ang monk, after all, had endured unspeakable sufferings. Indeed, all the ordeals which he had to
undergo throughout his journey have been recorded by your disciples.
Here is the complete account." The Bodhisattva started to read the
registry from its beginning, and this was the content:

The Guardians in obedience to your decree
Record with care the T'ang monk's calamities.
Gold Cicada banished is the first ordeal [see chap. 8];
Being almost killed after birth is the second ordeal [chap. 9];
Being thrown in the river hardly a month old is the third ordeal
  [chap. 9];
Seeking parents and their vengeance is the fourth ordeal [chap. 9];
Meeting a tiger after leaving the city is the fifth ordeal [chap. 13];
Falling into a pit and losing followers is the sixth ordeal [chap. 13];

The Double-Fork Ridge is the seventh ordeal [chap. 13];

The Mountain of Two Frontiers is the eighth ordeal [chap. 13];

Changing horse at a steep brook is the ninth ordeal [chap. 15];

Burning by fire at night is the tenth ordeal [chap. 16];

Losing the cassock is the eleventh ordeal [chap. 16];

Bringing Pa-chieh to submission is the twelfth ordeal [chaps. 18–19];

Being blocked by the Yellow Wind Fiend is the thirteenth ordeal [chap. 20];

Seeking aid with Ling-chi is the fourteenth ordeal [chap. 21];

Hard to cross Flowing-Sand is the fifteenth ordeal [chap. 22];

Taking in Sha Monk is the sixteenth ordeal [chap. 22];

The Four Sages' epiphany is the seventeenth ordeal [chap. 23];

The Five Villages Temple is the eighteenth ordeal [chap. 24];

The ginseng hard to revive is the nineteenth ordeal [chap. 26];

Banishing the Mind Monkey is the twentieth ordeal [chap. 27];

Getting lost at Black Pine Forest is the twenty-first ordeal [chap. 28];

Sending a letter to Precious Image Kingdom is the twenty-second ordeal [chap. 29];

Changing into a tiger at the Golden Chimes Hall is the twenty-third ordeal [chap. 30];

Meeting demons at Level-Top Mountain is the twenty-fourth ordeal [chap. 32];

Being hung high at Lotus-Flower Cave is the twenty-fifth ordeal [chap. 33];

Saving the ruler of Black Rooster Kingdom is the twenty-sixth ordeal [chap. 37];

Running into a demon's transformed body is the twenty-seventh ordeal [chap. 37];

Meeting a fiend in Roaring Mountain is the twenty-eighth ordeal [chap. 40];

The sage monk abducted by wind is the twenty-ninth ordeal [chap. 40];

The Mind Monkey being injured is the thirtieth ordeal [chap. 41];

Asking the sage to subdue monsters is the thirty-first ordeal [chap. 42];

Sinking in the Black River is the thirty-second ordeal [chap. 43];

Hauling at Cart Slow Kingdom is the thirty-third ordeal [chap. 44];

A mighty contest is the thirty-fourth ordeal [chaps. 45–46];

Expelling Taoists to prosper Buddhists is the thirty-fifth ordeal [chap. 47];

Meeting a great water on the road is the thirty-sixth ordeal [chap. 47];

Falling into the Heaven-Reaching River is the thirty-seventh ordeal [chap. 48];

The Fish-Basket revealing her body is the thirty-eighth ordeal [chap. 49];

Meeting a fiend at Golden Helmet Mountain is the thirty-ninth ordeal [chap. 50];

Heaven's gods find it hard to win is the fortieth ordeal [chaps. 51–52];

Asking the Buddha for the source is the forty-first ordeal [chap. 52];

Being poisoned after drinking water is the forty-second ordeal [chap. 53];

Detained for marriage at Western Liang Kingdom is the forty-third ordeal [chap. 54];

Suffering at the Cave of the Lute is the forty-fourth ordeal [chap. 55];

Banishing again the Mind Monkey is the forty-fifth ordeal [chap. 56];

The macaque hard to distinguish is the forty-sixth ordeal [chaps. 57–58];

The road blocked at the Mountain of Flames is the forty-seventh ordeal [chap. 59];

Seeking the palm-leaf fan is the forty-eighth ordeal [chaps. 59–60];

Binding the demon king is the forty-ninth ordeal [chap. 61];

Sweeping the pagoda at Sacrifice Kingdom is the fiftieth ordeal [chap. 62];

Recovering the treasure to save the monks is the fifty-first ordeal [chap. 63];

Chanting poetry at the Brambled Forest is the fifty-second ordeal [chap. 64];

Meeting disaster at Little Thunderclap is the fifty-third ordeal [chap. 65];

The celestial gods being imprisoned is the fifty-fourth ordeal [chap. 66];

Being blocked by filth at Pulpy Persimmon Alley is the fifty-fifth ordeal [chap. 67];

Applying medication at the Scarlet-Purple Kingdom is the fifty-sixth ordeal [chaps. 68–69];

Healing fatigue and infirmity is the fifty-seventh ordeal [chaps. 68–69];

Subduing monster to recover a queen is the fifty-eighth ordeal [chaps. 69–71];

Delusion by the seven passions is the fifty-ninth ordeal [chap. 72];

Being wounded by Many Eyes is the sixtieth ordeal [chap. 73];

The way blocked at the Lion-Camel Kingdom is the sixty-first ordeal [chaps. 74–75];

The fiends divided into three colors is the sixty-second ordeal [chaps. 74–77];

Meeting calamity in the city is the sixty-third ordeal [chaps. 76–77];

Requesting Buddha to subdue the demons is the sixty-fourth ordeal [chap. 77];

Rescuing the lads at Bhikṣu is the sixty-fifth ordeal [chap. 78];

Distinguishing the true from the deviate is the sixty-sixth ordeal [chap. 79];

Saving a fiend at a pine forest is the sixty-seventh ordeal [chap. 80];

Falling sick in a priestly chamber is the sixty-eighth ordeal [chap. 81];

Being imprisoned at the Bottomless Cave is the sixty-ninth ordeal [chaps. 81–83];

Problem of leaving Dharma-Destroying Kingdom is the seventieth ordeal [chap. 84];

Meeting demons at Mist-Concealing Mountain is the seventy-first ordeal [chaps. 85–86];

Seeking rain at Phoenix-Immortal Prefecture is the seventy-second ordeal [chap. 87];

Losing their weapons is the seventy-third ordeal [chap. 88];

The festival of the rake is the seventy-fourth ordeal [chap. 89];

Meeting disaster at Bamboo-Knot Mountain is the seventy-fifth ordeal [chap. 90];

Suffering at Mysterious Flower Cave is the seventy-sixth ordeal [chap. 91];

Capturing the rhinoceroses is the seventy-seventh ordeal [chap. 92];

Being forced to marry at India is the seventy-eighth ordeal [chaps. 93–95];

Jailed at Bronze Terrace Prefecture is the seventy-ninth ordeal [chap. 97];

Being freed of mortal bodies at Cloud-Transcending Stream is the eightieth ordeal [chap. 98];

The journey: one hundred and eight thousand miles.

The sage monk's ordeals are clearly on file.

After the Bodhisattva had read through the entire registry of ordeals, she said hurriedly, "Within our order of Buddhism, nine times nine is the crucial means by which one returns to immortality. The sage monk has undergone eighty ordeals. Since one ordeal, therefore, is still lacking, the sacred number is not yet complete."

At once she gave this order to one of the Guardians: "Catch the Vajra Guardians and create one more ordeal." Having received this command, the Guardian soared toward the east astride the clouds. After a night and a day he caught the Vajra Guardians and whispered in their ears, "Do this and this . . . ! Don't fail to obey the dharma decree of the Bodhisattva." On hearing these words, the Eight Vajra Guardians immediately retrieved the wind that had borne aloft the four pilgrims, dropping them and the horse bearing the scriptures to the ground. Alas! Truly such is

Nine times nine, hard task of immortality.

Firmness of will yields the mysterious key.

By bitter toil you must the demons spurn;

Cultivation will the proper way return.

Regard not the scriptures as easy things.

So many are the sage monk's sufferings!

Learn of the old, wondrous *Kinship of the Three* :[2]

Elixir won't gel if there's slight errancy.

When his feet touched profane ground, Tripitaka became terribly frightened. Pa-chieh, however, roared with laughter, saying, "Fine! Fine! Fine! This is exactly a case of 'More haste, less speed!'"

"Fine! Fine! Fine!" said Sha Monk. "Because we've speeded up too much, they want us to take a little rest here." "Have no worry," said the Great Sage. "As the proverb says,

You sit on the beach for ten days

And shoot past nine in one day."

"Stop matching your wits, you three!" said Tripitaka. "Let's see if we can tell where we are." Looking all around, Sha Monk said, "I know the place! I know the place! Master, listen to the sound of water!"

Pilgrim said, "The sound of water, I suppose, reminds you of your ancestral home."

"Which is the Flowing-Sand River," said Pa-chieh.

"No! No!" said Sha Monk. "This happens to be the Heaven-Reaching River." Tripitaka said, "O Disciples! Take a careful look and see which side of the river we're on."

Vaulting into the air, Pilgrim shielded his eyes with his hand and took a careful survey of the place before dropping down once more. "Master," he said, "this is the west bank of the Heaven-Reaching River."

"Now I remember," said Tripitaka. "There was a Ch'ên Village on the east bank. When we arrived here that year, you rescued their son and daughter. In their gratitude to us, they wanted to make a boat to take us across. Eventually we were fortunate enough to get across on the back of a white turtle. I recall, too, that there was no human habitation whatever on the west bank. What shall we do this time?"

"I thought that only profane people would practice this sort of fraud," said Pa-chieh. "Now I know that even the Vajra Guardians before the face of Buddha can practice fraud! Buddha commanded them to take us back east. How could they just abandon us in mid-journey? Now we're in quite a bind! How are we going to get across?"

"Stop grumbling, Second Elder Brother!" said Sha Monk. "Our master has already attained the Way, for he had already been delivered from his mortal frame previously at the Cloud-Transcending Stream. This time he can't possibly sink in water. Let's all of us exercise our magic of Displacement and take Master across."

"You can't take him over! You can't take him over!" said Pilgrim, chuckling to himself. Now, why did he say that? If he were willing to exercise his magic powers and reveal the mystery of flight, master and disciples could cross even a thousand rivers. He knew, however, that the T'ang monk had not yet perfected the sacred number of nine times nine. That one remaining ordeal made it necessary for them to be detained at the spot.

As master and disciples conversed and walked slowly up to the edge of the water, they suddenly heard someone calling, "T'ang Sage Monk! T'ang Sage Monk! Come this way! Come this way!" Startled, the four of them looked all around but could not see any sign of a human being or a boat. Then they caught sight of a huge, white, scabby-headed turtle at the shoreline. "Old Master," he cried with outstretched neck, "I have waited for you for so many years! Have you returned only at this time?"

"Old Turtle," replied Pilgrim, smiling, "we troubled you in a year past, and today we meet again." Tripitaka, Pa-chieh, and Sha Monk could not have been more pleased.

"If indeed you want to serve us," said Pilgrim, "come up on the

shore." The turtle crawled up the bank. Pilgrim told his companions
to guide the horse onto the turtle's back. As before, Pa-chieh squatted
at the rear of the horse, while the T'ang monk and Sha Monk took up
positions to the left and to the right of the horse. With one foot on the
turtle's head and another on his neck, Pilgrim said, "Old Turtle, go
steadily."

His four legs outstretched, the old turtle moved through the water
as if he were on dry level ground, carrying all five of them—master
and disciples and the horse—straight toward the eastern shore. Thus
it is that

In Advaya's[3] gate the dharma profound
Reveals Heav'n and Earth and demons confounds.
The original visage now they see;
Causes find perfection in one body.
Freely they move when Triyāna's won,
And when the elixir's nine turns are done.
The luggage and the staff there's no need to tote,
Glad to return on old turtle afloat.

Carrying the pilgrims on his back, the old turtle trod on the waves and
proceeded for more than half a day. Late in the afternoon they were
near the eastern shore when he suddenly asked this question: "Old
Master, in that year when I took you across, I begged you to question
Tathāgata, once you got to see him, when I would find my sought-
after refuge and how much longer would I live. Did you do that?"

Now, that elder, since his arrival at the Western Heaven, had been
preoccupied with bathing in the Yü-chên Temple, being renewed at
Cloud-Transcending Stream, and bowing to the various sage monks,
Bodhisattvas, and Buddhas. When he walked up the Spirit Mountain,
he fixed his thought on the worship of Buddha and on the acquisition
of scriptures, completely banishing from his mind all other concerns.
He did not, of course, ask about the allotted age of the old turtle. Not
daring to lie, however, he fell silent and did not answer the question
for a long time. Perceiving that Tripitaka had not asked the Buddha
for him, the old turtle shook his body once and dove with a splash into
the depths. The four pilgrims, the horse, and the scriptures all fell into
the water as well. Ah! It was fortunate that the T'ang monk had cast
off his mortal frame and attained the Way. If he were like the person
he had been before, he would have sunk straight to the bottom. The
white horse, moreover, was originally a dragon, while Pa-chieh and

Sha Monk both were quite at home in the water. Smiling broadly,
Pilgrim made a great display of his magic powers by hauling the
T'ang monk right out of the water and onto the eastern shore. But
the scriptures, the clothing, and the saddle were completely soaked.

Master and disciples had just climbed up the riverbank when suddenly a violent gale arose; the sky darkened immediately and both
thunder and lightning began as rocks and grit flew everywhere.
What they felt was

One gust of wind
And the whole world teetered;
One clap of thunder
And both mountains and streams shuddered.
One flash of lightning
Shot flames through the clouds;
One sky of fog
Enveloped this great Earth.
The wind's mighty howl;
The thunder's violent roar;
The lightning's scarlet streaks;
The fog blanking moon and stars.
The wind hurtled dust and dirt at their faces;
The thunder sent tigers and leopards into hiding;
The lightning raised among the fowl a ruckus;
The fog made the woods and trees disappear.
That wind caused waves in the Heaven-Reaching River to toss and
    churn;
That lightning lit up the Heaven-Reaching River down to its
    bottom;
That thunder terrified the Heaven-Reaching River's dragons and
    fishes;
That fog covered the shores of Heaven-Reaching River with a
    shroud of darkness.
Marvelous wind!
Mountains cracked as pines and bamboos toppled.
Marvelous thunder!
Its power stirred insects and injured humans.
Marvelous lightning!
Like a gold snake it brightened both land and sky.
Marvelous fog!

It surged through the air to screen the Ninefold Heaven.
So terrified were the pilgrims that Tripitaka held firmly to the scripture wraps and Sha Monk threw himself on the poles. While Pa-chieh clung to the white horse, Pilgrim wielded his iron rod with both hands to give protection left and right. That wind, fog, thunder, and lightning, you see, had been a storm brought on by invisible demons, who wanted to snatch away the scriptures the pilgrims had acquired. The commotion lasted all night, and only by morning did the storm subside. Soaked from top to bottom and shaking all over, the elder said, "Wu-k'ung, how did this storm come about?"

"Master, you don't seem to understand," said Pilgrim, panting heavily, "that when we escorted you to acquire these scriptures, we had, in fact, robbed Heaven and Earth of their creative powers. For our success meant that we could share the age of the universe; like the light of the sun and moon, we would enjoy life everlasting for we had put on an incorruptible body. Our success, however, had also incurred the envy of Heaven and Earth, the jealousy of both demons and gods, who wanted to snatch away the scriptures from us. They could not do so only because the scriptures were thoroughly wet and because they had been shielded by your rectified dharma-body, which could not be harmed by thunder, lightning, or fog. Moreover, old Monkey was brandishing his iron rod to exercise the nature of pure yang and give you protection. Now that it is morning, the forces of yang are evermore in ascendancy, and the demons cannot prevail."

Only then did Tripitaka, Pa-chieh, and Sha Monk realize what had taken place, and they all thanked Pilgrim repeatedly. In a little while, the sun was way up in the sky, and they moved the scriptures to high ground so that the wraps could be opened and their contents dried. To this day the boulders have remained on which the scriptures were spread out and sunned. By the side of the boulders they also spread out their own clothing and shoes. As they stood, sat, or jumped about, truly this was their situation:

The one pure yang body facing the light
Has put invisible demons all to flight.
Know that true scriptures will o'er water prevail.
They fear not the thunder-and-lightning assail.
Henceforth to Saṁbodhi they'll go in peace,
And to fairy land they'll return with ease.
Rocks for sunning scriptures are still found here,

Though no demon would ever dare come near.

The four of them were examining the scriptures scroll by scroll to see if they had completely dried when some fishermen arrived at the shore. When they saw the pilgrims, one of the fishermen recognized them and said, "Old Masters, aren't you the ones who crossed this river some years ago on your way to the Western Heaven to seek scriptures?"

"Indeed, we are!" replied Pa-chieh. "Where are you from? How is it that you recognize us?"

"We are from the Ch'ên Village," said the fisherman.

"How far is the village from here?" asked Pa-chieh. The fisherman said, "Due south of this canal, about twenty miles."

"Master," said Pa-chieh, "let's move the scriptures to the Ch'ên Village and dry them there. They have a place for us to sit and food for us to eat. We can even ask their family to starch our clothing. Isn't that better than staying here?"

"Let's not go there," replied Tripitaka. "As soon as the scriptures are dried here, we can collect them and be on our way."

The fishermen, however, went back south of the canal and ran right into Ch'ên Ch'êng. "Number Two," they cried, "the masters who offered themselves as sacrifice-substitutes for your children years ago have returned."

"Where did you see them?" asked Ch'ên Ch'êng. Pointing with their hands, the fishermen said, "Near the boulders over there, where they're sunning scrolls of scriptures."

Ch'ên Ch'êng took some of his farm hands and ran past the canal. When he caught sight of the pilgrims, he hurriedly went to his knees and said, "Venerable Fathers, now that you have returned, having accomplished your work and merit of acquiring scriptures, why did you not come straight to our home? Why are you loitering here instead? Please, please come to our home!"

"Wait till we've dried the scriptures in the sun," said Pilgrim, "and we'll go with you."

"How is it," asked Ch'ên Ch'êng again, "that the clothing and scriptures of the Venerable Fathers are soaking wet?"

"In that previous year," replied Tripitaka, "we were indebted to a white turtle for taking us on his back to the western shore. This time he again offered to carry us back to the eastern shore. When we were about to reach the bank, he asked me whether I had remembered to inquire of Buddha for him about how much longer it would take for him to achieve human form. I had actually forgotten about the matter, and he dove into the water. That was how we got wet."

After Tripitaka had thus given a thorough account of what had taken place, Ch'ên Ch'êng kowtowed and urged them to go back to the house. At length Tripitaka gave in, and they began to collect the scriptures together. They did not expect, however, that several scrolls of the *Buddha-carita-kāvya Sūtra* would be stuck to the rocks, and a part of the sūtra's ending was torn off. This is why the sūtra today is not a complete text, and the top of that particular boulder on which the sūtra had dried still retains some traces of writing. "We've been very careless!" said Tripitaka sorrowfully. "We should have been more vigilant."

"Hardly! Hardly!" said Pilgrim, laughing. "After all, even Heaven and Earth are not perfect. This sūtra may have been perfect, but a part of it has been torn off precisely because only in that condition will it correspond to the profound mystery of nonperfection. What happened isn't something human power could anticipate or change!" After master and disciples had finished packing up the scriptures, they headed for the village with Ch'ên Ch'êng.

The news of the pilgrims' arrival was passed from one person to ten, from ten to a hundred, and from a hundred to a thousand, till all the people, old and young, came to receive them. When Ch'ên Ch'ing got the news, he immediately set up an incense altar in front of his door and called for drummers and musicians to play. The moment they arrived, Ch'ên led his entire household to kowtow to the pilgrims so as to thank them once more for their previous kindness of saving their children. Then he ordered tea and maigre for them.

Since Tripitaka had partaken of the immortal victuals prepared for him by the Buddhist Patriarch, and since he had been delivered from his mortal frame to become a Buddha, he had no desire at all for profane food. The two old men begged and begged, and only to please them did he pick up the merest morsel. The Great Sage Sun, who never ate much cooked food anyway, said almost immediately, "Enough!" Sha Monk did not show much appetite either. As for Pa-chieh, even he did not resemble his former self, for he soon put down his bowl.

"Idiot, aren't you eating anymore?" asked Pilgrim.

"I don't know why," said Pa-chieh, "but my stomach seems to have weakened all at once!" They therefore put away the food, and the two old men asked about the enterprise of scripture seeking. Tripitaka gave a thorough account of how they bathed at the Yü-chên Temple first, how their bodies turned light and agile at the Cloud-Transcending Stream, how they bowed to Tathāgata at Thunderclap, and how they were feted beneath the precious tower and received scriptures at the treasure loft. He then went on to tell how the two Honored Ones, failing to obtain a gift at first, gave them wordless scriptures instead, how the second audience with Tathāgata had resulted in acquiring a canonical sum of scriptures, how the white turtle dove into the water, and how invisible demons tried to rob them. After this detailed rehearsal, he immediately wanted to leave.

The entire household of the two old men, of course, absolutely refused to let them go. "We could never have repaid," they said, "your profound kindness in saving the lives of our son and daughter except by building a temple to your memory. We have named it the Life-Saving Monastery so that we might offer you the perpetual sacrifice of incense." Then they called Ch'ên Kuan-pao and One Load of Gold, the son and daughter for whom Pilgrim and Pa-chieh originally served as substitutes on that occasion of child-sacrifice, to come out to kowtow again to their benefactors before they invited the pilgrims to view the monastery.

Leaving the scripture-wraps in front of their family hall, Tripitaka recited a scroll of the *Precious Permanence Sūtra* for their entire household. When they reached the monastery, food had already been laid out there by the Ch'ên family. Hardly had they been seated than another banquet was sent in by another family. Before they could even raise their chopsticks, still another banquet was brought in. There seemed, in fact, to be an unending stream of visitors and food vying for the pilgrims' attention. Not wishing to decline such sincere display of the people's hospitality, Tripitaka forced himself to make some show of tasting what was set before him. That monastery, by the way, was a handsome building indeed.

The temple's bright red-painted doors
Reflect the work of all donors.
From that moment one edifice would rise
With two porticoes adding to its size.
Screens and casements scarlet;
Seven treasures exquisite.

Incense and clouds interlace
As pure light floods the airy space.
A few young cypresses need water still;
Pines have yet to form clusters on the hill.
A living stream in front
Reaches Heaven with its tossing billows;
A tall ridge behind,
The mountain range through which the earth pulse flows.

After he had looked at the monastery from the outside, Tripitaka then went up to the tall tower, where he found the four statues of himself and his disciples.

When Pa-chieh saw these, he gave Pilgrim a tug and said, "Your statue looks very much like you!"

"Second Elder Brother," said Sha Monk, "yours has great resemblance, too. But Master's seems to look even more handsome."

"It's about right! It's about right!" said Tripitaka, and they descended the tower. In the front hall and the rear corridor, more vegetarian dishes were laid out for them.

Pilgrim asked the Ch'êns, "What ever happened to the shrine of that Great King?"

"It was pulled down that very year," replied the two old men. "Since this monastery was built, Venerable Father, we have been enjoying a rich harvest every year. This has to be the blessing you bestowed on us."

"It's actually the gift of Heaven!" said Pilgrim, chuckling. "We have nothing to do with it. But after we leave this time, we shall try to give you all the protection we can, so that the families of your entire village may enjoy abundant posterity, the peaceful births of the six beasts, and annually wind and rain in due season." All the people kowtowed again to express their thanks.

Before and behind the monastery, there seemed to have gathered a numberless crowd all wanting to offer fruits and maigre to their benefactors. With a giggle Pa-chieh said, "It's just my lousy luck! At the time when I could eat, there wasn't a single household that would give me ten meals. Today I have no appetite, but one family after another is pressing me with invitations." Though he felt stuffed, he raised his hands slightly and once more devoured eight or nine platters of vegetarian food. Though he claimed his stomach had weakened, he nonetheless put away twenty or thirty buns. The pilgrims all ate to their fullest capacity, but still there were other households waiting to invite them. "What contribution have these disciples made," said Tripitaka, "that we should receive such great outpouring of your affection? I beg you all to call a halt tonight. Wait till tomorrow and we shall be glad to be the recipients again."

It was already deep in the night. As he wanted to guard the true scriptures, Tripitaka dared not leave. He remained seated below the tower and meditated, so as to watch his possessions. By about the hour of the third watch, Tripitaka whispered, "Wu-k'ung, the people here have already perceived that we have finished our enterprise and attained the Way. As the ancients put it,

The adept does not show himself;
He who shows himself's no adept.

If they detain us too long, I fear that we may lose out in our main enterprise."

"What you say is quite right, Master," replied Pilgrim. "While it is still deep in the night and people are all sound asleep, let us leave quietly." Pa-chieh now had become quite alert, and Sha Monk was most understanding. Even the white horse seemed to know their thoughts. They all arose, silently loaded the packs on the saddle, took up the poles, and toted their belongings through the corridor. When they reached the monastery gate, they found it padlocked. Using his magic, Pilgrim opened the locks on both the second-level gate and the main gate. As they were searching for the way toward the East, a voice rang out in midair. "You who are fleeing," cried the Eight Vajra Guardians, "follow us!"

As the elder smelled a strange fragrance, he rose with the others into the wind. Truly

Elixir's formed, he knows the original face;
His healthy frame, easy and free, bows to his lord.

We do not know how he finally managed to see the T'ang emperor, and you must listen to the explanation in the next chapter.

They return to the Land of the East;
The five sages attain immortality.

Let us not say anything more about how the four pilgrims departed by
mounting the wind with the Vajra Guardians. We tell you instead
about the multitude in the Life-Saving Monastery at the Ch'ên Village,
who rose at dawn and went at once to offer fruits and other food to
their benefactors. When they arrived at the space beneath the tower,
however, they found that the T'ang monk had disappeared. Thereupon all of them hunted everywhere, but without success. They were
so upset that they did not quite know what to do except to wail aloud,
"We have allowed a Living Buddha to walk away!"

After a while, the entire household realized that they had no better
alternative than to pile all the food and gifts on the altar up in the
tower and offer them as sacrifices along with the burning of paper
cash. Thereafter they made four great sacrifices and twenty-four
smaller ones each year. Moreover, those who wanted to pray for healing, for safety on a journey, for the gift of a spouse, for wealth or
children, and to make a vow appeared daily at every hour to present
their offerings and incense. Truly,

The gold censer continued a thousand years' fire;
The jade chalice brightened with an eternal lamp.

In that condition we shall leave them.

We tell you now instead about the Eight Vajra Guardians, who employed the second gust of fragrant wind to send the four pilgrims back
to the Land of the East. In less than a day, the capital, Ch'ang-an,
gradually came into view. That Emperor T'ai-tsung, you see, had
escorted the T'ang monk out of the city three days before the full moon
in the ninth month of the thirteenth year of the Chên-kuan reign
period. By the sixteenth year, he had already asked the Bureau of
Labor to erect a Scripture-Anticipation Tower outside the Hsi-an pass
to receive the holy books. Each year T'ai-tsung would go personally to
that place for a visit. It so happened that he had gone again to the

tower that day when he caught sight of a skyful of auspicious mists
drifting near from the West, and he noticed at the same time strong
gusts of fragrant wind.

Halting in midair, the Vajra Guardians cried, "Sage monk, this is
the city Ch'ang-an. It's not convenient for us to go down there, for the
people of this region are quite intelligent, and our true identity may
become known to them. Even the Great Sage Sun and his two companions needn't go; you yourself can go, hand over the scriptures, and
return at once. We'll wait for you in the air so that we may all go back
to report to Buddha.

"What the Honored Ones say may be most appropriate," said the
Great Sage, "but how could my master tote all those scriptures? How
could he lead the horse at the same time? We will have to escort him
down there. May we trouble you to wait a while in the air? We dare
not tarry."

"When the Bodhisattva Kuan-yin spoke to Tathāgata the other
day," said the Vajra Guardians, "she assured him that the whole trip
should take only eight days, so that the canonical number would be
fulfilled. It's already more than four days now. We fear that Pa-chieh
might become so enamored of the riches down below that we will not
be able to meet our appointed schedule."

"When Master attains Buddhahood," said Pa-chieh, chuckling, "I,
too, will attain Buddhahood. How could I become enamored of riches
down below? Stupid old ruffians! Wait for me here, all of you! As soon
as we have handed over the scriptures, I'll return with you and be
canonized." Idiot took up the pole, Sha Monk led the horse, and
Pilgrim supported the sage monk. Lowering their cloud, they dropped
down beside the Scripture-Anticipation Tower.

When T'ai-tsung and his officials saw them, they all descended the
tower to receive them. "Has the royal brother returned?" said the
emperor. The T'ang monk immediately prostrated himself, but he was
raised by the emperor's own hands. "Who are these three persons?"
asked the emperor once more.

"They are my disciples made during our journey," replied the T'ang
monk. Highly pleased, T'ai-tsung at once ordered his attendants,
"Saddle one of our chariot horses for our royal brother to ride. We'll
go back to the court together." The T'ang monk thanked him and
mounted the horse, closely followed by the Great Sage wielding his
golden-hooped rod and by Pa-chieh and Sha Monk toting the luggage

and supporting the other horse. The entire entourage thus entered together the city of Ch'ang-an. Truly

A banquet of peace was held years ago,
When lords, civil and martial, made a grand show.
A priest preached the law in a great event;[1]
From Golden Chimes the king his subject sent.
Tripitaka was given a royal rescript,
For Five Phases matched the cause of holy script.
Through bitter smelting all demons were purged.
Merit done, they now on the court converged.

The T'ang monk and his three disciples followed the Throne into the court, and soon there was not a single person in the city of Ch'ang-an who had not learned of the scripture seekers' return.

We tell you now about those priests, young and old, of the Temple of Great Blessing, which was also the old residence of the T'ang monk in Ch'ang-an. That day they suddenly discovered that the branches of a few pine trees within the temple gate were pointing eastward. Astonished, they cried, "Strange! Strange! There was no strong wind to speak of last night. Why are all the tops of these trees twisted in this manner?"

One of the former disciples of Tripitaka said, "Quickly, let's get our proper clerical garb. The old master who went away to acquire scriptures must have returned."

"How do you know that?" asked the other priests.

"At the time of his departure," the old disciple said, "he made the remark that he might be away for two or three years, or for six or seven years. Whenever we noticed that these pine-tree tops were pointing to the east, it would mean that he has returned. Since my master spoke the holy words of a true Buddha, I know that the truth has been confirmed this day."

They put on their clothing hurriedly and left; by the time they reached the street to the west, people were already saying that the scripture seeker had just arrived and been received into the city by His Majesty. When they heard the news, the various monks dashed forward and ran right into the imperial chariot. Not daring to approach the emperor, they followed the entourage instead to the gate of the court. The T'ang monk dismounted and entered the court with the emperor. The dragon horse, the scripture packs, Pilgrim, Pa-chieh, and Sha Monk were all placed beneath the steps of jade, while T'ai-tsung commanded the royal brother to ascend the hall and take a seat.

After thanking the emperor and taking his seat, the T'ang monk asked that the scripture scrolls be brought up. Pilgrim and his companions handed them over to the imperial attendants, who presented them in turn to the emperor for inspection. "How many scrolls of scriptures are there," asked T'ai-tsung, "and how did you acquire them?"

"When your subject arrived at the Spirit Mountain and bowed to the Buddhist Patriarch," replied Tripitaka, "he was kind enough to ask Ānanda and Kāśyapa, the two Honored Ones, to lead us to the precious tower first for a meal. Then we were brought to the treasure loft, where the scriptures were bestowed on us. Those Honored Ones asked for a gift, but we were not prepared and did not give them any. They gave us some scriptures anyway, and after thanking the Buddhist Patriarch, we headed east, but a monstrous wind snatched away the scriptures. My humble disciple fortunately had a little magic power; he gave chase at once, and the scriptures were thrown and scattered all over. When we unrolled the scrolls, we saw that they were all wordless, blank texts. Your subjects in great fear went again to bow and plead before Buddha. The Buddhist Patriarch said, 'When these scriptures were created, some Bhikṣu sage monks left the monastery and recited some scrolls for one Elder Chao in the Śrāvastī Kingdom. As a result, the living members of that family were granted safety and protection, while the deceased attained redemption. For such great service they only managed to ask the elder for three pecks and three pints of rice and a little gold. I told them that it was too cheap a sale, and that their descendants would have no money to spend.' Since we learned that even the Buddhist Patriarch anticipated that the two Honored Ones would demand a gift, we had little choice but to offer them that alms bowl of purple gold which Your Majesty had bestowed on me. Only then did they willingly turn over the true scriptures with writing to us. There are thirty-five titles of these scriptures, and several scrolls were selected from each title. Altogether, there are now five thousand and forty-eight scrolls, the number of which makes up one canonical sum."

More delighted than ever, T'ai-tsung gave this command: "Let the Court of Imperial Entertainments prepare a banquet in the East Hall so that we may thank our royal brother." Then he happened to notice Tripitaka's three disciples standing beneath the steps, all with extraordinary looks, and he therefore asked, "Are your noble disciples foreigners?"

Prostrating himself, the elder said, "My eldest disciple has the surname of Sun, and his religious name is Wu-k'ung. Your subject also addresses him as Pilgrim Sun. He comes from the Water Curtain Cave of the Flower-Fruit Mountain, located in the Ao-lai Kingdom in the East Pūrvavideha Continent. Because he caused great disturbance in the Celestial Palace, he was imprisoned in a stone box by the Buddhist Patriarch and pressed beneath the Mountain of Two Frontiers in the region of the Western barbarians. Thanks to the admonitions of the Bodhisattva Kuan-yin, he was converted to Buddhism and became my disciple when I freed him. Throughout my journey I relied heavily on his protection.

"My second disciple has the surname of Chu, and his religious name is Wu-nêng. Your subject also addresses him as Chu Pa-chieh. He comes from the Cloudy Paths Cave of Fu-ling Mountain. He was playing the fiend at the Old Kao Village of Tibet when the admonitions of the Bodhisattva and the power of the Pilgrim caused him to become my disciple. He made his merit on our journey by toting the luggage and helping us to ford the waters.

"My third disciple has the surname of Sha, and his religious name is Wu-ching. Your subject also addresses him as Sha Monk. Originally he was a fiend at the Flowing-Sand River. Again the admonitions of the Bodhisattva persuaded him to take the vows of Buddhism. By the way, the horse is not the one my Lord bestowed on me."

T'ai-tsung said, "The color and the coat seem all the same. Why isn't it the same horse?"

"When your subject reached the Eagle Grief Stream in the Serpent Coil Mountain and tried to cross it," replied Tripitaka, "the original horse was devoured by this horse. Pilgrim managed to learn from the Bodhisattva that this horse was originally the prince of the Dragon King of the Western Ocean. Convicted of a crime, he would have been executed had it not been for the intervention of the Bodhisattva, who ordered him to be the steed of your subject. It was then that he changed into a horse with exactly the same coat as that of my original mount. I am greatly indebted to him for taking me over mountains and summits and through the most treacherous passages. Whether it be carrying me on my way there or bearing the scriptures upon our return, we are much beholden to his strength."

On hearing these words, T'ai-tsung complimented him profusely before asking again, "This long trek to the Western Region, exactly how far is it?"

Tripitaka said, "I recall that the Bodhisattva told us that the distance was a hundred and eight thousand miles. I did not make a careful record on the way. All I know is that we have experienced fourteen seasons of heat and cold. We encountered mountains and ridges daily; the forests we came upon were not small, and the waters we met were wide and swift. We also went through many kingdoms, whose rulers had affixed their seals and signatures on our document." Then he called out: "Disciples, bring up the travel rescript and present it to our Lord."

It was handed over immediately. T'ai-tsung took a look and realized that the document had been issued on the third day before the full moon, in the ninth month of the thirteenth year during the Chên-kuan reign period. Smiling, T'ai-tsung said, "We have caused you the trouble of taking a long journey. This is now the twenty-seventh year of the Chên-kuan period!" The travel rescript bore the seals of the Precious Image Kingdom, the Black Rooster Kingdom, the Cart Slow Kingdom, the Kingdom of Women in Western Liang, the Sacrifice Kingdom, the Scarlet-Purple Kingdom, the Bhikṣu Kingdom, the Dharma-Destroying Kingdom. There were also the seals of the Phoenix-Immortal Prefecture, the Jade-Flower County, and the Gold-Level Prefecture. After reading through the document, T'ai-tsung put it away.

Soon the officer in attendance to the Throne arrived to invite them to the banquet. As the emperor took the hand of Tripitaka and walked down the steps of the hall, he asked once more, "Are your noble disciples familiar with the etiquette of the court?"

"My humble disciples," replied Tripitaka, "all began their careers as monsters deep in the wilds or a mountain village, and they have never been instructed in the etiquette of China's sage court. I beg my Lord to pardon them."

Smiling, T'ai-tsung said, "We won't blame them! We won't blame them! Let's all go to the feast set up in the East Hall." Tripitaka thanked him once more before calling for his three disciples to join them. Upon their arrival at the hall, they saw that the opulence of the great nation of China was indeed different for all ordinary kingdoms. You see

The doorway o'erhung with brocade,
The floor adorned with red carpets,
The whirls of exotic incense,
And fresh victuals most rare.
The amber cups

And crystal goblets
Are gold-trimmed and jade-set;
The gold platters
And white-jade bowls
Are patterned and silver-rimmed.
The tubers thoroughly cooked,
The taros sugar-coated;
Sweet, lovely button mushrooms,
Unusual, pure seaweeds.
Bamboo shoots, ginger-spiced, are served a few times;
Malva leafs, honey-drenched, are mixed several ways.
Wheat-glutens fried with *hsiang-ch'un*[2] leaves;
Wood-ears cooked with bean-cured skins.
Rock ferns and fairy plants;
Chüeh[3] flour and dried *Wei*.
Radishes cooked with Szechwan peppercorns;
Melon strands stirred with mustard powder.
These few vegetarian dishes are so-so,
But the many rare fruits quite steal the show!
Walnuts and persimmons,
Lung-ans and lychees.
The chestnuts of I-chou and Shantung's dates;
The South's *ginko* fruits and hare-head pears.
Pine-seeds, lotus-seeds, and giant grapes;
Fei-nuts,[4] melon seeds, and water chestnuts.
"Chinese olives"[5] and wild apples;
P'in-p'os[6] and *sha-t'ang* pears;[7]
Tz'ŭ-kus[8] and young lotus roots;
Crisp plums and "Chinese strawberries."[9]
Not one species is missing;
Not one kind is wanting.
There are, moreover, the steamed *mille-feuilles*, honeyed pastries,
     and fine viands;
And there are also the lovely wines, fragrant teas, and strange
     dainties.
An endless spread of a hundred flavors, true noble fare.
Western barbarians with great China can never compare!

Master and three disciples were grouped together with the officials,
both civil and military, on both sides of the emperor T'ai-tsung, who

took the seat in the middle. The dancing and the music proceeded in an orderly and solemn manner, and in this way they enjoyed themselves thoroughly for one whole day. Truly

The royal banquet rivals the sage kings';
True scriptures acquired excess blessings bring.
Forever these will prosper and remain,
As Buddha's light shines on the king's domain.

When it became late, the officials thanked the emperor; while T'ai-tsung withdrew into his palace, the various officials returned to their residences. The T'ang monk and his disciples, however, went to the Temple of Great Blessing, where they were met by the resident priests kowtowing. As they entered the temple gate, the priests said, "Master, the top of these trees were all suddenly pointing eastward this morning. We remembered your words and hurried out to the city to meet you. Indeed, you did arrive!" The elder could not have been more pleased as they were ushered into the abbot's quarters. By then, Pa-chieh was not clamoring at all for food or tea, nor did he indulge in any mischief. Both Pilgrim and Sha Monk behaved most properly, for they had become naturally quiet and reserved since the Tao in them had come to fruition. They rested that night.

T'ai-tsung held court next morning and said the officials, "We did not sleep the whole night when we reflected on how great and profound has been the merit of our brother, such that no compensation is quite adequate. We finally composed in our head several homely sentences as a mere token of our gratitude, but they have not yet been written down." Calling for one of the secretaries from the Central Drafting Office, he said, "Come, let us recite our composition for you, and you take it down sentence by sentence." The composition[10] was as follows:

We have heard how the Two Primary Forces[11] which manifest
themselves in Heaven and Earth in the production of life are
represented by images, whereas the invisible powers of the four
seasons bring about transformation of things through the
hidden action of heat and cold. By scanning Heaven and Earth,
even the most ignorant may perceive their rudimentary laws.
Even the thorough understanding of yin and yang, however, has
seldom enabled the worthy and wise to comprehend fully their
ultimate principle. It is easy to recognize that Heaven and Earth
do contain yin and yang because there are images. It is difficult

to comprehend fully how yin and yang pervade Heaven and Earth because the forces themselves are invisible. That is why we know that the evidence of manifest images does not perplex the foolish, whereas the invisibility of hidden forms confuses even the learned.

How much more difficult it is, therefore, to understand the way of Buddhism, which exalts the void, uses the dark, and exploits the silent in order to succor the myriad grades of living things and exercise control over the entire world. Its spiritual authority is the highest, and its divine potency has no equal. Its magnitude impregnates the entire cosmos; there is no space so tiny that it does not permeate it. Birthless and deathless, it does not age after a thousand kalpas; half-hidden and half-manifest, it brings a hundred blessings even now. A wondrous way most mysterious, those who follow it cannot know its limit. A law flowing silent and deep, those who draw on it cannot fathom its source. How, therefore, could those benighted ordinary mortals not be perplexed if they tried to plumb its depths?

Now, this great Teaching arose in the Land of the West. It soared to the court of the Han period in the form of a radiant dream,[12] which flowed with its mercy to enlighten the Eastern territory. In antiquity, during the time when form and abstraction were clearly distinguished, the words of the Buddha, even before spreading, had already established their goodly influence. In a generation when he was both frequently active in and withdrawn from the world, the people beheld his virtue and honored it. But when he returned to Nirvāṇa and generations passed by, the golden images concealed his true form and did not reflect the light of the universe. The beautiful paintings, though unfolding lovely portraits, vainly held up the figure of thirty-two marks.[13] Nonetheless his subtle doctrines spread far and wide to save men and beasts from the three unhappy paths, and his traditions were widely proclaimed to lead all creatures through the ten stages toward Buddhahood.[14] Moreover, the Buddha made scriptures, which could be divided into the Great and the Small Vehicles. He also possessed the Law, which could be transmitted either in the correct or in the deviant method.

Our priest Hsüan-tsang, a Master of the Law, is a leader in Buddhism. Devoted and intelligent as a youth, he realized at an early age the merit of the three forms of immateriality. When grown he comprehended the principles of the spiritual, including first the practice of the four forms of patience.[15] Neither the pine in the wind nor the moon mirrored in water can compare with his purity and radiance. Even the dew of Heaven and luminous gems cannot surpass the clarity and refinement of his person. His intelligence encompassed even those elements which seemingly had no relations, and his spirit could perceive that which had yet to take visible forms. Having transcended the lure of the six senses, he was such an outstanding figure that in all the past he had no rival. He concentrated his mind on the internal verities, mourning all the time the mutilation of the correct doctrines. Worrying over the mysteries, he lamented that even the most profound treatises had errors.

He thought of revising the teachings and reviving certain arguments, so as to disseminate what he had received to a wider audience. He would, moreover, strike out the erroneous and preserve the true to enlighten the students. For this reason he longed for the Pure Land and a pilgrimage to the Western Territories. Risking dangers he set out on a long journey, with only his staff for his companion on this solitary expedition. Snow drifts in the morning would blanket his roadway; sand storms at dusk would blot out the horizon. Over ten thousand miles of mountains and streams he proceeded, pushing aside mist and smoke. Through a thousand alternations of heat and cold he advanced amidst frost and rain. As his zeal was great, he considered his task a light one, for he was determined to succeed.

He toured throughout the Western World for fourteen years,[16] going to all the foreign nations in quest of the proper doctrines. He led the life of an ascetic beneath the twin śāla trees[17] and by the eight rivers of India.[18] At the Deer Park and on the Vulture Peak he attained strange visions. He received ultimate truths from the senior sages and was taught the true doctrines by the highest worthies. Penetrating into the mysteries, he mastered the most profound lessons. The way of the Triyāna and Six Commandments he learned by heart; a hundred cases of scriptures forming the canon flowed like waves from his lips.

Though the countries he visited were innumerable, the

scriptures he succeeded in acquiring had a definite number. Of those important texts of the Mahāyāna he received, there are thirty-five titles in altogether five thousand and forty-eight scrolls.[19] When they are translated and spread through China, they will proclaim[20] the surpassing merit of Buddhism, drawing the cloud of mercy from the Western extremity to shower the dharma-rain on the Eastern region. The Holy Teaching, once imperfect, is now returned to perfection. The multitudes, once full of sins, are now brought back to blessing. Like that which quenches the fire in a burning house, the power of Buddhism works to save humanity lost on its way to perdition. Like a golden beam shining on darkened waters,[21] it leads the voyagers to climb the other shore safely.

Thus we know that the wicked will fall because of their iniquities, but the virtuous will rise because of their affinities. The causes of such rise and fall are all self-made by man. Consider the cinnamon flourishing high on the mountain, its flowers nourished by cloud and mist, or the lotus growing atop the green waves, its leaves unsoiled by dust. This is not because the lotus is by nature clean or because the cinnamon itself is chaste, but because what the cinnamon depends on for its existence is lofty, and thus it will not be weighed down by trivia; and because what the lotus relies on is pure, and thus impurity cannot stain it. Since even the vegetable kingdom, which is itself without intelligence, knows that excellence comes from an environment of excellence, how can humans who understand the great relations not search for well-being by following well-being?

May these scriptures abide forever as the sun and moon and may the blessings they confer spread throughout the universe!

After the secretary had finished writing this treatise, the sage monk was summoned. At the time, the elder was already waiting outside the gate of the court. When he heard the summons, he hurried inside and prostrated himself to pay homage to the emperor.

T'ai-tsung asked him to ascend the hall and handed him the document. When he had finished reading it, the priest went to his knees again to express his gratitude. "The style and rhetoric of my Lord," said the priest, "are lofty and classical, while the reasoning in the treatise is both profound and subtle. I would like to know, however, whether a title has been chosen for this composition."

"We composed it orally last night," replied T'ai-tsung, "as a token of thanks to our royal brother. Will it be acceptable if I title this 'Preface to the Holy Teaching?'" The elder kowtowed and thanked him profusely. Once more T'ai-tsung said,[22]

Our talents pale before the imperial tablets,
And our words cannot match the bronze and stone inscriptions.[23]
As for the esoteric texts,
Our ignorance is even greater.
Our treatise orally composed
Is actually quite unpolished—
Like mere spilled ink on slabs of gold,
Or broken tiles in a forest of pearls.
Writing it in self-interest,
We have quite ignored even embarrassment.
It is not worth your notice,
And you should not thank us.

All the officials present, however, congratulated the emperor and made arrangements immediately to promulgate the royal essay on Holy Teaching inside and outside the capital.

T'ai-tsung said, "We would like to ask the royal brother to recite the true scriptures for us. How about it?"

"My Lord," said the elder, "if you want me to recite the true scriptures, we must find the proper religious site. The treasure palace is no place for recitation." Exceedingly pleased, T'ai-tsung asked his attendants, "Among the monasteries of Ch'ang-an, which is the holiest one?"

From among the ranks stepped forth the Grand Secretary, Hsiao Yü, who said, "The Wild-Goose Pagoda Temple in the city is holiest of all." At once T'ai-tsung gave this command to the various officials: "Each of you take several scrolls of these true scriptures and go reverently with us to the Wild-Goose Pagoda Temple. We want to ask our royal brother to expound the scriptures to us." Each of the officials indeed took up several scrolls and followed the emperor's carriage to the temple. A lofty platform with proper appointments was then erected. As before, the elder told Pa-chieh and Sha Monk to hold the dragon horse and mind the luggage, while Pilgrim was to serve him by his side. Then he said to T'ai-tsung, "If my Lord would like to circulate the true scriptures throughout his empire, copies should be made before they are dispersed. We should treasure the originals and not handle them lightly."

Smiling, T'ai-tsung said, "The words of our royal brother are most appropriate! Most appropriate!" He thereupon ordered the officials in the Han-lin Academy and the Central Drafting Office to make copies of the true scriptures. For them he also erected another temple east of the capital and named it the Temple for Imperial Transcription.

The elder had already taken several scrolls of scriptures and mounted the platform. He was just about to recite them when he felt a gust of fragrant wind. In midair the Eight Vajra Guardians revealed themselves and cried, "Recitants, drop your scripture scrolls and follow us back to the West." From below Pilgrim and his two companions together with the white horse immediately rose into the air. The elder, too, abandoned the scriptures and rose from the platform. They all left soaring through the air. So startled were T'ai-tsung and the many officials that they all bowed down toward the sky. Thus it was that

Since scriptures were the sage monk's ardent quest,
He went on fourteen years throughout the West
A bitter journey full of trials and woes,
With many streams and mountains as his foes.
Nine merits more were added to eight times nine;
His three thousand works did on the great world shine.
The wondrous texts brought back to the noble state
Would in the East until now circulate.

After T'ai-tsung and many officials had finished their worship, they immediately set about the selection of high priests so that a Grand Mass of Land and Water could be held right in that Wild-Goose Pagoda Temple. Furthermore, they were to read and recite the true scriptures from the Great Canon in order that the damned spirits would be delivered from nether darkness and the celebration of good works be multiplied. The copies of transcribed scriptures would also be promulgated throughout the empire, and of this we shall speak no more.

We must tell you now about those Eight Great Vajra Guardians, who mounted the fragrant wind to lead the elder, his three disciples, and the white horse back to Spirit Mountain. The round trip was made precisely within a period of eight days. At that time the various divinities of Spirit Mountain were all assembled before Buddha to listen to his lecture. Ushering master and disciples before his presence, the Eight Vajra Guardians said, "Your disciples by your golden decree have escorted the sage monk and his companions back to the T'ang nation. The scriptures have been handed over. We now return to surrender your decree." The T'ang monk and his disciples were then told to approach the throne of Buddha to receive their appointments.

"Sage Monk," said Tathāgata, "in your previous incarnation you were originally my second disciple named Master Gold Cicada. Because you failed to listen to my exposition of the law and slighted my great teaching, your true spirit was banished to find another incarnation in the Land of the East. Happily you submitted and, by remaining faithful to our teaching, succeeded in acquiring the true scriptures. For such magnificent merit, you will receive a great promotion to become the Buddha of Candana Merit.

"Sun Wu-k'ung, when you caused great disturbance at the Celestial Palace, I had to exercise enormous dharma power to have you pressed beneath the Mountain of Five Phases. Fortunately your Heaven-sent calamity came to an end, and you embraced the teaching of Buddhism. I am pleased even more by the fact that you were devoted to the scourging of evil and the exaltation of good. Throughout your journey you made great merit by smelting the demons and defeating the fiends. For being faithful in the end as you were in the beginning, I hereby give you the grand promotion and appoint you the Buddha Victorious in Strife.

"Chu Wu-nêng, you were originally an aquatic deity of the Heavenly River, the Marshal of Heavenly Reeds. For getting drunk during the Festival of Immortal Peaches and insulting the divine maiden, you were banished to an incarnation in the Region Below which would give you the body of a beast. Fortunately you still cherished and loved the human form, so that even when you sinned at the Cloudy Paths Cave in Fu-ling Mountain, you eventually returned to our great teaching and embraced our vows. While you protected the sage monk on his way, you were still quite mischievous, for greed and lust were never wholly extinguished in you. For the merit of toting the luggage, however, I hereby grant you promotion and appoint you Janitor of the Altars."

"They have all become Buddhas!" shouted Pa-chieh. "Why am I alone made Janitor of the Altars?"

"Because you are still talkative and lazy," replied Tathāgata, "and you retain an enormous appetite. Within the four great continents of the world, there are many people who observe our teachings. Whenever there are Buddhist services, you will be asked to clear the altars. That's an appointment which offers you plenty of enjoyment. How could it be bad?

"Sha Wu-ching, you were originally the Great Curtain-Raising

Captain. Because you broke a crystal chalice during the Festival of Immortal Peaches, you were banished to the Region Below, where at the River of Flowing-Sand you sinned by devouring humans. Fortunately you submitted to our teaching and remained firm in your faith. As you escorted the sage monk, you made merit by leading his horse over all those mountains. I hereby grant you promotion and appoint you the Golden-Bodied Arhat."

Then he said to the white horse, "You were originally the prince of Dragon King Kuang-chin of the Western Ocean. Because you disobeyed your father's command and committed the crime of unfiliality, you were to be executed. Fortunately you made submission to the Law and accepted our vows. Because you carried the sage monk daily on your back during his journey to the West and because you also took the holy scriptures back to the East, you too have made merit. I hereby grant you promotion and appoint you one of the dragons belonging to the Eight Classes of Supernatural Beings."[24]

The elder, his three disciples, and the horse all kowtowed to thank the Buddha, who ordered some of the guardians to take the horse to the Dragon-Transforming Pool at the back of the Spirit Mountain. After being pushed into the pool, the horse stretched himself, and in a little while he shed his coat, horns began to grow on his head, golden scales appeared all over his body, and silver whiskers emerged on his cheeks. His whole body shrouded in auspicious air and his four paws wrapped in hallowed clouds, he soared out of the pool and circled inside the monastery gate, on top of one of the Pillars that Support Heaven.

As the various Buddhas gave praise to the great dharma of Tathāgata, Pilgrim Sun said also to the T'ang monk, "Master, I've become a Buddha now, just like you. It can't be that I still must wear a golden fillet! And you wouldn't want to clamp my head still by reciting that so-called Tight-Fillet Spell, would you? Recite the Loose-Fillet Spell quickly and get it off my head. I'm going to smash it to pieces, so that that so-called Bodhisattva can't use it anymore to play tricks on other people."

"Because you were difficult to control previously," said the T'ang monk, "this method had to be used to keep you in hand. Now that you have become a Buddha, naturally it will be gone. How could it be still on your head? Try touching your head and see." Pilgrim raised his hand and felt along his head, and indeed the fillet had vanished. So at that time, Buddha Candana, Buddha Victorious in Strife, Janitor of the Altars, and Golden-Bodied Arhat all assumed the position of their own rightful fruition. The Heavenly dragon-horse too returned to immortality, and we have a testimonial poem for them. The poem says:

One reality fallen to the dusty plain
Fuses with Four Signs and cultivates self again.
In Five Phases terms forms are but silent and void;
The hundred fiends' false names one should all avoid.
The great Bodhi's the right Candana fruition;
Appointments complete their rise from perdition.
When scriptures spread throughout the world the gracious light,
Henceforth five sages live within Advaya's heights.

At the time when these five sages assumed their positions, the various Buddhist Patriarchs, Bodhisattvas, sage priests, arhats, guardians, bhikṣus, upāsakas and upāsikās, the immortals of various mountains and caves, the grand divinities, the Gods of Darkness and Light, the Sentinels, the Guardians of Monasteries, and all the immortals and preceptors who had attained the Way all came to listen to the proclamation before retiring to their proper stations. Look now at

Colored mists crowding the Spirit Vulture Peak,
And hallowed clouds gathered in the world of bliss.
Gold dragons safely sleeping,
Jade tigers resting in peace;
Black hares scampering freely,
Snakes and turtles circling at will.
Phoenixes, red and blue, gambol pleasantly;
Black apes and white deer saunter happily.
Strange flowers of eight periods,
Divine fruits of four seasons,
Hoary pines and old junipers,
Jade cypresses and aged bamboos.
Five-colored plums often blossoming and bearing fruit;
Millennial peaches frequently ripening and fresh.
A thousand flowers and fruits vying for beauty;
A whole sky full of auspicious mists.

Pressing their palms together to indicate their devotion, the holy congregation all chanted:

I submit to Dīpaṃkara, the Buddha of Antiquity.
I submit to Bhaiṣajya-vaiḍūrya-prabhāsa, the Physician and
    Buddha of Crystal Lights.

I submit to the Buddha Śākyamuni.
I submit to the Buddha of the Past, Present, and Future.
I submit to the Buddha of Pure Joy.
I submit to the Buddha Vairocana.
I submit to the Buddha, King of the Precious Banner.
I submit to the Maitreya, the Honored Buddha.
I submit to the Buddha Amitābha.
I submit to Sukhāvatīvyūha, the Buddha of Infinite Life.
I submit to the Buddha who Receives and Leads to Immorality.
I submit to the Buddha of Diamond Indestructibility.
I submit to Sūrya, the Buddha of Precious Light.
I submit to Mañjuśrī, the Buddha of the Race of Honorable
    Dragon Kings.
I submit to the Buddha of Zealous Progress and Virtue.
I submit to Candraprabha, the Buddha of Precious Moonlight.
I submit to the Buddha of Presence without Ignorance.
I submit to Varuna, the Buddha of Sky and Water.
I submit to the Buddha Nārāyaṇa.
I submit to the Buddha of Radiant Meritorious Works.
I submit to the Buddha of Talented Meritorious Works.
I submit to Svāgata, the Buddha of the Well-Departed.
I submit to the Buddha of Candana Light.
I submit to the Buddha of Jeweled Banner.
I submit to the Buddha of the Light of Wisdom Torch.
I submit to the Buddha of the Light of Sea-Virtue.
I submit to the Buddha of Great Mercy Light.
I submit to the Buddha, King of Compassion-Power.
I submit to the Buddha, Leader of the Sages.
I submit to the Buddha of Vast Solemnity.
I submit to the Buddha of Golden Radiance.
I submit to the Buddha of Luminous Gifts.
I submit to the Buddha Victorious in Wisdom.
I submit to the Buddha Quiescent Light of the World.
I submit to the Buddha, Light of the Sun and Moon.
I submit to the Buddha, Light of the Sun-and-Moon Pearl.
I submit to the Buddha, King of the Victorious Banner.
I submit to the Buddha of Wondrous Tone and Sound.
I submit to the Buddha, Banner of Permanent Light.
I submit to the Buddha, Lamp that Scans the World.
I submit to the Buddha, King of Surpassing Dharma.

I submit to the Buddha of Sumeru Light.
I submit to the Buddha, King of Great Wisdom.
I submit to the Buddha of Golden Sea Light.
I submit to the Buddha of Great Perfect Light.
I submit to the Buddha of the Gift of Light.
I submit to the Buddha of Candana Merit.
I submit to the Buddha Victorious in Strife.
I submit to the Bodhisattva Kuan-shih-yin.
I submit to the Bodhisattva, Great Power-Coming.
I submit to the Bodhisattva Mañjuśrī.
I submit to the Bodhisattva Viśvabhadra and other Bodhisattvas.
I submit to the various Bodhisattvas of the Great Pure Ocean.
I submit to the Bodhisattva, the Buddha of Lotus Pool and Ocean
    Assembly.
I submit to the various Bodhisattvas in the Western Heaven of
    Ultimate Bliss.
I submit to the Great Bodhisattvas, the Three Thousand
    Guardians.
I submit to the Great Bodhisattvas, the Five Hundred Arhats.
I submit to the Bodhisattva, Bhikṣu-īkṣaṇi.
I submit to the Bodhisattva of Boundless and Limitless Dharma.
I submit to the Bodhisattva, Diamond Great Scholar-Sage.
I submit to the Bodhisattva, Janitor of the Altars.
I submit to the Bodhisattva, Golden-Bodied Arhat of Eight Jewels
I submit to the Bodhisattva of Vast Strength, the Heavenly
    Dragon of Eight Divisions of Supernatural Beings.
Such are these various Buddhas in all the worlds.
I wish to use these merits
To adorn Buddha's pure land—
To repay fourfold grace above
And save those on three paths below.
If there are those who see and hear,
Their minds will find enlightenment.
Their births with us in paradise
Will be this body's recompense.
All the Buddhas of past, present, future in all the world,
The various Honored Bodhisattvas and Mahāsattvas,
Mahā-prajñā-pāramitā!

Here ends *The Journey to the West.*

Abbreviations

Bodde	Derk Bodde, *Festivals in Classical China* (Princeton and Hong Kong, 1975).
Chou	Chou Wei 周緯, *Chung-kuo ping-ch'i-shih kao* 中國兵器史稿 (Peking, 1957).
CTS	*Ch'üan T'ang Shih* 全唐詩, 12 vols. (Ts'ui-wên t'ang 粹文堂 edition; repr. Tainan, Taiwan, 1974).
CW	*Chung-wên ta tz'ŭ-tien* 中文大辭典, 10 vols. (rev. ed., Taipei, Taiwan, 1973).
CYC	*Chung-yao chih* 中藥誌, 4 vols. (Peking, 1959–61).
de Bary	Wm. Theodore de Bary, ed., *Sources of Chinese Tradition*, 2 vols. (New York and London, 1960).
Fa-shih chuan	*Ta-T'ang Ta Tz'ŭ-ên-ssŭ San-tsang fa-shih chuan* 大唐大慈恩寺三藏法師傳. By Hui-li 慧立 and Yen-ts'ung 彥悰. *T*. 50, No. 2053.
Herrmann	Albert Herrmann, *An Historical Atlas of China*, new ed. (Chicago, 1966).
Hucker	Charles O. Hucker, "Governmental Organization of the Ming Dynasty," *Harvard Journal of Asiatic Studies* 21 (1958): 1–151.
HYC	*Hsi-yu chi* 西游記 (Peking, 1954). Abbreviation refers only to this edition.
JW	*The Journey to the West.*
Legge	James Legge, trans., *The Chinese Classics* (Taipei reprint of original Oxford University Press edition).
Needham	Joseph Needham, *Science and Civilisation in China*, vol. 1-5/4 (Cambridge, England, 1954–80).

Ōta   Ōta Tatsuo 太田辰夫 and Torii Hisayasu 鳥居久靖,
                       trans. *Saiyuki* 西游記, Chūgoku koten bungaku
                       taike 中國古典文學大系, 31-2 (Tokyo, 1971).
Schafer   Edward H. Schafer, *Pacing the Void: T'ang
                       Approaches to the Stars* (Berkeley, Los Angeles,
                       and London, 1977).
SPPY   *Szu-pu pei-yao* 四部備要.
SPTK   *Szu-pu ts'ung-k'an* 四部叢刊.
STTH   *San-ts'ai t'u-hui* 三才圖會 (1609 edition).
T.   Taishō Tripiṭaka.
Tai   Tai Yüan-ch'ang 戴源長, *Hsien-hsüeh tz'ŭ-tien*
                       仙學辭典 (Taipei, 1962).
THPWC   *Tun-huang pien-wên chi* 敦煌變文集, ed. Wang
                       Chung-min 王重民 et al., 2 vols. (Peking, 1957).
TPKC   *T'ai-p'ing kuang-chi* 太平廣記, 10 vols. (Peking,
                       1961).
TPYL   *T'ai-p'ing yü-lan* 太平御覽, 4 vols. (facs. of *SPTK*
                       edition. Peking, 1960).
TT   *Tao Tsang.*
Waley   Arthur Waley, *The Real Tripitaka and Other Pieces*
                       (London, 1952).
Welch and Seidel   Holmes Welch and Anna Seidel, eds., *Facets of
                       Taoism: Essays in Chinese Religion* (New Haven
                       and London, 1979).
Wilhelm/Baynes   *The I Ching, or Book of Changes.* The Richard
                       Wilhelm Translation rendered into English by
                       Cary F. Baynes, Bollingen Series XIX, 3d ed.
                       (Princeton, 1967).
YCCC   *Yün-chi ch'i-ch'ien* 雲笈七籤 3 vols. (facs. of
                       明正統道藏 edition. Taipei, 1978).
YYTT   *Yu-yang tsa-tsu* 酉陽雜俎 (*SPTK* edition).

References to all Standard Histories, unless otherwise indicated, are
to the *SPTK Po-na* 百衲 edition.

Notes

CHAPTER SEVENTY-SIX

1. Three Forces: *san-ts'ai* 三才, i.e., Heaven, Human, and Earth.

2. Clear Brightness: *ch'ing-ming* 清明, one of the Twenty-four Solar "Nodes," spaced at approximately fifteen-day intervals, that divide the Chinese year. Clear Brightness usually occurs around April 6 of the Gregorian Calendar. It is generally a time for sweeping family tombs in the countryside, offering sacrifices, picnicking, eating cold foods, and flying kites. See Bodde, pp. 296, and 394.

3. Mace . . . candareen: traditional monetary (silver) units in China, the mace (*ch'ien* 錢) is one-tenth of the Chinese ounce or tael (*liang* 兩), and the candareen (*fên* 分) is one-tenth of the mace.

4. The dread day of Red Sand: *hung-sha* 紅沙. According to calendrical literature, certain days of certain months bear the name of Red Sand, and such days are inauspicious (*chi* 忌) for marriages. See the *Ch'in-ting hsieh-chi pien-fang shu* 欽定協紀辨方書, *chüan* 36, 44a–b (Ssŭ-k'u ch'üan-shu chên-pên 四庫全書珍本; Taiwan Commercial Press facsimile edition).

CHAPTER SEVENTY-SEVEN

1. Substances and forms: the Buddhist technical term used in the original is *t'i-hsiang* 體相, substance and characteristics or phenomena. The first stands for the unity, the second for the diversity, of all things.

2. Six evils . . . desires: The six organs are the *liu-kên* 六根, the six *indriyas* or sense organs of eye, ear, nose, tongue, body, and mind. The six desires, *liu-yü* 六欲, are the lustful attractions coming from color, form, carriage, speech, touch (i.e., smoothness or softness), and features.

3. Six ways of rebirth: i.e., *liu-shêng liu-tao* 六生六道 or *liu-ts'ui* 六趣, the six directions of reincarnation. See *JW*, 1:513, note 7.

4. Thirty-six Halls: 三十六宮, the traditional number of halls or palatial chambers in the Han palace. See, for example, Pan Ku 班固, "Hsi-tu fu 西都賦," in *Wên-hsüan* 文選, chüan 1: "離宮別館三十六所" (1936 Commercial Press edition), 1:6.

5. Forms or features: *Hsing-sê* 形色, or *samsthānarūpa*, which are the

features or characteristics of form—long, short, square, round, high, low, straight, and crooked. These are what also awaken or stimulate the six desires.

6. Let *Oṁ* . . . Firmness: for the meaning of the spell, see *JW*, 3:445, note 7.

7. North Heavenly Gate: Dhṛtarāṣṭra, the deva who keeps his kingdom, 持國天王, is usually associated with the east. I have not emended the text.

8. Luminescent pearl: see *JW*, 1:271, for the description of Tripitaka's cassock.

9. Wall-climbing priests: in traditional Chinese fiction, such clerics are usually either thieves or adulterers.

10. Brocade-fragrance: *chin-hsiang* 錦香, usually a metaphor for the pomegranate.

11. Wondrous palm: *P'o-so* 婆娑, another name for the Bodhi tree under which the Buddha was supposed to have attained enlightenment. See the *Yu-yang tsa-tsu* 酉陽雜俎, *chüan* 18, 6a–b (*SPTK* edition).

12. Restrained the Bull Demon: see *JW*, 3:181.

13. Mahārāja Mayūra: the former incarnation of Śākyamuni, said to be a peacock, also manifests himself as a four-armed mahārāja bodhisattva riding a peacock. Hence I have retained the masculine gender in the translation.

14. Wisdom: literally *fa-mên* 法門, *dharmaparyāya*, those teachings or wisdom of Buddha venerated as the gate to enlightenment.

15. The head that had once supported a nest of magpies: during the time of intense meditation that led to his final enlightenment, the Buddha's appearance was said to so resemble a tree that magpies or other kinds of birds nested on his head and laid eggs in the nest. See the *Ta-chih-tu lun* 大智度論 (the *Mahāprajña-pāramitā Śāstra*), *chüan* 17, item 1509 in *T*. 25:188. Cf. also the "*Hsiang-mo pien-wên* 降魔變文," in *THPWC*, 1:377.

Chapter Seventy-eight

1. Causations: *yüan* 緣, *pratyaya*, the conditional or circumstantial causation which gives rise to every phenomenon in the world.

2. Great Canopy: *ta-lo-t'ien* 大羅天, the highest level in the Taoist Heaven. See the *YYTT*, *chüan* 2, 1a; *YCCC*, *chüan* 21, 1b.

3. Folk songs: an allusion to the alleged ancient tradition (dating from the Han dynasty) that folk songs were most expressive of the mores and temper of the people, especially in their discontent with bad governmental policies or wicked officials. Such songs or poems would be gathered by officials to be presented to the ruler, presumably for an admonitory purpose. See, for example, the "Chou Yü 周語," in *Kuo Yü* 國語, *chüan* 1, 5a (*SPPY* edition): 故天子聽政使公卿至於列士獻詩.

4. Medical supplement: see *JW*, 3:449, note 12.

5. Buddha of Medicine: 大醫王佛, the buddha who heals all sicknesses, including the disease of ignorance.

6. The Great: the original text is 摩訶, the Chinese transliteration for *Mahā*, meaning great or large.

7. Triratna: literally *san-kuei* 三皈, the three refuges of the Buddhist, being the Buddha, the Dharma, and the Saṅgha.

8. Five laws: the first five of the ten commandments, against the taking of life, stealing, adultery, lying, and taking intoxicating drinks.

9. The journey to the West . . . darkness: this is a pun on the popular phrase *shang hsi-t'ien* 上西天 (ascending the western Heaven), which means death.

10. Great knowledge . . . comprehensive: 大智閒閒, an allusion to book 2 of the *Chuang Tzu* 莊子, *chüan* 1, 11b (*SPPY* edition).

11. Two Eights: *êrh-pa* 二八; for a discussion of this term, see *JW* 2:429, note 20.

12. Three Nines: *san-chiu* 三九. Three times nine is twenty-seven. This is likely a reference to the alchemical theory based on the lunar month correlated with *I Ching* lore. At the end of the month (between the twenty-seventh and thirtieth day) the moon is almost completely obscure, but when the crescent first appears thereafter, the force of yang is said to grow once more. See *JW*, 2:176–77, for a fuller exposition.

CHAPTER SEVENTY-NINE

1. Babies: in the context of this episode, the word refers, of course, to the young boys Pilgrim has rescued. But the Chinese term, *ying-êrh* 嬰兒, with its inherent numerical ambiguity, may have also been used deliberately by the author to enhance the allegorical flavor of the story, since it is the standard metaphor for the state of realized immortality in internal alchemy.

2. Many hearts: a pun, since the Chinese term, *to-hsin* 多心, can also mean fickle or suspicious.

3. Hall of Careful Conduct: literally the Hall of careful or vigilant surveillance of one's personal conduct. The term, *chin-shên* 謹身, is an ironical allusion to book 6 of the *Hsiao Ching* 孝經: "謹身節用, 以養父母此庶人之孝也 (To keep careful watch over one's personal conduct and to spend frugally in order to care for one's parents—this is the filiality of the common people).

4. Lang-yüan: 閬苑, an abode of immortals.

5. P'êng and Ying: P'êng-lai and Ying-chou, two of the three famous mythical islands on which immortals live. For a brief description of their scenic splendor and inhabitants, see *JW*, 2, chap. 26.

6. Supreme Ruler of the East: *Tung-hua ti-chün* 東華帝君, the deity who inhabits the blessed island of Fang-chang. See *JW*, 2:8-10.

7. Anablastemic enchymoma: *huan-tan* 還丹. This is the general term for the regenerative and rejuvenating elixir made through cyclical processes in internal or physiological alchemy. See Lu Gwei-Djen, "The Inner Elixir (Nei Tan): Chinese Physiological Alchemy," in *Changing Perspectives in the History of Science: Essays in Honour of Joseph Needham*, ed. Mikuláš Teich and Robert Young (London, 1973), pp. 68-84; Needham, 5/4, 210-323; Judith A. Berling, "Paths of Convergence: Interactions of Inner Alchemy Taoism and Neo-Confucianism," *Journal of Chinese Philosophy* 6 (1979): 123-47.

CHAPTER EIGHTY

1. Seedtime rites: These are the sacrifices offered at the soil altars (*shê* 社), which, according to Bodde, p. 197, "have existed in China all the way from the Shang dynasty down to the twentieth century." The sacrificial days occur once in the spring and once in autumn. See Edouard Chavannes, Appendix, "Le Dieu du Sol dans la Chine antique," in *Le Tai Chang: Essaie de monographie d'un culte chinois* (Paris, 1910), pp. 437-525.

2. Heaven's plaque: this regulated verse, like the poems in chaps. 28 and 36 (See *JW*, 2:38, 165, and also the notes on 421-22, 427-28), is composed by means of a series of conventional names used for certain combinations in the traditional Chinese game of "dominoes" (bone tiles or ivory tiles, *ku-p'ai* 骨牌 or *ya-p'ai* 牙牌). Each line of the poem, in fact, has reference to one combination: thus line 1, *t'ien-p'ai* 天牌 (Heaven's plaque or sky tiles); line 2, *chin-p'ing-fêng* 錦屏風 (brocaded screens); line 3, *kuan-têng-shih-wu* 觀燈十五 (The Lantern Feast on the 15th of the first month); line 4, *t'ien-ti-fên* 天地分 (Heaven and Earth parting); line 5, *lung-fu-fêng-yün-hui* 龍虎風雲會 (dragon and tiger meeting wind and cloud); line 6, *yao-ma-chün* 拗馬軍 (to be opposed by horses and troops); line 7, *Wu-shan feng-shih-êrh* 巫山峰十二 (the twelve summits of Mount Wu); line 8, *tui-tzŭ* 對子 (lit., to face the master, but in the game, it means a pair). In the following diagrams, three of such combinations are illustrated:

1) "Heaven or Sky"

2) "Lanterns Feast"

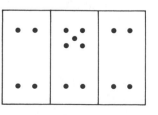

3) "Dragon and Tiger meeting wind and cloud"

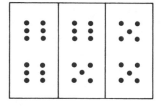

For other combinations, see Ch'ü Yu 瞿祐, "Hsüan-ho p'ai-p'u 宣和牌譜," in T'ao Tsung-i 陶宗儀 ed., *Shuo Fu* 說郛, *ts'ê* 154, vol. 33 (1647 edition); Cao Xueqin, *The Story of the Stone*, trans. David Hawkes (Bloomington, Ind., 1979), 2:586–87.

3. Big creature: *ta-ch'ung* 大蟲, another term for tiger in traditional vernacular fiction.

4. Bimbāna Kingdom: I follow Ōta's suggestion (2:284) that *p'in-p'o* 貧婆 (or 頻婆) may be the transliteration of Bimba or Vimba, a bright red gourdlike fruit, *momordica monadelphia*.

5. For this episode, see *JW*, 1:444–60.

6. Lead the horse: for the meaning of the clause, see *JW*, 1:455, and 529, note 4.

7. Floriate Canopy: *hua-kai* 華盖, a series of stars between Cassiopeia and Camelopardus. My translation of the term here follows that of Schafer, pp. 46–47. Although the lama priest here is ostensibly a Buddhist, the reason he gives for taking up the priestly vocation is similar to that of many Taoists. See Yoshitoyo Yoshioka, "Taoist Monastic Life," in Welch and Seidel, pp. 234–35.

CHAPTER EIGHTY-ONE

1. Temple: literally *t'ien-chieh* 天街, the street of Heaven. As an astronomical term, this could refer to either the Milky Way or the stars *kappa* and *nu* in Taurus. Another meaning is the street of the imperial capital. In this particular context, however, it seems more appropriate to use the term's less common meaning of the abode of Buddha, as found in the 梁元帝, "梁安寺刹下銘": 觀慧樓而下拜，望天街而興善 cited in *CW*, 2:1568, gloss 994.

2. *Triyāna* means: see *JW*, 1:506, note 2.

3. *Dharmamega: fa-yün* 法雲, the metaphor of Buddhist teaching as a fertilizing cloud.

4. *Dānapati: t'an-yüeh* 檀越, a patron or almsgiver.

5. *Litany of King Liang*: see *JW*, 2:430, note 1.

6. The gate beneath the moon: *yüeh-sha-mên* 月下門; the phrase may be an allusion to two lines by the T'ang poet, Chia Tao 賈島. See his "題李凝幽居": 鳥宿池邊樹僧敲月下門, in *CTS*, 9:6639.

7. Sha-lo tree: see *JW*, 1:528, note 9.

8. Stinky member: i.e., the penis.

9. Mythic, sea-filling bird: *t'ien-hai-niao* 填海鳥, this is Ching-wei 精衛, daughter of Yen Ti 炎帝, one of the five legendary rulers (Wu-ti 五帝) of high antiquity. She went swimming in the Eastern Sea and drowned. Her spirit became a bird, which frequently picked up plants and stones from the West Mountain and tried to fill the sea. See the *TPYL, chüan* 925, in 4:4112.

10. Turtle: *tai-shan-ao* 戴山鰲. The turtle or scorpaenid as a mythic creature is said to bear on its back Mount P'êng-lai in the Eastern Sea.

11. Lei Huan: 雷煥, a master of astronomy in the Tsin period, who was also the discoverer of two magic swords. See the *Tsin Shu* 晉書, *chüan* 36.

12. Lü Ch'ien: 呂虔, who came from the state of Wei 魏 in the Three Kingdoms period. He was famous for the cutlass or scimitar (*tao* 刀) that he wore. See the *Tsin Shu, chüan* 3, in the biographies of Wang Hsiang 王祥 and his brother, Lan 覽.

13. Kuan and Pao: this refers to the story of Kuan Chung 管仲 and Pao Shu-ya 鮑叔牙. Kuan was quite poor in his youth, but Pao was such a good friend that he frequently shared his wealth with Kuan. See the *Lieh Tzu* 列子, *chüan* 6, "Li Ming 力命."

14. Sun and P'ang: a reference to Sun Pin 孫臏, a master strategist from the State of Ch'i 齊 in the Warring Kingdoms period, and P'ang Chüan 龐涓, a general from the State of Wei 魏. For the story of how Sun out-foxed P'ang in a battle and drove the latter to commit suicide, see the *Shih Chi* 史記, *chüan* 65.

CHAPTER EIGHTY-TWO

1. Product of yin-yang copulation: i.e., water of nature.

2. Orchid-gland: *lan-shê* 蘭麝, the gland of the musk deer, used by Chinese as a kind of perfume.

3. *Fang-tan*: 方旦, I have not been able to discover the meaning of this term.

4. Dear: literally *ko-ko* 哥哥, elder brother, a term which in this context is used as one of endearment.

5. *T'u-mi*: written in Chinese as 荼蘼 and 酴醾, it is a climbing plant with white or yellow blossoms.

6. *Hsin-i*: 辛夷, *magnolia conspicua*.

7. *Mu-hsiang*: 木香, *rosa banksiae*.

8. *Shao-yao*: 芍藥, *paonia abiflora*.

9. *Yeh-ho*: 夜合, *magnolia pumilia*.

10. Yao's yellow or Wei's purple: 姚黃魏紫: according to Ou-yang Hsiu's treatise on the peony, there are some thirty varieties of this flower, some named by the families who plant them and some by the places where they are found. Thus the "Yellow of Yao" refers to a species with yellow

blossoms and dense leaves grown by a commoner household named Yao "姚黄者千葉黄花出於民姚氏家." The "purple of Wei" refers to another species with meat-red flowers grown by the household of a Minister Wei "魏家花者千葉肉紅花出於魏相仁溥家." See his "Lo-yang mu-tan chi 洛陽牡丹記," in *Ou-yan Wên-chung Ch'üan-chi* 歐陽文忠全集, *chüan* 72, 4a (*SPPY* edition).

11. Six loaves of liver and lung: this and the description of the heart in the next line are allusions to Problem 42 (四十二難) in the *Nan Ching* 難經, *chüan* 4, 5a–b (*SPTK* edition). There it is stated that "the heart weighs twelve ounces, and in the middle it has seven apertures and three hairs 心重十二 兩中有七孔三毛," and that "the lung, weighing three ounces . . . has six loaves or leaves 肺重三兩····六葉."

12. Scarlet thread: see *JW*, 2:424, note 5 of chapter 30.

13. Blue Bridge tide: 藍橋水派 refers to the legend of one scholar Wei 尾, who was to meet his girl friend beneath the Blue Bridge. The girl failed to appear, and when the tide rose, Wei drowned hugging the bridge's pillar.

14. Temple incense: an allusion to the love story of Ts'ui Ying-ying 崔鶯鶯 of the famed *Romance of the Western Chamber*. In both narrative and dramatic versions, the girl met her lover in a Buddhist temple.

CHAPTER EIGHTY-THREE

1. Holy babe: *shêng-t'ai* 聖胎, literally, the holy embryo. In the lore of physiological alchemy, this is, of course, the metaphor for the attainment of realized immortality.

2. Basic way: *mu-tao* 母道, meaning literally the way of the mother. In this context, however, it may also mean the basic or the fundamental principle.

3. For an extended treatment of Naṭa's birth and his relation to his parents, see *Fêng-shên yen-i* 封神演義 (*The Investiture of the Gods*), chaps. 12–14.

CHAPTER EIGHTY-FOUR

1. Priests: literally, 伽 = 加持, or *adhiṣṭhāna*, the dependence on a base or rule; hence, those who rely on Buddha for strength and support.

2. Letter-ten crossings: i.e., crossroads in the shape of the character ten (十, *shih*). I have translated quite literally to retain the numerical puns of the verse.

3. Eight Noble Dragon-Steeds: famous horses associated with various rulers. See *JW*, 1:508, note 7.

4. Su-hsiang: the name of one of the Eight Noble Steeds.

5. Truth: *hsiao-hsi* 消息; though the term means news or reports in

modern usage, its classical meaning has to do with the endless flux of yin and yang as exemplified in the growth and decline of the tide, the wax and wane of the moon, etc. It is thus another term for the fundamental reality of the universe.

CHAPTER EIGHTY-FIVE

1. This is a quotation of Chu Hsi's commentary on *Analects*, 1.11.1. See *Lun-yü chi-chu pu-chêng shu-shu* 論語集注補正述疏, *chüan* 1, 42a–b.

2. Twenty-eight Constellations: for the identity of these and other deities mentioned in this sentence, see *JW*, 1:509–10, notes 3, 5, 7, and 15.

CHAPTER EIGHTY-SIX

1. Dark Horse: *hsüan* 玄駒, another name for a large ant.

2. The following poem is apparently a catalog of various esculent plants, several of which still elude identification. For this segment of the translation, I have consulted Li Shih-chên, 李時珍, *Pên-ts'ao Kang-mu* 本草綱目, 3 vols. (Peking, 1975–78); Bernard E. Read and C. Pak, *A Compendium of Minerals and Stones used in Chinese Medicine, from the Pên Tshao Kang Mu*, 2d ed. (Peking, 1936); F. Porter Smith, *Chinese Materia Medica*, rev. G. A. Stuart, M.D., 2d rev. ed. Ph. Daven Wei (Taipei, 1969); K'ung Ch'ing-lai 孔慶萊, et al., eds., *Chih-wu-hsüeh ta tz'ŭ-tien* 植物學大辭典, 6th ed. (Shanghai, 1926), hereafter referred to as *CWH*; and *Chung-yao ta tz'ŭ-tien* 中藥大辭典 (Shanghai, 1977), hereafter referred to as *CYTT*.

3. Wild-goose-intestine: *Yen-ch'ang-ying* 鴈腸英, plant not yet identified.

4. Swallow: *Yen-tzŭ* 燕子, possibly a shortened term for *Yen-fu-tzŭ* 燕覆子, a southern name for the fruit of *Fatsia papyrifera* (Smith, p. 22). Or it may refer to *yên-tzŭ-hua* 燕子花, *Iris laevigata*.

5. Horse-blue: *Ma-lan* 馬藍, one of the several plants belonging to *Indigofera tinctoria* (Smith, pp. 217–18).

6. Dog-footprints: *Kou-chiao-chi* 狗脚跡, *Phyllanthus cochinchinensis* (*CYTT*, p. 1427).

7. Cat's-ears: *Mao-êrh-to* 貓耳朵〔草〕, *Gymnopteris vestita* (*CYTT*, p. 2209); it is also related to *hu-êrh-ts'ao* 虎耳草, *Saxifraga stolonifera* (*CYTT*, p. 1335).

8. *Pi*: 蓽, the fruit of *Piper longum*, or *Chavica roxburghii* (Smith, pp. 103–4).

9. Ashen-stalk: *Hui-t'iao* 灰條, possibly the same as *hui-t'iao* 灰藋, *Chenopodium album*.

10. Scissors'-handle: *Chien-tao-ku* 剪刀股, *Lactuca debilis*.

11. Cow's-pool-profit: *Niu-t'ang-li* 牛塘利, plant not yet identified.

12. Hollow-snail: *Wo-lo* 窩螺, possibly a reference to the 螺靨草, the "snail-shell grass" or *Drymoglossum earnosum* (Smith, p. 157).

13. Broken rice-*chi*: *Sui-mi-chi* 碎米薺. The full name should be 大葉碎米薺, *Cardamine hirsuta*.

14. *Wo-ts'ai-chi*: 萵菜藨, *Wo-ts'ai* is possibly another name for *pai-chü* 白苣 or *Lactuca sativa* (Smith, pp. 224–30); cf. *CWH*, p. 1207.

15. *Niao-ying*: 鳥英, plant not yet identified.

16. Wheat-wearing-lady: *cho-mai-niang* 着麥娘, possibly a variant of *Ch'iao-mai* 雀麥, *avena fatua* (Smith, p. 59).

17. Torn-worn-cassock: *p'o-p'o-na* 破破納 = 衲, plant not yet identified.

18. Little-bird: *chiao-êrh* 雀兒, possibly a reference to *Chin-ch'iao-êrh-chiao* 金雀兒椒 or "golden bird pepper," the fruit of *pai-hsien* 白鮮, *dictamnus albus* (Smith, p. 149). In the *CWH* (p. 991), however, there is the entry for *ch'iao-êrh-wo-tan* 雀兒臥單, *Euphorbia humifosa*, which is the same as *ti-chin-ts'ao* 地錦草.

19. Monkey's-footprints: *hu-sun-chiao-chi* 猢猻腳跡; the plant has not yet been identified, though it may refer to *hu-sun-t'ou* 猢猻頭, *Eclipta alba*.

20. Slanted *hao*: *hsieh-hao* 斜蒿, *seseli libanotis*, so named because the leaves are transversely veined (Smith, p. 405).

21. Green *hao*: *ch'ing-hao* 青蒿, *artemisia apiacea*.

22. Mother-hugging-*hao*: *pao-niang-hao* 抱娘蒿. The true name should be *pu-niang-hao* 佈娘蒿, *Sisymbrium sophia* (*CWH*, p. 521).

23. Bare Goat-ears: 羊耳禿, the true name being *yang-t'i* 羊蹄, goat-hoofs, *Rumex japonicus Houtt.* (*CYTT*, p. 965).

24. *Kou-chi*: 枸杞, frequently identified as *Lycium chinense* (cf. *CWH*, p. 659), but Smith (p. 286) thinks that it should be *nitraria schoberi*.

25. Black-blue: *wu-lan* 烏藍, plant not yet identified.

CHAPTER EIGHTY-SEVEN

1. Native light: *hsüan-kuang* 玄光 or *yüan-kuang*, 元光, generally regarded as the innate intelligence of man naturally endowed. Cf. *Huai-nan Tzŭ* 淮南子, *chüan* 2, 11b (*SPPY* edition): 外内無符而欲與物接騖其元光而求知之于耳目.

2. Prefect Shang-kuan: 即候上官 is a pun, since *Shang-kuan* can literally mean noble or superior official, or, as in the case here, a double surname.

3. A large countenance: one colloquial idiom of doing a favor is "bestowing face 賞臉 or 賞面子."

CHAPTER EIGHTY-EIGHT

1. For the *sung*, see *JW*, 1:278–79.

2. Sprinkling Flowers over the Top: these and what follows are names of movements or postures assumed in martial art.

3. Causes: *yüan-yu* 緣由, literally, developing causes.

4. Ubiquity: *yüan-t'ung* 圓通, literally, the universally penetrating or Buddha's supernatural power of omnipresence.

5. To the mean reverse: *Kuei-chung* 歸中. The word *chung* (middle,

center, mean) can refer to many things in Buddhism: e.g., *chung-kuan-lun* 中觀論, the *Mādhyamika Śāstra*, the principal work of the Mādhyamika or Middle School expounding the opposition to the rigid categories of existence and nonexistence; or *chung-tao* 中道, the mean between extreme oppositions such as the phenomenal and the noumenal, realism and nihilism, substance and nonsubstance, being and nonbeing, etc. In view of the poetic comment at the end of the chapter, moreover, *chung* may be a convenient allusion to *chung-yung* 中庸, the Confucian *Doctrine of the Mean* (see note 8 below).

6. Yang-shan: 陽羨, one of the top-grade teas.

7. A single canon: *i-tsang* 一藏, or a single catalogue. Popular tradition ascribes 5,048 *chüan* of Buddhist scriptures to the famous K'ai-yüan Catalogue (開元釋教録), and it is from this that the phrase, the number of a single canon (*i-tsang chih shu* 一藏之數), derives. Actually, the full catalogue lists 2,278 *pu* (部) of scripture, containing 7,046 *chüan*. The number of 5,048 is mentioned, as far as I can determine, once as follows: "於中一千一百二十四部五千四十八卷見行入藏." See No. 2154 in *T.*, 55:572.

8. See *Doctrine of the Mean*, chap. 1: 道也者不可須臾離也可離非道也.

CHAPTER EIGHTY-NINE

1. Dragon pulse: or earth pulse (*lung-mo* 龍脈, *ti-mo* 地脈). They stand for magnetic currents noted by geomancers as affecting the fortunes of lands and families.

2. Peach Blossom Cave: *t'ao-yüan tung* 桃源洞, an allusion to the legend of the Peach Blossom Spring (*t'ao-hua yüan* 桃花源), first made famous by the poet, T'ao Ch'ien (365?–427). The poem records how, at the edge of a river lined with blooming peach trees, a fisherman found a self-sufficient eremitic community, which lasted for several hundred years. See the *Ku-shih yüan* 古詩源, *chüan* 8, 116–26 (*SPPY* edition).

3. Four-lights shovel: *ssŭ-ming ch'an* 四明鏟. The name Four-lights may refer to one of the Taoist sacred mountains, so named because there are said to be four openings in the mountain, through which the lights of the sun, the moon, the stars, and the constellations shine. On the other hand, the phrase *ssŭ-ming* may also refer to four Shingon emblems—a hook, a cord, a lock, and a bell—which serve as aids to Yoga-possession by a bodhisattva or buddha.

4. Gibbon-Lion: *nao-shih* 猱獅. The word *nao* generally means a long-haired ape or gibbon. What this creature is is not certain. It may simply be a concoction of the *HYC* author.

5. *Suan-i*: 狻猊, another name for lion, or a fabulous beast which can devour tigers and leopards and travel five hundred *li* a day. See the *Erh-ya* 爾雅, *chüan* 11, 5a (*SPPY* edition); *Mu t'ien-tzu chuan* 穆天子傳, *chüan* 1, 7a

(*SPTK* edition); *TPYL, chüan* 889, 4a; the *STTH, ts'ê* 70, 3a–b.

6. *Pai-tsê*: 白澤, name of a lionlike fabulous beast, the shape of which is sewn on the front and back of a high ministerial robe in the Ming period.

CHAPTER NINETY

1. Masters and lions: the lines of the couplet are built on puns impossible to duplicate in English. The first line literally has masters (*shih* 師) and lions (*shih* 獅), to teach/impart (*shou* 授) and to receive (*shou* 受), etc. And the second line: bandits (*tao* 盜) and Tao (道), entangle (*ch'an* 纏) Zen (*ch'an* 禪), etc.

2. Three-cornered club: see *JW* 2:295, note 7.

3. An ax: for the sake of manageability, I have put the *fu* 斧 (ax) of the previous line here, for the *ku-to* 骨朵 of this line is another name for caltrop 蒺藜. See *STTH, ts'ê* 60, 25a–b.

4. Hour of the Tiger: 3:00–5:00 A.M.

5. Someone's teacher: the statement of the devarāja continues to pun on teacher (*shih*) and lion (*shih*); it is also an allusion to the oft-quoted observation of Mencius: "The evil of men is that they like to be teachers of others." See *Mencius*, bk. 4, pt. 1, chap. 23 (Legge's translation).

6. Pariahs: literally, *pien-i* 邊夷, border barbarians.

7. Nine: literally, *chiu-ling* 九靈, Ninefold-Numina.

CHAPTER NINETY-ONE

1. Leisure's released: the meaning of this line is uncertain.

2. Within the moon: not the satellite, but a circular gateway that has the shape of a moon. For a modern version of such a structure, see Audrey Topping, "A Chinese Garden Grows at the Met," *The New York Times Magazine*, 7 June, 1981, p. 41.

3. Summits: these are artificial hills.

4. Gold-Valley: an allusion to the Gold-Valley Garden (*chin-ku yüan* 金谷園), a luxurious garden resort built by Shih Ch'ung 石崇. See the *Tsin Shu* 晉書, *chüan* 33.

5. Felloe-Spring: an allusion to the *Wang-ch'un t'u* 輞川圖, a famous landscape painting done by the T'ang poet-painter, Wang Wei (699–759).

6. The most fragrant flower: *jui-hsiang hua* 瑞香花, or *Daphne odora*.

7. A vow: see *JW*, 1:283; cf. *JW*, 3, chap. 62.

8. With three *yang* begins prosperity: *san-yang k'ai t'ai* 三陽開泰, a variant form of the popular saying, *san-yang chiao-t'ai* 三陽交泰, Three *Yang* have reached the point of *t'ai*. The saying is based on the *I Ching*, where the *T'ai* hexagram is represented thus: ☰, the three unbroken lines underneath being three strokes of *yang*. Since this hexagram in calendrical literature is correlated with the first month, the saying usually signifies

renewal and a change of fortune which the new year ushers in. The Sentinels' action, moreover, plays on the homophonous *yang* 陽 and *yang* 羊 (goat or sheep).

9. Four ears: I am puzzled by the number, since each rhinoceros (see below) has only two ears, and three of them would have six.

Chapter Ninety-two

1. Fireflies: the whole line reads, The ancients said, "Grasses decayed etc." Which specific ancients the *HYC* author has in mind is uncertain, but fireflies are often associated with decayed or withered grasses in traditional writings. Cf. Chao-ming t'ai-tzŭ 昭明太子, "Liu-yüeh ch'i 六月啟," in *Chao-ming t'ai-tzŭ chi* 昭明太子集 (*SPPY* edition), *chüan* 3, 5a: 螢飛腐草光 浮帳裏之書; Li Shang-yin 李商隱, "Sui Kung 隋宮," in *Yü-ch'i-shêng-shih chien-chu* 玉谿生詩箋註 (*SPPY* edition), *chüan* 6, 7b: 於今腐草無螢火終 古垂楊有暮鴉.

2. Reverted Cinnabar: see *JW*, 1 and 2, chaps. 25–26

3. Female rhinoceros: *tou-hsi* 兕犀. Although the word *tou* was first used for a rhinoceroslike creature, it was later glossed consistently as a female rhinoceros.

4. Barbarian-hat rhinoceros: *hu-mao hsi* 胡冒＝〔帽〕犀, so named because the horns of the beast are located more toward the snout.

5. *To-lo* rhinoceros: 墮羅犀, supposedly the largest type of rhinoceros. For a description, see Liu Hsün 劉恂, *Ling-piao i-lu chi* 嶺表異錄記 (Taiwan Commercial Press facsimile edition), *chüan* 2, 6b. For further discussion of the rhinoceros in Chinese lore, see Chun-chiang Yen, "The *Chüeh-tuan* as Word, Art Motif, and Legend," *Journal of the American Oriental Society* 89 (1969): 578–99. *To-lo* may also be an abbreviation of *To-lo-po-ti* 墮羅鉢底 (*Dvāhapati*), an ancient kingdom on the upper Irrawaddy.

6. "Good's limit begets evil": The sentence says literally, the extremity of prosperity produces negativity. It refers to the Hexagrams of the *I Ching*, in which the *t'ai* 泰 (prosperity) is exactly the reverse of the condition of the *p'i* 否 (evil, negativity). In the cyclic view of the universe, the end of one phase gives rise to the other.

Chapter Ninety-three

1. Eight-word brick walls: see *JW*, 2:428, note 5.

2. For a modern account of this story, see *Dictionary of Pāli Proper Names*, ed. G. P. Malalasekera. Published for the Pāli Text Society by Luzac and Co., Ltd., 2 vols. (London, 1960), 1:963–66.

3. On the dialectical relation between our nature and the moon, see *JW*, 2, chap. 36.

4. On the construction of clepsydras in China and their principle of operation, see Needham, 3:315ff.

5. Brightest light: literally *chiu-hua* 九華, a term traditionally associated with decorated ornaments or appointments in the imperial palace: e.g. a *chiu-hua* fan or a *chiu-hua* drapery. There is also a *chiu-hua têng* 九華燈, a specially decorated lantern used for the Lantern Festival, whose light was supposed to be able to reach a hundred *li* all around when placed on top of a hill. This last allusion seems more appropriate for the meaning of the text here.

6. Hour of the Tiger: 3:00–5:00 A.M.

7. Hour of the Serpent: 9:00–11:00 A.M.

8. No leak: for the meaning of *pu-lou* 不漏 or *wu-lou* 無漏, see JW, 1:523, note 5.

9. Three perfections: *san-ch'üan* 三全, the preservation of the three vital elements of sperm, breath, and spirit (精氣神), is a constant theme in physiological alchemy. Cf. JW, 1:88.

10. Six organs: *liu-kên* 六根, the eyes, the ears, the mouth, the nose, the tongue, and the body.

CHAPTER NINETY-FOUR

1. The work of two-eights: for the meaning of this term in alchemy, see JW, 2:429, note 20.

2. The time of three times three: the term *san-san* 三三 is used to depict the correlation between the hexagrams of the I Ching and the lunar cycle. The *t'ai* 泰 hexagram shows three yin (broken) strokes on top and three yang strokes (unbroken) on the bottom (☷☰), whereas the *p'i* 否 hexagram is the exact opposite (☰☷). The *t'ai* is correlated with the waxing of the moon in the first quarter (前弦), and the *p'i* with the waning of the moon in the last quarter (後弦). For the dialectical relation between the moon and self-cultivation in physiological alchemy, see JW, 2, chap. 36 and notes; Needham, 5/4, 266ff.

3. For the meaning of baby and fair girl in alchemy, see JW, 1:525, notes 11 and 12.

4. Four Signs: *ssŭ-hsiang* 四相; in Buddhism, this term refers to the four *avasthā* or states of all phenomena—birth, being, alteration, and death. There are also variations of these states in the various schools. In the lore of divination (*shu* 術), however, the term refers to specific days during the four seasons (e.g., the day *ping-ting* 丙丁 in spring, *mao-chi* 戊己 in summer, *jên-kuei* 壬癸 in autumn, and *chia-i* 甲乙 in winter) when they are said to be days of prosperous signs 旺相之辰, fit for all kinds of activities such as building, repair, trade, planting, conception, and moving. Understandably these moments are also specially efficacious for alchemical undertakings. In the lore of physiological alchemy, the Four Signs or Emblems (*ssŭ-hsiang* 四相 = 象), moreover, refer among other things to the correlation of the Gold Squire (*chin-wêng* 金翁) with the secretion of the lungs (肺中之唾),

the Fair Girl (*ch'a-nü* 姹女) with the hole in the heart (心中之穴), the Baby (*ying-êrh* 嬰兒) with the spermal essence of the kidneys 腎中之精), and Yellow Hag (*huang-p'o* 黃婆) with the liquid in the spleen (脾中之液). Cf. the discussion in *JW*, 1:51. As the term is used in Sha Monk's declaration here, the meaning clearly points to one conferred by the context of physiological alchemy.

5. Leopard's-tail: *pao-wei* 豹尾, a bannerlike ornament hung at the back of an imperial chariot.

6. Carved dragons: *ch'ih-t'ou* 螭頭, dragons carved at the entrance to the court or palace.

7. Hour of the Serpent: 9:00–11:00 A.M.

8. The phoenix come, etc.: 引鳳來儀, a reference to book "I and Chih 益稷" of the *Shang Shu* 尚書 (Book of Historical Documents), where it says that "when the nine parts of the service according to the emperor's arrangements have all been performed [by tubes and reeds], the male and female phoenix come with their measured gambollings *into the court* 簫韶九成鳳 鳳來儀" (trans. Legge, 3:88).

9. *Mo-li*: 茉莉, *Jasminum sambac*.

10. *Li-ch'un* flower: 麗春花, *Papaver rhoeas*.

11. "Wood-brush" flower: 木筆花, *Magnolia conspicua*, so named because the flower, when first opened, resembles a Chinese brush.

12. *Fêng-hsien* flower: 鳳仙花, *Impatiens balsamina*, used in the north of China in combination with alum as a nail polish.

13. "Jade-pin" flower: 玉簪花, *Funkia subcordata*, so named because of its white, pearly blossoms and bracted stems.

14. Heaven-gate: a metaphor for the imperial gate.

15. *K'uei* 葵, malvaceous plants of all varieties.

16. *Wu-t'ung*: 梧桐, *Sterculia platanifolia*. Wells in wealthy and noble households often have carved, gilded railings; these are called golden wells.

17. The library's four treasures are brush, paper, ink, and ink-slab or ink-stone.

18. *Huai*: 槐, *Sophora japonica*.

19. Milk: 酥酪, literally, koumiss and cream. For the use of milk and dairy products in traditional Chinese diet, see Edward H. Schafer's article "T'ang," in *Food in Chinese Culture, Anthropological and Historical Perspectives*, ed. K. C. Chang (New Haven and London, 1977), pp. 106–7.

20. Mao Ch'iang: 毛嬙, a famous beauty of the fifth century B.C., said to be a mistress of King Yüeh.

21. Sister Ch'u: the ladies of Ch'u in the South are said to be particularly beautiful.

CHAPTER NINETY-FIVE

1. Numinous Source: *ling-yüan* 靈元, another name for Star Lord of Supreme Yin, the god of the moon.

2. *Kung*, etc.: these are the five tones of the Chinese pentatonic scale. According to the article "China" in *The New Grove Dictionary of Music and Musicians*, ed. Stanley Sadie, 20 vols. (London, Washington D.C., and Hong Kong, 1980), 4:260–61, these notes "are generally considered to be the earliest known Chinese pentatonic scale." They are also "the first five of the Pythagorean series. When arranged in an ascending order they are equivalent in terms of relative pitch to C-D-F-G-A." Cf. the discussion in Needham, 4/1, 160–228.

3. Three Primaries: *san-yüan* 三元. There are several explanations for the meaning of this term, the most basic being the abbreviated form of *san-ts'ai chih yüan* 三才之元, the three primary elements of Heaven, Earth, and Water emphasized in Taoist writings. Another name for these elements is *san-kuan* 三官. See the Biography of P'an Ni 潘尼 in the *Tsin Shu* 晉書, *chüan* 55. In the literature of divination, one *yüan* refers to a cycle of sixty years. Finally, in the literature of physiological alchemy, the term *san-yüan* refers to the primary element by which immortality is realized. Thus those who succeed by refining spermal essence (*ching* 精) and changing into breath (*ch'i* 氣) have worked on the human primary (*jên-yüan* 人元); those by refining breath and changing into spirit (*shên* 神) have worked on the Earth primary (*ti-yüan* 地元); and those refining spirit and returning it to the void (*hsü* 虛) have worked on the Heaven primary (*t'ien-yüan* 天元). See Tai, p. 25.

4. Toad Palace: *ch'an-kung* 蟾宮, another name for the Lunar Palace. For an informative account of the moon in Chinese mythology, see Schafer, chap. 9.

5. Cassia Hall: *kuei-tien* 桂殿, a hall in the Lunar Palace.

6. Vast Cold Palace: *kuang-han-kung* 廣寒宮, another name for the Lunar Palace, so named because the moon sheds light without heat.

7. Three rabbit holes: an allusion to the saying that the sly hare always has three holes.

8. White Lady: *su-o* 素娥 and the Blue Girl 青女, are goddesses of the moon.

9. Revealing cause: the Chinese, *liao-hsing* 了性 is an abbreviation of 了因佛性, the second of the three Buddha-nature causes. The first, 正因, is the direct cause of attaining the perfect Buddha-nature, and it is associated with the Dharmakāya. The second is related to Buddha-wisdom, while the third, 緣因, is the environing cause, associated with the merit and virtue of Buddha, which results in bringing salvation.

CHAPTER NINETY-SIX

1. A dream needn't be told: the line is an allusion to the common saying, 癡人説夢 (A silly person telling of a dream), meaning absurdity or nonsense.

2. Five-colored clouds: the *wu-yün* here is short for *wu-yün-t'i* 五雲體, a reference to the practice of one Wei Chih 韋陟 in the T'ang dynasty, who used to sign his name like a five-petaled cloud. Later, *wu-yün* or *to-yün* 朵雲 became a metaphor for letters. See his biography in *T'ang Shu*, 唐書, *chüan* 92.

3. *Hsiu-ts'ai*: 秀才, students who have taken their first degree in the civil service examination.

4. *A Guide*: *Shih-lin kuang-chi* 事林廣記, an encyclopedia of the Sung compiled between A.D. 1100 and 1250 and first published in 1325. My translation of the title follows Needham.

5. *Kung-ch'ê* notations: 工尺, according to *The New Grove Dictionary of Music and Musicians*, 4:264, was a form of notation similar to *solfeggio* in concept. It indicated "pitch and was the most popular form of notation for both vocal and instrumental music" from the thirteenth century to the twentieth. For illustrations of the *Kung-ch'ê* scores, see pp. 265 and 272. Cf. also the discussion in Wang Kwang-ch'i 王光祈, *Chung-kuo yin-yüeh shih* 中國音樂史 (Shanghai, 1934; reprinted in Taipei 1974), chap. 5, pp. 7ff.

6. Tenth-mile wayside station: see *JW*, 3:320 and appropriate note.

CHAPTER NINETY-SEVEN

1. External aid: *wai-hu* 外護. In Buddhism, this term refers to food and clothing provided for clerics, as contrasted with the internal aid of Buddha's teachings. It is used here as a metonym for the squire.

2. Three spirits and seven souls: *san-hun ch'i-p'o* 三魂七魄. Chinese thought from the earliest times has affirmed in man two kinds of souls. According to Needham, 5/2, 85ff., "the ouranic component, the *hun* soul, came from the upper air and was received back into it, while the chthonic component, the *pho* soul, was generated by the earth below and sank back to mingle with it after death." Around the time of the Later Han, "the number of *hun* souls was definitively fixed at three and the number of *pho* souls at seven." Needham finds it difficult to give a reason for the numbers, but he suspects a "macrocosmic or astrological" association.

3. Kung and Huang: these refer to Kung Sui 龔遂 and Huang Pa 黃霸, two model officials in the Han period noted for their administrative talents. For their biographies, see *Han Shu* 漢書, *chüan* 89. Their last names are frequently mentioned together in classical poetry.

4. Cho and Lu: these refer to Cho Mao 卓茂 and Lu Kung 魯恭, another two officials in the Later Han period noted for being able administrators. See their biographies in *Hou Han Shu* 後漢書, *chüan* 55.

5. No Alternative Bridge: see *JW*, 1:519, note 11.

CHAPTER NINETY-EIGHT

1. Yellow cranes bring letters: 黄鶴信 and 青鸞書. Immortals are thought to send their communications by means of magic birds like yellow cranes and blue phoenixes.

2. Feathered-one: *yü-shih* 羽士. From antiquity, it has been customary to refer to *hsien* 仙 immortals (and later, most Taoists) as feathered scholars or feathered-guests, *yü-k'o* 羽客. See Needham, 5/2, 96–113 for detailed discussion.

3. Former years: see *JW*, 1:186–87.

4. A diamond body: the incorruptible body in the Chinese here refers to the diamond incorruptible body 金剛不壞身 of Buddhahood.

5. Candana: see *JW*, 1:186, and note 21.

6. Six-six senses' sway: *liu-liu-ch'ên* 六六塵, the intensive form of the six *guṇas*, the six impure qualities engendered by the objects and organs of sense: sight, sound, smell, taste, touch, and idea.

7. In translating this catalog of Buddhist writings, I use the original Sanskrit or Pali titles whenever possible. The several titles that have eluded identification even after extensive research are given in literal translation of the Chinese.

8.. On the significance of this canonical number of 5,048, see note 7 of chapter 88.

CHAPTER NINETY-NINE

1. Double Three: for the possible meaning of this term, see *JW*, 1:505–6, note 15. Apart from its Buddhist connotations, the term *san-san* 三三 has also profound significance in alchemical lore, since the lunar cycle is correlated with the sixty-eight hexagrams of the *I Ching* (cf. *JW*, 2:428–29, note 18). In this correlation, the first quarter of the moon is represented by the *T'ai* 泰 hexagram ䷊ with its three broken (*yin* 陰) lines on top and three unbroken (*yang* 陽) lines on the bottom, whereas the last quarter of the moon is represented by the *P'i* 否 hexagram ䷋, with its positions of the *yin-yang* lines exactly reversed. The entire process of physiological alchemy, insofar as it is correlated with the lunar cycle, is thus called Double Three.

2. *Kinship of the Three: Ts'an-t'ung ch'i*: 參同契, the earliest book extant written on alchemical theory by Wei Po-yang 魏伯陽 in the second century. For an informative discussion of this text and its contribution to spagyrical development in Chinese antiquity, see Needham, 5/3, 50–75.

3. Advaya: *pu-êrh* 不二, no second or nonduality; the one and undivided reality of the Buddha-nature.

CHAPTER ONE HUNDRED

1. A great event: literally, the Grand Mass of Land and Water.

2. *Hsiang-ch'un* 香椿: *Cedrela odorata*.

3. The *chüeh* 蕨 and *wei* 薇 in this line are the several kinds of ferns (*Pteris, Osmunda, Vincetoxicum*), the young roots of which are eaten. In addition, some kinds yield rhizomes, which are ground into flour and eaten as a dessert.

4. *Fei*-nuts: 榧, *Torreya nucifera*.

5. "Chinese olives": *kan-lan* 橄欖, *Canarium*. These fruits are oblong and pointed, either green or shriveled, bearing no affinity with the true olive.

6. *P'in-p'o*: 頻婆 or *nai* 柰, a kind of *Pyrus malus* or crabapple.

7. *Sha-t'ang* pears: *sha-kuo* or *sha-t'ang-kuo* 沙糖果 is a kind of *Pyrus sinensis*, commonly found in southern China.

8. *Tz'ŭ-ko*: 慈菰, *Sagittaria sagittfolia*.

9. "Chinese strawberries": *yang-mei* 楊梅, *Myrica rubra*.

10. This "preface" was actually written by the emperor in the year 648, in gratitude for the newly completed translation by Tripitaka of the entire *Yogācārya-bhūmi Śāstra*. See the *Fa-shih chuan*, *chüan* 6, 10a–17b; Waley, pp. 92–95.

11. Two Primary Forces: *êrh-i* 二儀. In a text like the *Lü-shih ch'un-ch'iu* 呂氏春秋, *chüan* 5, 3a, the Two Primary Forces are that which beget the yin and yang (e.g. 太一出兩儀兩儀出陰陽). This and other ancient texts seem to imply that *êrh-i* may best be understood as Heaven and Earth (*t'ien-ti* 天地). In the *Great Commentary* of the *I-Ching*, however, *êrh-i* is traditionally regarded as referring to yin-yang. Cf. chap. 11 of the Commentary in Wilhelm/Baynes, p. 318: "Therefore there is in the Changes the Great Primal Beginning. This generates the two primary forces. The two primary forces generate the four images. The four images generate the eight trigrams."

12. A radiant dream: cf. the account given in Kenneth Ch'en, *Buddhism in China: A Historical Survey* (Princeton, 1964), pp. 29–30: "The dream of Emperor Ming (A.D. 58–75) of the Han Dynasty has often been connected with the introduction of Buddhism into China. Briefly, the episode is as follows. One night in a dream Emperor Ming saw a golden deity flying in front of his palace. On the morrow he asked his ministers to explain the identity of this deity. One of them, Fu Yi, replied that he heard there was a sage in India who had attained salvation and was designated the Buddha, who was able to fly, and whose body was of a golden hue. He went on to say that the deity seen in the dream was this Buddha. The ruler accepted his explanation and dispatched envoys abroad to learn more about this sage and his teachings. The envoys returned bringing back with them the *Sutra in Forty-two Sections*, which was received by the emperor and deposited in a

temple constructed outside the walls of the capital, Lo-yang."

13. The figure of thirty-two marks: the body of Buddha, a "wheel-king" or *cakravartī*, is said to have thirty-two *lakṣaṇas* or special physical marks or signs.

14. At this point, the *HYC* text varies from the *Fa-shih chuan* text (*chüan* 6, 15b0, which reads: 然而真教難仰莫能一其旨歸曲學易遵邪正於焉紛糺所以空有之論或習俗而是非大小之乘乍沿時而隆替. (However, the true Teaching is so difficult to uphold that there can hardly be a unified interpretation of its fundamental principles, whereas heterodox learning is so easy to follow that both the right and the deviant flourish at the same time. For this reason, the views on emptiness and being might have varied according to customs, while the division into Great and Small Vehicles might have arisen in response to the times). The two sentences in the *HYC* text prior to the reference to Hsüan-tsang may have been its author's own interpolation, or they may have come from another textual tradition.

15. Four forms of patience: *ssŭ-jen* 四忍, the four kinds of *kṣānti*: i.e., under shame, hatred, physical hardship, and in pursuit of faith.

16. Fourteen years: *Fa-shih chuan* (*chüan* 6, 16a) has seventeen years.

17. Twin *śāla* trees: beneath which Buddha was said to have achieved enlightenment.

18. Eight rivers of India 八水: Ganges, Jumna, Sarasvatī, Hiraṇyavatī, Mahī, Indus, Oxus, and Sītā.

19. The *HYC* text here is another interpolation. The *Fa-shih chuan* (*chüan* 6, 16a) reads: 爰自所歷之國總將三藏要文凡六百五十七部 (From all the nations he visited he acquired altogether six hundred and fifty-seven items of important writings from the Tripiṭaka).

20. Will proclaim: I use the future tense here to make the emperor's point of view consistent, since it is obvious that in the narrative, Tripitaka has not (and will not be) engaged in any work of translation.

21. *Fa-shih chuan* (*chüan* 6, 16a) reads: 朗愛水之昏波 (Illuminating the darkened waves upon the waters of affection).

22. The declaration of the emperor here was actually a note written in reply to a formal memorial of thanks submitted by the historical Hsüan-tsang. See the *Fa-shih chuan*, *chüan* 6, 16b–17b.

23. Bronze and stone inscriptions 金石: the *Fa-shih chuan* text has *po-ta* 博達, the learned.

24. Eight Classes of Supernatural Beings: 八部天龍 龍神八部. They are *deva*, *nāga*, *yakṣa*, *gandharva*, *asura*, *garuḍa*, *kinnara*, and *mahoraga*.

Index

(Boldface denotes volume numbers)